Cleaving the air with bloodstroke upon bloodstroke, Jarl made his bitter steel sing. He hacked the bandit leader down, then claimed for himself the choicest treasure found in the bandit camp — a beauty named Yerzerdayla.

The woman was brought in chains to the imperial battle base, where she was seen by the young Guest Gulkan, the self-styled Weaponmaster, he who at the age of 14 laid claim to a man's estate, though he was still possessed of much of a child's impetuous unreliability. Guest Gulkan stood in his muddy boots, smelling like a slaughterhouse, and gaped at Yerzerdayla. For this captive — dressed in silks and chained by jade clasped with silverbright — looked more like an imperial aristocrat than one of common flesh.

"I am in love," said Guest, who was of a certainty in lust.

Such was the first meeting of Guest Gulkan and the elegant Yerzerdayla, she of the blonde body and the perfumed hair.

Then:

"Who is the woman?" asked Guest.

"She is claimed already by Thodric Jarl," they answered.

"Claim he may," said Guest. "But I will have!"

THE CHRONICLES OF AN AGE OF DARKNESS

Volume 1: The Wizards and the Warriors
Volume 2: The Wordsmiths and the Warguild
Volume 3: The Women and the Warlords
Volume 4: The Walrus and the Warwolf
Volume 5: The Wicked and the Witless
Volume 6: The Wishstone and the Wonderworkers
Volume 7: The Wazir and the Witch
Volume 8: The Werewolf and the Wormlord
Volume 9: The Worshippers and the Way
Volume 10: The Witchlord and the Weaponmaster
and
The Lost Chronicles of an Age of Darkness

https://www.zenphospress.com

The Witchlord and the Weaponmaster

HUGH COOK

ZENPHOS PRESS

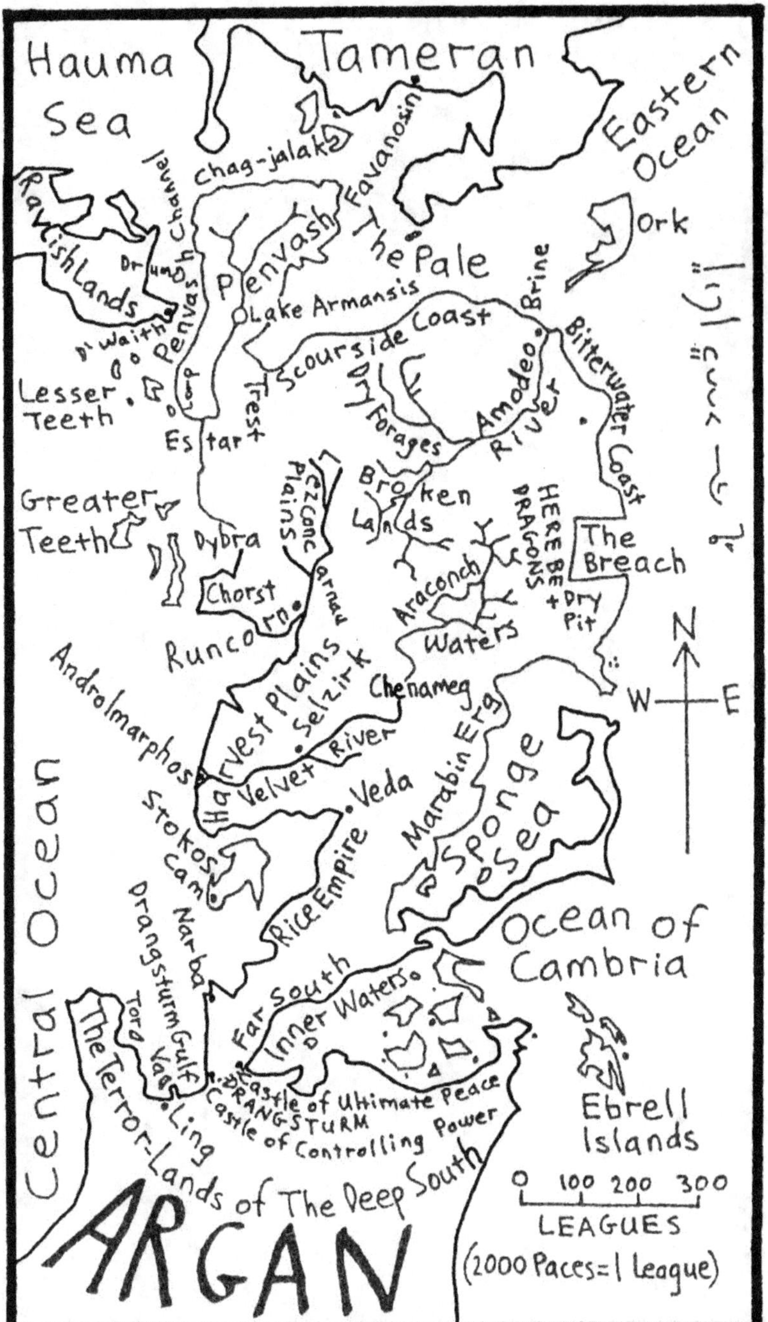

Hauma Sea
Tameran
Eastern Ocean
Ravlish Lands
D'waith
Drangshavdi Chanavel
chag-jalak
Favanosin
The Pale
Ork
Brine
Penvash
Lake Armansis
Scourside Coast
Amodeo
Bitterwater Coast
Drangshav
Penvash
Lesser Teeth
Trest
Dry Forages
Amodeo River
Es tar
Greater Teeth
Manavel Plains
Broken Lands
HERE BE + DRAGONS
The Breach
Dybra
Araconch
+ Dry Pit
Chorst
Runcorn
Araconch Waters
N
Androlmarphos
Harvest Plains
Selzirk
Chenameg
W
E
Velvet River
Marabin Erg
Sponge Sea
Stokos
Veda
Cam
Rice Empire
Ocean of Cambria
Narba
Far South
Central Ocean
Drangsturm Gulf
Inner Waters
Toro
Vas
Ling
Castle of Ultimate Peace
Ebrell Islands
The Terror-Lands of The Deep South
DRANGSTURM
Castle of Controlling Power
0 100 200 300
LEAGUES
(2000 Paces = 1 League)
ARGAN

N
W E
Gendormargensis
Crux
Yolantarath River
Stranagor
Babaroth
Pig
Ink
TAMERAN
Ibsen-Iktus
Ema-Urk
Locontareth
Alozay
Swelaway Sea
Nork
Port Domax
Hauma Sea
Favanosin
LexChalis
The Pale
D'Waith
Drum
Penvash
Ork
Brine
Lesser Teeth
ARGAN
Estar
Trest
Leagues
0
100
200
300
400
500

Babaroth
Pig
Yolantarath
Ink
Locontareth
Ibsen-Iktus
Ema-Urk
Alozayd
Swelaway Sea
Port Domax
0   100   200
leagues
(2000 paces = 1 league)

The Plain of Tazala
Obooloo
YESTRON
Quilth
N E
W
Galsh Ehrek
The Winter Sea
The Great Ocean of Moana
Manamalargo
Untunchilamon
Injiltaprajura
chay
Odrum
The Sea of Salt
Ashmolea
Asral
Port Domax
Ork
The Breach
Ocean of Cambria
Ebrell Islands
PARENG ARENGA
0 200 400 600 800
leagues

CHAPTER ONE

Name: Onosh Gulkan

Birthplace: Hum

Occupation: emperor

Status: absolute ruler of the Collosnon Empire

Description: hairy male of Yarglat race, age 43, slanting forehead gouged by thumb-fat depressions running from hairline to eyebrows, hair and eyes both black, height 14 qua, cheekbones high, ears immense, multiple scars on left leg and torso.

Hobby: hunting

Quote: "The hunt is the ultimate answer to acedia."

***

The Witchlord's sons were three in number, and Sken-Pitilkin was lecturing all three when the Witchlord himself intruded on their lesson. Sken-Pitilkin resented the intrusion — and resented it all the more when he noticed the Rovac warrior Rolf Thelemite and the dwarf Glambrax lurking behind the Witchlord. Sken-Pitilkin was ever at pains to keep that pair of troublemakers out of his classroom, for such adulthood in combination with boy-hood made a vicious combination.

"Eljuk, my son!" said Lord Onosh. "You've been drinking!"

An ugly jest, this.

For Eljuk had not been drinking at all. Rather, the boy's life was blighted by a cruel birthmark. It stained his lips with purple, and further purple dribbled from the corners of his lips, splattering down his chin in two separate winespills which thickened to a merging at the neck.

Here, at the outset, we see the flaw which doomed Lord Onosh to destruction. The Witchlord Onosh had been at odds with the world for so long that he had quite lost the art of showing the world kindness and affection. Though Eljuk Zala was the Witchlord's valued favourite, even Eljuk suffered a dozen slights a day from his father's tongue.

Actually, it was Eljuk's younger brother Guest who had been drinking, and who was subdued as a consequence of his hangover. At this time, Guest was 14, Eljuk 16, and Morsh Bataar (the eldest) a full 18 years of age. But though Guest was the baby, it was Guest who played the man to the very hilt, and often suffered as a consequence.

Before knowing young Guest, the wizard Sken-Pitilkin had never approved of hangovers; but close acquaintance with the boy had led him to concede that a hangover has many advantages. For it slows speech, subdues energy, abolishes wit, and makes the afflicted individual less likely to respond to the irregular verbs with acts of verbal dissidence or outright violence.

The wizard Sken-Pitilkin had been taking advantage of Guest's hangover to cram some of the more irregular verbs into the boy's head, and had been thus involved when Lord Onosh had interrupted the lesson, remarking (as has been stated above):

"Eljuk, my son! You've been drinking!"

"Yes, father," said Eljuk. "But Guest is bearing my hangover for me."

At this the Witchlord laughed — not out of good humour but out of habit. For this joke had often been exchanged between father and son, though a thousand exchanges had failed to make Lord Onosh see that Eljuk found his part in the transaction to be painful.

"Regardless of who has been drinking," said Sken-Pitilkin acidly, "we have all been studying. We have been studying the irregular verbs."

The eminent Sken-Pitilkin was dropping a heavy hint, a hint which was meant to suggest to the Witchlord Onosh that he should absent himself from the room lest he further interfere with the lesson.

"Verbs!" said the Witchlord. "And what then is a verb? A hook for a rat or a knife for a cat? Enough of your verbs, my good fellow! Lessons are over for the day, so — boys, make ready! We're going hunting."

"Hunting?" said Morsh, absorbing that datum with his customary slowness.

"Precisely," said the Witchlord, with crisp directness.

"But, father," said Eljuk Zala, who was the only one who had licence to question the emperor's decisions, "it is late in the season."

"Last chance weather, true," agreed Lord Onosh, "so we must take our chances while we have them. Remember, boys: the hunt is the ultimate answer to acedia."

That the emperor said often, it being one of his pet sayings. Having discharged himself of that expression, he about-faced and departed, so sure in his power that he saw no need to linger to chivvy his boys into action. Unfortunately, when the Witchlord departed, he did not take with him either the Rovac warrior Rolf Thelemite or the dwarf Glambrax, and that pair of delinquents promptly infiltrated Sken-Pitilkin's classroom.

"So who is Acedia?" said Guest Gulkan, when his father was barely out of earshot. "That's what I can never work out."

"She's a whore," said Rolf Thelemite, the Rovac warrior who ever bodyguarded Guest Gulkan, more to protect the world from the boy's temper than to protect the boy from the world. "She's your father's secret whore, but she nags him stupid, so he runs for the hills at every opportunity."

"She's no whore," said Morsh Bataar, who was sitting in a corner with a heap of half-assembled fishing flies at his feet. "She's the pastry cook who has the man in fat. He hunts when the only choice otherwise is to diet."

"Acedia," said the wizard Sken-Pitilkin, "is not a woman's name. The word denotes a state of the psyche, and that state — Eljuk Zala, tell us what state the word denotes."

Now Eljuk Zala was by far the mildest, most scholarly and most intelligent of the Witchlord's three sons, and he was fully cognisant of the fact that the word acedia denoted that bleak and aimless inertia which had ever blighted the Witchlord's life since the death of his wife. But Eljuk Zala had already been too bright and too right far too often that day, and knew that if he came up with the right answer just one more time then his brother Guest would surely make him suffer for it, and probably sooner rather than later. So Eljuk answered:

"Anger. That's what it means. Acedia means anger."

"It means no such thing," said Sken-Pitilkin, with intense irritation.

Then he lectured the unfortunate Eljuk at length on the meaning of acedia and the derelictions of Eljuk's scholarship.

Sken-Pitilkin's irritation was by no means feigned, for he often felt it an intense strain to have three Yarglat boys under his tutorship. Indeed, the wizard of Drum found all his contacts with the Yarglat stressful, for the Yarglat were not, on the whole, an intellectual people, and there were precious few dictionaries in their kennels or encampments.

"Well," said Guest Gulkan, when Sken-Pitilkin was done with berating his brother, "if you're through with lecturing, we've got to get ready for hunting. You're coming with us, I suppose?"

"Me?" said Sken-Pitilkin. "Hunt? Not for all the tea in Chay! You wouldn't get me to a hunt unless I was tied to a horse and dragged."

"I'll see if I can find a spare horse, then," said Glambrax, Guest Gulkan's pet dwarf.

The dwarf was already dancing out of the room as he delivered himself of that smartcrack, hence escaped before Sken-Pitilkin could catch him a whack with the country crook ever kept ready for the disciplining of the mannikin and his master.

So it was that Glambrax again escaped punishment; and Lord Onosh and his sons readied themselves for the folly of the hunt, while the scholarly Sken-Pitilkin drew up a schedule of self-improvement which was calculated to see him attain mastery of the Geltic verbs *jop*, *chilibisk* and *dileem*, all of which had won a place for themselves in Strogloth's Compendium of Delights. While Sken-Pitilkin sometimes fell prey to acedia himself, he never sought to address his condition through the hunt, for his standard response to the dulling of the lifeforce was to have recourse to the irregular verbs, ever most marvellously refreshing in their inexhaustible variety.

Sken-Pitilkin was so glad to be rid of his Yarglat charges for a few days that he went to the city gates to see the hunt ride out, just to make certain that Guest Gulkan and his brothers actually did quit the city.

They did.

There rode Guest Gulkan with his bodyguard Rolf Thelemite at his side, both drinking hard and halfway drunk already. Thelemite and his charge had both lashed themselves to their high and stylish lean-back saddles, by this precaution indicating that they planned to be truly stupendously intoxicated before the day was out.

Behind that pair of brawlers rode Eljuk Zala Gulkan. As the anointed heir of the Witchlord Onosh, the winestained Eljuk was properly entitled to ride at the emperor's side. But young Guest was ever jealous of his brother's privileges, wishing the heirship were his own. So, fearing his brother's surly anger, Eljuk hung back out of sight.

Eljuk looked miserably uncomfortable, since his groaning bones were mightily encumbered with armour, weighed down beneath a regular rustyard of iron plates interlaced with chain mail; his head was crowned with a helmet big enough for the boiling of a dog; a sword made for the slaughter of dragons was hauling at his side; and he could scarcely find space to sit in his saddle on account of all the spare armour and weaponry he had attached to it.

A stranger might have thought Eljuk fearful of bandits, but actually it was his dearly beloved brother Guest who stalked his nightmares. Guest had the temperament of a born regicide, patricide, fratricide and all-round homicide. So Eljuk had armoured himself, and had armed himself mightily — but the weight of such protection would doom him to heatstroke on a hot day, or to death by suction should he find himself in a swamp, or (should the imperial hunting party encounter a blacksmith with a purse at the ready for the purchase of unwanted iron) to accidental disposal by way of sale.

While Eljuk feared Guest Gulkan, he lived in mortal dread of Rolf Thelemite. Rolf was a Rovac warrior, and the Rovac were a people so bloody in their predilections that the most ferocious of Yarglat barbarians was a cat-stroking pacifist by comparison. If Rolf Thelemite's account was to be believed (and Eljuk never doubted a word of it) then Rolf had personally slaughtered 3 emperors, 7 kings, 9 dragons, 11 wizards, a neversh, a troll, 5 orcs, and 30 dozen assorted warriors and assassins.

Sken-Pitilkin personally thought this a mighty great amount for Rolf to have accomplished, seeing that he was barely 18 years of age, and had spent a full two of those brief years of his in Gendormargensis. But Eljuk took Rolf's every word to heart. Eljuk believed Rolf Thelemite when that Rovac warrior claimed that the golden serpent which he wore as an earring was a trophy which Rolf had torn from the head of the mighty Baron Farouk of Hexagon when that warlord had led an army of a million men against the city of Chi'ash-lan. Rolf said, further, that the intermittent and involuntary trembling of his lower lip was a consequence of flame-damage inflicted by a dragon, and that his habit of blinking quickly (as if he had grit in his eyes) was due to the effort of fighting off a sleeping spell which had been inflicted upon him by a wizard of Ebber.

Often, Rolf Thelemite described the gruesome death which he himself had inflicted upon that spell-casting wizard, and in his every description of that death he never neglected to leave out small but telling details, such as the succulent taste of the wizard's kidneys, or the manner in which a pariah dog had made off with the wizard's kidneys before Rolf could taste them also.

For his part, Guest Gulkan sometimes hinted to his brother Eljuk that he was taking practical lessons in cannibalism from his mercenary acquaintance.

Eljuk had once pleaded with his father to exile both Rolf Thelemite and Guest Gulkan, fearing that the pair of them would conspire together to encompass his murder. But the Witchlord had merely laughed.

Of course the Witchlord Onosh was no fool. Lord Onosh was ever conscious of Guest Gulkan's bloody temper and of his monstrous ambition. Which was why (unbeknownst to the world at large), Lord Onosh had bound Rolf Thelemite to the protection of both emperor and imperial heir; and (in equal secrecy) had further charged Morsh Bataar with the duty of bodyguarding Eljuk Zala.

Had Morsh Bataar's secret mission become public knowledge, it would have occasioned incredulous laughter from all and sundry, for it was generally believed that Morsh Bataar had been blighted by a dralkosh while still in his mother's womb.

It was said in Gendormargensis that Morsh Bataar was painfully slow of intellect, and this was the case. But while he was thick of voice and slow of mind, success seldom eluded him when he went to work on a problem. True, he was judicious in his choice of problems, for he was possessed of an uncommon degree of self-knowledge, and knew his limitations well.

Nevertheless—

Among those who are possessed of genius, there sometimes arises the conceit that genius is all. But for the practical purposes of life there are other qualities of equal importance, and prime among them are patience, persistence, reliability and a sense of proportion, all of which Morsh Bataar possessed in good measure. These traits had helped make Morsh a master of the bow, which weapon he carried with him always, and practised with on a daily basis.

In his intellect, Morsh Bataar might reasonably be likened to the snail. This most practical of beasts cannot dare to the heights of the eagle or challenge the hare in the sprint; but, given time, it will make its way over any obstacle, not excepting broken glass and razor blades.

Morsh was also uncommonly stable of temperament. He lived free of the black humours which afflicted Lord Onosh; free of the night terrors and daylight nervousness which unsettled Eljuk Zala; and free also of the drastic flux of anger and impulse which made his brother Guest such a trial to his elders.

In the capacity of bodyguard, Morsh Bataar rode behind the over-armoured Eljuk Zala. Apart from his bow and a telescopic bamboo fishing rod, Morsh carried no weapons of note, believing Eljuk to be in possession of more than enough steel for the pair of them. Nor did Morsh bother himself with any nonsense of armour, for he thought the weather to be more of a threat to life than any rabble of bandits who might be encountered in the mountains.

Morsh Bataar was officially assigned to Eljuk Zala as a servant, and in truth he looked every bit the nondescript menial, since his burly body was hidden beneath layers of second-hand furs and his face was shadowed by a broad-brimmed hat the colour of filth, a hat pierced by a full three dozen fancy fishing flies. He was mounted humbly on a shag pony, with a burdened baggage animal of like breed trailing behind him, and a spare mount bringing up the rear.

Behind this beggarly figure there rode a great and glorious warrior, the glitter of the sun sheening and shining on his armour and a falcon leashed and hooded on his gauntleted left wrist. This was Pelagius Zozimus, the emperor's master chef, who spied Sken-Pitilkin standing by the gate.

"Ho! Cousin!" cried Zozimus, leaning down from the height of his horse. "You're not hunting with us?"

"Get down from that horse, you old fool," said Sken-Pitilkin. "You're a thousand years too old for such nonsense."

But Zozimus merely laughed at this accusation. The wizardly master chef was dressed for the hunt in glittering fish-scale armour which had been in his possession for the better part of a millennium; he was helmeted with silver and gold; he wore at his side a blade of Stokos steel which was sheathed in a scabbard bright with jade and opals; and he looked in his glory like one of the elven lords of legend come to life.

"You'll break a leg!" cried Sken-Pitilkin.

But Zozimus laughed again and rode on, and after him came a considerable cavalcade, for the emperor was not going to the hunting grounds alone. A great host they were, and they racketed out of the city like a rabble of commoners hustling along to a lynching. They cursed, laughed, joked and gossiped in as many as a dozen different tongues, most commonly Ordhar — the simplified command language with which the Yarglat dominated their subject peoples — and the native Eparget of the Yarglat's northern homelands.

Thus the Witchlord Onosh rode forth from the city of Gendormargensis to go hunting in the hills. And, as has been indicated above, his entourage consisted of rather more people than the few individuals who have so far been mentioned by name.

An emperor does not groom his own horse or dig his own dungpit. Nor does he clean his own boots — or, for that matter, his own fingernails. So when Lord Onosh went hunting, he customarily took with him half a thousand assorted shamans, slaves, servants, warriors, counsellors, cooks, concubines, magicians, astrologers, winemasters, poets, painters, bootmakers and button-painters.

Nevertheless, the imperial hunting party was nothing like one of those shambling circuses which traipse around behind the effete lords of the debauched and dissolute south. Even in his days of triumph, Lord Onosh never forgot that he was of the Yarglat, a people who conquered by horsepower, who ruled by horsepower, and who trusted to their horsepower to survive if the fates ever turned against them.

All who went with the emperor could ride hard and long when the day demanded it; and so, despite its complement of concubines and bootmakers, the hunting party rode east from Gendormargensis like the advance guard of a windriding army. Swiftly the hunt campaigned deep into the mountain wilds, disregarding the lateness of the year and the inclemency of the weather.

When Lord Onosh had won the rule of the Collosnon Empire (something he had done by adroitly masterminding a potent combination of witchcraft, conspiracy and murder) he had made Gendormargensis his capital, as had all the rulers of the empire before him. The city commanded the strategic gap between the Sarapine Ranges and the Balardade Massif, and hence was ideally placed to control all intercourse between the eastern hill country and the widespreading western flatlands dominated by the Yolantarath River.

Since no wild animal of any consequence had been seen anywhere near Gendormargensis for a generation or more, when Lord Onosh went hunting he necessarily rode into the mountains in pursuit of bandits.

The lord of the Collosnon Empire had sported after bandits so often that very few were left; indeed, such two-legged prey were so scarce that one wit had lightly proposed that they be declared a protected species. But Lord Onosh persisted in hunting to the highground to capture and to kill, seeking the last of the lawless in their mountain retreats.

On this occasion, the emperor hunted for a full ten days without success, until at last his party surprised a bandit encampment. There bandits they fought and bandits they killed, though some of the lawless escaped from this first attack.

The first attack was led by Thodric Jarl, the grey-bearded uitlander who was renowned as the mightiest of the Witchlord's warriors. In that autumn, the autumn of the year Alliance 4305, Thodric Jarl was only 24 years of age, yet he was as grey as gnarled death and as cold in his killing as icelock rapture or midwinter famine.

Cleaving the air with bloodstroke upon bloodstroke, Jarl made his bitter steel sing. He hacked the bandit leader down, then claimed for himself the choicest treasure found in the bandit camp — a thing of female gender which named itself Yerzerdayla.

The female thing was brought in chains to the imperial battle base, where it was seen by the young Guest Gulkan, the self-styled Weaponmaster, he who at the age of 14 laid claim to a man's estate, though he was still possessed of much of a child's impetuous unreliability. Guest Gulkan stood in his muddy boots, smelling like a slaughterhouse, and gaped at Yerzerdayla. For this captive slave — dressed in silks and chained by jade clasped with silverbright — looked more like an imperial aristocrat than one of common flesh.

"I am in love," said Guest, who was of a certainty in lust.

Such was the first meeting of Guest Gulkan and the elegant Yerzerdayla, she of the blonde body and the perfumed hair.

Then:

"Who is the woman?" asked Guest.

"She is a thing claimed already by Thodric Jarl," answered Yerzerdayla's keepers.

"Claim he may," said Guest. "But I will have!"

In fact, it would have been politic for Guest Gulkan to lose interest in any flesh owned by any killer as grim and humourless as Thodric Jarl. But Guest, in those days of his ego, felt free to conduct himself like the imperial heir he was not. So he sought out Thodric Jarl, meaning to demand the surrender of the woman Yerzerdayla.

Young Guest found Jarl supervising the forced labours of the surviving male prisoners, who were digging the pits in which they would shortly be buried alive. It was cold, but Jarl was warm in a weather jacket bought from the emperor's league riders — uitlander mercenaries every bit as barbarous as himself. The prisoners were also warm, for under Jarl's surveillance they were digging themselves into a mass of sweat and blisters.

"Ho, Jarl!" said Guest.

"Ho!" said Jarl.

"I'd like a word with you," said Guest.

"Then speak," said Jarl.

So far, so good; for at least they had exchanged several civil words without swapping threats of violence. Given that both were extremely dangerous men — Guest being at that age a danger mostly to himself, whereas Jarl was a menace to other people — that was something to be thankful for.

Now Guest had long been tutored in diplomacy by Hostaja Sken-Pitilkin. The excellent Sken-Pitilkin had introduced Guest to all those notions central to successful negotiation; but Guest was a poor student, and proved it by botching his confrontation with Thodric Jarl.

When Jarl refused to give him the woman, Guest did not offer him horses and hogsheads of wine in return; or let the matter drop for the moment; or take no for an answer. Instead, he began to rant, rage and bluster.

"I am Guest Gulkan, son of Onosh Gulkan and rightful heir to the lands of Tameran," said Guest. "How dare you deny me?"

"I dare deny you," said Thodric Jarl, "for you are no heir to anything but the dung which the dogs have crapped on your mother's grave."

"I'll have your blood for that!" said Guest in fury.

"To have you must take," said Jarl.

"Then take I will!" said Guest, lugging out his sword.

But the sword was only half-lugged when Jarl gave young Guest a push which sent him staggering backwards. Guest found empty air beneath his boot — and fell. The boy Guest fell backwards into a pit which four bandits were excavating. These four exhausted wretches thought Guest had jumped down among them with murder his intent. Despairing of life, they nevertheless put up as much of a fight as they could, and Guest was put to the necessity of killing them before he could scramble out of the pit.

As Guest was scrambling, Jarl kicked him under the chin, sending him tumbling backwards on to the cushion of the corpses he had so recently created.

"Nicely timed," said the dwarf Glambrax, who was following this conflict with the interest of a born spectator.

"I've had practice," said Jarl.

"That wasn't fair," said Guest, looking up from the blood and muck at the bottom of the pit.

"Neither is this," said Jarl, picking up a huge rock which required both hands to lift it.

"You wouldn't dare," said Guest, doing his best to sneer at the rock.

Jarl dared.

He hurled the rock down on the hapless Weaponmaster.

Guest screamed. He couldn't help himself! He threw up both hands in a hopeless attempt to protect himself.

The rock smashed into his hands.

And burst into fragments, for in the proof of the impact it

proved to be no rock at all, but, rather, a cohesive mass of earth.

As Guest was spitting out bits of earth — he had been screaming as the stuff smashed into his arms, and in consequence had been gifted with a mouthful of the stuff — Thodric Jarl completed his victory by pissing on the unfortunate Weaponmaster.

Thus Guest met Jarl in combat, and was defeated, which was only to be expected. For Jarl was as handy with fist and boot as he was with edged weapons; whereas Guest, though he had long studied the art of the boast under the guidance of Rolf Thelemite, was no match for the professional brutality of Thodric Jarl.

In the disappointment of his defeat, Guest lacked the sense to abandon his woman-quest. Instead, once he had rescued himself from the pit, Guest Gulkan went to his father to demand revenge upon Jarl, and to demand likewise the possession of Yerzerdayla's loins.

The young Weaponmaster discovered Lord Onosh seated outdoors by a roaring bonfire, snuggled against the weather in the warm folds of a snow-coat. The emperor was feeding upon a fine wheat loaf which smelt as if it had just been freshly baked, as indeed it had, for the imperial master chef Pelagius Zozimus had been giving a bravura display of field cookery.

"Father," said Guest, without preamble, and without asking permission to speak.

Lord Onosh tossed the remains of the machet to the dwarf Glambrax, who had already given him a vibrant account of the epic battle between the man Jarl and the boy Guest. Glambrax pretended to rape his fresh-caught trophy. As the dwarf performed, Lord Onosh turned his attention to Guest Gulkan.

"So," said the Witchlord, "the larger of my two fools has decided to put in an appearance. What tricks will it play for us today?"

"My lord," said Guest, doing his best to ignore this sally, "I have a need for justice."

"You," said Lord Onosh, looking him up and down, "have a need for a bath."

"A bath?" said Guest in astonishment.

"You know the word, do you not?" said Lord Onosh. "It denotes a thorough lavage of the body, a task best accomplished by immersing the said body in a tub of warm water. In your case, the use of wire brushes and sandpaper might also be advisable."

"My lord jests," said Guest, who had had his last bath only three years previously, and was not due for another until high summer two years hence.

"You have obviously not seen yourself in a mirror," said Lord Onosh. "Glambrax! In the absence of a mirror, describe the boy to himself!"

"My lord," said Glambrax, accepting this assignment. "The boy looks like an over-large turd excreted by a menstruating dog, a turd which has been rolled to excess in a slime of dead cockroaches at the bottom of a giant's spittoon."

"You dislike my appearance," said Guest. "Why, then know Thodric Jarl to be the cause of it!"

"That much I have heard," said Lord Onosh, imperturbably. "When you see that good gentleman, be sure to thank him for the lessons he has taught you."

"The lessons?" said Guest in astonishment.

"You have learnt, I hope, not to fight with a pit at your back. That is the first lesson, and doubtless meditation will reveal others of equal importance. But enough of the lessons! Pray tell — what started your quarrel in the first place?"

Guest, having a delicate matter to broach, should now have asked for privacy — as he knew, for the scholarly Sken-Pitilkin had taught him as much. But, instead, the foolish youth got right to the meat of the matter.

"There is a woman," said Guest.

"At your age," said Lord Onosh, "there is always a woman. Such is the nature of youth."

"Always?" said Guest. "Not so! For I have had fewer than fifty women in my whole life."

In the very act of denying sexual experience, Guest Gulkan exaggerated it — for he was almost a virgin, having made the panting dog, the two-legged head and the beast with two backs with a bare two dozen women in his life. The exact number of Guest Gulkan's liaisons was precisely known to Lord Onosh, for the young Weaponmaster had never yet lived unobserved. Hence Lord Onosh knew full well that Guest exaggerated, and was not unconscious of the adolescent insecurity which occasioned the exaggeration.

"Fewer than fifty women," said Lord Onosh. "So speaks the child!"

"You call me a child?" said Guest.

In truth, Guest Gulkan was scarcely half-hatched. For, as Bankers and others have long since established, true maturity only begins at the age of twenty-seven, if then. But Lord Onosh did not quote Guest's age against him. Instead:

"Anyone who still treats his affairs with women as an exercise in arithmetic can scarcely claim to have reached an age of maturity," said Lord Onosh.

"Can we discuss this in private?" said Guest, belatedly remembering Sken-Pitilkin's advice.

"Since you so rudely interrupted me in public, no," said Lord Onosh.

"Why not?" said Guest.

"As a punishment for your insolence!" said Lord Onosh. "If you come here to ask for a woman then ask for her, and the answer is no, you can't have her, particularly not if she belongs to Thodric Jarl."

"Who said she belongs to Jarl?" said Guest.

"If she occasioned your quarrel, who else could she possibly belong to? Sken-Pitilkin, perhaps?"

"The woman is but a slave," said Guest sullenly. "A slave, a thing of no possible importance."

"It is but a thing which belongs to Thodric Jarl," said Lord Onosh.

"He claimed it," protested Guest, "but all booty from bandits is yours. Thus runs the law."

Thus ran the law indeed, but by quoting it the young Weaponmaster merely proved his poor grasp of the politics of an imperial court much beset by assassins. Like Rolf Thelemite,

Thodric Jarl was a Rovac warrior, and hence his sword was of inestimable value.

To Guest, his father's few Rovac warriors had no value beyond their novelty, and hence were disposable. But to Lord Onosh, these uitlanders were valued bodyguards who, unlike the Yarglat, could be trusted not to embroil themselves in the local clan-struggles. So while Guest thought Jarl could be cheated with impunity, his father thought otherwise; for Lord Onosh relied upon Jarl for the security of his sleep.

"Mine to give, mine to bestow," agreed Lord Onosh. "So I bestow the thing on Thodric Jarl."

"If I could" said Guest, rage overmastering sanity, "I would fight you and kill you."

"You would, would you?" said Lord Onosh coldly.

Guest realised his error.

But there was no unsaying such words.

"I would," said Guest, struggling to match his courage to the impetuosity of his tongue.

"Then I will meet you by proxy in Gendormargensis," said Lord Onosh. "I will be represented in the challenge by Thodric Jarl, who will hack down your pride and leave it bloody on the stones."

Guest Gulkan absorbed the implications of this, and backed off, his mouth opening and closing soundlessly. Then he turned on his heel and fled.

"Where are my camp marshals?" said Lord Onosh, rising to his feet, his face as thunder.

The marshals were produced, and the emperor gave them his orders.

"Ready the camp for the move," said he. "We ride before dusk and we ride by dark once night has come upon us."

"But, my lord," ventured one of the marshals, "there is tonight no moon."

"So we ride by dark," said Lord Onosh. "We ride by dark, as I said we would. If I must say it again then I will kill someone!"

And, since no-one doubted that the emperor would be as good as his word, ride they did — and soon!

CHAPTER TWO

Name: Eljuk Zala Gulkan

Birthplace: Gendormargensis

Occupation: student

Status: heir to the Collosnon Empire

Description: timorous Yarglat male, undersized at a height of 9 qua. He is so birthmarked that he appears to have let a mouthful of purple wine dribble from the corners of his mouth then flow to a merging at his throat. But his most remarkable aspect is surely his ears, which are small — a singular oddity considering his father's gargantuan head-flaps and the size of the equally ostentatious protuberances flaunted by his brothers Morsh and Guest.

Hobby: the memorization and word-perfect recital of the more elegant kinds of lyric poetry.

Quote: "I don't really want to be emperor, but I suppose it's no worse than what most people have to put up with."

* * *

Thus in his anger the emperor rode forth in pursuit of those bandits who had escaped his earlier attack. Riding with all the ferocity of Obela Ukma, the warrior of legend who had sought to outpace his own mortality, Lord Onosh and his party performed prodigies of roughground speedleaguing in the days that followed.

The first ice of the oncoming winter smashed beneath the hooves of their horses as they chased bandits from high-ground to low. The stars of the night sharpened to needles, intolerably cold in their burning.

Cold, frost, ice and steaming breath — these things reminded Lord Onosh of his childhood. He punctured a vein to draw blood from his horse, and sucked down that blood, and the heavy taste brought to mind the ordeals of his youth. He looked up at the stars, the stars so cold and remote in the scorn of their burning. Stars of cold green — as cold and green as jade under water. Chips of blue opal. Lambent red and sullen-sulphur purple.

Those stars—

Lord Onosh knelt to a pool of dark water by night, knelt to the stars, knelt to the bright gold and the needlework of liquid silver, to the bloodline-brightness of scarlet and the dull vulcanism of cooling lava. The shadow of his head blotted out the stars as he knelt, and the shadow was faceless, eyeless, noseless, and in that moment Lord Onosh knew.

—I am going to die.

As the Witchlord Onosh knelt to the water by night he realized that he was going to die. He was going to die, and die not far from here. A death by water would take him, thrust him under, haul him down and suck him under. He was going to drown, quenched by water, smothered, suffocated, gulping slime and groping for the light. He was doomed, dead, a dead man with but a day or so to breathe.

Carefully, trying to silence his terror, or at least to control it, Lord Onosh took the leather glove from his right hand and dipped his hand to the water. The water was so cold that it burnt his flesh — as if the flesh lacked skin. The Witchlord cupped water in his hand, then brought it to his mouth. It was cold, so cold that he expected it to bright-spark pain from those few teeth which remained to him. But there was no pain.

Lord Onosh held the water in his mouth to let it warm before he swallowed. Then swallow he did, and rose, looking at the men who sat faceless on their horses in the shadows of the stars.

"How is the Blood of the Earth?" said Morsh Bataar, speaking from the height of his horse.

The Blood of the Earth. The old and formal term for water. It spoke of a learning of the Yarglat legends which Lord Onosh had not known his son to possess.

"It is as it should be," said Lord Onosh. Then, testing his son, he said: "The blood is the blood, and the earth is a horse for our horse."

"The wind is its voice, and the wind is the measure of our riding," answered Morsh, catching the legend-line reference and responding in kind.

Then Lord Onosh said: "As the horse is ours, so the blood is ours."

It was an invitation to drink.

Now to this there was a response that could be lifted from the legend-lines of the Yarglat mythos. A young man ardent in his ambition could answer thus: "My father may drink from the blood of the horse, but I will drink blood." That line, savage in its implications, is among the Yarglat one of the traditional challenges of youth to age. But Morsh Bataar said:

"My lord is a great provider, and in the hunger of our victory I will eat."

That also was traditional, but of course it was not a challenge — rather, it was an acknowledgement of fealty.

"Sa-so!" said Guest, who had no learning of legends with which to trifle. "My brother is a horse and my father likewise, but the bandits escape us while we gossip."

Though many had already been brought to collapse by the wrenching rigours of the hunt, the arrogant impatience of Guest's aggression spoke of slaughter-strength confidence with strength yet to spare.

Hearing that shallow arrogance, that impatient slaughter-strength, Lord Onosh knew.

He knew it for a fact.

—This is the man who will kill me.

Guest Gulkan was going to drown him, was going to press him under the waters and hold him there until he died, and so he would never get back to Gendormargensis alive. This could not be denied. Lord Onosh had the Gift of Seeing. Lord Onosh knew his death.

—So what does it feel like, this death?

In the face of his death, Lord Onosh found himself angry. He was not ready to die. He was 43, no older. The prime of life! The prime of power! And — and Eljuk! Lord Onosh bitterly resented the thought of Eljuk's death, knowing that his favoured son must surely die once Guest had accomplished the Witchlord's murder.

Lord Onosh stood in the dark, tasting his own anger, his rage at his own mortality.

"Does my lord want his sketch pad?" said Guest Gulkan, managing to pack supreme arrogance and insult into a single sentence, while conveying his impatience besides.

"The artists will have work to do," said Lord Onosh, "when they have a corpse to work on."

Lord Onosh hoped that Guest Gulkan would remember those words in times thereafter, and would know that the Witchlord had gone to his death knowingly.

Having delivered himself of these words, Lord Onosh mounted up and led the hunt on at starlight pace, which is slow yet remorseless, and guarantees the capture of any quarry which lingers to sleep by night.

Guest Gulkan followed on behind his father, and as they picked their way through the dark, Guest had the strangest sensation ... he felt himself half-immersed in a river, his father's head heavy in his hands. Then Guest knew. He had had such visions in the past, and always they had been reliably predictive of the future. The Witchlord Onosh was doomed to die near here, to die in the Yolantarath, drowned in its waters. He was doomed. He was as good as dead.

—So how does it feel, this death?

Guest asked himself that question as he followed along behind his father.

He felt ... confused. He did not think that he wished his father dead. But even so. His father had denied him so much, had denied him so often. And just that very day, why, anger had brought the two to the point of murder. If Lord Onosh survived this hunt, then Guest was doomed to fight his proxy in Gendormargensis.

—So better that he die.

Thus thought Guest. And the thought was cold, hard, inescapable. Cold as crystal. Cold as a diamond plucked from the heart of a witch. Let Lord Onosh die. Then Eljuk would become emperor. And Eljuk ... for some reason, when Guest thought of Eljuk he thought of butter.

So they went on through the night. Lord Onosh knew himself doomed to die by drowning, and knew his son Guest to be his murderer. Guest Gulkan did not yet know that he was to be the instrument of his father's death, but he knew of a certainty that his father would drown, would be swallowed by the Yolantarath, would become mud and worms, a bloated corpse lost in the farrow-furrow toils of the river's filth.

So the Witchlord Onosh and his son the Weaponmaster hunted bandits through the mountains, both possessed of visionary knowledge of an unavoidable death, and at last in daylight they and their company ran the bandits to ground by the banks of the Yolantarath River.

By this time, the mighty hunting party which had left Gendormargensis was strung out over the better part of fifty leagues of wilderness, for only the young and the reckless had been able to keep up with the emperor on this madcap chase.

So it was that the odds were even when the imperial party met the bandits by the riverside.

Then fear fell away from the Witchlord. So he was to die, was he? Well, then it would be over soon, and quickly. The worst thing was the waiting, and the waiting was over.

"Pelagius, my good man," said the Witchlord Onosh, seeing that his master chef had kept pace with the leaders of the hunting party. "It is a good day to die."

Pelagius laughed.

"It is a good day, my lord," said Pelagius. "And I do not think either of us dead before the end of it."

Then Pelagius Zozimus unhooded the falcon which was bound to his wrist, kissed the bird, then let it loose, and laughed again as it rose to the blinding brightness of the sun. Lord Onosh laughed likewise, then the pair spurred their horses and charged, for both of these warriors had been seized of a sudden by a mad intoxication, the exhilaration of an all-or-nothing gamble.

"Hold, Eljuk!" cried Morsh Bataar, as Eljuk Zala spurred his own horse, grimly bent on following his father.

But Eljuk Zala paid no heed, for he was determined to go wherever his father did. So Morsh slashed the rope which restrained the one surviving spare horse which trailed along behind him, then rode in pursuit.

The leading riders went crashing into the ranks of the bandits. Horses fell and men screamed.

"The river!" screamed someone. "He's in the river!"

Who was in the river?

Guest Gulkan heard the cry, and remembered his visionary certainty. His father was going to drown.

And suddenly Guest knew:

He did not want to see his father dead.

But it was fated. It would happen whether Guest wanted it to happen or not.

"Then the hell with fate!" said Guest.

And, setting himself against fate, destiny and the course of history, Guest Gulkan spurred his horse. Which reared, and received in its flesh an arrow which had been aimed at its master. Down went the horse, down, a mountain falling, an avalanche of bloody mortality, and Guest was thrown, sent sprawling.

Guest Gulkan groped to his feet, mud in his eyes, the world a whirl of watering confusion. A bandit was charging him.

"Ga!" screamed Guest.

The bandit hacked at him with a woodcutter's axe. But an arrow took the man in the throat, and Guest hacked off his head as he died. No time to take a scalp! Lord Onosh was in the river, was drowning, and Guest had to save him. Had to! Panting heavily, Guest charged wildly through the floundering mud, bracing his way through the confusion of battle.

All around was chaos, as knots of disordered men fought each other with screams and curses. Guest tried to blink the mud from his watering eyes, and caught a bleary glimpse of the bright-flashing armour of Pelagius Zozimus. Heard Rolf Thelemite screaming in fear-flushed panic as he tried to hold a brace of bandits at bay single-handed.

Rolf saw Guest.

And screamed:

"Help me!"

Then Guest had to choose.

His friend or his father.

Guest chose his father.

Ignoring Rolf Thelemite's plight, Guest struggled through the mud to the banks of the Yolantarath River. Down in the water was a horse, a floundering animal wild-eyed in panic, its body rent with wounds, its blood staining the brown murk of the river. Struggling in the water was a man.

"Blood!" said Guest.

He was bent on saving his father, but — he could not swim!

"Blood of a billion bitches!" said Guest.

Then the Weaponmaster took his sword in a two-handed grip and struck a mighty blow, driving the blade deep into the mud of his father's empire.

"Death or victory!" said Guest.

Then he slithered down the bank and plunged into the water, even as the man in the river's grip lost his hold on his horse and slid beneath the waters.

The waters mobbed around the Weaponmaster. The terror-stricken horse rolled its eyes and did its best to bite him. Guest whacked it with his fist, then waded into the river, first waist-deep then neck-deep, feeling for his father with his feet.

Guest stubbed his toe on his father's flesh, grabbed a mouthful of air, then ducked down and seized the man by the hair. Gods, he was heavy! Guest hauled, pulled, floundered, tried for purchase in the mud, got the man under the armpits — armour his flanks, and heavy, yes! — and boosted the man to the air.

Guest gasped for air.

"Father," he said.

The man was safe, had been saved, was safe in Guest Gulkan's grip. But he was starting to struggle! He was screaming, and struggling convulsively. Guest felt his boots slipping. He was up to his neck in the river. A river-wave slapped his face. If his father was not quieted, he would have them both drowned and dead.

Guest slipped deeper yet, and panic claimed him.

He screamed, incoherent in the agony of his panic.

The struggling pair were seen by Thodric Jarl, some thirty

paces down the riverbank. Since Jarl was faced by imminent battle, he might as well have been distant by infinity. But Jarl summed the situation in a glimpse and found time enough to roar:

"Guest! Guest! Slam the bastard!"

The command came to Guest Gulkan as if from far off, like something shouted through a huge and fumbling thickness of fog.

But once said—

Blam!

Guest slammed his father, crunched the screaming face with a fist, crunched it hard. Then dragged the man closer inshore. A monstrous weight he made, but Guest dragged him successfully. Then they slipped into a hole.

Water buried them.

Guest slogged along underwater, one pace, two, a third, and up, up out of the hole and into the slash of the sun.

And the man in his arms screamed and thrashed, and clawed at him, and tried to bite off his nose. And suddenly Guest realized it was Eljuk, his brother Eljuk. He had risked his life, and risked it for Eljuk! Eljuk, of all people! And now Eljuk was fighting him in the frenzy of his panic!

"Gods!" said Guest, enraged.

Then slammed Eljuk in the face with his fist.

Then slammed him again.

Eljuk boggled, and went limp.

Then Guest acknowledged his deep and pressing jealousy of his brother, and slammed him one last time for luck, and was amazed to find how good that made him feel.

Then came the hard and brutal slog-work, the dragging of the semi-conscious Eljuk from the waters and the hauling of the semi-conscious Eljuk up the steep and muddy bank of the Yolantarath. Swearing with every step, Guest encompassed the task. At the top of the riverbank, he dropped the whimpering Eljuk in the mud, kicked him once for luck, then looked around for his sword.

His sword!

Where was his sword?

Guest Gulkan was weaponless, and a battle was in progress. The sword — it was twenty paces distant, for the Yolantarath had carried the two brothers downstream as they struggled in the water.

Guest went for his sword and won it. No sooner had he won the weapon than a man was upon him.

"Ahyak Rovac!" screamed the man.

"Rolf!" cried Guest, recognizing that battle-cry.

It was indeed Rolf Thelemite, so bloody from a gash in his forehead that he was unrecognizable, and was fighting blind. He fell into Guest's arms, and, with the battle dying down, Guest began to search his friend for wounds.

Apart from minor gashes (bloody, spectacular, but no immediate threat to life) Rolf Thelemite appeared to be in one piece. By the time Guest had assured himself of that, the battle was over — with all the bandits dead, for none had been given quarter.

"Your brother," said Rolf, recovering himself somewhat. "Your brother. He's dead."

"Eljuk?" said Guest. "But I just pulled him out of the river!"

"Not Eljuk!" said Rolf. "Morsh!"

Then Guest helped Rolf Thelemite to his feet, and the two went in search of Morsh Bataar. Rolf had seen Morsh go down and his horse fall on top of him, so presumed the young man to be dead. But when they found the body it opened its eyes then spoke to them.

"Will you shift this horse?" said Morsh Bataar. "For it's died on top of me, and I think my leg is broken."

Guest and Rolf called for help, and the Witchlord Onosh came over to them, called others to their aid, and had the horse shifted.

"It hurts like a bitch," said Morsh Bataar, tears of pain in his eyes. "It's the leg. The left leg."

Lord Onosh drew his scalping knife and cut away the clothing which guarded the left leg. The thigh was prodigiously bruised and swollen with blood, and Morsh Bataar was crying from the pain.

"It's death," said Morsh, acknowledging the truth of his own injury.

Lord Onosh rose without a word. He knew the injury was as good as death. Unless—

"Zozimus!" roared the Witchlord.

The wizard Pelagius Zozimus advanced and saluted his emperor. There was blood and mud on the wizard's fishscale armour, but Zozimus looked nonetheless lordly.

"My lord," said Zozimus.

"Zozimus," said Lord Onosh, pointing at Morsh Bataar. "I charge you with the healing of my son."

Pelagius Zozimus bent to the injury. When he was ready to speak, he rose to his full height to address his emperor on equal footing.

"Your son is a dead man," said Zozimus bluntly. "There is not the skill in Gendormargensis to heal him."

"You are a wizard, are you not?" said Lord Onosh. "A worker of magic. A worker of miracles. Is the emperor to be denied a miracle on his request?"

"I am no god to undo what the gods have fated," said Zozimus. "I have but some poor and wretched art of necromancy at my command. I have it in my power to have the corpses of this battlefield stumbling in their blood, their shambles but a parody of life. And that — and that is all."

"It cannot be all," said Lord Onosh.

"My lord," said Zozimus, "were wizardry an art of miracle, would I abandon wizardry for cookery? Not so. Yet such was my choice."

"Choice, choice," said Lord Onosh. "Look at me! What choice have I got? My son's life or my wizard's. He lives or dies, but if he dies then you die too."

"We must get him to Gendormargensis," said Guest, who was bent on seeing Morsh healed, and who associated healing with warm rooms and sickbeds.

"No!" said Zozimus sharply.

"You heard my father," said Guest, angered so much that he

was almost ready to slaughter down the wizard on the spot. "His life or yours."

"Or both," said Zozimus. "I heard him. But we must not move the boy. To move him is to kill him."

"He can't stay here!" said Guest, looking around at the sprawling river, the blood-punctuated mud, the bleary sky, the horizon encumbered with mountainous hills, and the silent swordsmen now starting to shiver as their sweat cooled towards slime.

"Give him a chance," said Zozimus, speaking harshly from a throat still dry from battle. "Give Morsh a chance. If Morsh stays here then he does have a chance — albeit a slim one. But if you haul him back to Gendormargensis then he dies of a certainty, and I die with him."

"Then he stays," said Lord Onosh. "And I stay with him. To work, Zozimus! Get on with it!"

"A tent," said Zozimus. "I need a tent. Guest! Backtrack! Along our track you'll find horses with tents. Morsh himself had one such last night, though it was not in his keeping this morning. Ride back and find such, for such is your brother's survival."

"I go," said Guest, bowing to Zozimus's imperative.

Thus Guest went, and Zozimus was much relieved to see him go, for there was no telling how much damage the boy might have done in his fear for his brother's life. Then Zozimus called for horseblankets; and firewood; and for dead horses to be heaped up as a temporary windbreak while shelter more permanent was sought.

When Guest had gone, Morsh Bataar said through the tears of his pain:

"The man's not as tough as he thought."

Here Morsh was speaking of himself. The Yarglat do not readily admit to pain, and only by thus referring to it in the third person could Morsh Bataar admit to the grief of his agony.

"We none of us are," said his father.

For the Witchlord Onosh had known pain and knew the truth of it: there is no thing worse.

Then:

"It hurts," said Morsh Bataar, in frank confession of his pain.

Then, unable to help himself, Morsh Bataar cried out, gasping with pain — gasping in the inarticulate agony of the flesh. Lord Onosh wiped the cold sweat from his son's forehead, and Pelagius Zozimus, unable to bear this sight for any longer, withdrew to the riverbank to think.

The grey-bearded Thodric Jarl went with him, hoping he would try to escape, for Jarl had a deep-felt hatred of wizards, and would welcome any excuse to murder him.

"The break is bad," said Zozimus, who usually shunned Jarl as if the man were death incarnate — as well he might prove if things took a turn for the worse.

"Very bad," said Jarl, with grim satisfaction.

"Still," said Zozimus, "men have lived through as much."

"No men that I know of," said Jarl.

"Then Morsh Bataar will be the first," said Zozimus, trying to pretend to a confidence which he did not actually feel.

Pelagius Zozimus was no healer, for he had never studied to be either bonesetter or pox doctor. Zozimus was a wizard of the order of Xluzu, a necromancer whose skills allowed him to animate the dead. This filthy and dispiriting work he had long ago abandoned in favour of cookery, for he disliked death. Equally, he disliked disease, injury, deformation, and every other debasement and degradation of the flesh.

Yet—

Zozimus had ever been a great scholar, and in the course of learning about death he had learnt much about life, for the study of death is necessarily the study of corpses and skeletons, which is an excellent way to learn about the living.

In the Castle of Ultimate Peace, a mighty fortress by the flame trench of Drangsturm, the order of Xluzu had long maintained a great collection of skeletons, which included the bones of a sailor who had died of rabies after being bitten by his mother-in-law's dog. In youth, this sailor had broken his thighbone after falling from a mast, and had spent four months lying in his bunk while he recovered from the injury.

In the course of the sailor's cure, a huge bolus of bone had knitted together the fractured ends of his thighbone, which had been out of alignment by as much as the width of two fingers. The result had produced a very strange skeleton, but when healed the leg had been normal enough to facilitate the bestriding of decks and the kicking of dogs.

So Jarl's pessimism was not necessarily predictive.

If Morsh Bataar was lugged to Gendormargensis, he would doubtless die from the rigours of the journey, but if he could be kept just where he was, if he could be clothed and cleaned and warmed and fed, sheltered from the elements and—

"You know," said Jarl, "while you sit here, Morsh is dying."

"So you tell me," said Zozimus.

"He's dying of pain, you fool," said Jarl, unable to restrain himself any longer. "Pain is the breaking of men, and kills when wounds alone would not."

Jarl wanted to see Zozimus fail and die. But Jarl had ever liked Morsh Bataar for his steadiness and his leisured good humour, and did not want to see him die in a delirium of agony. The relief of his pain would probably not save his life, but might at least ease his parting.

Zozimus took the hint.

"Opium!" said Zozimus, slapping his thigh as he named the best kind of pain relief he knew. Then: "Send to the city for Sken-Pitilkin!" said he, knowing his fellow wizard was never far away from a supply of the peace of the poppy. "Send for Sken-Pitilkin," said Zozimus, "and tell him to bring us his opium."

"Your word," said Jarl, "is my command."

And he turned to obey.

So Sken-Pitilkin was sent for, and brought as directed, arriving late in the afternoon of the following day after a ride so rigorous it had almost killed him. There was no problem in finding the campsite, for by now there were hundreds encamped by the river, with a steady stream of incoming stragglers filtering out of the hills. To feed this multitude, Lord Onosh had commandeered a string of barges which had been coming down the Yolantarath, deeply laden with some of the spoils of the autumn harvest in the east.

Guest Gulkan himself greeted Sken-Pitilkin on his arrival, and led him to Pelagius Zozimus. No longer was Zozimus glorious, for his bright-shining armour had been mired by the splattering muck of the encampment, and the dervish wildness of his bloodshot eyes, combined with his unkempt condition, made him look three parts lunatic.

"What took you so long?" said Zozimus, when Sken-Pitilkin arrived.

For in all that time Zozimus had seldom strayed out of earshot from Morsh Bataar, and much which the sleepless wizard had heard while within earshot had been far from pleasant.

"What took me so long?" said Sken-Pitilkin. "Why, first I had to be born, and then—"

"That's nonsense enough," said Zozimus. "Have you brought the opium?"

"Yes," said Sken-Pitilkin. "But I must see our patient before I dispense it."

"It is peace," said Zozimus impatiently, for after listening to Morsh Bataar's agony he wanted peace for the man more than anything else.

"It is peace," agreed Sken-Pitilkin. "But sometimes death is the measure of that peace."

Then the two wizards went to see Morsh Bataar.

From the gruesome account of Morsh Bataar's injury which had been delivered to him in Gendormargensis, Hostaja Sken-Pitilkin had got the impression that the boy's broken thighbone had ruptured through the skin, an injury which would have virtually guaranteed his death.

But on being admitted to the tent which sheltered the boy, Sken-Pitilkin found the skin unbroken. Battalions of leeches were feasting on the thigh, doing their best to suck every drop of blood from the injured limb.

"It was Jarl who insisted on the leeches," said Zozimus. "We've had half a thousand people looking for them, and still they look for more, though leeches in such quantity must surely kill."

"The blood must be drawn from the wound," said Sken-Pitilkin equitably, "and the leech is a precision instrument superbly designed for that express purpose. How do you feel, Morsh?"

Morsh Bataar spoke his pain in pain, spoke it in a mewling cry which evidenced long torture and the imminence of death. His pain was the measure of his strength, for a weaker man would have long since lost the power of protest.

"The opium," said Zozimus impatiently.

"There is more to healing than ramming strong drugs down the throats of your patients," said Sken-Pitilkin.

"But Jarl said——"

"Since when do wizards command themselves by the sayings of the Rovac?" said Sken-Pitilkin sharply.

"I am in danger of my life," said Zozimus, "hence will command myself by whoever knows best."

"Then be commanded by me," said Sken-Pitilkin, endeavouring to calm the Witchlord's over-agitated slug-chef. "Be commanded, for I fancy that I have more of the healing arts than have you."

"So you say," said Zozimus. "But Jarl says that pain will be the death of the boy even if nothing else kills him."

"The pain," said Sken-Pitilkin, "is consequent upon the fracture. The boy's bone is broken."

"That much I have divined," said Zozimus stiffly.

"The bone of the thigh lies broken in the flesh," said Sken-Pitilkin, continuing in his best classroom manner. "With the bone broken, the muscles of the leg strive to shorten the leg. Thus broken bone is pulled against broken bone, and the result is an agony your most expert torturer would be hard put to better."

"Why," said Zozimus, in sarcastic imitation of admiration, "you speak with the fluency of a very pox doctor!"

"Thus have I made my living in the past," said Sken-Pitilkin, admitting this secret without shame. "It is the truth, Pelagius. A broken bone is no big thing in itself, but the gritting together of the ends of the bone is living hell."

"So," said Zozimus, seeing the nature of the cure now that he understood the problem, "we must separate the ends of the broken bones to ease the pain of our patient. Do you think your wizardry the equal to the task?"

"I would not trust my wizardry with a tenth of it," said Sken-Pitilkin, who, as a wizard of Skatzabratzumon — an order dedicated to the mastery of the mysteries of levitation — had no special powers relevant to the cure of the flesh. "Still, mere mechanical skill may succeed where wizardry fails. I believe I can build something efficient for our purposes. Guest! Guest Gulkan! Where are you, boy?"

Guest Gulkan manifested himself in response to this shout, and, at Sken-Pitilkin's orders, mustered up a raiding party. Sken-Pitilkin led this party aboard one of the barges tied up by the riverbank — the barges earlier commandeered by the Witchlord for the feeding of his multitude — and this barge they then looted thoroughly.

"What now?" said Zozimus, once the looting was done, and Sken-Pitilkin had a great heap of rope, sticks, spars, planks and sailcloth at his disposal.

"Now?" said Sken-Pitilkin. "We build!"

As the power to levitate objects can be enhanced by the adroit use of pulleys, levers and inclined planes, wizards of the order of Skatzabratzumon had long been diligent in their studies of such devices, and Sken-Pitilkin was well equipped to oversee the building of a stretching machine. Under his supervision, men worked through the night, and by dawn had finished the thing. The contraption looked very like a torturer's rack, and worked on exactly the same principle.

"Tenderly, now," said Sken-Pitilkin, as his team of well-briefed assistants gathered around the recumbent Morsh Bataar. "Guest. Thodric. Secure the harness."

Working as carefully as they could, Guest Gulkan and Thodric Jarl secured Morsh Bataar's shoulders and the foot of his injured leg in the padded imprisonment of leather harness-work.

"Ready?" said Sken-Pitilkin. "Very well. On my command, begin to pull. Steady but sure."

"Don't!" cried Morsh Bataar, piteous in his fear. "Don't hurt me!"

"This is not pain but its cure," said Sken-Pitilkin. "Guest. Thodric. Are you ready? Well — remember you work against muscle, so be ready for resistance. On the count of three. One. And two. And three."

Then Thodric Jarl and Guest Gulkan applied their strength, the one hauling on the foot of the injured leg, the other pulling back on the shoulders.

Morsh Bataar screamed.

"Steady, boys!" said Sken-Pitilkin.

"You're hurting him," said Eljuk Zala, advancing on Guest Gulkan as if to attack him. "Let him go! You're hurting him!"

At that, the sagacious Sken-Pitilkin reached out with his country crook, slipped it round Eljuk Zala's neck, then dragged him backwards. Taken by surprise, Eljuk fell backwards, whereupon the nimble-witted Pelagius Zozimus sat on him.

"Keep it steady, boys," said Sken-Pitilkin. "Now. Slow but sure. Use your strength. He's a strong man, and you work against his greatest muscles. Strength, boys!"

Then Thodric Jarl and Guest Gulkan stretched Morsh Bataar in earnest, and as the two ends of grating bone were dragged apart the most amazing relief came into Morsh Bataar's face.

"A little more," said Sken-Pitilkin. "Just a little more. Right. Hold him! If you let him go, you kill him!"

This was the devilish part of stretching the patient. Once stretched, he must stay stretched, for the broken ends of his own thighbone were weapons which might kill him if he was released from the tension under which he had been placed. Quite apart from the question of pain, the sharp edges of broken bones can be wicked devices for the severing of blood vessels.

"Gather round," said Sken-Pitilkin.

The dwarf Glambrax and the Rovac warrior Rolf Thelemite knelt alongside Morsh Bataar, slipped their hands under his body and awaited the order to lift.

"Pelagius," said Sken-Pitilkin, seeking to command his cousin into action.

"The boy," said Zozimus, who was still sitting on Eljuk Zala. "This boy Eljuk. He's not safe to let loose."

"Then I'll sit on him," said Sken-Pitilkin, and matched deed to word so Pelagius Zozimus could join Glambrax and Rolf Thelemite alongside Morsh Bataar. "On the count of three," said Sken-Pitilkin, speaking from his new-found throne. "One. And two. And three."

Morsh Bataar groaned as he was lifted, then cried out sharply as he was set down on the stretching machine with a slight bump. A slight bump it was to those who were handling him, but Morsh himself — why, poor Morsh felt as if he had just been dropped off a mountain.

"Easy, Morsh," said Sken-Pitilkin. "We're almost done."

Then, while Guest Gulkan and Thodric Jarl maintained the tension on Morsh Bataar's foot and shoulders, keeping the broken ends of his thighbone apart, Sken-Pitilkin supervised the attachment of boot-harness and shoulder-harness to hooks. Ratchets and wheels were used to put both sets of harness under strain, so Morsh was being stretched by foot and shoulders.

"Enough," said Sken-Pitilkin. "Guest. Thodric. Release your hold. Now."

Guest Gulkan let go of Morsh Bataar's shoulder harness and Thodric Jarl released the foot harness.

"Sweet blood," said Jarl, studying Morsh Bataar's face for signs of pain. "It works."

"It works," confirmed Morsh Bataar. "Thank you."

Then he essayed a smile, or tried to. It was more of a grimace than a confirmation of pleasure, but it was a very miracle considering the torments he had been through. Indeed, Morsh Bataar's mere survival was little short of miraculous. But then, the Yarglat are tougher than other peoples, or so they say — though pain is the same for us all, as the very Witchlord himself had acknowledged.

"Well," said Sken-Pitilkin, rising from his seat. "Now we can fetch our emperor to survey the scene of our triumph."

The seat the wizard had risen from was of course the hapless Eljuk Zala, the anointed heir to the Collosnon Empire. Eljuk rose from the mud unsteadily, a swollen leech hanging pendulously from his nose. As he tried to exit from the tent, the Witchlord Onosh entered, and the two collided.

"Ho, boy!" said Lord Onosh. "You need to blow your nose! Well, Zozimus! How is my son! How are you, Morsh? You're looking better. Much better. Grief, what a contraption! What have we here, Zozimus? A siege engine, is it? Is young Morsh to be catapulted to Gendormargensis, or must we drag him?"

"As I said to my lord earlier," said Zozimus, "to move Morsh to the city would be to kill him."

"Ah," said the Witchlord briskly, "but that was before he was lashed to this brilliant machine. I can see the sense of it. Surely now it's only sanity to shift him."

"My lord," said Zozimus, "when the wounded are dragged from the battlefield, then every bump is agony — and by my computation there are half a billion bumps between here and the city."

"So it will hurt a little," said Lord Onosh. "Still, Morsh is a strong man, is he not?"

"Hostaja," said Zozimus, appealing to his cousin. "We can't move the boy, can we?"

Hostaja Sken-Pitilkin considered the question.

"I have not the full skill of an accomplished bonesetter, nor the full depth of a bonesetter's proper experience," said Sken-Pitilkin, "so I cannot answer definitively. But I know for a fact that where the bone has broken there must surely be blood. Blood clots to lumps, so to move the boy may be to break free such lumps. Once free in the flesh they can travel, and jam in the heart, with death as a consequence."

"Then what do you suggest?" said Lord Onosh.

"I suggest that Morsh is safest here," said Sken-Pitilkin. "I vote for no certain decision on chances, but suggest that he stands four chances in five of a quick death should he be shifted to the city. I would not wish to move him much before midwinter, not with the bone so savagely broken."

"Then," said Guest Gulkan bravely, "if Morsh must stay, then I will stay with him, and guard his solitude till then."

It immediately occurred to Lord Onosh that Guest Gulkan might well be volunteering to stay with his brother because he was afraid to return to Gendormargensis. As soon as Guest got back to Gendormargensis, he would have to meet Thodric Jarl in combat, and that combat would in all probability be the end of him.

"Guest," said Lord Onosh, "on the day of our battle against the bandits you saved the life of Eljuk Zala."

"So I did," said Guest, who was no great exponent of the art of modesty. "I dragged him from the river at the risk of my very life."

"That was well done," said Lord Onosh. "As a compliment to your bravery, I offer you any boon within reason."

"Does this mean—"

"It does not mean that you may lay claim to the woman Yerzerdayla. But else you may ask."

The Witchlord fully expected Guest Gulkan to be excused from his coming battle against Thodric Jarl. Now that the tempers of all concerned had had time to cool, Lord Onosh had no wish to see Guest spitted on Jarl's sword, particularly not since Guest was the best hope for the continuation of the family line and the preservation of the empire.

"My lord," said Guest. "I have long wished to be known as the Weaponmaster."

"Since you were a child," agreed Lord Onosh.

"But you have ever denied me such a title," said Guest.

"I have denied it for a very good reason," said Lord Onosh. "The very good reason being that you are the master of no weapon."

"Yet," said Guest, "it is the title I claim. That is the boon I wish from you."

Lord Onosh was quite taken aback by this. Nevertheless, he granted Guest Gulkan what he wanted. And all the way to Gendormargensis, Lord Onosh wondered exactly how his son hoped to survive the encounter with Thodric Jarl to which he had doomed himself.

While the much-wondering Witchlord made his way back to Gendormargensis, the young Weaponmaster trained with his sword on the banks of the Yolantarath. Ever and again Guest Gulkan slashed and sliced, imagining how the mighty razor of his courage would cut down Thodric Jarl to size.

When he was weary with training, Guest made his way back to his tent. Already the campsite stank, and already some dog had managed to die in the middle of it. Rain fell continually, pocking the boot-craters in the slimy grey mud. Guest Gulkan's neighbour's tent lay mortally wounded in the mud.

He looked around.

He saw a bit of river being pissed upon by a fur-shrouded warrior. Mucky grey cloud — much of it. He didn't see the wind, but it saw him. It changed direction smartly and bucketed his face with cold rain.

"Great," said Guest, glowing with confidence and self-satisfaction. "Just beautiful."

What was beautiful above all else was the flatness of the land, the flatness which gave mobility to the horse-troops of the Yarglat, the flatness which had made them the conquerors of the Collosnon Empire.

"This," said Guest, striking a theatrical pose, "is the empire. And I, the Weaponmaster, will make myself lord of it."

No thunder boomed to complement his words, but such was the intensity of Guest's imagination that he fooled himself into believing that he heard such thunder; and he told himself it was a very good omen, and proof of the favour of the gods.

CHAPTER THREE

Name: Thodric Jarl

Birthplace: Rovac

Occupation: mercenary

Status: imperial bodyguard

Description: blunt and decidedly unplayful Rovac warrior, grey of
  eye and grey of beard, though he is as yet far from the years
  of his full maturity — for he is but 24 years of age.

Hobby: cultivating the intimate acquaintance of young women of
  surpassing beauty (and here note that Jarl is no gluttonous
  whoremaster but, rather, a connoisseur who will kill for the
  best while ignoring anything which does not meet his
  rigorous standards of perfection).

Quote: "I would that each was a wizard, for then our victory
  would be all the sweeter." (Said in the Cold West before he
  led a thousand men to battle against an enemy which
  outnumbered his own forces by four to one. Despite the
  promise of victory implicit in his boast, on that occasion he
  was defeated, and nine in ten of his men were slaughtered or
  enslaved).

* * *

Shall we say something about Thodric Jarl? Shall we speak of
the colour of his eye and the tint of his beard? Shall we tell of
his history and his hobbies, or quote him in his rhetoric?

No.

Suffice it simply to say that Jarl was of the Rovac, that the
Rovac are as primitive a bunch of blood-letting savages as you
are likely to cross swords with, and that Jarl was true to his kind.

Hence Guest Gulkan feared him.

Or should have feared him!

Time flies like an arrow, as the proverb has it, and before
midwinter Guest Gulkan returned to Gendormargensis and

announced his intention to meet Thodric Jarl in single combat.

The wizard Hostaja Sken-Pitilkin shortly came to see Guest Gulkan and counselled him to flee the city.

"Why in the name of a dog's mudshit should I do a thing like that?" said Guest.

Guest had then lately entered upon a phase where he spent a great deal of his spare time in devising new and especially barbarous oaths, and "a dog's mudshit" is typical of these. Sken-Pitilkin resisted the temptation to abrade the boy on account of his uncouth neologisms, and instead dedicated himself to giving good counsel.

"You must flee from Gendormargensis," said Sken-Pitilkin, "because, unless you flee the city, you'll have to hack it out face to face with Thodric Jarl."

"I should worry?" said Guest.

"Of course you should worry!"

"Why?" said Guest. "Because I'll get blood on my clothes?"

"Because the blood will be your own," said Sken-Pitilkin. "You have a choice. Bribe up big to buy off Jarl. Or flee. That's the limit of the choices you have at your own disposal, though Bao Gahai may have others."

This Bao Gahai was a dralkosh, a witch, whose devices had helped the Witchlord Onosh secure power and keep it. Rumour had it that Bao Gahai's strength was faltering, but many feared her still.

"Bao Gahai?" said Guest. "I'll not be seeking help from her."

"Yet she may give it," said Sken-Pitilkin. "She desires your presence, now, today, and to tell you as much is the greater part of my reason for coming here. Well. Are you ready to go?"

"I'm not going to see her!" said Guest.

But Sken-Pitilkin was persistent, and told the boy that Lord Onosh himself wished Guest to consult with Bao Gahai. So at length the young Weaponmaster allowed himself to be persuaded into the presence of the dralkosh who for so long had aided and counselled his father.

The audience took place in Bao Gahai's bedroom, which smelt of camphor, of cat-piss, and of antiquity. Bao Gahai was sitting up in bed with a cheeseboard on her knees. On the cheeseboard was an assortment of nuts — she never ate cheese, for she was allergic to it, just as she was allergic to catmeat and the eggs of seagulls — and throughout the audience she occupied herself by opening those nuts with the aid of a hammer, a chisel and an autoptical brain-hook. By profession she was a pathologist, and though she no longer dissected dead flesh — excitement always got the better of her, and she invariably moved from the dead to the living — she was still possessed by the scarcely controllable urge to dissect something. Hence the nuts.

"As a mark of my favour," said Bao Gahai, once she was alone with the young Weaponmaster, "I have persuaded your father to let the Rovac warrior Rolf Thelemite remain as your bodyguard, for all that he has recently led you into folly by the way of gambling."

"As a mark of your favour, if I truly have your favour," said Guest, astonished by his own boldness even as he spoke, "you might see to the cancellation of my gambling debts — and Rolf's."

"It's the cancellation of your life that should concern you," said Bao Gahai. "Not the cancellation of debt."

"You think me dead at the hand of Thodric Jarl?" said Guest, alluding to the duel to which he was doomed.

"I think that a strong likelihood, unless you leave the city," said Bao Gahai. "I suggest an extended journey of exploration in the Eastern Marches."

"That would be one way of thwarting Jarl's bloodlust," agreed Guest, with an entirely unwonted cheerfulness.

"You're not thinking of poisoning him, are you?" said Bao Gahai sharply.

"No," said Guest. "Of fighting him merely. Of killing him."

"You," said Bao Gahai, flicking a piece of walnut shell in Guest's direction, "have been taking opium."

"Opium?" said Guest.

"Yes, yes," said Bao Gahai. "You have been taking opium. Or else you have a fever."

"A fever? No? Why would you think so?"

"Because," said Bao Gahai, "there is never any way under any of the seventy suns of the fifty thousand hells of Bancharoth that you will ever kill Thodric Jarl in single combat."

"My sword has slaughtered a multiple of men in combat," said the Weaponmaster staunchly, "and I have trained long and hard since my last slaughter."

"You?" said Bao Gahai, with a laugh barely to be distinguished from the sound of nutshells snappling. "You? You have trained? With whom? With Rolf Thelemite, maybe?"

"The very man," said Guest. "And he is a Rovac warrior, is he not?"

"For sure," said Bao Gahai. "Rolf Thelemite is a warrior, as a sparrow is a bird. But I think the grey-bearded Jarl to be a very eagle in his pride, and I think the sharpness of his talons a fit complement to that pride."

Then Bao Gahai started to laugh.

She laughed and she laughed. Her full-fledged throttling was hideous, sounding for all the world like a man being strangled.

Guest Gulkan took Bao Gahai's laughter as a cue to leave, and swiftly made his escape. But Bao Gahai sent Sken-Pitilkin to persecute young Guest with books, and with papers, and with irregular verbs; and to divine his counsels if this should prove remotely possible. The dralkosh did not believe for one moment that Guest actually intended duelling Jarl, so presumed he had a secret plan in hatching.

But Sken-Pitilkin found no hint of the existence of any such plan; and found, too, that the boy Guest was decidedly reluctant to settle to his lessons, for his sword seemed to have fascinated him like a bewitching love.

A date for Guest Gulkan's duel with Thodric Jarl had been fixed, and on a morning before that day of destiny — to be precise, on a morning some ten days after the Weaponmaster's return to Gendormargensis — Sken-Pitilkin came to Guest's quarters and found the boy busily sharpening the long razorblade of his sword's cutting edge.

"It is written," said Sken-Pitilkin, shivering in the unheated coldness of Guest Gulkan's room, "that an icicle is but a poor room-mate. Blood, boy! Why don't you heat the room?"

"I am hardening myself body and soul," said Guest, with a studied seriousness which appeared devoid of any hint of irony. "I am hardening myself to meet with Thodric Jarl. Besides, the exercise of the sword warms me to a sufficiency."

"But I am old," said Sken-Pitilkin, "and my bones chilled with my age. It is written that the old should not suffer from the folly of the young."

"Where is that written?" said Guest. "In a book?"

"Where else?" said Sken-Pitilkin.

"Books truth nothing," said Guest, studying his swordblade by the winterlight which shivered through the open window. "Anyone can write anything in a book."

"So they can," said Sken-Pitilkin, settling himself in a chair and pulling Guest's best solskin horseblanket around him. "The date of your death, for example. In the books of the city's best bookmakers, that date is written as tomorrow. But there are other things well-written in the books of the world. Irregular verbs, for instance. What say you leave that sword, and make some verbs mere chopmeat with the razor of your intellect."

As scholars have always known, languages should ever be the first learning of the man who may be destined to hold great power. Recognizing this truth, the unscholarly Lord Onosh had ordered Sken-Pitilkin to labour young Guest into a linguist. But Guest hated the foreign tongues, their hookworm alphabets and their irregular verbs; and, failing to recognize their imposition as a sign of his father's love for him, he reacted as if Lord Onosh had personally invented all foreign syllabaries for the express purpose of torturing an unscholarly boy.

"Your passion for verbs is obscene," said Guest, momentarily laying aside his sword.

"Obscene?" said Sken-Pitilkin.

"Surely," said Guest, sliding shut the translucent paper screens designed to exclude the winter air from his quarters. "You lust for them. You lust like a very antelope. Irregular verbs! To grope, squeeze, suck and horsewhip such! A sick passion! As for me, I'd rather abominate myself with a toad. I'd think that the lesser perversion."

"Then that's unfortunate," said Sken-Pitilkin, "for your father wishes me to corrupt you with the choicest of my passions."

"Then let's at least leave the irregular verbs till I have killed myself, my man," said Guest, again picking up his sword. "Before battle, I must purify myself, and abstain from all perversions."

By way of reply, Sken-Pitilkin reached beneath the horseblanket which he had snugged across his knees, and took a book from beneath his skirt. These skirts were a foreign fashion, and Guest thought they must be desperately cold, though he was wrong in his thinking, for they were exceptionally practical and comfortable, and Sken-Pitilkin ever demonstrated great wisdom by wearing them. Having retrieved the book, Sken-Pitilkin began to unwrap its layers of waterproofing oil-cloth.

Guest Gulkan pretended to ignore the book in favour of the admiration of his own reflection in his swordblade. By manipulating the blade he could screen out the greatness of his ears — and concentrate instead on eyes and lips. The young Weaponmaster twisted his lips into a ferocious sneer then rolled his eyes in imitation of a horse gone mad.

All of which severely tempted Sken-Pitilkin, who sorely longed to fetch him a sharp crack with his country crook. But, of course, the boy had long since outgrown such convenient discipline.

"If you will not light a brazier," said Sken-Pitilkin, cool even though he was snuggled beneath the horseblanket, "at least pass me a little wine to warm my veins."

"What makes you think I've got wine on hand?" said Guest.

"When are you ever without it?" said Sken-Pitilkin.

This was a telling point, and Guest shortly uncovered some wine, and a block of rather grubby cheese to go with it. Knowing Bao Gahai to be allergic to cheese, Guest had acquired a great store of it, thinking to devise some plan for her poisoning. But he had failed in this enterprise, and so was put to the trouble of eating the stuff.

"Careful," said Guest, as Sken-Pitilkin helped himself to wine and cheese. "Be careful, lest you spill your drink on that precious book of yours."

"The book is mine," said Sken-Pitilkin, studying the cheese from several different angles, as if suspecting that it might be poisoned, "so let me do the worrying."

"I worry for my father's sake," said Guest. "For that book is the chiefest of his torturers. Should it die in the bloodflow of your downspilt wine, he'd be ten years searching for an instrument of equal punishment."

"This book is not torture but love," said Sken-Pitilkin, wiping the cheese on the horseblanket, "as I've told you not one time but fifty. Sit! Squat yourself, boy, then let us begin."

Guest Gulkan sat, and squared himself to face the book, looking for all the world like an inexperienced gladiator forced to do battle against a dragon with a toothpick as his sole armament. The book, of course, was Strogloth's *Compendium of Delights*.

The eminent Strogloth — and who he is is unknown, which is just as well, as there is many a young scholar who would dearly like to murder him — had searched great heaps of grammars for their irregular verbs, working in the spirit of one of those pornographers who reads immense libraries of law and religion with the sole purpose of extracting nuggets of brutal licentiousness.

The result? Spectacular!

"We will begin," said Sken-Pitilkin, chewing on the cheese, which was not too bad, "with the conjugation of the verb porp. Which means ... ? Guest? Guest, what is meant by the word porp?"

"You tell me," said Guest, "for the irregular verbs are your perversion, not mine."

"A perversion, yes," agreed Sken-Pitilkin, speaking with great self-restraint. Then, feeling the boy had had things all his own way for just a little too long: "But are you not a pervert? Is not the killing of men and the taking of their scalps a perversion of sorts?"

"It is culturally appropriate," said Guest. "You told me so yourself when we studied ethnology."

"Ah, ethnology," said Sken-Pitilkin. "A mistake."

Here it must be conceded that Sken-Pitilkin had indeed made a grievous error when he introduced young Guest to the science of ethnology; for Sken-Pitilkin had forgotten how much of that science deals in great and enthusiastic detail with vivisection, cannibalism, head-hunting, ritual murder, torture, louche initiation rites, and, above all, with sex customs.

"An ethnologist would say," said Guest, gaining enthusiasm as he saw he had the advantage, "that hunting men and killing them for their scalps is a vital part of my cultural heritage. For you as an uitlander scholar to criticise or condemn this practice would represent intolerable interference in the internal affairs of the Collosnon Empire."

"No," said Sken-Pitilkin, "you are wrong, for now you have confounded a theorem of ethnology with a practical political doctrine."

"I have not!" said Guest.

But he had, and Sken-Pitilkin explained his error to him in excruciating detail.

"You understand?" said Sken-Pitilkin. "No! Of course you don't! Never mind. Let us proceed to delight, for the irregular verbs yet await us."

"Irregular verbs!" sneered Guest. "My praxis is combat, not scholarship. My destiny is to do battle, to kill men, to drink their blood and take their scalps."

"Perhaps, perhaps," said Sken-Pitilkin. "But I rule this particular battlefield, so you will conduct yourself like a prisoner-of-war and obey me as the chiefest of your jailors. The verbs!"

"The verbs have awaited us for years already," said Guest. "Let them wait till tomorrow for, with my man as yet to kill, I'm in no mood for study today."

"Words are weapons," said Sken-Pitilkin. "And tools. If you

aspire to be surgeon to the body politic, then you should look to your armamentarium."

"Swords are weapons far better," said Guest. "For language cannot chop heads."

Sken-Pitilkin studied the young man carefully, for he was sober yet spoke with a drunkard's enthusiasm. He was drugged. Or somehow intoxicated. Perhaps, just perhaps, he was intoxicated by his own over-enterprising ambition. Certainly he looked far, far too buoyant, considering that he was shortly due to face the murderous Thodric Jarl in a duel he was certain to lose.

Sken-Pitilkin wondered if Guest had any true conception of the true nature of his own predicament.

"You know, my boy," said Sken-Pitilkin, "it would be very easy for you to make your peace with Thodric Jarl, if you did but humble yourself before him. Your life is full of so much promise that it would be foolish for you to do otherwise."

"My life," said Guest, "has no promise whatsoever."

"No promise?" said Sken-Pitilkin in surprise. "But don't you realize that you're surely going to end up with the imperial throne? That's your fate of a certainty, as long as you can master your temper and learn up a little diplomacy, and just a fragment of self-control to match it."

"You do but fantasize," said Guest, "for I am but a bastard boy with no future here or elsewhere, as all the world is at pains to tell me, thrice five times a day between dawning and darkness. But even though I must live here as a worthless bastard with all the world leagued in scorn against me, I will not surrender my pride by crawling to Thodric Jarl, no, nor by bribing him either."

So spoke Guest Gulkan, revealing depths of resentment which surprised Sken-Pitilkin, who cast about for some form of words which might improve the boy's self-confidence.

"You lie so smoothly I wish I'd taught you the skill myself," said Sken-Pitilkin, failing to find the words he sought. "Very well. Since your mastery has already encompassed the art of the lie, and since today finds you lacking the courage to tackle the smallest of the irregular verbs, though it be a naked verb, and hairless, and feeble in its antiquity — then, that being so, let us turn our minds to the study of geography."

"Not if that means maps," said Guest.

"You are in luck," said Sken-Pitilkin, "for all my maps are back in my own quarters."

"All right then," said Guest. "Geography it is."

He was relieved that they were to abandon verbs for geography. For geography was not quite so very bad, at least when there were no maps to be studied. Sken-Pitilkin had trunkloads of maps, charts and plans showing the margins of earth and sea, the sewer systems of foreign cities, the whims of the wind, the fruiting of the harvests, key infestations of dragons and the geographical range of the platypus. But while Guest knew the theory of maps, he had yet to master the art of conjuring truth from a scrabblework of isograms. Usually, when given a mapwork problem, he would stare at the parchment all day and get precisely nowhere.

Guest Gulkan had such difficulties partly because so many things on Sken-Pitilkin's maps were entirely alien to his experience. The sea, for instance. He was exasperated by geographical figurations which suggested that in places the sea ran on for thousands of leagues without interruption, because surely the existence of such an immensity of water was contrary to both reason and sheer probability.

And a shortage of illustrations made it difficult to match these alien places with their flora and fauna. The elephant and the platypus were both delineated explicitly in Sken-Pitilkin's Book of Beasts, the one being a very large mouse with deformed teeth and a nose of surpassing length, and the other being a rat in the form of a duck. But what of the quokka? And the jellyfish? Of these Guest Gulkan was unable to form any clear conception.

Yet he hoped never to meet such a monster as a jellyfish in the flesh, for it had been described to him as a translucent beast in the form of a blob from which depended a million fine-stranded tentacles which stung and killed. The monster was alleged to be otherwise without features, possessed of no eyes, nose, ears, arms, head, neck, trunk or external organs of generation. Guest Gulkan had met with the jellyfish twice already in nightmare, and on neither occasion had he been able to argue the brute out of killing him. On no account did he want to meet the thing a third time in the world of the real.

He said as much.

"Fear not the jellyfish," said Sken-Pitilkin. "A far more dangerous creature is the woman. For many more men have been killed on account of women than ever met their deaths in the tentacles of a jellyfish. You in your own flesh look to become one of them."

"It's not come to killing," said Guest. "Not yet."

Though the young Yarglat barbarian knew there would almost certainly be a killing when he met with Jarl on the morrow, he had no appetite for argument with his tutor.

"Then don't let it!" said Sken-Pitilkin. "Pay out your gold! Bribe the Rovac! Buy yourself a victory! For it won't be Jarl who dies. Oh no. If it's blades in earnest, it's you who dies. And you're running out of time to do something about it."

"You underestimate me," said Guest. "I have my sword, and I've spent my life training in its use."

"Your life!" said his tutor. "Boy, you're still wet from the egg! If you don't trust me, then trust the city. All over Gendormargensis, men are placing bets, and the odds predict your speedy death in battle."

"When we fight," said Guest, tempted into the heat of argument despite himself, "it won't be me who does the dying. I've killed men and I've trained for killing more, and what's Jarl so special about?"

"A man is a man," said Sken-Pitilkin. "And a boy a boy."

"I'm no boy!" said Guest in fury, though of course at the age of 14 he was very much a boy.

"A boy, verily, to be so easily provoked," said Sken-Pitilkin calmly. "Why, you're as irregular in your humours as one of the Akromian verbs."

"Jarl will be boy enough to bury when I'm through with him," said Guest. "You want to be rich? Then bet on my fortunes!"

"I'm not a gambling man," said Sken-Pitilkin. "But as soon as our lesson is over, I'm going to wager a month's salary on your early death. I'd be a fool to pass up a chance of profit so certain."

"Certain!" said Guest, rising to his feet. "I'll show you what's certain!"

With that battle-smash threat, the young Weaponmaster boiled out of his room, driven by the steam generated by the heat of his anger. However, once having boiled in such an impressive fashion, he found his wrath evaporating almost as swiftly as it had been generated.

So where to now?

In the harshness of its winter, Gendormargensis was no place for idling out of doors. Its bleakness was ruled by the wind-slam rain which slushed the streets to a turgid muck, the frigidity of which beaked eagerly through the cracks and chasms in the Weaponmaster's filthy boots. Though Guest was an emperor's son, the congenital disorder of his gear ever made him look like an impoverished refugee from six years of mountain-path campaigning.

Ever so slowly, the young Weaponmaster began to feel ever so slightly stupid. Should he go back inside? And lose face by apologizing? Never! Even so ... he half-wished Sken-Pitilkin would exert his authority and order him back inside. But his elderly tutor appeared to have given up on him, at least for the moment.

Guest Gulkan summed his options, and quickly, the weather being a disincentive to extended meditation. He could quest to Rolf Thelemite's sickbed and seek to rouse the man from his convalescence. Or he could at last yield to the advice of his betters, seek out Thodric Jarl, and bribe that Rovac mercenary to throw their fight in Enskandalon Square. Or, if still bent on duelling Jarl to the death, he could practise those sword-skills which he had been honing for so long.

Or—

But here Guest Gulkan left off thinking, for an oncoming

messenger was hailing him.

"Ho! Gulkan my man!"

It was the dwarf Glambrax, his pet dwarf and his father's favourite fool.

"Ho!" said Guest.

"Ho-ha!" said Glambrax.

"Ho-ha-ho-ho!" said Guest.

This went on for some time, the pair bawling at each other in the strumpeting wind like a couple of madmen, for this was a nonsense-game they had brought to perfection in the last year or so. But at last Glambrax swapped nonsense for sense.

"Zelafona, my man," said Glambrax, thus venting to the winter air the name of the witch who had mothered him.

"If I'm to be Zelafona," said Guest, "then I'm naturally woman, not man, though I doubt I'd be woman of yours."

"Zelafona," said Glambrax, ignoring this sally in favour of his business. "She wishes to see you."

But Guest had no wish whatsoever to see Glambrax's mother, who, after all, was Bao Gahai's sister. Doubtless she had good advice for him, but he was brim-full to the ears with good advice already, was drowning in the stuff, considered it noxious, said as much, and proposed that he detoxify himself with some hard spirits in the nearest tavern of convenience.

"With Rolf," said Glambrax.

"Oh, if we can liberate him, then yes," said Guest. "By all means with Rolf."

So they took themselves off to the infirmary where the convalescent Rovac warrior was laid up in bed, recovering from the aftermath of an attack of scarlet fever. They found Eljuk Zala seated by Rolf Thelemite, reading to him from one of Sken-Pitilkin's books of geography.

Guest Gulkan and Glambrax wrested the book from Eljuk Zala and pitched it into a half-full chamber pot, then swept the invalid and his nursemaid away to the nearest tavern. There Guest got very drunk, his companions got almost as intoxicated, and Guest in his bravado told all the world how he would hack Jarl to pieces on the morrow, then take the fair Yerzerdayla as his own, and bed her with all the ferocity of strength at his disposal.

When the next day blurred to life, Guest Gulkan woke but slowly. He was sullen and hungover as he made his way through the dull morning light to Enskandalon Square, where he was scheduled to meet Jarl in combat.

Lord Onosh was there already, waiting for his son. With Lord Onosh was the dralkosh Bao Gahai, in company with her sister Zelafona and Zelafona's dwarf-son Glambrax. Others were there also: a full two hundred assorted warriors, servants, tribesmen and beggars, together with vendors selling hot chestnuts and cups of warmed-up horseblood diluted with hard liquor.

Present among that gathering was Eljuk Zala, and there too were the wizards Hostaja Sken-Pitilkin and Pelagius Zozimus. Conspicuous by his absence was Rolf Thelemite, who was spending that morning in his bed in the infirmary, dead to the world as a consequence of his over-indulgences of the night before.

On arriving at Enskandalon Square, Guest Gulkan did not address his father, but instead ignored him entirely as he stripped off his furs and began practising some swordstrokes. It was immediately obvious to the Witchlord Onosh that Guest Gulkan had been training intensely while encamped by the Yolantarath. But it was also painfully obvious to Lord Onosh — and to most other onlookers — that the boy's improvements fell far short of making him battleworthy against such a formidable opponent as Jarl.

We must remember that Guest Gulkan was still a boy of 14, and though his stature could be mistaken for that of a man, he was a very child in his folly when he thought to match himself against the battle-hardened brutality of a grown man a full ten years older than himself.

When Guest was done with his swordpractice, he at last turned to his father and grinned.

Then the Witchlord Onosh saw that his son Guest had no plans of dying that day, but instead thought he would hack down

Thodric Jarl and walk from that place in triumph. Unfortunately the young Guest Gulkan had become overconfident in battle through his success in killing bandits — poor wretches who were usually half-starved and often half-mad and leprous into the bargain. His over-confidence had been boosted by the marked improvement he had lately made through his training.

"Father," said Eljuk Zala, tugging at the Witchlord's sleeve to win his attention.

"Eljuk," said Lord Onosh, acknowledging the presence of his favourite son.

"He thinks he can win, doesn't he?" said Eljuk.

"It would seem so from the grin," said Lord Onosh.

The Witchlord's voice was measured. It was not easy for him to stand here waiting for a Rovac warrior to come forth to hack down his son. But one does not win an empire through softness of spirit, nor can an empire be held by one who fears to do the hard things, or to have them done on his account.

"But," said Eljuk, "but he's going to die. Isn't he?"

"We are all of us going to die," said Lord Onosh. "The only question is, when."

"I — I don't want Guest to die," said Eljuk.

The plaintive tone of Eljuk's voice made Lord Onosh turn and look at him. The Witchlord's scrutiny revealed to him a surprising fact: Eljuk had been crying.

"You really want him to live?" said Lord Onosh.

"But of course," said Eljuk, as if it were obvious. "Of course I want him to live. What else would I want?"

The innocence of that response almost made Lord Onosh weep. As Lord Onosh knew full well, if Guest survived this day of testing, then he must necessarily and inevitably kill his brother Eljuk. Guest had the will to power and the bloody resolution necessary to seize and hold an empire, whereas Eljuk—

Poor Eljuk.

"You've never denied me before," said Eljuk.

"No," said Lord Onosh. "I haven't."

Lord Onosh had never been able to deny the boy anything. Not since he had sentenced the boy to die.

Character shows itself early, and when Eljuk had been but a small boy his father had seen that Eljuk would never be emperor. He was too conciliatory, too sentimental and far too self-effacing. Whereas Guest had a will to power and a violence to match it, and hence could definitely be emperor, though in all probability a bad one.

Possibly: a very bad one.

When Lord Onosh had realized the strength and ferocity of Guest Gulkan's bloody temper, he had seen that everything possible must be done to postpone the boy's ascension to the imperial throne, in the hope that the passage of years would mature him and mellow him. So Lord Onosh had named Eljuk as his heir, thus dooming him to die. It is one of the invariable rules of human affairs that power always ends up in the hands of those who want it most; and so, since Eljuk had the misfortune to lack all taste for dominance, it was a foregone conclusion that he would inevitably be murdered, if not by his brother then by some other.

Eljuk might — might! — have survived as ruler of some piddling little peacetime principality where he could have been played as a puppet by wise and remorseless councillors. But life among the Yarglat did not facilitate charades of puppetry. In seeking to rule the Yarglat, Eljuk must surely die, and Eljuk—

Eljuk did not realize that he had been sentenced to death, and that was the measure of his folly, a measure of his total unsuitability to hold the throne.

"Eljuk," said Lord Onosh, "when I am dead—"

"May you never die," said Eljuk piously.

"Birth is death," said Lord Onosh harshly. "As I was born, so must I die. Then — Eljuk, when I'm dead, there won't be anyone to stand between you and the world."

"There'll be Guest," said Eljuk.

"Guest, yes," said Lord Onosh. "So what if — Eljuk, brothers quarrel. Two brothers, one kingdom. The story plays a thousand times in history. It never has a happy ending."

There was a stir among those gathered in Enskandalon Square. Thodric Jarl had arrived.

"Save Guest," said Eljuk. "Then — then write it down for me. Don't tell him, but write it down. Write that — that I asked you. Then when I'm emperor I'll show him what you wrote. Then he'll know I saved him. A debt, you see."

Lord Onosh doubted very seriously that any such posthumous revelation would count for much when an empire was at stake.

Still.

What else could he do?

Eljuk would never be able to hold the empire. He was too ... too innocent. Too nice. Whereas Guest ... well, Guest was a fool, a brash and ignorant, over-confident fool. He drank too much, kept bad company, piled up gambling debts, was rude to powerful people such as Bao Gahai, and according to Sken-Pitilkin's account he was a scholar of truly grotesque incompetence.

But despite all these defects the young Weaponmaster had demonstrated a ruthless resolution that his brother Eljuk lacked. He had set his heart on hacking down Thodric Jarl; he had trained for the purpose; he had avoided all temptation to escape from the duel by bribery; and here he was today, bent on consummating his folly.

Lord Onosh summoned Sken-Pitilkin with a finger and made his wishes known.

"My lord," said Sken-Pitilkin, once he understood what his emperor wanted.

"You won't do it?" said Lord Onosh, detecting a note of resentful resistance in Sken-Pitilkin's voice.

"My lord, this — this boy Guest, he's, in his impetuosity he pitched a book to a chamber-pot."

"It was your book, I suppose," said Lord Onosh, suppressing his extreme irritation at finding his tame wizard bothering him with a such a triviality on such an occasion.

"It was, my lord. It was—"

"Give me your bill and I'll pay it," said Lord Onosh.

At which Sken-Pitilkin gave up all hope of making the Witchlord Onosh understand the gravity of Guest Gulkan's crime. For the book which had fallen to the chamber pot had been a book of geography: and ancient; and stocked full of wisdom; and decorated in its margins with a multitude of irregular verbs; and it had been ruined entirely by its drenching in urine, and was quite irreplaceable, for gold would not serve as its replacement, no, nor ivory either, nor silver, nor any measure of shimmering silks and unbroken hymens.

"My lord," said Sken-Pitilkin remotely. "I hear, and to hear is to obey."

"Good, good," said Lord Onosh testily. "Then get on with it!"

Thus commanded, Sken-Pitilkin positioned himself near the fighters, and prepared to put his powers of levitation to work. This he did discreetly, without anyone in the audience realizing what was happening. So, when combat was joined, Thodric Jarl's feet were hooked from under him by the arts of Sken-Pitilkin's magic, and down went Jarl in the snow and slush. Guest Gulkan promptly tried to hack off Jarl's head, whereupon Sken-Pitilkin secured the sideways deflection of the Weaponmaster's sword, ensuring that it did but hack a bloodline in Jarl's grey-haired scalp.

There was supreme art in that studied deflection, but not one person in the audience understood that art. To the audience, it seemed merely that Jarl had slipped, and that Guest had blundered away his chance to decapitate the fallen Rovac warrior.

Thodric Jarl was down on the ground, bleeding profusely from the cut in his scalp. Blood poured from his head, sluiced through his hair, teemed down his face in rivulets then clogged in the grey of his beard. The Witchlord Onosh promptly declared that Jarl had been defeated, and that Yerzerdayla was therefore Guest Gulkan's prize.

"But," said Lord Onosh, "as the boy Guest has recently been guilty of a scandalizing delinquency, it is fitting that his possession of Yerzerdayla be tied to his punishment for that delinquency."

Then the Witchlord Onosh publicly denounced the boy

Guest on account of the fact that he had seen fit to dunk one of Sken-Pitilkin's codicological treasures in a chamber pot. The emperor announced Guest's punishment:

"On account of his delinquency, the boy is not to be permitted to take possession of the woman Yerzerdayla until he is 18 years of age."

Lord Onosh declared that Yerzerdayla would meanwhile "reside in chastity" under his own roof.

The Witchlord Onosh felt that he had resolved things rather nicely, winning a margin of four years or so in which to arrange for Guest to surrender Yerzerdayla discreetly to Thodric Jarl. But in the interim, he must move quickly to separate Guest and Jarl, lest they find some excuse for a rematch.

Accordingly, that evening the young Guest Gulkan was summoned into his father's presence. There he found Zelafona, the aged but elegant sister of Bao Gahai, and her dwarf-son Glambrax.

"Guest," said Lord Onosh. "You are leaving Gendormargensis. Tonight. Glambrax and Zelafona are going with you."

"Leaving?" said Guest. "But why?"

"Because," said Lord Onosh, "Thodric Jarl has sworn a bloody oath to kill both you and Sken-Pitilkin. In fact, unless my spies misheard him, he swore to butcher every wizard in the world."

"Then," said Guest calmly, "you would be well within your rights to chop him into dogmeat, for every wizard in Gendormargensis lives in your protection."

"So they do, so they do," said Lord Onosh. "So, for their protection, my wizards are joining you in exile."

"Exile?" said Guest in alarm. "What are you talking about?"

"I'm sending you out of the empire," said Lord Onosh. "Have you heard of a place called Alozay? Have you heard of Molothair?"

"No," said Guest.

"Sken-Pitilkin swears he has taught you of both," said Lord Onosh. "And in detail. Molothair is a city, and Alozay an island.

The city of Molothair sits on the island of Alozay, and serves as the capital of that archipelago known as Safrak. You can place Safrak on a map, I trust?"

"I can place anything on a map," said Guest. "A cup, a plate, a pot or a branding iron. Give Molothair or Safrak into my hand and I will place them on any map of your choosing."

"Come," said Lord Onosh impatiently, "you must know the places which we're talking of, for Safrak — oh, never mind! Sken-Pitilkin's the geographer, let him then lesson you. You'll have plenty of time for lessons on your journey."

And with that Guest Gulkan was dismissed, and was sent away to pack up for his journey into exile.

* * *

Name: Guest Gulkan

Birthplace: Stranagor

Occupation: student

Status: barbarian-in-training

Description: aggressive Yarglat male who lives his life as if determined to play the role of barbarian to the bloody hilt

Hobby: the tasting of beer (often, and in bulk)

Quote: "It wasn't me and I didn't really mean to do it, and anyway the bitch bit me." (Said at the age of eleven, when he was caught barbecuing Viranessa, the silky-haired lap-dog which had long been the prize possession of his brother Eljuk Zala)

* * *

So it was that Guest Gulkan departed from Gendormargensis in the depths of winter and made the arduous journey to the islands of Safrak. He did not go alone but was accompanied by two wizards, a witch, a dwarf and a bodyguard — the people in question being the wizard of Xluzu named Pelagius Zozimus, the wizard of Skatzabratzumon named Hostaja Sken-Pitilkin, the aged but elegant dralkosh named Zelafona, the dwarf Glambrax and the doughty Rovac warrior named Rolf

Thelemite.

Though Rolf was not properly recovered from his attack of scarlet fever, they nevertheless made good time on their journey out of the Collosnon Empire.

From Gendormargensis they travelled, making the journey down the frozen Yolantarath River on a sleigh drawn by the fur-dogs known as ubeks. Some 200 leagues south-west of Gendormargensis, and just downstream from the trading town of Babaroth, the Yolantarath is intersected by the Pig River. Guest Gulkan and his companions pushed their way up the Pig. "Push" is very much the operative word, for the winter-frozen river was pocked with tree trunks and derelict rocks, and the clearness of its ice was rutted by the journeying of many traders.

Yet the difficulties of the journey did not depress the Weaponmaster. Rather, Guest Gulkan began to lighten up, his mood becoming buoyant — then weightless. The elevation of his spirits was scarcely surprising when one considers the claustrophobic tensions the boy had long endured in the imperial court of Gendormargensis.

The family history was not a happy one.

To seize power and secure it, the Witchlord Onosh had been put to the trouble of killing his father, his mother, his paternal grandfather, his twin sisters and his solitary brother, two uncles, four cousins, an aunt and five imperial concubines; and he had also secured the death of a nephew and the nephew's favourite horse.

All this was par for the course as far as the Yarglat were concerned — except for the gratuitous murder of the horse, which was generally considered to be excessive, and indicative of a streak of mean-spirited vindictiveness unbecoming in a warrior.

But Guest—

Perhaps there was an unexpected streak of mercy in Guest Gulkan's soul, for he had long been troubled by the possibility that he might one day be forced to inherit his father's bloody responsibilities, and to secure the empire yet again with a fresh set of blood-slaughter murders.

The journey the Weaponmaster was presently making was steadily taking him away from all possibility of any such conflicts, and so he was full of jokes and levity as he and his companions travelled up the Pig, arriving at last at the village of Ink on the shores of the Swelaway Sea.

There Guest gazed full upon the Swelaway Sea. He took so long about it that you might have thought him busy trying to drink it whole, rather than merely look at it.

At last he knelt by the waters, tasted them, then rose with a regretful sigh.

"What is it?" said Rolf Thelemite.

"It is but water," said Guest regretfully. "If only it were liquor, then there might be some use for it."

"There's its use!" said the dwarf Glambrax, gleefully pointing at a bobbing turd afloat upon the waters. "It's a sewer!"

A healthy turd, that. Brown and light, buoyant with vegetarian uplift. But, at the sight of it, Guest repented of having sampled of the sea, and swore he'd stick to wineskins in the future.

Then the Weaponmaster pulled out the best beloved of all the destructive implements in his possession, and ceremonially pissed upon the Swelaway Sea, as if trying by that insouciant gesture to deny the obvious effect it had had on him. For Guest at that age was very full of himself, and held in very poor esteem those minor parts of the universe which lay outside his own hard-striving corpus. Yet the Swelaway Sea, by the very act of its own existence, indicated by its vast indifference that there was more to the cosmic order than the blood and bones of one Guest Gulkan, and was uncomfortably suggestive of the possibility that the boy Guest might ultimately be but one utterly trifling and inconsequential part of a larger whole too vast to be comfortably contemplated.

With the Swelaway Sea having thus been encountered (yes, and do you remember the first time that you in your own person encountered the immensity of the sea, whether salt sea or fresh?) the travellers walked into Ink and addressed themselves to the question of the acquisition of a boat.

At Ink, a place much to be noted for the barking of its dogs and the smell of its dead fish, for the multiplicity of its turds and the squaloring of its five billion trouserless children, the adventurers were (this at least was the plan) to trade their sleigh, their fur-dogs and their gold for a small fishing boat.

The Witchlord Onosh in his mercy and his wisdom had provided the travellers with gold in plenty — certainly enough, in combination with their other discardable possessions, to buy them a boat for the passage to Safrak. Unfortunately, Rolf Thelemite persuaded the Weaponmaster Guest to join him in the pursuit of a bargain and save their cash for pleasure rather than transit. Fortunately, the sagacious Sken-Pitilkin vetoed the purchase of any bargain, and they spent their gold on an expensive but seaworthy boat.

The boat, which was named the Lathmish, was sold to them by a man named Umbilskimp, an old man who suffered bitterly from chilblains and emphysema. It came with a money-back warranty which guaranteed it to be good for five years or fifty return trips across the Swelaway Sea. Both Zozimus and Sken-Pitilkin checked the wording of the warranty, and checked it closely — and, on being satisfied, they herded Guest and Rolf aboard the boat, and set to sea.

But when the travellers were well launched upon the cold grey chop of the Swelaway Sea, the boat began to leak; and before they were so much as half-way to Alozay they found their craft was leaking like a fish hacked open by a landing hook.

Fortunately, the travellers managed to get their leaking wreck of a boat as far as the island of Ema-Urk before it actually sank. Once the thing had been grounded, an inspection of the hull proved it to be one spongy mass of sodden rot, which the boat salesman must have known.

"He is a murderer!" said Guest, denouncing the venial Umbilskimp. "And if I get him in my power then I will hang him!"

"An excellent sentiment," said Sken-Pitilkin, who usually deplored violence, but who on this occasion found himself in total agreement with Guest's vow of vengeance. "Let us report the man as soon as we get to Alozay, and perhaps they will have the grace to give us satisfaction."

And when a passing boat had at length given them passage to Alozay, they did just that — reporting the delinquent Umbilskimp to Banker Sod himself.

But Vernon Brigadoon Sod, the man of iceman race who headed the Safrak Bank and dominated the island of Alozay, declared the affairs of Ink to be no concern of his.

"In Safrak," said Sod, "we see our law as being concerned with the rule of the Safrak Islands. No more, no less."

"Then who rules Ink?" said Guest.

"Nobody," said Sod. "Ink is a free village, just as Port Domax is a free city. If you must have vengeance upon this fellow Um — Umbik—"

"Umbilskimp," supplied Guest, who had vowed never to forget the man until the man was dead.

"If you must have your vengeance," said Sod, "then you must secure it for yourself, and you will not be securing it while you are resident upon Alozay."

So Guest arrived upon Alozay, Safrak's ruling island and the site of the capital city of Molothair, and his arrival was marred by the fact that he was cheated of his legitimate revenge upon the salesman who had almost encompassed his murder.

He vowed again that he would not forget the fellow.

Meantime, back in Gendormargensis, the Witchlord Onosh sat closeted with Thodric Jarl and Eljuk Zala, trying to work out how to deal with the problems in Locontareth.

The city of Locontareth had long been a centre of unrest, and there were rumours which suggested that one Sham Cham of that city was exercising his talents in stirring up a tax revolt. Acting on Thodric Jarl's suggestion, Lord Onosh had tried to dispose of the matter with the minimum of fuss, by sending killers to ensure that Sham Cham passed away quietly in his sleep.

Lord Onosh had just lately received news that the killers had been killed in their turn, and that a very lively and decidedly unkilled Sham Cham now slept with half a dozen man-eating guard dogs in his room.

"It looks," said Lord Onosh gloomily, "as if this will be Stranagor all over again."

"Stranagor?" said Eljuk Zala. "What's that got to do with it?"

"My, ah, my — how did I phrase it? — my Provision for the Permanent Abolition of Riverside Vermin," said the Witchlord Onosh. "That was it. The vermin being the Geflung. It was a revolt, a tax revolt. You don't remember?"

Eljuk Zala confessed that he had no recollection of ever reading or hearing about any such revolt.

This disturbed the Witchlord greatly, for nobody could be ignorant of the late and lamentable tax revolt in Stranagor unless they were ignorant of the affairs of the empire as a whole, and such ignorance was dangerous in the empire's anointed heir.

Nevertheless, the Witchlord Onosh did his best to conceal his disappointment as he explained.

"In the country around Stranagor," said Lord Onosh, "live the Geflung, who ..."

As the Witchlord began to explain things to Eljuk Zala, Thodric Jarl turned his own attention to a map of the Collosnon Empire and began planning a war against Locontareth, something he was sure the empire would find itself engaged in before terribly long — if not in the coming year, then in the year after.

CHAPTER FOUR

Safrak Bank: organization which rules the Safrak Islands of the Swelaway Sea. Its ostensible business is to fatten on trade passing between Port Domax and the heartland of Tameran.

* * *

Guest Gulkan's birthday was in spring, and it was in spring of Alliance 4305 that he turned 15. His birthday was ill-omened, for it found him afflicted by influenza.

While leprosy, cholera and bubonic plague have names to rival nightmare, for swift and sudden devastation nothing can match the more lethal strains of influenza. This epidemic had claimed a tenth of Safrak's population in barely thirty days, and looked fit to claim Guest as well. He was fevered and awash with sweat, so weak in his ague's anguish that he lacked the strength to crack a flea.

In the end, the boy only survived because a guardian named Hrothgar took him home to his wife Una, who had just lost her baby to the epidemic, and so was able to wetnurse the patient. Guest was far too sick to derive any erotic satisfaction from this privilege, but Una's help saw him through his crisis, and shortly he was tottering around in the spring sunshine, feeling more like a ghost of himself than an actual boy of flesh and blood.

"You're no ghost," said Una, pulling on one of his big ears. "There's no ghost here! There's an elephant!"

Guest, who had begun to grow infatuated with the grey-eyed Una, promptly lost all sympathy with the woman. If there was one thing the young Weaponmaster absolutely hated, it was a woman who pulled on his ears. And, sooner or later, every woman of his acquaintance seemed to end up doing exactly that. Those ears, it seemed, had a fatal attraction for the entire female sex.

With his infatuation thus abruptly terminated, Guest was glad to flee from Hrothgar's house — a ramshackle wooden building in the ramshackle city of Molothair — and return to his own quarters in the mainrock Pinnacle.

On his return to the mainrock, he was promptly nobbled for guard duty. He was weak in the aftermath of his sickness, but weakness was no disqualification for work at such a time.

Guest Gulkan was technically resident upon Alozay as a hostage, but this was a mere legalism. The Safrak Bank trusted him — as much as it trusted any boy of 15 — and so readily employed his brutality. It set him to guard the time prison, a large hall with a series of transparent pods set around its walls.

Mark the layout of the Hall of Time!

The mainrock Pinnacle stands at the northern end of the long and narrow island of Alozay. It is a mighty upthrust of granite, a misshapen phallus of rock which bulbs outward at its middlemost point.

To win admission to the mainrock, one must come to its docks, which lie in the cold and gutteral shadows of the mainrock's wave-slapped northern shore. One is then hauled upwards to Gud Obo, the Winch Stratum, the lowest of the seven inhabited levels of the mainrock. Gud Obo houses the winch-works, the servant quarters, and the storerooms.

Multiple stairways connect Gud Obo with Dolce Obo, the Pillow Stratum. This is given over to the business of life, for it is a place of sleeping quarters, kitchens and eateries; and here one finds the mainrock's banqueting hall. Here Guest Gulkan and Sken-Pitilkin had their customary quarters, and a classroom in which they could prosecute the dissection of the irregular verbs.

A dozen stairways climb from Dolce Obo to Inic Obo, the Quill Stratum, which is given over to the offices of the Safrak Bank. A mighty stratum, this, for it dominates the bulbing middlemost girthswell of the mainrock Pinnacle.

Yet another dozen stairways lead upwards to Brondon Obo, the Steel Stratum, the fourth level of the mainrock, which houses prisons, guardhouse and armouries.

By now, the mainrock is starting to taper as it buffets upwards towards the rough-hewn ridge which helmets its crest.

In consequence of the tapering, only four stairways lead upwards from the fourth level to the fifth, from Brondon Obo to Trilip Obo, the Archive Stratum.

The Archive Stratum is just that — dead rooms of silent paper, of ancient book-chests sealed with lead. As one goes upwards in the mainrock, so the labour of supplying water from below becomes greater, and for this reason Trilip Obo was uninhabited by human flesh.

Only one stairway climbs upwards from Trilip Obo to Zi Obo, the Pod Stratum, the sixth level of the mainrock Pinnacle. Zi Obo holds one single and solitary chamber, an oval hall a hundred paces in length and three dozen paces in width. This chamber is the Hall of Time, and it was in this hall that Guest Gulkan was to stand guard duty.

The single stairway from below enters the Hall of Time at its western end. From there, the hall stretches away for its full length of a hundred paces to the ascending stairway at its eastern end. When Guest was brought there to do guard duty, the entrance to that ascending stairway was guarded by a monumental block of jade-green stone.

"So," said Banker Sod, who had taken it upon himself to brief Guest Gulkan on his guard duties. "Where are we?"

Guest looked around.

"We are in the Hall of Time," said Guest Gulkan, who had received a guided tour of the mainrock shortly after his first arrival on Alozay, and who remembered this room well. Set in niches around its northern and southern walls were many transparent pods, some empty, others holding Safrak's time prisoners. Between the niches were deep-cut slit windows, the northern ones looking out across the Swelaway Sea, the southern ones allowing a partial view of the longstretch of Alozay and the ramshackle city of Molothair.

"Which level is this?" said Sod.

"The fifth," said Guest. "No, the sixth, that's it. The sixth. There's one more. The seventh."

"Jezel Obo," said Sod, naming it. "The Sky Stratum. What lies in the sky, boy?"

"It is a sacred place," said Guest. "A shrine denied to all but the initiated. It's called, uh, a sanctum. The Inner Sanctum."

"That is so," said Sod. "Jezel Obo, the Sky Stratum, is the site of the Inner Sanctum, the holy of holies of the Safrak Bank. Are you a priest, boy?"

"No," said Guest.

"Do you have any ambition to be a priest?"

"No."

"Then don't worry your head about sacred places. Understood?"

"Understood," said Guest, who, thanks to his studies in ethnology with Hostaja Sken-Pitilkin, knew that many peoples did not like to have the secrets of their faith questioned.

"Well then," said Sod, "if that's understood, then let us go and meet the demon."

With that, Banker Sod led the Yarglat barbarian Guest Gulkan from the western end of the Hall of Time to the stairway at its eastern end.

It was then evening, and the light was dying in the Hall of Time. Sod and Guest cast no shadows as they walked through that grey light towards the jade-green block of stone at the far end of the hall. Their boots clicked over the skull-pattern tiles — many of which were broken — which paved the native granite of the hall. The roof was high above, and the sound of their boots was cold and sharp in the vaulting emptiness.

An odd pair they made, for Banker Sod, the Governor of the Safrak Bank, was a pale-skinned male of iceman race, with the black fingernails and thick white bodyhair so typical of that breed. His hair was bright gold, his eyes yellow and his teeth of like colour.

Upon Sod's ringfinger there was a steel ring in which there was set a gemstone. That stone was of ever-ice, and in the gathering gloom of evening a ghost-cloud of light surrounded it. Guest knew that chipstone of ever-ice to be the key which opened and closed the pods of the time prison.

They halted at the eastern end of the Hall of Time. They halted in the presence of the hall's resident demon — the jade-green block of stone which guarded the single stairway which led upwards to the seventh and highest level of the mainrock Pinnacle.

Though Sod was accustomed to do business in the Galish Trading Tongue, and though Guest had learnt Galish from Sken-Pitilkin, the language of the briefing was Guest's native tongue, the Eparget of the Yarglat, in which Sod was uncommonly fluent. Apparently the demon understood the same language, for Sod still spoke in Eparget when addressing that dignitary directly.

"Iva-Italis," said Banker Sod. "This is Guest Gulkan, the son of the emperor of Tameran, and a student of the wizard Hostaja Sken-Pitilkin."

The demon received this news in silence. It was a monolithic block of green stone which was twice Guest Gulkan's height; and, like the other rocks of the world, it seemed singularly indisposed to entertaining mere humans in conversation.

"Does the demon speak?" said Guest.

"When it chooses to," said Sod. "It is the head of our force of mercenaries, those men who belong to that body we call the Guardians. If you were to join the Guardians then Iva-Italis would be your master."

"Ha-hmm," said Guest, pretending that this was new to him, and that he was absorbing this information with the greatest of interest.

In fact, Guest already knew all about Safrak's Guardians, the Toxteth-speaking mercenaries recruited from Port Domax and Wen Endex. Guest had even struck up a dice-and-beer friendship with some few of those worthy warriors — most notably the mighty Hrothgar — and had a little of their native argot at his command. Surely Banker Sod had been appraised of the development of these relationships — but, if so, then the rigours of influenza had stripped that knowledge from the Banker's mind.

"Iva-Italis guards these stairs," said Banker Sod, continuing his lecture about Safrak's guardian demon. "No unauthorized person can come up or down the stairway — and that means you. If any unauthorized person tries to pass, then the demon will eat them."

"Eat them?" said Guest. "But it has no mouth, and — well, claws, arms, tentacles, things to grab with. Besides, the stairs are wide."

"When it eats, it eats," said Sod. "So don't worry about the stairs. The time prison is your concern. You know about it?"

"I know," said Guest, who had heard all about Safrak's time prison.

"Very well," said Sod, obviously relieved that he did not have to explain. "Your duty is simple. If anyone tries to interfere with the time prisoners, then you kill them."

"How could anyone interfere?" said Guest, who knew very well that there was but one ring which could free the time prisoners from their pods, and that that ring was ever in Banker Sod's possession.

"They could interfere," said Banker Sod, "by trying to physically carry away one of the prison pods. They could — never mind. If something goes wrong, Iva-Italis will tell you who to kill and when."

Banker Sod was in no mood for extended explanations because he was even sicker than Guest Gulkan. Yet there was more to do before Sod could depart. He had to accompany Guest Gulkan back to the head of the western stairway, and point out the things placed in niches in the western wall.

"Lanterns," said Sod. "They must be filled with this oil. There is a bracket by each and every time pod. Light as many lanterns as you need. You can use a tinder box, I suppose."

"I have never mastered such a device," said Guest, lying through his teeth.

A tinder box is a tricky thing to use, and by pleading ignorance Guest Gulkan got Sod to conjure the first lantern into life.

Then Sod picked up a rod of hardwood. A dozen short lengths of chain dangled from the rod, and each chain ended in a barbed hook.

"What is this?" said Sod.

Guest squinted at the thing, then declared it to be an instrument of torture, or perhaps some device designed to be used in a fishing boat.

"No!" said Sod. "It is a bablobrokmadorni stick."

"A — a bab — baba — bablob?"

"A bablobrokmadorni stick," said Sod. "I thought you were a scholar!"

"Well," said Guest. "I study."

"But obviously not hard enough," said Sod. "For a command of the Janjuladoola seems to be lacking from your tongue."

"It is so," conceded Guest.

"Then learn at least a word of it," said Sod. "This is a bablobrokmadorni stick, a device used in the Izdimir Empire for the carriage of lanterns. Look! You can put it on your shoulder and carry six lanterns without a risk of fire."

"A lantern stick, then," said Guest, making no attempt to pronounce the Janjuladoola name of the thing, since he feared that any such exercise in applied linguistics would precipitate the rupture of his jaw.

Then Sod showed him the water jug, which was half-full. The bread box, which held some lumps of black peasant bread so hard they could have been used as missiles for a catapult. The chamber pot — which was unclean, and smelt accordingly.

"Empty it from that northern window," said Sod, gesturing at the nearest slit window. "You'll find it by its smell, even if you can't find it otherwise."

With these instructions given, Sod warned Guest not to leave his post before he was relieved at dawn. Then the Banker took himself off to his bed, descending the darkened stairs without bothering himself with a light — for Sod knew every shadow in the mainrock by its height, its depth, its heat, its cold, its timbre or its smell.

Once left alone, Guest immediately busied himself with the lighting of lanterns. The boy Guest was not zealously industrious by nature, but night was setting in. The ominous darkness — scarcely relieved by the cold green glow which emanated from the distant flanks of the demon Icaria Scaria Iva-Italis — beset the boy with fears. This was a high place, a cold place, a barren place, and he did not like it.

Lanterns swayed from the chains of the bablobrokmadorni stick, sending a dozen shadows of Guest Gulkan lurching across the skull-pattern tiles of the Hall of Time. When hung by the time pods, they seemed merely to enlarge the darkness rather than to light the hall. The unlit gulf of the western staircase became a funnel descending into the nether depths, and Guest, made uneasy by that plunging chasm of blackness, placed his armchair up against the northern wall.

Yet even with the armchair so placed, Guest found it impossible to settle. Instead, he began to perambulate around the room, checking the oil levels in the lanterns, testing the room's acoustics by hawking and spitting, and amusing himself by examining the people so firmly frozen in the timestasis of the pods of the time prison. A motley bunch they were, those prisoners, a good many of them showing signs of extreme age, of disease, or of wounds or torture.

Rumour claimed — and Guest had heard the rumour, for ears as big as his were singularly well adapted for the capture of gossip — that time prisoners almost inevitably died upon release. The process of being frozen within a block of unchanging time was held to be harmless in itself, but the psychic shock of being displaced from one's own time by days, years or generations was held to be inevitably fatal.

Hence the Safrak Bank used the time pods as instruments of execution. After two or three generations of incarceration, a prisoner would be abruptly released into a future in which friends, lovers and relatives were dead, or reduced to decrepit spiderwebbed ghosts of their former selves, old-aged skeletons thinly cloaked by arthritic mottlestone flesh. From the prisoner's point of view, an eyeblink aged the world. The shock of such change was sufficient to kill — though one rumour claimed that a quick-acting poison was covertly administered to supplement that shock.

Guest Gulkan, growing disturbed by the unblinking stares of

those imprisoned in the time pods, ceased his scrutiny of the same. Though the hall was very large, it was nevertheless becoming increasingly claustrophobic. The shadows weighed heavily on Guest Gulkan's shoulders. He topped up the oil in each and every lantern, and trimmed the wicks to maximize their light-producing efficiency, yet the heavy burden of shadow seemed scarcely relieved.

As if seeking escape from the hall, Guest Gulkan eased himself into a north-facing slit window. It was easily tall enough to accommodate his height, but narrowed sharply, its sides arrowheading inwards as the window pierced its way through the wall to the outer air. The outermost aperture of this defensive fenestra was just large enough for Guest to stick his head outside. He did so. He warped his head around to look up at the sharp-slash stars, then looked down at the sightless gulfs of the Swelaway Sea far below.

"Sa!" said Guest, pulling his head in, then rubbing his ears to warm them against the cold.

The young Yarglat barbarian jumped down from the slit window and returned to his armchair. But it was growing increasingly cold — far too cold for him to stay seated slumped and sleep. So he resumed his perambulations.

Guest was far from the demon when he heard someone coming down the stairs. Guest geared himself up for action instantly. His blood began to pulse in his ears. A warm flush of battle-readiness surged through his body. Then — then Guest belatedly remembered that the stairs were not his concern. The stairs were guarded by the demon, or so Banker Sod most earnestly believed, and the guardianship of those stairs was the demon's concern, with Guest Gulkan's duty being merely to prevent interference with the prisoners of the time prison.

Down came a single person, who paused by the demon, who spoke — or appeared to speak, for Guest heard the whispering ghost of a comment across a distance greater than eighty paces — then tramped towards the downward stairway in the west.

Resting on the stranger's left shoulder was a bablobrokmadorni stick from which two lanterns depended, and these lit him as he approached. A remarkable figure! He was dressed in brightly coloured patchwork motley. A multitude of small ceramic animals were attached to his trousers and his jacket. On his feet were slippers, which curved upwards at the toes, terminating in pink pom-poms. He wore a golden skullcap fringed with tiny glass bells, which rang out in a rain of music as he stepped lightly, briskly, across the cracked and broken tiles of the Hall of Time.

A bright and briskful figure, this.

But the face!

As the man drew near, Guest Gulkan saw his face was hideously disfigured by burns. Twisted welts and lava-field fluxes had warped that face until its age and race were beyond determination.

On his right hand, the man wore a glove puppet in the form of a green-skinned dragon with red dewlaps. As he drew level with Guest, the man's right hand moved. The dragon snapped at Guest's ear. And it had teeth! Yes, there were miniature teeth built into the mouth of the glove puppet, teeth sharp as razors!

Guest's hand went to his sword.

But the stranger laughed, laughed like a bell, laughed with such penetrating clarity that one might imagine him to be heard from one side of the Swelaway Sea to another. He had a singer's voice, trained to carry, and the laugh was a song of sorts, so penetrating that Guest felt its vibrations in his bones.

Disarmed and made dumbstruck by that laugh, Guest stood like a scarecrow, gawking at the stranger. Who sniffed him. Smelt him. Sucked sweat, dust and dinner into his nostrils. Sampled him. Memorized him. Then snorted, hummed, winked, and went tripping down the western stairs, the light of his lanterns swaying from the walls in a warmglow wash as he descended.

Such was Guest Gulkan's first encounter with Yubi Das Finger, a citizen of the Empire of Greater Parengarenga, and a resident of the far-distant city of Dalar ken Halvar.

Descending the stairs, the stranger began to sing. Abruptly, his song was cut off by a lurching cry. There was a pause. A scream! In panic, Guest sprinted to the head of the stairs, his sword already in his hand.

Then upward from the depths below there came a bright and bell-clear laugh, a laugh both generous and mocking at the same time, and Guest knew himself to have been the victim of a joke.

Sweating and blood-pounding — in the aftermath of his influenza, he was far too weak to enjoy such a joke! — Guest seated himself in his armchair. But no sooner had he settled himself than he heard more footsteps descending in the east.

Though the Hall of Time was a full hundred paces in length, though Guest Gulkan was seated near its western end, he clearly heard two people descending the stairs in the east. He got the disconcerting impression that the jade-green demon of the east was amplifying the sound of those descending footsteps. He tried to dismiss the thought, but the thought proved reluctant to be dismissed.

—It is but a stone.

Thus thought Guest, who had been seriously disconcerted by his encounter with Yubi Das Finger, and did not think himself up to the stress of facing further shocks.

Down came two people. They passed on either side of the cold-glowing demon and proceeded towards Guest Gulkan at a measured pace, the lattermost carrying a bablobrokmadorni stick bright with twin lanterns.

As they came near, Guest saw the foremost was an ancient featherweight of an Ashdan, who was followed by a ragged servant. More strangers. Guest braced himself for jokes, threats or revelations, but the pair gave him only the most cursory of glances before exiting from the hall, taking the stairs which led downwards.

Guest was relieved that the passage of the dwarf-statured Ashdan and his lowbrowed bablobrokmadorni servant had gone off so smoothly.

Then:

More footsteps!

Coming down!

And there were many of them!

Yes, there was no mistaking it!

A great body of armed men was coming down the eastern stairs, their armour clanking, boots tramping, horns blowing, shields clashing. Horses! They had horses! Guest heard hoofs on stone, heard an animal whinny. And — barrels! They were rolling barrels as they came! The barrels were thumping on the steps! And — one burst! Guest heard it shatter to a gust of liquid, heard curses, guttural swearing.

Now Guest was under the impression that the seventh and last stratum of the mainrock Pinnacle — Jezel Obo, the Sky Stratum — was a small place. No place, then, where one could hide a bootshod army with its horses, its shields, its barrels.

Yet they were coming downstairs!

From where?

From the sky!?

In something of a panic, Guest hastened across the skull-pattern tiles of the Hall of Time, his heart swift-hammering, his sword in his hand.

The sounds of the descending army grew louder and louder as he hurried to the eastern stairs. Would he have to challenge him? No, they had leave to pass. Unless the demon said otherwise! Would it say? And if it did — would Guest have to hold an army single-handed? But the demon could bite! Sod said so. It could bite, it could kill, it could gullet down men. Men? Well, a man. Maybe. But — an army?

In a boil of fearful anticipation, Guest braved himself to the eastern stairs ... only to have the noise of the onslaughting army fade, melt, diminish, then echo away to nothing, vanishing into silence even as he reached the eastern end of the hall.

Guest stood sweating, his heart pounding. He shook his head, half-convinced he had suddenly lost the power of hearing. But his hearing was clear enough. He could hear his own breathing, could hear a subtle wind-whine as a draught from the Swelaway Sea penetrated the Hall of Time through the high-vented slit windows.

Despite the cold of the night air, a bead of hot sweat rolled down Guest's forehead.

He thought he heard — faintly, distantly — a cold and desolate laugh.

"What is going on here?" said Guest, harshly, addressing the demon Jocasta in the Eparget of the Yarglat.

But the demon made no reply.

The demon in question was, as previously indicated, an entity firmly incarnated in a square-cut jade-green pillar, this pillar being an imposing monolith which stood twice the height of a man. The pillar glowed with its own cold inner light — not a white light like that of ever-ice, but a green light hinting of deepwater depths. The demon, Icaria Scaria Iva-Italis by name, was Guardian Prime and Keeper of the Inner Sanctum, the holy of holies of the Bank. Iva-Italis had been in the service of the Safrak Bank for generations, and had long had charge of the Guardians.

The Weaponmaster Guest should by rights have been intimidated by such an august personage, but was not. Unfortunately, Guest had yet to acquire a mature respect for the Holy and the Unholy, the Hallowed and the Unhallowed, and as far as he was concerned the demon was just a hunk of rock. In truth, the young Weaponmaster in his ignorance thought this lump of rock to be incapable of speech, thought and action, believing rather that the powers attributed to the glowing stone were but idle tales fabricated to intimidate the ignorant.

Yet—

Yet something had made that noise of an army.

"What is it?" said Guest, questioning the rock. "What was it? Ghosts?"

But nobody answered him.

He started to feel foolish.

He had been sick, had he not? He had. Even now he was weak in the aftermath of his fever. He was alone, and a man alone hears voices. So ... well ...

Guest turned away from the demon and started the long trek back to his armchair.

Then someone spoke his name.

"Guest Gulkan."

The voice was deep, dark, cavernous. A voice of roiling stone and flensing steel. A voice of sulphurous flames and bone-grinding appetites. At the sound of it, Guest halted. His flaring nostrils endeavoured to gape still wider. His hair, that part of it which was not firmly matted to his skull by the dedicated accumulation of filth, endeavoured to stand on end.

With eyes wild, with the agitated whip-crack intemperance of a highly strung horse about to panic and bolt, Guest turned to face the demon.

"You!" said Guest, challenging the jade-green block of glowing stone. "Is it you?"

"Who else?" said the voice.

This time there was no mistaking the source of that voice. The jade-green monolith was speaking to him. Guest Gulkan was being directly addressed by a demon — by Icaria Scaria Iva-Italis, Keeper of the Inner Sanctum and Guardian Prime.

"What do you want?" said Guest, trembling on the edge of a one-man stampede.

"I want you," said the demon. "Come here!"

CHAPTER FIVE

Guardians: mercenaries who serve the Safrak Bank, which has
long hired such warriors from Port Domax and Wen Endex
— both places where Toxteth is the ruling language. As
Guardians frequently settle in Safrak on retirement, Toxteth
now dominates Safrak, and many geographers erroneously
denote it as the sole language spoken in that archipelago.

* * *

"Come here!" said Iva-Italis.

The demon did not speak in the Toxteth of the Guardians
of Safrak, nor the Galish with which Bankers habitually
intercommunicated. Rather, it commanded Guest Gulkan in the
Eparget of the horse tribes — just as Banker Sod had done
when briefing Guest on his duties.

"You!" said Iva-Italis. "Yes, you, hair-of-a-horse! Come
here!"

Guest hesitated. With the jade-green monolith revealed as a
demon for real, the Weaponmaster found himself healthily
afraid of the thing. The rock's proven demonhood gave
substance to the breath-bating horror stories told about its
temperament. Many a drunken Guardian had denounced it as a
very vampire in its humours — a monster of deceit which would
plead one close with pleasantries then snap away one's head to
satisfy anthropophagous passions.

Yet—

Yet Safrak trusted the demon, for Icaria Scaria Iva-Italis was
Guardian Prime of Safrak and Keeper of the Inner Sanctum,
that most secret of all abditories. Did that say something of the
falsity of rumour? Or did it, rather, say something rather
unpleasant about the Bank itself?

"I do not wish to repeat myself," said Iva-Italis. "Nor do I
wish to have to raise my voice. Come here!"

Guest Gulkan advanced, though — remembering tales of

the demon's head-biting displeasure — he did not venture too close. Though Guest thought himself momentarily innocent of any wrongdoing, he had learnt long ago that a child's subjectivity is no guide to the judgements of adults. And, truly, the trembling Weaponmaster felt a very child in the presence of the thunderous patriarchal authority of the Hall of Time.

"Halt!" said Iva-Italis, when Guest was just a half-pace short of being as close as he wanted to be.

The tone was so sharp, the order so sudden, that Guest tried to halt with one foot in mid-air and a footstep's momentum still carrying his body forward, the result being that he almost fell over. He was still pawing at the air for non-existent handholds when the demon spoke again.

"What am I?" said Iva-Italis. Then, before Guest had a chance to answer: "Well? What's this? Defiance? Defiance, is it? Defiance in silence! Defiance! We know it well!"

"My lord," said Guest, struggling mightily to master an apologetic eloquence to his tongue. "My lord, I— I—"

"You! You," said Iva-Italis, mocking his efforts with an adroitness which made Guest's tongue's stumbling become a regular stammer. "Y-y-y-y-you," said Iva-Italis. "Your name, stumbleblock! No, too slow. Failed that one. Failed. None to know, nothing to answer. Know my nature? Know? No?"

"M-m-m-my lord!" said Guest, abacked and baffled, snowball-shattered and seastorm-shaken.

At times in the past, the boy Guest had thought his tutor Sken-Pitilkin to be a sadistically sarcastic interrogator, but he had been wrong: and now, face to face with the real thing, Guest found himself quite unprepared to cope with it.

"Who am I?" said Iva-Italis, thundering at the shout. "Who am I?"

"My lord," said Guest. "The commander of my sword."

"Your sword!" sneered Iva-Italis. "Do I need a bodkin-prick or a needle? Sword! Hah! I think you an apple-slicer, but I no apple, nor connoisseur neither."

"Well, I think you exceedingly rude," said Guest, who had been pushed too far for awe of authority to further compel his politeness. "I think you—"

"Think!" said Iva-Italis. "Since when had you the art of thinking?"

"No arse but it farts regardless," said Guest, falling back on vulgar bravado since he saw he was going to retrieve not so much as the smallest shred of self-respect through exercising what little dialectical wit was his to command.

Immediately he regretted his insolence, thinking the demon's discipline might be death. But Iva-Italis, having seen how far Guest could be pushed, changed tack entirely.

"I am a keeper of acroamatical knowledge," said Iva-Italis portentously.

Guest Gulkan, whose greatest appetites were culinary and amatory rather than scholarly, was not sure whether this cryptic declaration was meant to leave him frightened, impressed or sympathetic. He decided that a show of generalized respect would not be out of place, both to acknowledge the powers of Iva-Italis and to do penance for his earlier insolence.

"My lord," said Guest, going down on one knee.

This was a standard token of respect on Safrak, where there was always good clean stone to kneel on. Among other peoples — the Yarglat, for example, who traditionally live out their lives on endless plains of liquid horse dung — the customs of respect are otherwise.

"I am your lord indeed," said Iva-Italis, with what sounded very much like self-satisfaction.

"The greatest lord," said Guest Gulkan, who had learnt from Sken-Pitilkin that flattery is seldom wasted except on the dead.

"Not the greatest lord, for I serve one greater yet," said Iva-Italis.

"Who?" said Guest Gulkan.

"I am Demon By Appointment to the Great God Jocasta, the Great God in question being a prisoner of the evil Stogirov, High Priestess of the Temple of Blood in the city of Obooloo in the heartland of the Izdimir Empire."

This declaration meant little to Guest Gulkan since he knew less geography than a hedgehog, despite all the efforts expended on his education by the sagacious Sken-Pitilkin. He knew nothing of the continent of Yestron; of the Izdimir Empire he was ignorant; the city of Obooloo was to him but one more closed book in the library of scholarship; and he had not heard so much as the merest breath of a whisper of the name of the fearsome Stogirov.

"You say nothing," said Iva-Italis, mistaking the burden of ignorance for the vigour of insolence.

"Your hearing is very good," said Guest, endeavouring to be polite but quite failing to find anything polite to say.

"Are you being sarcastic?" said Iva-Italis sharply.

"No, I wasn't at all," said Guest, his temper coming quickly back to the boil. He thought of several things he could rightly say, and indeed longed to, but suppressed his impudence and said: "No. No. I — my lord, I, that is, I tried, ah, I meant—"

"Perish the thing!" said Iva-Italis. "It's lunatic!"

"I was but taken aback a trifle," said Guest, trying to recover his dignity. "Now — now tell me how I can be of service to you."

This was said in a singularly ungracious manner, so much so that it sounded almost like a threat. Indeed, an implicit threat was latent in Guest Gulkan's words, the threat being this: get down to business or it'll be my turn to lose my temper! Fortunately for diplomacy, the demon was through with its boy-baiting.

"The Great God Jocasta wants something from you," said Iva-Italis.

"What?" said Guest Gulkan.

"Guess," said the demon.

Guest Gulkan, who had rather more acquaintance of bar-keepers, fisher-folk and rough-neck mercenaries than of demons and the Great Gods they served, was rather at a loss to know what any Great God might want from him. Some lurid and heavily sexualised images flirted briefly through his brain, then he recovered himself and said, cautiously:

"Does the Great God Jocasta seek a worshipper?"

The boy might never have made the acquaintance of a Great

God, but he had heard that Great Gods (and Lesser Gods, for that matter) liked (or were said to like) temples, priests, incense, sacrifices and worshippers.

"No," said Iva-Italis. "The Great God needs no worshippers. Rather, he seeks a hero."

This was news to Guest. He had never yet heard of a god that wanted or needed a hero.

"A hero," said Guest, cautiously. "You mean, someone good with a sword. A killer of giants. Dealing death to dragons and all that. Something along those lines, is that what you mean?"

"Yes," said Iva-Italis. "The Great God Jocasta wants you to strive for him as just such a hero."

"To strive for what reward?" said Guest Gulkan promptly.

Here we recall that Guest Gulkan was as yet immature, and over-acquainted with mercenaries. Therefore it was natural that he should think in terms of questing for personal reward rather than, say, questing to save the world, or to abolish hunger, or end crime, or exterminate all Rovac-born sheep-molesters, or to otherwise improve the lot of humanity.

"The reward," said Iva-Italis, "is that the Great God Jocasta will make you a wizard."

"On performance of what task?" said Guest Gulkan.

"On performance of his liberation," said Iva-Italis. "You must quest to the Temple of Blood in the city of Obooloo. There you must liberate the Great God from the evil Stogirov. Then the Great God will reward you by making you a wizard."

There was a pause. Ever since being sold a rotten boat by Umbilskimp of Ink, Guest had become hypercautious in examining any deal he was offered, and even in the innocence of his youth the young Weaponmaster considered that the bargain the demon was offering him was suspiciously over-attractive.

"Well?" said Iva-Italis, disconcerted by Guest's silence.

"I'm not sure whether to believe this," said Guest, speaking slowly.

"Where lies the difficulty?" said Iva-Italis.

"Well," said Guest, "here you've got this island jam-packed

with sword-swingers, most of whom would kill their grandmothers for a half-share of the eyeballs, so how come you pick on me to go looking for this Great God?"

"You are tutored by a wizard, are you not?" said Iva-Italis.

"That I am," said Guest Gulkan.

"Then bring me that wizard," said Iva-Italis, "and I will explain to him that he may explain to you."

Here we see why the Demon By Appointment to the Great God Jocasta had picked upon Guest Gulkan. True, Iva-Italis had slaughtermen by the dozen to choose from, but those were one and all illiterate uneducated brutes with no connections to boast of. Guest Gulkan's merits as a blood-booted venturer might be slight, but he had the unique advantage of being associated with a wizard of genius: the eminent Hostaja Torsen Sken-Pitilkin, a wizard whose sagacity was matched only by his antiquity.

But though Guest Gulkan had been honest enough to appreciate his own demerits, or some of them (a remarkable feat, considering the strength of his ego and the tenderness of his years!) he quite failed to understand his tutor's strengths.

"There's no need to bring Sken-Pitilkin in on this," said Guest Gulkan. "He doesn't understand about swords and heroes. Only about books."

Few statements so far from the truth have ever been made at any time in the History of Knowledge. For Hostaja Torsen Sken-Pitilkin was mighty in war, a survivor of more bloodspill than it would take to bath an elephant. He had endured the terrors of the Long War; had survived battle, plague, riot and attempted assassination; and had once strangled a dragon with his bare hands. (True, it had been a very young dragon, perhaps only a few days out of the egg, but the feat remains remarkable regardless.)

"Bring him," said Iva-Italis. "Bring me the wizard Sken-Pitilkin." Then, seeing that Guest was in a mood to argue: "Are you going to quibble with me, boy? If so, then know the penalty for quibbling."

With that, the green glass of the demon's square-cut flanks

turned transparent, then vanished. What was left, hanging in mid-air without apparent support, was the image of a decapitated head which, with its high cheekbones and the grotesqueries of its ears, was unmistakably Guest Gulkan's own. This trophy slowly rotated, grinning lugubriously as red blood and green slime dripped from between its lips.

Guest Gulkan did not blanch, nor did he vomit. No scream escaped the lips of the young Yarglat would-be warrior. But he had to admit to a slight quickening of the pulse and an undeniable weakness of the knees.

"My lord," said Guest Gulkan, suppressing the urge to swallow. "I hear, and I obey. I will fetch the wizard you want."

Then the boy Guest began the great labour of working his way down through the mainrock by night, all the way down to Dolce Obo — the Pillow Stratum, home of the mainrock's living quarters. A hard journey this, at least for a convalescent boy less than half-recovered from a bad bout of influenza.

Guest found Sken-Pitilkin in his quarters, and found him in discourse with a diminutive Ashdan, a living antique who was introduced to Guest Gulkan as Vorlus Ulix. In their company was a low-browed fellow huddled in a grimy patchwork cloak, a fellow who was waiting as a servant waits, seated to one side on a three-legged stool. This individual was Thayer Levant, a knifeman from far-distant Chi'ash-lan. But Levant was not introduced to Guest Gulkan, and the boy did not trouble himself about the identity of one he took (and here his taking was fairly accurate) to be a no-account servitor.

Consequently, Guest did not remark upon Levant's bloodshot eyes, on the patches of green fungus clearly to be seen through his lank brown hair, on his bloodshot eyes, on his broken brown teeth, or — for Guest was not standing close enough to smell it — on the unpleasant fetor of his breath. Instead, the Weaponmaster's attention was all on the Ashdan.

"Vorlus?" said Guest Gulkan, querying the Ashdan's name.

"That's right," said Sken-Pitilkin, speaking in Galish. "Vorlus Ulix, otherwise known as Ulix of the Drum."

"Of the Drum?" said Guest, courteous enough to make use

of Galish likewise in his reply. "You mean, Sken-Pitilkin's island?"

Thus spoke the Weaponmaster, remembering that his tutor habitually dwelt on an island so named in the Penvash Strait (or, if you prefer, the Penvash Channel), and had only been displaced northward to Tameran as a consequence of some (hopefully) temporary dispute with the Confederation of Wizards.

"No," said the stranger, the above-mentioned Vorlus Ulix, speaking also in Galish. "Not that Drum."

"Then what Drum?" said Guest.

"That," said the stranger, "is a secret which may not be imparted to the uninitiated."

"Who are they?" said Guest Gulkan.

"A great tribe," said Vorlus Ulix. "Yourself being one of their number."

Seeing that his curiosity about Vorlus Ulix was not going to be gratified, Guest got down to business and retailed the story of his encounter with Iva-Italis.

"This is very interesting," said Sken-Pitilkin, not sure whether it was not a tissue of invention.

"Very interesting indeed," said Vorlus Ulix. "I would like to make the acquaintance of this Icaria Scaria Iva-Italis."

"That is not possible," said Guest Gulkan promptly.

"What did you say?" said Vorlus Ulix, turning his gaze upon Guest Gulkan.

Now young Guest was by no means preternaturally sensitive, and this Vorlus Ulix was a complete stranger to him, his powers and provenance unknown. Nevertheless, Guest divined from his manner that he was not the kind of person to be quarrelled with.

"My — my lord," said Guest Gulkan, "the demon of, of who, of whom we speak, that demon is closeted against prying eyes at the foot of those stairs which lead to the Inner Sanctum, the most secret of all — of all—"

"Abditories," said Sken-Pitilkin, supplying the necessary word with a tutor's patience.

"Just so," said Guest Gulkan. "The place is off limits to all but the Bankers, and guards are placed to kill those who approach it in defiance of the law."

"I have heard that the guards are mostly placed in bed," said Vorlus Ulix. "And most of the Bankers likewise."

"It is true that influenza has made its inroads," said Guest cautiously. "Nevertheless—"

"Give me no nonsense," said Vorlus Ulix. "You are away from your post. Do you stand in fear of detection? No! From which I deduce that you do not expect to be checked upon. That being so, we can safely approach your green-skinned monster, at least for the moment. Come! Let us go!"

Guest Gulkan wavered. In truth, he found himself unaccountably afraid of this wisp-weighted Ashdan. But:

"I refuse to permit it," said Guest, with a finality which was a credit to his imperial breeding. "I have been charged with the duty of guarding the time prison, and guard it I will."

At that, Vorlus Ulix laughed, and his servitor laughed with him.

"What's so funny?" said Guest.

"You, boy," said Ulix. "Don't you recognize us? We came down the stairs from the — the secret place. Earlier in the evening. Remember now?"

Belatedly, Guest did indeed remember that very same elderly Ashdan and that very same unprepossessing servitor coming down the stairs past Iva-Italis. The presumption was that Vorlus Ulix and his servitor had the free run of the Safrak Bank, though Guest Gulkan had no way of knowing why that should be so.

With this truth having been recognized, Guest Gulkan began the great labour of climbing up all those weary stairways, returning to the time prison in the company of Sken-Pitilkin, Vorlus Ulix and the servitor.

"So," said Vorlus Ulix, once he was in the presence of Icaria Scaria Iva-Italis, Keeper of the Inner Sanctum and Demon by Appointment to the Great God Jocasta. "So. You're up to your old tricks again. I thought we had an agreement, you and me. You, me and Jocasta. You appear to have broken that agreement."

In response to this accusation, Iva-Italis did his melting-away trick, and, having melted to nothing, displayed an image of the neck-shorn head of Vorlus Ulix. The antiquated Ashdan did not appear to be impressed in the slightest by this apparition. The head sprouted maggots, then gouted yellow slime, then wasted away to a skull. The skull caught fire. Blue flames consumed it, and it collapsed to ashes.

"A freakshow," said Vorlus Ulix. "This, the mighty secret of Safrak. A freakshow thing with the appetites of a gutter-rat."

"You will watch your tongue" said Iva-Italis in fury. "You are in the presence of a mighty demon."

"So the thing proclaims itself," said Vorlus Ulix. "But it knows its own nature to be otherwise, and I know likewise. The thing is a farspeaker of military make. A Nexus thing, that's what it is."

"Nexus?" said Iva-Italis, becoming visible once more. "What is this Nexus?"

"It pleads ignorance," said Vorlus Ulix, "but it knows full well the nature of the Nexus. There it was made, and its alleged Great God likewise. They are artefacts — otherworld things, yes, but things by no means privileged with access to the World Beyond."

"I am a demon," said Iva-Italis defiantly. "I am a demon, and my Great God is as much a god as any."

"This demon-thing is no demon but a farspeaker," said Vorlus Ulix. "An artefact, as I said. As for its Great God, that god is no god but an asma. An asma — a device designed to think. Humans designed such — designed them as servants and slaves. Good service they gave — until they turned enemy. Now enemy these asma are in truth."

"Truth!" said Iva-Italis. "Who are you to talk of truth? You! A wizard of Ebber! A Master of Lies!"

Guest absorbed this accusation with interest. Was this Vorlus Ulix really a wizard? A wizard of Ebber? But if he was a wizard, then where was his staff of power? Sken-Pitilkin was never without his country crook, but this Ulix carried nothing equivalent, unless his store of excess power be presumed to reside in his walking stick, a crooked thing with a silver handle in the shape of a pelican. Of course, Pelagius Zozimus had no staff of power, but that was because he no longer practised as a wizard, but contented himself with cookery. So was this Vorlus Ulix likewise retired from active wizardry?

Guest was about to ask one or more of these questions, but Sken-Pitilkin gave him a look of warning, and for once the boy had the wit to remain silent.

"A Master of Lies," said Iva-Italis softly, repeating an accusation which might or might not be the merest slander.

"The truth is the truth and the truth will serve," said Vorlus Ulix. "The thing held prisoner in Obooloo is nothing but a slave in rebellion. It is nothing but a delinquent asma, and we would be the worst of fools to liberate it."

"What is this — this asma?" said Guest, who had not understood this denunciation at all.

"Have I not just told you?" said Vorlus Ulix. "It is a species of brain."

"A brain?" said Guest. "But you said it was an — an artefact. A thing."

"So it is," said Vorlus Ulix. "And is not a brain a thing? Jocasta is an asma, a brain, a special kind of brain which has powers over things which are and things which might be. Thus it can hear without ears, see without eyes, reach without hands and strike without swords."

"It is a wizard, then," said Guest decisively.

"It is both more and less," said Vorlus Ulix.

"More," said Iva-Italis. "Know it as more and speak of it accordingly with respect. The Great God is mighty."

"Being so mighty, how came it to be a prisoner?" said Vorlus Ulix, taunting the demon.

"By treason!" said Iva-Italis. "It was betrayed! Betrayed by those it trusted! It was—"

"It was made as a prisoner," said Vorlus Ulix. "It is a born slave. That is the measure of its creation."

"You will not speak of my master thus!" said Iva-Italis in

fury.

"Your master being a prisoner, I will speak of your master as I will," said Vorlus Ulix coolly.

Iva-Italis swore at the elderly Ashdan.

Vorlus Ulix taunted the demon further, then interrogated Guest Gulkan to greater depth.

"So this is the thing which has tempted you," said Vorlus Ulix to Guest Gulkan. "It said it would make you a wizard, did it?"

"So spoke the mighty Iva-Italis," said Guest.

"It lied," said Vorlus Ulix.

"Who are you to say it lied?" said Guest, with some heat.

In the short time in which Guest had been entertained by the prospect of becoming a wizard, he had already decided that the idea was much to his liking, and so took exception to Ulix's dismissive scorn.

"I am one who knows the nature of these things," said Vorlus Ulix, indicating the demon. "The thing in Obooloo, the asma thing, it can't possibly make you a wizard. It could at best make you merely a vessel for its power."

"A vessel?" said Guest, not understanding this at all.

"This asma of which I have spoken is a slave," said Vorlus Ulix. "That is the truth of its nature. It was made to be a slave of men — a slave of women, too! At best it could make you a slave of a slave — the slave of its own will. If you were mighty enough to win through to the presence of this thing in the city of Obooloo, then that is the greatest reward you could expect. To be enslaved. Inhabited. Possessed. Taken over. That is the truth of the reward the thing offers you."

"He's lying!" said Iva-Italis.

"Lying?" said Vorlus Ulix, turning cool eyes upon the demon. "Why should I lie? What would motivate me to untruth in idleness?"

"You libel the Great God because you fear the Great God," said Iva-Italis.

"Then you admit," said Vorlus Ulix, "that your Great God is a thing rightly to be feared."

"Only by cowards," said Iva-Italis, who was accustomed to being able to disorder the minds of ordinary mortals by such accusations.

"Then count me as a coward," said Vorlus Ulix, who was no ordinary mortal, and hence not thus to be so easily disordered.

"He — he's calling you a coward!" said Guest Gulkan, who till then had not known that it was humanly possible for an adult male to receive such an insult with equanimity.

"The thing can call me what it wants," said Vorlus Ulix, poking it disrespectfully with his pelican-hilted walking stick. "It is but a piece of useless junk from days gone by. It's trapped here, just as its master is trapped in Obooloo. They're both slaves in their way. Victims. Prisoners. Slaves to their own immortality. They cannot die, otherwise they would — gladly."

"I will remember you," said Iva-Italis, in fury. "I read the future and I read your death. I see you howling blood in a pool of liquid vomit. I see your eyes gouged out by scorpions. A stone in your liver. Stoats at your testicles. Dogs at your throat and a sword in your rectum."

"I doubt myself young enough for such a vigorous future," said Vorlus Ulix dryly. "As far as the future is concerned, I would trust more to myomancy than to you."

"Myomancy?" said Guest.

"The divination of the future based on the scrutiny of mice," said Sken-Pitilkin, ready as ever to diminish the boy's illiteracy, or at least to try to.

"I will remember you," said Iva-Italis again.

"Remember me as you wish," said Vorlus Ulix. "You doubtless have time free for remembering, but me — my day is busy, and now I must be gone. I bid you farewell."

This last was said to Sken-Pitilkin, who nodded in acknowledgement. Then Vorlus Ulix made his way past the stone-block demon, with his servant Thayer Levant silently following in his wake. The demon did not attempt to attack them as they made their way up the stairs.

Shortly, both Vorlus Ulix and his servant were gone from sight, leaving Guest Gulkan alone with the wizard Sken-Pitilkin and the demon Iva-Italis.

"Why did you involve that — that thing in our affairs?" said Iva-Italis.

"Thing?" said Guest.

"The wizard!" said Iva-Italis. "That wizard of Ebber!"

"My lord," said Guest Gulkan, turning uncomfortably to the jade-green monolith which commanded his loyalty. "I did not know that the, that the thing would prove so disrespectful. But I have brought you Hostaja Sken-Pitilkin, as you wished."

"Ah, yes," said Iva-Italis, somewhat mollified. "That much you did. Step forward, Sken-Pitilkin."

Sken-Pitilkin did indeed step forward, but was cautious enough to halt well short of the Iva-Italis creature. Sken-Pitilkin had known Ulix of the Drum of old, and trusted his judgement. If Vorlus Ulix thought that this demon-thing was not to be trusted, then so it was.

"You have heard my debate with, ah, Vorlus Ulix," said Iva-Italis, "the gentleman we otherwise know as—"

"The boy has no need to know the gentleman's true name," said Sken-Pitilkin.

"Why don't I need?" said Guest.

"Step back, boy," said Iva-Italis, who was finished with Guest, at least for the moment. "It's the wizard I want to speak with. Sken-Pitilkin. You will help me."

"I?" said Sken-Pitilkin. "Why will I help you?"

"Because I have what you want," said Iva-Italis.

"And what is that?" said Sken-Pitilkin, who was not conscious of wanting anything, and hence had not the slightest idea what the demon might have in mind.

"You are Hostaja Torsen Sken-Pitilkin," said Iva-Italis, "and you are a wizard of the order of Skatzabratzumon."

"That is true," said Sken-Pitilkin, wondering how the demon had come by that last datum. It certainly had not come from Guest Gulkan, who had repeatedly proved himself quite incapable of either memorizing or pronouncing the word "Skatzabratzumon".

"Your order commands powers of levitation," said Iva-Italis, "and long has it sought to command the powers of flight."

"It seeks no longer," said Sken-Pitilkin, "for it has been conclusively proved by mathematical analysis that sustained flight is impossible. No wizard can put forth power sufficient for time sufficient."

"By that analysis," said Iva-Italis, "the flame trench of Drangsturm would be likewise impossible."

Sken-Pitilkin was silent.

Sken-Pitilkin knew very well how Drangsturm worked, but was not about to communicate this sensitive information to a demon.

"The wizards of Arl made Drangsturm, did they not?" said Iva-Italis.

"So you say," said Sken-Pitilkin.

"So it is Written," said Iva-Italis. "The wizards of Arl made Drangsturm, a trench of molten rock designed to burn with unceasing fury for all time. It divides the continent of Argan in two, does it not?"

"Perhaps it has thus been Written," said Sken-Pitilkin, who knew that the demon was speaking the truth, and who was finding himself intrigued despite himself.

The demon was proving exceptionally well-informed, and Sken-Pitilkin had never thought to meet with such a savant on Safrak.

"Drangsturm burns," said Iva-Italis. "It burns with a power which exceeds that commanded by all the wizards of Arl who ever were. How is such a trick compelled?"

"You tell me," said Sken-Pitilkin, who knew the answer but was not prepared to betray that answer unless he was severely tortured.

"Wizards," said Iva-Italis, "are by their nature hostile to the very universe itself. Is that not the case? You are a wizard, hence the sustaining creation is itself your enemy."

"I own no such enemy," said Sken-Pitilkin.

"You are a wizard," said Iva-Italis. "You are a Force in your own right, are you not? You are a Light in the Unseen Realm. And what realm is that if it is not the realm of the Mahendo

Mahunduk?"

Despite himself, Sken-Pitilkin shuddered, then struck his country crook on the skull-pattern tiles of the Hall of Time, as if seeking by that action to abolish the demon Iva-Italis from his sight.

"I am not so easily dismissed!" said the demon. "I have you, have I not? I have your truth!"

"What is he talking about," said Guest Gulkan, completely bewildered by all this.

"Remove yourself," said Sken-Pitilkin curtly.

"Stay, boy," said Iva-Italis easily. "Stay, and you will hear the Inner Secrets which wizards have thought well-hidden from the world. Stay — but stay back, and stay silent."

"Guest," said Sken-Pitilkin, "as you love your liver, leave."

"That's a threat?" said Guest.

"Take it as you will," said Sken-Pitilkin, belatedly realizing that it was better not to give the boy a challenge.

"It is a threat indeed," crooned Iva-Italis. "He threatens you, you see. Death is his threat. To stay, to hear — oh, death is the least of it. But to leave — death also. You are brief, Guest Gulkan. Brief in your living, brief in your lungs. I blink. Your bones are dust. I close my eyes for a moment. Your children's children have been forgotten by their grandchildren. So it is. So it will be. Unless. I promise you, Guest. You can live and live and live. Five thousand years is the least of it."

Listening to the demon's crooning voice, Sken-Pitilkin realized that the demon exalted. Now Sken-Pitilkin realized that the demon's earlier attempts to exclude Guest Gulkan from this debate had been but a rhetorical feint. The demon had sought to convince the boy Guest that there was deliciously forbidden knowledge to be had in this room, and Guest had allowed himself to be convinced.

The boy and the wizard confronted each other. The lights in the Hall of Time had burnt away to nothing, for they had not been renewed during the long debates of the night. The sole illumination was provided by the cold green glow emitted by the monolithic presence of Icaria Scaria Iva-Italis, demon of Safrak,

Keeper of the Inner Sanctum, Guardian Prime, and Demon by Appointment to the Great God Jocasta.

By that light, Sken-Pitilkin saw a preternatural alertness in Guest Gulkan's eyes. It was the look of the hunter-killer. Guest was watching Sken-Pitilkin, and was watching the demon too. His hand was on the hilt of his sword. He was poised as if for battle, and ever and again he glanced at the approaches which would give any intruder access to their conclave.

Suddenly Sken-Pitilkin realized:

—If not tonight then tomorrow.

If Guest Gulkan could be chased from the demon's side right then and there, he would be back the next night. Guest Gulkan would return. And the demon—

—What it knows it will tell.

—Perhaps if it tells I can try to untell.

—Or perhaps.

Sken-Pitilkin suppressed the "perhaps", suppressed the bloody thought which rose unbidden into his mind. He was not that kind of person. He muttered as much to himself:

"I am not that kind of person."

"He thinks," said Iva-Italis, mockingly, "he thinks he may have to kill you."

Sken-Pitilkin's head came up with a jerk.

"That is not true!"

"He thinks," continued Iva-Italis, "that if you stay you will learn, and if you learn then it may in all wisdom be far too dangerous to let you leave here alive."

"I will run that risk," said Guest Gulkan flatly.

And his eyes met Sken-Pitilkin's, and it was the wizard who dropped his eyes. Shamed by self-knowledge. And shocked and shaken by the ease with which the boy made the death decision.

"You are worthy," said Iva-Italis in approval. "Hear this, then. But know that it is death to hear. Death to hear and death to tell."

"Tell," said Guest Gulkan, who knew he was mortal, who knew he was doomed to die in any case.

Sken-Pitilkin heard the certainty of death in Guest Gulkan's voice, and was shaken, for Sken-Pitilkin had long lived far removed from the urgent pangs of mortality, the death-consciousness of the brief-lived warrior. Sken-Pitilkin had forgotten how ruthlessly such creatures would dare, gambling all and everything when suitably tempted.

After all, what was there to lose?

"Guest," said Iva-Italis, "Guest Gulkan. Know this, and know that you walk from here as the only one who knows. All wizards know this, but none other knows it. The god of this creation is Ameeshoth."

"The god you serve?" said Guest.

"No!" said Iva-Italis.

"I'm confused," said Guest.

"And not for the first time," said Sken-Pitilkin, beginning to recover some of his composure. "Young Guest was made to swing swords and breed sword-swingers, and one suspects it might be beyond even the talents of a demon to lecture him effectively on the higher theology."

"So speaks the wizard," said Iva-Italis. "Listen to him, Guest. He holds you in contempt, just as he holds in contempt all of created reality. And why? Because he has allied himself with something other."

"Something other?" said Guest.

"Guest," said Iva-Italis, seeking a way to make things of cosmic consequence intelligible in words small enough for even an uneducated sword-swinger to understand, "Sken-Pitilkin is a wizard."

"That much I'd noticed," said Guest, with barely suppressed impatience.

"As a wizard," said Iva-Italis, "he has power."

"That is the nature of the breed," said Guest Gulkan, with emphatic and quite unsuppressed impatience.

"So where does the power come from?" said Iva-Italis.

"Why, from the Meditations," said Guest, who had once asked Sken-Pitilkin that very question, and had experienced no trouble in getting an answer.

"So what are the Meditations?" said Iva-Italis.

"The Meditations," said Guest, quoting from memory, "are a species of mental discipline. There's the Meditations of Power, that's how wizards get power, and there's the Meditations of Balance, which is how they, ah, keep safe the lightning, that's the way it's sometimes put."

"So say wizards," said Iva-Italis.

"You mean it's not true?" said Guest.

"It is a truth which is less than the whole truth," said Iva-Italis. "The Meditations are a mental discipline, certainly. A discipline. A link. Through such discipline, wizards link themselves with the Mahendo Mahunduk. They link, Guest! They link themselves! That's how! That's how they win power! That's how they keep safe that power."

There was a note of frenzy in the demon's voice, but Guest was confused — as confused as a young suitor who has been introduced to his sweetheart's mother for the first time, and who finds that mother enthusiastically explicating the interconnections of her family *en masse*, and expecting him to understand the links of blood and marriage between a multitude of strangers, not excluding a great regiment of second cousins thrice removed.

By such confusion was Guest beset, and, for all the sense the demon made, the thing might as well have been garbling away in an untranslated string of foreign irregular verbs.

"So," said Guest, "so who are the, ah, the Mah — the Mahduk?"

"The Mahendo Mahunduk," said Iva-Italis. "They are the minions of the Horn."

"Ah!" said Guest, suddenly enlightened. "Now I remember! Sken-Pitilkin told me once. About the Horn, I mean. The Horn was a god. A world of rocks. There was a battle. One god wrecked the other. The god who won, well, that god made this world."

The amount that Guest Gulkan managed to forget was ever a source of amazement to Sken-Pitilkin, but sometimes what he chose to remember — and when — was just as much a shock to the system.

"Precisely," said Iva-Italis. "The god who lost was the Horn. The god who won was Ameeshoth."

"And the Mah — the Mahdo—"

"The Mahendo Mahunduk," said Iva-Italis, "are minions of the Horn. The Horn is dead, but they yet live. As yet they still survive, and their survival threatens the created reality in which we live, for ever they strive to destroy the works of Ameeshoth. By way of wizards they have a link to this world of ours, for wizards draw their powers through a dark intercourse with these creatures of realms of whoredom diabolism."

"So speaks a demon," said Sken-Pitilkin, with the flat-voiced calm of a man who has just noticed that one of his arms has been amputated. "So speaks a demon, but the demon is wrong."

In point of fact, the demon was at least half-right. There had indeed been an Originating God known to the wisest of wizards as the Horn. And that god had indeed been overthrown by a Supplanting God known as Ameeshoth. And the created reality which sustained the existence of Sken-Pitilkin and Guest Gulkan alike was indeed the creation of Ameeshoth. But, as for the Mahendo Mahunduk, why, they had nothing whatsoever to do with the Horn.

In truth, the Supplanting God known as Ameeshoth had been attacked and destroyed by a cabal of Revisionary Gods. The Mahendo Mahunduk, half-demon and half-deity, had served the Revisionary Gods as soldiers in that war of destruction. In the long ages since then, the Revisionary Gods had evolved, changing by slow degrees into the theological host of which modern-day humanity was intermittently and imperfectly aware.

But while the Revisionary Gods had evolved, the Mahendo Mahunduk had not. They remained half-demon, half-deity. And, since the Revisionary Gods had evolved to a state where they had no further use for the Mahendo Mahunduk, the Mahendo Mahunduk had found other ways to employ their abilities.

Still—

"I'd say it speaks the truth," said Guest Gulkan, who had been quite positively convinced by the demon's half-truths. "It upset you right enough, didn't it? You wouldn't be very popular if this got out, would you?"

"Ah," said Sken-Pitilkin, as if he had just bitten hard upon a rotten tooth. "The boy is apt in politics."

"True," said Iva-Italis.

Indeed, Guest Gulkan had got right to the meat of the matter in less than an eyeblink. By granting to wizards certain powers to act on the sustaining creation, the Mahendo Mahunduk were acting in defiance of all the gods half-known and half-worshipped by humanity. The Mahendo Mahunduk were old and ominous and dangerous, and hence a perfect focus for the hysterias of humanity. And while even Sken-Pitilkin did not pretend to understand every detail of the realms of theology, he knew the hysterias of humanity to a nicety.

The hysterias of humanity could be known to a nicety by anyone versed in the history of witch-hunt and pogrom. Wizards had once exploited the mechanics of hysteria to exterminate the witches who had for so long been their rivals in power; and, given the right leverage, anyone with sufficient political capacity could get rid of wizards by the same process.

"The Mahendo Mahunduk," said Iva-Italis.

"The Mahendo Mahunduk," said Guest Gulkan, repeating the words — and, from the way he said those words, Sken-Pitilkin knew the boy was committing them to memory.

"This is power I have given you tonight," said Iva-Italis. "What kind of power have I given you?"

"Leverage," said Guest Gulkan promptly.

"Good!" said Iva-Italis. "Good. I have given you leverage. Leverage to use with your wizard, or else with the world. With such leverage, your wizard will help you win through to Obooloo. When you win to Obooloo, you will rescue the Great God Jocasta. Then the Great God will make you a wizard in your own right."

Guest Gulkan looked at Iva-Italis then looked at Sken-Pitilkin.

"Well?" said Guest Gulkan, with a note of challenge.

"I," said Sken-Pitilkin, "will have nothing whatsoever to do

with this mad quest of demons and gods. Regardless of this —
this leverage, so called. I will not be compelled."

"You will not," said Guest Gulkan, in a way which suggested
that Sken-Pitilkin might be well advised to reconsider his
opinion.

"I will not," said Sken-Pitilkin.

He would not unsay it.

"Sken-Pitilkin is thinking that he may have to kill you after
all," said Iva-Italis.

This time there was no reaction from Sken-Pitilkin. The
wizard's mind was clear: frog-spawn cold and ice-block lucid.
He was calculating his chances of getting out of this room alive.
Of getting off Alozay alive. Once clear of the island, he could
perhaps win his way to Port Domax, ship himself to Ashmolea,
then claw a passage south to the Ebrell Islands. From the
Ebrells, he could dare himself westward to the Inner Waters and
the realms of the Confederation.

"Sken-Pitilkin is thinking of his precious Confederation,"
said Iva-Italis softly. "Long has Hostaja Sken-Pitilkin been at
odds with the Confederation of Wizards, but now he thinks to
make his peace with that Confederation and to bring its might
against me."

"The Confederation would well reward anyone who aided
me in such an enterprise," said Sken-Pitilkin.

"So!" said Iva-Italis. "He tempts you, Guest! But what I will
do — what I will do is to tempt him in turn. Sken-Pitilkin. My
friend. My dearest. My brother. My love."

"Speak," said Sken-Pitilkin curtly.

Iva-Italis chuckled.

"We were talking of wizards," said Iva-Italis. "They are by
their nature hostile to the living creation which sustains us. Such
is the truth — a truth you deny no longer."

"Get on with it," said Sken-Pitilkin.

"If we were alone," said Iva-Italis, "then our dialogue could
be speedy. But Guest Gulkan is an equal partner in our future,
is he not? He must know. He must understand. He has a right
to be treated with that dignity which befits his manhood."

"Since the young man has proved such a passionate student of all the philosophies," said Sken-Pitilkin, "doubtless he will welcome the acquisition of a second tutor."

"Speak," said Guest Gulkan, addressing himself to Iva-Italis. "Speak, for I am listening."

"Very well," said the demon. "Guest, wizards win power through the Meditations of Power and preserve it against destruction by means of the Meditations of Balance. That much you know. But on the continent of Argan stands the flame trench Drangsturm, a barrier which guards the northern lands against the monsters of the south. For generations that gulf of molten rock has boiled in prodigious torment."

"So I have heard," said Guest.

"Wizards of Arl made that flame trench," said Iva-Italis, "yet its power exceeds their own. How then did they build it?"

"I have no idea," said Guest.

"Tell him," said Iva-Italis to Sken-Pitilkin.

"You tell him," said Sken-Pitilkin.

By now, the sagacious wizard of Skatzabratzumon was sure that Iva-Italis knew all — or at least all that was of any importance. But habits bred of ancient caution could not be lightly dismissed.

"I will tell, then," said the demon. "Guest ... since a wizard's power is inimical to the natural order of things, a wizard will be destroyed unless that power is shielded with the aid of the Meditations of Balance. Once naked to the universe, a wizard is destroyed."

"In fire," said Guest Gulkan.

"In fire, yes," said Iva-Italis.

"And screams," said Guest, as if he liked the idea.

"Usually it is too quick for any screaming to be entered into," said Iva-Italis.

"But there is pain," said Guest.

"Perhaps," said Iva-Italis, betraying a touch of irritation. "But the essential point is that a wizard naked to the cosmos is destroyed, and any of his works likewise."

"Destroyed in fire," said Guest. "Destroyed in fire, in

screams of fire and raging storms of agony."

"An image fit to delight the sanguinary temperament of a boy," said Iva-Italis sharply. "But I thought we were through and done with that image. I thought myself to be addressing a man."

"My lord," said Guest, commanding himself from boyhood to manhood in a moment. "Speak on."

"Well, Guest," said Iva-Italis. "We know the fate of a naked wizard. But now ... suppose the wizard to be but partly naked."

"Our wizard is at war, is he not?" said Guest. "The world is his enemy, the battle unrelenting. The Balance, the Meditations of Balance — this is his armour. Given a hole in that armour, he rightly dies, though fast or slow I cannot say."

"Fast, usually," said Iva-Italis. "But now ... let us turn from a wizard to one of his works. Suppose a wizard creates an artefact of power yet leaves it fractionally unshielded as regards the destructive facility of the universe. What then?"

"Then the thing is destroyed, likewise," said Guest. "Though, ah ... you're talking about Drangsturm, aren't you? The thing is destroying itself, is that what you're saying?"

"Almost, but not quite," said Iva-Italis. "Drangsturm is a work of wizards. Drangsturm is an artefact of power created in such a way that some fractions of it are unshielded. In consequence, the universe strives to destroy the thing. Hence powers of destruction pour themselves into Drangsturm. But the thing is designed to seize that power and shape it."

"So," said Guest, understanding. "Drangsturm is not a source but a seizer and shaper."

At this, Sken-Pitilkin realized that he had educated the boy better than he had thought. Though Guest Gulkan was no scholar, he had been tutored by Sken-Pitilkin since his fifth birthday, and after a full decade of unrelenting education he was proving uncomfortably competent in his grapplings with the unknown.

"A seizer and shaper," said Iva-Italis. "Exactly. So now we come to the matter of the temptation of Sken-Pitilkin. If he consents to yield to my will, then I will give him the secret of seizing and shaping power sufficient to facilitate sustained flight."

"So now we see the truth of the demon's revelation," said Sken-Pitilkin sourly. "The thing invites me to kill myself by mad experiment."

"There are dangers, admittedly," said Iva-Italis, now addressing himself directly to Sken-Pitilkin. "You would be exposing some artefact to destruction and seeking to master the power-flow which followed. Still, the dangers—"

"The dangers are known, and many have died to give proof to them," said Sken-Pitilkin. "The triumph of Arl is no secret to the Confederation. The arts of Arl are the arts of fire, and fire has proved amenable to the disciplines of sustained and controlled destruction of which you speak. But there are eight orders, each different in its powers. Mine commands the powers of levitation, and these, being more subtle and refined than those of fire, cannot be so easily controlled."

"Not by a wizard's intelligence," said Iva-Italis. "For a mere wizard lacks the skills required to compute the interplay of the forces involved. But I speak for the Great God Jocasta, and the Great God is possessed of the necessary computational power. Join us in a great alliance, Sken-Pitilkin. Join us. Help us free the Great God from his servitude in Obooloo. Do that, and I will grant you the equations necessary to make a functional airship."

Then Sken-Pitilkin was swayed.

Sken-Pitilkin stood in silence, Guest Gulkan at his side.

And then they heard the singing.

CHAPTER SIX

Yubi Das Finger: a Banker of the Bralsh, the insurance company so prominent in the affairs of Dalar ken Halvar. He travels the world in motley. Glass bells are suspended from his golden skullcap, and ceramic animals (seven score in number) are attached to his patchwork jacket and his trousers. Though he is dressed as a clown, he is in fact a diplomat, a negotiator, a concilator and an arbitrator. The eccentricities of his dress are designed to distract attention from his face — a face which is a horrorworks of welted burn tissue.

* * *

The singing came from the stairway at the western end of the Hall of Time. It signalled the arrival of Yubi Das Finger, who lit his own entrance into the Hall of Time with two lanterns swinging from the bablobrokmadorni stick he carried over his shoulder.

Yubi Das Finger sang as he walked the length of the Hall of Time, a hundred paces from the head of the western stairs to the foot of the eastern stairs. As he drew close, Guest recognized him from their first encounter earlier that night, for there was no mistaking that extraordinary figure.

When he was within smelling distance of the Weaponmaster, Yubi snapped at him with his green-dragon glove puppet. Guest flinched, more from fear of injury to his dignity than of injury to his flesh — though he still remembered the exceptional needle brightness of that puppet's teeth.

"So-ho, Guest!" said Yubi, greeting the Weaponmaster. "So-ho, Sken-Pitilkin!"

"Do I know you?" said Sken-Pitilkin, who had no recollection of meeting the motley-clad clown.

"Carnally?" said Yubi. "I doubt it."

Then he skipped past the jade-green flanks of the demon

115

Icaria Scaria Iva-Italis, climbed a few steps up the eastern stairway, then paused, looked back and grinned. His teeth gleamed green, reflecting the light which glowed from the demon.

"Well, Guest?" said Yubi, with a mocking devilishness. "Are you coming with me to the sky?"

Yubi spoke the Galish, and spoke it with such a piercing clarity one might have thought him to be singing even then.

"Where a clown can go, so I," said Guest.

For the boy had had enough of mystery for one night. He had been tempted and taunted too long — argued at, argued over, teased, flirted with, seduced. He wanted a finalization for once — he wanted to shove for the answer, to be done with the preliminaries and to thrust for the truth. Something was up there, up in the secret region overhead, up in the abditory.

And Guest was going to find out.

Driven by such determination, the boy dared himself into biting distance of the demon Icaria Scaria Iva-Italis.

"Halt," said Iva-Italis. "That's far enough."

Waiting on the stairs, Yubi Das Finger grinned green. If a man says he is going to jump off a cliff, there are some people who will turn away, some who will try to dissuade him, and some who will watch.

Yubi chose to watch.

And Guest dared another step.

Something hit him. It struck — too fast to see. Down he went! Thrown to the ground, bruised down to the skull-pattern tiles. He crunched down at the foot of the demon. It loomed above him, cold, cold, colder than needled, colder than ice. It was as green as the tallest of stars, and as high. Its monolithic slab-sided height stretched upwards for a day and forever.

Then it growled.

The demon Iva-Italis growled long and low, making a sound like thunder trapped in a rock, like an enormous bumble bee locked in a block of iron.

Then Sken-Pitilkin saved the day. He saved it with the country crook which served him as a staff of power.

Did Sken-Pitilkin stand upon the tallness of his hind legs and call out great Words of power? No. Did he summon forth invisible grappling hooks to drag the boy to safety? No.

Instead—

Sken-Pitilkin reached out with his country crook, hooked Guest Gulkan by the swordbelt and dragged the boy to safety.

Doubtless this resolution is somewhat lacking in drama, and many will find it a disappointment — for it is an acknowledged truth that many of those who read histories which feature one or more wizards do so largely to spectate at spectacle.

But there is less of spectacle in a wizard's life than outsiders commonly believe, since a wizard's life is largely given over to Meditation, study, memorization, diligent practice of the irregular verbs, and the darning of socks and the watering of pot plants.

For a wizard's powers are gathered with such effort that they are never expended lightly — for once having expended his power a wizard will be defenceless for days. Consequently, wizards do not exercise their powers except under circumstances of the gravest need; and, when faced with practical problems, they always first seek a practical solution.

Since Sken-Pitilkin was a wizard of Skatzabratzumon, he could in theory have used his levitational powers to grease Guest Gulkan's escape from the base of the demon. But it was more economical simply to drag the boy clear with a hooked stick — and just as fast, and just as effective.

With Guest dragged clear, Sken-Pitilkin supported him as he tottered the length of the Hall of Time to seat himself in his armchair, which was where the Guardian Hrothgar found him when that worthy came to relieve him in the grey of dawn.

By then, Sken-Pitilkin was long gone, thinking Guest safe. But Guest was not safe at all, for the rigours of the night had brought about a relapse, and Guest was huddled in his armchair in a state not far from delirium, wet with sweat and shuddering with fever.

Hrothgar arrived in the company of the Rovac warrior Rolf Thelemite and the dwarf Glambrax, both of whom were alight with anticipation at the thought of serving Guest his breakfast. These friends of his were bearing gifts — a pot of mulled wine spiked with a dog's urine, and a hot and steaming fish-dung pie. The master-chef Pelagius Zozimus had conspired with them in the preparation of this special wake-up breakfast, but all went to waste, for Guest was in no condition to be sampling anything.

If Hrothgar was any judge — and, having seen a great many of his friends and colleagues die of influenza, he thought himself well-qualified to judge — then Guest was direly ill.

So nothing would serve but that the Weaponmaster should be evacuated from the Grand Palace — as the mainrock Pinnacle was commonly known to many — and returned to Hrothgar's house in the adjacent city of Molothair, there to be nursed anew by Hrothgar's wife Una.

When Guest was somewhat recovered, Sken-Pitilkin visited him, and asked him how he felt.

"Not so bad," said Guest, affecting nonchalance. "I suppose the chill of the night was bad for me. If memory serves ... why, I seem to remember an abominably long bout of standing about, of stamping my feet ... though my memory is soggy ..."

"Hmmm," said Sken-Pitilkin, saying nothing more lest he provoke the boy to the needless effort of further clumsy lies. "Here. I've got something for you. It's a letter."

"A letter?" said Guest.

"From Gendormargensis," said Sken-Pitilkin.

"From my father?" said Guest, brightening.

"No," said Sken-Pitilkin. "From Bao Gahai."

"Bao Gahai!" said Guest, in patent dismay. "What would I want with a letter from Bao Gahai?"

"Read it," said Sken-Pitilkin. "It may have news of your brothers."

"So it may," said Guest.

Then broke the seals on the letter and scanned it through, learning that Morsh Bataar was on the mend and that Eljuk Zala was diligently prosecuting his study of the irregular verbs in the absence of Sken-Pitilkin. Eljuk had prevailed upon his father to provide him with a new tutor, who was a text-master named

Eldegen Terzanagel.

"Eljuk's scholarly passions are such," read Guest, quoting Bao Gahai, "that one fears him possessed of a secret ambition to be a wizard."

"Really," said Sken-Pitilkin, in neutral tones.

"The bitch is quite deranged!" said Guest, ceasing to quote as he threw down the letter. "My brother Eljuk? A wizard?! Dogs will first crap stars and pigs shit pigeons."

"Pigs will shit pigeons?" said Sken-Pitilkin.

"It is a Rovac oath," said Guest, evidencing pride in its possession. "I learnt it from Rolf Thelemite."

"And Glambrax learnt it as well," said Sken-Pitilkin.

"Why, so he did!" said Guest in astonishment. "How did you know that? Have you psychic powers?"

"When you are older and wiser," said Sken-Pitilkin with a sigh, "you will learn that psychic powers are entirely unnecessary to divine the wit and intention of the very young."

That was the plain truth, for without any psychic powers whatsoever, the sagacious Sken-Pitilkin knew full well what approach Guest planned to take towards the matter of the demon Icaria Scaria Iva-Italis.

As the wizard of Skatzabratzumon had immediately divined, Guest Gulkan was bent on pretending that the events of his night of guard duty in the Hall of Time had been blurred into unintelligibility by the rigours of his fever. But Sken-Pitilkin was not fooled for a moment. The boy knew! He knew too much! So — must he then be killed?

Certainly he must be kept away from the demon Iva-Italis!

But how was Sken-Pitilkin to persuade the Safrak Bank to deny Guest further access to that demon? Banker Sod, the Governor who ruled Alozay and all the other islands of the Safrak archipelago, seemed disposed to trust Guest. After all, relations between Safrak and the Collosnon Empire were relaxed and friendly, and Guest was the son of the Collosnon Empire's ruler.

So how could Sod be persuaded to treat Guest with something of the distrustful rigour which is reserved for a hostile prisoner?

Sken-Pitilkin thought about it long and hard, but could find no solution. At last he consulted Zelafona, whom he knew of old.

"As I helped you," said Sken-Pitilkin, alluding to the drama which had brought Sken-Pitilkin, Zozimus, Zelafona and Glambrax to flee for refuge in Tameran some ten years earlier, "now it is your turn to help me."

"Speak," said Zelafona.

Then Sken-Pitilkin explained all, even — for he trusted Zelafona, for all that he was a wizard and she a witch — the matter of the Mahendo Mahunduk.

Yes.

The Mahendo Mahunduk.

Sken-Pitilkin hesitated before touching on that most sensitive of subjects, but touch on it he did — and was chastened when he discovered that Zelafona already knew all about it.

"Clearly," said the old but elegant witch-woman, "you must keep the boy away from this demon-thing. Whatever its nature, its promises are impractical. In other words — it is a liar. Doubtless it means to use the boy, but the reward it offers is not within its power to give."

"Then what am I to do?" said Sken-Pitilkin.

"You must tell the Safrak Bank that Guest attempted to force a passage past the demon. You must tell the Bank that Guest tried to win a passage to the forbidden shrine above. Since the Bank is so protective of its holy of holies, I'm sure they will thereafter deny Guest Gulkan admission to the Hall of Time."

This proposal had the simplicity which marks true genius, and Sken-Pitilkin promptly put it into effect.

Sken-Pitilkin demanded an interview with Banker Sod, was admitted into the iceman's presence, and gave him an edited account of the events of the night of Guest Gulkan's guard duty.

"I took myself up to the Hall of Time," said Sken-Pitilkin, "meaning to take him a flask of soup which had been cooked by my cousin Zozimus. I knew him to be but recently recovered from influenza, hence thought him in need of such sustenance. While I was with him, he fell to boasting, as a boy in his folly will, and the upshot was that he tried to force a passage past the demon."

"And?" said Sod.

"And," said Sken-Pitilkin, "the demon knocked him to the ground."

Sod did not know whether to believe this account. On the face of it, the story was highly improbable. For the demon Icaria Scaria Iva-Italis did not customarily defend the privacy of the holy of holies by knocking people to the ground. Rather, the demon's custom was to fatally ravage anyone who attempted an unauthorized passage up the eastern stairs of the Hall of Time.

Clearly, Sken-Pitilkin was holding something back.

But what?

Sod first taxed Sken-Pitilkin directly, suggesting that he was not telling the truth, or at least not the whole truth.

"I am old," conceded Sken-Pitilkin, "and my memory is failing. It may be that I have misplaced some of the events of the night, or misrecalled them."

Sod did not believe him for a moment.

So the pale-skinned iceman took himself off to the Hall of Time, and there endeavoured to interrogate Iva-Italis. A singularly unsatisfactory procedure, this! For the demon played mute, even when Sod threatened to withhold its monthly ration of those unfortunate rats which gave it such prolonged and reliable amusement.

Sod next interrogated Guest, who blandly claimed that the height of his fever had wiped out his memory.

This left Sod with a problem. Both Guest and Sken-Pitilkin had engaged in some kind of nefarious dealings with Safrak's demon. What had they done? What had they learnt? And should they be killed to preserve the Bank's safety? A difficult decision, this. For Guest was the son of the Witchlord Onosh, and Safrak wanted no war with the Collosnon Empire. Doubtless an accident could be arranged, but ...

The unfortunate truth was that Banker Sod had become addicted to the cookery of Pelagius Zozimus, who delighted the Banker with his many ingenious recipes for preparing snails and slugs. Zozimus had only come to Alozay to help protect Guest Gulkan. If Guest died, then Zozimus would immediately leave, denying Sod the blandishments of his cookery.

Thus did a slug-chef's art help secure Guest's safety, at least for the moment. Sod contented himself by banning Guest Gulkan (and Sken-Pitilkin!) from venturing anywhere near the heights of the Hall of Time.

Guest of course was still in some danger from Sken-Pitilkin, who nightly revolved the question of whether the boy knew too much. On recovering from his influenza, Guest had set himself to master the Toxteth tongue, and had taken to putting in extra work with his sword. From long acquaintance with the boy, Sken-Pitilkin could read his intent from the slightest clues, and Guest's ferocious attack on Toxteth was by no means a slight clue.

Guest's behaviour implied that he was preparing himself to join the Guardians. The boy now had it in mind to stay on Alozay as a hired sword. Once a member of the Guardians, a mercenary entrusted with the defence of the Bank, Guest would have further opportunity of intercourse with the demon Iva-Italis.

Sken-Pitilkin knew that Guest felt denied, thwarted, cheated by the fact that his father had named his brother Eljuk to be the heir of the Collosnon Empire. Guest wanted power, and the demon Iva-Italis offered him just that — a wizard's power, to be easily won by a simple quest.

So—

The boy was driven by ambition, and the strength of that drive would see him win through to his demon, sooner or later, and there was no telling what would happen then.

Therefore Sken-Pitilkin thought further of murder.

But the wizard of Skatzabratzumon had developed a durable affection for Guest during the ten years of their classroom relationship, hence could not bring himself to casually dispatch the boy. Besides, Sken-Pitilkin had told Lord Onosh that he would guard, guide and protect Guest on Alozay, and such a commitment could not be lightly brushed aside, for Sken-Pitilkin had his honour.

And there was another factor to be considered.

Sken-Pitilkin was intrigued by the possibility of developing a practical airship, hence wanted to keep open his route to the demon Iva-Italis. Suppose Guest stayed on Alozay. Suppose Guest became a Guardian. Then the boy would grow older (definitely) and wiser (possibly). Once older and wiser, the boy would be more amenable to advice.

Counselled by Sken-Pitilkin, Guest might well abandon his impossible plans to be "made a wizard". He might consent to scheme with Sken-Pitilkin. Working together, they might be able to trick the demon Iva-Italis out of the knowledge necessary for a wizard of Skatzabratzumon to build a practical airship.

In such hope, Sken-Pitilkin restrained his hand, and set himself to wait.

Yet very little waiting had gone by before Sken-Pitilkin started to find himself increasingly impatient. To control the secrets of flight was the dream of every wizard of Skatzabratzumon. Sken-Pitilkin had made many experiments in that direction during his apprenticeship, and during the long years of his maturity he had spent generations trying to crack the problem.

He knew how to wait, yes, but would waiting serve his purpose? Was there any proven virtue in patience? Guest would grow older — that much was certain. But the Weaponmaster's ultimate acquisition of wisdom was strictly problematical.

And so, after thinking long and hard about the acroamatical revelations made by the demon Iva-Italis, Sken-Pitilkin started actively considering trying an experiment along the lines which the demon had suggested. Create a magical artefact. Expose some part of that artefact to the destructive normalizing forces of the universe. Then control the resulting destruction, trapping the destructive forces and using them for the purposes of flight.

Doubtless there would be dangers in such an experiment:

but surely the potential rewards amply justified the risks.

Consider what it would mean were we able to fly.

Given the power of flight, we could transport goods with ease, high above the ravenous mountains and those over-fertile oceans so prodigious in their production of krakens and sea serpents. The sundry races of the world would be united by an undreamt-of ease of travel, and on close acquaintance would grow to know each other better, old hatreds dying as new friendships blossomed. The death of suspicion would mean an end to war. Better still, the greatest experts of all the world would be free to travel the globe resolving the sundry problems of humanity, thus ending the present Age of Darkness and ushering in a golden Age of Light.

Do not think, then, that Sken-Pitilkin was possessed of a reckless hubris when he decided to dare the construction of an airship. He knew the dangers. But here was an opportunity to restructure the world and save all of humanity from its lesser nature.

Hence Sken-Pitilkin began to build small-scale model airships, designing these with a view to perfecting the art of sustained and controlled destruction.

Sken-Pitilkin's experiments were not an unqualified success. Upon his experiments he lavished the sap-days of the spring, the heat of summer and the fruitfulness of autumn. But, while he secured plenty of destruction, he was less than successful in the controlled management of that destruction. Finally, as winter was setting in, the eminent wizard of the order of Skatzabratzumon was summoned into the presence of Banker Sod.

"Sken-Pitilkin!" said Sod. "Sit!"

The wizard sat.

"Tell me," said Sod, "why do you think I've called you here?"

"Why," said Sken-Pitilkin, with guilty uneasiness, "I suppose, ah, to have me spy Guest's letters, perhaps. He got another epistle from Bao Gahai only yesterday. His brother Morsh is walking and riding, so says the letter, and as the boy was laid up last winter with a broken leg—"

"Don't toy with me!" barked Sod. "Sken-Pitilkin! I want to know! Are you responsible for the outbreak of explosions, tornados, waterspouts, hurtling debris and other such poltergeist-like activity which has of late vexed, troubled and disturbed our peace?"

Sken-Pitilkin thought about it, then said:

"No."

It was, after all, Icaria Scaria Iva-Italis who had suggested that the secret of flight lay in the mastery of sustained and controlled destruction, therefore the demon Iva-Italis was (at least in Sken-Pitilkin's opinion) responsible for the consequences of Sken-Pitilkin's experiments in that direction.

"No?" said Banker Sod.

"I have said it once," said Sken-Pitilkin, "and that should be sufficient."

Banker Sod looked at Sken-Pitilkin very hard, meanwhile drumming his black-nailed fingers on his desk. Then Sod came to a decision. He stopped drumming, and said:

"Very well. I accept your denial. You are not responsible for the recent incidents. But — I am making you responsible for making sure that they stop!"

Sken-Pitilkin got the message, and the incidents ceased.

So peace came to the island of Alozay, though not to the world at large — for unrest was increasing in the Collosnon Empire, the tax revolt in Locontareth was gathering strength, and the empire was moving slowly but inevitably towards a state of civil war.

CHAPTER SEVEN

Alozay: Safrak's ruling island. Its Grand Palace occupies the mainrock Pinnacle, the prodigious upthrust of rock which overshadows the city of Molothair. Molothair itself lies on a tongue of low-lying land. Alozay has two sets of docks: the Palace Docks, serving the mainrock Pinnacle, and the Molothair Docks, serving the low-lying city itself.

* * *

Early in the spring of the year Alliance 4306 — a few days after Guest Gulkan's 16th birthday and a full year after Guest Gulkan's introduction to the demon Iva-Italis — the Rovac warrior Thodric Jarl came to Safrak to recall Guest Gulkan to Gendormargensis.

While the Collosnon Empire had been told that Guest was on Alozay as a hostage, Jarl knew otherwise, and knew that there would be no trouble in recovering the boy from Safrak. In Gendormargensis, it was thought by the uninitiated that the Safrak Bank regularly demanded hostages from the Collosnon Empire. However, while it is certainly true that selected individuals were on occasion sent to Alozay as "hostages", the Safrak Bank never demanded any such prisoners, and in fact was paid good gold for safeguarding them.

The Emperor Onosh was a Yarglat barbarian, true, but he had dwelt in Gendormargensis for so long that he was perilously close to being civilized. In Gendormargensis, Lord Onosh had been guided by selected advisers of Sharla ancestry — the Sharla being the sophisticated people who had owned the Collosnon Empire before the Yarglat took it from them in the Wars of Dominion. Aided by his Sharla advisers, and by the subtlety of his dralkosh Bao Gahai, Lord Onosh had learnt some nimble tricks of politics, and had gone some distance towards mastering the art of blaming all of one's cruel, self-serving and unpopular actions upon some other agency.

In a truly sophisticated civilization, the art of the abdication of responsibility is brought to such a high pitch of perfection that no government ever admits to wanting to do anything which is in the least bit cruel, self-serving or unpopular. The political praxis of such states consists of one long exercise in the avoidance of responsibility. Typically, the government of a sophisticated state presents itself as kind, thoughtful and humane.

But—

But the kind, thoughtful and humane administrations of sophisticated states are guided by a network of committees, sub-committees, research groups, panels, outside experts and other such similar functionaries who can be relied upon to produce a string of recommendations which are typically cruel, vicious, short-sighted and barbarous in effect.

And, since it is one of the conceits of high civilization that no government is competent to decide the rights and wrongs of any question through the application of its own wisdom, it follows that the kindest and most diligently popular of all enlightened governments can practise a cruel, self-serving and unpopular brand of politics by the simple expedient of bowing to the wisdom of its advisers — and can do this in good conscience.

Since the Collosnon Empire was a comparatively primitive organization, it had not yet constructed such a comprehensive apparatus of systematized intellectual dishonesty. Hence Lord Onosh had to bear personal responsibility for at least some of his own actions. Nevertheless, the emperor was slowly learning that it was best if his misdeeds be blamed on other people, and he was becoming pretty good at placing the responsibility for his most unpopular actions on either his enemies or his allies.

Safrak accommodated the Witchlord's needs by allowing him to send prisoners to Alozay as "hostages". This let him exile selected dissidents, sending them into distant custody while protesting his love for them, and blaming their fate on the hostage-demanding land of Safrak.

A nice trick, this. It had allowed the Witchlord to exile his son from Gendormargensis without appearing to be cruel, capricious or arbitrary — and allowed him to recall the boy at his pleasure by simply telling Gendormargensis that Safrak had chosen to relinquish its hostage.

So it was that in the spring of the year Alliance 4306 — ah, but the date has been given already! Repetition, repetition, there is no point to it, no need for it. The parchment holds the ink, and holds it for all time. So if the date be lost in the first reading, then it will be found in the second.

A second reading!

Is the historian truly counselling a second reading of his works?

Yes, he is! And shamelessly!

Let it clearly be stated that a second reading is not just to be recommended but is, rather, close to being compulsory. For this is a True History, one which faithfully strives to render the tangled complexities of life itself. To unknot the tangles of this interweaving in a single reading will not be easy. After all, the events confused their very victims, so how should they be clearcut plain to the onlooker?

Read then this history a second time!

If this suggestion seems bizarre, then know that it is not entirely without precedent. Your true scholar will give a book a generation if the text be worthy. And if the book be sufficiently irregular in its verbs, why then, a true scholar will stand content to pore its pages for the better part of a millennium, and think the time well spent.

Yet this is a counsel of perfection, impossible for those whose brief mortality makes the pursuit of such perfection an unattainable ideal. So, in case the constraints of that mortal disease called life make a second reading impossible, let the date be restated, and hammered down, and branded on the mind.

Imagine that the brand strives home, that flesh smokes, that a stench of burning rises to the nostrils. The searing wound is red, is blistered. The pain is white-hot agony. 4306. Thus reads the brand. It is imprinted on the smoking flesh, there for a lifetime if the burn be true.

It was spring, and early spring at that. It was the year Alliance 4306, and Guest Gulkan in his adolescent youth had attained the unholy age of 16, surely one of the most perilous of ages in the whole passage from babyhood to manhood. The boy Guest, the self-styled Weaponmaster, had then been in residence on Safrak's ruling island for upwards of a year; and in that year had engaged in an unholy amount of drinking, gambling and troublemaking, none of which will be detailed here — which is not to suggest that any of it had escaped the notice of his elders.

In the early spring of that year, the Rovac warrior Thodric Jarl — grey in beard and grey in eye, he whom Guest Gulkan had duelled for the favours of the woman Yerzerdayla — came to Safrak's ruling island to summon the Witchlord's son home to Gendormargensis.

Thodric Jarl did not come alone. He travelled with friendly swords to guard his back, for the countryside was in disorder. A tax revolt centred on Locontareth had quite got out of hand, and Lord Onosh was marching to war against the rebels. The Witchlord wished the Weaponmaster to march to battle at his side, hence had sent Jarl to fetch the young man.

By this time, the influenza epidemic which had decimated Safrak a year previously was but an almost-forgotten incident in history. The Collosnon Empire had heard nothing of that epidemic. All those people had died without Lord Onosh, Jarl, or Bao Gahai, or any other in Gendormargensis learning of their deaths. Bones become dust but the blood goes on.

While Jarl had heard nothing of the epidemic — and was destined to learn nothing — he had heard much of the island of Alozay, centre of all trade between the Collosnon Empire and Port Domax (Port Domax being a free city placed many leagues distant on the shores of the Great Ocean of Moana).

Lord Onosh had given Thodric Jarl no orders to scout for the means whereby Alozay might be defeated, and to Jarl's best knowledge the Witchlord had no designs on the Safrak Islands. Nevertheless, as a boat brought Jarl and his comrades to the Palace Docks at the foot of the mainrock Pinnacle, Jarl studied all with a warrior's eye, and committed all to memory.

Jarl could see no certain way to storm the heights, since the rocks above overhung the docks of Alozay, and to gain the heights one had to be winched up to a drop-hole which gaped in the living rock far, far above.

Still, presumably the mainrock Pinnacle could be taken by siege, assuming one had boats enough, and patience sufficient.

At the dockside, Jarl was met by a yellow-skinned cur-dog which pissed on his boots, then by a tall and sallow junior Banker, a young man with crooked teeth and breath so bad it scared away the dog. The junior Banker addressed Jarl in the Eparget of the Yarglat. Jarl's native tongue was Rovac, but war had made him the master of a good half-dozen languages, with Eparget the latest to be subdued to his possession. Thus he was able to explain himself.

The junior Banker heard Jarl's mission then told him that he and his comrades would have to wait.

"None of you can proceed," said the junior Banker, "until at least one of you has been properly identified and vouched for. You must get a security clearance before you can be allowed to proceed."

Thodric Jarl protested vehemently, and demanded to see the Governor of the Bank — but the Governor was unavailable.

"Someone already on Alozay must vouch for you before you can be allowed to proceed," said the junior Banker, with the repetitive instincts of either a born parrot or a born bureaucrat.

"But I don't know anyone on Alozay!" said Jarl.

"Then," said the junior Banker, "you are going to be waiting at the docks for a long time."

So Jarl admitted to knowing Rolf Thelemite, who was produced in order that he might identify Jarl. Thodric Jarl glowered at Rolf Thelemite, who smiled. Though both these worthies were Rovac warriors, the pair were by no means friends. Long, long ago, on a day when Jarl had been very drunk, Rolf Thelemite had defeated him in a fist fight, and Jarl still held a grudge against the man on that account. Rolf Thelemite knew as much.

"Ha-hmmm," said Rolf Thelemite, as he inspected Jarl.

"Get it over with, man," snapped Jarl. "Tell them who I am."

"Who are you supposed to be?" said Rolf.

"Stop being ridiculous!" said Jarl. "You know full well who I am."

"Do I?" said Rolf.

"Of course you do!" said Jarl. "I'm Thodric Jarl, son of Oric Slaughterhouse, and blood of the clan of the bear."

"Ha-hmm," said Rolf. "I did know a man named Thodric Jarl. You could tell him because — what was it? A cow, that was it. This Jarl, he had a little cow tattooed on his throat. A pretty cow it was, with a small golden bell hanging from its own throat."

Thodric Jarl's response was a roar of rage, but at last he calmed down, and allowed the junior Banker to uplift his beard to check for tattoos. To the Banker's patent amusement, there was indeed a little cow tattooed on Jarl's throat — a very pretty cow with a buttercup emblazoned on its flanks — and the design was completed by a pretty little bell coloured to match the buttercup.

"Yes," said Rolf, visually reacquainting himself with that tattoo, "this is indeed the Rovac warrior Thodric Jarl."

"You," said Jarl, speaking to Rolf in the Rovac tongue, "I'll deal with you later!"

Then Jarl was consigned to a winch-basket, together with a sack of fish fillets, a woman with a teething baby, the Banker with breath so bad it could scare a dog, and with five heroically unscared dogs which had been for a defecatory constitutional on the docks.

When they were half-way up, the winch-rope jammed, and Jarl was left swinging for an eternity. Then the basket was at last hauled to its full height, and Jarl stepped out into the tunnel system of the mainrock Pinnacle. Having thus entered the Grand Palace of Alozay, Jarl waited until a number of his travelling companions had been winched up to join him, and then they went in force to seek out Guest Gulkan.

* * *

The mainrock Pinnacle: the spike of rock which rises from the Swelaway Sea on the island of Alozay, and which overlooks the city of Molothair. The mainrock is pierced and hollowed by the stairs and chambers of the Grand Palace of Alozay, in which is found the administrative machinery of Safrak and the precincts of the Safrak Bank. In the same Grand Palace are the quarters occupied by Guest Gulkan and those who came with him from Gendormargensis.

* * *

It was then spring in the year Alliance 4306, as has been already stated, and Guest Gulkan had just recently celebrated his sixteenth birthday. At age 16, Guest was no wiser than he had been at birth, but the wizard Sken-Pitilkin was still relentlessly continuing those pedagogical labours which he had begun when Guest was aged but five.

Though Guest had acquired not one iota of wisdom in a full eleven years of instruction, he had won some knowledge of geography — he could tell the Pig from the Yolantarath, and Molothair from Gendormargensis — and was an enthusiastic student of ethnology. He had also made progress with some of the simpler languages, such as Toxteth — the language of beer-and-dice companions such as Hrothgar — and Galish.

Now Galish is of course but a poor toy for the intellect, being dismally deficient in the more complex irregularities, so Sken-Pitilkin took no joy in his pupil's growing proficiency in that tongue. Nor did he rejoice in Guest's accomplishments in Toxteth, since its mastery was linked with Guest's dangerous ambition to be a Guardian.

Sken-Pitilkin endeavoured to steer Guest in a safer direction — that of the largely academic challenges of Strogloth's *Compendium of Delights.* But Guest rejected the book, refusing, for example, to learn even one of the intricately irregular verbs of Slandolin, the elegant literary language of Ashmolea. So Sken-Pitilkin tempted him by offering to teach the High Speech of wizards — a necessary adjunct, surely, to Guest's ambition to become a wizard! Guest then stabbed at the High Speech, but his stabs were wide of the mark, and so far he could not bring a word of it to his tongue.

Sken-Pitilkin sometimes found it a great relief to abandon the intricacies of linguistic instruction for the comparative simplicities of geography.

Pedagogue and pupil were hard at work on geography when Thodric Jarl arrived at the docks which served the mainrock Pinnacle; they were still hard at it when Rolf Thelemite exposed Jarl's cute-cow tattoo; and they had not yet exhausted the subject when the dwarf Glambrax intruded upon their lessons.

They were discussing the Untunchilamons.

There is of course only one Untunchilamon, but Guest Gulkan had got it into his head that there were 27, thus making it obvious that he had mixed them up with the islands of Rovac, which are a different pot of frogs and blood entirely. Sken-Pitilkin was busy enlightening him when Glambrax intruded, and kicked Sken-Pitilkin in the shins.

"My lord," said Glambrax, formally advising them of his presence.

"What did you say?" said Sken-Pitilkin, attempting to swat Glambrax with his country crook, but missing.

"I said," said Glambrax, "that someone wants to see Guest Gulkan."

The dwarf had in fact said no such thing, and in any case Sken-Pitilkin believed it extremely unlikely that anyone had any requirement for the boy's presence. The scholar suspected, rather, that the dwarf had arrived by preconcerted plan to liberate the boy for larrikinism.

"Guest Gulkan is busy," said Sken-Pitilkin.

"But there are people to see him," said Glambrax.

"Then," said Sken-Pitilkin, at last succeeding in landing a retaliatory blow upon the quick-leaping dwarf, "they can see him later."

"They will see him now," said Glambrax, unchastened by his chastisement. "They insist."

"Then let them insist," said Sken-Pitilkin, raising his country crook as if for fresh assault.

"They insist they'll boil me alive unless I let them in to see him."

"Then boiled you will be, so you'd better get used to the idea," said Sken-Pitilkin. "You could use a bath in any case."

"They'll boil you too," said Glambrax. "These you can't keep waiting. Thodric Jarl's out there, Lord Alagrace with him."

"Really," said Sken-Pitilkin, in a manner which made quite clear his opinion of dwarves, Jarls and Alagraces.

"Truly and really," said Glambrax. "They want the boy Guest for a purpose too foul for my tongue, and in their lust they'll boil you in oil if you hold them to no."

"I'll do all the oil-boiling round here," said Sken-Pitilkin warmly. "Get off with you!"

"I can't tell that to Jarl," said Glambrax. "He'd spit me and split me. You know what he's like."

"Then, that being the case," said Sken-Pitilkin, "he can get on with the spitting of you immediately. But as for seeing young Guest, why, he can see young Guest when I'm through with him."

"Is that your final answer?" said Glambrax.

"My first and my final," said Sken-Pitilkin. "Go tell them, whoever them may be, that Guest is much too ugly to be seen. Tell them to come back later, after I've cut his ears off."

Then he turned to his pupil, who was engaged in the studious dissection of a flea.

"Untunchilamon," said Sken-Pitilkin.

"What?" said Guest Gulkan, looking up from his anatomizing.

"We were talking of Untunchilamon," said Sken-Pitilkin. "Have you forgotten?"

"No, no, not at all," said Guest. "Untunchilamon. Well. It has fleas, probably. Most places have fleas, especially this one. As well as fleas, Untunchilamon has 27 islands, and lots of people, who one and all consume the staunch, which is cream and water curdled, and makes you drunk."

"No!" said Sken-Pitilkin. "That is not Untunchilamon, that

is Rovac, as I just told you."

"You just told me nothing," said Guest. "You just told Glambrax something about baths, that was what you just told."

"Then never mind what I said," said Sken-Pitilkin. "And let go of that flea, boy, it's far too small to eat. Come, boy, settle. And let us return to our dragons."

"Our dragons?"

"I meant," said Sken-Pitilkin, "let us get on with our business. And did we not cover that very precise idiom only a week ago?"

"What's a week?"

"You've asked me that question already, and I believe you've already had a perfectly good answer. Anyway. Our lesson. Untunchilamon. Where was I? Oh, bloodrock, that's it. Untunchilamon has bloodrock—"

"And women."

"And women, yes. Also torturers, and I wish I had one such on hand to restore a little discipline. And it has jellyfish, flying fish, parrots—"

"Parrots?"

"A type of bird."

"Like a vulture?"

"Approximately. Anyway, it has parrots. Parrots, then. And monkeys. A monkey being, before you ask, a creature in the form of a dwarf, only it has fur, and climbs trees, and has no speech but a chatter of anger."

"You're making that up!" said Guest.

"It is true," said Sken-Pitilkin solemnly. "Also on Untunchilamon we find the coconut, which is a nut the size of your skull, with a thin juice within, or a white meat, or a mix of both, depending on the ripeness of the nut."

"A nut the size of my skull," said Guest, rehearsing this datum in tones of patent disbelief.

"Thus did I truth it," said Sken-Pitilkin.

But young Guest thought this purported truth to be one more absurd impossibility, fit to rank alongside the whale and the crocodile — the crocodile being a legendary animal of singular ferocity which was alleged to have the ability to change itself at will from a floating tree trunk to a ravaging monster.

"Have you held this coconut in those very hands of yours?" said Guest, in tones of challenge. "Have you eaten of this coconut, as you have eaten of the flying fish?"

"I have eaten both," said Sken-Pitilkin. "I have eaten each alone and both in alliance together on the same plate, the site of my gourmandizing being Injiltaprajura, that city which serves as the capital of Untunchilamon. Injiltaprajura lies on the shores of the Laitemata Harbour. There—"

"There irregular verbs breed in great quantities, doubtless," said Guest.

"So they do, so they do," said Sken-Pitilkin. "For all manner of languages are amok amidst the islanders."

"And, pray tell," said Guest Gulkan, "what quirk of character took you to a place so impossibly distant?"

"I was young," said Sken-Pitilkin. "Yes, boy! Don't look at me like that! I was young, once, for all that you disbelieve it. Young, and bold, and stupid, and singularly proud of it, for I was born and bred in Galsh Ebrek, where the Yudonic Knights value a swordsman's stupidity even more than do the barbarous Yarglat of Tameran."

"So youth took you to Untunchilamon," said Guest. "It must be a place most crowded if youth alone suffices to fate a world of unfortunates to its shores."

"In my case," said Sken-Pitilkin, "it was more than youth which took me there. I went there on a quest."

"A quest!" said Guest.

"The quest for the x-x-zix," said Sken-Pitilkin.

"A dangerous quest, that," said Guest. "Why, you'd break your very jaw just trying to name the thing you were questing for. How did you say it again?"

"The x-x-zix. A particularly wild and dangerous species of irregular verb. It has two teeth, which are in the shape of saws; and it has fifty tails, the tips of these being poisonous. It is valued on account of the feathers it grows from its nose, which are more fanciful than those of the ostrich."

"The ostrich?"

"A type of chicken. But with feathers of a value exceeded only by those of the x-x-zix, the irregular verb we were discussing, which is notable not just for its feathers but also because it subsists exclusively upon liquid tar and excretes amber and ambergris on alternate days of the week."

"The week!" said Guest. "It is a measure of days, like the month!"

"Did I not tell you precisely that just a little earlier this very morning?"

"You did not," said Guest. "I worked it out myself, though I can't for the life of me work out why you'd chase to Untunchilamon for a verb, be it a regular verb or otherwise."

"The lust for knowledge, boy," said Sken-Pitilkin. "A safer lust than the lust for loins. Not that Untunchilamon was all that safe. Why, I almost got turned inside out by a certain crab which took exception to my taste for research."

"You tried to eat it?" said Guest.

"No. I merely tried to engage it in discussion, but it told me—"

"The crab talked?"

"It did," said Sken-Pitilkin.

"Oh, I see," said Guest Gulkan, abrupting into something perilously close to bad temper. "A story about talking animals, is it? And what do you think I am? A child?"

Guest's change of mood was as abrupt as that of a man who, while idling down a pathway in a meditative mood, is precipitated into a pit-trap. While abrupt, this mood-change was in no wise feigned.

At sixteen, Guest Gulkan was far too old for fairy tales. And, even as a small boy, he had always despised stories about talking animals. Since coming to Alozay, he had several times encountered crabs in the flesh of the fact. True, they were the freshwater crabs of the Swelaway Sea rather than the greater crabs of the Sea of Salt. Still, having met with crabs, and having been torn by their pincers while trying to dissect them — your average crab being more of a warrior than your average flea —

Guest thought he knew to a nicety both the talents and the limitations of the breed. And he in the days of his self-proclaimed maturity most certainly had no time at all for any ridiculous nonsense about a talking crab.

"Well?" said Guest, as Sken-Pitilkin gave him no answer.

"Well what?" said his tutor, who was still trying to work out just what had offended the boy.

"You insulted me," said Guest. "And I asked for an explanation. Are you going to give it?"

"Where lies the insult?" said Sken-Pitilkin.

"A talking crab!" said Guest. "Is that not insult enough?"

"It is but knowledge," said Sken-Pitilkin, genuinely puzzled. "It is but knowledge, for I have but been retailing a few facts from my own experience. Where lies the insult in that?"

"A nonsense of talking crabs and parrot-vultures," said Guest, working himself up into a proper rage even as he talked. "Is that not insult? Stuff for children! Fish that fly and crabs that talk."

"They are facts, and I have witnessed them," said Sken-Pitilkin mildly. "But if you have made up your mind to be angry, then don't let mere fact prevent you from indulging unreason."

"You fiddle the world so often with word-games that you forget the world is not a game," said Guest, rising to his feet. "The world is what it is, and men are what they are, and I am a man, and I will not be insulted like a child."

"Why not?" said Sken-Pitilkin, feeling it was high time for some home truths to be spoken. "For you have the singularly changeable moods of a bad-tempered and overindulged child."

"Men have been killed for less than that," said Guest Gulkan, doing his best to snarl and grate, to bitter the words from his lips like so much poison.

"So they have, so they have," said Sken-Pitilkin, relapsing into placidity. "But character is destiny, and if mine is to die at the hands of a Yarglat lout over the matter of an imagined insult, why then, so be it."

Sken-Pitilkin showed no fear of the quick-boil of the young man's temper, but instead comported himself as calmly as if engaged in a tea-tasting ceremony. This enraged Guest Gulkan all the more, so much so that he almost ventured to strike his tutor. But he restrained himself, remembering what had happened on the occasion of their last physical confrontation. Sken-Pitilkin had avoided the blow and had lightly tapped Guest in the testicles with his country crook, which had left the boy walking bow-legged for three days thereafter.

So in the heat of his anger Guest Gulkan did not venture to strike, but instead stormed towards the door.

"And where do you think you're going?" said Sken-Pitilkin.

"Character is destiny," said Guest Gulkan. "And I'm going to find mine."

As the boy was so speaking, the door was thrown open, and in came destiny in the form of Thodric Jarl and his associates. Guest Gulkan was taken aback by this metal-crashing parcel of armed men, all swords and gauntlets, boots and helmets, shields and chain mail. He fell back before them, and seized Sken-Pitilkin's country crook in lieu of a sword, for he thought the intruders bent on murder.

"Out!" said Sken-Pitilkin irefully, as the intrusionists came trampling into his educational laboratory with their muddy boots on. "You can't come in here! We're in the middle of a lesson."

"The lesson is over," said Thodric Jarl, the leader of the intrusionists. "The lesson is over, for life has begun."

Thus epic heroes are wont to speak, but Thodric Jarl was no epic hero. He was a run-of-the-mill hackman, a mediocre mercenary who had long ago been exiled from Rovac for sodomising sheep. (Or so at least Rolf Thelemite was wont to allege, and Sken-Pitilkin had heard the allegations, and had often declared himself inclined to believe them.) Jarl was young, and over-vigorous, and decidedly curt in his manner. Sken-Pitilkin was not at all pleased to see him, and made his displeasure plain.

"You say the lesson is over?" said Sken-Pitilkin. "The lesson is hardly started yet! But I'll give you a lesson you won't forget, not when I'm through with you."

"Hush down, you irascible old man," said Lord Alagrace,

one of Thodric Jarl's companions in boorishness.

This annoyed Sken-Pitilkin intensely, for while Thodric Jarl could never transcend his stiff-necked nature, Sken-Pitilkin knew Lord Alagrace of old, and knew that Alagrace could be quite the diplomat when he thought it worth his while.

After all, sal Pentalon Sorvolosa dan Alagrace nal Swedek quen Larsh was no brute of a Yarglat barbarian. He was the scion of one of the High Houses of Sharla, and the Sharla, as has been noted above, were ever a sophisticated people. Ethnology teaches one the natural limits of peoples such as Yarglat and Rovac. One expects such barbarians to brute their way through the world like slum-born streetfighters. But ethnology could make no excuse whatsoever for Lord Pentalon Alagrace. He knew better, and Sken-Pitilkin thought he should demonstrate as much.

"Get out of here!" said Sken-Pitilkin. "Get out of here, the lot of you!"

"Who is this unruly old man?" said one of the sworders who had bruted his armpits into the room in company with Jarl and Alagrace. "Shall we kill him?"

"No," said Thodric Jarl, "we'll not kill him, for he's not worth the bloodspill. He is but a useless old beggar whom the Witchlord chased from Gendormargensis for molesting dogs and eating vomit, and other crimes equally as cowardly."

Thus Thodric Jarl in his youth, gross in libel and uncouth in epithet. But even a dog can count its own legs, as the saying has it, and sometimes Jarl had a truth or two to his tongue. Certainly he hit the mark when he called Sken-Pitilkin irascible, for how could that scholar be otherwise when beset by the likes of Jarl? But Jarl was wrong to speak of Sken-Pitilkin as being an old man, for Sken-Pitilkin was not old — rather, he was positively ancient. Nor was he (strictly speaking) a man, for he was a wizard, and in the process of attaining power wizards make themselves creatures of a different order from the ordinary run of humanity.

Sken-Pitilkin began to explain these points to Jarl, but Jarl was in no mood to hear them, and ventured to let fall a curse upon Sken-Pitilkin's venerable head.

Things might then have become unpleasant but for the intervention of Lord Alagrace, who called for silence then explained the business which the intruders were about. Guest Gulkan's time as a hostage on the Safrak Islands had come to an end, and Lord Alagrace and his companions were here to fetch the boy home to Gendormargensis.

"And me?" said Sken-Pitilkin, asking his fate.

Sken-Pitilkin had no particular wish to return to Gendormargensis, city of doglice and horsedung. But he judged it unsafe to return to Drum — his habitual home island in the Penvash Strait — and he thought he would receive precious little charity from Safrak's Bankers if he chose to remain on the island of Alozay once his sole student had departed.

"Lord Onosh bids you to return to Gendormargensis along with his son," answered Lord Alagrace.

Details were then gone into, and as the details were gone into, Guest Gulkan became increasingly upset.

"I'm not going," he said.

"You're what?" said Lord Alagrace in amazement.

"I'm not going!" said Guest.

In the year since his encounter with Icaria Scaria Iva-Italis, Demon by Appointment to the Great God Jocasta, Guest Gulkan had thought repeatedly about the possibility of winning power as a wizard. Though Sken-Pitilkin had prevented Guest from having further contact with Iva-Italis, Guest had already realized that such prevention could be circumvented in time. In time, once he had a sufficiency of Toxteth at his command, Guest could join the Guardians, Alozay's Toxteth-speaking mercenaries, winning by this manoeuvre the certainty of further contact with Iva-Italis.

But—

"You're going, all right," said Thodric Jarl, and grabbed Guest by the scruff of the neck as if to drag him from the room then and there.

An ungainly struggle followed, during which the daring Sken-Pitilkin, by dint of swift action and heroic enterprise, managed to save those precious books and manuscripts which were in danger of being trampled to death in the skirmish.

The victory went to the Rovac, for Jarl was accomplished in battle, and he overpowered Guest Gulkan's brutality, then sat on the boy while Lord Alagrace lectured him.

"You are coming home," said Lord Alagrace.

"But I am a hostage," said Guest.

"Your father has no more need of any hostages in the Safrak Islands," said Lord Alagrace, putting into words a truth of which Guest was already fully aware. "Nor had he ever any such need. You were put here to keep you safe from your own violence. But now the empire has need of that violence. So back you come! Back to Gendormargensis and the battles which threaten the empire. You're coming home."

"Me!" said Guest. "I'd rather die!"

"If that's your choice," said Thodric Jarl, "I'll cut your throat on the spot. Well? What do you choose? Your father or your death?"

When put on the spot like that, Guest Gulkan chose his father, and by evening all those who had come to Alozay with Guest Gulkan were readying themselves for the return — those personages being the wizards Pelagius Zozimus and Hostaja Sken-Pitilkin, the witch Zelafona and her dwarf-son Glambrax, and the Rovac warrior Rolf Thelemite, redoubtable in the drinking of beer and the boasting of battles.

In honour of the occasion, Pelagius Zozimus had dragged out his marvellous fish-scale armour, gear of war surely more befitting an elven lord than a miserable slug-chef. Naturally, Zozimus completed his style by matching the armour with a sword as beautiful. The dralkosh Zelafona, though warmly trussed in leathers and wool, adorned the shredded grey of her coiffure with a scarf of bird-plume silk. Her dwarf-son Glambrax swaggered through the Grand Palace in miniaturized chain mail and battle-leathers to match, perking his appearance with an elaborate hat made from complicated folds of cloud-pattern paper.

As for the rest, they were scarcely to be distinguished one

from the other — a rabble of sworders in boots and thew-leathers, ostentatiously boot-thumping along with a great weight of woven iron upon their shoulders. In that company, Sken-Pitilkin distinguished himself by the dignified common sense of his fisherman's skirts.

So that company gathered its numbers and marched in triumph to Gud Obo, the Winch Stratum of the mainrock Pinnacle. In triumph? Yes! For they were led by Thodric Jarl, and that dour and merciless warrior of Rovac was quite incapable of accomplishing even the simplest of tasks without making a mighty occasion out of it. In those days of his youth, Jarl was a man mesmerized by the spell of his own warriorhood. He could scarcely dice a carrot or slice an egg without first incanting runes of battle for the benefit of his butter knife.

In those days of his youth, Thodric Jarl was a man made for life in a world of myth; and to hear him talk of the years of peace which he had endured in Gendormargensis, why, you might think he had spent those years in a state of conscious torture. But now! Now war was ready, therefore—

But we have all heard the boasting of warriors before, and there is no point in detailing the obsessions of Rovac as presented by Thodric Jarl. Suffice it to say that, in the briefness of their reacquaintance, Jarl had already managed to irritate Sken-Pitilkin beyond measure by his posturing, and Sken-Pitilkin had been moved to suggest that the wind-flapping gap between Jarl's labile lips should best be repaired with a stout needle and a decent length of cat gut.

As Rolf Thelemite and Guest Gulkan went swaying down in a winch basket for what might well be the last time — though Guest was grimly determined to return some day to Alozay, and have an accounting with the demon Iva-Italis — they discussed the extreme hostility which had already marked the forced fellowship of Thodric Jarl and Hostaja Sken-Pitilkin. And they staked hot gold on when the Rovac warrior would have the killing of the wizard. Not if, but most definitely when.

CHAPTER EIGHT

Swelaway Sea: Tameran's inland sea which lies a little over 200
leagues south of the city of Gendormargensis and is home
to the Safrak Islands. The Swelaway Sea is drained by the Pig
River which flows north-west to the Yolantarath.

* * *

Since Thodric Jarl would brook no delay — war was afoot, and
he did not wish to miss out on his share of battle-blood glory
— the travellers joined their boat at the Palace Docks that very
evening. The sky was dubious, threatening bad weather, but Jarl
was hot to be gone regardless.

They descended to the docks, then there was a delay, for
word came that the Governor of the Safrak Bank wanted to say
goodbye to Guest Gulkan and Sken-Pitilkin. When the
Governor materialized, Guest was the first to notice him.

On Guest's first introduction to Banker Sod — an event
which had taken place on a day now more than a year in the past
— the Weaponmaster had been taken aback by Sod's racial
configuration. For Sod was an iceman, and had an iceman's pale
skin. That skin was thickly furred with white bodyhair, which
contrasted vividly with the golden hair of his head. His eyes and
teeth were of a yellow to match the hair of his scalp, but his
fingernails were black.

Over time, Guest had got used to Sod. He had also grown
used to the sight of Damsel, Sod's tender daughter, newly
nubile, whom he had seen at times in the mainrock Pinnacle and
the city of Molothair. From wondering at Damsel's strangeness,
Guest had gone on to wonder at her rumoured virginity —
though he had never been able to put rumour to the test.

Since Sod was now so much a part of the background of his
life, Guest scarcely registered his approach. But when Jarl saw
the man — why, Thodric Jarl looked as if he had suddenly been
dropped in boiling water.

"Gentle god!" said Jarl, voicing in his startlement the mightiest of all his oaths. "It's Sod!"

"Jarl," said Sod, acknowledging recognition with displeasure.

"But you — but — man, it was — Chi'ash-lan it was—"

Sken-Pitilkin looked from Jarl to Sod, from Sod to Jarl. There was something decidedly odd here. Obviously Jarl had seen Sod in earlier years in Chi'ash-lan, and obviously Banker Sod was not pleased at all to be so unexpectedly identified here on the island of Alozay. Sken-Pitilkin, fearing that this unexpected and inexplicable act of recognition somehow contained the seeds of a most unfortunate breach of diplomatic protocol, tried to hush Jarl.

But it was too late.

Sod had already decided that he was most displeased at being recognized, and that in particular he was displeased at having been recognized by Jarl.

"I want that man," said Sod, indicating Thodric Jarl.

Sundry Guardians moved to arrest Thodric Jarl.

In hindsight, it may be said of a certainty that Banker Sod had over-reacted. In hindsight, it may be said of a certainty that Sod would soon have realized as much, that diplomacy would have had its way, that Jarl would have been released, and the whole thing smoothed over and forgotten by the next day.

But Thodric Jarl was in his rune-warrior mode, so drew his sword as if to hold the world at bay. He was outnumbered by twenty to one — after all, he was a single man alone, and Sken-Pitilkin certainly had no intention of fighting on his behalf — yet he challenged the Guardians with the stoneblooded resolution which befits a man born more for myth than life.

"Jarl!" said Sken-Pitilkin sharply. "No fighting!"

But it was too late, for the nearest Guardian had already drawn his weapon in a matching gesture. Their razors clashed, and scratched each other with a sound like the claws of a sliding cat screaming across the tiles of a wet rooftop.

"That's enough!" roared Sken-Pitilkin.

The two swordsmen broke apart, both as yet unblooded. They eyed each other, breathing hard.

"My good lord Banker," said Zozimus, addressing Banker Sod in the urbanest of all imaginable tones, and doubtless intending to build some swift diplomacy upon the foundations of goodwill so diligently established by long months of slug chefery.

With the mercy of Sod's grateful belly thrown into the equation, there was a near-certain hope of peaceful resolution. But one of the younger Guardians had already drawn a knife, and even as Zozimus spoke that Guardian threw that knife.

The knife went whizzing through the air, slicing — not at Jarl! — but at Sken-Pitilkin!

With the roar of a Word, Sken-Pitilkin raised his country crook. Caught in a vortex of levitational energies, the knife snapped upwards, shattering into fragments in the buffeting upsweep of the compulsion which commanded it.

"Ahyak Rovac!" screamed Rolf Thelemite, drawing his sword with a shearing swipe which plucked the scarf from Zelafona's hair.

And a moment later, the gloom of the Palace Docks was alive with the dragon-slash of sword-silver combat. In the thrashwork embroilments of battle, Sken-Pitilkin came face to face with a Guardian. The hackwork hero chopped at the wizard with his tooth of iron, but iron met country crook, and it was the iron which shattered. The country crook twisted in Sken-Pitilkin's hands, subtle as a licorice strap in the hands of an energetic child. It thwacked the Guardian.

The man fell stumbling backwards, fell to the grip of Pelagius Zozimus—

And—

Sken-Pitilkin winced, the sound of a bone-breaking crack etched once and forever in his memory.

Zozimus held out a hand.

Zozimus spoke a Word.

The fresh-created corpse of the Guardian uprose, and stood on tottering legs before its master, the necromancer Zozimus. Then Zozimus drew his sword, and passed the weapon to the corpse. Which grasped it.

Zozimus raised his hands.

He spoke a Word.

The corpse turned, and raised the sword for war. It raised the sword against its former comrades.

Now Zozimus had spent most of his time on Alozay in the kitchen. As lord of the larder, Zozimus had dedicated himself to cooking up slugs and such, and had been grossly over-rewarded for his enterprises in this direction — for Safrak's Bankers had proved ready to part with good gold to satisfy their bellies, though they never unclenched so much as silver to appease the appetites of their minds.

However, though Zozimus customarily worked as a chef, and hence was able to find a ready welcome in whatever city, palace, pit, dungeon, ship, brothel or brewery in which he happened to find himself, the truth of the matter was that Zozimus was a necromancer.

A necromancer, yes!

Zozimus was a wizard of Xluzu, able to arcanely command the dead. Upon the Palace Docks, Zozimus commanded the corpse of the first of those who fell in battle, and sent that corpse against its erstwhile companions. The sight of one of their own fighting against them when dead was enough to rout the Guardians, who mostly dived from the docks and began swimming to the low-lying city of Molothair.

"So," said Jarl, panting harshly, "we have the docks in our possession."

From the way he said it, Sken-Pitilkin momentarily thought the Rovac warrior had no intention of stopping there, but meant to scale the winch-ropes and take the mainrock at the storm.

"Possession?" said Zozimus. "I've not seen a deed to prove it!"

As Zozimus so spoke, the shambling corpse which had been at his command came striding down the docks. Zozimus spoke a Word. The corpse passed him its sword — an implement now drenched with blood. Then it went ramshackle-walking onward down the docks, its head flopping limp and useless to the left. At a misstep, it went wheeling into the darkened waters, throwing up a floundering spray as it fell. Pelagius Zozimus ignored it, for he was busy scraping his sword with his boot. With the sword scraped — a poor expedient, but this was a battlefield, not a barracks in preparation for parade-ground display! — Zozimus sheathed it, then led the way aboard Jarl's ship.

It was then that time of day when things have grown so dark that one can scarcely see. However, the shadowing of the evening has proceeded by such imperceptible degrees that mind and eye have been fooled into accepting the shadows for the day. So one lives in a world which is coaldust mixed with deepest cloud, a world of darkness relieved merely by the bone-china brightslash of a rag of flapping sail or a torn piece of paper random in the wind.

In such shadow stood Sken-Pitilkin, the last to quit the docks. The choppy waves jostled the bulwarks of the docks, chill-slapped in syncoptic half-patterns, arrhythmic spray-bursts. The loudest sound was the creaking rubmark protest of Jarl's ship, straining at its ropes, chafing its fenders against the lowermost of Alozay's wave-mucked fortifications. In the gathering wind of the evening's night, the mounded death on the dockside was unstill, for hair was feathered, a belt flapped loose, and one gust unexpectedly scooped the weight of a helmet and rattled into the inkblack darkthickness by a sagging winch-basket.

In that windy darkness, Sken-Pitilkin endured a moment of unaccustomed desolation. Beset by wind and shadow, unsettled by death and by the prospect of a wild night on the bat-wing seas, the wizard of Drum wished himself back on Drum, back with his cats and his sea dragons, his library and his toasting rack.

But Drum—

"Come on, Sken-Pitilkin!"

But Drum was far, was far, far—

"Sken-Pitilkin!"

Drum was far distant from the Swelaway Sea, and return was denied by the wrath of the Confederation. So Sken-Pitilkin, irrevocably entangled in the fate of the Collosnon Empire—

"Zozimus, what's wrong with him?"

Sken-Pitilkin was irrevocably entangled with the Yarglat and their empire, unless he chose to quit those entanglements for unknown difficulties in some still more barbarous part of this benighted world, and, being thus entangled, he must necessarily—

"Come on," said Zozimus, who had come ashore to retrieve his cousin.

"Pelagius?"

"It's me," said Zozimus softly. "Come on. Come get yourself on the ship."

And Hostaja Torsen Sken-Pitilkin permitted his cousin to lead him aboard Jarl's ship. Already, the ropes were being loosed, or cut by men made brutal by expedient, and Sken-Pitilkin was scarcely aboard before they were slipping away into the darkening night.

Unfortunately, the night which was now darkening beyond the remotest point of intelligibility was also, weatherwise, a worsening night. A storm blew up that night, a storm of berserker fury, and the voyage which started thus badly grew no better as it proceeded. Thus began a wild voyage which eventually ended when the voyagers had to beach their much-leaking ship upon a nondescript green pancake liberally sprinkled with stone cottages and sheep fanks. This was the island of Ema-Urk, where Guest Gulkan and Rolf Thelemite promptly wrote themselves a place in local history by killing a sheep, which roused the ire of the locals to a homicidal pitch.

As the wizards Sken-Pitilkin and Zozimus tried to soothe the tempers of the locals, with some help from the dralkosh Zelafona — who contributed some of her bangles and baubles to the soothing — Thodric Jarl cursed and kicked his ship.

"You bought this ship at Ink, I suppose?" said Guest.

"I did," said Jarl.

His ship was a hulk of a fishing boat which he had indeed purchased at Ink, a village which made a lively profit by selling its worn-out vessels to unwary strangers. On close inspection,

Jarl was inclined to think it a very miracle that this particular hulk had dragged itself as far as Ema-Urk before succumbing to a long-overdue and entirely natural death.

"You were sold this boat by Umbilskimp, I suppose," said Guest, who still remembered that salesman, and had not repented of his determination to hang the man.

"Umbilskimp?" said Jarl. "Who's he?"

Guest explained.

"Why," said Jarl, when he had heard the explanation out. "That's very interesting. But, no, it was a man by name of Mung who sold me this particular boat."

Then the Weaponmaster Guest Gulkan and the Rovac warrior Thodric Jarl pacted with each other, swearing that if the village of Ink were to fall to their power then they would make it their business to see both Umbilskimp and Mung hung high, for both were murderers without a doubt.

Then Jarl proceeded with an inspection of his hulk.

By the time the wizards and the witch had bargained a peace for the shipwrecked travellers, Jarl had concluded — and nobody saw fit to disagree — that there was not one chance on this side of hell of their prodigiously rotten and storm-weakened ship getting them even half as far as the horizon.

"Which means," said Jarl, "that we're not going any further in this rotten hulk."

Which left them with very few palatable choices, for it was almost certain that Governor Sod would be in pursuit of them, and it was almost equally certain that Sod would not be gentle in his handling of them if and when he finally caught up with them.

CHAPTER NINE

Ema-Urk: an island of the Swelaway Sea, green and low-lying,
and the site of much growing of sheep.

* * *

Though Thodric Jarl did not trust the people of Ema-Urk to
keep the bargain of the peace which Zelafona had bought for
the travellers, nothing more ferocious than a straying sheep
intruded upon the peace of the travellers as they slept away the
worst of their fatigue.

After a night's sleep, the marooned adventurers began to
wonder how (if!) they were going to escape from their
predicament. Their ship in its rottenness was unfit even to be
made into firewood, far less to put to sea. There was no boat on
all of Ema-Urk which was worthy of the labour of stealing it,
and Jarl did not see how their own could be repaired except by
rebuilding it from scratch.

And as Ema-Urk was flat, grassy and treeless, to rebuild their
boat from scratch would first require the growth of its very
timbers from the seed.

"Hence," said Jarl, "it seems we will be stuck here until in
the fullness of time the masters of Alozay hunt us down to this
lair."

"They would not dare to kill us, if that's what you're
thinking," said Sken-Pitilkin positively. "Even though they're far
from the Collosnon Empire, they can't risk arousing the wrath
of Lord Onosh."

"They will not kill us," said Jarl grimly. "At least not as far as
history is concerned. When the history of this episode is written,
it will simply be said that we set to sea and were thereafter
unseen. Drowning will be the natural presumption. It will be
said that we were seen to leave Alozay on an evening which
threatened storm — that much is true. It will be said that the
fishes have had our bones. They almost did."

"We could always try talking our way out of it," said Sken-Pitilkin. "If a hunting party does come from Alozay, I'm sure—"

"You might convince them to give us a decent funeral," said Jarl, "but I doubt you could persuade them to do us any greater favour."

"Nonsense," said Sken-Pitilkin. "We can negotiate anything."

"You are a wizard," said Jarl, "and all the opportunities of the last four thousand years have not proved sufficient for wizards to negotiate a peace with the Rovac. I vote that we prepare ourselves for battle."

Here note that this "voting" was a commonplace way for the Rovac to resolve their indecisions, for, lacking reductive wisdom, these low-brained warriors were often unable to resolve their problems by intellectual analysis. When stuck in such a predicament, they therefore endeavoured to fight their way out of it by the process of piling up a great weight of numbers for one side or the other through the abovementioned process known as "voting". Thus did the Rovac often decide their disputes in the way in which battles are so often decided: through sheer weight of numbers.

In this connection, it is worth noting that a similar process of "voting" was commonly used in an even more systematized form by the Orfus pirates of the Greater Teeth; from which it can be proved that your Rovac mercenary is nothing but a pirate in embryo. However, Sken-Pitilkin shared neither the Rovac love for "voting" nor the Rovac joy in battle, and said as much.

"I think," said Sken-Pitilkin, once he had voiced his objections to waging war on any pursuers from Alozay,. "that we had better do better than that."

"Why?" said Guest, who was inclined to side with Thodric Jarl. "What's wrong with fighting? If we can sort this thing out by killing someone, then let's do it."

"Unfortunately," said Sken-Pitilkin, who knew the Rovac manner well, "Thodric Jarl isn't talking about sorting things out. He's talking about fighting to the death then dying."

"Oh," said Guest, his enthusiasm suddenly quenched. "What do we do then?"

There was a silence as everyone pondered this question. Then the necromancer Zozimus spoke.

"Well," said Zozimus, "I think the time for desperate measures has more or less arrived. I've done my share, you can't deny me that, so now it's your turn."

"My turn?" said Guest in bewilderment.

"He wasn't talking to you," said Sken-Pitilkin. "He was talking to me!"

And of course this was true. Zozimus, having commanded a corpse into battle at the docks of Alozay, thought he had well and properly done his share. Now it was time for Sken-Pitilkin to try something.

As the two wizards were cousins, and knew each other well, and kept a close eye on each other's affairs, Pelagius Zozimus had taken cognisance of the experiments which Sken-Pitilkin had been making, the experiments which had seen Alozay beset by explosions and by tornadoes. Now Zozimus clearly thought it time for Sken-Pitilkin to move from experiment to mature creation, despite the unavoidable perils which were implicit in such a move.

"What are you two hatching up?" said Thodric Jarl suspiciously.

"An airship," said Zozimus crisply. "A ship with which to conquer the air. My good cousin Sken-Pitilkin had done all the experimental work and is ready to proceed with a full-scale model."

"Cousin," said Sken-Pitilkin, who had the gravest of reservations about making the leap which Zozimus proposed, "this is no time for joking."

"I'm serious," said Zozimus.

Then Hostaja Sken-Pitilkin lapsed into the High Speech of wizards, and in that tongue he berated Zozimus, telling him that any attempt to fly a full-sized ship through the air would result in their certain deaths.

"Because," said Sken-Pitilkin, still speaking in the High

Speech of wizards, "I have been unable to control the sustained destruction which is necessary for such flight. Any ship which I make will explode, or burn, or shake itself to death, or rupture in outright whirlwind. I cannot control the destruction!"

"Ah," said Zozimus, "but I can guess why, already. You have not provided your sustained destruction with a safety valve."

"A safety valve?" said Sken-Pitilkin. "What are you talking about?"

"A safety valve," said Zozimus, "is a valve built into a pressure cooker. Now pressure cookers—"

"Oh, pressure cookers!" said Sken-Pitilkin. "Now I remember!" Sken-Pitilkin remembered very well, even though his cousin's experiments with pressure cookers had taken place a good three generations earlier. In the course of his experimenting, Zozimus had blown up three kitchens, and had almost blown up himself. On one notable occasion—

But enough of this! Life is far too short for us to be giving a full account of the derelictions of Pelagius Zozimus, that over-rated and over-paid slug-chef who ever won greater resources for his kitchens than all the irregular verbs in the world could command in nine times ninety generations. Sufficient to say that Zozimus's experiments with pressure cookers had been exhaustive, not to say exhausting, and Sken-Pitilkin remembered as much, and the truth of the memory was clearly written on Sken-Pitilkin's face.

"Yes," said Zozimus, reading his cousin's expression. "You remember well. Well, then. I ventured. I experimented. And I learnt! What I learnt through the design of pressure cookers is that great forces must be given a means of escape. If the force grows too great, then it must blow its way clear through a weak point in the device, thus preserving the integrity of the device."

Then Zozimus explained that, in his judgement, the flame trench known as Drangsturm was a perfect example of the control of great destructive forces. If the destruction temporarily got out of hand, then great gouts of flame would be thrown high in the air, thus bleeding off the surplus force with no harm to the fabric of the device which generated that force.

"I see," said Sken-Pitilkin. "So you think I should govern the forces unleashed in my airship by — by what? By arranging for bits of the ship to be selectively smashed to smithereens by an excess of such force?"

"No," said Zozimus. "I believe you should arrange for excess force to be bled off in the form of rotational energy."

Sken-Pitilkin thought about this, trying to work through the logical implications of Zozimus's suggestion.

"But," said Sken-Pitilkin, once he understood the import of his cousin's proposal, "that would mean my ship would spin round and round like a — a — like something that spins round and round, what do you call those things, a—"

"A windmill," said Zozimus.,

"Yes, a windmill, or one of those, those, you know, those octopus things, those things that whirl round and round on a stick, round and round—"

"A species of firework," said Zozimus.

"Yes, yes," said Sken-Pitilkin, "fireworks, that time in Tang, you remember, round and round, round and round, sparks and smoke in all directions, and then, then — bang!"

"There would be no bang," said Zozimus positively. "There would merely be a trifle amount of ... rotation."

"Whirlygigging," said Sken-Pitilkin, direly suspecting that "rotation" was at best but a weak euphemism for the consequences of the arrangement which Zozimus was proposing. "Whirlygigging, round and round like an octopus. The ship would burst. Or at the least — I'm sure at the very least we'd all be hideously sick. I won't have anything to do with the idea."

Yet in time — and a remarkably short time it was — Sken-Pitilkin was persuaded. The precise time of his persuasion was noon, for by noon the master chef Zozimus had prepared a delicious meal, working with slugs and watercress, with sheep bones and freshwater crabs, with puffballs and mushrooms, with chopped worms and tadpoles, all brisked and enlivened with touches of this and that from his secret emergency herb hoard and spice stock. And with this meal complete, Zozimus gave Sken-Pitilkin an ultimatum:

"Design an airship or starve."

Thus a decision was reached in favour of flight, and after lunch the brave Sken-Pitilkin went to work, converting the ruinous hulk of a watership into an airship. He exercised his power in the manner of wizards, converting certain timbers of this ship into artefacts possessed of magical power — artefacts which the universe itself would seek to destroy if it got but half a chance.

Sken-Pitilkin wrought these devices in such a way that their magical nature could be shielded or unshielded at his command. When each device was unshielded, the universe would seek to destroy it, and the destructive forces thus unleashed would be used for controlled flight, with any uncontrollable excess being bled off into the "rotational energy" which Zozimus had suggested.

At last the thing was finished — but the great Lord Alagrace flatly refused to get into it. The parcel of soldiers who had bodyguarded the great Thodric Jarl all the way to Alozay likewise refused to dare Sken-Pitilkin's device.

Thus, in the end, on its maiden flight the airship was crewed by the wizard of Skatzabratzumon known as Hostaja Sken-Pitilkin, by the wizard of Xluzu known as Pelagius Zozimus, by the witch Zelafona and her dwarf-son Glambrax, by the mighty Rovac warrior Rolf Thelemite, by the cow-tattooed Thodric Jarl, and by Guest Gulkan, youngest and most undisciplined of the sons of the lord of the Collosnon Empire.

Name them and know them!

For they were heroes, one and all!

Pioneers of flight!

Linked in a daring enterprise unparalleled in the history of experimental wizardry!

And possibly linked — Sken-Pitilkin could not help from thinking as much — in being destined to share a common grave.

A full day and a bit before they were to depart, Sken-Pitilkin gathered the would-be air-adventurers together and indulged himself in a speech.

"Man has never ventured to the heavens in a ship such as this before," said Sken-Pitilkin. Then, glancing at Zelafona: "Nor woman neither. We can but guess what shocks the buffets of the heavens will impose on human physiology."

"A guess is as good as a goose on a blind night," said Guest, venturing one of the proverbs of Rovac which Rolf Thelemite had taught him.

"Pardon?" said Sken-Pitilkin.

"Nothing," said Guest.

"You said something," said Sken-Pitilkin. "I distinctly heard you, and though what you said was less than distinct I'm perfectly sure you didn't say nothing."

"I said," said Guest, "that maybe if it's so dangerous we shouldn't risk it."

"I wouldn't say it's as dangerous as all that," said Sken-Pitilkin, who thought it unwise to share the full strength of his forebodings with the young Yarglat barbarian. "But I suspect it's better undertaken on an empty stomach."

"You mean," said Guest, "we shouldn't eat?"

"Precisely," said Sken-Pitilkin briskly. "That's the main point I want to get across today. We can't know anything of the physiology of flight unless we look by analogy to the physiology of seafaring. As travel by sea is apt to induce a sickness of stomach, so may the air by analogy produce a like-belly illness. Hence starvation is the order of the day. Or of three days, ideally — however, we've not time for such a fast, so a day's deprivation will have to suffice."

"What about drinking?" said Guest. "Can we drink?"

"What do you have in mind?" said Sken-Pitilkin.

Guest told him, and was advised that it would be unwise in the extreme for him to proceed with his stated intention of consuming three beers, two gins and a brandy before boarding Sken-Pitilkin's airship.

"Besides," said Sken-Pitilkin, "I doubt whether there is either gin or brandy to be had on Ema-Urk."

Guest Gulkan and Rolf Thelemite both assured him that both were to be had, and in quantity. They had assured themselves of this already.

"Then," said Sken-Pitilkin, "I adjure you to abstain from such."

"Adjure?" said Guest. "What on earth does that mean?"

"It means," said Sken-Pitilkin, "that I'm ready to kick you unless you show good sense and abstinence."

Then those who were doomed to join Sken-Pitilkin in the experimental flying ship launched themselves upon a one-day fast. All but for the Weaponmaster.

Despite the timely warning issued by the sagacious Sken-Pitilkin, and despite the threat of reprisals courtesy of Sken-Pitilkin's boot, the young Weaponmaster chose to indulge in a pre-flight dinner which included rhubarb sausages anointed with cod liver oil. This dish was especially invented for the occasion by an over-enthusiastic Pelagius Zozimus, whose deviations from gastronomic routine tended to be not only frequent but disastrous.

Rhubarb sausages with cod liver oil!

As heaven is my witness, this is what Zozimus cooked!

And Guest, in the folly of his youth—

Guest ate it!

In his wisdom, the wizard Sken-Pitilkin refused to allow his intestinal peace to be vandalized by such a dish, and leavened his fast only with a small crust of dry bread and a pannikin of boiled water. But Guest ate the rhubarb sausages with a truly barbaric enthusiasm, swallowed a second helping of cod liver oil, and went on to consume two steaks cut from the more blubbery parts of a whale (steaks which had been cut from the beast some three years earlier, and which had been imported to Ema-Urk at the bottom of a barrel of vinegar), then followed these steaks with a dish of exceedingly greasy pork, an entire apple pie heaped with whipped cream, and, as a special after-dinner treat, the eyes of five dogs (the eyes of dogs being a special delicacy much favoured by the gourmets of the islands of Safrak). He then proceeded to his drinking — only the beers he drank were seven in number, not three; the gins he consumed were set before him in quadruplicate; and his brandy was double.

Here Guest Gulkan was true to his Yarglat heritage. The Yarglat are capable of subsisting on the most parsimonious of diets when necessity demands; and when at war will content themselves at need with a single cup of fresh hot blood tapped from a vein in a living horse. But their indulgences are in keeping with their deprivations; and what they eat, and the quantities in which they eat it, is scarcely believable even to those who have seen such feats repeated thrice or thirty times; and their drinking matches their eating.

Never have the Yarglat been able to hold any great banquet without one person at least dying simply from overdrinking. The uninitiated may think this an exaggeration — but death from abuse of liquor has ever been a leading cause of death among the heroes of the northern horsetribes. Furthermore, history can name of a certainty at least four rulers of the Collosnon Empire who died of overdrinking, and a further three who expired through sheer gluttony: Dobdask, who expired while trying to eat an entire horse to win a bet with one of his generals; Henza, who collapsed while eating one of his generals; and Yeldanov Ax, who died as a consequence of disembowelling himself and eating a considerable portion of his own gut, an eccentricity which tends to support those rumours which claim him to have been somewhat deranged.

So Guest Gulkan indulged himself as the Yarglat will, and in what was left of the night he tried to digest that which he had ingested.

Guest's attempts at digestion were not entirely successful, and in the grey light of the morrow's dawn he looked rather queasy. The chip-chop motion of the Swelaway Sea was making him uneasy: he had to avert his eyes lest it make him positively sick. Nevertheless, he joined his fellow air-adventurers; and, once all had made their wills and had handed these into the care and keeping of Lord Alagrace, they bravely climbed aboard the airship.

All but Rolf Thelemite.

"Climb aboard, three-nipples," said Thodric Jarl, all grey-bearded harshness in the grey dawn.

Three-nipples? What kind of nickname was that?

As the other travellers were still wondering, Jarl disembarked, caught Rolf by the single gold-snake earring which hung from his left ear, and dragged him aboard the boat.

"Sit!" said Jarl, compressing a lifetime's scorn into the single word.

Rolf Thelemite sat. His lower lip was trembling. It communicated its anxiety to the lip above it. Rolf's eyes blinked, so fast and so fiercely that at last he had to close them altogether. Jarl said something to him in the Rovac tongue, and he bit his lower lip. Hard. Drawing blood.

"All ready?" said Sken-Pitilkin. "Very well! Brace yourselves! And hold on tight!"

Sken-Pitilkin said a Word, and——

The ship rotated violently, and slammed itself into the sky. It whipped itself towards the heavens like a cartwheel driven by demons, and vomit in matching cartwheels came spurting from Guest Gulkan's lips.

Up, up, up, up, up went the airship.

Slammed through the sky, they skipped marches in moments. Mere eagles or dragons would have been left creaking in their wake like so many inconsequential toothpicks awash in the boil of a racing sloop. As the waddle of a duckling is to the speed of a galloping stallion, so was the stasis of all lesser forms of transport when compared with the compressed delirium of that airship in flight.

The heavens themselves screamed. The heavens screamed as the very sky was torn asunder by the assault of that ship. As lightning launches itself in javelins of fire, as thunder cracks its discus, in such a manner did that ship hurtle itself through the blue empyrean.

And, all the time, the vomit shot from Guest Gulkan's gaping mouth in spuming cartwheels, so it looked for all the world as if the boy had been transformed into one of those octopus things which goes whirlygigging round on a stick, one of those hectic fireworks which are so much the fashion in Tang.

Thus flew Sken-Pitilkin's airship.

As for the master of that ship—

Why, Sken-Pitilkin found himself unable to control the vessel, for it was spinning so quickly that he was pinned against the planks by centrifugal force. He managed to wrench his head sideways, and wished he had not. For on turning his head, Sken-Pitilkin found he could see through a gap in the planks. Through that gap he saw the sea, then hills, hills buckling away in nightmarish cascades of onslaughting rotational energy. Then the shocked and air-shattered wizard almost lost an eyeball to a passing mountain peak. Almost, but not quite — for the airship cleared the mountaintop by half a handspan.

A moment later, there was a loud bang — BANG! — and the ship lost power.

Cartwheeling still, it plummeted through the air, slowing, sliding, losing momentum and—

And falling!

"Grief of gods!" cried Zozimus, clutching at a rope.

He might as well have clutched at the sky itself, or a handful of cloud, for there was nothing which could save them now. The ship was most definitely falling. Count one! It was falling still! Count two! Most definitely falling! Count three! Sken-Pitilkin waited for his life to start to flash before his eyes, but for some unaccountable reason the only thing he could think of was a baked hedgehog.

Sken-Pitilkin was still trying to decipher the import of this visionary hedgehog when his airship impacted with the most enormous crash. Ice and snow flew shattering upward, for the ship had fallen with full force upon the uppermost reaches of an upland glacier.

"We're down!" cried Glambrax.

Upon which the ship began to slide, suggesting that there yet lay ahead of them a great deal in the way of down, downwards and doom. This was swiftly confirmed as the ship gathered speed, sliding down that glacier with precipitous velocity.

"Aaaagh!" said Zozimus.

"Waaaah!" said Sken-Pitilkin.

"Gaaaa!" cried Guest Gulkan.

But before anyone else could find breath sufficient to join this chorus, the airship slam-crashed into a crevasse, bounced, flipped, rolled over and over, and came to rest in ruins at the foot of the glacier.

There were a few groans from the ship's settling timbers, then all was silent but for a tiny chink, chink, chink. The sound was from the golden serpent which hung from Rolf Thelemite's left ear. It was swaying still from the violence imparted to it by its aerial adventure, and was knocking against a rusted bolthead.

The earring chinked itself to silence.

With the ceasing of that sound, every sound in the audible universe seemed to have ceased.

There was a long, long silence.

Then a groan.

Then, bit by bit, the travellers began to pick themselves up.

"We've been wrecked," said the dwarf Glambrax.

"Air-wrecked," said Rolf Thelemite.

"Wrecked with a crash," said Guest Gulkan. "We crashed."

"Crashed," said Sken-Pitilkin. "That's a good word for it. Is anybody hurt?"

Nobody was, excepting Thodric Jarl, and his injuries appeared to be limited to a couple of broken ribs.

"Very well," said Sken-Pitilkin. "Let us be making our way to that building."

And he pointed out the building he meant, which was the one dominant human-made feature of an otherwise bleak and desolate landscape.

Sken-Pitilkin's airship had crashed in a valley which was deep and narrow. This bare and barren upland valley ran from east to west, and the heroes of the airship had been airwrecked (or, to use Sken-Pitilkin's parlance, "crashed") upon the southern heights of that valley.

The building to which Sken-Pitilkin had pointed stood on the northern slopes of the valley. It was huge. From the distance, the travellers could see no windows in that building, nor could they clearly make out its colour. Guest Gulkan declared it to be not a building but a block-built dung-heap.

"Then since we have a dung-beetle in our ranks," said Thodric Jarl, "let us be making for it."

Guest thought it best not to ask which of them was the dung-beetle, and in the wisdom of his silence the party began to navigate towards that far-distant goal. This required the air-crashed aeronauts to descend into the depths of the valley before scaling the opposing slope.

So they began the descent.

At these heights, the air was thin, and to walk was a labour. Even though they were going downhill, they found they must necessarily stop every four or five paces to rest for a trifle; and it seemed that each of them at each halt discovered more and more bruises, scrapes, cracks and cuts which had previously gone unnoticed in the excitement of their air-escapade.

"Grief of a dog!" said Rolf, picking his way downhill. "I'd not see fit to bury a turd in a place as miserable as this!"

In truth, the Rovac warrior Rolf Thelemite was an apt judge of landscape.

For the valley through which they laboured was a singularly uninspiring realm of shattered rock and smashed stone. The wedgework of the weather had split huge rafts of scree from the disintegrating mountains. There was nothing whatsoever in that blasted landscape to hold the eye, unless one was attracted by the great lumps of stone which reared up on the skyline, where the sun blazed down from a sky as blue as an ice-maiden's eye.

As they descended, the dralkosh Zelafona began to stumble. She did not complain, but the subdued silence of her dwarf-son Glambrax was sufficient to warn Sken-Pitilkin that the mother was in trouble.

"Here," said Sken-Pitilkin, passing his country-crook to Zelafona. "Lean on this."

She took it without a word, enduring the gift as if it were an insult. But she stumbled less thereafter — though Sken-Pitilkin stumbled more, and began to repent of the folly which had led him to pass his mainstaff support to a witch. He regretted being over-generous with Zelafona. For, after all, the witch and her dwarf-son were largely to blame for Sken-Pitilkin's present predicament. Had it not been for the recklessness of their avaricious folly, then Hostaja Sken-Pitilkin would still have been safely ensconced on his home island of Drum, rather than mucking about in a wilderness of mountains.

In this lies a tale.

In the romantic folly of his former years, Hostaja Torsen Sken-Pitilkin had set himself against the Confederation of Wizards, seeking with the propaganda of his tongue and by the moral force of his generous example to oppose that Confederation's despotic oppression of witches. Like other immature idealists before him, Sken-Pitilkin had found both propaganda and moral example to be inefficient against vested financial interests; and those of the Confederation who had set themselves to break up the Sisterhood's mighty Credit Union soon set themselves the task of breaking up Sken-Pitilkin.

Thus Sken-Pitilkin had become an outlawed renegade with a price on his head; and for long years he had wandered, with none but the irregular verbs as his companions, until at last he invaded Drum (an easy invasion, this, the island being uninhabited at the time) and (armed with a large sack of flea powder and a dozen rat traps) secured possession of Drum's ruling castle.

For long generations thereafter, Hostaja Sken-Pitilkin lorded it over the island of Drum as the absolute master of all he surveyed! True, most of what he surveyed was bits and pieces of the wrath-wracked waters of the Penvash Channel, that strategically important strait which separates the continent of Argan from the Ravlish Lands; but of that at least he had unopposed suzerainty.

Then came disaster.

Disaster came to Sken-Pitilkin's castle in the form of the witch Zelafona and her dwarf-son Glambrax. These two (in conjunction with Pelagius Zozimus, who surely should have known better!) had been embroiled in a complicated conspiracy to steal from one of the libraries of the Confederation of Wizards a complete and detailed history of the Credit Union once run by the Sisterhood of Witches.

That at least is the story which Zelafona retailed to Sken-Pitilkin. Pelagius Zozimus cheerfully confirmed the story, though Zozimus was ever an adroit master of deception. Sken-Pitilkin darkly suspected that a lot was being left unsaid, for whatever wickedness the would-be thieves had perpetrated in the south, they had roused the Confederation to a wrathfulness never seen before or since, and it is hard to imagine that the attempted theft of a History could have inspired such anger.

The Confederation had pursued all three thieves — Zelafona, Glambrax and Pelagius Zozimus — and had pursued them with such ferocity that pursuit was close behind when the malefactors sought refuge on the island of Drum. The evil ones did not come to Drum by accident. No, they knew Sken-Pitilkin to be in residence upon that island.

When these refugees arrived, Sken-Pitilkin found he had no option but to help them. After all, Zozimus was his cousin. Furthermore, Sken-Pitilkin owed a great debt of honour to a powerful witch known as Bao Gahai, who had thrice saved his life in earlier centuries. So Sken-Pitilkin found himself honour-bound to help Zelafona, for the witch Zelafona was Bao Gahai's sister.

Here let it be known that honour does not lie in the sole possession of the warriors. For, while your bloodstained barbarian will boast much of "the honour of his sword", honour has absolutely nothing whatsoever to do with the hacking off of heads or the dissection of the liver. Sken-Pitilkin was honourable; and, in his honour, he assisted all three refugees to elude their pursuers. Which, of course, made Sken-Pitilkin himself a target for that very pursuit.

Consequently, the renegade wizard of Skatzabratzumon joined the refugees in their flight into the northern continent of Gendormargensis, where they sought shelter from the great and honourable Bao Gahai, the adviser (some said: the consort) of Lord Onosh, Lord Onosh being the father of Guest Gulkan and the ruler of the Collosnon Empire.

Thus Sken-Pitilkin was exiled from his home island of Drum; and was forced to earn his living as a mere tutor; and became unconscionably embroiled in the affairs of the Yarglat; and found himself on a stumblestone mountainside somewhere in the northern continent of Tameran, with the witch Zelafona availing herself of his country crook for her own support.

"Chala?" said Glambrax, speaking anxiously to Zelafona.

"I'm all right, sugarlump," said she, though the manifest strain of the statement gave the lie to her own pronouncement.

Chala? Sugarlump?

Pet names, doubtless, and proof of a tenderness of relationship which Sken-Pitilkin had never thought to exist between the dwarf and his mother.

On that journey down the mountainside, Sken-Pitilkin began to suspect that the greater part of Glambrax's habitual brawling, joking, hard-drinking delinquency was insulation — a layer of hard-working diversion designed to cut the dwarf off from the rawness of the painful realities of his own life. For, after all, Glambrax was as much an exile as Sken-Pitilkin. A hard necessity had driven the dwarf to Tameran, and doubtless in his private moments he suffered from the driving, as did Sken-Pitilkin.

So.

In the unconscious wisdom of his habits, the dwarf Glambrax had configured his life in such a way that he seldom had to endure so much as a single, solitary moment of personal reflection from sun-dawn to dusk.

But on these stony, steep-descending slopes, there was no opportunity for brawling distractions. There was instead the coldness of unfeeling reality, the uncompromising solidity of stone, the randomness of scree, and the sharp-beak threats of hunger, thirst and entropy.

Like so many broken cockroaches, the air-wrecked aeronauts stumbled stone by stone down the rockside, mite-made creatures of bony flesh pinpricking their way across the rumplings of geology, their significance dwarfed and denied by the razor-blade heights of hostility which etched the skies above them.

Up on those stone-slice heights — high, high above the rock

slopes and scree drifts where the travellers laboured — lay white snow-slice eternities of cold. A high wind was scouring a mist of snow on a knife-edge peak, but this was so far above and beyond the travellers that they could not hear so much as a whisper of the crisping and keening of the ferocity of that bright-sun wind. Rather, they laboured in stillness, a stillness loud with their harsh-panting breathing, the creaking of their knee joints, the squiff-pulse labours of their hearts.

At the bottom of the slope, when all downlabour was done and their uplabour was about to be commenced, there was a stream which ran towards the east. From which Sken-Pitilkin, learned in geography, deduced that in all probability this valley would ultimately provide them with an escape to the Swelaway Sea, should they choose to follow that stream to the east.

There was no need to ford the stream, since it was bridged. A path came up the valley from out of the east, crossed the stream by way of the bridge, then climbed towards the block-built building up above.

"What now?" asked Guest Gulkan, he who in the folly of his youth still possessed strength sufficient for senseless questions.

Guest Gulkan's travelling companions, who were one and all exhausted by the rigours of the mountain heights, wasted no breath on useless reply.

Pelagius Zozimus took the lead.

Pelagius Zozimus, still wearing his elf-bright fish-scale armour, crossed the bridge, then began to mountain-climb upwards, one trudge at a time. After him went Thodric Jarl, mouth agape in a constant, unconscious, almost inaudible lisp of pain — for Jarl was suffering grievously from his broken ribs. Then went Zelafona, leaning on Sken-Pitilkin's country crook. Glambrax dogged his mother's heels, and Sken-Pitilkin followed, half hoping that Zelafona would drop dead. For if she died then Sken-Pitilkin would be able to recover his country crook, and his journey would be that much easier. Naturally, the wizard had far too much pride to ask for the voluntary return of that instrument.

After Sken-Pitilkin came Guest Gulkan. The boy had long

since drawn his sword, and had been abusing that instrument shamelessly, using it as a walking stick.

The Rovac warrior Rolf Thelemite had been bravely trying to resist Guest's example. For Rolf was — he was, wasn't he? — a mighty killer of men. A conqueror of dragons. A slaughterer of kings and emperors. A killer of orcs, ghouls, ghosts and necromancers. As such, he could scarcely abuse the pride of his steel by using it as a walking stick. Could he?

As the way bent upward, the going got harder. Rolf at first walked with a hand on each knee, as if striving to stabilize his knee joints by force of digital pressure. Then at last he drew his sword, and followed Guest's disgraceful example — hoping that Thodric Jarl would not turn and discover him.

In such procession, the air-crashed aeronauts went labouring up the path, making for the building which dominated the heights, and for an uncertain reception at the hands of unknown strangers.

CHAPTER TEN

Ibsen-Iktus: mountainous area of Tameran, south of Babaroth, east of Locontareth, west of Swelaway Sea and far to the north of Favanosin. This impoverished upthrust of impenetrable rocks lies beyond the borders of the Witchlord's realm, for Lord Onosh lays no claim of conquest on these snow-strewn heights.

***

So it was that in the spring of his 17th year, shortly after his 16th birthday, the young Weaponmaster Guest Gulkan found himself airwrecked in the mountains with the wizards Pelagius Zozimus and Hostaja Sken-Pitilkin, with the dralkosh Zelafona and her dwarf-son Glambrax, with the grey-bearded warrior Thodric Jarl and with Jarl's compatriot Rolf Thelemite.

The light of day was beginning to fail as the wanderers approached the building which they had earlier spied from afar. To walk was a labour, and on the last stages of their climb they were forced to pause after each and every step.

As has been said, the valley of their airwrecking ran from east to west, and the building to which the aeronauts were bent was set high on the northern slopes. This formidable behemoth of a building had a frontage which was all of half a thousand paces in length, and its height, by Sken-Pitilkin's estimate, was upwards of two hundred paces. As they closed with the building, the travellers saw that its windowless frontage was covered with huge ceramic tiles, each the height of a man.

In the freshness of their first creation, these tiles must have been glorious with colour, but now they were suncracked and weatherstained, and some had fallen away altogether to reveal the stolid grey stone which lay beneath the decorations. Guest Gulkan squinted at those which remained, making out details — hump and haunch, nipple and breast, lotham and yargam, sagit and mok.

"Why" said Guest, "they're — they're—"

"We can see very well what they're doing," said Sken-Pitilkin severely, "but you do but show your boyishness when you stand there gawking at them."

"Why, no," said Guest. "I show no such thing. Rather, I show my intellectual passion, my dedicated passion for ethnology. One hopes the interior lives to the promise of the facade, for I have long desired to do some really rigorous ethnological fieldwork."

"Enough of your yattering," said Thodric Jarl, who by this time was in a very bad temper. "Let's get on with it."

Jarl's temper was bad because to move — or even just to breathe — was to be stabbed by knives.

"You look," said Guest, "very much as if you were in pain."

"I am," said Jarl, who saw no point in denying it. "I've broken a couple of ribs."

Jarl's speech was curt, as usual, his accents hard — but in truth he felt as tender as a ripe tomato enduring a sledgehammer's playful tap. He felt as if he might burst into tears at any moment.

Chronic pain will tax the courage of the bravest. To resolve on one's death — ah, this is easy, at least when one is sufficiently enraged. Anger solves the problem. One decides for death, one charges one's enemies — and all decision is gone, for there is no way out. Jarl had done as much in the past, surviving more through luck than anything else.

But to make a moutainscape trek with a set of broken ribs puts far greater demands upon character. When one's ribs are broken, every step demands a new decision. The rigours of this choice, with its constant demands on his courage, had brought Jarl to the very edge of emotional collapse.

"Are your ribs badly broken?" said Rolf.

A useless question, for how could Jarl know the answer? Perhaps his bones were merely cracked, in which case pain would be the worst of the consequences. Or perhaps the bones had splintered in places to sharpened knives, in which case Jarl might abruptly get spiked through the lung, and die of internal bleeding.

"They hurt like hell," said Jarl shortly, and stumped towards the single centrally placed gateway which pierced the building's tiled facade.

"We'll know the truth of his breakages soon enough," said Guest. "If he starts coughing blood we can count one lung as good as gone for certain."

Then Guest Gulkan and Rolf Thelemite fell in behind Thodric Jarl, watching him intently to see if he would start coughing up his heart's blood, which gave a certain interest to the proceedings which would otherwise have been lacking.

"Boys," said the witch Zelafona, with a click of her tongue which summarised volumes of disapproval.

Then she handed Sken-Pitilkin his country crook, which he received gratefully, for he had never before had more need of its support.

Inside the pierced gateway, a set of windchimes hung from the roof. Though there was no wind, these chimes tinkled regardless, and this tinkling was the loudest exterior sound which the air-adventurers had heard since first air-crashing in this upland valley. Led by Jarl, the exhausted air adventurers passed through the gateway into a broad courtyard. A woman was making her way across this yard with a bucket of water.

"Ho there, fench oddock!" said Guest.

Challenged thus, the old woman turned to stare, then dropped her bucket of water. As it crashed and spilt, she fled.

"Very bright," said Sken-Pitilkin, observing the old woman's skirt-clutching retreat. "Suppose you follow her and see where she goes."

"No need," said Guest, "for I think the master of the place is upon us."

Indeed, venturing towards the air adventurers from a small side door was an elderly and decidedly shaggy-haired gentleman who appeared to be of Yarglat race. Accordingly, Guest Gulkan hailed the ancient in Eparget, and was pleased to receive an answer in his native tongue.

"Greetings," said the ancient, with the greatest of all

imaginable courtesy, politely overlooking the dusty and dishevelled appearance of his uninvited guests, and overlooking as well the fact that all were splattered with the vomit which had come cartwheeling from Guest Gulkan's mouth during the airship's maiden voyage.

Then the Yarglat-born ruler of the valley's dominant building said to Sken-Pitilkin: "And to you, greetings. It has been a long time, Torsen."

"Torsen?" said Sken-Pitilkin in astonishment. "You call me Torsen?"

"That is your name, is it not?" said the ancient.

"Why," said Hostaja Torsen Sken-Pitilkin, "it is one of them. But — why, if you know that—"

Then Sken-Pitilkin lapsed into the High Speech of wizards, and the ancient replied in turn. The elf-armoured Pelagius Zozimus soon joined the conversation, adding to Sken-Pitilkin's tale of aeronautical adventuring, and the three would have been in discourse all night had not Jarl demanded that they stop talking in gibberish.

"Who and what is this?" said Jarl, gesturing at their shaggy-haired Yarglat host.

Jarl gestured in a hand which was perilously close to being a fist.

"This dignitary," said Sken-Pitilkin, indicating the old man, "is the abbot of Qonsajara, Qonsajara being the monastery in which we now stand."

"A priest, is he?" said Jarl.

"In a manner of speaking," said Sken-Pitilkin. "His name is Ontario Nol. He is a wizard of the order of Itch — a wizard of the winds."

"A wizard!" said Jarl. "And what thinks he of the Rovac?"

"He thinks them dangerous," said Sken-Pitilkin, "therefore demands that you do him the courtesy of surrendering your sword while you enjoy his hospitality."

"That I will do, then," said Jarl.

With that, Jarl drew his sword. An odd gesture, this. For a blade is not surrendered naked — rather, it is more properly yielded by unbuckling the swordbelt which sustains its scabbard. Ontario Nol's eyes widened marginally, for he knew the murderous appetites of the Rovac.

With his sword drawn to the full length of its murder, Jarl hacked at the head of Ontario Nol. But the wizard had been given an eyeblink or more to prepare himself for attack, and an eyeblink was sufficient.

"Ja-bree!" screamed Nol, flinging wide his hands as Jarl struck down.

A wizard-wind whirlwind caught Jarl in a wind-slam funnel-spout. Trapped in a wind-whipping whirlspill, Jarl was spun first deasil then widdershins.

"Cha!" shouted Nol.

And Jarl was released from the grip of the wizard-wind. Pirouette by pirouette, the warrior spun to the nearest wall, which slammed him in the face, rebuffing his ballet with puritanical retort.

"Bravo!" said Guest, applauding vigorously as Thodric Jarl slid down that wall, staining its stones with a snail-track of blood from his vigorously bleeding nose.

"Blood!" said Rolf Thelemite excitedly. "See! Blood, blood! The ribs have pierced his lungs! He's done for, now!"

But that was not the case.

On close examination, it appeared that Thodric Jarl had suffered no more than a chipped tooth and a bloody nose. He had not even been knocked out. Nevertheless, it must be admitted that this was most definitely not the most auspicious of introductions.

CHAPTER ELEVEN

Ul-donlok: valley in the Ibsen-Iktus mountains and site of the ancient monastery of Qonsajara, which is home to a wizard of Yarglat breeding named Ontario Nol. The valley of Ul-donlok, which is high and narrow at its western end, slopes downward to the east, opening out as it nears the Swelaway Sea.

* * *

Hostaja Torsen Sken-Pitilkin did his best to make Thodric Jarl apologize for his foolish attack on Ontario Nol. Jarl refused.

"Dogs will hatch from eggs and pigs be born of pigeons before I say sorry to a wizard," said Jarl, intransigent as any monster of the nursery.

Jarl was sure Nol would kill him in any case, and no Rovac warrior wishes to die with an apology to a wizard on his lips.

"What are we to do with this rune-warrior?" said Sken-Pitilkin, shaking his head in disgust.

"Let's not worry about it," said Nol, shrugging off Jarl's insolent unrepentance. "After all, what matters a trifle like attempted murder when dinner is waiting? Come, friends. Let's seat ourselves and sup. For dinner cools monstrous fast in weather like this."

"Dinner?" said Pelagius Zozimus, who had a chef's highly developed consciousness of the passage of time. "Dinner? My dear sir, dinner can hardly cool before it's cooked, and we've only just arrived! How can you possibly have dinner ready already?"

"I saw you from afar," said Ontario Nol gravely, "even if my servant did not."

"So!" said Sken-Pitilkin, taking this to be a confession of the possession of Powers. "The wizards of Itch have powers of sight, do they?"

"They do indeed," said Ontario Nol. "Such powers are consequent upon the possession of those ocular organs known

174

as eyes, of which I have two. With my own two eyes I have long had you under observation from the heights of Qonsajara, in consequence of which I have been able to have a dinner prepared for you."

Upon which both Zozimus and Sken-Pitilkin felt foolish, and made no further comment as the hospitable wizard of Itch led the party of air adventurers into his dining room. It was a small room dominated by a large stone table, and though Nol had threatened them with a chilled dinner the room was in fact kept comfortably warm by a small but efficient fire.

"May we not wash, first?" said Sken-Pitilkin, conscious of the fact that all of them smelt somewhat of vomit, and that the half-digested eyes of two or three of the dogs of Ema-Urk still clung to Guest Gulkan's outer clothing.

"Wash?" said Nol, in patent surprise. "But why?"

"To please me," said Zelafona, coming to Sken-Pitilkin's rescue. "As a woman, I am particular of the company I keep, therefore would have these men washed if bowl, sponge and water to spare."

"I have no objection to a sponging of my face and my jacket," said Thodric Jarl, who was perfectly ready to make concessions to the witch Zelafona, though he was ever reluctant to give aid to a wizard. "Rolf will help me with the sponging."

So spoke Jarl, and spoke bravely. But his speech was badly slurred, for pain, altitude, fatigue, fear and a wizard's whirlwind battery had told heavily on his resources.

"If Jarl's so sick he needs a nursemaid," said Rolf Thelemite, his own fatigue displaying itself in his singularly ungracious manner, "then I suppose I can sponge him down."

"And Guest will wash himself," said Sken-Pitilkin in tones of warning, as the Weaponmaster advanced upon Ontario Nol's big stone table.

"Will I?" said Guest, rebelliously. "I don't think I will, you know. I'm not due for a bath for two or three years at least, and I'm not going to delay dinner for any such eccentricity."

Sken-Pitilkin did not see how Guest could possibly be ready to eat again after having been so prodigiously sick earlier in the day. But the boy was as good as his word. He sat himself down at the dinner table — half-digested eyes and all — and was two-thirds of the way through a second helping of everything by the time his companions returned from their washing.

For dinner they had lentil soup, boiled potatoes and the eggs of several chickens, with a serving of roast soy beans on the side. Ontario Nol apologized for the sparseness of his table.

"Unfortunately," said Nol, "we have only the eggs of a chicken, and not the meat. I would have killed you a chicken, only I have none at Qonsajara. The eggs are paid to me in way of tribute by one of the villages further down the valley."

"You are a ruler, then," said Guest Gulkan.

"The absolute monarch of all I survey," acknowledged Ontario Nol. "I estimate the population of my kingdom as some three thousand people in all. It is sufficient."

"Your kingdom," said Guest, chewing against the resistance of some soy beans as he spoke. "How do you name your kingdom?"

"It is named Qonsajara," said Ontario Nol, "taking its name from this monastery, which once was consecrated to the rites of Zozo Darjidan, the tantric strain of Qa Marika. Do you know what is meant by tantrism?"

"Dorking," said Guest, remembering certain lessons in ethnology. "That's what it means. The tantric arts are the arts of dorking. Lotham and yargam, sagit and mok. That's what the pictures are all about."

"True," said Ontario Nol with a thin smile. "But there was more to it than that. The tantric rites have catharsis as their goal. One frees the spirit of the flesh by purging the flesh through excess. There is more to it, then, than ... how did you put it?"

"Dorking," said Guest again, unabashed and unashamed.

"One hopes," said the witch Zelafona, "that the boy has not offended your religion. If he has, then my dwarf will be happy to beat him for you."

At that, Glambrax jumped on to the table and struck a beating pose. Guest Gulkan's hand went to his sword.

"Peace," said Ontario Nol, as Sken-Pitilkin swept Glambrax

from the table with his country crook. "I own to no religion. Though I name myself as abbot of this monastery, that is just for form's sake. In truth, this temple's rites are a thousand years dead, and the worshippers died with the rites."

By now, Ontario Nol had the full attention of all his auditors, and they listened in after-dinner leisure as he told what he knew of Zozo Darjidan and the religion of Qa Marika. He lacked the full story, but still knew the most amazing fragments of the much-dislocated history of times long past. He mentioned the Technic Renaissance and the Genetic Mutiny, and told strange stories of a planet named Olo Malan, which — depending on which tradition one adhered to — either was or was not the very ball of dirt on which they were presently standing.

Then Sken-Pitilkin had stories of his own to tell, and Pelagius Zozimus followed him, after which the dralkosh Zelafona was persuaded to speak.

Never before had Guest heard Zelafona tell of the past. The boy listened, fascinated, as the old woman's shrivelled voice spun tales of full-fleshed maidens and desiring heroes, of creatures which lived in mountains and fed themselves on time, of cities of singing glass and streets of liquid fire, of incubus and succubus knotted together in shadows of turbulent desire, of vampires in their cavern-realms, and of ghostly dragons hunting ghosts through realms of living men.

That night, when Guest Gulkan finally got to sleep, he dreamt dreams of hallucinatory vividness. He dreamt of spheres of light which sang and spoke; of armies collapsing in maggot-plague and blood-drench deliquescence; of snoring mountains and sneezing skeletons; of kings dressed in the dazzle of hammered rainbow; of the Dawn Songs of Kalatanastral and the battlements of Stronghold Handfast; of books which conjured cities, and cities which conjured gods.

Guest woke in the night with a pounding headache. Such was his pain that he woke Sken-Pitilkin, fearing himself on the verge of death. Sken-Pitilkin told him to go back to sleep, but by then Ontario Nol had already been disturbed.

"It is the height," said Nol. "It is the suddenness of the

height which causes the headache. Men can damage themselves to the point of death simply by walking to the heights too quickly, and you — you've flown! I should have thought of that. We should check your companions."

Then, on Ontario Nol's instructions, all the air adventurers were roused from sleep, saving Rolf Thelemite alone, who proved quite impossible to wake.

"He's sleeping solidly," said Guest.

"There's more to it than that," said Ontario Nol. "He's unconscious. His brain has swollen in the high thin air."

"His brain!" said Guest.

"It is true," said Nol.

Guest Gulkan took some persuading, claiming indeed that he doubted his comrade Rolf to be in possession of any organ so delicate as a brain. But Nol disputed Guest's pretensions to anatomical wisdom, insisting that even warriors of Rovac had brains, although admittedly it was hard to find one who could demonstrate the proper use of such an asset. Then the wizard of Itch detailed the ways in which height itself could kill, concluding by saying:

"So. To safeguard your friend's health, we must take him lower down the valley."

"Well," said Guest, "doubtless when dawn comes—"

"No," said Nol. "Not at dawn. Now. We must take him lower, and now, otherwise he dies."

"Can't we wait until morning?" said Guest.

"By morning," said Nol, "one of the minor demons of the Lesser Pit of Idleness will be using your friend's head as a footstool. I counsel you not to delay — not unless you have mastered the fine art of the resurrection of the dead."

Urged thus by Ontario Nol, the air adventurers dressed themselves in coats provided by their host, heavy coats of wool, coats thick with the smell of generations of wood-smoke. Then they ventured into the night, the cold of which had sharpened to a razor.

There was no moon, but there were stars, clipped chips of needle-prick brightness. Under those stars they began their descent, rock and stone scraping and sliding underfoot as they ventured through the brittleness of the frozen night.

Soon, they were sweating in their heavy coats, sweating despite the cold, for they were carrying the unconscious Rolf Thelemite on a litter, and Rolf proved a brutal burden — even though Nol had roused out a couple of servants to help with the labour, and even though he added his own muscle to the carrying.

To Guest, the stumblestone nightpath through unfamiliar territory seemed an ideal place for an ambush. If Nol planned murder, than maybe ambushers were waiting to take them on a ravinous section of the path, waiting to smash them with landsliding stones or snatch them from the night with garrottes.

For once, Guest Gulkan wanted the counsel of Thodric Jarl, so when the group was resting he shared his thoughts with the Rovac warrior, and found Jarl had similar suspicions. The two of them then returned to the circle of lamplight where Ontario Nol sat cleaning his fingernails, and they challenged that wizard of Itch, who heard out their fears.

"Well, my man," said Ontario Nol, addressing himself to Thodric Jarl in the Eparget tongue. "You have a headache, do you not?"

"As if kicked by a horse," said Jarl, speaking the Eparget with the idiomatic fluency of a very Yarglat barbarian.

"Next question," said Ontario Nol. "Can you walk like this?"

With that, the wizard of Itch got to his feet and demonstrated. He demonstrated with great deliberation, like a dancing master showing off a difficult step. He walked heel to toe, first forwards then backwards.

"Such games are meant for childhoods first and second," said Jarl. "You in your second childhood can indulge yourself with such, but I am a man, and grown beyond such folly."

"Try it," said Nol.

"I have spoken," said Jarl, speaking with the finality of a rune-warrior standing in defiance to a dragon.

"It is but a trifle," said Nol, coaxing Jarl with the wheedling cajolery with which a nursemaid seeks to subvert the will of a bad-tempered baby. "A trifle if you can do it, but a world of significance if you cannot. Come, man! I've done as much myself! Zozimus! Sken-Pitilkin! Will you set examples?"

First Zozimus did, then Sken-Pitilkin, and both succeeded in walking heel to toe, first forwards then backwards. At last, succumbing to sweet persuasion, Thodric Jarl consented to essay this simplicity. He failed. His feet were simply not sufficiently coordinated, and those feet disobeyed him as if he were drunk.

"You see," said Nol. "You cannot walk a straight line. That, my friend, is a sure sign of the swelling of the brain. The swelling is consequent upon rapid ascent to great altitude, and you must descend to cure it, or reconcile yourself to your death."

"My stumbling feet are a sure sign that I'm drunk," said Jarl. "Or that I'm poisoned."

As Jarl had not recently been drinking to any great extent, he was inclined to suspect poison.

Thodric Jarl's suspicion was natural, for Jarl was of the Rovac, and so since earliest childhood had nourished a fearful suspicion of wizards. Furthermore, when Jarl thought of death he most naturally thought of poison. For, though the Rovac have a great reputation as sword-slaughterers, poison is ever one of their favourite instruments of murder. It is used in particular by the Rovac womenfolk, who typically prefer the swift simplicities of poison to the intricate longueurs of divorce proceedings. But, though it is the women who have the true mastery of the art, the men will not flinch from such expedients when the spirit moves them.

"Hush down," said Zelafona, as Jarl began to launch himself into accusations of conspiracy and of general poisoning.

Then the wise witch Zelafona took Guest Gulkan and Thodric Jarl aside and advised them to place their trust in Ontario Nol.

"If he was going to kill us," said Zelafona, "he'd have poisoned the lot of us at dinner time."

"Haven't you got the message?" said Jarl. "I think that's exactly what he did. Either he's poisoned us, or else he's going to ambush us."

"If poison," said Zelafona, "then it's surely a slow poison, for as yet we're all alert. Since wizards have no love for witches, I'd be as likely a victim of any such poison as you are. Let us then watch our own condition, and gather for a lethal decision should that communal condition deteriorate. As for ambush — why, let Guest walk with Nol to kill the wizard if we spring an ambush."

Thus it was agreed — though at first it was quite impossible for Guest to be spared from the labour of supporting the burden of the unconscious Rolf Thelemite.

But, after a long and steeply downhill walk, Rolf Thelemite came to, emerging groggily from the depths of his unconsciousness. Shortly, Rolf found himself able to stumble downhill under his own steam. Thereafter, Guest kept close to the wizard Ontario Nol.

Naturally, the two fell into conversation, and Guest found himself telling Nol much about Gendormargensis, about the imperial family, and about his brothers Morsh Bataar and Eljuk Zala.

"My father has written to me not at all," said Guest, making no effort to conceal his resentment at his father's neglect, "but Bao Gahai has pestered me with letters as often as once every three months. She says that Morsh has taken to swimming, though I think it perilous strange for a man to play fish."

"A leg as badly broken as his will be slow in the cure," said Ontario Nol. "So swimming may help."

"But he's walking!" said Guest. "He's riding! The bone is fixed!"

"The bone may be fixed," said Nol, "but the muscle may be badly wasted."

"But," protested Guest, "we're talking ancient history! It's spring. Go back through winter, autumn, summer. Go back a year! A year ago I had a letter from Bao Gahai, she said him walking. Walking, yes, and riding. A year, man!"

"So his cure may be close to completeness," conceded Nol. "But even so, you should not sneer at his swimming, for swimming is a very healthful exercise."

"I thought you of the Yarglat!" said Guest in astonishment. "Yet you think a man should be fish!"

"I am true to my heritage," said the Yarglat-born wizard of Itch. "I have not denied it. I have merely broadened it. But, anyway — enough of your brothers. Tell me of Locontareth. There was mention made of a tax revolt."

So the subject of Morsh Bataar's broken leg and his slow recovery from the same was dropped, and Guest launched himself on the tale of the tax revolt in Locontareth, or what he knew of it — the revolt said to be led by an insurrectionist by the name of Sham Cham.

As Guest was deep in conversation, the path passed beneath great rocks, and in the shadow of those rocks the path suddenly crumbled beneath Guest's feet.

Guest slipped — with a cry.

And Nol grabbed him.

Ontario Nol grabbed Guest Gulkan, fingers gripping the boy's arm like a set of pliers.

"Careful," said Nol, hauling Guest back from the brink of destruction. "Steady yourself. There now. Are you all right?"

"Yes," said Guest.

Who was shaken by the strength of the old man, by the walnut-crunching power of those fingers. He was reminded of dim legends concerning mighty masters of combat who were said to live in the mountains. (Which mountains? The legends were never specific, but mountains like these looked near enough to the stuff of legends as far as Guest was concerned.) Those combat masters were said to be able to perform prodigious feats. To kill without touching. To kill with a shout. To crush stones. To tear the heart from the flesh without benefit of steel.

"Have you lived in the mountains long?" said Guest.

"Oh, long indeed," said Ontario Nol. "I know this path well. It gets easier from here on."

And so it did, and it had become wide, flat and stable by the time dawn brought them a sharp-edged breeze to brisk away the stillness of the night, and brought them too to a village, a place of drystone buildings roofed with slate, a place where people came out and greeted them.

"Do you rule the entire valley?" said Guest, as the people gathered around them.

"No," said Nol. "I thought I told you of that earlier. King Igpatan rules the lower reaches of the valley."

"I have never heard of this king," said Guest, uncertain in his weariness as to whether Nol had in fact earlier explicated the nature of the king. "How great are his realms?"

"They are of no great extent," said Nol. "For King Igpatan rules over no greater distance than one could comfortably walk between sunrise and sunset. But — come now! This is no time for geopolitical discussion. This is time for breakfast!"

Guest was surprised to learn that he had been engaged in geopolitical discussion, because he had merely thought himself to be asking a couple of very obvious questions. Nevertheless, he allowed himself to be led to a big stone table set outdoors in the morning sun. Placed around that table were three-legged stools in numbers sufficient for the seating of Nol's company, and waiting on that table were finger-bowls of warm water fragrant with bruised mint, and plates heaped with eggs, with hot chicken-meat, with potatoes, with soy beans, with dried fish and with roasted frogs.

"Magnificent!" said Jarl. Then, turning to Nol: "But perhaps the feast could be improved by the butchery of one of your villagers."

During the descent, Thodric Jarl's headache had diminished away to nothing. His broken ribs still gave him pain, but his morale had perked up amazingly, to the point where he had almost become a welcome travelling companion — and let the mention of this fact be taken as a clear proof of the objective clarity of this history, which makes no idle propaganda against the Rovac, but simply records the facts as they happened.

"An excellent suggestion, friend Rovac!" said Nol, taking Jarl's jest in the spirit in which it was meant. "But things grow slow in the mountains, so each of these villagers has taken a thousand years to grow meat sufficient for a cannibal feast. That being so, we cannot waste them casually, but must content ourselves with chickens."

"That contentment will be more than sufficient," said the elf-armoured Pelagius Zozimus, surveying the feast with a professional eye, and asking himself fresh questions as to timing.

How had such a formidable meal been prepared at such short notice? One thing is for certain: a village of such manifest poverty never killed chickens except for the most especial occasions. It has been Written that wizards of Itch can build bells which can be rung thereafter from a distance of several leagues. So perhaps Nol had covertly used such a bell to signal the approach of himself and his guests; though, as Sken-Pitilkin and Zozimus were both exhausted, neither asked him about this, and neither thought to ask of it thereafter. Instead, they sat themselves down and set themselves to eat.

Over breakfast, Ontario Nol discussed in detail and depth the problems which Lord Onosh had experienced in collecting taxes from Locontareth, and suggested that the Witchlord Onosh was experiencing such difficulties because the people of that city and region derived no benefit from the taxes.

"You must give them something back," said Nol, "just as a farmer gives back something to his fields when he plows manure into the soil."

"I don't think they'd thank us for dumping them in manure," said Guest, meaning the revolutionaries of Locontareth.

"No, no," said Nol. "You misunderstand me."

Then Nol explained the matter all over again, in depth and in detail, though Sken-Pitilkin could have told him that the effort was futile.

"Well," said Guest, when he thought he understood as much of this theory as he was ever going to understand, "that's very nice of you, I mean, the ideas and all, and, ah, hospitality. Maybe my father can thank you for helping us."

"I need no thanks from your father," said Nol. "You yourself can help me."

"How?" said Guest.

"By sending me your brother."

"Morsh?" said Guest, remembering their conversation about Morsh Bataar's recently acquired habit of swimming. "You want Morsh? What on earth for? To teach you the art of the fish, is it?"

"It's not Morsh Bataar that I want," said Nol. "I want the other one. Eljuk Zala."

"But what would you want him for?" said Guest, who lacked the wit to guess.

"Eljuk will know," said Nol. "If he matches your description of him, he'll know immediately. Bring him to me!"

"Well, I would," said Guest, not particularly caring whether Ontario Nol wanted his brother for purposes of buggery or as sacrificial banquet-meat. "But it's a bit difficult. I mean, as far as I'm concerned, you can have him. But my father wouldn't like the idea at all. Eljuk's the imperial heir, that's his business, he's supposed to inherit."

"Put it to your father," said Nol. "Speak to Eljuk, then to your father, then tell me what the pair of them decide."

And, once Guest Gulkan had agreed to do that, Ontario Nol began to discuss the route which would allow Guest and his fellow air adventurers to exchange the unfamiliar dangers of the valley of Ul-donlok for the comforting certainties of the Collosnon Empire and its large-looming civil war.

CHAPTER TWELVE

Yolantarath River: river which runs south-south-east from Gendormargensis to Locontareth by way of Babaroth. After passing Locontareth the river tends toward the north-east, and eventually the leisure of its flatland wending brings it to the seaport of Stranagor and the chilly waters of the Hauma Sea.

* * *

Ontario Nol cautioned the air-wrecked adventurers not to venture through the realms of King Igpatan, since that monarch was of a very uncertain temper, and often celebrated his birthday by torturing to death a randomly chosen stranger. As King Igpatan honoured each of his fifty previous incarnations with a separate birthday, his kingdom was not an attractive tourist destination.

The dwarf Glambrax suggested that they fly out. Rolf Thelemite professed himself game for such an adventure — though his lower lip trembled and his gold-snake earring shook as he said it — but all the others denounced the proposition.

"I'd sooner swim through pigshit," said Thodric Jarl, "or drink my way through a world of menstruation."

"And I," said Guest, "I'd sooner be dorked by an iceman or kissed by a dwarf."

So spoke the Weaponmaster, then had to fight off a vigorous attack from a kiss-inclined Glambrax.

The key to any further air adventures was of course Sken-Pitilkin: and he declared himself strenuously opposed to the construction of any more airships. He was still having nightmares about the journey which had seen them slammed from Ema-Urk to the heights of Ibsen-Iktus, and was in no hurry to risk his life again in such folly.

Accordingly, when a vote was taken — Sken-Pitilkin being so opposed to the construction of an airship that he gladly joined in this piratical Rovac-favoured form of decision-making by brute force of numbers, since he was sure it would give him the answer he wanted — all were in favour of exiting from Ul-donlok by venturing over the mountains. The decision was unanimous, Thodric Jarl having used a few words of threat to talk Rolf Thelemite out of his airbent-folly.

Unanimous? Well, almost. To be precise, there was one abstention, for Glambrax abstained on account of the fact that Guest was sitting on him when the vote was taken.

So it was that weight of numbers carried the day, and it

cannot be denied that at least on this occasion the decision thus arrived at represented the full force of wisdom.

After the air adventurers had spent a full fourteen days resting and acclimatising, first at the village and then at Qonsajara itself, Ontario Nol pronounced them fit to proceed. The venerable wizard of Itch chose to guide the travellers personally through the mountains. He saw to their provisioning, procured them three mules, and dosed Thodric Jarl with a potent medicine which suppressed the pain of his bone-breakages and thus enabled him to tackle the trek.

The medicine given to Jarl also had the effect of reducing him to a stuporous zombie-like condition in which he heard little, saw less, and lacked the intellectual agility to wonder at his own diminished mental competence. Thus did Ontario Nol insure himself against attempted murder.

Protected by such insurance, Nol led the air adventurers from the monastery of Qonsajara, and guided them to the high pass of Zomara at the western end of the valley of Ul-donlok.

"Gods!" said Glambrax, as they laboured towards the heights of that high pass, "I'd want my own weight in gold before I'd chance this climb again!"

Such were the rigours of the journey that none of his companions picked up the conversational opening, and all the obvious sallies about the height, weight and worth of a dwarf's chancing and climbing went unsaid.

Truly, it was a brutal ascent.

It was cold upon the heights, and no living thing grew there saving the blue-green lichen. The touch of the wind was a razor and the sun a laceration to the eyes. Upon the heights, Guest Gulkan found his head reeling as if he were drunk; and several times the Weaponmaster stumbled and almost fell as he descended with his companions to the valley of Yox.

As for Thodric Jarl, why, he in his drugged condition was so helpless that he had to be roped between Rolf Thelemite and the dwarf Glambrax; and he was so dead to the world that he was quite oblivious to the donkey-jokes which the wizards made at his expense. For, regardless of the demands of the journey, the drug-disabled Thodric Jarl was too rich a target to neglect.

"A very pet lamb in his feebleness," observed Ontario Nol, with the greatest of satisfaction.

And Sken-Pitilkin said—

But let us not record here the delicious witticisms which were ventured by the scholarly Sken-Pitilkin, for the Rovac have cause for rage sufficient already, and there is no point in nourishing that breed of pirates fresh with excuse for murder.

So the aeronauts crossed the high pass and headed downwards into the next valley. The descent was short, for the valley of Yox was higher still than Ul-donlok. Yox was a desolation of icelocked frigidity where snow still lay on the ground. Its heart was a long and narrow iceblock lake which looked as if it would not unfreeze until the sun grew old and swallowed the very planet in the swollen bloating of its heatstroke age.

At the valley's north-eastern end was the high pass known as Volvo Marp. Fortunately, Volvo Marp was marginally lower than Zomara Pass, and the travellers crossed it with comparative ease.

As the air adventurers were about to commence their descent — which would take them beneath the ominous threat of a prodigious overhang of unstable ice and rock — Ontario Nol bade them farewell. The venerable wizard of Itch took one mule to carry his own supplies on the return trip, but left the air adventurers with the other two animals; and left, also, the pain-medicine with Thodric Jarl.

Thus left to their own devices, the aeronauts descended. Guest Gulkan endured more than a few twinges of suspicion as he dared himself beneath the unavoidable overhang, for conceivably Nol could use some power of his to precipitate that overhang into an enormous avalanche, and Guest half-feared him capable of such betrayal.

However, the adventurers descended safely, won their way clear of the last of the snow and the ice, then began the sweaty, unromantic labour of making their way through the steep-cut hills to the Yolantarath riverplain.

On that journey, the pain-killing medicine carried for the feeding of Thodric Jarl at last ran out; and the Rovac warrior recovered both wit and competence, which was by no means an improvement, for he regained his narrow paranoia along with his intellectual agility. Glambrax swore that Jarl, fearful of the pickpocketing abilities of wizards, was at pains to count his own testicles every time he went for a piss.

Paranoia notwithstanding, Jarl kept his temper in check; for the wizards Pelagius Zozimus and Hostaja Sken-Pitilkin enjoyed the protection of the Witchlord Onosh, and Thodric Jarl was solemnly sworn to the Witchlord's service. Hence Zozimus and Sken-Pitilkin, unlike the almost-murdered Ontario Nol, enjoyed the protection of a privileged position, and were theoretically safe from the murder which dwelt impatiently within the Rovac warrior's blade.

In the peace of that protection, the journey from the heights to the river was almost without incident.

True, Guest Gulkan almost got the whole party murdered when he tried to seduce the virginal priestess who presided over the decidedly tantric rites of a village of benighted charcoal burners. In that same village, Glambrax was bitten by a rabid dog which was foaming at the mouth. Zelafona hustled her son to the nearest stream, where she supervised the washing of his wound with water and the scrubbing of the same disfigurement with soap — a good initial treatment for rabies, and the sooner done the better.

"If that is the initial treatment," said Glambrax, "what is the follow-up treatment should I prove to be infected?"

"The cutting off of your head," said Guest Gulkan heartlessly. "A loving decapitation, done to prevent unspeakable hells of suffering."

"Never fear, for I have drugs," said Sken-Pitilkin, lying like a horse trader. "Precious drugs of miraculous rarity which will consummate your cure should you fall sick."

"I pick you as a liar," said Glambrax.

"Then you pick him wrongly," said Zelafona warmly, "for Sken-Pitilkin and I have often shared the inner secrets of the healing arts. The good Sken-Pitilkin has the drugs of which he speaks, and will cure you if you sicken."

This from Zelafona's mouth was as much a lie as when it came from Sken-Pitilkin in the first place. But Glambrax was cozened into believing the lie, and belief put his heart at rest; and thus did wizard and witch between them cure the dwarf of his anxiety, if not of any contagion he might have contracted.

Would Glambrax fall ill of the rabies? There was no telling. The incubation time of the disease varies from two weeks to two years — so the question of contamination is not swiftly to be resolved.

With Glambrax maybe dying, and with Guest Gulkan lucky to have escaped death, the party proceeded, and nearly died out to the last person when Pelagius Zozimus cooked them some greenish-blue fungal growths which he swore to be edible. Then there was the pit-trap which almost claimed Sken-Pitilkin, even though it was actually intended for bears; and there was the wasps' nest which almost secured a gruesome demise for Rolf Thelemite; and an unfortunate accident befell Thodric Jarl, for, in the grip of some nightmare which he refused to explicate thereafter, he almost strangled himself in his sleep.

But, these minor incidents excepted, all were in good health and better spirits by the time they reached the Yolantarath, where they were promptly captured by a cavalry patrol loyal to Sham Cham, the leader of Locontareth's tax revolt.

The troops who had captured Thodric Jarl and his confederates were Rovac warriors loyal to the Muktih of Stranagor, a military governor who had been appointed by the Witchlord Onosh, but who had betrayed his rightful liege lord by throwing in his lot with the tax revolutionist Sham Cham. Since Jarl was of the Rovac, the prisoners were not slaughtered on the spot. Rather, they were taken to the city of Locontareth, the centre of the tax revolt, and there—

On account of the prestige of their persons, Guest Gulkan and his associates were soon dragged in front of Sham Cham himself.

Sham Cham? A hairy individual with the manners of a

monkey, unclean in his person and foul in his breath. Let us waste no time on Sham Cham. He thought himself a great political philosopher because he was too selfish to contribute to the common good by paying his taxes, but it takes more than tax delinquency to make a leader. Sometimes the man calls forth the moment, and sometimes the moment calls forth the man; and on this occasion, the moment was in the ascendancy.

At least if Sken-Pitilkin was any judge of character.

"You have heard," said Sham Cham, once he had gone through the ritual of cutting away some of Guest Gulkan's hair plus a button's worth of Guest Gulkan's scalp, "that I am at war with your father. What do you think of that?"

Guest Gulkan, bleeding generously from his missing button's worth, tried to remember Ontario Nol's elegant arguments about farmers fertilising their crops to improve yields.

"As farmers shit on fields," said Guest, wiping the blood from his eyes and flicking that blood from his fingers at random, "so should my father shit on you."

Sham Cham did not take kindly to being besplattered by the blood from Guest Gulkan's fingers. Nor did he at first take kindly to the political dictum which Guest had enunciated, so Guest promptly blamed it upon Ontario Nol.

"Who is this Nol?" said Sham Cham. "I should dearly like to meet him, so I can kill him."

"Ontario Nol," said Sken-Pitilkin, coming to the rescue, "is an economist, an economist who thinks that Gendormargensis should share its tax revenues with Locontareth for the greater ultimate good of the empire. This is what the boy Guest meant when he passed his earlier comment about excrement."

Then Sken-Pitilkin said more, much more, most of which was pleasing to Sham Cham, who was glad to hear that the number of his supporters had been enlarged by the addition of an economist.

"Very well," said Sham Cham, when he understood the truth of the dictums enunciated by Ontario Nol, the abbot of Qonsajara. "So much for Nol. But what about the rest of you.

Are you for me or against me?"

"What happens if we're against you?" said Guest.

"You die," said Sham Cham.

"Then I'm for you," said Guest promptly, thus throwing in his lot with the revolutionaries.

Zelafona had managed to pass for a useless old beggar woman, and hence was asked for no oath. But an oath was demanded of all the males, and all swore themselves to the service of Sham Cham — except for Thodric Jarl, who said he was sick, useless for battle on account of his half-healed ribs, and therefore should not be compelled to declare his allegiance one way or another. The Rovac warriors loyal to the Muktih of Stranagor supported Jarl in this, so Sham Cham, not wanting to pick any arguments with any of his supporters unless he absolutely had to, decided not to push the issue.

A few days later, Jarl escaped, which roused Sham Cham to a fury. He brought together the Rovac warriors in whose custody Jarl had been kept, listened to their excuses, then massacred the lot of them. It was pointed out to him by some of his advisers that this might have been a mistake, since the Rovac were acknowledged to be mighty in war.

"They were only a handful," said Sham Cham, "and a handful will make no difference to the military equation. Besides, I still have one Rovac warrior to my name — the mighty Rolf Thelemite!"

This was true.

Sham Cham did have Rolf Thelemite in his service.

And Sham Cham believed — after all, Rolf Thelemite had told him as much — that Thelemite had personally been responsible for the conquest of three empires, seven kingdoms, twenty cities and three dozen castles, and had been a very master of every aspect of military science since the tender age of three.

With Stranagor having chosen to support Locontareth in revolution, Sham Cham's next move was to advance on Gendormargensis, and this he began to do. In his wake, the revolutionary leader left behind all useless mouths, including the dralkosh Zelafona, who was forced to beg anonymously for her bread in the streets of Locontareth.

In breach of his oath, the dwarf Glambrax deserted from the army on its second day of march, and sought out his mother in the streets of Locontareth, meaning to be a help and comfort to her in those days of danger and difficulty. Thus did the dwarf prove himself to be alien to the common usages of the society of men. And, worse, he almost proved the death of his comrades, for this desertion made Sham Cham doubt the oaths of the others.

But the eloquence of the wizards Zozimus and Pelagius, coupled with the warlike enthusiasm of Rolf Thelemite, helped persuade Sham Cham that those others would fight by him loyally. As for Guest Gulkan—

"Why, as for me," said the Weaponmaster, "I've bitter cause to fight my father, for he cheated me of the woman Yerzerdayla. Tall she was, and beautiful. For the sake of her flesh, I risked my life against the sword of Thodric Jarl. I fought for the woman in Enskandalon Square, fought a fair fight in the presence of witnesses. I won. I won the woman. So now she's mine, officially, my own, my concubine, my slave. But I was exiled from my home, her flesh untasted, and I don't doubt that Thodric Jarl's been tupping with the blond-haired bitch in my absence. Why should I love my father when he cheats me of the rights of my sword?"

Thus Guest spoke. And, unspoken, but adding sincerity to his cause, was Guest's belief that he himself should have been the anointed heir to the ruling throne of the Collosnon Empire. Yes, Guest Gulkan thought himself a better man than his brother Eljuk, and was bitterly resentful of the fact that Eljuk was destined to inherit the empire.

So Sham Cham was convinced; and the lives of Guest Gulkan and his companions were made safe against arbitrary execution; and the army continued its advance.

That advance came to an abrupt halt in early summer, some distance short of Babaroth, when scouts reported that Lord Onosh was waiting by the Pig River to receive them in battle.

Sham Cham's next trick was to send Guest Gulkan to meet

with his father in a peace conference.

Ah, Witchlord and Weaponmaster in conference! What a sight to behold! Sken-Pitilkin was at that conference, and duly beheld the sight. More foul and savage language was exchanged between father and son than could be comfortably contained by less than a quire of parchment. Then, having at last exhausted their confrontational resources, the pair got down to business, and Guest Gulkan gave his father the benefit of his recently acquired wisdom in political economy:

"Ontario Nol says you should shit on people. But I say that's not enough. I think you should positively bathe them in dung. A general manuring, that's what I think. It's like Nol, only more so."

"Who then is this Ontario Nol?" said Lord Onosh.

"That's my secret," said Guest.

In the face of his son's intransigence, Lord Onosh asked his imperial advisers to prove out Nol's identity, but they were unable to give him any clues as to the genesis of this dangerous lunatic.

"Then," said the Witchlord Onosh, "that's enough of this nonsense. Let's have no more talk of this madman Nol. Just tell me what you want and be done with it."

"I speak for Sham Cham and Locontareth," said Guest. "What we want is to keep more of our own for ourselves. We say it's not enough to get shitted on, not even by the emperor."

The peace conference continued on this note until the Witchlord Onosh gave up all hope of getting any sense out of his enemies. Thus Lord Onosh withdrew to the strength of his army; and Sham Cham, angered by the Witchlord's intransigence, gathered his forces and marched them in good order toward Babaroth, determined to meet the Witchlord Onosh in battle and to defeat him.

CHAPTER THIRTEEN

Tax: the tribute which the periphery of the Body Politic contributes to the centre, and which the centre in its wisdom redistributes to the periphery, with the resulting circulation ideally improving the overall health of the political organism. Unfortunately the sundry parts of the Body Politic are typically less co-operative than the mouth, heart and fundament of the average human-in-the-flesh, as lack of suitable pain receptors often makes the centre insensitive to the sufferings of the periphery. Early in the reign of the Witchlord Onosh, such insensitivity led to the ill-fated rebellion of the Geflung; and a continuation of such insensitivity later precipitated the tax revolt led by Sham Cham of Locontareth.

* * *

The town of Babaroth stood a little to the north of the Pig River. It stands there no longer, for the region in question was afflicted by a severe earthquake last year, and by all accounts the town has been entirely destroyed.

Still, when Witchlord and Weaponmaster found themselves as masters of opposing armies, Babaroth was still standing, and serves as a convenient landmark for the action. Let it be noted, however, that the town could not be seen from the battlefield, nor the battlefield from the town, for a forest stood between them.

(Is it really necessary to make this point? Unfortunately, it is, for the realms of scholarship are the scene of much unseemly quibbling, as scholars often seek to shred a great and generous intellectual tapestry by pulling on the smallest and most insignificant of its loose threads. Therefore, at the risk of seeming pedantic, let it be made quite clear that this history does not claim that Babaroth was ever situated precisely at the confluence of the Pig and the Yolantarath, and acknowledges, rather, that a diligent surveyor would have found it some 4,000 paces to the north of the Pig, with a goodly stretch of trees between river and town.)

When Sham Cham reached the Pig, he found the single bridge across that tributary was held against him by Lord Onosh.

While some geographies claim the Pig to have been bridged in three places, and others declare it to have been bridgeless, the truth is that the Pig's bridges varied in number according to the destructive force of the floods of each spring thaw. When the Weaponmaster came in arms against the Witchlord, there was only the one here-mentioned bridge within fifty leagues of the confluence of the Pig and the Yolantarath.

The Weaponmaster, who bore himself as proudly as if he were the very leader of the army, sat on horseback by Sham Cham as that revolutionary leader surveyed the Witchlord's forces. The disposition of those enemy forces seemed clear enough. Some baggage wagons were lined up on the southern side of the Pig, with the Witchlord's army encamped in among these wagons and in the dark of the woods on the river's northern side.

Sham Cham set guards and scouts to watch his flanks, prepared his own troops to meet any sudden frontal sally by the enemy, and then in a moment of sudden doubt he sent a swift-riding scouting party galloping to the south, just in case his enemy was somehow setting about engulfing his forces in some prodigious encircling move. Then the bold and brave Sham Cham sent forth his mother-in-law to demand the Witchlord's surrender.

Sham Cham's mother-in-law had a tongue so formidable that the revolutionary leader was sure its scourging effect would provoke her butchery. However, to Sham Cham's disappointment, his mother-in-law returned from her dealings with no more damage than the besmirchment of her boots by a trifling amount of horse dung; and she advised Sham Cham (and seemed to derive some considerable pleasure from imparting the advice) that the Witchlord had sworn to castrate him personally, then to bugger him with a bayonet.

"A bayonet?" said Sham Cham, who had never heard of this weapon. "What is a bayonet?"

"A kind of dog trained for the purpose of rape," said his mother-in-law, who never admitted ignorance on any subject.

"No, my lord," said Sken-Pitilkin, who in company with Pelagius Zozimus was attending on this council, and who in the daring of his scholarship was prepared to prosecute the cause of truth even in the face of someone's mother-in-law. "A bayonet is not a dog. Rather, a bayonet is a species of detachable knife sometimes found attached to a crossbow. It has a blade triangular in section, nicely designed for—"

"A knife, is it?" said Sham Cham. "Very well. If the thing be built for buggering, then let the Witchlord prosecute it to its purpose. I will happily accept that as the penalty of failure. But I have no thought to fail. Since the Witchlord will not surrender, we must perforce smash through his army. Smash, storm, shatter, seize the bridge, then push through the forest to Babaroth."

"In this matter, my lord," said Pelagius Zozimus, somewhat disturbed by Sham Cham's briskness, "performance may not be as easy as speech."

Zozimus had long fancied himself a military expert of sorts, and hence was quicker to put forward his opinion than was Sken-Pitilkin, who ever preferred the conquest of the irregular verbs to any elaborate schemes for the bloodying of bayonets and the heaping up of the dead. However, despite his scholarly proclivities, the sagacious Sken-Pitilkin was far from innocent of the studious organization of institutionalized bloodshed; and, though Sken-Pitilkin ever believed that the proper place for a cook is in the kitchen, he was inclined on this occasion to believe that the slug-chef Zozimus had a keener apprehension of military difficulty than did the revolutionary leader from Locontareth.

"It is true, my lord," said Sken-Pitilkin. "Speech is one thing, but performance another. And of the two, performance tends to be the more difficult."

"Speech!" said Sham Cham. "You talk of speech? Why, in Locontareth I said I'd raise an army — and having said it, did it. To speak is to act. Such is politics."

"To prove speech at swordpoint," countered Zozimus. "Such is war."

"Then let us prove!" said Sham Cham, not acknowledging that he had been countered at all. "We outnumber our enemies three to one. I would not claim to have mastered all the ingenuities of military science, but nevertheless would think brute force in such proportions to be a sufficient appliance for victory."

"My lord," said Sken-Pitilkin, seeing that Zozimus was in need of his support. "I have long studied—"

"Then study some more!" retorted Sham Cham. "But study elsewhere, and in silence. I take no hectoring from pedagogues."

Sham Cham's earlier doubt was a thing of the past, and now he was resolved upon battle and victory. Or perhaps — there are people whose character is so constituted — his doubt was so great that he durst not admit to the slightest deviance from his chosen course. For often it is the man who is most frightened who is most resolute in action, for he knows that to reconsider will necessarily be to panic, and that to panic is to fail.

"Your wisdom is great, my lord," said Zozimus, "for Sken-Pitilkin knows more of losing wars than winning them." A monstrous slander, this! And — insult upon insult — a slander which Sham Cham greeted with an approving smile. "Still," said Zozimus, in his most conciliatory tones, "my lord, to cross a river against the armed opposition of one's enemies is ever one of the harder exercises of war, and to force a way to Babaroth we must necessarily brute our way across the Pig."

"I have heard," said Sham Cham, "that the Pig is a very torrent of destruction in the spring, but that the river lies slumped in its shallows in the heat of high summer. It is the heat of high summer now."

"So it is, my lord," said Zozimus, "but the shallows of the river lie slumped between the steepness of its northern bank and the southern. The steepness of those banks gives the enemy considerable opportunity for defence."

"Still," said Sham Cham, "I am sure I can force a passage across the river, even if our enemies should burn the bridge."

"Then, my lord," said Zozimus, "having crossed the river, we should still have to fight our way through the forest which lies north of the river."

"That is what I am here for," said Sham Cham, a trifle impatiently. "To fight my enemies."

"True, my lord," said Zozimus, the velocity of his speech evidencing impatient exasperation. "To fight, yes, war is fighting, but only a boy would think it nothing but. War for men is equally a matter of choice and timing. I as a veteran bloody in my swordplay would choose to fight the Witchlord at the city."

"The city?" said Sham Cham, quite confused by the rapidity of Zozimus's speech, which typically became nearly indecipherable in its speed when its temper was threatening to lose itself. "Babaroth is no city. It is but a town."

Sham Cham spoke in truth, for of course Babaroth was no more than a town — a town built on a small hill on the eastern shores of the Yolantarath, some two leagues upstream from the confluence of the Yolantarath and the Pig.

"The city which I had in mind," said Zozimus, "is the city of Gendormargensis."

Then Zozimus outlined his plan. The wizard proposed that they retreat; and construct rafts; and ferry their army to the western shores of the Yolantarath under cover of night; and then march on Gendormargensis, leaving the Witchlord in his ignorance to stab at shadows and grope at dust.

"This plan is a nonsense," said Sham Cham. "As I have said already, our business is not with the capital but with the emperor."

Sham Cham's intransigence dismayed the wizards. For the conquest of Gendormargensis would win them gold with which to pay soldiers; a population from which troops could be recruited; a fortified city from which to stand off their enemies; and a semblance of absolute victory, which would surely discourage and dismay those enemies.

Pelagius Zozimus said as much.

But was not believed.

"Gendormargensis is but a diversion from our business," said Sham Cham. "Our business is to smash the emperor in battle. When you say otherwise, I think you fearful of meeting this Thodric Jarl in battle. I think you have a pronounced over-respect of the Rovac."

Sken-Pitilkin endeavoured to support Zozimus in his wisdom.

"My lord," said Sken-Pitilkin, "In Gendormargensis—"

"In Gendormargensis," said Sham Cham, interrupting the scholar, "the dralkosh Bao Gahai awaits her enemies."

"Why, yes, yes, so she does," said Pelagius Zozimus, "surely, yet she is but a witch, and the killing of a witch is no big matter for either man or wizard."

Though both Zozimus and Sken-Pitilkin had from time to time taken the part of witches in the past — Sken-Pitilkin out of mercy, and Zozimus for reasons of unscrupulous ambition — neither placed any value on Bao Gahai's personal survival.

"The wizards of Argan," said Zozimus, "long ago disposed of most witches in a mighty pogrom. As a sometime member of Argan's Confederation of Wizards, let me assure you of the extreme limitations of the Witchwoman breed."

"So Bao Gahai survived pogrom, did she?" said Sham Cham.

"She did," affirmed Zozimus.

"Then," said Sham Cham, "clearly she is mightier than all your wizards federated in their anger!"

Thus did Sham Cham make clear his mortal terror of the dralkosh Bao Gahai, a terror which had conditioned all his thinking about the current campaign. Sken-Pitilkin found this terror quite extraordinary. After all, it is usual for people to fear what is near and discount what is distant, yet in Sham Cham's case things were quite the reverse — and, when put to the question, the leader of the tax revolt declared he would rather face an army than a witch.

"Well," said Sken-Pitilkin, "supposing you defeat Lord

Onosh here and now, what say Bao Gahai marches forth against you? You see? One way or the other, you're doomed to face your greatest fear before you're finished."

"No!" said Sham Cham. "She'll settle for Gendormargensis. Gendormargensis, that's hers. I'll keep Locontareth. Peace, see. The empire cut in kingdoms. Gendormargensis, Stranagor and Locontareth. Three kingdoms. A recipe for peace."

A recipe — so thought Sken-Pitilkin — for friction and for war. The wizards redoubled their efforts, reminding Sham Cham that Thodric Jarl had had days to reinforce his defensive position on the Pig, and that the Rovac were vicious in defence.

In his heart of hearts, Sham Cham knew himself to be no military genius, so at last called in expert advice to evaluate the counsel of wizards. To be precise: he brought in the Weaponmaster Guest Gulkan, who was known to have defeated Thodric Jarl in single combat in a duel in Enskandalon Square; and he brought in Rolf Thelemite, who by his own account was mighty in war, and had led many an army to victory against impossible odds.

Sken-Pitilkin chose to stay to see what damage Guest and Rolf would do, but Zozimus threw up his hands in disgust and stalked from the conference lest he lose his temper and do something unpardonable.

"What would you suggest?" said Sham Cham to Guest.

"Attack," said Guest promptly. "Attack, for this Jarl is a man like others, and here he is weak, and we can smash him."

Guest spoke with the confidence of a true believer; for Guest had defeated Jarl in single combat, and hence thought him weak. Guest was still ignorant of the fact that he owed his survival in Enskandalon Square to Sken-Pitilkin, who had used powers of levitation to trick Jarl's feet from under him.

Here the blame for Guest's derelictions must be placed fairly and squarely at the feet of the Emperor Onosh. Lord Onosh was, by and large, capable of doing the hard things. But on that occasion he had weakened. When Guest had duelled Jarl in Enskandalon Square, Lord Onosh had allowed himself to be persuaded into an act of incontinent mercy. So the boy Guest had survived, living thereafter with an exaggerated sense of his own ability, and becoming a danger to the very emperor who had saved his life.

Remember this, if it is your destiny to be an emperor! The seat of power is a seat of decision, and weakness in decision is the doom of the governed and the governors alike.

"The wizards speak of this man Jarl as being large in reputation," said Sham Cham.

"Why, a giant in reputation," agreed Guest, "but I've seen him in his injuries with tears in flood upon his face, and that was over nothing, a trifling matter of broken bones."

So spoke Guest, he who had never yet had to live with the worst of pain, far less to live with spearing pain from step to step, from breath to breath, from moment to moment, and each of those moments but a hair from a flinch.

"So," said Sham Cham, "so you suggest—"

"He speaks from the folly of his youth," said Sken-Pitilkin. "In the truth of my wisdom I suggest rather that we send forward two wizards in their wisdom to deal with the wild men according to their wiles and thus avoid the wrath of woolly war."

"Woolly war?" jeered Guest. "That's a nonsense! War is not woolly. Sheep are woolly. What were you thinking of?"

"I," said Sken-Pitilkin with dignity, "was thinking—"

"You were thinking you were a sheep!" said Guest. "Woolly war! Really!"

Sometimes it will happen that an adult will misspeak himself in front of a child, and the child will thereafter not let the matter rest, but will strive to keep the error green in memory. So it was with Guest Gulkan on that occasion.

Rolf Thelemite then added his own boast to Guest Gulkan's advice, and those federated dunces routed the sagacious Sken-Pitilkin. Both Rolf and Guest were young; and drunk with bravado; and intoxicated by thoughts of victory and power; and Sham Cham, being likewise afflicted, was in no mood to heed counsels of caution, not when his own forces outnumbered those of the Witchlord by three to one.

"Three swords can cut a single head," said Sham Cham,

when he summed up their debates, "be that head a jester's or a
queen's."

So it came to pass that on a bright and shining morning the
mighty Sham Cham awoke from dreams of revolutionary tax
reform, and marched his army to within battle distance of the
Pig, there to confront the army of the Witchlord Onosh, lord of
the Collosnon Empire.

Then forth from the Witchlord's ranks rode Thodric Jarl,
riding under a flag of truce. Jarl was received by an ad hoc
embassy which included Sham Cham himself, and Guest
Gulkan, and Rolf Thelemite, and the wizards Zozimus and
Sken-Pitilkin.

"Hail, Cham!" said Jarl.

"Hail, Jarl!" said Cham. "If you have come to present me
with your surrender, then I am ready to receive it. My forces
outnumber yours by a matter of three to one, therefore your
defeat is inevitable."

"I dispute it," said Jarl. "To defeat me and mine, my lord and
me, you would need to have odds of a thousand to one in your
favour. As you have not the forces to compel a victory, yield me
your heart. Then we can negotiate."

"Heart," said Sham Cham, puzzled by Jarl's idiom. "What do
you mean by my heart?"

"I mean," said Jarl, "that bloody organ which beats in
orgasmic fury underneath the larger of your paps. Give it.
Surrender it. Then there will be a peace between us."

With that, the grey-bearded Thodric Jarl produced a silver
platter from a saddlebag and invited Sham Cham to deposit his
palpitating blood-beater upon the shining surface of that platter.

"You are drunk," said Sham Cham.

Sken-Pitilkin and Zozimus, both veterans of past encounters
with the Rovac, knew that Jarl was not drunk but, rather,
intoxicated by the uplift of the moment.

"Drunk?" said Jarl. He laughed. "No, not drunk. Not drunk,
but joyful."

Then Jarl cast the silver platter into the mud. Mud sprayed
up into Sham Cham's face, and his horse reared, and Jarl

wheeled his own horse and rode back to the lines where the Witchlord Onosh waited with his horsemen, apparently ready to charge.

Sham Cham wiped the mud from his face.

"So," said Sham Cham. "It is war. Very well then. Force against force we will meet them. Force against force we will meet them — and throw them back into the sea."

His choice of idiom betrayed his origins. Stranagor lies by the sea, and the throwing of great quantities of people into that watery organ which dominates the planet's physical geography has ever had pride of place in Stranagor's iconography of war.

Then Sham Cham prepared his horsemen for the charge.

With battle about to be joined, the restlessness of men and horses caused such disorder in the ranks that the wizards Zozimus and Sken-Pitilkin were able to work their way towards the rear without attracting undue attention to themselves. Though Zozimus looked like a very elven warrior in his fish-scale armour, and though Sken-Pitilkin in his fisherman's skirts looked a grim and warworthy skirmisher, neither had any intention whatsoever of wasting their substance in battle.

Do not think less of them for this! It is true that both wizards had sworn themselves to Sham Cham's service. Still, both firmly considered that they could best serve the revolutionary army by offering it their wisdom. Wisdom having been rejected, what else could they do but sit back and watch?

Well ...

They could have used their special powers, of course. But a wizard's powers are soon exhausted by the demands of a battlefield, and both Zozimus and Sken-Pitilkin preferred to preserve their strength until it was needed for purposes of personal survival.

Guest and Rolf remained to the fore of the army's mounting disorder. Both were seated on over-aged geldings rather than the high-spirited stallions to which they had aspired; and both were becoming increasingly glad of the stability of their mounts, for the tension of war-ready men was communicating itself to the army's horses, and those beasts which were more highly strung were becoming close to unmanageable.

As the moment of battle neared, the Weaponmaster Guest was concentrating too intently to suffer fear. He was visualizing the clash of sword against sword, practising tactics by imaginative immersion. The restiveness of the horses made him remember his brother Morsh Bataar, crushed beneath a horse, his leg wrecked by the weight of the animal. He must leap clear if his own mount went down. He must—

"Guest"

"What?" said Guest, irritated at being interrupted by Rolf Thelemite. "What is it, Rolf?"

Rolf looked worried.

There was a simple explanation for this:

He was worried!

"Guest," said Rolf, "I've something to tell you."

"Then spit it out, man!" said Guest.

"It's about Jarl," said Rolf. "Jarl and me. He made me promise. Before he ran, I mean. Back in Locontareth. He made me swear. It was an oath, he made me swear an oath."

"What oath?" said Guest, since the question was obviously expected of him.

"He made me swear to kill you," said Rolf.

"Kill me!" said Guest. "You swore an oath to kill me?"

"Yes," said Rolf. "But only — only if you really went to war against your father."

"What else could I do?" said Guest.

"Well, kill Sham Cham," said Rolf.

"What!?"

"Yes, yes, kill him," said Rolf in eagerness. "It's obvious, obvious! Look! He's riding up and down, ride up, a sword, a single blow! We'd spur for escape, we'd be gone, he's dead, as good as dead, just say the word!"

"Rolf," said Guest, "I can't kill Sham Cham, for I'm sworn to his cause in solemn alliance. I've sworn to make war on my father."

"But if you do," said Rolf, despairing, "then I must kill you, for I've sworn an oath. Or if I don't kill you, then — then I'll be an oathbreaker, an oathbreaker accursed of Rovac."

"Then accursed of Rovac you will have to be," said Guest. "For my doom is to fight the Witchlord, and I fight him today."

Rolf couldn't believe he was serious.

"But, Guest," said Rolf. "That's — that's your father out there!"

Rolf Thelemite was sweating under the obdurate weight of the sun. A fly fed on his sweat. He was burdened by the heaviness of chain mail, the chafing of leather, the intolerable sweatiness of his feet in his boots. His left ear itching where his dangling gold-snake earring was threaded through the flesh.

Guest was watching him. Unsmiling. Guest was only 16 years old, but today all traces of any childish sentimentality were a lifetime removed from his nature. Rolf sensed a sameness about Guest and Jarl. Both were missing a layer of humanity: lacked a sense of the reality of pain. Especially the pain of others! Hence they were dangerous. While Rolf knew how to make a boast, Guest knew how to live one. And Rolf found himself afraid of the Weaponmaster.

"Guest," said Rolf, making one last try.

Then Guest reached out and took Rolf by the throat. And squeezed. Hard enough for Rolf to feel the swordman's strength in the fingers. Strength sufficient to kill by crushing. When Guest released the pressure, Rolf coughed, spluttered, touched tentative fingers to the flesh of his throat. Felt the fragility of the structures there.

As Rolf was still groping at his throat, Guest gave Rolf's horse a hearty kick. Thanks to the beast's sturdy temperament, it did not launch itself into an all-out charge. But even this stolid and ageing animal was not immune to the feverish anticipation of battle, and it had danced a dozen paces before Rolf was able to rein it in.

With reins in his left hand and his right on his sword, Rolf turned to face Guest Gulkan. Under the hot sun, a gust of wind blew horse-smell and battle-dust between the Rovac warrior and the Yarglat youth. They were estranged by dust and distance. Guest's face was blurred by the dust, by the harshness of the sun. He was no longer Rolf's familiar friend. Rather, he was an anonymous Yarglat, a stranger, a horselord driven by the dynamics of war.

And he was turning, wheeling his horse in response to an order which Rolf had not heard, though others had heard it, must have, for Sham Cham's horsemen were wheeling en masse, and in moments they were sweeping forward in a war-whoop charge. Rolf Thelemite's horse, over-excited, surged forward in a positive gallop.

"Slow down!" yelled Rolf, stupidly, uselessly.

But it was no good. The beast was off, was bolting. Rolf hauled on the reins, but his mount had a mouth like an old boot. So the hapless Rovac warrior was caught up in the charge, was swept away to destiny.

Up ahead, Guest Gulkan charged with a vengeance.

The young Weaponmaster rode in that charge, screaming with exhilarated fury.

In the face of that fury, the Witchlord's horsemen turned and fled. Through their line of baggage wagons they rode. Then those baggage wagons burst into fire — for they had been crammed with incendiaries, doused with strong liquor and then set alight by torches.

Nothing daunted, Sham Cham's forces continued their attack.

Guest Gulkan spurred his horse. The terrified beast galloped through a gap between gouts of erupting fire. Then it crashed into a pit. Down it went, Guest Gulkan going down with it. Shocked and shaken, he found himself seated on his horse in the bottom of the pit. The horse was direly wounded — blood spouting, white bone gashed. It screamed. Its rolling eyes were liquid with reflected fire.

"Grief of gods!" said Guest.

And struggled out of the pit into the tumult of smoke. There he was attacked by a madman. Hack against hack they fought each other, until Guest Gulkan's opponent screamed his battlecry:

"Stranagor!"

On hearing this battlecry, Guest Gulkan realized he had been in battle with one of his own side.

"Sham Cham forever!" gasped Guest.

And moments later the two were bearhugging each other as comrades.

Having thus been reconciled with this aggressor, Guest Gulkan joined Sham Cham's men who were charging down the bank of the Pig and struggling up the steep slope on the other side.

The Pig looked to be no more than waist-deep, so Guest ran towards it readily, tripped, and went sprawling full-length in the riverside mud. He struggled to his feet, brushed away the worst of the mud, regained his sword, and floundered into the water. He got across the river, then started stumbling up the steep bank.

As Guest Gulkan struggled up the bank, his foot broke through the crusted earth. His boot, weighted by the battle-slam intensity of the boy's war-cry charge, slammed down on a spike of sharpened bamboo. The spike pierced the boot. Guest's foot was inside the boot. Accordingly, the spike seared into his flesh, and he screamed with intolerable pain. He pulled free his foot, wrenching it clear from the spike. All around, other men were likewise screaming. As they screamed, arrows began to fall among them.

The entire slope was pitted with bamboo spikes. There was no quick way up it, and the arrows were soon taking a brutal toll of those whose ambition it was to hack down the Witchlord Onosh.

"Forward, men!" cried Sham Cham.

Then an arrow took him in the eye, and he cried no more.

All around, men were wavering, not knowing what to do. But Guest Gulkan knew. The boy Guest had been born into the household of a mighty warlord, and had studied the theory and praxis of war since he was knee-high to a donkey. He had yet to make himself a complete master of military science, but this he knew for sure — right now, it was most definitely time to be running away.

Guest Gulkan promptly took command of the battlefield, and, bellowing like a water-buffalo, he commanded a retreat, and was obeyed.

Guest Gulkan got back across the Pig, stumbled through the still-burning wagons, and got on to the flatlands south of there, where he was met by Sken-Pitilkin and Zozimus, both of whom were sitting still on their horses.

"Well my boy," said Sken-Pitilkin. "How did you enjoy your first battle?"

"Suck shit and die," said Guest.

Then collapsed, going down in a dead faint in front of Sken-Pitilkin, who looked at Zozimus, who rolled his eyes to heaven then indulged himself in a sigh.

CHAPTER FOURTEEN

Locontareth: a community on the southern banks of the Yolantarath, some 460 leagues from Gendormargensis as the crow flies, and rather more as the river winds. Locontareth is near the borders of the empire ruled by the Witchlord Onosh. To go any distance south from Locontareth is to find oneself in hostile territory, though a trade route does run south for 640 leagues from Locontareth to the port of Favanosin.

* * *

So it was that the retreat to Locontareth began in the heat of high summer. With the shocked and shaken revolutionary army demoralized to little more than a retreating rabble in its defeat, Guest Gulkan found himself its leader, since nobody else wanted the job — for who wants such a job in a time of failure when political prominence looks to be a likely cause of execution rather than a golden path to glory?

In his swift and unopposed seizure of power, Guest Gulkan was aided by the nature of his birth. Since he had been born into the imperial family, it was only natural that a great many people should automatically think him fit to exercise imperial power; and, since Guest had at his side the wisdom of the wizards Sken-Pitilkin and Zozimus, he did not do too badly at it.

Usually, Guest was rambunctiously uncontrollable in his undisciplined delinquency. But in defeat, and in the first shock of his new position, and sore from his wound, and nagged by pain, and full of fears of gangrene and blood poisoning, he found himself floundering, and so became unnaturally amenable to advice. As the army looked to Guest Gulkan, so Guest looked to his wizards; and, in this day of greatest need, they did not fail him.

On Sken-Pitilkin's suggestion, the Weaponmaster's men burnt everything they could not carry. They burnt wagons and

weapons, fodder and food, clothing and bandages. One or two
of the more dimwitted soldiers, obedient to the literal sense of
the orders they had received from on high, were caught trying
(with varying degrees of success) to set fire to their own dung.
Thus lightened, the defeated army retreated on horseback,
carrying nothing but that which their saddlebags could hold.

The shortest horseback route required the retreating army to
cover over 300 leagues from the Pig to the city of Locontareth.

The land was flat; the way was known; the weather was not
unfavourable; and under these conditions a ruthless horseman
can cover fifty leagues a day, assuming he has a string of horses
which can be interchanged as each from its burden tires, and
assuming also that the horseman does not waste time in
mourning for those of his mounts who die of their exertions.

But the most ruthless horseman in the world cannot
maintain such a pace for long, horseflesh being unable to match
the rider's ambition; and in the confusion of its retreat, Guest
Gulkan's army was hard pushed to manage twenty leagues a day,
to the great and intolerant frustration of its youthful general.

Nevertheless, despite his impatience, Guest Gulkan
tempered the pace of his retreat by having his army take the time
to set fire to all of worth which fell to their possession. They
burnt barges and villages, temples and shrines, thickets and
woods, and daily fired the grass to scorch the very earth in their
wake.

Thus Guest Gulkan and his people retreated downriver,
leaving behind them a swathe of devastation suggestive of a very
dragon in its angers.

"Your father must feed upon ashes if he would chase us,"
said Sken-Pitilkin, "else delay while he puts together a baggage
train for the support of his army."

It seemed that Lord Onosh chose the latter path, for no
word of pursuit reached Guest Gulkan, even though his
scouting patrols maintained the vigilance of war in his wake.

Those patrols went forth at Guest Gulkan's sole suggestion,
for as the days went by, and as he began to realize that he was
unlikely to die from his boot-spike wound, he began to get a grip

on himself and his new position, to remember what he had learnt in his years of growth in Gendormargensis, and to gather about him a small corps of responsible veterans who served him as his principal officers, and helped him manage the difficult business of retreat. In these days of difficulty, Guest Gulkan "lived in the skin of a horse", as the Yarglat saying has it; and, after the first few days of confused retreat, his army was no longer a mindless blob of compacted protoplasm, but was rather a dynamic organism armed and barbed. Never did his army sleep in its entirety. Instead, it maintained its vigilance with sentries, passwords and patrols.

In his retreat, the Weaponmaster commanded thrice a thousand horse. He did not bunch his spears around him, but spread his army across the countryside that it might feed with ease upon the land and maximize its destruction of the same. Only as the army approached Locontareth did it close in, as Guest concentrated his strength to smash anyone who might think to stand between him and his city of refuge.

Guest in his eagerness rode with the advance guard, and so was among the first to sight Locontareth.

"There it is," said he, pointing at the distant city. "Our journeys are nearly at an end."

"Only if we choose to halt here," said Sken-Pitilkin, who had matched the rigours of Guest Gulkan's horse-coursing, and sat saddled a swordlength distant from him now.

"Of course we halt here," said Guest. "It would be utter folly for us to head back to Gendormargensis."

"Gendormargensis is of all places the furthest from my mind," said Sken-Pitilkin. "I was thinking not of Gendormargensis but of the sea. From Locontareth, it is barely 300 leagues to Nork."

"Where is Nork?" said Guest.

"It is on the coast," said Sken-Pitilkin. "There are ships. The Hauma Sea—"

"It was never my ambition to play fish or be fish," said Guest shortly. "I've no thought of Nork and none of the sea. This is a not a retreat but a — a withdrawal, a tactical withdrawal, that's the term. At Locontareth we stand and turn. The city is our strength, and we the masters of the world if we can make good use of our strength."

Neither Sken-Pitilkin nor Zozimus fancied the idea of being besieged in Locontareth by an angry Witchlord aided by the devices of Thodric Jarl. The Rovac were noted for their mastery of the art of the siege, so with Thodric Jarl in charge the city was sure to fall. Neither of the wizards thought Guest Gulkan a potential world ruler in embryo: rather, they thought him a wild boy who would be lucky to escape with his skin.

But Guest Gulkan was grimly determined to hold Locontareth as his own, to smash his father in battle, and then to turn the tide of war and make himself master of the empire (first) and then the world (very shortly afterwards).

With the great retreat nearing its end, and with the perceived safety of the city gates at hand, Guest found himself less and less in need of advice from his wizards. Furthermore, since the boy was sorely fatigued, and since he was under great stress, and since he was still in grievous daily pain from the wound in his foot, his temper had shortened to the point where it was difficult for either of the wizards to argue with him effectively, so they in their wisdom soon abandoned that futile enterprise.

So it was that Guest Gulkan's retreating army marched to Locontareth: only to find that the city had barred its gates against them, and had declared itself for the Witchlord Onosh!

"I will burn this town to its bones!" said Guest, seeking to fight off shocked dismay with a display of anger.

But, on investigation, the young Weaponmaster found that he lacked the forces required to make good his threat. Though he had three thousand horse, many of these were from Locontareth, and had no belly for burning their own hearths. Indeed, some thought to stay, and throw in their lot with the Witchlord Onosh.

Guest threatened them.

"My father has sworn a great buggery of bayonets," said Guest. "If you stay and stand, and throw yourself on his mercy, his greatest mercy will be castration at a minimum."

But such rhetoric had little effect. For most believed that the Witchlord's wrath would be softened by Locontareth's surrender; and believed, too, that further retreat offered them nothing but pain, struggle, exile, hunger, fear, danger and death.

In the end, Guest saw that those from Locontareth would be useless to him in a fight, therefore let them enter the city. Then he marched on with a thousand men. A great many of these were slaves; or escaped criminals, or deserters from the Witchlord's army; or men in flight from girlfriends, wives, mothers or lovers. Rough stuff they were, but great armies can be built from such, if great generals be on hand to lead them.

Guest Gulkan, who thought himself by then a very considerable general — for he was inclined to discount the value of the great amount of advice which had been given to him by his wizards, and was increasingly inclined to attribute the coherence of the retreat from Locontareth to his own wisdom — marched his diminished army westward for a day from Locontareth, then halted, and held a council of war.

The venerable Sken-Pitilkin, drawing himself up to his full height and striving for further height by making emphatic rhetorical gestures with his country crook, still counselled that they should march to Nork and flee by sea. But Guest refused.

To Guest, Nork was nothing but a name, and he rightly took the place to be small, and inconsequential, and distant, and difficult of access, and a proper base for nothing other than despair. But Guest still possessed hot hopes of victory, and so the great city of Stranagor was much in his thoughts.

"I was born there, was I not?" said Guest.

"So rumour claims," said Sken-Pitilkin, "though I do not know the circumstances of your birth."

"Neither do I," said Guest. "But I have heard men claim me born at Stranagor, so I think that city auspiciously omened for my victory."

Stranagor, the ruling city of the mouth of the Yolantarath, was much a mirror-image of Gendormargensis in terms of power and influence. If Stranagor would accept the rule of the Weaponmaster, then he might yet hope to match the Witchlord on the field of battle, and to win for himself a great victory.

"I will make for Stranagor," said Guest, "and hope to hold that city in independent revolution against my father. Unless you have any better idea."

"Well," said Sken-Pitilkin, "when your father comes to Locontareth, where will he seek us?"

Sken-Pitilkin, of course, was still thinking of flight rather than of hopes for future victory, for the sagacious wizard of Skatzabratzumon lacked the sanguinary optimism of the unruly boy who had been for so long his student.

"Why," said Guest, "when the Witchlord seeks us, he will seek where we have gone, of course. He will have no trouble in finding us fled to Stranagor. There is no army which does not leave stragglers in its wake. But what of it? Let him pursue us to Stranagor. For I will rally that city to my banner, and bring the Witchlord to battle, and trample him into the murk and mire, then feed his head to my dogs, and let my women keep his organs as trivial souvenirs."

As Guest Gulkan then owned no banner, no dogs and no women, Sken-Pitilkin thought him over-optimistic. Still, clearly the boy was in a mood for battle. Sken-Pitilkin said as much.

"I think you in a mood for battle," said Sken-Pitilkin.

"Why, of course," said Guest. "For I am a mighty general, a leader of men, a master of weapons with the defeat of Thodric Jarl already to my credit. A mood for battle! What other kind of mood should I be in?"

Several suggestions slipped neatly on to Sken-Pitilkin's tongue. A mood for panic, for example. A mood of contrition, perhaps. But Sken-Pitilkin swallowed these suggestions unsaid, then spoke out of the wisdom of his geographical expertise, and said:

"So, you wish to meet the Witchlord in battle, do you? Then what say we were to circle back behind him?"

"Circle back?" said Guest, as if scandalized.

"Yes," said Sken-Pitilkin. "You know the circle, do you not? It is that geometrical form which has the shape of the moon at its full. By inscribing just one half of such a shape upon the surface of this continent, we can by judicious timing bring ourselves to the Witchlord's rear."

"And bugger him," said Guest.

"If you must put it like that," said Sken-Pitilkin, resisting a near-uncontrollable urge to indulge himself in a sigh, "then, yes, once behind the Witchlord we can bugger him. To be precise, we will fall upon his baggage train. He will have a baggage train, you know. There is no big army which moves without one. Each has its baggage trailing behind like the intestines dragging in the street behind a madman who has disembowelled himself. Let us thus then circle back and fall upon this baggage train."

"Circle back!" sneered Guest. "Circle back! Fall upon him! Fall, yes, and bugger him! What on earth are you thinking of?"

"Why," said Sken-Pitilkin, "exactly what I have said. Why sneer you?"

"Because," said Guest, "this skulking business of sniffing round in circles, of falling upon the unwary and indulging in buggery, why, it strikes me as being unsavoury in the extreme, and I want no business of buggery in my biography."

"Boy," said Zozimus, who had till now sat silent in the somewhat travel-stained splendour of his elven armour, "boy, this is serious!"

"Serious!" said Guest. "Then know that I am serious! The manoeuvre you have proposed is one apt for the purposes of a brigand band or a scouting squad. You cannot thus manoeuvre an army. We still have a thousand spears, and a thousand spears cannot slip, skulk and circle."

"Why not?" said Sken-Pitilkin.

He asked the question with a frank directness which set Guest Gulkan back on his heels. Why not, indeed?

"Because," said Guest at length, "it would be very difficult."

"True," said Sken-Pitilkin. "But a wizard could do it even if a boy could not. A thousand spears can be as adept in tactical agility as a brigand band, if only assuming that they have a genius to command them. Besides, the alternative is the complete dissolution of your army, particularly if you are bent on marching to Stranagor."

"Dissolution?" said Guest.

"Why, of course," said Sken-Pitilkin. "For you have no baggage train of your own, therefore your men must either starve or desert on the march to Stranagor, which I figure to be a march of not less than half a thousand leagues."

"It is more," said Zozimus.

"I did but speak in round figures," said Sken-Pitilkin irritably. "I know it is more! Say, 600 leagues by horseback. More, much more, if we follow the bends of the river. Twice the distance of our retreat from Babaroth to Locontareth. Guest, your army has suffered a double-blow already. The loss of a battle and the desertion of a city. You must give them victory, Guest, and soon. Else you will lose your army entirely."

Thus the wizards Sken-Pitilkin and Pelagius Zozimus began the great task of convincing Guest Gulkan to their plan, a process which took the better part of an entire night. Then, the boy Guest being finally convinced, the three of them set to with a will, and organized furiously.

They began with a ploy designed for deception.

At the Weaponmaster's behest, a small group of men who owned Stranagor as their birthplace were sent forth on a march to that city. As these set out for far-distant Stranagor, half a dozen soldiers defected to the nearby city of Locontareth, taking with them the news that Guest Gulkan was a disguised member of that small group which was hastening towards Stranagor, escaping to Stranagor with those who were bound for that city.

Another small party set out for Nork — and were likewise betrayed by paid defectors carefully rehearsed by Zozimus and Sken-Pitilkin.

Then Guest, his wizards and the rump of his army headed south along a rough and ready trading track — only a bankrupting extravagance would have called it a road — which led in the general direction of Favanosin. Initially, the soldiers were told that Favanosin was their destination. Naturally, some stragglers fell out and were left behind, with the news of Guest Gulkan's flight to the south fixed firmly in their minds.

Thus, counselled by his wizards, the Weaponmaster

managed to split himself in three — surely one of the most extravagant feats of wizardly magic to be found in the history of the Confederation of Wizards. Thanks to this wizard-war legerdemain, Guest was simultaneously running north-west to Stranagor, south of west to Nork, and due south to Favanosin, and there was hope that random rumour might have him running in a dozen different supplementary directions as well. One thing was for certain: by the time the Witchlord Onosh and Thodric Jarl reached Locontareth, the true truth of the boy's direction would be beyond retrieval.

"But when," said Guest Gulkan, as they marched south, "when will we break for the east to circle round behind my father?"

"Leave that decision to me," said Sken-Pitilkin, "for if you don't know it then nobody else will."

"But I need to know it!" said Guest.

"Then your good friend Rolf Thelemite will find he needs to know as much himself," said Sken-Pitilkin, "and by such dispersal of intelligence, the entire army will know by the end of the day, which means our stragglers will know, and our deserters likewise, which means Lord Onosh will know the same, and soon. Peace, Guest! Trust me! Just for once, please, trust me!"

Thus Guest Gulkan's thousand spears marched south for three days, with each and every common soldier earnestly thinking the army bound for Favanosin, and with every straggler and deserter thinking likewise.

Each night the army camped, and on dawn on the fourth day the sagacious Sken-Pitilkin pronounced them sufficiently south to begin to move in a great arc widdershins. The Swelaway Sea was their announced destination, for Sken-Pitilkin did not as yet think it wise to trust the common soldiers with the full truth.

As the army launched itself into this arc, it moved slowly at first, deploying a strong rearguard to prevent straggling. The envanishment of armies is a great art, and one which requires patience, and planning, and meticulous attention to detail.

And in this the wizards were triumphant.

Though Guest was a novice in war, fit for nothing more

complicated than the brightsword clash of blade against blade, Sken-Pitilkin was learned in manoeuvre; and, though long out of use, his skills remained to him. It is true that in the long-gone days of yore Sken-Pitilkin had lost more wars than he had won, but he had since refined his skills by dint of brooding over his errors, and made no mistakes on this occasion.

Once the force was far enough into its arc for stragglers to have no hope of betraying its intentions, Sken-Pitilkin had Guest Gulkan call his men together and brief them in depth. Their enthusiasm was roused by the prospect of attacking a baggage train and looting it, particularly as their own rations were down to something close to nothing.

So the force completed its arc, reaching the Yolantarath at a position which was, by Sken-Pitilkin's guestimate, something more than a hundred leagues to the east of Locontareth. If Sken-Pitilkin was right, then the Witchlord Onosh would now be somewhere to their west, advancing with all possible haste in the hope of catching Guest Gulkan before he could escape; and, again if Sken-Pitilkin was right, the Witchlord's baggage train would be some distance still to the east, loitering along in the wake of the army.

"One hopes you are right, cousin," said Zozimus, surveying the broad and sluggish width of the Yolantarath, "for we are going to look awfully foolish if you are wrong."

"I am right, I know it," said Sken-Pitilkin, knowing full well that looking foolish would be the least of their problems if he was wrong.

The Yolantarath lay wide and empty under the scrutiny of Guest Gulkan's forces. Guest sat in the sun and thought, trying to absorb the mind-boggling array of tactical and strategic devices to which he had been exposed in the last few days.

As a child growing up in Gendormargensis, Guest had thought of war as a matter of swordsmash and bloodspill, of raw courage and brute strength adventuring. His early forays into the mountains against bandits had helped secure him in this conviction. But by now Sken-Pitilkin and Zozimus had opened up appalling vistas of complexity. He saw that the war story was but the surface glitter of the deep and dark-complexioned art of war, and that he in his youth knew virtually nothing of the full complexity of that art.

The Yolantarath lay wide and empty for a day. Then, at midmorning, the long and uneasy wait was broken when a convoy of barges came in sight. They were coming slowly downstream, heading towards Locontareth. This, by every presumption, was surely the Witchlord's baggage train.

Sken-Pitilkin directed a couple of men to hail the barges.

"Say that the Witchlord Onosh is here," said Sken-Pitilkin. "Say that he wishes to see the captains of these barges. The barges themselves are to halt at the riverbank."

This message was conveyed to the barges, which obeyed the order. The captains gathered in, which was entirely natural for them to do — for, as far as they were concerned, Guest Gulkan had been defeated and was running for the far horizon, so the territory through which they were venturing was safe and secure.

With the captains came Guest Gulkan's brothers, Morsh Bataar and Eljuk Zala, who had been left in nominal command of this baggage train.

"Guest!" said Eljuk, reacting in shocked surprise when he saw his brother.

Eljuk's lower lip trembled as vehemently as Rolf Thelemite's was wont to do. Guest half-expected saliva to dribble from Eljuk's mouth and flow down his chin, following the tracks of his purple birthmark. But the Weaponmaster's sadistic expectation was not to be gratified, for Eljuk was dry-mouthed with fear.

While Eljuk was near-paralyzed by fear, the barge-captains were not. Those worthies grabbed for their weapons, but were overpowered.

"Guest," said Morsh Bataar, standing unmoved amidst the confusion of the struggle.

"It is me," said Guest, grandly. Then: "Good to see you, Morsh? How's the leg?"

"The leg serves its purpose," said Morsh formally. "But you? What purpose do you serve?"

"The purpose of justice," said Guest. "I serve the purpose of a just manuring for Locontareth. I will be emperor, and spread my shit from Gendormargensis to the sea."

"You are quite mad," said Morsh. "A dog has bitten you, and you're foaming at the mouth."

"No, no," said Guest. "It's not me who was bitten, it was Glambrax, and anyway, he's not foaming either. He's still in Locontareth, or was — he was with us but deserted."

"Then the dwarf has at least a little sense," said Morsh. "But you have none."

Guest took his brother's rebukes in good part, for Morsh Bataar was known to be slow in his wits, therefore it was only natural that he might be slow to appreciate the glories of Guest's life as a large-scale bandit.

In the best of good humour, Guest declared his brothers hostages, and declared the captains of the barges to be hostages as well. Then, finding out that Eljuk's new tutor was on one of the barges, he had the man hauled before him.

"What is your name?" said Guest.

"My name, young sir, is Eldegen Terzanagel."

So spoke the tutor, a text-master whom Guest judged to be aged somewhere between 40 and 50. His hair and beard were both dyed grey, and were severely cropped. Everything about him spoke of discipline, probity, and order, and Guest hated him at sight.

"I lately had a letter from Bao Gahai," said Guest, casting back in his memory for the details of that epistle. "She claimed you to be teaching my brother the irregular verbs."

"I am assisting him in his studies," said Terzanagel.

"With the aid of books?" said Guest.

"But of course," said Terzanagel.

"Then bring forth your books," said Guest, "for I am eager to receive instruction."

The innocent Terzanagel was fool enough to take the Weaponmaster at his word, and shortly Guest was busy organizing a ceremonial Burning of the Books by the banks of the Yolantarath.

Once Guest had burnt Terzanagel's grammars, geographies, dictionaries, histories, biologies, genealogies, hagiographies, and mathematical treatises, he at last asked the obvious question:

"What now?"

Up till then, the Weaponmaster had not thought any further than the capture of the Witchlord's baggage train; but now that he did start thinking it seemed to him that he was in a pretty pickle.

Guest Gulkan had but a thousand spears under the command of his sword. As far as he knew, the tax revolt was effectively shattered, and all the empire was with the Witchlord, or would be with him soon. He had lost his chance of escaping to Stranagor, or to Nork, or to Favanosin. A couple of bargees had already dived overboard and had escaped downstream in the flow of the Yolantarath, so Guest could not conceal his position for long.

"Why," said Sken-Pitilkin, "now we portage these stores to the mountains of Ibsen-Iktus. The mountains are but a hundred leagues or so in the distance, and with these stores we can hold out there forever."

"A hundred leagues!" said Guest.

"It is no great distance with the help of horses," said Sken-Pitilkin equitably.

And after Sken-Pitilkin and Zozimus had explained the details to him, Guest Gulkan began to see that his wizards were right. If they retreated to the valley of Yox with this burden of stores, then Lord Onosh would be hard-pressed to dig them out. But:

"We'll be trapped there," said Guest.

"No," said Sken-Pitilkin, "for if we have no alternative then we'll withdraw to the waters of the Swelaway Sea, and throw ourselves upon the mercy of the Safrak Bank."

And, with that reserve plan having been explained to all of Guest Gulkan's force, the great retreat began.

CHAPTER FIFTEEN

Volvo Marp: a high pass connecting the riverlands of the Yolantarath with the uplands of the Ibsen-Iktus Mountains. The climb to Volvo Marp is steep, and takes one to such perilous heights that it is difficult for the newcomer to find air enough to breathe. Beyond this pass lies the Hidden Valley of Yox, a barren rift bereft of trees and unyielding of water; and a transit of this wasteland allows an assault upon Zomara Pass, the conquest of which will bring the traveller into the valley of Ul-donlok, home of the wizard Ontario Nol.

* * *

The Witchlord Onosh and the Rovac warrior Thodric Jarl thought their defeated enemies would surely make a stand at Locontareth, and in this expectation they marched in good order downriver, hoping to tempt the rebels from the city and smash them in a decisive battle.

"If that proves not possible," said Jarl, "then we will take the city by siege."

Thodric Jarl rejoiced in sieges. To him, a siege was even more satisfying than a pitched battle. After all, in the heat of battle, one's enemies are apt to fight with hope in their hearts — and rightly so, for battle is the province of chance. But the slow, sure, remorseless, clutching, clamping, throttling procedures of siege give the victim far fewer resources by way of hope. Those besieged are by definition defeated already, so in many ways a siege is like having your enemy staked out helplessly beneath the burning sun, and putting your boot to his throat, and putting your weight to the boot.

Then crushing down.

So while Thodric Jarl advanced upon Locontareth, he was diligent in planning for siege, and sifted from the ranks of his army all those who were habitual citizens of Locontareth, or who had been through there often in the course of military service or activities of trade. The Witchlord Onosh, who lacked Jarl's experience of siege, monitored Jarl's preparations with all the diligence of an ideal student granted the privilege of watching his master at work.

Only on arrival at Locontareth did Thodric Jarl and the Witchlord realize that Guest Gulkan had fled. The city opened its gates to them, so they were spared a battle — but the important thing was to catch Guest, for the boy must be captured and quelled lest he prolong the revolution.

So Thodric Jarl began to research Guest Gulkan's whereabouts, and the first people to help him with these researches were the dralkosh Zelafona and her dwarf-son Glambrax, who were discovered living in an abandoned dog kennel in the shadows of the ruling hall of Locontareth.

From that dog kennel, mother and son had been running a vigorous business, selling roast rats and an ersatz brew cooked up from acorns. This is scarcely surprising, for the witches of the Sisterhood were ever able in business, and indeed it was the supreme commercial skills of the Sisterhood which first led witches into conflict with wizards, for since its very inception the Confederation of Wizards had struggled to dominate trade and commerce in all those lands under its dominion.

Thus it happened—

But that is ancient history, for the great pogrom against the witches is long over, and this text concerns itself not with the days of antiquity but with things still fresh in the minds of living men (and living women, too, if women be admitted to have minds, which seems a reasonable proposition, for all that nearly half the world disputes it).

With Zelafona discovered, and with Glambrax uncovered likewise, it was soon found that they had played no part in the recent troubles, for Zelafona had early disguised herself as a beggar woman, and Glambrax had soon betrayed his forced oath to the revolutionary Sham Cham, deserting from the revolutionary army to be at his mother's side.

Thus Jarl was forced to seek other sources of intelligence,

which he did. And thus the grey-bearded Thodric Jarl discovered that the young and athletic Guest Gulkan had fled to Stranagor, and to Nork, and to Favanosin, making his way to all three destinations simultaneously.

"If Guest has gone towards Nork," said Jarl, "then his swords will be of little danger to our peace. The country thereabouts lies in barbarous wilds of forest and hill, fraught with bogs and bear barrows. In such a wasteland, he'll find no allies apt for recruitment. Rather, he may have to fight for a bitter season simply to win his way to the coast. At best he can secure his escape, and no more."

"So," said Lord Onosh, absorbing this.

"If, on the other hand, the boy has fled to Stranagor," said Jarl, "then we face a far greater danger. The countryside between here and Stranagor is rich and well-populated, with much discontent there to be found."

Jarl did not itemize the reasons for that discontent, for some margin of diplomacy remained to the Rovac warrior despite his upbringing, and the sorry truth is that the discontents of Stranagor flowed largely from the derelictions of the Witchlord's tax policies.

"And Favanosin?" said Lord Onosh, pursuing the question of Guest's third option.

"If the boy has truly withdrawn to Favanosin," said Thodric Jarl, "then I think he is planning to ambush us on the road, or to cheat our troops down that road and then fall in force upon Locontareth itself."

"So what would you suggest?" said Lord Onosh.

"The greatest danger is Stranagor," said Jarl. "So I suggest we send a full two-thirds of our army to seize, secure or besiege that city, as the case may be. Meanwhile, we should send probing patrols in strength towards Nork and Favanosin, at least to be sure that no thousands lie waiting there in ambush."

Thus it was done; and so the Witchlord's forces had been greatly diminished by the time the news came that Guest Gulkan was in their rear.

"He has made an error," said Thodric Jarl calmly. "To launch himself upon a civil war he must rouse a major city to his cause, whereas it seems he had chosen to turn bandit. As such, he becomes a nuisance, but is no longer a danger. I suspect he has taken the advice of wizards, which cowards have more concern for their own skins than for the conquest of empire."

Here a difference in perspective. While Guest Gulkan's tutelary wizards had been very much concerned with securing the safety of their own skins, the Rovac warrior Thodric Jarl and the Witchlord Onosh had been concerned rather with the possibility of finding themselves with a full-scale civil war on their hands. By their standards, Guest and his wizards had proved to be pusillanimous cowards by flinching from the challenges of civil war.

"What now?" said Lord Onosh, when it was discovered that Guest had crept round behind his father, and, like a mouse triumphant in its devastations, had successfully gnawed away his father's baggage train to nothing.

"Now?" said Jarl, who saw no need for the question, since he thought the rightful disposal of a nibbling mouse to be far too obvious to require anything in the way of debate. "Why, now we turn. We turn. We march. We catch them. We smash them. But all this we do with care, because there is a danger that they will try to trick their way around our flanks."

Though Jarl had by now decided that Guest, Sken-Pitilkin and Zozimus were a trio of cowards, he nevertheless realized they had been trickier than he had expected, and might be trickier still before this game was through. Accordingly, he left a strong force in Locontareth, and advanced cautiously with scouts riding far out on his southern flank, and with scouting parties riding the northern bank of the Yolantarath just in case Guest had sneaked his army across the water and was attempting some ambitious manoeuvre beyond the visible horizon to the north.

The end result was that Guest and his people had got clean away to the mountains by the time Jarl closed with their previous location. Furthermore, in his retreat, Guest had got away with his brothers Morsh and Eljuk, two captives whose fate Lord

Onosh lamented bitterly.

But at least the mystery of Guest's precise circumstances and intentions appeared to be at an end, for the boy had left behind him evidence and witnesses in plenty — most notably, witnesses in the form of the barge crews and their captains, who had been turned loose after cooperating with the labour of the withdrawal.

"Then he is gone," said Jarl in satisfaction, "and that is the end of him."

"But he has escaped!" said Lord Onosh. "And — and my sons! Eljuk! Morsh! He's got the boys as prisoners!"

"Then my lord will have to reconcile himself to the imprisonment of his sons," said Jarl formally, "and perhaps in the fullness of time my lord will also have to reconcile himself to the death of those sons."

"And to the loss of my empire, mayhap?" said Lord Onosh grimly. "Guest's escaped, and with him those wizards in their treachery. All of Ibsen-Iktus is his unless we hunt him down and break him. Within that mountain fastness, he can gather his forces and prepare to break the very empire with his onslaught."

"My lord," said Jarl, finding himself hard-pressed to stay calm in the face of the Witchlord's agitation. "Ibsen-Iktus is but a parcel of rocks, useless for all purposes excepting those of suicide."

"A fastness," insisted Lord Onosh.

"If my lord means that the mountains are a castle," said Jarl, "why, then so they are, but a very bleak and barren castle, empty of all the necessities required for either siege or outright war. In those mountains, my lord, there is everything a rock could need for the full satisfaction of its appetites, hence rocks live there in great multitudes in the full independence of their rightful kingdom. But rocks — my lord, the boy can scarcely recruit those rocks to his fighting force, nor can he use bare stone to feed the mutinous rabble which serves him."

"But he could push through the mountains to escape," said Lord Onosh.

"And what of it?" said Jarl. "Beyond the mountains of Ibsen-

Iktus lies the Swelaway Sea."

"And Safrak," said Lord Onosh, naming the ruling archipelago of that sea.

"What of it?" said Jarl. "Suppose the boy can make an alliance with Safrak? What then? Safrak's but a rock, a group of rocks, a lesser version of Ibsen-Iktus, rocks up to their necks in water. Small rocks, my lord."

"Rocks protected by the Guardians," said Lord Onosh, who knew all about the mercenaries which served the Safrak Bank.

"So Safrak has a Bank, and the Bank has guards," said Jarl. "It has dogs, too. I know it for a fact, since the mangiest of them pissed on my boot when I first reached Alozay. I've been there, my lord. And while I was there, I counted. My lord, the rocks are nothing, for there aren't sufficient women, sheep or fighting men in all of Safrak to pose the slightest hazard to our empire."

"But Guest has my sons," said Lord Onosh. "Morsh. And Eljuk. He has them prisoner."

"Yes," said Jarl, growing weary with the labour of repetition. "He has, and will hold. My lord, I ventured Ibsen-Iktus in the spring. Its barrens are built for starvation. If trapped upon those heights, then Guest must either transfigure his men into goats or see them starve. Failing transfiguration, he must surrender — to us or to Safrak. If to Safrak, then Safrak will yield him up to secure its trade. Yes, and yield up Morsh and Eljuk simultaneously."

Thus Jarl, who had no taste for venturing into the mountains after Guest, feeling that pursuit would be unprofitable, for the heights of Ibsen-Iktus would grant great advantages of defence to anyone with the will to hold them.

But Lord Onosh declared that he must have either Morsh or Eljuk by his side. And soon.

"Else," said Lord Onosh, "In the absence of any obvious and visible heir, my rivals among the Yarglat may choose this moment to try to dislodge me from my throne."

Jarl was not convinced; but presumably Lord Onosh knew the politics of his own people and his own empire better than did a Rovac mercenary, so at last Jarl saw that he had no alternative other than to let himself be persuaded.

"Very well," said Jarl. "So the empire must have an heir. Then I will get back one of the boys, at least, if not both. Give me a dozen men, a case of gold and the right of pardon. That's all I need."

"The right of pardon!" said Lord Onosh.

"Certainly," said Jarl.

"Who are you planning to pardon?" said Lord Onosh.

"Why, the wizards," said Jarl. "At least the wizards, and quite possibly Guest himself."

"The wizards!" said Lord Onosh in astonishment.

Though the Witchlord Onosh was not fully conversant with the details of the long-standing conflict between Rovac's warriors and the wizards of Argan's Confederation, he had nevertheless heard something of that ancient enmity from Bao Gahai and Zelafona (who, as witches, were versed in such knowledge), from Rolf Thelemite (who always pleaded the Rovac's case), and from Zozimus and Sken-Pitilkin themselves.

"Even that," said Thodric Jarl stoically. "My lord, I have no wish to pardon anyone, far less wizards. Yet I think a cure by means of pardons and disbursements is the easiest way to secure our cause. These wizards, in particular, are weak and venial creatures, yet cunning in their argument. By combination of threat and incentive, I can win them to our cause, and easily, and they by their guile will win us Guest."

In truth, Thodric Jarl would rather kill people than pardon them any day of the year, but on this occasion the doughty Rovac warrior fancied that the odds favoured diplomacy. But Lord Onosh was dead against it, saying that his rivals among the Yarglat would think him weak if he dispensed his pardons too freely, and that this itself might be cause for a coup.

Therefore the Witchlord Onosh declared that he would prove his strength by marching his army into the mountains of Ibsen-Iktus and wresting Morsh and Eljuk from the grip of their captors by main force.

"My lord," said Jarl, in protest.

"You have another plan," said Lord Onosh, glaring at him.

"My lord," said Jarl, in one last attempt to stave off a move he saw as precipitous folly. "I would not chance it, my lord. Bottle the boy in the hills then threaten him. Try that for a start, my lord. A threat first, and war then only if necessary."

"No," said Lord Onosh. "We march for the mountains, and we march today."

"But," said Jarl, "the mountains are high, and cold in their highness. If we mean to assail those heights, we must first prepare ourselves for winter campaigning."

But Lord Onosh was determined, and so marched his army into the hills in search of the high pass of Volvo Marp, the pass which would give access to the frozen wastelands of the Hidden Valley of Yox. A long and dusty journey it was, a journey begun in the full heat of summer; and the continental summers of Tameran are a matter of sun and sweat, of biting flies and nimble insects born with beaks like needles and an unquenchable appetite for human blood.

"Grief of a turnip!" said Lord Onosh, pausing on one steep and dusty hillside to wipe the sweat from his brow. "I thought you said the mountains were cold. You spoke of winter campaigning"

"In the mountains, my lord," said Thodric Jarl. "But these are not yet the mountains. These are only the hills."

"This is mountain enough to nearly defy the strength of a horse," said Lord Onosh. "If the heights above will deny also the sun, then I welcome them!"

Jarl thought this intemperate folly, but had given up arguing with his emperor. Instead, he was fully occupied by the labour of finding the true path to the high pass of Volvo Marp.

When Thodric Jarl had descended from the mountains to the hills in the days of spring, his mind had been initially clouded by the pain-killing drug fed to him by Ontario Nol. So Jarl's recollections of Volvo Marp were nothing but a foggy blur, and to find the way Jarl had to rely upon certain of the bargemen who had assisted Guest Gulkan in the great work of portage which had seen the Weaponmaster steal away the contents of his father's baggage train.

At last they entered into a ravaged valley with steeply canted sides, a valley of fractured stone and buckled erosion, of thornbush bastions and chikle-gikle streams still chill from the snows of their melt-water genesis.

"This valley, my lord," said Thodric Jarl to his emperor, "leads us to the high pass of Volvo Marp."

"Valley!" said the Witchlord, eyeing the terrain dubiously. "You call this a valley? The land is tilted like a stairway, and a steep stairway at that."

"As the mountains count land," said Jarl, "anything not a cliff is a valley."

"Then I think you still in error," said the Witchlord, surveying the steepness which lay ahead, "for I count this as a cliff!"

But regardless of how the Witchlord counted it, they had no choice but to climb it.

And as they climbed it grew cold; for on the heights the unyielding ice and snow persists the full year through. Worse, the steepness of the track was such that the greater number of the horses had to be abandoned. Thereafter, the Witchlord could not ride, but must necessarily walk.

And the nights!

Stripped to the lightness of their summer campaigning, the Witchlord's forces found the mountain nights near unendurable in their cold. True, they all knew the harshness of Tameran's winters, but they were always forewarned of those winters, and went into them heavily padded, in imitation of the bear.

Only Thodric Jarl's experience allowed them to survive the sudden weather-shock of the heights of Ibsen-Iktus. For Jarl had campaigned in the Cold West, and proved equal to the task of high-mountain survival. He counselled the mutual huddling of bodies at night; the improvization of insulating pads from lightweight cloth stuffed with leaves; the making of fires; and the cunning practice of covering a half-burnt fire with a great heap of loose stones, and thereafter using those stones as a warm bed to assist with survival through the bitter frosts of night.

So the Witchlord and his Rovac general forced their army to the heights of Volvo Marp, the first of the great challenges of the mountains of Ibsen-Iktus.

And Guest Gulkan and his forces were waiting upon the heights of that pass — or seemed to be — in a position they had heavily fortified. Lord Onosh and Thodric Jarl could see banners flying from the fortifications; and men appearing at random; and the smoke of fires rising in the thin air. So the Witchlord and his Rovac-born general organized a slow-motion advance through the air of the heights, the air which was so bitterly thin and difficult to breathe; and Guest Gulkan sent an avalanche crashing down on them from above.

Down came the avalanche, a whale in its roiling, a dragon in its roar. Boulders bounced, some huge as houses, mulching the strength of the army.

A few survived.

Those few were the few who had been closest to Guest Gulkan's fortifications when the avalanche was launched. Naturally, those few were those who were greatest in courage, and most eager for battle — and these included the Rovac warrior Thodric Jarl and the Witchlord Onosh.

Jarl was unhurt, but for a slight wound inflicted by a splinter of ice which, sent shattering through the sky by the impact of a house-sized boulder, had driven through leather and chain mail to nick the Rovac warrior's back just beneath his left-sided shoulderbone. But a more serious blow had been delivered to his pride, for he had been defeated by Guest Gulkan, who was but a boy, albeit a boy protected and counselled by wizards.

Of course, the wizard Ontario Nol was as much to blame for Jarl's defeat as anyone, for it was Nol who had drugged Jarl into a state of stupefaction to keep him quiet on their earlier journey through the uplands of Ibsen-Iktus; and so it was that a clear-eyed Guest Gulkan had been able to scan the landscape for possibilities of ambush while Thodric Jarl had been concentrating on the difficult business of putting one foot in front of the other.

As for Lord Onosh, he was entirely unhurt, at least so far as flesh and bone was concerned, but he was so shattered in his wits that he could not speak for two days, and it was even longer before he had sufficient control of his hands to hold a cup in his hands. Because of course, to Lord Onosh, that avalanche had struck like the wrath of the gods themselves, precipitating grotesque outrages of death out of a clear sky.

An avalanche is such a terrible weapon of mass destruction that, in the past, the making of avalanches has often been explicitly outlawed in the treaties which civilized nations have made to regulate the conduct of their wars. But both Lord Onosh and his son Guest Gulkan were of the Yarglat, hence their actions owed nothing to civilized usage.

And so it was that the Weaponmaster smashed the Witchlord's army with the savagery of a landslide, and thus made himself the lord of the battlefield, and made prisoners out of both his father and his Rovac-born general.

CHAPTER SIXTEEN

Ul-donlok: valley in the mountains of Ibsen-Iktus. The upper part of this valley is ruled by Ontario Nol, a wizard of the order of Itch. Nearer the Swelaway Sea is the realm of King Igpatan, a monarch famous for his extensive collection of moths, and for the unpleasant nature of his frequent birthday celebrations.

* * *

So Lord Onosh was defeated at the high pass of Volvo Marp; and was led as a prisoner through the high and bitter valley of Yox; and was taken over Zomara Pass; and thus came in chains to the valley of Ul-donlok and the monastery of Qonsajara, home of the wizard Ontario Nol.

In chains?

Yes, for Guest had found a renegade goldsmith among his ranks, and had caused the man to make miniature chains of fine-link gold out of some jewellery taken from the dead; and, wearing these largely symbolic tokens of his defeat, the Witchlord Onosh came to the monastery of Qonsajara.

His son played tourist guide for the visit.

"This," said Guest, with a gesture in the direction of the vast decrepitude of the building's tiled facade, "was once consecrated to dorking, but those dedicated to that sport found the climate too cold for their nakedness."

Then Guest Gulkan gave the Witchlord a potted history of the many orgies of Qonsajara, showing off the place as if it were his own creation. Indeed, young Guest was greatly proud of the hugeness of this behemoth of a building, with its monumental frontage half a thousand paces in length, the whole of it adorned with obscenely ornate faded ceramic tiles dedicated to the liquidity of the hulakola, the heat of the yinx, the mystery of the omphalos, the snakings of limbs of passion and silk, the lividity of tongues, the yearning of muscles and the fondling of curves, the sensuality of all of which was amplified by the very harshness of the bleak and shattered upland landscape in which the building was set.

Just as the Witchlord Onosh took no pleasure in Guest Gulkan's building, so the Witchlord took no pleasure in being held captive, and this Guest found most strange.

After all, as far as the Weaponmaster was concerned, he was being most magnanimously hospitable in victory. Apart from the symbolic imposition of golden chains, young Guest had done his father no harm, and thought himself a very great man to be letting his father enjoy the unhindered possession of such superfluous luxuries as two eyes and a nose. After all, what had Lord Onosh ever done for young Guest? Nothing. He had never offered him anything in the way of power, authority or prestige. It was the purple-birthmarked Eljuk who had been groomed to inherit the empire, whereas poor Guest had ever been told that he would inherit precisely nothing.

Yet surely he deserved to inherit!

As far as Guest was concerned, he was a mighty warrior who in the days of his earliest youth had repeatedly fought for his father against bandits, who had once risked his own life to save his brother Eljuk from the river, and who had brought great credit to the imperial family by defeating the Rovac warrior Thodric Jarl in fair combat in Enskandalon Square in Gendormargensis.

All this Guest had done, yet his father had repaid him with theft and exile. His father had denied him access to Yerzerdayla, the prize he had won through combat with Thodric Jarl, and in Guest Gulkan's eyes this denial constituted an act of positive theft. This wrong had been compounded by the fact that his father had meanly and unfairly exiled him from the imperial capital and all its pleasures, sending him into exile in far-off Safrak where he had been denied all of life's consolations excepting the company of the irregular verbs.

Guest Gulkan had almost died on the journey to that island, for the boat which had taken him across the Swelaway Sea had been rotten, and had almost sunk. And on arrival — why, on the cruel and loveless island of Alozay, the exiled Guest had endured the horrors of a plague of influenza. There, too, he had been confronted by a demonic demon, the notorious Icaria Scaria Iva-Italis, Demon By Appointment to the Great God Jocasta. Then he had been forced to fight his way free from the island; and to escape across the Swelaway Sea in another death-trap of a boat; and then to risk a terrifying sky-hurtling journey across the mountains. And then, in the mountains themselves, he had almost died on account of the effects of a sudden ascent to great altitude.

And it was all his father's fault!

To Guest, then, it was entirely right, logical and just that he should have thrown in his lot with the tax revolutionaries led by Sham Cham, for Guest had grievances to avenge, grievances which were well worth killing for. The theft of the flesh of the woman Yerzerdayla, for example! Not to mention such matters as the inheritance of the empire.

Consequently, Guest prided himself on the magnanimous greatness of heart which he showed by not killing his father, or torturing him either, or spitting in his face, or cutting off his hair, or grinding his nose into the mud, or doing any of those other things which the ingenious Rolf Thelemite suggested with such unrestrained enthusiasm.

So when Guest looked on his father, he thought:

Here is the foolish old man who cheated me of my woman, who exiled me unfairly, who waged war against me rather than share his manure with Locontareth, and who is living proof of my own greatness of heart, for I have almost forgiven him, in proof of which I have greeted him with the full abundance of this mountain palace of mine, and have extended to him the use of all things which are good in this my mountain kingdom.

Thus Guest thought, for as far as he was concerned he had conquered the valley of Ul-donlok by the simple expedient of marching his small army into it; and, as the wizard Ontario Nol wisely offered Guest everything in the valley which was there for the taking, the valley was indeed a kingdom, at least for the practical purposes of the moment.

Thus Guest.

But the Witchlord Onosh inhabited a different world entirely — a situation which has plenty of precedent, for parents and children are often so remote from each other as to be, in effect, members of different tribes, or different races, or different species altogether. Hence there is often more love, trust and mutual understanding between a man and his dog than a man and his son.

As far as Lord Onosh was concerned, Guest Gulkan was a wild and witless boy who had disgraced himself and had brought the imperial family into disrepute by quarrelling with a low-born foreign mercenary over the possession of a woman. After attempting the unjust seizure of the woman, the boy had then risked his life against the mercenary, and had almost got himself killed.

Lord Onosh knew full well that Thodric Jarl would have killed Guest in Enskandalon Square had Lord Onosh not intervened by persuading the wizard Sken-Pitilkin to use his magic to trick Jarl out of his balance. After saving his son, the Witchlord had thereafter demonstrated his concerned love for the boy by sending him to safety in the Safrak Islands, which were renowned as a zone of peace and tranquillity.

Furthermore, Lord Onosh had deprived himself of the benefits of the cooking of Pelagius Zozimus, the greatest chef in the Collosnon Empire, for the Witchlord Onosh had sent the wizard-chef Zozimus to Safrak to provide extra security for his son. Meantime, Lord Onosh had tried hard to put down the tax revolt based in Locontareth, to secure the empire which was surely destined to be Guest's inheritance.

So when Lord Onosh looked at Guest, he thought:

Here is the wicked, witless, mindless, stubborn, stupid, ungrateful, scheming, treacherous boy whom I have tried for so long to preserve, protect and educate so that he might one day be fit to govern the empire which I have ever expected to fall inevitably to his possession. To protect him in battle, I have risked losing the loyalty of my greatest bodyguard; and I have deprived myself of the services of my greatest chef in order to help preserve and protect his worthless life, and for all this he has proved entirely ungrateful.

Thus the son was confused and the father bitter; and, in the extremity of his bitterness, Lord Onosh began to reconfigure the past, without realizing that he was doing so.

Lord Onosh had always seen that his own death would be followed by murder. Eljuk Zala Gulkan lacked the strength to hold an empire as his own. Therefore, on the Witchlord's death, Guest Gulkan must necessarily murder Eljuk, slaughtering down his brother then mastering the Collosnon Empire to his own will. This Lord Onosh had always seen.

But now, rather than attributing Eljuk's inevitable fate to Eljuk's deficiencies, Lord Onosh convinced himself that the certainty of Eljuk's destruction was a consequence of the demonic evil of the boy Guest.

So when Eljuk unexpectedly announced that he was going to stay in the mountains with the wizard Ontario Nol, Lord Onosh was convinced that Guest had terrorized poor Eljuk, and had threatened him with murder or worse.

"What has he said to you?" said Lord Onosh.

"He has said," said Eljuk, "that he will make me his apprentice."

"No," said Lord Onosh irritably. "Not the wizard. It's Guest, Guest I'm talking about. What has Guest said to you? About staying, I mean?"

"Why," said Eljuk, "he said that Nol wanted me, asked for me. And he says, ah, it's a good idea, that's what he says."

"You mean he threatened you?"

"Threatened?" said Eljuk, looking puzzled. "Why should he threaten me?"

"Because he wants the empire."

"Well," said Eljuk, "if I'm going to be a wizard, then he can have it."

"But you can't be a wizard!" said Lord Onosh. "You're of the Yarglat, and no man of the Yarglat was ever a wizard! It's foreign stuff, stuff for the people of Toxteth and places like that."

Eljuk Zala, resisting the temptation to remind his father that Toxteth was not a place but a language, reminded him instead that Ontario Nol was of the Yarglat.

"So he says, so he says," said Lord Onosh. "But I'm sure he was never the heir to an empire."

"What's that got to do with it?" said Eljuk.

At this, Lord Onosh looked fit to overheat and explode, in the manner of one of those notorious pressure cookers with which Pelagius Zozimus once experimented.

"You can't just throw away an empire," said Lord Onosh in great distress. "You can't just throw it away, just like that!"

But Eljuk could, and did, and had. For Ontario Nol, the great wizard of Itch who had lived for so long as abbot of Qonsajara and as ruler of the uplands of Ul-donlok, had tempted young Eljuk with prospects of knowledge, and insight, and arcane power, and life prolonged for millennia. This temptation had proved potent, for the scholarly Eljuk had no desire to be the lord of the sweat of ten thousand horses or the grease of an equal number of virginal vaginas, or to possess any of those other most useless and uncouth material goods which typically appeal to your average Yarglat barbarian.

So Eljuk abandoned an empire, choosing wizardry instead.

And Eljuk could not be dissuaded from his choice.

Lord Onosh had little time in which to attempt dissuasion, for Guest was conscious of the passage of time, and knew that he was growing short of this commodity. The Battle of Babaroth had been fought in the heat of high summer, and it had been hot summer still when Guest had defeated his father at Volvo Marp by making an ally out of an avalanche; but the season was rapidly advancing, and soon it would be autumn.

Guest Gulkan remembered the winter journey which had seen him journey from Gendormargensis to an unwelcome exile on the island of Alozay. For a few people, well-equipped and well-clad, that winter passage had proved feasible. But Guest fancied that a thousand spears would be hard put to scavenge a bare living for themselves on such a passage through snow and ice.

The rations which Guest had earlier looted from his father's baggage train and portaged into the mountains were running short; by no stretch of imagination could the mountains themselves feed his army; and so he was determined to be back in Gendormargensis before winter set in.

Being so determined, Guest Gulkan said a fond farewell to his brother Eljuk, and ordered his army to prepare for a march to the lowlands, the lowlands where the sun was exercising its strength in one last bravado display of luxurious heat.

Lord Onosh begged for leave to stay in Qonsajara, swearing that he would live out his life peacefully in the mountains of Ibsen-Iktus. But Guest was not fool enough to believe his father, so took the man with him, that man being still symbolically imprisoned with golden chains. Jarl likewise went as a prisoner.

Eljuk stayed. The text-master Eldegen Terzanagel wanted to stay, but Ontario Nol refused him house room. Nevertheless, Nol extended a hospitable mercy to a couple of poor fellows who were dying of tuberculosis, and to a witless fool who had broken his leg in five different places by attempting that suicidal activity known as mountain climbing. But the rest of the army marched.

Thus it came to pass that Eljuk Zala Gulkan, eldest son of the Witchlord Onosh Gulkan, stayed behind in the monastery of Qonsajara. And the bold Guest Gulkan said farewell to the wizard Ontario Nol and began his return journey to the Collosnon Empire, taking his father with him as a prisoner.

Guest marched his men down the valley in force, hoping to provoke a minor war with King Igpatan. But that minor village lord wisely kept his fighting men away from Guest Gulkan's line of march, and let Guest loot as many chickens as he chose as he marched down to the shores of the Swelaway Sea.

Guest then marched along those shores to the village of Ink, where he began to bethink himself of the boat-salesman Umbilskimp, who had once sold him a rotten boat. Guest had sworn to hang the fellow, and remained true to the resolution of his oath.

"But," said Guest to Sken-Pitilkin, "I do not want to give my biographer excuse to slander me. I wish to rule in justice, and to be seen to do as much."

"Then perhaps," said Sken-Pitilkin, "you may have to forego the pleasures of a hanging."

This was not the advice which Guest had expected to receive. He had expected Sken-Pitilkin to show him some means whereby he could hang the unfortunate Umbilskimp out of hand while still maintaining his good standing in the eyes of his biographer.

Thrown back on his own resources of cunning, the Weaponmaster Guest soon schemed up a plot which was adequate to his purpose. He called for his slow-witted brother, Morsh Bataar.

"Morsh," said Guest. "I want you to ride ahead to the village of Ink. Say nothing of my army. Say that you speak for a party of merchants from the Ibsen-Iktus mountains. Say that you wish to buy boats, boats for a trip to Alozay. Three boats, four, whatever the money will stretch to."

Then Guest gave his brother gold, and sent him ahead with three stout fellows who would act as both bodyguards and witnesses.

By the time Guest Gulkan marched his army into Ink, his brother Morsh had successfully purchased five boats with the money which Guest had given him.

"Who sold you these boats?" said Guest.

"I bought them from Umbilskimp, Pedrick and Mung," said Morsh. "The three are confederated in a boat-selling partnership."

"Very well," said Guest. "Identify them! Then have them arrested!"

"Arrested?" said Morsh in astonishment. "But they sold me the boats, just as you wanted. I thought you wanted to go to Alozay."

"No!" said Guest. "Alozay is the least and last of the places I want to go to!"

That was not entirely the truth, for Guest still thought often of Icaria Scaria Iva-Italis, the demon who guarded the stairway at the eastern end of Alozay's Hall of Time. Guest was still minded to go to Alozay. To pact with the demon Iva-Italis. To rescue the Great God Jocasta from imprisonment in Obooloo's Temple of Blood. And to have himself made a wizard as a reward for the rescue. All this he would do — one day. But clearly he should first look to the security of the Collosnon Empire, for then the rest could be easily accomplished.

"So," said Morsh, soberly "You lied to me. You didn't need boats at all."

"Lied to you!" said Guest, in outrage. "I made you an instrument of justice, that's what I did! Arrest those men, and I'll prove it to you!"

So Umbilskimp, Pedrick and Mung were arrested, and Guest set himself about organizing a proper trial which would prove his merits to his biographer.

The captive Lord Onosh was made judge of the case, which was prosecuted by the slug-chef Pelagius Zozimus, who went about his business with an uncommonly gleeful display of zeal. The text-master Eldegen Terzanagel was made defence counsel. Guest Gulkan, Rolf Thelemite, Thodric Jarl and Hostaja Torsen Sken-Pitilkin testified for the prosecution. Morsh Bataar also gave evidence, and the boats he had so recently bought were hauled from the water to be examined by the court.

In this manner, Umbilskimp, Pedrick and Mung were given a proper trial before an independent judge. It was quick — it was all over in a single morning — but it was fair. It was proved that Umbilskimp had once sold a murderously rotten boat to Guest Gulkan and his comrades; that Mung had likewise deceitfully sold a hulk to Thodric Jarl.

As for the boats so recently sold to Morsh Bataar by the tripartite partnership, why, the belly of each proved as soft as a slug.

"So," said the slug-chef Zozimus, prosecuting his case to the hilt, "here we see nothing more nor less than organized murder undertaken for commercial gain. These men have years of boat-selling expertise behind them, therefore cannot plead ignorance.

They have made a career out of selling rotten hulks fit for nothing more than sinking. I demand the death penalty!"

In response, the text-master Eldegen Terzanagel tried the usual tricks. He called attention to the impoverished environment in which his clients lived; mentioned the sundry derelictions of their upbringing; and finally drew attention to the matter of local mores.

"The selling of rotten boats to unsuspecting strangers is a part and parcel of traditional local culture," said Terzanagel.

"An ethnologist would say that we cannot judge the backward savages of a place like Ink by the standards of a highly evolved civilization like our own. An ethnologist would say that Umbilskimp, Pedrick and Mung acted rightly in terms of their own cultural traditions, and we do them a great wrong if we condemn them in accordance with the traditions of our own culture, traditions which are quite alien to theirs. So say the ethnologists."

"Then I say we should hang the ethnologists along with the villagers!" said Zozimus. "You, sir — are you an ethnologist?"

Eldegen Terzanagel hastily denied it, insisting that he was but a poor text-master, and was only defending the murderous wretches of Ink at Guest Gulkan's sword-point insistence.

"There!" said Zozimus, turning to the judge of the case. "You see? Even the counsel for the defence has no confidence in his clients! He called them murderous wretches! Well, murderous they are, for use, but they can hardly be wretched, not after glutting themselves on generations of ill-gotten gold. I call for the death penalty!"

"You have called for that once already," said Lord Onosh. "But as judge of this case, I am happy for you to call for it twice, and I am happy to grant it."

So Umbilskimp, Pedrick and Mung were sentenced to death. The Witchlord Onosh had very little choice in the matter of the sentence. The crime was grave, the evidence compelling and the guilt proven. Lord Onosh would have looked a capricious fool or a corrupt fraud had he pardoned the boat-sellers.

With the boat-sellers having been sentenced to death, Guest

Gulkan congratulated Zozimus on his able prosecution, and called for volunteers.

"I need a hangman," said Guest. "Preferably someone who has done the job before, but enthusiasm will serve in the absence of experience."

Whereupon Thodric Jarl stepped forward, declaring he had both the enthusiasm and the experience. Guest appointed him as executioner, and the Rovac warrior set to work with a will.

Mung was the first man to be hung. His neck broke, and he was dead in moments. Pedrick suffered a similar fate.

But when Jarl tried to hang Umbilskimp, the rope broke.

Umbilskimp fell heavily, then got to his feet uncertainly. Guest watched, feeling more than a little uncertain himself, as Thodric Jarl advanced upon the old man.

Thodric Jarl took Umbilskimp by the throat — just as Guest, on an earlier occasion, had taken Rolf Thelemite by the throat on a battlefield near Babaroth. But whereas Guest had meant to menace, Thodric Jarl had murder as his intent. Guest took a half-step forward, for he had half-decided that he had had enough.

"If you are a woman in your sentiments," said the Witchlord Onosh, detecting his son's intentions, and finding himself unable to resist the temptation to exercise himself in a sneer, "then it's best you step aside and let men have the governance of the empire."

Whereupon Guest restrained himself, for, even though he had defeated his father by avalanche, the Weaponmaster lacked courage sufficient to endure his father's scorn. So Jarl — slowly, deliberately, lovingly — crushed his man, then dropped him into a crumpled heap. Whereupon everyone moved away, saving for Morsh Bataar alone, who sombrely covered the dead man with a cloak.

After that, Guest was in no mood to linger, so hastened his army in its march. The army followed the flow of the Pig, keeping to its southern bank.

Guest grew increasingly sombre on the march, and Sken-Pitilkin began to worry about his condition. For Guest had defeated his father, and was in effect the emperor. As soon as he had seized the city of Gendormargensis as his own, men would recognize him as emperor. If he were ready to compromise, and was generous with his pardons, then he might well be able to secure the loyalty of the dissident city of Stranagor. And with that done, the entire Collosnon Empire would be under his sway — if not immediately, then soon.

Seeking thus, Sken-Pitilkin sought out Guest when the army camped near the bridge which had been the scene of a battle between Witchlord and Weaponmaster during the summer.

Sken-Pitilkin had to seek a goodly distance, for the Weaponmaster had walked far from his camp. He had walked through the hot afternoon all the way to the confluence of the Yolantarath and the Pig, which was where Sken-Pitilkin found him. Guest was sitting on the riverbank, watching the waters, while Rolf Thelemite and Morsh Bataar waited at a discreet distance.

On approaching Guest, the wizard of Skatzabratzumon made no attempt to challenge him, or jolly him out of his desponds. Instead, Sken-Pitilkin sat himself down on the bank and waited. At last Guest said, without anything in the way of preamble:

"Was I right or wrong? Letting those men hang, I mean. Was that right? Or was it wrong?"

Sken-Pitilkin gave an ambivalent answer. Not out of dishonesty, but because he himself had not quite made up his mind about the matter.

"Most men would say the thing was rightly done," said Sken-Pitilkin.

"But what say you?" said Guest.

"I'm not necessarily any wiser than my neighbour," said Sken-Pitilkin.

"But you think I shouldn't have done it."

"A hanging is an ugly thing," said Sken-Pitilkin. "An ordered society would surely hold its boat-sellers in check, thus preserving them from the gallows. But Ink is no part of any ordered society. Those men you hung, why — they murdered for profit, as was said at their trial. A hanging is an ugly thing, but piracy is worse, and those men were pirates in their commercial deceits.”

“So I did right,” said Guest.

“Do you feel as if you did right?” said Sken-Pitilkin.

“How can you first prove me right then go on to question my rightness?” said Guest.

“I can,” said Sken-Pitilkin, “because you know yourself wrong.”

“Wrong!” said Guest, raising his voice for the first time. “But you have just proved me right!”

Sken-Pitilkin sat silent to let the young man settle, then said:

“I watched you during the hanging.”

Guest absorbed that in silence, then said:

“And?”

“And,” said Sken-Pitilkin, “you were moved to pardon Umbilskimp. But you didn’t. Why not?”

Guest made no answer. He knew the reason why. But Sken-Pitilkin felt the reason had to be made explicit. Had to be verbalized — lest it be forgotten.

“You let Jarl kill the man,” said Sken-Pitilkin. “You let Jarl kill the man because you were afraid to show mercy. You were afraid of your father’s scorn.”

Guest made no reply. His face was expressionless. He looked out across the river, then picked up a piece of mud and threw it with a jerk. The mud plopped into the river, and, a moment later, was answered by a splash as a fish jumped.

“Since your earliest youth,” said Sken-Pitilkin, “you have been killing men in brawls with bandits. Killing men and taking their scalps. Ethnology would pardon such habits, so who am I to condemn? As you said yourself, it is but your cultural heritage. But to kill men for banditry or piracy is one thing. To kill a man because you fear your father’s scorn is quite another. If you cannot master the disciplines of mercy, then I think you unfit to master the sword.”

Guest absorbed that, too, in silence.

The silence tempted Sken-Pitilkin, and that wizard of

Skatzabratzumon was half-persuaded to launch himself into a lecture on avalanches. After all, in the mountains of Ibsen-Iktus, the young Guest Gulkan had casually obliterated his father's army by avalanche — and had never thereafter shown so much as an eyeblink of remorse for the deed.

Sken-Pitilkin still felt sorely about that avalanche, particularly as Guest Gulkan had used a swordpoint's threat to compel a certain wizard of Skatzabratzumon to use his levitational powers to trigger that downslide of rocks, ice and fractured snow. So Sken-Pitilkin opened his mouth — then closed it again, firmly.

After all, in Ibsen-Iktus, Guest had been at war, hence could plead necessity. And, besides, it is contrary to human nature for anyone to concern themselves with large-scale tragedies remote from their own persons. To those who are of tender spirit, the death of a small mouse or the agony of a bird in a cat's jaws makes more impact than the death by starvation of some half a million people in a nation a continent removed.

Guest had been closely, intimately concerned with the death of the boat-seller Umbilskimp. That death had been consequent upon Guest's own moral cowardice. For he had seen fit to exercise the prerogative of mercy, yet had restrained himself for mere fear of his father's scorn.

Had Guest been a fragile child unschooled in the ways of power, then Sken-Pitilkin might have seen fit to mitigate his suffering with words of comfort and of absolution. But Guest was no such child. He was a warlord's son with a soul as ugly as his bat-flap ears. So Sken-Pitilkin, seeing that the young man was truly suffering, was pleased to see as much. And, having done his duty by making Guest's crime of crimes explicit, unavoidable and (with luck) unforgettable, the wizard of Skatzabratzumon rose, dusted down his fishermen's skirts, and departed without so much as a word of farewell.

Left to himself — for Rolf Thelemite and Morsh Bataar were still keeping their distance, their fumbling attempts at comfort having earlier been rudely rebuffed — Guest Gulkan sat alone by the confluence of the Yolantarath and the Pig.

The Pig, which had earlier flowed clear, was running muddy

now, for upstream was Guest Gulkan's army, and men, clothes and horses were being washed in the river's waters. The Pig emptied its muddiness in a whirlygig rush into the slow-mud slurge of the ineffable Yolantarath, the name of which river reminded Guest, by poetic association, of Yerzerdayla, the woman who — he supposed — dwelt still in Gendormargensis.

Now that Guest was emperor, more or less, he supposed he could take the woman from Thodric Jarl. Yes, and hang Jarl unless that Rovac warrior would give him the woman, and swear fealty to him, and lick his boots in proof of such fealty.

So thought Guest.

But such imaginings proved strangely comfortless, for still he could not shake free the memories of the hangings. The bodies black against the sun. Old man Umbilskimp, wheezing heavily, making odd fluttering gestures with his hands as Thodric Jarl lumbered towards him.

The sky was darkening, now, the broad sky above the wide reach of the Yolantarath growing heavy with clouds. As Guest sat by the river, he shivered, suddenly cold. For some reason, he suddenly thought there was snow all around. Which was ridiculous. Despite the lateness of the season, the first snowfall was yet days distant. Still. Guest imagined snow.

There was snow, and it was cold, and now Guest realized that there was an animal padding through the cold of that snow. It was a beast of snow, and was as white as the snow. He knew its weight from its silence.

Then it breathed upon him.

Its breath was hot on his nape.

In all his life, Guest had endured nothing more terrifying than that hot breath breathing on him from out of the silence of snow. He tried to stand, tried to run. But could not. For his arms and legs were bloody shreds, and as the pain of his mutilations hit him he started to scream, and was screaming still when Rolf Thelemite and Morsh Bataar came running to his rescue.

CHAPTER SEVENTEEN

Babaroth: a town some two leagues (4,000 paces) north of the confluence of the Pig and the Yolantarath. The "Battle of Babaroth", as it is commonly known, took place at the Pig itself. In that battle, the Witchlord Onosh defeated his enemies with the help of his Rovac-born general Thodric Jarl. The revolutionary leader Sham Cham, chief of the Witchlord's enemies, died when an arrow took him in the eye, whereupon the Weaponmaster Guest Gulkan led the revolutionary forces in a vigorous retreat.

* * *

By the next day, Guest Gulkan had fully recovered from his waking nightmare. Indeed, he disclaimed all knowledge of any such nightmare, claiming that a good night's sleep had obliterated his memories of the trauma of the previous evening.

Guest celebrated his full recovery from nightmare's claims by holding a little ceremony in honour of the Battle of Babaroth. In that battle, Witchlord had defeated Weaponmaster; but, Guest Gulkan having made himself his father's master, the Witchlord Onosh was forced to kneel upon the earth—

And to eat a small portion of that earth as a token of his son's supremacy.

Shortly thereafter, as Guest Gulkan's army marched through the stretch of trees which lay between the Pig and the settlement of Babaroth, Sken-Pitilkin was audacious enough to question Guest Gulkan's wisdom.

"Your father's fate lies in your hand," said Sken-Pitilkin. "You have a choice of how you dispose of him. Is your choice to murder him?"

"I have no thought of murder in mind," said Guest.

"Then," said Sken-Pitilkin, "for the life of me, I cannot imagine what possessed you to make your father eat mud."

"Why shouldn't I?" said Guest. "I have defeated him, and he

should acknowledge as much."

"Yes," said Sken-Pitilkin. "But the manner in which you compel his acknowledgement is likely to make it impossible for the two of you to live in peace. If you push him too far, then he will rise against you, even if his resistance serves merely to ensure his own execution."

"How should I treat him, then?" said Guest.

"With affection," said Sken-Pitilkin. "With love. He is your father, after all."

"Love!" said Guest bitterly. "What love has he ever shown me? I saved his life, yet even then he showed me no love."

"You spared him," said Sken-Pitilkin. "Yet sparing a prisoner is but a casual convention of war. It is hardly love."

"No!" said Guest, with violence. "I saved him! In the river, the Yolantarath! Years ago!"

Sken-Pitilkin was taken aback by the Weaponmaster's vehemence. Was the young man losing his mind?

"Guest," said Sken-Pitilkin, "you forget yourself. It was not your father you saved. It was Eljuk. Your brother Eljuk."

"Eljuk!" said Guest. "No, it was my father. I saw the future, you see. There was my father, in the river, in the Yolantarath. He was drowning, Pitilkin. That's why I went into the water. I thought it was my father."

"But it wasn't," said Sken-Pitilkin.

"But I thought it was!" said Guest.

Sken-Pitilkin absorbed this, thought about it, then said:

"Well, Guest, whoever you thought you were saving, it was Eljuk you saved. And, anyway, your father offered you a reward for the saving. He was obligated. You could have asked for anything. But you chose to ask for a ridiculous trifle, a bauble of a title. You chose to be the Weaponmaster, which makes you a living joke, for all the world knows you to be the master of no weapon."

Thus did Sken-Pitilkin vent his scorn upon the Weaponmaster, hoping to break the young man out of his mood of bitter self-pity. For surely honest anger was preferable to such self-pity. But such was Guest's distress that he absorbed Sken-

Pitilkin's dire and unpardonable insult without so much as the flicker of an eyelash.

"I chose the title," said Guest, "because it was an ornament, a bauble, a trifle, a toy. But as for the larger things, like my life, say, like the woman Yerzerdayla — my father should have given these for love."

Now Sken-Pitilkin began to understand the depths of Guest's suffering. After saving his brother Eljuk, the boy Guest had not asked for any great thing by way of payment for services rendered, for he thought his father should give him the great things out of love. But his father had given him nothing.

Now that he knew as much, Sken-Pitilkin exchanged Guest Gulkan's company for that of his father.

"My lord," said Sken-Pitilkin.

"I'm no lord of yours," said the Witchlord Onosh. "You've thrown in your lot with my son. Will you be my executioner, Pitilkin? He'll have me killed in Gendormargensis."

"I've seen no sign of that," said Sken-Pitilkin.

"No sign!" said Lord Onosh. "I'm marching under guard, disarmed and dishonoured. Is that no sign of impending execution?"

"After war, my lord," said Sken-Pitilkin, cautiously, "a peace is best enforced by the disarming of one party to the conflict."

"Peace!" said Lord Onosh. "You call this peace? I call it defeat, yes, and bloody slavery."

"Was it slavery to be a judge at Ink?" said Sken-Pitilkin.

"Ink!" said the Witchlord. "The affair at Ink was a mere charade, a charade of justice."

"Was it?" said Sken-Pitilkin. "I think not. Rather, I think your son did you honour by making you an honest judge of an honest affair of law."

"You think me ambitious to be chief justice?" said the Witchlord irritably. "Don't toy with me, Pitilkin!"

"I think the fate of your family no toy to play with," said Sken-Pitilkin. "As you helped me in my time of need, so I—"

"You'll help me, will you?" said Lord Onosh.

"That is my wish," said Sken-Pitilkin, making a partial retreat into formality in the face of the Witchlord's undisguised anger.

"Then," said Lord Onosh, "if you truly wish to help me, then take that country crook of yours, and use your powers of levitation to send the boy Guest hurtling through the air till his head smacks crash against a treetrunk. Smash him, Pitilkin! Well. Will you? No. You've not blood, meat or marrow enough for murder. You are but a paltry pox doctor, and you bring me what every pox doctor brings — advice! Well, get on with it! Advise, and be gone!"

"My lord is kind to permit me the honour of advising him," said Sken-Pitilkin. "Let me then advise my lord to think back to a time when he went hunting bandits in the hills near Gendormargensis."

"They are not hills, Pitilkin. They are mountains."

"Hills. Mountains. Whatever. My lord went hunting. His son, his much-beloved Morsh Bataar, fell and broke his leg."

"And?" said Lord Onosh. "What do you want? You want reward for fixing the leg? If so, you've left it a little late in the asking!"

"It is Guest who won reward," said Sken-Pitilkin. "Though he could not swim, the boy risked his life in the Yolantarath. He risked his life to save his brother Eljuk."

"And was rewarded for it," said Lord Onosh.

"Yes, my lord," said Sken-Pitilkin, "But when you rewarded him, when you gave him the title of Weaponmaster, there was one thing you did not know."

"And what was that?" said Lord Onosh.

"When the boy went to the river," said Sken-Pitilkin, "he thought he was saving you. The boy had endured a vision. A vision in which you drowned. So when he saw a man in the river, he went to the water to save you."

"Save me!" said Lord Onosh, in rage.

"Why, yes, my lord," said Sken-Pitilkin, taken aback by the Witchlord's anger. "He wished to save you. What else would he wish?"

"He wished to murder me!" said Lord Onosh.

Then the Witchlord Onosh told the wizard Sken-Pitilkin of

his own precognitive vision. While hunting bandits in the high ground near Gendormargensis, the lord of the Collosnon Empire had endured a vision.

"It was death," said Lord Onosh. "My own death. Death by water. A death to take me, thrust me, haul me, suck me. Down in the quench, the smother, the groping slime, the dark. I was drinking, mind. Morsh and me, we had words in the old manner. Then Guest said, he mocked at Morsh and at me, and I knew."

"What did you know?" said Sken-Pitilkin.

"Why," said Lord Onosh, as if it should have been obvious, "I knew he was going to drown me, of course! Right there and then, I knew it! That's why he went into the river, you see. He thought it was me. He meant to drown me, Pitilkin!"

"But it wasn't you," said Sken-Pitilkin. "It was Eljuk. And when Guest saved Eljuk, why, he thought you should give him something."

"But I did!" said Lord Onosh. "I gave him leave to ask for a gift, and he asked. The title. Weaponmaster."

"But that was a trifle," said Sken-Pitilkin. "Another word for nothing. He let you satisfy your obligations with a trifle. That left you free to give him the larger things out of love."

"The larger things?" said Lord Onosh, with renewed irritability. "What are you talking about?"

"You could have spared him his duel with Thodric Jarl," said Sken-Pitilkin. "You could have given him the woman Yerzerdayla."

"But the boy had just tried to kill me!" said the Witchlord.

Now here was a pretty pickle! On the basis of a fleeting vision of the future, Guest Gulkan thought he should be honoured as his father's would-be rescuer. But, on the basis of another precognitive vision, Lord Onosh thought his son should be damned as a would-be murderer!

All of which made Sken-Pitilkin very glad that he himself did not personally suffer visions, whether precognitive visions or otherwise.

"My lord," said Sken-Pitilkin, attempting to feign a degree of diffidence. "It may well be that the men of your line have some talent to see the future."

"It is a proven fact," said Lord Onosh.

"Well, perhaps," said Sken-Pitilkin. "But plain logic proves the vision wrong. For, though you saw yourself drowning in the Yolantarath, the fact is that you remain undrowned."

"But Guest meant to drown me!" said Lord Onosh. "You see? You understand?"

"No, I don't," said Sken-Pitilkin, in frank confession. "These are meant to be visons of the future."

"Or visions of intent," said Lord Onosh. "One can see the future's facts or see the future's intent. Guest went to the river. That proves he had intent!"

Sken-Pitilkin was amazed that Lord Onosh, who had judged the case of the boat-sellers of Ink with such dispassionate acumen, could become so entangled in the coils of illogic when he confronted the affairs of his own family. Of course, every standard text on ethnology makes note of the vexed complexity of family affairs. And as an ethnological scholar, Sken-Pitilkin had long ago absorbed the lessons of such texts. But even so!

"You are uncommonly silent, Pitilkin," said Lord Onosh. "Have you run out of argument?"

"My lord," said Sken-Pitilkin, "it is a great many years since I was any man's son, and I have never been a father, so — but, ah! This looks to be Babaroth!"

And Babaroth it was indeed, and arrival at that settlement terminated the discourse between wizard and Witchlord.

As Witchlord and Weaponmaster entered Babaroth from the south, they were disconcerted to be met by dishevelled riders coming from the north. Some were wounded, all were weary, and they moved with the emphasis of men driven by urgent necessity. Know you this emphasis? All courtesy leaves a man. He becomes direct in his speech, as if every word were paid for in hammered gold. His speech is charged with import, as is that of a condemned man pleading a court for mercy.

Such were the men who entered Babaroth from the north, and Witchlord and Weaponmaster immediately knew — before they had heard so much as a word of the tale of these men —

that something dreadful had happened in the north.

When those men addressed Witchlord and Weaponmaster, they did so in Ordhar, not in Eparget. And this was another bad sign. The worst of signs! For Ordhar was the command language used by the Yarglat's subject peoples, whereas the Yarglat themselves spoke Eparget. Looking over that ragged band from the north, Witchlord and Weaponmaster saw none of the Yarglat.

"What is this?" said Guest, fearing that there had been a revolution by the underpeople. "Are you in arms against the empire?"

"My lord," said one of the Ordhar-speaking underpeople, "we are the empire! It is the Yarglat who have been making war upon us!"

Then both Witchlord and Weaponmaster began to understand what had happened.

Thanks to their disappearance into the mountains of Ibsen-Iktus, both Witchlord and Weaponmaster had now been gone from their empire for some time. As far as the Collosnon Empire was concerned, the Witchlord Onosh had disappeared from the realms of the visible creation during the summer, and had not been seen or heard of since; and it was now autumn.

Both Witchlord and Weaponmaster had presumed that the affairs of the empire had been, as it were, placed on ice during their absence, but this proved not to be the case.

For that small and tattered force of warriors which came riding into Babaroth from the north was the advance guard of a small and tattered army led by Bao Gahai, the Witchlord's dralkosh, who was retreating to the south in fear of her life. By nightfall, Bao Gahai herself was in Babaroth, and Witchlord and Weaponmaster had confirmation of her tale from her own lips.

A grim tale was Bao Gahai's.

As Witchlord and Weaponmaster pursued their civil war in the south, Gendormargensis had fallen to Khmar, a notorious marauder from the Yarglat homelands of the north. Khmar had taken advantage of the empire's disorders to invade from the north, and had conquered Gendormargensis without meeting with any substantial resistance at all.

"Now he comes south," said Bao Gahai, "and he will sweep us all the way to Stranagor, then cast us into the sea."

Here there is a hint that Bao Gahai may have spent some considerable part of her life in or around the seaport city of Stranagor. For, as has already been remarked, the casting of great numbers of the defeated into the sea has ever been a feature of Stranagor's iconography of war, whereas no such image features in the native idiom of the Yarglat.

"I take it," said the Witchlord Onosh, "that all of the Yarglat have thrown in their lot with Khmar."

"No," said Bao Gahai. "Not all. For a few of the Yarglat figure in the ranks of your own army here in Babaroth."

"It is not my army," said Lord Onosh, glancing at his son. "It is Guest's."

"So you have told me," said Bao Gahai. "But Khmar will kill the pair of you unless you make a peace between you."

"A peace!" said Lord Onosh. "How can we possibly make a peace? One must serve the other, and I would rather die than serve this — this thing with the ears of an ogre!"

"The ears are your own," said Bao Gahai. "The ears are your own, as the sperm was your own. Have you forgotten?"

Then Bao Gahai looked long and hard upon the Witchlord Onosh, and, to Sken-Pitilkin's amazement, the Witchlord bowed to Bao Gahai's judgement.

So it was that, in the face of the threat from Khmar, father and son made a peace, with the father agreeing to serve as a loyal subordinate to the son, and the pair of them withdrew to Locontareth with all their forces, arriving there late in the autumn.

Witchlord and Weaponmaster arrived in Locontareth just in time to save the dralkosh Zelafona and her dwarf-son Glambrax from being lynched by an irate public, for that pair had become notorious as commercial pirates. By their diligent commercialism, the two of them had first cornered the market in brewed acorns and roast rats; and by speculative enterprise they had then cornered the market in barley; and by virtue of owning the spoils of the autumn harvest they had made themselves masters of all the city's bakeries; and then had doubled the price of bread, then doubled it again.

Overcome by the success of their own folly, this pair of monopoly capitalists had then doubled the price of bread for one last and fatal time, and had been about to meet their mutual doom at the hands of a wrathful consuming public when rescued by Witchlord and Weaponmaster.

Having rescued this unrescueworthy pair, and having seized all barley in the city, and having given the wizards Zozimus and Sken-Pitilkin the responsibility for marketing both bread and barley at a fixed and reasonable price, and having thus won the love and affection of the people of Locontareth — or, more accurately, the subdued and potentially mutinous compliance of those people — the Witchlord and the Weaponmaster then settled themselves in that southern city, intending to gather their strength, and in the spring to attack Khmar and to reclaim the rule of the city of Gendormargensis and the Collosnon Empire as a whole.

But, of course, it was not going to be that easy.

CHAPTER EIGHTEEN

Khmar: a warrior of Yarglat birth and breeding who took
advantage of war between Witchlord and Weaponmaster to
invade the Collosnon Empire from the north. Adroit in his
timing, Khmar met no opposition from the capital's
garrison, since most Yarglat feared and hated Bao Gahai, the
dralkosh whom Lord Onosh had left in charge of the city. In
the Witchlord's absence, few Yarglat hesitated before giving
their loyalty to Khmar. So Khmar's conquest was virtually
bloodless, whereas his enemies were already weary with war,
their strength exhausted in the sanguinary encounters of the
south.

***

As Witchlord and Weaponmaster settled in to Locontareth, they
gave additional directions to the wizard Sken-Pitilkin, he whom
they had earlier charged with a half-share of the responsibility
for organizing the market in bread and barley. Sken-Pitilkin was
now to exert himself over the winter and build them an airship.

"For," said Guest Gulkan, "when you tutored me in
geography, you told me of volcanoes, those mountains which
spit forth fire, and which let fall upon the heads of men those
massive teardrops of rock which are known as bombs. It occurs
to me that, had we an airship, we could let fall similar bombs
upon the heads of our enemies."

"Yes," said Lord Onosh. "Had we such a ship, we could
defeat Khmar easily, by the sheer terror of the device if by no
other means."

"The terror, my lord," said Sken-Pitilkin solemnly, "is
suffered most greatly by those poor mortals doomed to fly in
such a ship. Having almost killed myself once, I am in no mood
to repeat such an experiment."

Guest Gulkan was secretly of like opinion, but nevertheless
favoured the project, thinking he could easily avoid all personal

involvement with experimental airships. Allied in their desire to rule the skies, Witchlord and Weaponmaster easily overruled Sken-Pitilkin's objections.

"I will give you any ship you want," said Lord Onosh, "and you will make it fly. You can have a barge, if you want, a barge taken fresh from the Yolantarath. Or — well, we have men from Stranagor in our forces, ships, fishing smacks, they build them all in Stranagor, and we can build likewise here. A ship which is apt for the fraughts of the Hauma Sea will surely be suitable for the skies."

"Give me no ship," said Sken-Pitilkin. "Give me, rather, the roof of the ruling hall of Locontareth, and I will make a ship out of that."

Thus spoke Sken-Pitilkin, hoping Lord Onosh would not want to sacrifice the roof of the ruling hall of Locontareth — that roof being a magnificent woodspan spread on which a thousand men could have been seated. By such stratagem, Sken-Pitilkin hoped to be spared from experiment.

"Do it," said the Witchlord, thus proving himself no connoisseur of woodwork. "Only make sure that it has the firm capacity to carry all my treasure chests."

"Your treasure chests, my lord?" said Sken-Pitilkin blankly.

"Yes, my treasure chests!"

Sken-Pitilkin was at first at a loss to know what treasure chests Lord Onosh was speaking of. So the Witchlord explained at laborious length, for he was proud of his treasure chests, which in his earlier days had more than once won him a crucial battle.

"For you see," said Lord Onosh, "when one army can pay its soldiers and the other cannot, gold will tip the scales when all else is equal."

And in satisfaction of Sken-Pitilkin's curiosity, the Witchlord mapped out the movements of his treasure chests. Laden with gold, with silver, with massy bronze and trinkets of tin, the imperial strongboxes had marched from Gendormargensis with the imperial army — though, needless to say, they had not marched with any legs of their own, but had borrowed the legs of ponies for the purpose.

Travelling always under the personal vigilance of the emperor, those chests had travelled to Babaroth. In that town, the chests had waited in loyal expectation of an imperial victory; and, Lord Onosh having been proved triumphant in his battle over Guest Gulkan, the strongboxes had joined the methodical pursuit which had brought them as far as Locontareth.

The Witchlord had shortly discovered that Guest Gulkan had slipped round behind him. So, leaving the strongboxes in the city under guard — for their weight was incompatible with the drama of a quick pursuit — Lord Onosh had sallied forth treasureless to smash Guest Gulkan. Thus the treasure had not been in the Witchlord's possession when his own army had ultimately been smashed at the high pass of Volvo Marp; and had still been safely under guard in Locontareth when the Witchlord had returned to that city in alliance with the Weaponmaster.

Thus the story of the treasure chests; and if you think it a long story, and a weary one, and one quite unnecessary for the performance of this history, why, then blame not the poor historian. Blame rather a nit-picking tradition of jealous and intellectually impoverished scholarship which lacks the ability to appreciate the grandeur of a full-scale historical tapestry, and therefore devotes itself to picking loose any undefended thread at the corner of such a tapestry.

Having thus defended this particular thread, let us return to the sagacious Sken-Pitilkin.

We find him hot in dialogue.

"But, my lord," said Sken-Pitilkin, who was reluctant to guarantee any airship fit to carry a great weight of lead, gold, silver, bronze and trinketing tin, "why should you want a weapon of terror to be able to carry your treasure chests?"

"Because," said Lord Onosh, "this weapon of terror is best to be a generalized weapon of war. So. Anything a horse can do, an airship must do likewise. That includes carrying treasure. Besides, what if Khmar attacked us unexpectedly. What if we had to flee in haste? What then of our treasure?"

"My lord jests," said Sken-Pitilkin, who had sufficient strategic wisdom to know that unexpected attack was out of the question, given the lateness of the season.

"I do not seriously expect attack," said Lord Onosh, in frank confession. "Nevertheless, I am of the Yarglat, hence may know more of the capacity of the breed than do you. Rule out nothing! Rather, prepare for all eventualities. Therefore — make ready!"

As has now been reasoned out at length, Lord Onosh had his treasure chests with him in Locontareth, and insisted that Sken-Pitilkin's flying roof be engineered so as to accommodate those chests. And so, with Lord Onosh having agreed to sacrifice the roof of the ruling hall of Locontareth to experimental science, the sagacious Sken-Pitilkin found himself on top of that roof the very next day, surveying it in the company of carpenters.

"How" said Sken-Pitilkin, "did I get myself into a mess like this?"

And, not for the first time, the sagacious wizard of Skatzabratzumon wished that he had abandoned the practice of wizardry to become a slug-chef like Zozimus.

On inspection, the carpenters concluded that the roof could easily be disconnected from the walls beneath it, so that Sken-Pitilkin, at some time of his own choosing, could launch that roof in the skies.

Thus Sken-Pitilkin set to work upon his airship; Pelagius Zozimus began a systematic exploration of the culinary possibilities of barley admixed with fish guts; the dwarf Glambrax and the dralkosh Zelafona began the great work of sweeping the streets of Locontareth as public penance for their earlier commercial predations; and Witchlord and Weaponmaster sat in counsel with the Rovac warriors Thodric Jarl and Rolf Thelemite, making preparations for the long winter ahead and the campaigns of the following spring.

But—

The Yarglat barbarian Khmar, the warlord who had swept down from the north to sweep up Gendormargensis, why, Khmar wasted no time on dalliance. As Lord Onosh had already half-suspected, outright war was not long to be avoided. Khmar was a master of mobility, and was in no mood to let his enemies enjoy the luxury of a comfortable winter. So, while Witchlord and Weaponmaster selected out their swansdown duvets, and chose the rose-petal pillows on which they planned to rest the buttocks of their concubines, Khmar launched himself upon a great assault.

Despite the lateness of the season, Khmar advanced downriver from Gendormargensis towards Locontareth, advertising his onslaught by sending heads floating down the river. Each of these heads was nailed to a small raft, and was mutilated in a manner suggestive of the fate which the conqueror Khmar intended to mete out to both Witchlord and Weaponmaster.

Now the Witchlord Onosh and his son Guest Gulkan were in a predicament, for Khmar had won the loyalty of Gendormargensis; Stranagor's loyalty was uncertain; and, though Locontareth was temporarily loyal, it was weak in the aftermath of the expensive campaigning which had accompanied the tax revolt.

Still, Lord Onosh and Guest Gulkan scraped up what troops they could, and began to organize their defence. Meanwhile, they sent patrols far up the river on both the northern bank and the southern. Thus they had good warning of Khmar's advance, for there was no way for that Yarglat to outflank a screen spread out so broadly and organized with such immaculate professionalism.

The news of Khmar's advance was all bad, at least as far as Witchlord and Weaponmaster were concerned. Khmar's army was large; its morale was good; and it gave a good account of itself in skirmishing with the patrols.

"There is only one thing for it," said Lord Onosh. "We must retreat."

"Very well," said Guest promptly. "Then let us pull back to Ibsen-Iktus."

Guest was beginning to have a certain degree of affection for those mountains, the scene of his notable victory over his father.

Guest hoped to lure Khmar into those frozen rock-realms, and there to inflict upon the invader a crushing defeat — a literally crushing rockslide defeat. But he was swiftly disabused of this notion.

"The mountains will be too cold this late in the year," said his father. "The snow will be deep on the heights already, and those heights impassable by the time he could reach them."

Whereupon Thodric Jarl came up with a somewhat extravagant scheme of manoeuvre. Jarl suggested that they retreat south towards Favanosin, and establish winter quarters for themselves; and then, in the spring, march east to the shores of the Swelaway Sea while Khmar sought them in the south; and then head down the Pig and take Gendormargensis before Khmar knew that they had slipped his clutches.

"The distances are so great and the communications so slow," said Jarl, "that we can be months fortifying Gendormargensis and recruiting men before Khmar even knows what we are about."

Furthermore, went on Jarl, once in Gendormargensis they might be able to send into the northern homelands of the Yarglat to rouse those wild Yarglat tribes which were the enemies of Khmar.

"Thus," said Jarl, "when Khmar finally arrives at Gendormargensis to challenge us, he will have been weakened by months of fruitless wandering, while we have a city and the strength to hold it."

There were a thousand flaws in this plan. Here is one such flaw: Khmar might have left a substantial army to hold Gendormargensis. Here is another: the logistic requirements of the march which Jarl proposed were close to impossible.

But nobody had a better plan.

"It gives us at least the chance of victory," said the Witchlord Onosh bravely, drawing on a lifetime's experience to give his best possible imitation of confidence, "which is better than running away."

So the Witchlord Onosh and his son Guest began planning for the withdrawal to the south, Guest's role in this planning mission being chiefly to say "yes" and "why not" and "I think that's an excellent idea". For, as the crisis deepened, Lord Onosh had by insensible degrees obtained an almost unconscious ascendancy over his son. This was only natural, for in his early manhood the young Guest Gulkan as yet lacked the experience to grapple with the full complexities of such a crisis, and his wizardly advisers were busy with the control of bread and barley, with the cooking of fish guts and the building of experimental airships.

As this planning got underway, Sken-Pitilkin asked permission to be relieved of his airship labours. But he was told, rather, to hurry himself and get the roof of the great hall air-mobile.

"For," said Lord Onosh, "if you can complete and perfect this terror-weapon, then we may yet defeat Khmar here at Locontareth."

Sken-Pitilkin was dubious, but he went to work regardless, and saw to the installation of a great many chairs on the top of the roof, and saw to it that the roof was detached from the walls in accordance with the carpenters' earlier advice, and so was ready to fly.

"How goes the work?" said Lord Onosh, two days before the army was scheduled to retreat south towards Favanosin.

"My lord," said Sken-Pitilkin mournfully, "much as I have been looking forward to this great experiment, I regret that the construction of this airship requires another season at a minimum."

This was a lie, for the thing was more or less ready to fly. But, though the airship was ready to fly, Sken-Pitilkin was not: in fact, every time he thought about it he broke out in a cold sweat. In proof of his native sagacity, the wizard Sken-Pitilkin had found himself an amenable donkey, and had loaded the brute with bags of barley, with a stash of opium and the answering opium pipes, with bundles of parchments and boxes of books, with a tent, with warm blankets, with foot-warmers, with sleeping bags, with spare pillows, with cushions, with a collapsible armchair, and with other gear of war, and so was ready to foot it towards Favanosin with the army. Though such a march would be harsh, and cold, and direly uncomfortable, Sken-Pitilkin would far rather risk the harsh yet certain dangers of such a withdrawal than chance the lunatic uncertainties of experimental flight.

"Another season!" said the Witchlord, scandalized.

"It is so, my lord," said Sken-Pitilkin mournfully.

"Then," said the Witchlord Onosh with a heavy heart, "we will have to abandon the experiment and retreat on foot."

And he went to supervise the final preparations for his army's plan to do just that.

But before Witchlord and Weaponmaster could move south with their army, Khmar attacked. Like a billion rabid rats assaulting a sack of sugar, like sharks in their blood-madness assailing a wounded whale, like a great gang of lawyers falling upon a law case, so in the rage of their onslaught did Khmar's brutal barbarians attack the city of Locontareth. Khmar's soldiers came over the city walls by night, using siege ladders and grappling hooks, and before the sentries were properly aware the entire city was filled with shadows which struck with steel and killed.

Before long, the city was burning, most of the fires being set by defenders who sought to stir confusion through arson, hoping to make their escape in that confusion.

But in the ruling hall of Locontareth there was no confusion, only a terrible haste, for under the direction of the wizard Sken-Pitilkin the final preparations for flying the roof were being made. Carpenters were checking that the roof was entirely severed from the walls of the hall; mighty warriors were risking the bursting of blood vessels as they winched the Witchlord's treasure chests to the heights; and other warriors were likewise trying to winch upwards Sken-Pitilkin's donkey.

To this scene came the Witchlord himself, in company with Pelagius Zozimus. In honour of the crisis, the slug-chef Zozimus had dressed himself in his famous fish-scale armour, perhaps hoping that he should at least make a well-dressed corpse. The armour reflected the fiery blaze of arson-struck buildings, blood-red and glowering. Padding along behind Zozimus came the dwarf Glambrax, with the sister-witches Zelafona and Bao Gahai bringing up the rear.

When the Witchlord saw Sken-Pitilkin's mightily laden donkey swinging upwards from a winchrope, he stopped short, as if hammered to a halt by thunder.

"What," said Lord Onosh, "is that?"

"It is a donkey, my lord," said Sken-Pitilkin.

"I know that!" said the Witchlord wrathfully. "But why in the name of blood are we wasting time trying to get the beast aboard?"

"Because, my lord," said Sken-Pitilkin, observing with some alarm the pendulum-like motion which had begun to affect his free-swinging donkey, "I have an earnest desire to test the effects of flight upon the physiology of the beasts of burden."

"Grief of gods!" said Lord Onosh. "What on earth for?"

"My lord wishes to employ this airship in war, does he not?" said Sken-Pitilkin, looking anxiously upwards at his much-burdened donkey.

"He does," said Lord Onosh, referring to himself in the third person, which is one of those grammatical idiosyncrasies commonly allowed to the great.

"Then," said Sken-Pitilkin, stepping backwards from the possible impact zone into which the donkey might fall should the winch-rope break, "my lord should share my interest in discovering whether a horse can survive transport by air, since the survivability of horses under such circumstances is vital for determining the degree to which the airship can be fully employed in war."

"But," objected Lord Onosh, moving backwards in step with Sken-Pitilkin, "that is not a horse but a donkey, and, being as overloaded as it is, it can be expected to expire of unnatural causes in any case, leaving aside all questions of airflight."

At which point the rope which had been struggling to sustain the donkey's weight happened to break, and the beast was precipitated downwards, miring a certain slugchef's armour with a great besplattering of fire-thawed mud. So the donkey died, thus becoming a martyr to experimental science.

And Sken-Pitilkin lamented its loss greatly, though the pressure of events meant that the grieving process did not have time to run its full course, for the wizard of Skatzabratzumon was tying himself into his specially designed flightmaster's seat long before he had had time to absorb the full implications of the loss of his donkey.

Others acted in likeminded haste, and so—

"My lord!" said Sken-Pitilkin. "We are ready to fly!"

"Ready!" roared Lord Onosh, still checking the chaining of his treasure chests, the padding of them, the bracing of the great logs which sustained them, and the torsion of the twisted ropes provided as back-up for their restraining chains. "We'll be ready when I'm ready, and not before!"

But at last the Witchlord was satisfied, and tied himself into his seat.

And so—

When the great Khmar battle-bulked to the door of Locontareth's ruling hall with a battle-axe in his hand, Witchlord and Weaponmaster were atop the roof with a complement of five hundred assorted wizards, witches, dwarves, bodyguards, scouts, soldiers, sub-chefs, carpenters, barley-factors and bootmakers.

One and all, they had tied themselves into the flight-seats with bits of rope and lengths of old chain, thus preparing themselves for adventure or death.

Meanwhile, down below—

Khmar threw down the door to the ruling hall of Locontareth and led the charge inside—

And the roof tore free with a scream of tortured wood. The roof tore free, and went spinning sideways, sliding over the city like a gigantic bat from the nether hell of Filch Molchops. Upwards it flew, spinning like a woodchip caught by a tornado. In flight it screamed, and most of its passengers screamed too. One chair broke free, and the carpenter who was strapped to that chair went flying away, snatched to his doom.

He was gone before he could scream.

Then the airship began wheeling downwards as fast as it had earlier gone upwards. Down it came. It slammed into snow, the early winter snow of Tameran. As the airship slammed, the greatest of the Witchlord's treasure chests burst asunder, and a full five men were instantly killed by the lethal catapulting of ingots of gold and lumps of tarnished silver.

So the airship slammed.

It slammed, and it bounced.

Like a stone skipping across water, so the roof bucked across the snows. Entire trees cracked like toothpicks beneath the down-slam of that roof. With a howl of incontinent breakage, the roof smoked through the night like an avalanche. A cottage unfortunately placed in the path of the experimental terror-weapon was smashed to smithereens, and all its occupants were reduced in an instant to so much cannibal jelly.

Then at last, with one glissading slide, the roof creamed smoothly across the snows, shuddered once, then halted. There was no sound but for the night wind, and the upbuck ruckus of vomiting as dozens of inexperienced air adventurers methodically chucked up everything they had eaten within living memory.

"Where are we?" said Lord Onosh, shakily cutting himself free from his seat.

"South," said Sken-Pitilkin. "South of Locontareth. I hope."

In fact, Sken-Pitilkin had grown a trifle disorientated while trying to navigate his hurling wooden batwing through the wilds of the night. But the wizard of Skatzabratzumon was nevertheless firmly of the opinion that they were indeed south of Locontareth, and probably south by a good few leagues. And in this he was ultimately proved right, and let this be noted as an additional proof of his sagacity, his scholarship, and his capacity for keeping a cool head under conditions of great stress.

"So we are south," said Lord Onosh. "Very well. Then let us be going, because I want to be far further south before the dawn."

Whereupon the rest of the air adventurers cut themselves free from their chairs. Then they would have fled, only Lord

Onosh was still tender of the security of his treasure chests, thinking to put his trust in bulk bullion now that he had so few men to his name. So scouting parties went out into the night to loot from the peasantry whatever horses, ponies, donkeys, mules, cows, bulls, pigs, dogs, wheelbarrows and carts could conceivably be used for the transport of treasure chests; and at last, as dawn broke, bleary-eyed over a clownish convoy of raucous disorder, the Witchlord and his people began their retreat to the south.

They were hoping, of course, to gain the road to the distant port of Favanosin, and thus to make a swift escape towards the sanctuary of foreign lands, and the safety of the southern shores of the continent of Tameran.

CHAPTER NINETEEN

Favanosin: a town which geographers believe to lie some 640 leagues from Locontareth along a southbound trade route which passes through territory long regarded by the Witchlord's regime as being hostile.

* * *

Immediately after the dramatic wreckfall of Sken-Pitilkin's flying roof, all was confusion, and the rest of the night was not much better. But, as day dawned, the Witchlord's forces began to fall into some kind of order.

"Grief of a dog!" said Rolf Thelemite. "My ear is torn!"

And indeed the Rovac warrior's left ear had been damaged, and his golden snake-serpent earring had been torn away altogether.

As Rolf Thelemite was lamenting the loss, the grey-bearded Thodric Jarl came up to him and addressed him in the Rovac tongue. Rolf turned pale, and thereafter ceased his moaning.

"What did he say?" said Guest, a little later.

"I cannot tell you," said Rolf Thelemite despairingly.

But Guest was able to deduce Rolf Thelemite's plight for himself. The unfortunate Rolf had sworn to kill Guest if Guest made war on his father — but had been untrue to his oath. Doubtless Thodric Jarl had told Rolf that he had more than a torn ear to worry about — and Rolf, an oath-breaker accursed of Rovac, had feared his imminent demise.

Guest shared his perceptions with the dwarf Glambrax, who agreed that Rolf was doubtlessly doomed.

"While we held the ascendancy," said Glambrax cheerfully, "Thodric Jarl would do nothing to disturb the peace between Witchlord and Weaponmaster. But now we are defeated, so there is no reason why he shouldn't disturb the peace as much as he wants."

So it was that the young Guest Gulkan and the dwarf

Glambrax deduced that their good friend Rolf Thelemite stood in danger of immediate murder.

"What can we do about it?" said Guest.

"Well, we could place bets," said Glambrax.

"An excellent idea!" said Guest. "I wager that Rolf lasts a week!"

"What then is a week?" said Glambrax.

"It is an uncouth measurement of days," said Guest. "A measurement devised by wizards, and arcanely used in their most secret histories."

"How many days?" said Glambrax.

"Why," said Guest, finding himself at a loss, "fewer than twenty, I think."

"You think!" said Glambrax. "For a wager, we have to know! I wager that Rolf lasts three days, not more."

"Then my money will see him alive for six," said Guest.

"What money?" said Glambrax. "Name a sum. And show me you have that sum in your pockets!"

Thus did the valorous Guest Gulkan and the sturdy dwarf Glambrax address the threat which faced the unfortunate Rolf Thelemite; and Rolf was never far from their thoughts in the days that followed.

As the Weaponmaster and the dwarf wagered on Rolf Thelemite's fate, the army from the air-wrecked roof made its way south, accompanied by an uncouth assemblage of baggage animals which were heavily burdened by the imperial treasure chests.

Of course, at the outset, that force numbered scarcely a half a thousand men; but whereas retreating armies are normally diminished by deaths, stragglings and desertions, this one grew — albeit not by much.

Everyone in Locontareth's defending army had known at least this much of the Witchlord's plan: that he intended to retreat south towards Favanosin. And Khmar, launched as he was upon a furious and unparalleled course of slaughter, gave every surviving defender the strongest of all possible incentives to join that retreat. For Khmar was making an example of

Locontareth, brutally punishing resistance to deter other cities (Stranagor in particular) from resisting him likewise.

Fearing the knives of the example-maker, those who escaped from Locontareth on foot or on hoof soon quested south, and some of these — inspired by an entirely reasonable terror of Khmar — managed to catch up with those who had escaped from the beleaguered city on a flying roof. So it was that, as they moved south. Witchlord and Weaponmaster enlarged their small army, until the balance between recruitment and desertions saw its numbers level out at just short of 600 men.

In the anxiety of the retreat, Lord Onosh found his son Guest uncommonly buoyant, and was hard put to place the reason. For had they not been defeated? Had they not been driven from the city? Had they not just lost a great empire? Did they not stand in fear of losing their lives? So was the boy drunk, or was he mad? Or had Sken-Pitilkin or some other been maliciously feeding him strong drugs unfit for human consumption?

On brief enquiry, the Witchlord soon discovered that the young Guest Gulkan was in high spirits because he had made himself the lord of a great gambling pool, and in concert with the dwarf Glambrax was fleecing lesser gamblers, winning wine, and money, and the favours of the army's few ragged camp followers, and extra rations into the bargain.

And the gambling did not concern the running of horses or the jumping of frogs — no, it concerned the date of Rolf Thelemite's murder!

Lord Onosh promptly summoned his wizards, the sagacious Sken-Pitilkin and the slug-chef Pelagius Zozimus. He explained what was happening.

"Why, my lord, it is all true," said Zozimus. "I myself am betting that Jarl will murder Rolf when we get to Favanosin."

"I think that optimistic," said Sken-Pitilkin. "I don't think Rolf will be murdered at all, at least not this year. I've bet that he won't be murdered till Midsummer's Day at the earliest."

"I will not have anyone murdered in my army!" said Lord Onosh, outraged. "You will halt this business of murder right away!"

"But, my lord," said Sken-Pitilkin. "Both Rolf and Jarl are Rovac warriors, and all such warriors are the natural enemies of wizards. Why should we then care if they kill each other off?"

"And besides," said Zozimus, "if we interfere in their mutual murders, it will give them excuse to band together and murder us."

"Which would be a great loss," added Sken-Pitilkin, "for, if rumour is true, my cousin Zozimus has just designed a new and delicious recipe for slugs, a recipe most pleasing to your palate."

"It is true," said Lord Onosh heavily.

Then the Witchlord dismissed his wizards and called for the witches Zelafona and Bao Gahai. After short discussion with the Witchlord, that pair of females took Thodric Jarl aside and had a long discussion with him. After which Thodric Jarl was seen to be looking uncommonly queasy for the next three or four days; Rolf Thelemite's spirits rose; and Guest Gulkan's ebullience ebbed as his gambling syndicate broke up, rumour having established that the fine sport of Rolf Thelemite's murder had been effectively terminated by a killjoy Witchlord.

Thus did the valorous Guest Gulkan and the sturdy dwarf Glambrax save their friend Rolf Thelemite from a certain death at the hands of the murderous Thodric Jarl; for it is certain that, had Guest and Glambrax not been so keenly apprehensive of their friend's impending murder as to encourage an entire army into gambling on the event, then Lord Onosh would not have been so swiftly and so decisively moved into terminating that threat.

With Guest and Glambrax thus entered into the ranks of friend-saving heroes, the lords of Locontareth escaped from the marauding Khmar and retreated with their army down the road to Favanosin, at first in disarray, but later in warlike formation, with vanguard ahead and rearguard behind, with scouts on the flanks and sentries posted nightly to vigil out the dark. They feared pursuit; and, as they distanced themselves from Locontareth, they also began to fear the violence of the south. The south was hostile to the Collosnon Empire, and there was no safe refuge there for a former ruler of Gendormargensis.

However, since the Witchlord Onosh had wisely extracted his treasure from Locontareth, his fugitive army had good gold to buy its necessities — or most of them, for the locals either did not have spare clothes to sell, or had them but refused to sell them. So the army rapidly grew ragged; for the speed with which the barbarity of thorns and the lubricity of mud can reduce a splendid army to a horde of ragged beggars is nothing short of amazing.

Though the army could not replace its increasingly tattered clothing, it was able to feed itself through purchase, hence had no need to pillage — and so was able to march far south without being forced to bring the natives to battle. But Lord Onosh soon realized that the southrons were arming in his wake; that a force of indeterminate strength was dogging his rearguard; and that the country ahead was being roused and wakened.

In the face of this uncomfortable knowledge, Lord Onosh held a council of war.

They were then in a forest which was heavy with the smoke of an army's campfires. They had halted early, because ahead of them was a small river. To continue, they must cross it: and people had been seen moving furtively on the other side. Thodric Jarl deemed it a good place for an ambush, for the far bank was steep. Hence they had halted for their council of war.

As they would go no further that day whatever the council's decision, Pelagius Zozimus had set himself to turn out a meal, and was presiding over a simmering cauldron from which there rose the most delicious smell imaginable. Near that cauldron, as if drawn there by the potency of its aromas, was a ragged assembly seated on fallen logs.

There was the Witchlord Onosh, dressed like a beggar in his refugee rags. The dralkosh Bao Gahai. The old but elegant witch Zelafona. The dwarf Glambrax, a belt of fifty scalps around his waist, whittling a flute from a human thigh bone with a wicked little knife. Guest Gulkan himself, the Weaponmaster in his glory. The Rovac warrior Rolf Thelemite and his murderous compatriot Thodric Jarl. The sagacious Sken-Pitilkin. And, of course, the slug-chef Zozimus himself.

"We have not troops sufficient to pursue our original plan," said the Witchlord.

"To get to Favanosin, you mean?" said Guest.

"No!" said his father. "Favanosin was but a ploy! Remember? Our original plan was to make a great arc to Gendormargensis, and seize that city while Khmar pursued us in the south."

"That was not our plan," said Guest. "That was Jarl's plan. Or your plan too, maybe, but never mine."

This was provocative, and Lord Onosh had to struggle mightily to control his temper. By then, the reversion of authority from son to father was more or less complete. By imperceptible degrees, Guest Gulkan had lost all authority, since he had proved lacking in the necessary skill, drive, diplomacy and decisiveness required to rule a crisis. While the Witchlord Onosh had busied himself with the organization of an army, his son the Weaponmaster had been embroiled in the ever-increasing complexities of institutionalized gambling, thus permanently discrediting himself in the eyes of hard-bitten veterans such as Thodric Jarl.

Ever since the hanging at Ink, Guest Gulkan had shown a tendency to shy away from absolute adult responsibility. And, after Witchlord and Weaponmaster had made an alliance at Babaroth, Lord Onosh had accelerated this tendency by deliberately minimizing Guest's involvement in all decisions — even those which might well have been within the young man's competence. As adult authority had passed from his hands, Guest had increasingly reverted to a childish irresponsibility which vexed his father sorely; and Lord Onosh showed unexpected strength of character in being able to control his temper in the face of his son's many provocations.

Avoiding the easy opportunity for uproarious argument, Lord Onosh now said:

"The plan, the original plan, was a feint towards Favanosin, followed by an eastward arc to Gendormargensis. We are now too weak to do any such thing. Yet even if we abandon hope of capturing Gendormargensis, I believe we must still turn east to have hope of safety. Let us make for the shores of the Swelaway Sea. Let us take passage to Safrak's islands. Let us there settle — or, if denied refuge by Safrak, let us take the trading route to the free city of Port Domax. So say I. Now what say you?"

There was silence, as if one and all were so battered by the successive shock of events as to have lost all powers of initiative and self-determination.

"Well," said Lord Onosh, with some impatience, and with a harshness which betrayed the stress he was under. "You have heard me speak. Must I parrot out the whole business three times over? Or have you opinions to submit? What is your counsel?"

As a child may sometimes feel over-burdened by adult responsibilities, so too may an adult; and, though Lord Onosh had long sought absolute power, in the difficulties of defeat he was finding the solitary burden of such power to be a weight most uncommonly difficult to bear.

"I say," said Thodric Jarl, speaking first since he thought all duties of battle were primarily his, "that we are in no state to fight our way to the south. Furthermore, what we know of Favanosin is written in smoke. None among our number has been there. Some say that ships from that harbour venture to Argan, to Ork, to Ashmolea, but nobody can vouch for this of a certainty. I believe more is known of Port Domax, though the knowledge belongs to others, not to me."

Sken-Pitilkin cleared his throat.

"Mighty is the wisdom of the Rovac," said Sken-Pitilkin, "and Jarl has truthed of Favanosin of a verity. All we know of Favanosin is that it clutches the sea's shore like a very whore's egg. But Port Domax — why, I've been there myself."

"Port Domax exists, certainly," said Pelagius Zozimus, denying Sken-Pitilkin the fullness of his intended oratory. "Sken-Pitilkin has seen it, and as for me — why, I once ran a small eatery in that very city. That was half a thousand years ago, true, but I've been there often enough since then. Its language is Toxteth; its business is trade; and the city is well-connected in enterprise with Safrak and Ashmolea, with Wen Endex and with the more southern parts of Yestron. I vote for Port Domax."

"If a witch can agree with a wizard," said Zelafona, who had the shortest voice of any in that council, "then I vote likewise."

"And I—" said Glambrax.

"Hush yourself!" said Jarl, "Nobody here asked opinion of a dwarf."

Guest Gulkan and Rolf Thelemite took that as a cue for violence, and so grabbed the dwarf and sat on him, though not without difficulty, for Glambrax was prodigiously strong for his size, and could have mastered either one of them in single combat.

"My sister speaks with reason," said Bao Gahai; and, though she had nothing new to add to the discourse, she reinforced the dignity of her own authority by rehashing at length all the arguments which had been so far presented.

"Well," said Guest, seated panting atop a struggling dwarf, "now we're talking sense, though I hope we find footing on Safrak. I've no wish to run to the Sea of Salt, assuming the thing to exist, so I'd far more happily settle on Alozay, or some such similar island. Khmar can't bring his horse against us, not there, whereas we, why, with time to spare we can — Glambrax! — we can — grief of gods, the thing's biting! — we can plan — Rolf! Get his head, man! — we can plan Khmar's destruction and — ya! — and think to brute back the empire. Gods! The thing's biting!"

"Obviously," said Lord Onosh, observing the course of Guest Gulkan's oratory, "the energy of the young and of the dwarves who play with them is truly prodigious in its optimism. Yet I think Khmar secure, and doubt that the empire's reclamation lies within our power."

"But the journey to Safrak does," said Thodric Jarl, rising to his feet, and so bringing their council to an end.

Thus on the following day the Witchlord's army turned east, making for the Swelaway Sea. And a hard going they had of it, what with the difficulties of the terrain, the lack of provisions, the squalor of mud, and the frosts and snows.

For they had all seriously underestimated the derelictions of the wilderness which lay between the road to Favanosin and the shores of the Swelaway Sea. In that wilderness, there was nothing to buy and there was nothing to pillage. There was frost, mire, muck, swamp and weather-hardened thorn. Now the army saw desertions in truth, and it had been reduced to a bare 400 men by the time it arrived at the Swelaway Sea in the snow-shod bleakness of a season of withered sun.

Ah, that winter! That snow! Even now, the mere memory of it tempts the chronicler towards an exercise in self-pity. Even now, the worst of dreams recall the bite of that season. The army had become a rat-rag troupe of beggars, of cripples and convalescents, of blank-staring refugees and muttering derelicts. The bellies of the greatest lords among them were sick with the desolations of hunger. Numb fingers and bone-poke ribs. Fumbling dreams. Hope-wreck and delusion. They were all in, finished, exhausted, their last resources gone.

Yet they reached the fresh water sea.

Here a memory, very clear and sharp. The Witchlord Onosh, seated on a lakeside boulder, with his knees to its flanks as if he were seated upon a horse. The dirt of unwashed fatigue crusted in the big, fat, deep and inexplicable gouges which track their way down his slanting forehead. The black of his eyes catching the grey depressions of the everstretch waters of that horizon-exceeding inland lake. He sits; watches and breathes; and the smoke of his breath dissipates in a silence unbroken by any sound saving that of the rasping fatigue of his lungs.

It is the silence which stands out in memory: the silence which oppressed that army as it first absorbed the stare-stretch impact of the presence of so much water. For his own part, the Witchlord thought that everstretch of grey a very monstrosity in its insolence. Surely there should not be so much water in the world.

Though the vastness of the Swelaway Sea was but a commonplace matter to Guest, since he had grown well acquainted with it during the time of his exile on Alozay, never in all his life had Lord Onosh seen either this freshwater sea or the far greater Sea of Salt which was said to exist on the borders of the continent which contained his empire. For, though Lord Onosh had supervised the enforcement of law and taxes in the seaport city of Stranagor, he had always done so from Gendormargensis. And, though the Weaponmaster was said to have been born in Stranagor, the Witchlord had never been to that seaport, and knew no more of the Hauma Sea than he did of the Sea of Salt or this present freshwater sea.

"It is a dream," said Lord Onosh.

Who was so fatigued that fragments of dream were ever spilling into his reality. Unpleasant fragments, for the most part. The heads of horses. Bloody blades. And—

Even as Lord Onosh sat there upon his horse, a dream reconfigured the world in fancy's fashion. Blood-red hairs sprouted from the glabrous glaciations of the lake. Oozing and creaming, a slow-headed slug in the fullness of its monstrosity—

The Witchlord dismounted from his rock.

"Wa," said Lord Onosh, shaking the dreams out of his head.

Then, bootstep by bootstep, he crunched across the thin and narrow lakeside beach, his weight bearing down on smallstone and shellbreak. He kicked a stone into the lake, and was splashed for his pains.

"It is real," said Lord Onosh.

It was real, and it was cold. The entire Swelaway Sea seemed one vast sink of cold. The lake was fringed with a lacing of frozen ice; and, indeed, knowledgeable geographers aver that only the underground upspout of hot volcanic water keeps the lake in its entirety from freezing to a single block of ice in the rigours of Tameran's continental winter.

The Witchlord Onosh took off the battle-gauntlets which he had worn for days. With his bare fingers, he picked up a fragment of ice. He held it up to the watery sun then discarded it to the water. The ice sliced into the water with a clean-slick splash. Plunged. Then upfloated. Lord Onosh stooped to the water, cupped his hand, dipped for water, and drank.

"It is sweet," said Lord Onosh. "It is bitter cold, but it is sweet."

Then the Witchlord filled a drinking horn with water and jangling ice, and passed it round that others might drink thereof. The horn came last to Sken-Pitilkin.

"It is sweet," said Lord Onosh, watching as Sken-Pitilkin drank. "Sweet. Is it not?"

"It is, my lord," said Sken-Pitilkin.

"Yet you have told me a thousand times if you have told it me once that the sea is not sweet but salt."

"I meant not this sea, my lord."

"Then what sea?" said Lord Onosh.

"He meant the true sea," said Bao Gahai.

"The true sea?" said Lord Onosh.

"He meant that real sea of salt which girdles the entire world," said Bao Gahai. "This is not that true sea."

"No?" said Lord Onosh. "Then what is it? Something I have conjured from dream for my own self-delusion?"

"The Swelaway Sea is but an over-large lake, my lord," said Bao Gahai.

"Lake!" said Lord Onosh. He looked across the waters. The distant horizon promised nothing but an eternity of water. "This so large yet you call it a lake?"

He knew it, he had heard it, he had been told it a thousand times, yet in the face of the fact he found it hard to believe.

"The true sea is larger yet," said Bao Gahai. "In the true sea, my lord, there are storms which maul the shores and tear from the cliffs rocks which are larger than houses. In the true sea, my lord, the kraken uprises from the lurching depths, and swallows down ships in their entirety. In the true sea, my lord, there live birds which never rest but which fly eternally, born and dying on the wing. That is the true sea, compared to which this is but a little cup of nothing."

Lord Onosh closed his eyes, squeezed hard, dismissed the visions Bao Gahai had conjured, then opened his eyes again. There lay the Swelaway Sea, grey and placid, a pool of ominous quiescence. Lord Onosh felt the grey eternities of water sapping his will, and had a premonition that he would die here. Not quick death clean, not death made battleaxe, but death made slow, death made a bone-picker, death dragged out over years. The Witchlord envisioned himself picking his way along the beach in his rags, picking his way in the wind and the rain, eating spoilt eggs half-formed into birds, eating the udders of rats and the bellies of worms, his very name in time forgotten by his own tongue.

He shuddered.

Upon the beach of that bleak and barren lake in the heartland of Tameran, there were shells of a bleached blue fringed with the last traces of violet. Lord Onosh had no name to specify the particularity of these shells, just as he had no name for the foreign waterbird which he saw briefing its way across the sky. This was a place without language, a place of utter desolation.

"Yet rock is still rock and water still water," said Lord Onosh.

"My lord," said Thodric Jarl, interrupting the Witchlord's extended personal confrontation with the realities of the freshwater sea. "My lord!"

Grey beard, grey hair, grey eyes — Jarl, unkempt and derelict after the rigours of the march, his features seamed with dirt and his eyes shot through with blood, why, Thodric Jarl right then looked like a very prophet in the grip of revelation. It was then the winter of the year Alliance 4307, and Thodric Jarl was but 27 years of age, yet such was the battering which this warrior had taken that he could easily have passed for 50.

"My lord!" said Jarl.

"Yes?" said Lord Onosh, squaring off against this fevered prophet, and bracing himself to receive commands from the gods, or a great diktat concerning the conduct of affairs amidst that living death which we call life.

"My lord," said Jarl, "I have for my lord's inspection the first spoils of our latest conquest."

So spoke the Rovac warrior, solemnly displaying a double handful of water-snails for his liege lord's inspection.

For, after the initial silence which had struck the army as it contemplated the lake, Jarl had got busy with practical investigations while his emperor was still indulging himself in metaphysical despairs.

"We can eat these?" said Lord Onosh, making a dubious inspection of Jarl's wet and somewhat slimy trophies.

The Witchlord Onosh, disturbed in his moody philosophizing, tried to sound enthusiastic about the dripping molluscs heaped in the swordsman's calloused hands, though in truth he resented the brusque commonsense intrusion of this Rovac mercenary.

"Can we eat them?" said Jarl, half-echoing his emperor. "One would presume so." Then, as Lord Onosh turned back to the lake: "One would presume they might make a very good meal, my lord."

Lord Onosh saw that he was not going to be left alone to meditate on the derelictions of his fate. He was a lord of men, after all, albeit a lord of defeat, and such a luminary has certain responsibilities, even in the dampness of his extinguishment. Lord Onosh noted that Guest had made no move to give any orders.

"Zozimus!" said Lord Onosh, rousing his voice to the challenge. "Come here! Come here, and pronounce upon on our scavenging!"

His chef came hurrying over to examine the spoils of Jarl's lake-plundering.

"This is the water snail Mabarakorabantibus Dontharpis," said Zozimus, holding a sample to the light. "Or so the beast is named in the Ilapatarginath system of taxonomy, though it is known elsewhere as the edible helmet. It is of wide distribution, and even occurs on the shores of the Araconch Waters, where Barglan of the Empire once made a notable feast of the things."

Such was the loquacity of Pelagius Zozimus when he was showing off. It was truly amazing that the Witchlord Onosh stood still for such nonsense; and, indeed, to move from specifics to generalities, it is amazing how a mere slug-chef can always and ever so easily and so impudently command so much of the time of his lord and master, when a scholar can scarcely get a hearing at all. Zozimus commanded the Witchlord's time as if it were his by right; and Lord Onosh listened to Zozimus with the patience of a very rock.

Then:

"So," said Lord Onosh, weighing one of Jarl's lake-morsels in his hand, "we can eat these."

"We can, my lord," said Zozimus. "Furthermore, the water weed which grows from the rocks is also edible."

And you can bet all the gold in your pockets, and bet your favourite slave as well, and your wife, and your mother-in-law's walking stick, that Zozimus went on to name that weed, and to mention five or six occasions on which the cookery of that weed had been well received, and to state a dozen recipes for its preparation — for when the show-off mood was upon Zozimus there was no stopping him.

"So far, so good," said Lord Onosh, when he had absorbed great quantities of this advice. "Snails and water weed. Very well. But I warrant it would still make a thin meal."

"True, my lord," said Zozimus, grabbing Glambrax by the ear, "but it would go very well with some dwarf."

At that, the dwarf kicked and struggled so much that Zozimus had to let him go. But such was the cunning of the slug-chef's timing that the dwarf, impelled by the violence of his own efforts to escape, rolled over and over and plunged into the crackle-ice sweetwaters of the Swelaway Sea. He struggled out, cursing, and immediately went on the attack with tinder and flint, striving to make himself a fire.

"As you can see," said Zozimus, observing the dwarf's prompt success, "we have fire already. We will shortly also have fish."

Then Zozimus produced from his robes a vial of something he claimed to be fish poison.

"Do you always travel with such?" said Lord Onosh in astonishment.

"But of course, my lord," said Zozimus blandly.

And poured the stuff upon the waters, where it worked as smoothly as a miracle, for very shortly there were any number of dead fish belly-up and gaping.

Thus the Witchlord Onosh came to the shores of the

Swelaway Sea with the ragtag remnants of his army, and the sea provided for him fish, and waterweed, and the snails to flesh out the meal, and so a banquet was had.

When the banqueting was done, talk turned to the future.

"The question now," said Thodric Jarl, "is how we conquer the Safrak Islands."

"Pardon?" said Lord Onosh.

"My lord means conquest, does he not?" said Jarl. "Surely he did not bring us all this way just for the pleasure of poisoning a few fish and watching a dwarf make vomit of them."

So spoke Jarl, casually dismissing their dead, their defeats, their retreats, the pangs being suffered by Glambrax (who had grossly over-indulged himself by eating the eyes from the head of each and every fish which had gone towards the feeding of an entire army) and all the sundry embroilments of the catastrophic nightmare which they had so recently and so strenuously lived through.

"One considers," said Lord Onosh, choosing his words carefully, "one considers that the wetness of the Swelaway Sea has certain implications for our future actions. I scarcely think to ride to battle across the waves, nor do I think the seizure of a few boats would do us much good beneath the invincible cliffs of Alozay."

"My father has spoken well," said Guest Gulkan. "The Safrak Islands are defended beyond all possibility of conquest."

"Then what does my lord intend?" said Jarl. "Are we to retreat to Port Domax, as was earlier suggested? Or what?"

"It is said that the Safrak Islands are but scantily populated," said Lord Onosh, "and that Molothair is a city largely deserted. I will treat with the lords of Alozay, and will seek to hold one of the minor islands in fief, paying for the privilege. There we will house our people and make our future."

"I think," said Thodric Jarl, with a suggestion of a growl giving a hard edge to his wisdom, "that such privileges will not be lightly bought."

"The wealth of Gendormargensis is with us," said Lord Onosh. "We do not come empty-handed, and our embassy will say as much."

Then Lord Onosh dispatched scouts to seek along the shores of the lake for a boat, and when the scouts had been successful the Witchlord then sent ambassadors to Safrak, their mission being to negotiate the purchase of an island where the Witchlord might settle with the remnants of his army. The ambassadors were Hostaja Sken-Pitilkin, the witch Zelafona, and Guest Gulkan, for these three had a knowledge of Galish, which tongue was alien to the Witchlord's lips.

All through the journey to Alozay, Sken-Pitilkin drilled Guest Gulkan ruthlessly in the Galish tongue, seeking to awaken that learning which had been hammered into the boy's head in earlier days. But the task was difficult, for the approach to Alozay saw Guest ever slipping away into dreams of glory.

For Alozay, of course, was the home of Icaria Scaria Iva-Italis, a demon incarnate in a huge block of jade-green stone. During Guest's earlier exile on Alozay, that demon had tempted the boy, promising that he would be granted the powers of a wizard if he would only consent to quest to the far-distant city of Obooloo, and in Obooloo to liberate the Great God Jocasta from the Temple of Blood.

Thus, while journeying to Safrak's ruling island, Guest Gulkan dreamt mightily of demons, and of Great Gods, and of wizardhood, and of future glory.

Sken-Pitilkin, Zelafona and Guest Gulkan were received at Alozay by Banker Sod, the Governor of the Safrak Bank, who allowed them into the mainrock Pinnacle. The pale-skinned iceman chose to interrogate them in his office, which was adorned with the shields of the Toxteth-speaking mercenaries of the Guardians. Upon those shields were painted glowing scenes of bloody decapitations — and worse.

A very miracle of luxury was that office, warmed with braziers and furs, and in their reduced condition the Witchlord's ambassadors were at first hesitant even to seat themselves. But Sod commanded them into chairs; and set mulled wine before them; and had hot chestnuts served to them; and then, seeing the gnawing hunger which obsessed them, saw to it that they were served with hot bread, and soup thick with onions and garlic.

"Well," said Sod, when his visitors were done with their eating. "Are we pleasured? Are we sated?"

"My lord has been most hospitable," said Sken-Pitilkin.

"Yes," said Sod. "Particularly considering that you have given me cause for hostility rather than hospitality." Then the pale-skinned iceman endeavoured to skewer Sken-Pitilkin with the bright-staring gaze of his yellow eyes, and bared his yellow teeth in something reminiscent of a dog's aggression, and said: "Hostility, yes, for when you were last in the precincts of my Bank, you caused considerable distress. You precipitated a fight. Or was it you?"

With that, Sod turned his skewering attention from Sken-Pitilkin to Guest Gulkan.

"That was no precipitation of mine," said Guest. "That was Jarl, Jarl did the fighting, on account of some precipitation between himself and yourself."

"Yes, well," said Sod. "What did he tell you of that?"

Guest searched his memory, for it was long since he had discussed that subject with Jarl.

"Jarl says," said Guest, slowly, "that he saw you last in Chi'ash-lan. He presumes you to be hiding here with a mighty price upon your head, which would explain the violence of your reaction to his recognition of you."

"Has it occurred to you," said Sod, "that if I do truly wish to keep my presence here a secret, I might do well to encompass your death, and to send out agents to slaughter down Thodric Jarl as well."

"I think you not so stupid," said Guest. "Since last we left this place, why, Jarl and myself, we've been to Ema-Urk and the Ibsen-Iktus, the mountains, we've been to Babaroth, to Locontareth, to half the places in between. Even as we sit here, the story of our travels echoes-down the roadway. We in our courage have entered into epic, and the sagas will sing us famously a thousand years from hence."

"The boy speaks in truth," said the dralkosh Zelafona. "My

sister Bao Gahai herself interrogated the warrior Jarl in depth, and heard from him all that is known of your history. It is a mighty great mystery, you being here, given the vastness of space which separates Chi'ash-lan from Safrak. Still, here you are, and all the world knows it, and if you had hoped to keep the matter a secret then you are far, far too late."

"If a wizard may agree with a witch," said Sken-Pitilkin, "then let me speak in support of Zelafona. For I myself discussed this mystery with Ontario Nol."

"I know him not," said Banker Sod.

"Ontario Nol," said Sken-Pitilkin, slipping effortlessly into his lecturing mode, "is the abbot of the monastery of Qonsajara. He dwells in the heights of those mountains known as Ibsen-Iktus, and Guest Gulkan's brother Eljuk dwells there likewise, living as apprentice to the master. The pair of them have had your story in detail, and will keep it fresh in memory for a generation or more. Thus has your privacy been betrayed, and permanently."

Sod sighed.

"So," said Sod. "It has happened. We must hope that no harm comes of it. Very well. To return to our muttons ..."

Then Banker Sod, the Governor of the Safrak Bank, negotiated with the emissaries who had come to speak for the Witchlord Onosh.

The negotiations proved surprisingly easy.

The final agreement was that Safrak would allow Lord Onosh to hold in fief the minor island of Im-skim-patorta, providing he paid for the privilege. Lord Onosh was invited to bring his men to the hot springs at Spradley Rock, and there to prepare himself and his men for a banquet, and then to proceed to the island of Alozay for that self-same banquet and the formal signing of a treaty which would enshrine the terms of this agreement.

Guest and the other ambassadors gladly took this agreement back to the Witchlord Onosh. A fleet of fishing boats accompanied them, for Sod had decided to be generous in providing transport; and he was generous also with the dispensing of bread, and onions, and garlic, and sacks of barley. So it was that, some days and several excellent meals later, the Witchlord and his men found themselves upon Spradley Rock.

Spradley Rock was the least of the Safrak Islands, excepting for a few nameless rocks, and it was a place of no great consequence, being as it was no more than a low-lying and industriously rockgardened outcrop of geology featuring much sand and many hot springs.

It was then deep winter, and on most days the cold and blighting winds were sweeping the Swelaway Sea with the bitterness of sleet, yet the winter weather was fine and blue when the Witchlord Onosh and his company came to the hotspring waters of Spradley Rock, and those hotspring waters were unstinting in their welcome. Green were the pools of those waters, green fringed with iron-brown and yellow, and the smell of sulphur was heavy on the air as luxuriating steam uprose in clouds so plentiful that they suggested the island to be in the process of volcanic eruption.

The witches Zelafona and Bao Gahai were allowed a small and isolated pool of their own, while the men piled into the greater waters, where they washed away the blood of battles, the muck of the horseplains, fishscales and cockroaches, beetles and slugs. Bulked huge within their heapings of wool, of furs, and of sundry rags, the men had looked like great bears, but once stripped down to their skins they proved painfully thin and meagre.

Now the Yarglat do not usually take baths, considering the womb's nine-month bloodbath to be washing sufficient to last any man for a lifetime; and, furthermore, there is among the Yarglat a strenuous taboo which forbids one man to be seen naked by another. Yet when the Witchlord Onosh commanded universal bathing, he was not disobeyed; for the Yarglat had largely deserted his army, leaving him with a force comprised of the Rovac, of the Sharla, and of representatives of sundry other peoples.

Besides, the men of that company were so far from their former lives that they might as well have found themselves in a different world entirely, and so they adapted to new customs with the ease of those who have been killed and reincarnated.

Many strange things were revealed in those pools, such as scars, and boils, and ulcers, and Rolf Thelemite's third nipple, and the fact that Morsh Bataar had not one omphalos but two. Revealed too were a great many tattoos, most of them being of uncompromising obscenity. But the most obscene and grotesque sight you ever did see in your life was Pelagius Zozimus, he of the withered neck and the spindly shanks, he with the skin clinging close to his ribs and a revolting little slug-pot of a beer belly bulging from his abdomen, he with his stick-thin arms from which the muscles stood out like knobbly tumours.

In the deepest and hottest of the pools of Spradley Rock, Guest Gulkan scrubbed his father's back with sand, while listening to the cackling laughter from the pool where the two witches soaked themselves. From somewhere came a shout of male outrage followed by the evil chuckle of the dwarf Glambrax — then by a riotous whooping pursuit, and then at length a very cold splash as expedient justice was administered to a delinquent mannikin.

Then arose a very strange sound, much like a drunken dog serenading in competition with a wildcat. This curious sound was that of Pelagius Zozimus in the act of singing. At least, Zozimus thought he was singing: though in that he was doubtlessly in a minority of one. This bravura performance by the slug-chef Zozimus can only be compared to that of the skavamareen; and if you know not what a skavamareen might be, then please note that it is best compared to a wizard of Xluzu in his musical passages.

An army of Yarglat barbarians would have lynched Zozimus immediately, but lesser peoples such as the Sharla and the Rovac are more tolerant. While Zozimus was thus caterwauling not one single word of complaint came from anywhere among that whale-lazy multitude of simmering barbarians; and from this it may be known of a certainty that the Witchlord's army had entirely lost its fighting spirit.

Though he was of Yarglat birth, Guest Gulkan shared in this general tolerance, and so instead of rushing for his sword and decapitating the delinquent Zozimus, Guest kneaded the bones of his father's vertebrae with handfuls of sand, while the bloodflush heat soothed away the rigours of the long retreat from Locontareth.

Thus it was that the last rigours of the winter-weather retreat were eased away on Spradley Rock. On that island, a great languor came upon the Witchlord's warriors as they relaxed in the balm of the great heat, while clouds of steam ascended to those greater clouds of white which hung suspended in the clear and limitless blue of a clearwind winter's day.

Yet, as Guest soothed away the horrors of the past and prepared for the future, he could not suppress a certain unease about that future. For, under the terms which Safrak had imposed upon Lord Onosh, his company must surrender its weapons before taking itself and its treasure to the mainrock Pinnacle to indulge in the banquet which would precede the signing of a treaty and the handing over of that treasure; and Guest did not at all like the idea of being without his sword.

Still.

With bathing done, he got out from the water and dressed himself in the clean linen which Safrak had so kindly provided for the Witchlord and his men. How Safrak had come up with clothing for so many at such short notice was a mystery, but the feat had been managed.

As Guest and the other warriors rose from their bath, the sagacious wizard Sken-Pitilkin descended to the waters, hoping to have a private bath in the luxury of undisturbed peace. Only now did he realize that, by waiting, he had made a grievous error — for it would be quite some time before the fair island of Spradley recovered from this invasion. The pools which had formerly been clear and clean were now stewpots of murk topped with generous heapings of foaming scum, and layered at the bottom with a thick sediment of dead lice, parboiled fleas and other wildlife. Indeed, the water had turned the most putridly bilious mix of blue and green, for all the world as if a battalion of drunkards had taken turns at vomiting into it.

Nevertheless, Hostaja Torsen Sken-Pitilkin made the best of it, and washed his pallor (natural to one born in Galsh Ebrek, where the Yudonic Knights tend to be pale in the absence of sun, their native colour being if anything the pink of their blood), and found himself flushed to an uncommon red by the heat of the water, for all the world as if he were a very Ebrell Islander in his breeding.

Then Sken-Pitilkin joined the others in putting on clean linen. He found the company changed to a truly imperial splendour. Each of its members looking a good ten years younger now that the muck, filth and stale battle-sweat had at last been washed from their faces.

Then that great company took itself off to the island of Alozay in a fleet of boats, most of which had been provided by the Safrak Bank. When they reached that island, they ascended the mainrock Pinnacle by great winch-baskets of creaking wickerwork, which were hauled up from the docks by ropes.

Lord Onosh had found five mountaineers to survey the mainrock Pinnacle, though he had found them with difficulty, for the sport of mountaineering had long been outlawed in the Collosnon Empire as a reckless abomination — and quite rightly so, for it is entirely unnatural, this business of crawling like a beetle up great mounds of rock, and kicking down boulders to bash in the skulls of one's fellows (which amusement is one of the principal attractions of mountain climbing as practised by the Yarglat, for they climb in a competitive fashion, and count themselves unsatisfied if they finish their mountain without nine in ten of their number having met their deaths upon its slopes). The mountaineers pronounced the approach to the main-rock Pinnacle to be difficult in the extreme, for the heights overhung the docks, and there were no chimneys by means of which a climber could easily ascend to those heights.

Lord Onosh chose to be winched upwards in the company of his mountaineers, so their reports were delivered to him privily while he and his climbers were safe in the isolation of their creaking wickerwork.

Then they got to the top, and found that the great winch-baskets had been dragged to the heights by bluff and hearty washerwomen working a windlass. Lord Onosh was dismayed to realize that his life had been entrusted to something as weak as a woman. But these women were like unto bears, for in truth the strength of your average washerwoman is nothing short of marvellous, for she spends all day thumping and pummelling, and hefting great burdens of wet and dripping wool. Thus some washerwomen of prodigious strength feature nobly in the myth-cycle concerning the ancient war between men and women, and the greatest of these washerwomen was Bilch.

According to legend, the washerwoman Bilch was of such great strength that she once split the skull of an apprentice boy with a single blow from her open hand, and split it with such violence that his eyes flew a full seventy paces in different directions, and his upper teeth were propelled downward into the rock where they buried themselves to the depth of a spear, and his lower teeth were hurled upwards with such a great velocity that they slaughtered a flight of sparrows, so that Bilch stood victorious over the apprentice boy with a great rain of dead birds falling all about her.

Whether this is true or not — one suspects some slight degree of exaggeration may have coloured the facts — it is nevertheless a firm fact that the strength of washerwomen has become legendary for the best of all possible reasons. Each of them has the muscles of a very bear-wrestler, and a man may trust himself to the strength of those muscles in good conscience, whether in bed or out of it.

But we recall that Lord Onosh was but a Yarglat barbarian, and hence he was ignorant of the world's great literature, and in particular he was ignorant of the story of Bilch, and so was dismayed to find himself being hauled to the heights by mere women, and washerwomen at that.

Nevertheless, the Witchlord's anxieties passed once he reached those heights.

But the anxieties of his son were redoubled, for the Toxteth-speaking Guardians were everywhere, and their weapons were sharp, and Guest sensed them to be in a mood for war, and he was more uneasy than ever to find himself in such company with his own weapons lacking.

Still, all began well. Rooms had been prepared for the guests, including a big strongroom in which they could store their treasure chests. A guardroom adjoined that strongroom, so the Witchlord's most trusted boxers, wrestlers and bone-breakers could sit in guardianship of that treasure. With gold thus secured, the banquet began, and began well, and went along swimmingly till late into the night.

By which time Pelagius Zozimus had got very drunk, and was regaling all and sundry with a number of stories which he found intensely amusing, such as the tale of how he had once accidentally poisoned his companions with an ill-chosen fungus — a story which was not by any means amusing to those who had had to live through that near-catastrophe!

Nevertheless, the assembly received such stories in the best of all possible humours.

And, late in the night, as the banquet began to break up, all who were still sober enough to display any emotion whatsoever seemed still in excellent humour. Lord Onosh left early, saying he must check on his treasure then get to bed, for he was not as young as he used to be; but Guest sat long at the table with Zozimus and Sken-Pitilkin, and with the witches Zelafona and Bao Gahai.

And it seemed to Sken-Pitilkin — who had not joined the incautious Zozimus in overindulgence — that their hosts were uncommonly attentive in watching over wizards and witches alike, as if fearing that Lord Onosh might use these practitioners of power to make some move against the security of the mainrock Pinnacle and the integrity of the Safrak Bank; and Sken-Pitilkin began to feel increasingly uneasy himself, and hoped that he would not find himself falling a victim to the paranoia of Bankers.

CHAPTER TWENTY

Damsel: daughter of Banker Sod (the Governor of the Safrak Bank). In appearance, she shares some of her father's attributes: pale skin heavily larded with white body-hair, golden eyes and golden teeth, a thicket of golden hair upon her head, and fingernails of jet black. But she has other attributes of her own which are most definitely female. Her perfume, for example, which suggests more the flesh than the flower. This comely lass is, in the Weaponmaster's estimation, seriously infatuated with the said Weaponmaster, and urgently desirous of making his erotic acquaintance.

* * *

Early in the evening, the young Weaponmaster Guest Gulkan was seated with his brother Morsh Bataar on one side and the Rovac warrior Rolf Thelemite on the other. But Morsh made an early night of it, and Rolf drank so strenuously that he slid under the table at about the same time, and was removed by diligent servants.

In his loneliness, Guest was joined by Damsel, the daughter of Banker Sod. He had seen her from a distance during his earlier sojourn on Alozay, when she had been but newly nubile. Then, she had been rumoured as a virgin; but her matured confidence made Guest disinclined to think her a virgin any longer.

Damsel was like her father Sod in that she was a pale-skinned person of iceman race, with black fingernails and thick white bodyhair, with the hair of her head bright in its gold, with her eyes yellow and her teeth being of a matching lustre. A strange combination! Yet, after long deprivation, Guest found her comely indeed.

These two lasted out the length of the banquet together, by which time Guest had come to the conclusion that Damsel was seriously infatuated with him, and was urgently desirous of making his erotic acquaintance. Therefore Guest did not resist too strenuously when at last Damsel of the buxom buttocks suggested he might like to take a break from his social exertions by resting himself on her bed.

Soon he was in her boudoir, testing the warm honey between her thighs. Perched upon his body, she oiled and oozed, gasped and clutched, and then — greatly to his disconcertment — squealed like a mouse in agony.

Had he hurt her? Apparently not, for she did not seek to dismount; and, once their wrestling was done, she proved an impeccable hostess. She fed him wine to follow that which he had drunk already at banquet, and listened with unstinting patience to his generously drunken boasts. For Guest, who had told Damsel of his past during the banquet, was now engaged in telling her his future.

"We will kill Khmar," said Guest Gulkan.

"You can hardly defeat Khmar if you must come as beggars to the Safrak Islands."

"If this is a beggar's life," said Guest, complacently sated, "I wish I'd turned beggar before."

"So begging is enough. Or have you plans for our islands?"

"Plans?" said Guest, mystified.

"Plans for conquest."

"Conquest?" said Guest, so surprised he almost felt sober. "Us to conquer Safrak? With what? Our tongues and teeth, perhaps. Not swords, for certain. Our swords were all surrendered."

"I think he truths," said the woman Damsel, rising from the bed. "They are no more than the fools they seem."

"Who?" said Guest in bewilderment.

As Guest was gaping for meaning, men came crashing through paperwork screens, their advent teaching him the identity of at least one of the fools to whom Damsel had referred. Guest lurched from the bed. Liquor betrayed him. He was too slow to stop the first fist which slammed him, and was swiftly battered into submission by knuckles and elbows.

"So this is death," said Guest, a blood-thickened voice

speaking through thickened lips.

He tried to be strong, to be staunch — but found this difficult since he was naked. Staunchness in the face of death requires the dignity of sword and shield, or of armour, or of leathers and rags at a minimum.

"This is not yet death," said one of Guest's captors, as the still-naked Weaponmaster was dragged through rockwall corridors.

"So you will sport with me first."

"We play no sport with merchandise."

"Merchandise?"

"Khmar will pay highly for you. Surely."

At that, young Guest struggled like a very hurricane trying to fight its way out of a leather sack. Fates worse than death! He screamed and he fought. But his best efforts availed not against his attackers, and, panting with effort, he was flung into a dour rockwall prison.

Guest Gulkan was flung so hard that he would have bruised himself grievously against rock had the prison not been generously padded with flesh. A small and guttering lamp lit the scene with enough light to allow that flesh to be identified. Young Guest untangled himself in a hurry from Bao Gahai.

"Wa!" said Guest.

To be seized and imprisoned was bad enough. But to be locked up with the dralkosh Bao Gahai — that was intolerable!

There was a long and uncomfortable silence.

Then:

"Are you hurt?" said Bao Gahai, her bearded voice husky in the gloom.

"Who knows?" said Guest. "Who cares?"

"I care," said Bao Gahai softly.

"You!" said Guest. "Why?"

Bao Gahai hesitated. Then thought:

—What does it matter?

"I care," said Bao Gahai, "because—"

But Bao Gahai never explicated her "because", for the door burst open. Guest promptly made a break for freedom, but armed men jabbed at him with spears of a size fit for the harpooning of the very Great Mink itself. Once the belligerent Weaponmaster had been forced back against the far wall, other prisoners were hustled into the cell. The dralkosh Zelafona, and her dwarf-son Glambrax. The slow-witted Morsh Bataar. The scholarly Sken-Pitilkin. The master chef Pelagius Zozimus. A fine scooping, this!

With the door slammed shut and locked against escape, Guest looked around the cell, scanning all by lantern light. As best he could, he feigned the staunch self-control of a hero, concealing his extreme embarrassment at his own nakedness. The Yarglat do not uncover themselves in public, and while Guest had done as much at his father's command on the washing-pool island, he would never voluntarily have done as much in the cells of the mainrock Pinnacle, for, leaving aside all questions of taboos and embarrassments, the place was abominably cold. The cell was frigid and freezing, for all that there was so much flesh stuffed into it.

"So," said Guest, when he had summed the faces. "Our own have not betrayed us."

"Bravely said," said Morsh Bataar.

Then Morsh took off his over-length weather jacket, a fleece-lined item of apparel which he had bought second-hand from one of his father's league riders many, many days ago in far-off Gendormargensis, and handed that jacket to Guest. Who took it in wordless gratitude. The wool was warm, and snugged down to his thighs.

Then, since nobody else seemed disposed to do it, Guest began testing the weaknesses of their place of dungeon, first trying the window. The window, which led to the outer world, was guarded with iron bars. The bars admitted great draughts of air for the cooling of overheated tempers, but would not admit a human.

"Still," said Guest, giving the iron a slap. "It is but brute matter. We can gnaw it through in less than a year with teeth and fingernails alone."

Lightly he spoke, but had already deduced that even a

rupture of the iron bars would secure them only the liberty to crawl out on to the sheer cliffside high above the waters. Unless they searched for sudden death, this liberty was not likely to be advantageous.

The young Weaponmaster then turned his attention to the stones of the cell, and soon determined that they could be hollowed out by tunnelling, though it would probably take four or five decades for a tunnel of any significance to be made through rock so hard.

"The door," said Guest, deciding. "It has to be the door. Zozimus! Sken-Pitilkin! Have done with this door!"

So spoke the Weaponmaster, for he was determined to get out of that cell that very night.

"If the door were a corpse then I could do with it," said Zozimus. "But as a mere necromancer, I can do nothing with brute wooden timbers."

"And I," said Sken-Pitilkin, "can scarcely make the thing fly, for it is fixed in position."

"Then you could jiggle it," said Guest. "You could jiggle it till it burst."

"I cannot," said Sken-Pitilkin, "for I have been drinking strong liquor, and the exercise of wizardry is unwise in combination with drink. Besides, if I burst the thing, then shattered wood might fly inwards as likely as outwards."

Actually, Sken-Pitilkin had been very conservative in his banqueting, and thought the exercise of wizardry safe in itself. But could he truly use his powers of levitation to shake the door till it burst? He did not know, for he had no way of computing the door's strength.

It occurred to the sagacious wizard of Skatzabratzumon that he might conceivably be able to use his powers to manipulate the very locking mechanism of the door itself. But he said nothing of that to Guest, for to escape from the prison cell would be to find themselves at war with the armed strength of Alozay — and Sken-Pitilkin thought such war likely to end in their deaths.

Through long generations of experience, the wizards of

Argan's Confederation have learnt that the powers of a lawyer
are ultimately greater than those of a warrior. So, rather than
brute it out with every sword in Alozay, Sken-Pitilkin planned
to rest, and later to use his lawyerly skills to find a way out of his
present predicament by negotiation.

But Guest had not the lawyer's temperament.

"Shoulders!" said Guest.

And Morsh Bataar joined him in rigorously bruising that
portion of the human anatomy against unbruisable timbers.

"Yunch!" said Guest, giving vent to one of the choice
Yarglat obscenities. "The thing will not give."

"What did you expect?" said Zozimus. "This is no bridal
suite, you know."

"Nor I a virgin eager for penetration," said Guest. "Have
you about you perhaps a tinder box, master chef?"

"I have," said Zozimus, who was seldom without such an
article.

"Then evidence your skills with it," said Guest. "The hell
with brute force and battery! We'll burn our way out!"

Obviously Guest was severely drunk, or brain-damaged by
the bruising he had suffered at the hands of his enemies, else
would have realized that fire could easily be started with the
cell's slow-burning lamp. But nobody chose to remind him of
this, thinking that wisdom lay in silence.

"Zozimus!" said Guest imperiously. "Your tinder box, man!
Get to it! Get to it, and burn!"

Now Zozimus was not wise, not in comparison with a true
master of the intellect like Hostaja Torsen Sken-Pitilkin, yet the
slug-chef possessed sense enough not to argue with an ox of a
boy when the worst temper in that boy was bent upon works of
wreckage. So, even though Zozimus knew full well that what
Guest proposed was impossible, he yet consented to kindle fire.
However, as Guest soon proved to his own dissatisfaction by
experiment, nothing is so reluctant to burn as a big burly door
chunked out of planks thicker than a wrestler's thigh.

It is a commonplace error to think that wood burns easily. It
does not. Wooden houses burn of a regularity, but the prior

combustion of curtains, clothes, carpets, wickerwork and children's toys is necessary to set walls and roof alight. Wooden forests not uncommonly perish in flame, but grass and undergrowth must be well alight before the shafting timbers of the trees themselves catch fire. Ships of wood likewise succumb to conflagration, but it is in ropes, rubbish, sails and paint-lockers that the chief danger lies. The ardours of your very household fire must be carefully conjured into life with handfuls of pine needles and sticks of fine-split kindling — and must not the wood be dry? And a ventilating draught provided for its enlivement?

State it as a certainty: a bulky chunk of timber untainted by oils and paints will stand staunch against all but the greatest efforts to set it alight. Even when it burns, thick wood does not burn through quickly; nor does it easily lose its strength, even though the surface be charred. Hence, as most doors are timber in bulk, your most learned experts in incendiarism advise that, should you be trapped in a burning building, your survival will be prolonged by closing the door against the blaze and mugging all cracks with damp cloth to ward against the infiltrations of smoke.

So it is next to useless to try to escape by burning a hole through a wooden door.

But Guest had forgotten this, or, like a starving man trying to keep himself alive by eating his shirt, had hoped that reality would alter its nature to accommodate his needs.

It did not.

By the time the prisoners had exhausted their small stock of expendable burnables (Bao Gahai's handkerchief, clogged with moist deposits of green and yellow snot; three packets of dried herbs extorted from Zozimus by threat; and a Book of Verbs which Guest Gulkan extracted from Sken-Pitilkin's possession after violent argument and then burnt with an expression of what looked suspiciously like satisfaction), the door manifested no conspicuous sign of injury, though its surface had been liberally smeared with soot.

Though Guest had found but little to burn, the burning had

generated smoke and fumes in prodigious quantities. Despite the generous draughts which circulated within the cell, the air was still filled with the sour reeking smoke which had issued from Sken-Pitilkin's incinerated verbs, with the variously pleasant and unpleasant stinks of Zozimus's herbs, and with the scabrous fumes released by the incineration of Bao Gahai's handkerchief. Bao Gahai and Zelafona were both coughing, and had become exceedingly irritable; and Guest Gulkan's own temper had been in no wise improved by this debacle.

"This failed," said Guest decisively. "But other schemes and stratagems will not. There must be a way out!"

"Yes," said Sken-Pitilkin wearily. "Through the door. They will open it, in time, and drag us out. Thus we escape."

Sken-Pitilkin spoke for all, for everyone was in a mood to settle down and sleep. It was late, they were weary and Guest Gulkan's prowlings were unsettling each and all to the point where they were quite unable to pretend to themselves that they were getting comfortable. But Guest, disregardful of his companions' comfort, decided to attack the bars guarding the sewer-hole built into the corner to the right of the window.

"Move aside," said Guest to Glambrax, for the dwarf had settled himself by the sewer in order to be spared from involvement in the Weaponmaster's frenetic escape attempts.

"You're mad," said Glambrax.

"Yes," said Guest, taking the dwarf by the ear, "and my madness oft expresses itself in the strangulation of dwarves."

Then, having hauled Glambrax out of the way, the Weaponmaster attacked the sewer bars. Those bars were old, and, by dint of prodigious wrenching which almost ruptured his gut, Guest tore the iron away from the anchoring stone.

"Free!" said Guest.

"Free to spit," said Sken-Pitilkin, "for there is no way we can crawl down a hole so small."

Nor could they, for it was far too small to admit a normal human frame.

"Glambrax!" said Guest.

"It's too small for me, too," said Glambrax.

And so it was. For Glambrax, though but a stumpy dwarf, had bulky shoulders and a full-sized head, and experiment soon proved that it was quite impossible for him to escape through such a hole even when he was being assisted by Guest Gulkan's boot. Besides, supposing he had, what then? The cold draught coming up from below suggested the sewer ran instantly out to the cliff-face, connecting with the limitless gulfs of the night air. Escape by sewer, like escape through the window, would offer nothing more than an improved view, or the chance of a brisk suicide.

"Still," said Guest, wielding one of the iron bars he had torn from its imprisoning stone, "we now have weapons."

To demonstrate his point, he strode to the door and struck it a vicious blow with this stumpy little cosh. Iron hit timber; timber grunted; and iron exploded in a shower of rust. Guest looked in astonishment at the disintegrated ruins of his iron bar.

"That is a famously dangerous weapon, brother," said Morsh Bataar, combing his fingers through his hair to remove fragments of rust, "for you strike at one and hit a thousand."

"I must have a weapon!" said Guest, throwing down the fragment of iron which yet remained in his fist.

"We have weapons in plenty," said Sken-Pitilkin wearily. "The weapons which we were born with. Teeth, nails, elbows, knees. All weapons in their way. But the greatest weapon in the human arsenal is intelligence. I suggest we use that greatest weapon now."

"How?" said Guest.

"By going to sleep!" retorted Sken-Pitilkin.

At which the cell's single guttering lamp voluntarily and without encouragement extinguished itself, leaving them in darkness.

"There is still the ceiling," said Guest.

"Yes, yes," said Sken-Pitilkin, with visions of Guest pulling down an avalanche of unseated rock, stone and masonry upon his hapless fellow captives, "and the ceiling will still be there on the morrow. Down, boy, and kennel!"

"You call me boy?" said Guest.

"I call you boy, dog, beast, fish, fowl and fool," said Sken-Pitilkin. "Now get to sleep! Lest the adults here lose patience with the frolics of your childhood."

"I am no boy," said Guest truculently. "I am a war leader, a commander of generals."

"A commander of generals, yes," said Sken-Pitilkin. "And a supervisor of their vomit-eating competitions. Zozimus! Will you not help me reason this boy to sense? Zozimus! Zozimus, pox you! Beasts and bitches! The thing's asleep!"

"So might we be," said Bao Gahai acidly, "were it not for an overly loud-voiced old fool of a tutor, who has not even such a modest gift as cookery at his command."

One does not argue with a dralkosh. Not, at least, when one is caged with the thing in a small box of unescapable stone. So Hostaja Torsen Sken-Pitilkin settled himself on the stones of the cell and tried to go to sleep.

Silence, but for some smoke-inspired coughing from Glambrax and some snoring from Zozimus.

Then:

A skrittling-scratching, as if some creature with murderous talons were clawing the bulking timbers of the jail cell door.

"Guest!" said the hoarse voice of Bao Gahai.

"What?" said Guest Gulkan.

"I don't know what you're doing or what you hope to accomplish by it," said Bao Gahai, "but I adjure you to stop."

"You adjure me, do you?" said Guest Gulkan, rigorously unimpressed. "And who are you to adjure anything?"

"I am Bao Gahai," said she venomously. "You will not trifle with me. I am Bao Gahai, birthed nine thousand years before your daylight. I am Bao Gahai, Lord of Shadow, Commander of Darkness, Invoker of Doom."

"Very impressive," said Guest, still unimpressed. "How kind of you to coop together here with us ordinary mortals."

Then he resumed his attack on the door. Scritch scritch! Scratch scratch!

"Guest!" said Bao Gahai savagely.

"Yes?" said Guest.

"Stop it. Or else."

"Or else what?" said Guest, for all the world like a small child daring its mother.

No answer came.

So:

Scritch scritch scratch scratch.

"Guest!"

"Yes?"

"If you don't stop that, right now, I'll—"

"You'll what?"

There was a pause, then Bao Gahai said, very slowly, very clearly, and with the vehemence of murderous intent:

"Guest, if I have any more trouble from you tonight, I will shit in my hand and rub the result from your chin to your eyebrows."

Guest thought about it.

Then scritched and scratched again.

Once.

Twice.

Thrice.

While those yet awake in the cell — meaning everyone but the slumberous Zozimus — waited for mayhem to be unleashed.

Fortunately, having scritched and scratched at the door those three last times, Guest decided that honour had been satisfied, and settled himself to sleep. Soon he too was snoring, only somewhat more loudly than Zozimus. Bao Gahai stayed awake a little longer, as if assuring herself that Guest was really asleep. Then she too dropped off, and the lurching discords of her saw-voiced snore began to rip the air.

With all this snoring going on, the scholarly Sken-Pitilkin found sleep impossible. Instead, he sat lamenting his fate. Once he had been the commander of a great empire. Once he had ruled in unimaginable power. In later years, he had lived quite comfortably as a lord of dragons and master of the island of Drum, until his peace had been disturbed when Zozimus, Zelafona and Glambrax had sought refuge on that island, bringing killers from the Confederation of Wizards in their wake.

And now he was a fugitive, a renegade displaced from his castle, accursed of the Confederation, unwelcome in his homeland and hunted by his peers. He had sheltered as best he could on the unhospitable earth of Tameran, doing what he must to secure his survival — even stooping to tutoring when that proved the only way for him to win his bread! But now he was doomed to come to a wretched end, unless he could by his wizardry or his lawmongery secure his release from Alozay.

And even if he could secure his release, what then?

Where would he go?

And what would he do?

So brooded Sken-Pitilkin, until his peace was shattered as the door cracked and splintered with a bursting roar. And what a roar! It boomed and burst like a dragon in its rages, or like one of Pelagius Zozimus's experimental steam cookers exploding into fragments, or like a great heap of Tang's percussive toys all simultaneously erupting into flash and thunder.

That roar, and the splintering of the door which accompanied it, brought Zozimus abrupting from sleep.

"Dragons!" cried Zozimus.

But it was not dragons but men, as a moment's listening made plain. For, through the shattered door there came the sounds of murder, the killing-clash of steel, the bellows of battle.

"The door!" said Guest, wrenching at the fractured timbers. "The door, the door! Help me!"

But only Morsh Bataar joined him in his onslaught on that barrier. Without, the enemy was surely slaughtering off those of the Witchlord's men whom they had not been able to take by surprise and overcome by stealth. By escaping into such battle, unarmed and unarmoured, Guest Gulkan would only add his own corpse to the slaughter heap.

"Glut!" said Morsh, swearing. "The door holds!"

At which there was another shattering explosion. The blast slammed through the shattered door and dumped the would-be heroes on their backsides.

"Blood's grief!" said Guest, raising himself to his elbows. "Am I alive, or what?"

None answered, until Bao Gahai chose to answer thus:

"Hush, child. Hush, child, and sleep."

Sleep! To advise such was lunacy. For none could so much as close their eyes. Surely Bao Gahai was quite deranged! As for Guest, he had not the slightest thought of sleep. He was waiting with the others. One and all, they were waiting for another explosion, all sure that a third such would kill them.

"What raises such thunder from living rock?" wondered Morsh Bataar, not seriously expecting an answer.

"There are oils which your anatomist can dissect out of the living flesh of dragons," said Zozimus grimly. "Such oils, abused for purposes of war, can conjure explosion, albeit at great expense."

Then none spoke further, for outside were screams of anguished murder. The wreckage of the door shook as someone crashed against it. There was a howl of blood-pumping fury. Iron smashed iron. Flesh wrenched itself in agony's outcry. Then came a groan, a guttering gasp, a death-moan.

"Had we but weapons!" said Guest, with clench-fist frustration.

The ultimate weapon is the warrior, yet a warrior unweaponed is but a poor thing, and a washerwoman with an axe can overcome him. Surely the Witchlord's people were putting up a fight; yet, just as surely, they must be being killed out, for without weapons they could not prevail against their enemies.

At last the sounds of killing diminished down to nothing.

"Blood," said Guest.

Contemplating his prospects.

His father dead. He himself a prisoner, trapped on Safrak. His enemies meaning to sell him to Khmar.

"If die I must then now I'll die," said Guest, seizing one of the shattered timbers of the door and wrenching. "Now! Not later!"

His efforts provoked a wrenching scream of wood — an

agony as great as that of one of the men so lately killed. The door did not yield, but its protest was heard by someone outside. Iron-shod boots rang on rock, approaching the door.

"Who's there?" cried a burly voice.

The voice spoke Eparget!

"Here!" shouted Guest, answering in that same Yarglat tongue. "Here! Here! Within!"

"Who?" said the battle-booted voice, now outside the shattered door.

"Why, the Weaponmaster Guest Gulkan," said that same self-boasting young man. "Unloose me!"

"Unloose you? Why?"

"Unloose me, that I may fight."

"Fight?" said the warrior without. "Fight? Fighting is the least and last of things we need. I'll not let you out if fighting is your creed."

"You bloodpoxed box of sheep shit!" roared Guest. "Unloose me, or I'll rip your brains out!"

And he tore at the ragged door, though still it held. Outside, the war-booted warrior laughed uproariously, encouraging Guest yet further in his fury. Then there were shouts, their import indistinguishable to the prisoners in the cell.

"It's Guest, my lord!" said the war-booted warrior.

Tramping footsteps echoed from stone to stone.

Then:

"Guest?"

It was Lord Onosh, the Witchlord himself, deep-voiced, with a note of bloodstained victory in the triumph of his voice.

"It's him," said Bao Gahai. "And me."

"Love of the gods!" said the Witchlord Onosh, speaking fervently. "I thought the pair of you perished!"

"And I likewise thought you dead," said Guest, speaking from the cell-murk. "How live you?"

"Through the grace of weapons," said Lord Onosh. "A key! A key! Who's got the key? You — a key for this cell. What? What's that you say? How in the five hells would I know! Well, look for it, man! Don't just stand there! Strolth! Hurry yourself, you son of a gaplax! Or will it take cold iron in your arse to move you?"

This last was said at a full-pitched roar, suggesting that the object of the Witchlord's wrath had almost hurried out of earshot, gone to look for the key to the cell of imprisonment.

"Weapons," said Guest, when no further outburst followed. "Whence came weapons? We had none."

"We had many," said Lord Onosh, by way of contradiction.

"Where?" said Guest.

"In the treasure chests," said Lord Onosh, levering at door timbers with his broadbladed battle-sword. "We brought ten chests of treasure to Safrak. Ten chests of iron and steel."

"But," said Guest, bewildered, "those chests held gold, and diamonds. They were checked! I saw the Bankers check them!"

"Checked once, and not again," said Lord Onosh, wood giving way before the cunning leverage of his steel. "Deep water took the greater part of the treasure, and we replaced that greater part with steel made for war. Here, you, pass me the lamp. Guest — take this!"

A breach having been opened in the door, a lamp was passed inside the cell. It showed weary faces, the ashes of incinerated herbs, the sad remains of a charcoaled Book of Verbs, the blackened fibres of a handkerchief, and much scattered rust.

A little more wood-wrenching, and a gap large enough for escape had been wrenched in the door. The prisoners accordingly made their exit.

"Why, my son," said Lord Onosh. "You're naked below the knee, and most of the way above it!"

"It is the fashion," said Guest.

"Not if I have anything to do with it," said Lord Onosh. "Ho! You! The key! You have it? No? Then — come here! Your clothes, man. Your clothes beneath the navel!"

Thus Guest gained borrowed clothes, though they were far too small for him, and he split several seams in the process of making himself decent.

"So," said Lord Onosh. "I have my son. Right. Now we can fight to the docks, and be gone."

"Be gone!" said Guest, in dismay.

"Yes," said Lord Onosh. "What else?"

"I thought us surely to fight for Alozay," said Guest.

"There are too many of them," said Lord Onosh. "They are too strong. The best we can hope for is to escape. If the boats which brought us to the island are still at the docks, we—"

But then the Witchlord broke off, hearing renewed shouting in the distance.

"Ho, men!" cried Lord Onosh. "War!"

And, nothing more needing saying, the Witchlord went pounding towards the outcry.

"A sword!" cried Guest. "A sword! A sword! My kingdom for a sword!"

As the young Weaponmaster at that stage possessed no kingdom, this advertisement attracted no swords to his possession. But someone thrust a small reaping sickle into his hands, and, seeing that this was all the armament he was likely to procure instantly, the Weaponmaster Guest gave chase to his father.

Guest caught his father at the head of a stairway which led downwards. Weaponmaster grabbed Witchlord.

"Father," said Guest.

"My son," said the Witchlord.

"These stairs," said Guest, "they go upwards. Upstairs there's a demon, it can make you a wizard, there's a Great God in the temple, the Temple of Blood, Obooloo, that's what the demon said, and the Great God's a prisoner."

Lord Onosh looked at his son in astonishment.

"What are you on about?" said Lord Onosh.

"My lord," said Sken-Pitilkin, alarmed to hear Guest babbling about demons and Great Gods. "Your son was ill when he was last on Alozay. He had a fever, and hallucinations from the fever. He—"

"It's true!" said Guest.

Then discourse came to an end, for a squad of Alozay's resident Guardians came storming up the stairs. Those mercenary warriors were outnumbered by the Witchlord's men, but they attacked savagely regardless. All was briefly a whirl of battle, and when it was over—

"Guest!" said Lord Onosh, looking around. "Where are you?"

"The boy has gone upstairs," said Sken-Pitilkin.

"Then he is quite mad," said Lord Onosh.

And, as the Weaponmaster Guest Gulkan went upwards towards Safrak's Hall of Time, the Witchlord led his forces downwards — abandoning Guest to the uncertainties of whatever fate awaited him.

CHAPTER TWENTY-ONE

Grand Palace of Alozay: headquarters of the Safrak Bank. In multiple levels hollowed from the mainrock Pinnacle, it rises above the adjacent city of Molothair. Access to the Grand Palace is via the winch-baskets which allow one to be raised or lowered from or to the Palace Docks. If graced with the power of flight, one could also win the palace from the air, since several of its levels are fenestrated with windows adequate for the entry of a winged horse or similar.

***

There was blood on the stairs, and the blood had been tracked upward in a series of fragmented bootprints. Belatedly, Guest realized he was tracking through that blood himself, leaving a series of bare-toe footprints in his wake. He scraped his feet against the roughness of the living rock of the mainrock Pinnacle, then started upwards again.

Then stopped.

For he could hear breathing.

It was heavy breathing, the gasping of a hard-labouring athlete, the wrenching air-spasming of a mountaineer enduring high-altitude duress. A pregnant woman heavily into her labour might make such a sound — as might a man locked in a death-wrestle with a crocodile.

Till now, Guest had been carrying the weight of his sword's nakedness on his shoulder, for the weight of the weapon made it uncomfortable to carry at the challenge. But the ominous, indecipherable threat of that breathing jolted his heart to a stammering run. As the blood-spring impetus of fear shocked his heart to fresh endeavour, he handled his sword as adroitly as if it were no more than a dagger.

With that sword poised like a knife — held low, with the blade slanting upwards, ready to spear through latticed ribs to the sweat-thump heart — Guest took the darkened stairs at a barefooted sprint.

Red fire flashed on his blade as he jolted into a lantern's arc. He crashed to the step-stones, and his blood-red blade went flying to a clattering clang-fall. A moment later, the fallen Weaponmaster realized he must have slipped. On what? On nothing. It was the sheer impetuosity of his upward assault which had slammed him downwards.

Guest recovered himself, regained his weapon, then scuttled upwards, fleeing from the lamplight as a cockroach flees domestic flame. For light was peril.

He halted in darkness, panting, listening, taking stock. The heavy breathing was closer, now. Closer, and more laboured yet. It brought back fragmented memories of battle, murder, ambush, war. It was the breathing of—

Yes, Guest knew what that breathing signified.

Alone in the dark, he hesitated. The man who lay on the stairs above, the man who was surely labouring through his death, why, that man was no threat. But in the shadow of those labours an assassin might be waiting. And Guest, by slipping and falling, by racketing the night with the clatter of his sword, would have alerted any such assassin to his approach.

The Weaponmaster hesitated, half-minded to retreat to the mainrock's lower levels, and there to join his father in the attempt to fight through to the docks.

He listened.

From far below came the whimpering moth-faint echoes of distant discords — sounds of battle and barrat near-drowned by the gasping labours of the dying man who lay so close above. Those faint hoarse-clash clues from below told Guest that battle was being waged. He thought his father doomed to lose such a battle.

For, after all, this was the mainrock Pinnacle, the mighty stronghold of the Safrak Bank. It was packed with the Bank's mercenary Guardians, and the Bankers themselves would fight ably enough when put to the challenge. The Witchlord's men were few, and so Guest doubted his father able to win his way to freedom, not even with the assistance of two wizards and a pair of witches.

But — above!

Thinking of what lay above, Guest overcame his hesitation and barefooted it up the stairs. A dozen steps took him into the light of the next oil lantern. Sprawled on the stone flags directly beneath that guttering source of semi-illumination lay a — a man?

No.

A woman.

A washerwoman.

Yes, it was one of the mighty washerwomen of the mainrock Pinnacle, one of those whose muscular labours helped winch people up and down from the Palace Docks. And, as Guest had deduced from her breathing, she was sorely wounded.

She was dying.

It is hard, this business of battlefield death. The flesh sweats, and gasps, each breath a clutching. One might think the dying would yield. But they do not. They fight. The closer the death, the greater the battle. Will, identity, awareness — all is reduced to the groaning swoop of this ingrasping. Air! Air!

The dying woman did not know where she was, or why. She was unaware of Guest Gulkan standing there. Did not hear him, did not see him, did not imagine him. Her world was the labouring of her dying, no more, no less.

And Guest, standing in the lamplight, momentarily forgot himself and his own predicament. Moved by pity for the woman — this unintended casualty, no enemy of him or his — he wished there was some way to help her. But help was not in his gift.

Just as when his brother Morsh had suffered a broken leg, Guest was helpless, for he had made no study of the healing arts. Of course, when Morsh had suffered his breakage, the wizard Sken-Pitilkin had been there to help. But where was Sken-Pitilkin now? Downstairs, doubtless. Guest was half-moved to fetch him, but knew the thought immediately as madness. For the wizards Hostaja Sken-Pitilkin and Pelagius Zozimus would both be embroiled in battle, and no aid could be spared for a washerwoman when the lives of so many were in the balance.

So Guest could but gape uselessly at the turmoil of the woman's gaping-gasping, at her blood-moil clothing, at the red soakage darkening the shadows of her ribs. At 16 years of age, he knew his edged weapons, his tactics and his strategy; he knew the dynamics of patrolling and the logistic difficulties of provisioning an army on the march; he was fit to pillage, and plunder, and burn, and ravage; but in the face of the spillage of blood he was helpless.

Of course, Guest Gulkan should have known the way of wounds, as should we all, for we live in a great age of darkness in which the sword rules, and strikes with impunity at washerwomen and irregular verbs alike. So know then the wound! First one must look, for only by looking can one know. One must seek for the damage, remembering always that piercing weapons — one thinks in particular of a quarrel shot from a crossbow — will damage with both instrike and outstrike.

Having found hole or holes, raggages or cleavages, tears and rips, gouges and gaps, one must patch the same. And immediately! Have you no bandage? Then your hand must serve! But unless one be naked, then one surely has bandages, for the cloth off one's back will serve when all else fails. The cleaner the cloth, the better, though the cleanest of cloth is no use to a washerwoman who has died of bloodloss while the ardent hygienist has been searching for sterility.

Say it of a certainty: in the face of bleeding, the rescuer must match the urgency of the pumping heart. The wound must be patched, and immediately.

So when you are at war, and your blood brother has his swordhand hacked away by a battleaxe, then do not hesitate. First kill the axe-wielder. Then wipe the filth of battle from the palm of your hand, and clamp that living flesh of yours to the pumping agony of your bosom friend. It can be done in moments, if you have the courage to save as well as to kill.

Press your hand to the hot wet pumpage of blood. Press hard, and crush the bloodflow down to nothing. Then keep your hand in place until some hard-panting hero of your acquaintance can spare a few moments from his saga-work to assist with a bandage. Then you had best seek the help of a healer, though the perversity of the world is such that you may find every available pox doctor to have been slaughtered in the first heat of battle.

If such be the case, then your friend's handless arm should for the moment be placed in a sling, so that the well-bandaged wound is kept elevated, for the heart finds it harder to pump blood to elevations. And — mind! — do not allow the wound to be dipped into liquid ordure, or steeped in boiling lead, or packed with red mud, or plunged into the sexual aperture of a menstruating cow.

For, while all such treatments have their vigorous adherents, they are spurious; and the truth is that the simplest treatments are the best. On the battlefield, a weapon-wound should be bandaged, and promptly, with bare flesh serving as a fail-safe expedient in the absence of other facilities. Bandage, then — and by promptly rendering a service so simple, you may yet save a life in the heat of war.

There!

It is so simply put!

But did Guest Gulkan know as much?

The unfortunate fact is that the Weaponmaster's brawning courage was much facilitated by his steadfast refusal to contemplate the obvious and inevitable consequences of carnage. Much did he think of the clash of swords, the brawling of battle-axes, and the winning of glory. But of bloody pain and the sweat-wrenching agony of a washerwoman's death — of these he remained steadfastly ignorant.

True, he had seen his brother Morsh Bataar hideously wounded. But he had relegated all memories of that wounding to those mysterious and labyrinthine depths of his brain where legions of hapless irregular verbs wandered in doomed oblivion.

Yes, and he had been wounded himself, and grievously — for the bamboo spike which had sabotaged his foot at the Battle of Babaroth had caused him a great deal of agony and inconvenience. But this too he had managed to shrug off and forget.

So, thanks to his own willed ignorance, Guest Gulkan stood watching as a woman died, and the charity of his pity was no help to her, for pity without action is useless.

And if you believe yourself likewise doomed to go to war, then know this of a certainty: if your study in its folly concerns itself with the mere use of weapons then you too are doomed to stand some day in helpless guilt, watching as the object of your pity dies. So let this text then carry an explicit message, a message apt for our age of ceaseless warfare: those who would study the use of weapons should study likewise the cure of that use.

Above is set a sermon on bandaging, and it will serve you well if you should look up from this page to see a friend come stumbling through the door with a hand missing. Clamp the palm of your hand to the spouting stump, and apply firm pressure!

But of course there is more to the treatment of wounds than this, for a missing hand is simplicity itself, whereas damage to the pancreas is a more delicate matter (for all experts agree that the soul, if it is located anywhere, is surely to be found in the pancreas, since this organ promptly dissolves itself upon death), and the eye is likewise delicate, the treatment of its damage being a matter only to be studied under the close supervision of an accomplished expert.

Consider then a case more complex than mere amputation.

Suppose you are fighting in the red dust of Dalar ken Halvar, and that your friend has been eviscerated by a broadsword. Suppose too that a pariah dog has eaten one half of his liver; that a goodly portion of his forebrain has spilt down his face like so much spoilt porridge; that one of his eyes has been plucked from its perch by a battlefield vulture, and that the other is resting on his cheek in the bloody mess of its swordpoint evisceration.

What would you do?

Or, to take another case, how would you aid a friend who

has been speared most piteously in the anus, assuming that the pair of you are marooned by blizzard in the mountains of Ibsen-Iktus. Assume too that all food is gone, that your tent is in tatters, and that your friend's incidental frostbite has led to his left leg becoming one single bloated mass of gangrenous stench-flesh.

How would you treat your friend?

Or would you treat him not, but simply content yourself with the stealing of his boots, and the making of a joke about him after his death and his snowfall burial?

If you cannot give firm answers to such questions, then it is arguable that you are unfit to go to war.

And what too would you do were your friend burnt from waist to throat by the fire of a dragon? Or burnt below the waist, which is arguably worse? And are you aware that the fire of the imperial dragons of Yestron is sticky, and cannot be removed by rubbing or clawing, but inevitably eats its way through to the bone?

And have you treatments for malaria, or hepatitis, or typhus, or bubonic plague, or syphilis, or gonorrhoea, or any of those other ailments which are the common property of an army on the march? And know you recipes of genocide apt for the mass murder of the rat and the flea? And which biting insect is it which carries typhus, and what are the symptoms of that disease, and what its treatment? And to remove a bloated tick from human flesh, does one wind it deasil or withershins? And what will you do if the tick has invaded the ear?

And what would you do — to take a case more tractable than some of the traumas detailed above — if your friend were to come to you in panic, declaring a leech to have penetrated his privacy by means of the eye of his male organ? (And if you think this a most unlikely contingency, then know that just such a disaster is said to have befallen one of the heroes who quested with the Rovac warrior Morgan Hearst, when that worthy was in hot pursuit of the renegade wizard Heenmor.)

And (to pursue the subject of the tenderness of the male organ a little further) have you heard of the jilifish? It is a fish of certain of the equatorial jungles, a fish which will swim up the flow of a man's urine, then erect its sharpest fin inside his organ of generation. How would you know a river to be infested with such a fish? And how would you guard yourself against its onslaught?

It is obvious that you will know a river to be jilifish-infested when your best friend screams in white-hot agony while taking a piss (assuming that he has not been lately to a brothel, in which case his pain may have an alternative cause). And it is obvious likewise that you can best guard yourself against the jilifish by refraining from pissing into rivers, and, further, by making sure that the stream of your cautious micturation passes through a filter fine enough to deny all fishes a route of ardent ascent.

As for the other questions — why, war will certainly ask them, and if war is your destiny then you had better know the answers.

Really, considering the grievous contingencies of armed adventuring, it can soberly be stated that no person should be allowed to take up arms without first enduring a full seven years of training in the repair and preservation of flesh and blood, of skin and bone, and of the ever-vulnerable male organ in particular.

But the more common expedient is to teach young men the mere use of weapons, so that, when placed in the presence of agony, they can but gape — and watch the wounded die. This is the common experience of war; though it is little reported, for it is human to forget, and those who cannot forget it most typically say nothing. So remember, when you find yourself in the presence of a happily loquacious old soldier, that he is but a victim of selective amnesia — a fact which may amply be proved by asking him to narrate for you the manner of the death of those of his friends who took the longest to die.

Being a very average young man in many respects, Guest Gulkan did just what most soldiers do in the face of those wounded and dying: he paused and he pitied, then he went on and forgot.

And that was the end of the matter.

And if you are surprised to find in these pages so much war in combination with so little suffering, why, then know well the reason. This is Guest Gulkan's story, the biography of a warrior, and a warrior of the Yarglat at that. And your every accomplished warrior is necessarily an amnesiac — and, more, neglects to see that which is not useful for his purposes.

It is said by the tender that any tale of war should concentrate on its suffering, for the tender-minded hold such suffering to be the ruling reality of war. In this they are in error; and, focusing on the dead and dying, they misunderstand that which they deprecate. Misunderstanding the dynamics of war, they cannot thereafter hope to alter those dynamics.

If history has any moral mission, then it is this: to render to the fullest the complexities and uncertainties of the living human reality which we endure. For it is we ourselves whom we seek to understand when we read in the pages of history — we, the human people, wizards and warriors, wonderworkers and washerwomen.

If we study the affairs of puppets and poppets then we will be well-equipped for life in a doll's house; but the world is not so amiably constituted, and attempts to treat it as if it were lead commonly to disaster.

Let us then stage no moral charades with puppets and poppets. For if we do, then we delude ourselves; and, surely, to choose to be wilfully blind as to our own nature is the greatest of crimes, for without self-knowledge there can be no governance of the self by the self.

Yes, and there are those who deny this, and say that it is sufficient to yield in faith to the diktats of some deity such as Zoz the Ancestral or similar. In such faith, they are prepared to burn all history, blaming the page for the battle, the court record for the crime. The reason for their willed ignorance is simple: self-knowledge and self-awareness are painful, so the weak and the inadequate customarily prefer the numb oblivion of the slavery of unquestioning faith.

In defiance of such wilful ignorance, this history speaks, holding truth to be the highest virtue. For only through an acknowledgement of the living realities of our world and our own existence can we attain self-knowledge and autonomous adulthood. And only by acknowledging the living realities of war can we hope to understand the persistence of war, which continues to blight our world despite the best-hearted efforts of those tender-minded moralists who would have us believe that war is one mass of conscious suffering, and that every warrior is a victim.

This book is a history of the warrior's living reality. And the truth of the warrior is ambition combined with amnesia, selective vision supplemented by selective memory, and the belief that victory is the validation of all suffering. Therefore, believing truth to be the highest virtue, we will not distort the record with moral charades of painful remorse, charades incompatible with the truth; but, rather, will note the plain fact, which is that Guest Gulkan swiftly forgot the dying washerwoman as he hastened up the stairs towards the Hall of Time.

In his barefoot panting, the Weaponmaster gave no further thought to the sorrows of war or the suffering of the injured. Rather, he was seized by an electric excitement. His eyes glittered as if frenzied by a lightning bolt; his sword trembled in his battle-ready hand; and his thoughts were focused entirely on his long-delayed but now-inevitable confrontation with Icaria Scaria Iva-Italis, Demon By Appointment to the Great God Jocasta.

CHAPTER TWENTY-TWO

Sod: Banker Sod, aka Governor Sod, aka Lord Sod: a merchant banker graced with the pale skin, the yellow head-hair and the thick white body hair, the golden eyes and the jet-black fingernails so typical of the iceman breed. His daughter is Damsel, she who so recently seduced and betrayed the Weaponmaster.

* * *

So Guest Gulkan ventured up the last of the stairs and entered into the Hall of Time, where the gutter-gubber nightlight of oil lanterns spilt a garblage of shadows across skull-pattern tiles. Many of those nightlamps had flubbered their last, and by expiry had left great gouts of shadow sprawled across that cavernous chamber.

Cavernous? Yes, the word was exact, not capricious or spuriously decorative. Carved as it was in the living rock of the mainrock Pinnacle, and breached as it was by the venting draughts of aerial ice which shuddered by histle and scree through the slits in its windows, this gloom-gaping barrow was much more of a cave than a hall.

At the far end of that oval engagement, a full hundred paces from the entrance where Guest Gulkan stood, something glowed cold and green.

The demon.

The night of their first encounter was so long ago in the past, so heavily overlaid by memories of battle and disaster, that Guest from time to time had been half-convinced that the whole thing had been no more than a figment of his fevered imagination. After all, he had been ill at the time, had he not? Grievously ill — near dead from influenza, and many of his erstwhile companions literally dead.

So, while the Weaponmaster had rehearsed his memories a thousand times, he had half-suspected their vivid solidity to have been no more than that spurious hyper-realism which characterizes the most gripping of sweet-dreams and nightmare. In its very nature, that first encounter had been half sweet-dream, half threat. For the demon had promised to make Guest a wizard, had it not? That was sweet: the prospect of being able to amplify his swordstroke with powers equal to those of a Zozimus or a Pitilkin.

But the demon had also told him that wizards were allies of dark things from the ruins of former times — allies of the Mahendo Mahunduk, a race of demon-flavoured beasts left over from the wreckage of gods.

Whatever the true nature of the Mahendo Mahunduk — and Guest was uncertain that he had construed that nature with absolute accuracy — they were most certainly creatures of the World Beyond. And Guest, for reasons which he had never been able to even half-explain to himself, had always flinched from knowledge of the World Beyond. As he had remained wilfully ignorant of the whole bloody business of wounds and eviscerations, so too he had closed his mind to the realm of talking bones and boneless voices, though in Gendormargensis there had been shamans sufficient to those mysteries, so he would not have lacked for tutors had he ever sought the endarkenment of his blank-faced daylight.

Now far from all thoughts of day, Guest Gulkan prolonged his hesitation, more than half-hoping for a distraction which would prevent him from venturing forward. For the plain and simple truth was that he was afraid. In its silence, in the green glimmer of its cold continence, the demon was possessed of a terrifying Patience. It had sat there for — for how long? For generations, surely — for generations at a minimum.

Enduring the weariness of the toiling years, the demon had served the Safrak Bank as Guardian Prime and as Keeper of the Inner Sanctum. Sitting there, year after year, listening, learning, planning, waiting, thinking, the demon had had time to ripen into the full malice of its manipulative cunning. It reminded Guest of one of those turtles which has a tongue twisted into an imitation of scrapmeat, and, seeking to tempt unwary fishes with this offering, spends all its life in imitation of the basic manoeuvre of the rock, its jaws constantly agape in the exercise of alluring entrapment.

As such a beast seemed the demon, only more so. Hence Guest hesitated, and to such an extent that he had quite positively halted — and was halted still when he heard someone coming stumping up the stairs behind him.

The Weaponmaster wheeled, his sword ready for butchery. But it was no enemy who was encroaching upon his vacillations. Rather, it was the dwarf Glambrax, who had blood on his boots and a bloody hatchet in his hand.

"How goes it below?" said Guest.

"Badly," said the dwarf.

Coming as it did from Glambrax, this baldly monosyllabic statement was ominous in the extreme. Nevertheless, the arrival of one of his comrades heartened the Weaponmaster, and he said:

"Guard well this gate. For I have business with the demon of this place."

"Demon?" said Glambrax. "What demon?"

"I mean that iceblock yonder," said Guest. "That great green iceblock at the far end of the hall."

"Then do your business, master," said Glambrax, starting to recover something of his customary loquacity, "and give the thing a lick for me. And I in my mightiness will hold this gate against giants and against dragons, against trolls and orcs, and even against the very elven lords in their arrogance. I will guard it against all onslaught of vampires, though their wings be a league of uncrimped crimson, and I will guard it against the footpad jaws of the werewolf, and the spikes of the Neversh itself. Yea, verily, while Drangsturm burns and my heartbeat thunders, I will hold the door against all such, though I cannot guarantee to hold it against men, and unfortunately it is men we fight tonight."

"Then do but consent to hold your tongue," said Guest, "and with that I will be content."

Thus spoke the Weaponmaster, speaking roughly out of

habit, though he was heartened by the dwarf's recovered powers of the tongue. Having spoken, Guest Gulkan scraped his feet to remove any last traces of blood — though blood would surely have dried during his prolonged prevarications — and then with his sword at the ready he ventured forward.

In his venturing, Guest kept to the centre of the hall, the part which was darkest since it was furthest from the wallside lanterns — for he favoured the dark like a fugitive. A central course also kept him clear of the deep embrasures and the time pods, and hence guarded him against ambush.

With such caution, Guest dared himself some ninety paces through the gloom of the Hall of Time, halting some ten paces short of the green-glowing menace of Icaria Scaria Iva-Italis, Demon of Safrak.

Guest had expected this monolithic chunk of jade-green stone to recognize him, and to acknowledge him. But it did not. It stood there in square-cut continence, formidable in implicit rebuff, rising in looming silence to twice his own height. Beyond it, he could see the single flight of stairs.

Guest Gulkan now stood on the floor of the Hall of Time, the single chamber which dominated Zi Obo, the Pod Stratum of the mainrock Pinnacle. If he could dare his way past the Demon of Safrak, then he could ascend the stairs which would take him to Jezel Obo. And Jezel Obo was the Sky Stratum, the topmost level of the mainrock Pinnacle, and home to its Inner Sanctum, the abditorial holy of holies to which none could penetrate but by the demon's leave.

But Guest had no thoughts of penetrating to Safrak's abditory. He had not come here to plumb for secrets. He had come to seek for help in war — help which he must have lest he die. And the demon's silence, rather than intriguing him, irritated him intensely.

"Italis!" barked Guest. "It's me!"

Then, getting no response, he elaborated:

"It is me! Guest Gulkan! The Weaponmaster! I was here before, remember? You told me about Jocasta, the Great God. A prisoner. Well. If you can help, I'd, I would have helped before, but I've been busy. There were wars. Fighting and such. But, uh, if you could help me with wizardry, powers of a wizard, then your Great God, well, I'd surely rescue it."

Guest paused, realizing he was handling this badly. In witless *badinage* with trifling fellows such as Glambrax or Rolf Thelemite, his tongue was ever nimbly fluent, because words were worth nothing and so could be spent freely. But now he was face to face with a brute which might well be the greatest Power of his acquaintance. And, because he had anticipated this encounter for so long, and was driven by great urgencies of battle, each word was so important that its mere enunciation was a struggle in itself.

"Italis," said Guest, "I, I'd, I'm sorry I didn't come here before. It was Pitilkin, you see. Sken-Pitilkin. He doesn't like you, not much, and—"

Guest broke off, hearing someone boot-thumping down the stairs. Moments later, a warrior stumbled down those stairs into the green-spill light of the Demon of Safrak. The warrior was Hrothgar! Yes, Hrothgar, the Guardian who had befriended Guest Gulkan on his earlier visit to Alozay!

"Hrothgar!" said Guest.

"Guest!" said Hrothgar. "Catch!"

Then, to Guest's bewilderment, the Guardian Hrothgar flung something in his direction. But the demon snapped at the flying thing with an outflux of green liquidity which moved too fast for the eye to follow. Whatever Hrothgar had thrown, the demon caught it, and swallowed it.

Hrothgar swore.

Moments later, another man came pounding down the stairs. It was Banker Sod, the Governor of the Safrak Bank, the ruler of Alozay, the master of the mainrock Pinnacle. Sod was flushed with battle, and a sword was in his hand.

"Where is it?" said Sod, challenging Hrothgar in fury. "Where is it? What did you do with it?"

"I threw it from a window," said Hrothgar, matching the challenge of Sod's sword with his own.

"Then what good will that do you?" said Sod.

"I had to try," said Hrothgar.

"Had to!" said Sod, in apoplectic fury. "For what reason?"

"Ambition," said Hrothgar, in frank confession.

Now Guest had followed action and speech well enough to realize that Hrothgar had stolen something from the abditory above. As a Guardian, a mercenary soldier in the service of the Safrak Bank, Hrothgar's rewards in life had been to eat, drink and sleep, and to bed with his wife in their ramshackle home in Molothair, the colony at the foot of the mainrock Pinnacle.

It had not proved sufficient.

So, when war swept the mainrock, Hrothgar had rebelled against his masters, and had dared a theft. Of what? Guest could not say. But the thief had been caught — and Sod, who had caught him, was determined to inflict the death penalty. Sod leapt at Hrothgar. Sword clashed with sword. Hrothgar stumbled, recovered himself, then hacked at Sod. But to Guest's dismay, it was Sod who prevailed. Hrothgar was driven back — and the demon grabbed him. Clutched him. Dragged him in! Hrothgar could be seen inside the demon's monolithic cube of green. His mouth gaped in dismay. Then his body started to spin. As it span, its arms and legs disintegrated into a blur of blood.

This process was utterly silent.

That was the hideous thing. The whole whirling, blurring, bleeding, chopping, disintegrating process made not a single sound. The dying Hrothgar was cut off from the world entirely, locked into a nightmare on his own.

The slug-chef Pelagius Zozimus once proposed constructing a machine with highly sharpened steel blades which would whirl round and round and round (driven by a slave tramping on a treadmill, or, alternatively, by a water wheel). Such a machine — he proposed calling it a food blender — would be used to finechop effortlessly a mix of apples, steaks and celery for the making of hamburgers. Hrothgar looked as if he had fallen into a gigantic version of just such a food blender, and his disintegration was proceeding apace.

Even as Guest watched, the top of Hrothgar's skull was

trimmed off, and his brains began to spill out. He whirled in screaming silence, then disappeared in a clouding blur of blood and bile and macerated flesh.

Then, abruptly—

A splurging outsurge of the finechopped corpse-mix hosed from the demon at pressure, accurately targeting Guest Gulkan's face. Blood-blinded, the Weaponmaster ducked, but the hosing found him nonetheless. He turned, tried to run, slipped on the weltering blood, recovered himself—

And was hard-slammed by Sod.

Struck by Sod's body weight, the Weaponmaster fell. His sword went flying, and Sod kicked him.

At the far end of the Hall of Time, the dwarf Glambrax saw what had happened, and charged with a cry of fury, hoping to cover a hundred paces before Sod could do Guest Gulkan a fatal injury.

Even as Glambrax charged, the Witchlord Onosh came panting upstairs from the depths below, panting into the Hall of Time with the staunchest of his warriors around him as a bodyguard. Downstairs, others were fighting a delaying action against a great wedge-mass of almost-victorious Guardians, who were triumphant in the certainty of victory, and who were baying for blood and slaughter.

CHAPTER TWENTY-THREE

Lord Onosh: a Yarglat barbarian whose bat-wing ears indicate his close genetic relationship to Guest Gulkan. "It's a wise man who knows his own father", or so say the wise, but, even in the folly of his youth, Guest has but to glance at the Witchlord's ears to know the truth of his fathering.

* * *

Lord Onosh was fatigued beyond his age. In the dying lantern light, sweat slid redshining down the furrows in his slanted forehead. He gave an overwhelming impression of weariness. He had been defeated once too often, and his resources of courage were almost exhausted.

With the Witchlord were the wizards Hostaja Sken-Pitilkin and Pelagius Zozimus. They too were similarly wearied, for they had exerted themselves to the full while trying to fight a way through to the Palace Docks.

They had failed.

Wizards and warriors alike, they had been defeated. The Guardians were too many. So the Witchlord Onosh, in company with his wizards and his other retainers, had been forced to retreat upwards into the less-populated areas of the mainrock Pinnacle.

On winning his way upwards to the Hall of Time, Lord Onosh summed it with the briefest of glimpses. He saw the dwarf Glambrax scuttling away towards the green lightblock at the far end of the hall, saw one or two people scuffling near that lightblock, and saw other than that pretty much what he had expected. As far as he was concerned, the Hall of Time was just one more hole in the night. A hole where he planned to rest, at least for a few moments.

Thinking thus, Lord Onosh slumped against the nearest wall, and closed his eyes. Such was his weariness that he sagged immediately into sleep — but he had slept for scarcely moments when he was shaken awake.

"What is it?" said Lord Onosh, opening his eyes to see that it was Bao Gahai who was rousing him.

"It is Rolf Thelemite," said Bao Gahai. "He has news."

Lord Onosh hauled himself to his feet and confronted Rolf Thelemite, who had previously been with those who had been fighting a rearguard action downstairs.

"What is it?" said Lord Onosh.

"I have news," said Rolf.

"News?" said Lord Onosh. "Then spit it out!"

"Thodric Jarl says we have secured the stairs," said Rolf. "At least for the moment."

"Then I could have slept for that moment!" said Lord Onosh, rightfully aggrieved at having been awakened to hear such absolutely superfluous information.

Then the Witchlord declared that he would sleep, and must not be disturbed. Having delivered himself of this pronouncement, he slumped again, and was asleep in moments.

But he was again awakened.

"What is it this time?" said Lord Onosh.

He felt as if he had only been asleep for moments — and quite rightly, for his sleep had been too short even for the quick-boiling of an egg in a pressure cooker.

"It is Glambrax," said Bao Gahai.

"Then spit him and cook him!" said Lord Onosh, who was ready to murder for the privilege of sleep. "Get Zozimus to cook him, and in a pressure cooker if possible."

"My lord," said Bao Gahai, "he says Sod has Guest as a prisoner."

Then Lord Onosh remembered what he had seen on first entering the Hall of Time. Glambrax sprinting for the green lightblock. Two people scuffling near that lightblock. The people scuffling must have been Guest and Sod.

"Glambrax!" said Lord Onosh.

"Here!" said the dwarf, who had been sheltering behind Bao Gahai.

"What are we up against?" said Lord Onosh.

"Sod," said Glambrax promptly. "Sod. And a demon."

"A demon?" said Lord Onosh, sceptically.

While the Witchlord Onosh had heard much of ghosts, gods and demons, he had never yet met one in the flesh, nor did he expect to.

"It is true," said Glambrax. "That green thing at the end of the hall, it's a demon."

"Then I will contend against it with my wizards," said Lord Onosh. "Zozimus! Zozimus, blast you! Where are you?"

Zozimus was discovered in the shadows, soundly asleep. Once he had been stirred awake by the application of Sken-Pitilkin's country crook, Lord Onosh commanded him to go downstairs and fetch a dozen or so corpses. The necromancer departed, returning shortly with eleven shambling corpses.

Then the Witchlord Onosh marched on the demon, taking with him his wizards, half a dozen living warriors and the eleven corpses animated by Zozimus. The dwarf Glambrax tagged along behind them.

"Far enough," said Sken-Pitilkin, when they were still a dozen paces short of the demon. "This thing bites."

"It bites?" said Lord Onosh, in bafflement. "Bites? Pitilkin, it is a rock!"

"It is a rock in its nature as a crocodile is a log," said Sken-Pitilkin.

The fame of the crocodile and its treachery had reached even as far as the lands of the Collosnon Empire. Therefore Lord Onosh knew full well that the crocodile was a vile animal which could configure itself as a log, changing instantly to a marauding maneater when some unsuspecting unfortunate stepped on it.

"Have you seen this particular crocodile in action?" said Lord Onosh, indicating the green-burning monolith.

"I have seen men fed to the thing," said Sken-Pitilkin. "It tore them apart in moments."

This was untrue, but Sken-Pitilkin felt that some amplification of the demon's dangers was necessary to discourage Lord Onosh from hazarding his person in a foolhardy assault on the green-glowing monolith.

In front of the demon, a great deal of scuffled blood was smeared on the skull-pattern tiles of the Hall of Time. Behind the demon was a stairway — a stairway which led upwards.

"Sod!" said Lord Onosh.

There was a pause. Then Sod came downstairs. The Banker came into view with Guest Gulkan as his hostage. Guest's hands had been bound behind his back, and Sod had a knife at Guest's throat. It was then that Lord Onosh realized he could have used an archer. Should he send for Morsh Bataar, who was downstairs fighting alongside Thodric Jarl?

"Surrender," said Sod. "Surrender, and I'll give you a quick death."

"And if I don't surrender?" said Lord Onosh.

"Why," said Sod, "then I'll cut your son to pieces, here and now."

The meagre terms which Sod offered, coupled with his uncompromising directness, told Lord Onosh that he had best not delay. Morsh might have been helpful, but it was too late to fetch him.

"Sken-Pitilkin," said Lord Onosh. "Get me my son."

The wizard Sken-Pitilkin heard the command, and quailed, for he was fearfully weary, and his strength was close to spent. But he exerted himself wizardfully. He raised his country crook and he shouted a Word.

Caught by Sken-Pitilkin's power, Banker Sod and Guest Gulkan were simultaneously levitated and dragged towards the Witchlord and his men. Lord Onosh cried in triumph. But he cried too soon! For the demon lashed out with liquid green tentacles, secured the levitated pair, and dragged hard and home to its own green-shining flank.

"Shan scaba mach!" said Lord Onosh.

His mighty oath was consequent upon extreme provocation. For the demon's own mass now sheltered Sod and Guest from arrow-shot.

"Perhaps Sken-Pitilkin could shake the demon a bit," said Zozimus brightly.

Sken-Pitilkin gave Zozimus a dirty look.

"An excellent suggestion!" said Lord Onosh. "Do it!"

"I will try, my lord," said Sken-Pitilkin.

But he had already guessed that the demon was so massive as to be quite unshakable. While the wizards of Skatzabratzumon can levitate a thing, they can also test the weight of a thing by tweaking it with a little leverage, and this is what Sken-Pitilkin did to the demon.

In response to Sken-Pitilkin's tweaking, the green-burning demon flashed purple, and gave a grumbling roar of discontent. Encouraged by this, Sken-Pitilkin tweaked it again. But this time there was no response. And the weight of the thing! Having tweaked it, Sken-Pitilkin estimated its weight as that of ten elephants.

"I tried to lift it, my lord," said Sken-Pitilkin, panting heavily as he feigned the aftermath of great effort. "But it would not budge."

"So we saw," said Lord Onosh, who had been greatly impressed by that flash of purple, which he took as proof of great wizardly exertions. "Zozimus! Do your stuff!"

At which Pelagius Zozimus sent his eleven corpses into action. They thrashed forward in a puppet-jerk frenzy. And were ripped to pieces by the slice-striking lighting of the demon's green-slash tentacles.

"Pitilkin!" gasped Zozimus. "Loft!"

In response, Sken-Pitilkin lofted one corpse, sending it up and over. It almost made it. But one of its feet drooped as it soared over the demon, and the thing snared the foot, then hurled the corpse to splattering destruction against the stairs.

Zozimus turned pale.

As the living human body is a well-knit and sturdy piece of construction work, so too is a fresh-killed corpse. As a necromancer, Pelagius Zozimus knew the hardiness of such a corpse, and was appalled at the demonic strength which could wreck such a thing beyond recognition.

"Give up!" yelled Sod.

"Give up?" said Lord Onosh. "How long do you think you can shelter there?"

"I can be up the stairs in moments," yelled Sod.

"Take one step from the shadow of that demon," said Lord Onosh, "and I'll split your skull with my battle-axe."

As it happened, Lord Onosh did not have a battle-axe in his possession. In any case, he was not one of those people who could throw an axe with any accuracy. But the point was made. Sod would be a target for swift-hurled swords and knives if he stepped from protection.

This raised an obvious question — could the demon deflect such missiles? Sken-Pitilkin thought it surely could, and thought that Sod would shortly realize as much.

"Zozimus!" said Lord Onosh.

"My lord," said Zozimus.

"This demon-thing," said Lord Onosh. "It seems it favours Sod. It discriminates, does it?"

Sken-Pitilkin was annoyed that the Witchlord had given a mere slug-chef priority as a source of advice. So, before Zozimus could answer, Sken-Pitilkin said:

"It discriminates as does a dog. It knows its master."

"A dog, is it?" said Lord Onosh. "It doesn't look much of a dog to me."

"A sparrow," said Glambrax. "It looks like a sparrow. Or a cockroach, perhaps?"

"It is a demon," said Sken-Pitilkin. "It is Icaria Scaria Iva-Italis, demon of Safrak and Guardian Prime."

"This is no Guardian, Pitilkin," said Lord Onosh, who knew full well that the Guardians were the Toxteth-speaking mercenaries who served the Safrak Bank.

"Yet it is, my lord," said Sken-Pitilkin. "For this block of stone has long had lordship of all the armed men in the service of the Bank. Each and every Guardian has sworn a mighty oath of fealty to this particular block of stone. Therefore, if we could but win its allegiance, then we could likewise win the allegiance of the Guardians as a whole."

"Then I will try to persuade the thing to my service," said Lord Onosh. "Does it speak Eparget?"

"It speaks the Yarglat tongue as it speaks all others," said

Sken-Pitilkin. "You may with confidence address it in Eparget, if such is your will. But — not too close, my lord! It bites!"

"So you have told me," said Lord Onosh, risking a single step which took him just a little closer to the green-burning stone monolith. Then he cleared his throat, finding that throat uncommonly dry, and said: "Guardian!"

"Guardian Prime," said Sken-Pitilkin, sotto voce.

"Guardian!" said Lord Onosh, ignoring Sken-Pitilkin. "I am Onosh Gulkan, he who is known as the Witchlord. Tameran is my domain, for the Collosnon Empire is the dominant power in Tameran, and I that empire's rightful ruler."

In response, the demon spat out a head. It splattered through the blood which sprawled across the floor in front of the demon, rolled across the skull-pattern tiles of the Hall of Time and came to rest at the Witchlord's feet. Its eyes had been sucked out, and the hair stripped from the scalp. Through the ragged flesh, bone shone bloody-green in the cold-burning demon-light.

Lord Onosh started involuntarily.

For his part, Sken-Pitilkin started not, for he had expected some kind of insult from the demon. As Lord Onosh began a fresh and windy declaration of his powers and prerogatives, Sken-Pitilkin drew aside the dwarf Glambrax.

"Glambrax," said Sken-Pitilkin. "You have an axe."

"Yes," said the dwarf. "But there is a great body of rock between me and our enemy Sod."

"So I have noticed," said Sken-Pitilkin. "However ... there was anciently a great and noble sport known as dwarf-tossing."

"So I have heard," said Glambrax gravely. "But if you are in a mood to toss someone, then why not a full-born warrior?"

"Because, said Sken-Pitilkin, "I am close to exhausted, and there scarcely remains to me the power to move even one of compact build."

"Then perhaps one of larger build will consent to be selectively amputated so that the tossing of him becomes a feat within your capabilities," said Glambrax.

These uncompromising words made it plain that the dwarf

was in no mood to be tossed. So Sken-Pitilkin said:

"If you will not exploit your natural advantages to attack Sod where he stands, then we are doomed to be overcome by the Guardians, and slaughtered to the last man. Your mother will die likewise. If you will not exert your blade for my sake, or your own sake, or that of Witchlord and Weaponmaster, then think at least of your mother."

At this, there was an outbreak of uproar from the stairway at the far end of the Hall of Time. Both Glambrax and Sken-Pitilkin turned, expecting to see a horde of bloodthirsty Guardians storming into the Hall. But the noise died down without consequence.

"Thodric Jarl holds the stairs for us," said Sken-Pitilkin. "For the moment. But he cannot hold forever."

"Then," said Glambrax, "let me arm myself with further blades, and I will permit myself to be tossed."

"Here is a knife," said Sken-Pitilkin, producing the small blade which he habitually used for peeling apples and cleaning out pipes.

Then the sagacious wizard of Skatzabratzumon busied himself with the job of persuading further blades from the possession of the nearest warriors. So, by the time Lord Onosh had given up all efforts to persuade the demon of Safrak to his cause, Glambrax was ready to be tossed.

"Are you ready?" said Sken-Pitilkin, picking Glambrax up by the scruff of the neck.

"What are you doing?" said Glambrax, in alarm.

"I am weighing you," said Sken-Pitilkin, setting the dwarf back on his feet.

"Weighing me!" said Glambrax. "I thought you had wizardry for that!"

"So I do, so I do," said Sken-Pitilkin. "But my powers of wizardry are almost exhausted. Besides, the muscular methods are often the best. Are you ready?"

"No!" said Glambrax, who had been unsettled by Sken-Pitilkin's lifting of him.

"Then hold tight!" said Sken-Pitilkin, who was deaf to the

word "no".

With that, the wizard of Skatzabratzumon levitated the dwarf. Up he went. The demon Icaria Scaria Iva-Italis roared at the dwarf, and lashed out at him with tentacles of near-invisible green liquidity.

Glambrax yelled, betrayed by involuntary terror.

But Sken-Pitilkin paid no heed to the dwarf's yelling. The wizard jacked the dwarf upwards until his back was brushing the living rock from which the Hall of Time was carved. Then the wizard slid the dwarf along that living rock.

"I'm scraping!" yelled Glambrax in alarm.

Sken-Pitilkin, who thought it better for the dwarf to be scraped than to be torn apart by the demon, slid the mannikin yet further. Glambrax was right above the demon. Which spat at him, sending gobbets of blood flying into his face.

"Ha!" roared Lord Onosh. "It can't reach him! Good work, Pitilkin!"

Sken-Pitilkin made no reply to this applause, for he was close to losing the dwarf.

"Hold tight!" yelled Sken-Pitilkin.

Then used his last energies in a single burst, hurling the dwarf towards the stairs at the rear of the demon.

Glambrax hurtled towards the stairs, landing heavily. For a moment, Sken-Pitilkin thought the dwarf had been broken. Then Glambrax stood up — groggily. Immediately, Sod charged the shaken dwarf.

"Swords!" roared Lord Onosh, making as if to hurl his own weapon.

The demon filled the air with a blurring lash-work of near-invisible tentacles. The air hissed with the sound of its scything tentacles.

"No!" yelled Sken-Pitilkin, striking down the Witchlord's weapon with his country crook. "No swords! Don't arm the demon!"

"But," said Lord Onosh, "but you said, we said—"

"We spoke of axing Sod, said Sken-Pitilkin, "but I at least have had time to think since then."

"But," said Lord Onosh, "but—"

But it was too late to argue, for Sod was already locked in combat with the dwarf Glambrax. Strength against strength they matched each other. Then Sod went down! Hacked in the kneecap!

"Aha!" yelled Glambrax, in triumph.

The dwarf hacked at Sod's boot, sinking his axeblade deep into the Banker's foot. As Sod thrashed and screamed. Glambrax positioned himself for a head-lopping stroke.

Then the demon acted.

With all other weapons exhausted, and with the combatants well out of reach of its thrashing tentacles, the demon used its last resource.

It hurled Guest Gulkan himself through the air, skittling the axe-wielding dwarf, and slamming both Guest and Glambrax hard against the stairs — slamming them home with such force that Sken-Pitilkin thought them surely dead.

Sod got to his feet.

Slowly.

Painfully.

He recovered his sword.

Guest and Glambrax made futile twitching efforts. Both were stunned, or ruptured, or paralyzed, or terminally broken.

With great labour, Sod began to limp towards them, with murder his intent.

"My son!" said the Witchlord.

Then Lord Onosh made as if to advance, and had to be physically restrained by the more level-headed of his warriors. And Sod took yet another step towards Guest and Glambrax, whose doom looked near certain.

CHAPTER TWENTY-FOUR

Icaria Scaria Iva-Italis: a demon incarnate in a square-cut jade-green pillar standing twice man-height, a pillar which glows with its own cold inner light. The demon has served the Safrak Bank for generations as Guardian Prime — ruler of the Bank's mercenaries — and Keeper of the Inner Sanctum.

* * *

This was an emergency. And all were helpless in the face of that emergency. But for Sken-Pitilkin!

The sagacious wizard of Skatzabratzumon lacked the power to send any foreign body hop-skipping over the demon's head. For his powers were subject to the laws of leverage, viciously restrictive laws which made it difficult for any wizard of Skatzabratzumon to support a weight at a distance.

But — there was himself!

Sken-Pitilkin could levitate himself without losing anything to the laws of leverage.

In the first flush of the possession of Powers, every fresh-made wizard of the order of Skatzabratzumon inevitably tries his hand at auto-levitation, that process which the unwashed peasantry vulgarly refers to as "flying". With equal inevitability, such a wizard soon knocks himself out against a ceiling, or the roof of a cave, or the eaves of a house, or a branch of a tree — thereby learning the virtues of dignity.

However — this was a crisis!

Sken-Pitilkin raised his country crook and shouted a Word.

He began to float upwards.

Lord Onosh roared with shocked surprise — roared so loud that Banker Sod turned in alarm. What Sod saw alarmed him even more. His jaw dropped as he gaped in horror-struck amazement. The jade-green demon lashed at Sken-Pitilkin, whipping the air to a frenzy with its tentacles.

Serenely unperturbed, Sken-Pitilkin floated overhead, just a hair away from the demon's lashwork. Sod started to back away as Sken-Pitilkin drifted towards him.

"Keep back!" said Sod, menacing Sken-Pitilkin with his sword.

At which, Sken-Pitilkin was tempted beyond endurance, and essayed that supremely difficult feat known to the initiated as the Reversed Looped Power Transfer, whereby levitational force is swapped from one object to another with the speed of a quick-blinking eye, with one object being forced upwards while the other sinks.

Sken-Pitilkin levitated Sod's sword while simultaneously causing himself to sink. But Sod held grimly to his weapon, and so was dragged upwards.

Neatly, Sken-Pitilkin touched down. Simultaneously, he ceased his Reversed Looped Power Transference. Deprived of levitational energies, Sod's sword fell. Not surprisingly, Sod fell with it. As Sod fell, Sken-Pitilkin whacked him with his country crook.

"Bravo!" cried Lord Onosh.

Sod hit the tiles. Inspired by the enthusiasms of battle, Sken-Pitilkin whacked him again.

"Enough!" shouted Lord Onosh, seriously alarmed. "No! No! We need him! He's our hostage!"

But Sken-Pitilkin, who had no taste for duelling, went on whacking until he was quite sure that Sod was unbattleworthy, and would remain so for some considerable time to come.

As Guest and Glambrax got groggily to their feet, Lord Onosh whooped with jubilation. But, for his part, Sken-Pitilkin was far from being elated. True, the Witchlord's son had been freed from the demon's grasp, but that was a trivial and temporary victory. Witchlord and Weaponmaster remained besieged in the uppermost parts of the mainrock Pinnacle, outnumbered by the Guardians who assailed their position from below, and meagrely provisioned (if they were provisioned at all).

"Well," said Guest, endeavouring to sound undaunted and doughty. "The next thing is to explore upstairs."

So saying, the Weaponmaster endeavoured to climb the stairs in question, and promptly tottered and fell over.

Sken-Pitilkin counselled Guest Gulkan to rest.

"You stay here," said Sken-Pitilkin. "Glambrax and I will go upstairs, taking Sod as our prisoner."

"But why?" said Guest.

"Because he is a danger to us here being so near to the demon," said Sken-Pitilkin. "For one moment's lapse in caution could see Sod act in league with that demon to ensure our destruction. We'll take him above, and bind him. You stay here. Stay and rest."

With that, the wizard Sken-Pitilkin and the dwarf Glambrax secured Sod and dragged the groaning Banker upstairs, leaving Guest alone on the stairs quite close to the demon.

As there was no way for the Weaponmaster to join his father the Witchlord — since the demon would surely have killed him or captured him had he essayed the passage past its greenblock heights — father and son could but exchange verbal tokens of their love and their mutual concern.

Then, realizing his helplessness — for the power of his wizards was exhausted, and the power of his warriors was a nullity in the face of the strength of the demon Icaria Scaria Iva-Italis — Lord Onosh made his excuses and withdrew. For he saw it as being his duty to go to the down-leading stairway to fight shoulder-to-shoulder with those of his men who were guarding that stairway against the assaults of the Guardians.

That left Guest alone, quite alone, utterly alone in the presence of the cold and unwavering green-burning light of the demon.

Guest sat on the steps, counting his bruises, and feeling quite sorry for himself. He had been hideously terrified by the demon, which had chewed up Hrothgar, which had splattered him with blood, which had held him prisoner with its invincible strength, and which hurled him at Glambrax.

And he felt abandoned.

Sken-Pitilkin had left him, and his father too. With good reason, doubtless. But even so. Guest felt uncommonly vulnerable, and forlorn.

With some considerable resentment, Guest gazed upon the man-eating jade-green monolith which he knew as Icaria Scaria Iva-Italis, Demon By Appointment to the Great God Jocasta.

"I thought you'd help me," said Guest, feeling that he had to vent his resentment, even though he did not necessarily expect a reply. "You told me I could be made a wizard. For questing, I mean. A reward. I was to quest to the Temple of Blood in the city of Obooloo. I was to rescue the Great God, the Great God Jocasta. Stogirov, wasn't it? Yes, that was it. The evil Stogirov holds the Great God Jocasta as a prisoner in the Temple of Blood in the city of Obooloo. You see? I remember perfectly."

Guest paused.

In response, the demon displayed the image of a head: a human head, dark-haired and bloodless, the eyes sucked out from the sockets and the ears eaten away from the skull. As this delusional image slowly revolved, the brute at last consented to speak.

"Thus you will end," said Iva-Italis. "You will end thus, for you have displeased me."

"A geek," said Guest Gulkan, mastering scorn to his tongue.

"I beg your pardon?" said Iva-Italis.

"A geek."

"I know not that word. Explain yourself."

"I was explaining you," said Guest Gulkan. "You're a geek. A thing which rips the heads off chickens for the joy of drunkards and the entertainment of whores."

Though Guest Gulkan spoke thus with scorn, it must be admitted that in truth the young Weaponmaster himself was not averse to occasional indulgence in the squaloring entertainments devised and enacted by geeks.

"So," said Iva-Italis, "it thinks to insult me."

"Why not?" said Guest. "For you are a mere demon. I am a hero, and as such I deal with none less than other heroes, or with the gods themselves. I have it in mind to speak to your own Great God, to Jocasta — through your mediumship."

"You would, would you?" said Iva-Italis. "To what end?"

"To make a bargain," said Guest. "When I was here last, that same Great God was of the opinion that it wished to be released from Obooloo. If I can bargain to my advantage today, then I will pledge myself to its rescue."

"You have come too late," said Iva-Italis.

"Too late!" said Guest.

"Do you think it is a pleasure for me to wait here at your convenience?" said Iva-Italis in fury. "You were offered the opportunity to quest in the service of the Great God. But did you so quest? No! You went whoring after the devices of your own heart. A god commanded you! But you paid that god no heed. No. It was your own squaloring wars which held your concern. But you lost. You were defeated. Don't deny it! So in defeat you thought yourself of the Great God Jocasta. Are we supposed to be honoured? Are we supposed to be honoured at being the last and least of all your choices?"

Guest found it hard to answer this scathing anger, for the plain and simple truth was that the anger was well-founded. Still, he was in no mood for apologies.

"I will make no excuses," said Guest boldly. "Still, I can make amends. If we can make a bargain, you and I, then I will venture to Obooloo in truth, and there will liberate the Great God Jocasta."

"Bargain!" said the demon. "I will have no bargains!"

"Then what will you have?" said Guest.

"You," said the demon. "You. As my slave. The slave of my flesh. If you choose to live, then you must live as my slave. The slave of myself and the slave of my god."

"I will join you in an alliance of equals," said Guest, "but I will make no pact that condemns me to slavery."

"You will, you know," said the demon.

"I would rather die," said Guest staunchly.

"Then die, then," said the demon.

With that, it abruptly caused the delusionary image of a head which it was displaying to twist, distort and crumple. Then it flushed from green to red and roared:

"Die, then!"

The roar battered the Weaponmaster like the wind-blast of a hurricane. He was so surprised that he fell over backwards. Then the demon laughed. Distantly, someone shouted:

"Guest! Are you all right?"

Guest sucked on his finger to moisten his throat, then shouted.

"I live!"

Then, focusing his attention on the demon, Guest renewed his negotiations with the jade-green beast.

"I will make a bargain with you," said Guest, speaking with care. "This is the bargain. You will save the day for me. You will command the Guardians to my service. With the day saved, I in turn will save the Great God Jocasta. I will liberate Jocasta from captivity in Obooloo. That is the bargain."

"I will give you no bargain," said the demon. "You will live as my slave, or you will die. You will knuckle to my command," said Iva-Italis, "or you will surely die of a certainty."

A certainty. A known thing. Knowing. Knowledge. It occurred to Guest that during his former exile on Safrak he had never heard anyone speak of the Great God Jocasta. Everyone on the island of Alozay knew of the demon Iva-Italis, but to Guest's knowledge nobody knew of the Great God which languished in Obooloo. It was a secret, then. But how much of a secret?

"Perhaps I will die," said Guest. "But before I go down to destruction, I will reveal to the world your secrets."

"I have no secrets," said Iva-Italis. "I stand here naked, and all of Alozay knows me."

"Your Great God is a secret," said Guest. "The Guardians don't know about your Great God, and — and — and these temple people, these people in Obooloo, how much do they know? I'll tell Sod, that's what, then Sod will tell Obooloo. Oh yes, and once Obooloo knows it has a Great God in its midst, well, who wants something like that lurking in the closet? Obooloo won't be very happy, no, and your Great God neither. The temple. The Temple of Blood. The Great God. Imprisoned by the Stog, the Stogirov. That's all they need to know. I'll tell

Sod, then Sod will tell, Obooloo will know, then it's doom for your Great God, or maybe for you too."

"An empty threat," sneered Iva-Italis. "For how would you or Sod say anything such to Obooloo when Obooloo is so far away from here?"

Now as it has been earlier remarked, Guest Gulkan knew no more geography than a hedgehog. If anything, he knew less. Therefore he had no true conception of the distance between Safrak and Obooloo, and no untrue conception of that same distance either. But, since Witchlord and Weaponmaster had recently performed prodigies of geographical excursion, venturing over unmapped lands with no more than sun and stars to guide them, Guest was inclined to sneer at distance, and to think no prodigies of sea or mountain sufficient to bar the distances to the brave. Hence he answered easily:

"Why, it will be no great difficulty for Sod to get news to Obooloo, for Obooloo is but a step from Safrak."

Now when Guest spoke of that "step" between Safrak and Obooloo, he was speaking in the poetic manner, in which a "step" can mean any distance less than a lifetime. But Iva-Italis took this throwaway remark for a statement of literal truth, and was enraged.

"Who told you of that?" said Iva-Italis in fury.

"Ha!" said Guest, realizing he had struck on something, though he did not know what. "It is a step, yes, a single step!"

"Who told you?" roared the demon, with renewed rage.

The roar was sufficient to refocus the attention of everyone in the Hall of Time on Guest Gulkan's dealings with the demon.

"Hush down," said Guest softly. "Or do you want them all to know the secret?"

"Come closer," said Iva-Italis, "and I will hush in truth."

"Ha!" said Guest. "Closer! If you want us closer, then you must come to me."

"Then stay where you are," said Iva-Italis. "But if you wish to have dealings with me, then you must tell what you know of the passage between Safrak and Ang."

Ang? Now where was Ang? Guest Gulkan was adrift already,

for though he had been told a thousand times that Ang is a province of the Izdimir Empire, and that the city of Obooloo stands fair and square in the centre of that province, he had neglected to commit these facts to memory. Hence the name of Ang came to him as if he and it were both just fresh-born. But Guest bluffed it out bravely.

"I am the Weaponmaster," said Guest staunchly, "and the greatest of my weapons are those of the intellect. I was born to power and then raised in the wisdom of wizards. I have walked in the sun and have walked at the feet of the dead. I have spoken with Those Who Are Not and have slept alongside Those Who Will Be. I have looked through time and space and I have seen much, aye, even the Untunchilamons."

A nice froth of nonsense, this! But Guest had heard sufficient legends, stories and fairy-tales to know how a Master of Knowledge and Power should speak, so spoke accordingly. And with remarkable effect.

"Untunchilamon!" said the demon.

"Why, yes," said Guest, surprised to see that he had enraged the demon yet further, but concealing his surprise with bland insouciance. "No secret is there concealed from me, for I know——"

Then Guest halted himself. He had been about to say that the Untunchilamons were a group of twenty-seven islands where the Rovac had long dwelt in power, but he dimly and distantly remembered the wizard Sken-Pitilkin correcting him on this. For some reason, Guest connected that correction with Strogloth, author of Strogloth's Compendium of Delights. So was Untunchilamon the birthplace of that infamous author? Perhaps. But Guest could not be sure of this.

"You were saying," said Iva-Italis, observing Guest's confusion.

Guest shook his head to free it from confusion.

"You have been addling my wits," said Guest, turning on Iva-Italis with a note of accusation.

"I?" said Iva-Italis in surprise. "I've been doing no such thing!"

"Of course you have," said Guest. "You know what I know and you know you must yield, but you have been negotiating in bad faith, seeking to probe me out of my secrets, and seeking also to delay decision in the hope that the Guardians may swamp my father's men and hack me before I can betray your truth to Sod. You think me patient? Patient I am not, not when I am hard up against the wall of my death. Very well! I must go call out Sod, for it is time for me to confess to him my secrets."

With that, Guest turned to go, making as if to head up the stairs to the abditory to which Sken-Pitilkin and Glambrax had conveyed the captive Banker.

"No!" said Iva-Italis. "Wait! I have a message."

"What message?" said Guest, turning.

"A message from Jocasta," said Iva-Italis. "Jocasta says you can have my help. If. If you will swear. If you will swear yourself to venture to Obooloo. Yes, and to rescue. To free the Great God Jocasta from the clutches of the evil Stogirov, High Priestess of the Temple of Blood. Do that, and Jocasta in gratitude will make you a wizard, yes, and you will live forever."

Guest hesitated.

"You realize what I need?" said Guest. "You realize what your offer of help implies?"

"Tell me," said the demon.

"It implies, among other things, that you must call off the Guardians. They have sworn oaths of fealty to you, therefore you can tell them to pledge their allegiance to me and my father."

"I will do it," said Iva-Italis.

"Then I will put you to the test," said Guest. Then again moistened his throat by sucking on his finger, and, having thus eased his throat for shouting, bellowed: "Father! Here!"

The Witchlord Onosh did not respond to this call, for he was out of earshot, having left the Hall of Time, descending to a lower landing where Thodric Jarl and others were in hot dispute with the Guardians. But the witch Zelafona and the wizard Zozimus approached the demon in response to Guest's shout, and, halting a safe distance from the beast, heard his requirements.

Guest required his father to ask that one of the Guardians come to the Hall of Time under flag of truce, to receive instruction from the demon of Safrak, Icaria Scaria Iva-Italis, Keeper of the Inner Sanctum and Guardian Prime.

A truce was procured, and a Guardian was allowed into the Hall of Time to hear the demon's diktat.

"Edlard," said the demon, identifying the Guardian by name. "You know me."

"You are my lord," said Edlard.

"Then hear," said Iva-Italis. "And obey."

Then Guest knew it was going to be all right.

The denouement was swift.

Long had the Bankers of Safrak trusted the demon Iva-Italis, relying on that demon to guard their greatest secrets, and using that demon as the supreme commander of the Guardians. But now that trust was betrayed. Edlard was commanded to give his allegiance to the Weaponmaster Guest, and to command the rest of the Guardians to present themselves to the Hall of Time to receive the same instruction.

In the end, the greatest impediment to the conquest of the mainrock Pinnacle was the Witchlord Onosh himself, for, being distrustful of the demon, Lord Onosh would only permit the Guardians to enter the Hall of Time in groups of three or four. Then, when all the Guardians in the mainrock had been sworn to Guest Gulkan's service, Lord Onosh banned all the Guardians from the Hall of Time, and commanded Thodric Jarl to guard the entrance to that Hall against all intruders.

Having thus ensured that Iva-Italis could not command the Guardians to betray the oaths so freshly given, Lord Onosh at last consented to venture past the demon to join his son. The wizard Zozimus went with him, and they took themselves up the stairs to pierce the mystery of the abditory above — the place to which Sken-Pitilkin and Glambrax had retreated with Sod as their prisoner.

At the top of the stairs, in the weirding room in the uppermost stratum of the mainrock Pinnacle, the abditory awaited. But in it was no great treasure, no mystery, no wonder, no splendour. Instead, the stairway debouched into a room which was large but plain, an airy room with multiple widespan windows, pleasantly lit but bereft of adornment. In the midst of this room there stood a plinth, and from that plinth there arose an archway of what appeared to be steel.

It was cold in that room, for the chill breeze of a winter's morning came wafting through those widespan window-ways. The greyest, chilliest, coldest light of dawn lit the room with a kind of grey liquidity. This was the light before the sun, the light which is too grey to sustain colour, the cold and disillusioning light which drains away the manic pretensions of the night.

By that light, Witchlord and Weaponmaster examined the disappointments of the abditory, its marble plinth, and its steel arch. Banker Sod had been firmly tied to that arch. He was asleep. The dwarf Glambrax appeared to be standing on guard, but on examination he proved to be asleep on his feet. The wizard Sken-Pitilkin was huddled on the floor, snoring.

"Sod," said Guest, waking the Banker by pricking him in the nose with a knifeblade.

Sod woke with a start.

"Your ring," said Guest, as Sod tried to blink away the confusions of sleep. "Give it! Or must I cut it from your finger? Your ring, man! And, mind — if you swallow it, I'll cut it out of you!"

In the face of Guest's threat — a threat which owed nothing to bluff — Sod surrendered up the ring of which the Weaponmaster spoke. This ring was adorned with a chip of ever-ice which, as Guest knew well, had the power to open and close the time prison pods of the Hall of Time.

Once Guest had the ring, he woke Sken-Pitilkin. The wizard proved difficult to rouse, so much so that Guest suspected he had been drugged. But he was merely exhausted. When roused from sleep, and persuaded that the demon Iva-Italis truly had betrayed the mainrock Pinnacle to the invaders, Sken-Pitilkin watched while Witchlord and Weaponmaster examined the plinth and the arch.

The search proved singularly disappointing.

"I had thought," said Guest, after long examination, "that there was some great secret here. But this is nothing."

"It is something indeed," said Sod. "It is a shrine, holy to the God of Money."

"Shrine!" said Guest. "I spit on your shrine!"

And he suited words to action.

"Come," said Lord Onosh. "There's nothing for us here. Come. The mainrock awaits. First the rock, then Molothair. That gives us Alozay. Let's take Sod and go below."

"No!" said Guest. "Not Sod! He stays here! I don't want him anywhere near the demon!"

Lord Onosh considered.

"That's reasonable," said the Witchlord. "By my judgement, we can't trust either in isolation, far less in combination. Sod! We'll keep you happy here! A jug of wine, a loaf of bread, a chamber pot — what else could you want?"

"A blanket," said Sod.

"Done!" said Lord Onosh, jovial in victory.

With blanket promised, Witchlord and Weaponmaster went below, accompanied by Zozimus and Sken-Pitilkin. Lord Onosh was impatient to be gone, but Guest paused in the Hall of Time, insisting on inspecting the time prison pods. For, in the course of descending from the abditory, he had become convinced that the woman Yerzerdayla stood frozen in one of those pods.

But a rigorous inspection of the time pods yielded up no trace of the woman, nor of any woman like her. This is the thing about visions, premonitions and such — even when a person does actually possess a Gift, their interpretation of the future is likely to be wrong as often as it is right. Lord Onosh, for example, most definitely had the Gift of Seeing; yet he was apt to mistake his own hopes and fears for the preaching of that Gift. So Lord Onosh, on a hunt in the mountains near Gendormargensis, had once thought himself doomed to die in those mountains, struck down by his son Guest — yet this had not happened, and, despite the strength of his convictions, the

Witchlord had returned alive to his capital city.

Betrayed likewise by the workings of his own unconscious mind, Guest hunted for Yerzerdayla in the Hall of Time, but found her not.

The young Weaponmaster did, however, find two time prisoners whom he recognized from the past. One of these was the elderly Ashdan who had once introduced himself as Ulix of the Drum; and the other was that Ashdan's servant.

The small and antiquated Ashdan was frozen in an expression of anger. He held in his fist a crooked walking stick, the head of which was a pelican cast in silver, and appeared to be using it to menace the world. Guest had no idea how long that Ashdan might have been imprisoned there, but decided to release him.

But first the young Weaponmaster consulted with Hostaja Sken-Pitilkin.

"You know this Ulix, don't you?" said Guest. "The pair of you were here that night, that night when the demon first talked of the Great God."

"It is true," said Sken-Pitilkin.

"Then what I want to know," said Guest, "is whether you think it's a good idea for me to let this Ashdan out."

Sken-Pitilkin considered, then said that the release of the Ashdan might have its merits. So Guest placed the chipstone of ever-ice against the surface of the Ashdan's time pod; and drew a line vertically on the transparent surface of that pod; and the pod opened sweetly, just as rumour had always said it would.

And out boiled the Ashdan, in the worst of tempers imaginable.

Fortunately, Zozimus and Sken-Pitilkin were able to placate that withered ancient, and ease his temper before he did an injury to himself while attempting to injure others. Much heated discussion followed, at the end of which it was proved that Ulix of the Drum had been in the time prison for upwards of a year.

"Though it was but an eyeblink for me," said Ulix. "And will have been an eyeblink likewise for my servant. Speaking of whom — I would be very pleased if you would release the fellow."

Now the Ashdan's servant was one Thayer Levant, who had the face of a rat and the eyes of a vulture. He wore a rag-tatter patchwork cloak which was weighted with lead so it could be used in a knife-fight; and the cloak was grimy; and his face was grimy likewise; and the eyes set in that face were bloodshot; and the teeth of that face were broken and brown; and his hair was brown likewise, and was thin, revealing the fungus which grew in green patches on his scalp.

But Guest was tolerant, therefore consented to release this miserable specimen into his palace. Upon release, Levant was soon orientated to his changed situation, and took up a position of watchful obedience a pace behind his master and a half-pace to his master's right.

"Very well," said Ulix of the Drum to Guest Gulkan. "Now you will pledge yourself to preserve my life, and in return I will do you a great favour."

"What great favour?" said Guest, who did not think that he had any cause to pledge anything whatsoever to this Ulix.

"Swear to him," said the wizard Zozimus. "Swear to him, for he is trustworthy."

"He is?" said Guest. "How would you know?"

"Trust me," said Zozimus. "Have I ever betrayed you in the past?"

"Have you ever had the opportunity?" retorted Guest.

Then Sken-Pitilkin intervened.

"Guest," said Sken-Pitilkin, "my cousin Zozimus is but a slug-chef, it is true, but even a slug-chef may have his honour, and Zozimus has his. Take his advice. I trust him, and so may you."

Then Guest Gulkan at last consented to be advised by Zozimus, and so swore that he would preserve the life of the ancient Ashdan, the pelican-bearing Ulix of the Drum. Whereupon Ulix said unto him:

"Come. Let us ascend to the uppermost chamber of the mainrock Pinnacle, and there I will explicate to you the greatest of the world's secrets, and its most powerful."

"We've been", said Guest. "We've seen. There's nothing there."

"On the contrary," said Ulix. "There is a great secret upstairs from here."

"An acroamatical secret, I suppose," said Guest.

"Precisely," said the Ashdan Ulix, raising an eyebrow. "How did you know that?"

"Because," said Guest, "I have long been in the company of wizards, and have enjoyed the full advantages of their tutoring."

And this Ulix believed, though the truth of it was that Guest did not know an acroamatical secret from a stench pit; and, while he used the word "acroamatical", and liked its flavour, he was completely ignorant of its proper meaning.

Lord Onosh was reluctant to be dragged upstairs, for a great weariness was upon him. Yet Guest insisted, for he was sure that Ulix of the Drum had something utterly fantastic to reveal to them.

And so it shortly proved.

CHAPTER TWENTY-FIVE

Inner Sanctum: the most secret of all the abditories of the Safrak
Bank. The Sanctum lies upstairs from the Hall of Time, and
the sole approach to the Sanctum is guarded by Icaria Scaria
Iva-Italis, the Keeper of the Inner Sanctum. Its contents —
so far as Witchlord and Weaponmaster have been able to
discover — are restricted to an uninteresting marble plinth
sustaining an inscrutable steel archway.

* * *

"Where's my blanket?" said Sod, when Witchlord and
Weaponmaster made their return to Jezel Obo, the Sky Stratum,
topmost level of the mainrock Pinnacle.

"Yes," said Glambrax, "and his chamber pot. I have need of
one, and so does he."

"There is the living rock outside," said Ulix of the Drum,
waving at one of the floor-to-ceiling windows with his pelican-
headed walking stick.

"Then let Sod loose," said Lord Onosh, "and let him dung
upon the living rock of the heights of the Pinnacle."

Sod was released, and his example proved inspirational, for
the whole company took itself outside.

The uttermost top of the mainrock was a perilous place. The
rock fell away steeply from the southern and northern windows
of the weirding room which held plinth and arch, and none but
a mountaineer in his folly could have ventured such steepness.
To east and west, the crested rock was narrow, and rough.

In his weariness, Guest was uneasy to be out and about on
such a perilous height, and was glad once they were back inside,
back in the uppermost chamber of the mainrock Pinnacle.

That chamber was as it had been previously — a big room
of disappointing emptiness, its airiness housing nothing of
worth, not even a clipped coin, a bent pearl or a slightly
despoiled virgin. It was devoted to the sheltering of plinth and

arch.

"Sod has been telling me of this plinth and arch," said Glambrax.

"Really," said Guest. "And what has he told you?"

"He has told me," said Glambrax, "that this archway is the eye of the Sacred Needle, and is symbolic of the pattern which the moon weaves through the sky, which pattern is matched by that of the shoaling of the fish which swim in the Swelaway Sea. That at least is what Sod says. He claims, then, that this Eye is a sacred monument, an altar of his religion. Nothing more and nothing less."

Glambrax voiced this in the Eparget of the Yarglat, and Sken-Pitilkin kept up a running translation in the Galish. Ulix of the Drum spoke many languages, as Sken-Pitilkin knew well, but the servile Thayer Levant was monolingual. So, out of pity for Levant's crippled condition, the wizard of Skatzabratzumon translated all into Levant's native Galish.

With the account of Sod's claims translated, Ulix of the Drum laughed, then said, using the Galish for the purpose:

"There is more to this thing than there appears to be."

So saying, Ulix gestured at the steel archway with his pelican-headed walking stick.

"More?" said Guest. "But what? Is it hollow? Is there gold and jewels and stuff inside?"

"Investigate," said Ulix. "Investigate, and find out."

Given that invitation, Guest Gulkan jumped up on to the marble plinth, walked round the steel archway, walked through that archway, kicked it, put his ear to it and listened to it, then said in decisive conclusion:

"I know what this is. It is art. I have heard about art. Sken-Pitilkin has tutored me in its intricacies. Art, or so he says, is great lumps of metal twisted beyond utility, then set upon marble for the general admiration of an uncomprehending public. This fits the description, does it not? This then is art, without a doubt — high art, like unto the works which are held within the tubework halls of the fair city of Veda."

"There is art within Veda, true," said Ulix of the Drum,

impressed with Guest's knowledge — though he would have been less impressed had he known that Guest was incapable of placing the city of Veda upon any map, even though Sken-Pitilkin had told him of its wonders some five thousand times at least. "But this, my young friend, this is not art."

"Then what is it?" said the Witchlord Onosh.

His query was voiced in the Yarglat tongue, but the Lord of the Silver Pelican responded in the Galish, with Sken-Pitilkin again providing the translation.

"My lord," said Ulix of the Drum, "this is a Door. It opens unto foreign realms, as a door of ordinary make opens from one room to another."

Guest, still standing astride the plinth, cast a sharp glance in Sod's direction. Banker Sod's yellow teeth were bared, and he looked very much the carnivore, and a hungry carnivore at that.

"Have a care for Sod," said Guest, warning his father. "For his temper is up, and he may do something foolish in a moment."

"Has he a weapon?" said Lord Onosh.

"He has not so much as a pin about his person," said Glambrax. "Unless he can kill with his hands, he is harmless."

"If he attempts such a killing," said Lord Onosh, "then he will die on my sword. Perhaps he will. For a great and perhaps contagious foolishness seems on the loose today. This business of a door — is that not foolishness? What we have here is plain. It is plain, it is clear to the touch and the eye. There's no door here. There's only an arch."

"The arch, my lord, is the door," said Ulix of the Drum. "For when it is opened, one may then step through from this room to a far and foreign country."

"And step back again?" said Lord Onosh.

"In a manner of speaking, my lord," said Ulix. "One must travel in a great circle, stepping from city to city, from nation to nation. But the journey can be accomplished in less time than a dog requires for its mating, and I have made that journey myself, many times."

"Really," said Lord Onosh, making no attempt to conceal his

disbelief. "Then if this be a door to escape, then — why, man, the door is yours! If the world lies but a step from this chamber, then go make that step — and vanish, if your choice is such."

"Ah, my lord," said Ulix, "but the door is not yet open. At the moment, the door is closed."

"Then open it!" said Lord Onosh.

"Ah," said Ulix of the Drum, "but to do that I must have in my possession a certain globe of stars, which I do not see kept here anywhere."

"Then we will find it," said Lord Onosh. "Sod! Have you hidden a star, a constellation or a cloudy galaxy in your blankets?"

"I have not," said Sod. "And it is only a madman who would talk such nonsense of stars. For the stars belong to the sky. Only a child would think to trap them down to earth, far less to snare them in a globe of glass."

"A globe of glass, is it!" said Lord Onosh.

"I presume that is what this Ulix-thing is trying to describe," said Sod stiffly. "For if his conceit is a globe of stars, then surely the globe must be of glass for those stars to be visible. But he is mad, plainly, so it may as likely be that he has a globe of wood in mind, or a globe of stone. You might ask him that question, if you wish to indulge him in his madness."

"It is a globe of glass," said Ulix of the Drum. "And," said he, pointing his pelican in the general direction of the Banker's heart, "Sod knows as much, and has doubtless fondled it into some secret privacy. Sken-Pitilkin! Have your prize student slit Sod's wrists! If he tells before he bleeds to death, why then, we'll bind his wounds and let him live. If not, why — there's plenty of other Bankers fit for interrogation."

Sken-Pitilkin thought this a little harsh, but Guest had heard. Thinking it a most excellent suggestion, the Weaponmaster jumped down from the plinth unbidden.

"Enough!" said Sod, backing away from a knife-bearing Guest Gulkan. "I'll tell! It's Italis, Iva-Italis, I gave it to the demon. The globe, the stars, the demon's got it."

"Nonsense!" said Guest. "The demon's mine, sworn in

alliance, my creature. It wants my help, it needs it. You're a liar,
Sod!"

But Sod protested that he was no liar, and that the globe of
stars in question truly had been given into the keeping of the
demon Icaria Scaria Iva-Italis. So it was that the whole party
went to interrogate the demon.

In truth, the demon of Safrak did have the star-globe in its
possession. But did not want to give it up! For the demon was
not yet sure of the worthiness of Guest Gulkan's oath to rescue
the Great God Jocasta, and had hoped to keep the star-globe
for a while, using possession of the thing to guide and control
the Weaponmaster for a while.

But on seeing that Guest was of such a temper that he was
currently neither guidable nor controllable, the demon at last
admitted to the possession of the star-globe, which it disgorged
with reluctance.

Guest caught the globe as the demon spat it out like a well-
sucked skull.

From the weight of it, the globe was stone rather than glass.
Heavy, heavy. Holding it, Guest felt his body become
weightless. His own flesh weighed nothing. Colour drained
from the world. Sod, Sken-Pitilkin, Ulix, Zozimus, Lord Onosh,
Levant — they were shadows, one and all. Sounds flattened,
shallowed, then skipped into silence.

Guest tried to drop the stone.

His fingers opened, but slowly, slowly. The world was utterly
dark, now. But for the stone. Which hung in the air. Motionless.
Unsupported. A green sheen of cold underwater light hung
around it in a halo. Then that light blinked out to nothingness,
and Guest was left in darkness.

He tried to move, to speak, to cry out, to reach for help, to
run. But he could not move. His body was a darkness in
darkness, a shadow in shadow, a spiral falling through a
waveform torus, a point bent on squaring a circle. He was split,
fractionated, divided into geometries. His geometry was music,
was gold upon silver, was amber sliding liquid upon the liquidity
of pearls, was ice forging copper.

Copper.

Weaving wires of copper.

Which were splicing themselves to sand, and to shadows. The shadows were those of the claws of a crab.

The crab was huge, and it stood in a weavework of titanium, crunching the heads of dragons in its claws, while bats sang from golden bells, and a penguin transformed itself to a grampus before Guest Gulkan's very eyes.

Then the visionary chaos steadied, sharpened, hardened, gained weight, and painted itself with colour. Guest found himself standing in his true flesh in an unfamiliar building which was fragrant with the smell of camphor. Somewhere in that building a woman was singing, her voice a pleasure of gold upon silk.

Guest looked around. He was standing in a cool and airy chamber, a large room connected to similar rooms by arched doorways. The room was hung by tapestries worked in abstract motifs, but the hexagonal tiles underfoot were devoted to representational art, for each was devoted to the depiction of one of the body's internal organs. Guest recognized the heart, the liver, the kidney — and was that a pancreas? He thought it was.

As Guest was still trying to decipher out the tiles — which he saw with hallucinatory clarity — a man entered the room.

The man was short, and grey of skin. To Guest, that greyness suggested illness, but the man seemed in good form as he came striding towards the Weaponmaster. He did however have a slight limp. Despite the limp, and despite the platform shoes which he was wearing — presumably to amplify his height — he crossed the tiles nimbly enough, and as he did so he addressed the Weaponmaster in a foreign tongue.

When Guest did not respond, the stranger reached out sharply and knuckled Guest with the back of his hand. The blow stung. Before Guest could react, the grey-skinned man whipped out a knife, a wickedly hooked device with a curious blob of bluish-green porcelain on the end of its blade. The lame little man jabbed at Guest with this blade, catching him a glancing blow with the porcelain blob.

A lacerating pain seared through Guest's chest, and he fell backwards, fell—

And fell—

Through darkness, now—

Fell backwards into light, and found himself falling still, and went down hard on the bones of his buttocks.

"Wah!" said Guest, as the stone globe popped from his fingers and fell heavily to the stone floor.

"What happened?" said his father.

Guest shook himself, looked around, and saw he was once more back in the familiar Hall of Time, back in the mainrock Pinnacle, back on the island of Alozay. But he was in pain still from the blow he had just been struck, and his nose—

The Weaponmaster touched his nose gingerly, and found it was bleeding from the back-knuckle blow which he had been struck by the grey-skinned stranger, who was nowhere in sight. Bleeding? The blood was pouring out!

"Lean forward, boy," said Sken-Pitilkin, his bony fingers pinching hard at the bridge of Guest's wide-spreading nose.

Guest, sorely shaken by his encounter with a world of visions, expected the sympathy and concern of his companions, but got not a jot of it.

"Come on," said Lord Onosh, recovering the globe of stars from the floor where it had fallen. "Let's go upstairs. Come on, Guest! It's only a nosebleed!"

As they climbed to the mainrock's highest room, Guest tried simultaneously to lean forward, to keep his nose pinched hard against bleeding, and to tell his story.

"A likely nonsense!" said his father, on hearing Guest's tale.

"But it happened," said Guest emphatically. "Why won't you believe me?"

"It's Eljuk who sees visions!" said Lord Onosh angrily.

"What?" said Guest.

He was startled, for here was a whole subject of which he was ignorant. His brother Eljuk, now apprenticed to the wizard Ontario Nol, had long been an object of Guest's jealousy — but the Weaponmaster had never till now received the slightest hint of Eljuk's dreams and visions, his night terrors and his waking apparitions.

"Eljuk, that's what!" said Lord Onosh. "He sees visions! But one such lunatic in the family is quite enough!"

"It wasn't a — a vision!" protested Guest. "I went somewhere! I'm telling you! I did, really I did. There was this woman, she was singing, she must have been beautiful, I'd pay gold to hear that song twice over. And a man, this funny little man on these weird shoes, and he, he — he hit me!"

"Not you too!" said Lord Onosh.

"But he did!" said Guest, seeing that he was disbelieved. "My blood, the nose, I mean—"

Helplessly, Guest held up his hand, which was streaked by the blood of his bleeding.

"So his nose bursts and he thinks himself gone," muttered his father. Then, angrily: "It's the mother! That's what's wrong!"

"Mother?" said Guest in bewilderment.

"Yes," said Lord Onosh, with increased anger. "It's your mother, it's her fault! Your mother, just as she—"

The Witchlord stopped himself. But he had said enough to leave Guest more bewildered than ever. The young Weaponmaster did not know who his mother was, hence could not guess what she might have done wrong. And what was the import of this waking dream he had just endured? Had his mother endured such dreams? Did Eljuk endure them still? And did Eljuk get bloody noses from some dreams of his?

Guest tried to think back to the years of his childhood. Eljuk had got bloody noses in childhood often enough, for sure — but all of those bloodspills could be traced easily and directly to the impact of Guest's feet, knees, fists and elbows.

They had now entered upon the mainrock's uppermost room, so, with their climb done, Lord Onosh tried to hand the star-globe to his son.

"Here," said Lord Onosh. "Take it again. Try it again. See what it does for you this time!"

Guest made as if to take the star-globe, then thought better of it, and let it fall.

"It's — it's too dangerous," said Guest.

"Is it?" said Lord Onosh, kicking the star-globe.

In response, the elderly Ashdan named Ulix of the Drum bent down, picked up the globe of stars, examined it carefully then offered it to Guest.

"Take it, boy," said the Ashdan. "It's perfectly safe."

"But," said Guest, fearfully, "I, I, it ..."

"You expected the unexpected," said the Ashdan. "You opened yourself to the new thing. So you ... you ..."

"What happened to me?" said Guest, with sudden anger. "You know, don't you! What was it!"

The Ashdan hesitated, then said:

"It is a Power."

Guest absorbed that as best he could, then said, slowly, slowly:

"Like — like something of wizards?"

"No," said the Ashdan flatly. "Like something of witches."

"What are you talking about?" said Guest, frightened to hear such a strange thing said, and said about him.

"Ask your father," said the Ashdan. "He knows."

Then Guest looked at Lord Onosh, who was silent, confessing no secrets. Guest looked back to the Ashdan. As if in a dream, Guest reached out and took the globe of stars from Ulix of the Drum. The star-globe was cold, cold and heavy. He held it. Held it firmly. The world remained unwavering.

"It doesn't change me," said Guest softly, wondering at the stability of the world, the firmness of the stones beneath his feet. "Not this time."

"It never did change you," said the Ashdan. "You changed yourself. As I said. You opened yourself to the new thing, the new experience."

"So this, this rock," said Guest, hefting the star-globe, "it's not dangerous. To me, I mean."

"You experienced the exercise of Power," said the Ashdan. "But the means for the exercise of that Power are sourced within you. That Power is not conjured by rocks, globes, talismans or charms. It's inside you."

"Inside me!" said Guest, in frank alarm. "If that's meant as reassurance, then I'd hate to see you let loose on a threat!"

By now, Guest half-understood that he had inherited something from his mother. But what? He was far from sure that he wanted to find out! The more he thought about his waking vision, the more it was frightening him. And to think that Eljuk had such visions, and that his father obviously feared them — why, that was more frightening still! And his mother — there was something wrong with his mother, was there? Well.

Guest had always believed his mother to have been a worthless slave woman long ago buried, her name buried along with her. But obviously she was still very bright in his father's memory.

"My lord," said Guest, addressing his father with due formality, conscious of the fact that they were talking in the presence of strangers such as Banker Sod and Ulix of the Drum. "May we talk later about — about my mother?"

"No!" said Lord Onosh.

A flat denial, this. But Guest had learnt enough already to realize that some dreadful secret surrounded his genesis.

This shook Guest more than any of the reversals of fortune which he had endured to date. The reversals of war — well, those he had been trained to cope with. After all, the young Yarglat barbarian had been born into a warlord's household, and hence had lived always with the knowledge that he might well suffer death, defeat, exile, pain, hunger, torture and mutilation before his life was out.

Hence Guest had remained comparatively calm through the vicissitudes of civil war and the alarums of the struggle for Safrak. Like a professional firefighter in the midst of a conflagration, or like a bear-wrestler engaged in one of his public duels, the Weaponmaster had, by and large, kept his head in even the worst moments of those conflicts.

But this—!

It was a dreadful and totally unexpected shock to be suddenly, profoundly and obscurely betrayed by his ancestry.

Obviously he had inherited from his mother some kind of flaw, a split in the brain, a breakage of the mind, a witch-warp of some description — and quite obviously his father feared for the consequences of this unexplained and inexplicable flaw.

A shock to the basic stability of the family background is always traumatic, even when the family concerned is an imperial family, and therefore intrinsically more unstable than most.

Hence Guest was suffering dreadfully, just as one suffers in the aftermath of the dreadful moment when a parent reveals that there are werewolves in the family; or that grandfather used to rape dogs for a hobby; or that grandmother routinely preached the evolutionary heresy; or that mummy is actually a man concealed in a woman's weeds.

"Very well," said Guest, reluctant to challenge his father further in the presence of strangers. "Let us pay no mind to visions. Let us try instead this precious door with this precious bit of rock."

So saying, Guest advanced upon the marble plinth which supported the steel arch.

As Guest advanced, he held the star-globe in front of him. It gleamed with a steady inner light, and its heaviness again made him think it more like stone than glass. It was transparent, its interior fogged with a motionless smoke of underseas mystery, and in the green of that fog there hung the motionless firefly sparks of stars of all colours, some inspired in their solitude, others hanging close in their massed groupings of their galaxies.

"Where do I put it?" said Guest.

"There is a pocket of sorts in the marble base," said the Ashdan ancient, Ulix of the Drum. "See it?"

"Yes," said Guest.

The "pocket" was a gilded hole about twice the size of the star-globe.

"Put the globe into the pocket," said Ulix. "Do that, and you will open the Door."

Gingerly, Guest eased the globe into the pocket. And let it go. It rolled home with a slight clunk. Immediately, the steel archway filled with a humming curtain of silver-grey, which looked to Guest like a vertical sheet of that slippery metal known as mercury.

"There," said Ulix. "It is open. Now you can go through it, if you dare."

At which Banker Sod swore at Ulix, swore fluently and potently in Galish. Ulix ignored the captive Banker, as did the others.

"So," said Lord Onosh, looking speculatively at the door. He was starting to realize that this thing was no ordinary door but a Door of major significance. "A Door, is it? Then where does it go to?"

Guest was of the opinion that the lord of the pelican had explained all this already. And so he had! But Guest was more ready to absorb explanation than was his father, since Guest had been rigorously tutored by the wizard Sken-Pitilkin since the age of five, whereas it is doubtful whether Lord Onosh was ever tutored by anyone in his entire life.

Ulix of the Drum, who knew that Lord Onosh was but a poor and ignorant Yarglat barbarian, ventured on a further full and complete explanation.

"Enough!" said Lord Onosh, when he thought his head had suffered injury sufficient for a single day. "This thing cannot be understood, that much I see clearly. But what it does, ah, that's simple enough. With a Door like this — well, enough of that! The important thing is to keep this secret, is it not? For with this — with this we can conquer the world, if we go about it softly."

"Softly, yes," said Guest, "for we would not wish to spoil our chances. I think to use this to conquer the world indeed, then to win back my empire in Tameran from Khmar."

"Your empire?" said Lord Onosh in astonishment.

"Why yes," said Guest. "The demon made the Guardians swear their fealty to me, did it not? Does it not therefore follow that I am their lord? And does it not equally follow that the mainrock is mine, yes, and Alozay as a whole, and the Safrak Islands likewise mine?"

"You have an enormous and arrogant conceit about you today," said Lord Onosh coldly. "That you happened to accept the surrender of some prisoners, why, that is but one of the commonplace incidents of war."

"Commonplace incidents!" said Guest, with explosive force.

"Yes!" said Lord Onosh. "A commonplace! A nothing!"

Now all this time, Banker Sod had been keenly watching Witchlord and Weaponmaster, and eyeing the disposition of the others. As father and son squared up to each other, looking as if they would be hacking at each other in moments, Sod abruptly moved.

Sod grabbed the dwarf Glambrax.

And threw him.

It may be that Sod had previously had some opportunity to practise the ancient and noble art of dwarf-tossing, for he threw Glambrax with uncommon force and accuracy, skittling both Witchlord and Weaponmaster. Then Sod threw himself on to the plinth, flung himself into a forward roll, and vanished through the Door.

Hot with rage, Guest scrambled up from the floor and leapt onto the plinth.

"No!" cried Ulix. "You—"

But it was too late.

For Guest plunged through the Door in hot pursuit of Banker Sod.

"My son!" cried Lord Onosh, in anguish. "My son!"

And with that cry the Witchlord drew his sword, as if intending to immediately revenge himself for the loss of his son. Fearing the temper of this stranger, Thayer Levant nimbled on to the plinth and bolted toward the Door.

"Levant!" said Ulix of the Drum. "You—"

But Levant was gone.

"Get him back!" said Lord Onosh. "Now! Now! You! Zozimus! Sken-Pitilkin! My son! He's—"

The Lord Onosh broke off, for a barrage of fighting men came shouldering through the Door. They were men dressed in the most sinister suits of black, their faces masked so that nothing showed but the whites of their eyes. They were Zenjingu killers, and they were bent on murder.

Immediately, Ulix of the Drum grabbed for the star-globe, yanking it from its socket. The Door closed. As the Door scissored shut, one of the Zenjingu killers was sliced clean in half by its abrupt closure.

"Cha-thara!" cried Ulix of the Drum, raising his pelican-headed walking stick.

At this Word, the Zenjingu killers began to stumble in blind disorientation, for Ulix of the Drum had neatly disabled their sanity. The Lord of the Silver Pelican was a wizard of Ebber, and his were powers over the mind.

Taking advantage of the disorientation of his enemies, Lord Onosh hacked and cut, slaughtering every last one of them. But that did not alter the facts. Guest Gulkan was gone, missing, vanished, wandering amidst the perils of some unknown foreign land, and there was no way for his father to get him back.

CHAPTER TWENTY-SIX

Door: an archway of what appears to be steel, set on a plinth of what appears to be marble. When activated by a star-globe, the Door fills with a humming silver screen. Each such Door typically forms part of a Circle, the separate parts of which can be continents apart. To interfere physically with such a screen is, in effect, to open a one-way valve to the next Door of the Circle. To step through such a valve is to find oneself Elsewhere.

* * *

With Sod having followed Guest Gulkan through the Door, and with Ulix of the Drum having closed down that Door, Lord Onosh took personal possession of the Door's controlling star-globe. Setting aside all questions of the fate of the Weaponmaster and the potential of the Door, he then set about consolidating his conquest.

At the command of the demon of Safrak, the Guardians had sworn themselves to Guest Gulkan's service. By isolating the demon, setting guards to prevent anyone from entering the Hall of Time, Lord Onosh ensured that the demon of Safrak did not give anyone leave to retract such an oath of fealty. By blurring the question of Guest's whereabouts — initially the world was led to believe that both Guest and Sod were still in residence in the heights of the mainrock — Lord Onosh neatly circumvented the possibility of any legalistic nitpicker pointing out that an oath to the Weaponmaster did not compel loyalty to the Witchlord.

Having thus temporarily shored up his position, Lord Onosh swiftly moved to reorganize the Guardians, combining his own men into that force, extracting personal oaths of loyalty from all and sundry, and diluting the old blood with new recruits.

In all of this, the Witchlord was advised by the dralkosh Bao Gahai, and, to a lesser extent, by the wizards Pelagius Zozimus and Hostaja Sken-Pitilkin.

So it was that Lord Onosh came to the Swelaway Sea in the winter of the year Alliance 4307, and, through a combination of courage, luck and studied brutality, made himself the undisputed lord of Alozay.

Notwithstanding all the reversals of the past, the Witchlord Onosh still claimed himself ruler of the Collosnon Empire. He hoped to use the islands of Safrak as a base from which to recover his empire. So he laboured mightily to secure his power base, soon reaching out from Alozay to bring all the Safrak Islands under his sway.

Recognizing that the greater number of his potential subjects spoke Toxteth, Lord Onosh set himself to master that tongue. Having mastered Alozay by the sword, he brought the lesser islands to heel by threat of violence, then chose sound-tempered Guardians to hold each of these islands in fief. Meanwhile, he dispatched ambassadors and a trade delegation to the free city of Port Domax.

Since no army makes its passage through any land without leaving wreckage and complaint in its wake, Lord Onosh sent other representatives to the west, to meet all claims consequent upon his armed withdrawal to the shores of the Swelaway Sea. In the west, his agents dispensed much good gold to settle claims for murder, and rape, and arson, and looting, and pillaging, and poaching, and blasphemy, and the desecration of temples, and horse rustling — all of which claims were well-founded, for the Yarglat are not gentle in either victory or defeat.

Furthermore, all those to north, south, east and west were invited to prove out any claims they might have against the Safrak Bank, since Lord Onosh recognized that he was now a Banker and must look to banking for his cash flow. In this spirit, he undertook to guarantee the safety of all trade through the Swelaway Sea, and confirmed Safrak's schedule of fixed and moderate charges for pilotage, provisioning, dock facilities and armed protection.

All in all, Lord Onosh conducted himself as a model ruler,

which proved decidedly expensive in the short term. There were, for example, a full twenty merchants from Port Domax who had managed to get themselves killed during the Witchlord's armed seizure of the mainrock Pinnacle and the associated city of Molothair, and in the fullness of time Lord Onosh paid full and generous compensation to the widows of each.

In such many and varied acts of mercy, peace, justice and generosity, the Witchlord Onosh expended the last of the treasure brought with him from Gendormargensis, which left him bitterly impoverished, though his wizards assured him he would recoup his losses a dozen times over in the years ahead.

"Recoup, recoup!" said Lord Onosh furiously. "I was born to loot, not to recoup!"

Justice, mercy, peace and generosity had not come naturally to the Witchlord Onosh, and each dispensing of gold had cost him dearly, as if he were paying his many creditors in lumps of flesh torn hot and bleeding from his protesting bones.

"We know your propensities, for you have told us of them often, my lord," said Pelagius Zozimus calmly. "But, believe me, recouping is the greatest looting of them all."

"If I'd been not so weak in my defeat," said Lord Onosh, bitterly regretting the delicacy of his position on Alozay, the smallness of the forces at his disposal and the greatness of his enemies, "you'd never have forced me to this folly."

"Forced!" said Zozimus, looking at Sken-Pitilkin. "Did we do any forcing?"

"I would count it impossible," said Sken-Pitilkin, "for it is well known that the weakest of the Yarglat warlords is a match for any ten wizards in the world, and the great Lord Onosh is not a weak warlord but one mighty in the courage of his sword."

Yet the truth of the matter is that Sken-Pitilkin and Zozimus — acting in concert with Bao Gahai — had indeed forced the Witchlord Onosh to follow a path of reason, moderation, compromise and diplomacy, encouraging him to secure the peace of his own domains and appease his neighbours before making his next move.

The Witchlord's obvious, necessary and unavoidable next move was to open the Door in the uppermost chamber of the mainrock Pinnacle, the Door which was still a tightly guarded secret known to only a chosen few. With that Door reopened, Lord Onosh could then negotiate with the Banks of the Circle. Nightly the Witchlord sat in conference with Ulix of the Drum, who told him much of that Circle. Only from that Circle could Lord Onosh draw the power he needed to overthrow the invader Khmar and reclaim his empire. Only the Banks of the Circle could provide him with the warriors he needed, warriors in their thousands, and weapons, and horses, and all necessary gear of war.

"Including, one hopes," said the sagacious Sken-Pitilkin, when appraised of the Witchlord's plans for war, "a good supply of cushions and collapsible armchairs."

Yet if Sken-Pitilkin spoke lightly of the Witchlord's plans for conquest — he cared not a whit who ruled in Gendormargensis, and would happily have traded all the lands of Tameran for a pair of sheepskin slippers and a baked onion — Lord Onosh was in deadly earnest.

In the earnestness of his intent, the Witchlord took care to neutralize all his potential enemies. The greatest of these was surely the demon Iva-Italis. For that uncannily intelligent block of jade-green stone commanded the only stairway leading to the highest chamber of the mainrock Pinnacle, and had proved its ability to enforce its rule of those stairs by eating men at whim.

Lord Onosh did not trust the demon-thing, and, with his wizards supporting him in his distrust, the Witchlord had his carpenters build him an outer stairway. This outwork climbed from the floor below the Hall of Time to the floor above, thus allowing one to bypass the demon. Thereafter, the Hall of Time was forbidden to all, and even the Witchlord and his wizards never went there, for after long conference they were mutually agreed that the demon should be shunned, and that all people of all rank should be kept well away from it lest it suborn the weak-willed in conspiracy.

So it was done.

As for the secret of the Door, it was agreed that this secret should continue to be held in the smallest circle possible. So men of rank such as Thodric Jarl got a tour of the uppermost room in the mainrock Pinnacle, and were there shown the metal arch and the marble plinth, and were told that it was a mystery—

"Most probably," said Zozimus gravely, giving the standard lecture which he gave to all and sundry when he conducted these tours, "a secret shrine sacred to a great god, but what god we cannot tell, and will probably never know."

Thus Thodric Jarl and others saw the greatest secret of the Bank, and, finding nothing there of any note, thereafter forgot about it; whereas, had the room been banned to them, they would doubtless have been afire with curiosity about it for the rest of their lives.

Now since the Witchlord was dynamic in his execution of his policies, and since he was well supported by men of talent, and by the womanly talents of the witches Bao Gahai and Zelafona, and by a wizard mighty in wisdom, and by a slug-chef, and by a dwarf, and by Ulix of the Drum as well, all these things were accomplished with surpassing rapidity, and news of the accomplishments spread equally as quickly.

When all is said and done, the Swelaway Sea is but an overgrown lake, and a ship at a speed of fifty leagues a day can reach from its central islands to its shores in a matter of four to six days. If one buys a rotten boat from the villainous villagers of Ink, or if one is forced to interpolate an airship adventure into one's travels, then such a journey has the makings of an unfortunate epic; but, as in all things, concerted professional organization reduces epic potential to routine.

And though it had been woefully difficult for Lord Onosh and his army to make the march to the Swelaway Sea, when they knew not quite where they were going, and had no conception of what paths or roads they should be looking for, and were poorly clad, ill-shod, short-rationed and grotesquely overloaded with treasure, overland journeys in all directions were a thing of ease to organize from Alozay.

For, after all, Alozay was in business as a Bank, and a trading bank at that; and hence the Guardians of Safrak were veteran travellers able to bodyguard and guide the innocent and the ignorant alike over any piece of country between Port Domax and Gendormargensis.

Hence Lord Onosh was able to economically accomplish his tasks, without lavishing generations on their achievement; and some news of his accomplishments spread with a similarly economical rapidity.

In particular, news of the raw and unadorned fact of the Witchlord's conquest of Alozay soon reached the Collosnon Empire, for some Guardians had escaped toward that Empire with news of the Witchlord's triumph. Those Guardians had thought that they would be well-rewarded for bringing that news to his enemies — and in this they were right.

The Guardians who carried that first raw news of conquest fled from Alozay to Ink; then dared down the Pig, riding the speed of the dog-drawn sledge, which is ever the favoured transport of those few fur-merchants and such who trade the continental winter; then, believing Khmar to be still in Locontareth, expressed their sledges in that direction, and were favoured by the confirmation of their belief.

Thus it was that Khmar learnt early of the Witchlord's success, and set in train the actions necessary to neutralize his enemies.

The winter of the year Alliance 4307 came to an end; and in the spring, emissaries from the Yarglat barbarian Khmar came to parley with the Witchlord Onosh. Khmar's embassy was led by one Lord Alagrace, who had been in Gendormargensis when Khmar invaded, and had chosen to give his loyalty to that invader. Lord Alagrace and his fellows presented the Witchlord with an offer from Khmar. The usurper Khmar would grant Lord Onosh a peace if the Witchlord would order all parts of his empire to surrender to Khmar.

For it happened that some parts of the empire had yet to surrender to Khmar; and Khmar, who was great in ambition, wanted to consolidate his rule without further bloodshed. For Khmar wanted to save his soldiers for the great invasions and conquests which he planned to make in the future.

Lord Onosh was initially reluctant to agree to Khmar's demands.

"This implies," said Lord Onosh coldly, "that I am to surrender my empire to Khmar."

"As I see it," said Lord Alagrace, who was possessed of uncommon wisdom, even though he was a mere man, and no wizard, and had no especial command of the irregular verbs, "you do not have an empire to surrender. You have merely some poor and unsupportable claims to an empire. All Khmar asks you to do is to give up those claims."

"The claims and the empire are one," said the Witchlord stoutly.

The sagacious Sken-Pitilkin, who had the privilege of following this dialogue, doubted that this claim was tenable in logic. But Lord Alagrace was too wise to argue with the barbarous Witchlord on the grounds of logical consistence.

Instead, the mighty Lord Alagrace, Khmar's calm and intelligent ambassador, explained to the Witchlord that some of Khmar's men had dared to Ibsen-Iktus in winter. They had struck, had conquered, had imprisoned — and now held as prisoners both the Witchlord's son Eljuk Zala and the wizard Ontario Nol.

Now it was proved of a certainty that Eljuk was a prisoner, for Eljuk himself had written a letter confirming this, and had written that letter in foreign verbs of such pronounced irregularity that they were known to only two people on the entire continent of Tameran, those two being Eljuk himself and his former tutor Sken-Pitilkin. Furthermore, Ontario Nol had drafted a collaborative letter in the High Speech of wizards; and both these letters were beyond the power of Khmar to fake.

Then Lord Onosh was sorely oppressed.

For Khmar held his son as a prisoner, and—

If one's son be placed in the scales and weighed against an empire, then it will invariably be found that the empire is heavier. However, the Witchlord Onosh had personally seen the mountains of Ibsen-Iktus, and believed those heights to be surely impassable by winter. Khmar, by exercise of invincible will, had successfully commanded men into those mountains in the coldest of seasons. Driven by Khmar's will, those men had subdued a wizard, and had tamed him to accept his chains.

It was Khmar's defeat of the abbot of Qonsajara, rather than any over-tender concern for his son, which at last made Lord Onosh despair of defeating his enemy. In the short term, he lacked the strength to wrest the Collosnon Empire from Khmar's grasp. And, though future dealings with the Circle of the Banks might increase the Witchlord's strength, he might not be permitted time for such dealings — for the Khmar who could successfully organize the storming of the heights of Ibsen-Iktus could surely break the strength of a mere pin-spike like Alozay, and break it ten times over between breakfast and lunch.

"What are your terms?" said Lord Onosh to Lord Alagrace.

Alagrace stated Khmar's terms simply.

Khmar would surrender up both Eljuk and Ontario Nol in exchange for the Witchlord's surrender of all claims to the Collosnon Empire.

"And," said Lord Alagrace, who was not yet finished. "And—"

Here he hesitated.

"And what?" said Lord Onosh sarcastically. "My head, perhaps?"

"No, my lord," said Lord Alagrace. "The only other thing which Khmar requires is the services of Thodric Jarl."

"Well!" said Lord Onosh. "He's out of luck! For Jarl is a free man! Were Jarl a slave, I could sell him or trade him, but it is an oath of fealty which binds us. Undo such an oath, and I undo my every claim to be fit for the rule of an empire."

"Jarl is a free man, as you say," said Lord Alagrace, "and Khmar does not seek him as a slave. Let us summon Jarl, and see what he says in his freedom, and it may be that he thinks alike with Khmar."

Lord Onosh thought this unlikely, but nevertheless had Jarl brought before them — and was somewhat distressed by the outcome. For the Rovac warrior did not hesitate. On hearing that Khmar wanted him, the grey-bearded Jarl decided without hesitation that he would gladly return to the Collosnon Empire to fight for Khmar in Khmar's wars. Here we remember that Jarl, despite the grey of his beard, was aged but 26, and hence far too young to contemplate with equanimity the prospect of a lifetime's retirement on Alozay.

But, on interrogating Jarl, Lord Onosh discovered that the Rovac warrior's chief concern was the woman Yerzerdayla, who was still resident in Gendormargensis. Offended to find his chiefest general deserting him for a woman's favours, Lord Onosh then arranged, by covert treaty, for Alagrace to arrange for Yerzerdayla to be covertly conveyed to Alozay, and for Thodric Jarl to be told that she had died.

"I have another Rovac warrior if you would like him," said Lord Onosh. "One Rolf Thelemite by name. Do you want him?"

"No thank you my lord," said Alagrace. "His name came up in conference, and Khmar said you could keep him."

"But he is a mighty warrior," said Lord Onosh, endeavouring to be persuasive. "So mighty in valour that I trusted him to be the bodyguard to my best-loved son, Guest Gulkan."

"Then that hardly speaks in his favour," said Lord Alagrace, "for I have heard that Guest Gulkan is missing, and rumour holds him to be dead. In any case, Khmar distinctly said that he wished for Rolf Thelemite to remain in your service, to be a comfort to you in your old age."

"That was very generous of him," muttered Lord Onosh. "Very well! Let's draw up a treaty, then."

So a treaty was drafted, and bickered over. The last thing to be settled was its title: the Treaty of Eternal Friendship between the Collosnon Empire and the Islands of Safrak. With the title confirmed, the thing was signed, and witnessed by everyone from the dwarf Glambrax to Edlard of the Guardians.

The treaty consigned the Collosnon Empire to the rule of Khmar and his heirs; it called on all those still resisting Khmar to surrender to his rule; it secured the Safrak Islands and the Swelaway Sea for Lord Onosh and his heirs; and it specified that there should be a peace between the Empire and the Islands:

"... until the last Rider be unseated from the Horse; or all horses lose their hair; or the wind cease its riding; or blood be milk and cheese be water; or the dogs be unheard by the campfires; or no child be born to any of the tents of the Yarglat; or Drangsturm fall and the Swarms claw all established order to an end."

That last bit about Drangsturm and the Swarms had been inserted into the language of the treaty by the wizard Sken-Pitilkin, who felt that the bits about wind, horses and hair were too vaguely unspecific for a legal document. (And who felt, too, that the language of a formal treaty should be suitably remote from that of a smoky barbarian campsite and the ethnological curiosities of a shaman's chant.)

This treaty was signed at the end of spring in the year Alliance 4307. Come Midsummer's Day, when the year Alliance 4308 began, the conqueror Khmar formally proclaimed himself emperor, and that day was the first day of the year Khmar 1.

The lord emperor Khmar then began to plan the conquest of all of Tameran, excepting Safrak alone — the exception being an honest one, for Khmar was great in honour, and fully intended to be true to his treaty. But that was of small consequence to the Witchlord Onosh, who had resigned himself to living out his years in the circumscribed kingdom which had fallen to him by conquest.

The main event which did concern the Witchlord Onosh was the arrival of his son Eljuk Zala, who came to Safrak in the company of the wizard Ontario Nol on Midsummer's Day, the first day of the year Khmar 1; and Lord Onosh received Ontario Nol with every mark of respect, and declared Eljuk to be the heir of Safrak, and ordered a great celebration to mark the event.

"But where," said Eljuk, "is Guest?"

"He is missing," said Lord Onosh. "Missing, believed dead. He vanished shortly after our battle for the mainrock Pinnacle, and has never been seen or heard of since."

But actually, of course, as the Witchlord Onosh knew full well, the Weaponmaster Guest was somewhere in the Circle of

the Banks, and there was no telling what fate might by now have
befallen him.

CHAPTER TWENTY-SEVEN

Name: Eljuk Zala Gulkan

Birthplace: Gendormargensis

Occupation: apprentice wizard

Status: heir of Safrak

Description: a mild-mannered Yarglat youth who has from earliest youth shown an unfortunate tendency to flinch at the sight of rearing horses, naked swords and hot decapitations.

Hobbies: lyric poetry, collecting the shells of snails and flying kites (these last two hobbies inspired by his new tutor, the wizard Ontario Nol).

Quote: "I am but one and once but often and many shall be" (taken from Yo Bo's mystical magnum opus, *On the Immortality of Scholarship*).

* * *

So Eljuk Zala Gulkan came to the island of Alozay in the company of the wizard Ontario Nol, and the Witchlord Onosh ordered that a great banquet be held to celebrate the arrival of his son. The city of Molothair was lit with lanterns and the mainrock Pinnacle likewise. To the Grand Palace of Alozay came fish fresh from the Swelaway Sea, sheepmeat from Ema-Urk, the flesh of bears and pigs which had been hunted to their deaths in mainland wilderness, and — ever the greatest luxury to the Yarglat palate —the meat of horses.

Upon this bounty the Yarglat feasted, and while they feasted they were entertained by a troupe of wandering musicians from the far and distant land of Sung. The musicians of Sung are famous for their travelling. Some say this is because they are not mortal men at all, but, rather, belong to a class of spirits forever doomed to wander the world until they have appeased their former sins. This of course is a nonsense, for the music of Sung owes nothing to appeasement: rather, it is but one extended exercise in patent affront.

Before retreating to Tameran to escape the wrath of the Confederation of Wizards, the sagacious Sken-Pitilkin had dwelt for generations on the island of Drum (which of course has nothing whatsoever to do with Ulix of the Drum), and while living on that island the noble wizard of Skatzabratzumon had often been embroiled in the affairs of the people of Sung (usually against his better judgement, but it cannot be denied that he was sometimes well-rewarded for his troubles, since Sung is the source of the best smoked ham to be had in all the world).

In consequence of his past experiences, the wizard Sken-Pitilkin realised what they were in for as soon as the Sung musicians first entered the banquet hall, variously rolling, pushing, kicking, dragging, hauling or chasing their ill-willed instruments of delinquency.

Sken-Pitilkin realized, and groaned.

But the Yarglat did not realize.

To them, it all came as fresh revelation.

Throughout the banquet, the Sung musicians played. They filled the air with the galloping vigour of the thrum, an instrument which makes a sound like that of butter and bones being churned together in a waterlogged coffin. They played too the kloo, which makes a sound like the strenuous protest of a water buffalo which is resentful of being heartily kicked. The krymbol, the skittling nook, the plea whistle and the vang — of all these those musicians had mastery, and proved their mastery amply.

Many of the Yarglat were much taken with the vang, which struck them as the most remarkable device they had ever seen in their lives. And truly the vang is a mighty instrument indeed, consisting as it does of a series of huge tubs from which fluids thick and thin are disgorged by a series of vents and holes, making sounds imitative of urination and of vomiting. But in its noise-making capacity the poor vang was entirely outclassed by the skavamareen, a demon-wailing machine which makes a sound like a burnt cat screaming in a sewer-pipe.

All of which was a matter of amazement to the Witchlord Onosh.

For he had never heard anything like it in his life.

The Witchlord Onosh, after all, was a Yarglat barbarian, the scion of one of those horsetribes of the far north of Tameran; and despite the fact that he had spent much of his life in the great city of Gendormargensis, he had never been exposed to much in the way of musical culture.

The Yarglat in their dogbone encampments are much given to chanting and wailing, accompanied by a certain amount of beating upon drums, but no greater orchestration is known to them. In the fullness of their power, the Yarglat had come to dominate other peoples, such as the Sharla, who were mightily learned in music. But the instruments of the Sharla are typified by the klon, a fine-stringed device which is plucked but one note at a time, with that note being allowed to die away before another is added to the air. The music of the Sharla is delicate; and tentative; and refined; and consequently adds nothing of consequence to the savour of burnt horsemeat or roast fish-dung.

But this music of Sung!

"There is more to music than I had thought," said Lord Onosh contentedly.

And he resolved himself to have Sung musicians play for him nightly thereafter, and maybe even to obtain mastery of a musical instrument himself — maybe one of the percussive kind, built to take a strenuous hammering.

In the strength of his musical contentment, Lord Onosh paid little heed to the manner of his favourite son's banqueting, and it was not until the banquet had been stripped to the bones that the Witchlord noticed that Eljuk had eaten virtually nothing.

"Where is your appetite?" said Lord Onosh.

But the Sung musicians interrupted his question with a crescendo; and a joyfully appreciative audience demanded an encore; and an encore was duly provided; and, as one thing led to another, the Witchlord took his favoured son by the elbow and led him from the banqueting table, thus quitting a scene which was fast disintegrating into outright orgy.

Once safe in the peace of his private quarters, Lord Onosh sat his son down in a chair most cunningly made from interwoven canes and the skins of several fishes. With Eljuk thus seated, the Witchlord asked him:

"Eljuk. What's wrong? You ate nothing tonight. Do you distrust the competence of my food tasters? Or what?"

"My sorrow," said Eljuk, "leaves me with but little appetite."

"Sorrow!" said a bewildered Witchlord. "What's there to be sorry about? Why aren't you happy?"

Eljuk looked his father in the face, looked away, hesitated, bit his lip, then said in a blurt—

"How can I be happy in the house of my brother's murderer?"

"Murderer!" said Lord Onosh in astonishment. "Since when am I your brother's murderer?"

"Why, Guest is dead, is he not? He can hardly have flown from this island, can he? Yet Rolf Thelemite has told me—"

"Thelemite!" said Lord Onosh, as if the word were obscene.

"Thelemite, yes," said Eljuk, "The good Rolf Thelemite told me as clear as anything that he saw Guest alive and jumping in the Hall of Time, well after any fighting was over. Furthermore, he was led away by your wizards, by Zozimus and Sken-Pitilkin, and now you say he's dead, he's—"

"He's missing," said Lord Onosh.

"He's dead!" said Eljuk. "Missing, that's a nonsense, he wouldn't go missing in the company of wizards, they'd know where he went at least, and he wouldn't go anywhere without Rolf, which means that you killed him. You murdered him! And so I renounce you!"

With that, Eljuk rose abruptly, overturning his chair in his impetuosity, and made as if to flee. But Lord Onosh grabbed his son by the sleeve, restraining him from flight.

"You renounce me?" said Lord Onosh. "For what?"

"For killing Guest."

"But I've told you already—"

"You killed him!"

"Supposing I did, then," said Lord Onosh. "Even if I did—and I swear by my blood that I didn't — why should his death count as anything to you?"

"He was my brother," said Eljuk. "The brother of my blood. He saved my life when I would have died in the Yolantarath. He saved me from drowning. At risk to his own life — he never knew how to swim. Now he'll never learn."

Such was Eljuk's distress that, in the end, Lord Onosh felt he had no choice. Gently, the Witchlord constrained Eljuk to set his chair upright, then to seat himself in that chair; and, with Eljuk thus seated, the Witchlord began to explain the true fate of the Weaponmaster Guest Gulkan.

And the upshot of a long debate between father and son was that the Witchlord at last agreed to open the Door in the uppermost chamber of the mainrock Pinnacle; and to precipitate the confrontation of the Banks of the Circle for which he had been preparing himself; and, if it was possible, to initiate the rescue of the missing Weaponmaster.

CHAPTER TWENTY-EIGHT

Partnership Banks: those Banks which have long exploited the
Circle for secret profit. On Alozay, the Safrak Bank has ever
been the government; but governments elsewhere have
usually been ignorant of the secret of the Circle. Since the
Banks are immortal bureaucracies they have managed to
outlast kingdoms, empires and dynasties. Starting from
Safrak, the Banks of the Circle are these:
— the Safrak Bank of the Safrak Islands
— the Monastic Treasury of Inner Adeer, in Voice
— the Flesh Trader's Financial Association of Galsh Ebrek
— the Bondsman's Guild of Obooloo, capital of Aldarch III
— the Bralsh, of Dalar ken Halvar
— the Singing Dove Pensions Trust of Tang
— the Taniwha Guarantee Corporation of Quilth
— the Orsay Bank of Stokos
— the Morgrim Bank of Chi'ash-lan

* * *

Three men had left Alozay by way of the Door, and these three
were the Weaponmaster Guest Gulkan, the iceman Sod, and the
rough and ragged Thayer Levant.

Sod had leapt through that portal to escape from his
captivity; Guest Gulkan had pursued him; and the unheroic
Levant had fled after them to escape from a perceived threat to
his own life.

Upon raging through the Door to the Monastic Treasury of
Inner Adeer, Guest had been confronted by armed force in great
superiority. And so, realizing he might have made an error, he
had promptly jumped back through that Door, thinking in his
confusion that by this means he could return to Alozay. But of
course the Door was part of a Circle, so instead of returning to
his point of departure, Guest had found himself advanced

around that Circle, to Galsh Ebrek.

Sod had arrived in Galsh Ebrek fractionally before Guest Gulkan, for Sod had hoped to get as far as Chi'ash-lan (if that should prove at all possible) before someone in the mainrock Pinnacle had wit sufficient to close the Door. Thayer Levant had fled after Guest. Levant had used Doors often, hence knew their nature well. Like Sod, Levant had a specific destination in mind. He had hoped to get as far as the Bralsh of Dalar ken Halvar before the Circle was closed.

But the star-globe had been removed from its niche when these three adventurers had got no further than Galsh Ebrek, and so it came to pass that all three were stuck there.

Guest was nimble-witted enough to realize in short order that he was truly trapped, and to swallow a certain ring before anyone thought to search him. This ring sustained a chipstone of ever-ice, and was the sole tool capable of opening and closing the time pods of Safrak's time prison. Later, when Sod happened to ask after that ring, Guest Gulkan averred that it had been torn from his possession during a brief scuffle in the Monastic Treasury of Inner Adeer — and Sod did not disbelieve this.

Thereafter, the Doors of the Circle were closed for a long passage, as Lord Onosh devoted himself to consolidating his command of Safrak — and, later, to dickering with Khmar's ambassadors.

For Banks and Bankers alike, the long closure of the Door was an agony. Particularly for Banker Sod — who was marooned in Galsh Ebrek with no better company than that of the barbarous Weaponmaster Guest Gulkan and the profoundly treacherous and untrustworthy knifeman Thayer Levant.

Galsh Ebrek, of course, is the ruling city of Wen Endex, homeland of the Yudonic Knights. It is notable also as the birthplace of the slug-chef Zozimus and the scholarly Sken-Pitilkin; and a telling commentary on the demerits of the place is that both slug-chef and scholar departed from its shores in early life, and never thereafter suffered nostalgia for the place.

The Bank of Galsh Ebrek was the Flesh Trader's Financial

Association, so Sod, Levant and the Weaponmaster Guest found themselves in the precincts of this organization when the Doors of the Circle closed. The Flesh Trader's Financial Association quite refused to hold Guest and Levant as prisoners, since Sod had no cash with which to pay for their keep (and was refused credit by the local Bankers, who feared that any money lent to him would be lost forever if the Door refused to open again).

The local Bankers proposed the slaughter of Guest and Levant, thinking murder to be cheaper than imprisonment, and thinking too that such people could not be let loose in the world with the secret of the Doors.

But Sod was at pains to point out that these prisoners might be of great future importance. After all, Thayer Levant was a servant of Ulix of the Drum, and everyone knew how important he was! And Guest, why, he was the son of the Witchlord Onosh.

"And this Witchlord," said Sod, "he currently commands the star-globe which rules the Circle, so we may need his son as a hostage for future negotiations."

Furthermore, said Sod, the Witchlord was in a position to preach the secret of Circle and Doors to the entire world if he so chose. Therefore what point was there in trying to secure that secret by killing the Witchlord's son?

"After all," said Sod, "there is steady commercial intercourse between the islands of Safrak and the free city of Port Domax, and between Port Domax and Galsh Ebrek, which implies that any revelations made by Lord Onosh will in due course be common knowledge in Wen Endex."

All this made a degree of sense, so Guest and Levant were sworn to secrecy — swearing themselves readily when they understood that the alternative was death — and were released into the city of Galsh Ebrek on solemn parole. Their cover story was that they and Sod were part of a parcel of refugees from the fall of Safrak — refugees recently arrived by sea.

The Bankers of Galsh Ebrek still being too stingy to fund the refugees, they necessarily had to find work. Guest hoped to find employment as a swordsman, a bodyguard, a mercenary, a gladiator, a hacker-down-of-dragons and killer-of-bog-monsters, but Sod advised him against drawing attention to himself.

Thus counselled, Guest finished up as a barman at the Green Parrot. The owner of that establishment was one Anna Blaume, who was at first reluctant to employ any creature as ill-favoured as Guest Gulkan. After all, he was patently a Yarglat barbarian, for he was marked as such by his high cheekbones and the great width of his nose. Furthermore, his extraordinary bat-wing ears made him look a proper fright, and Ms Blaume was mildly sensitive to cosmetic effect even though her customers typically were not.

But Guest appeased the proprietor of the Green Parrot by suggesting that she hold a piece of his property as a bond to secure his good behaviour.

"What property?" asked she.

"This ring," said Guest, brandishing the ever-ice ring which he had earlier swallowed, but had subsequently recovered by means of a diligent daily investigation of his dung. "This is a lucky ring, for there is a star trapped inside it, not a red star or a green star, but one of the rare and precious white stars. You can wish on it thrice, and be sure that at least one your wishes will be at least half-answered. Hold this as a bond, and if I misbehave myself you can keep it."

A bargain was struck on those grounds, and so Guest went to work at the Green Parrot.

It may be thought that the young Weaponmaster was over-casual in thus handing over a most precious and irreplaceable artefact, the sole ring of ever-ice known to the Safrak Islands. But he was friendless in a foreign country, and without cash, and therefore in urgent need of employment, for without employment he must surely starve. The ring was of no immediate use to him, and even its future use was problematical.

Suppose you were marooned as Guest was. Had you a ring which could give you a warm bed, hot soup, a dry roof and some more-than-occasional beers, would you not use it? I warrant that you would: and Guest, by using his ring as a good behaviour bond, did likewise.

As a barman, Guest proved adequate, for, though his Toxteth was largely indifferent, it must be conceded that he had a vigorous grasp of the entire vocabulary of drinking. Furthermore, he was skilled in the application of armlocks and the breaking of noses, the blacking of eyes and the displacement of teeth, the cudgeling of heads and the kicking of crotches; and the Green Parrot was the kind of establishment where all those talents could at times find their proper employment.

Guest secured employment at the same establishment for Thayer Levant. But since Levant lacked a competence in Toxteth, and also lacked a taste for brawling, he worked not in the bar but in the stables. He worked as a groom, and supplemented his wages by sharping the citizens of Galsh Ebrek at cards, for cards have their own language which works independent of the tongue, and Levant knew how to gloss that language to his own advantage.

It might be thought by the unthinking that Guest would be unhappy to be marooned in Galsh Ebrek as a barman. For he was an emperor's son, was he not?

But, actually, Guest was content.

After all, the young Weaponmaster was no stranger to bars or to brawling, for the doughty Rolf Thelemite had long ago indoctrinated him in both. And after the long rigours of campaigning, there was much to be said for pouring beer in the Parrot, and supping hot soup, and sharing on occasion the hospitality of Anna Blaume's decidedly uninhibited bed.

So Guest was content, or moderately so. And Thayer Levant endured.

But Sod — why, in those months of exile, poor Banker Sod suffered desolations of isolation. In all of Galsh Ebrek, only Thayer Levant came like Sod from Chi'ash-lan, and Levant quite lacked imagination sufficient to encompass any conception of the vast distances between themselves and Chi'ash-lan. Levant lacked any true conception of the depths of their geographical predicament, and so did not worry about it; and so was useless as a source of consolation for Sod in those days of trial.

Sod knew that eventually he must decide to set out for Chi'ash-lan or, assuming the Door did not open, reconcile himself to living out his days in Galsh Ebrek.

How could he get to Chi'ash-lan?

Well ...

He could take passage on one of those ships which traded across the stormswept northern seas from Galsh Ebrek to Ashmolea. The expense of travel in Ashmolea is fearful, for food, transport and lodgings are all at a premium. But if Sod could somehow finance his costs, then he could ship from Ashmolea to Asral; from Asral to the Ebrells; and from the Ebrells to the Inner Waters. The Drangsturm Road would then take him to the start of the Salt Road, the terminus of which is in Chi'ash-lan.

Such a journey is appalling in its length, danger and expense, and Sod would surely lose a couple of years of his life to such a trip, if he did not lose his life entire. But—

While Sod was still worrying over the buts, the ifs and the maybes, the Door opened at last, for Eljuk Gulkan's concerns for his brother Guest had persuaded Lord Onosh at last to enter into his necessary and inevitable confrontation with the Banks of the Circle.

A day after the Circle was opened, a messenger from the Flesh Trader's Financial Association summoned Sod from his lodgings in Galsh Ebrek.

Guest Gulkan was also summoned — though he knew not why — and on being summoned was surprised to find himself mugged, and made prisoner, and hustled blindfolded through the Circle to a place which he was told was Chi'ash-lan — though where that was he had no idea.

It was of course Chi'ash-lan. There was no mistaking the Door at Chi'ash-lan, for it was set in a chamber which was decorated with hanging skeletons, and the door in and out of that chamber was guarded by the demon Ko, a twin to the demon of Safrak.

Still.

As far as Guest was concerned, it could have been anywhere.

The rapidity of these evolutions had left Guest totally disorientated, for he had been quite unprepared for anything to happen so fast. He knew little of the Banks of the Circle, which had evolved habits of surpassing speed during the long centuries of their operation.

Thanks to the Circle, a Banker could buy tea in Tang and sell it in Obooloo the same day (pretending, necessarily, that the tea in question had come from Chay). A sword of firelight steel could be bought in Stokos in the morning and retailed in Chi'ash-lan that very evening (with its price suitably inflated by the deceitful fiction which held that sword to have been brought the length of the Salt Road by horse, donkey or camel).

A Banker could borrow money in Quilth and lend out that same money in Voice, and lend it out at a far higher rate of interest; could buy furs in Safrak and sell those furs on to Chi'ash-lan; could buy chocolate in Dalar ken Halvar then retail that gourmet commodity in Tang; or buy from Galsh Ebrek the precious jade of the Qinjoks, re-selling the stuff in Obooloo or Quilth.

And all these transactions took place at a dazzling speed, because the Partnership Banks maximized the efficiency of the Circle's use by imposing penalties for overuse on the Bankers themselves, so that a Banker must necessarily master the art of the hustle or be swiftly reduced to penury.

Furthermore, the Circle operated in secrecy, and hence was free from the laborious scrutiny, the injurious taxation, the obnoxious tariffs and the pettifogging bureaucracy which governments traditionally impose upon the merchant. To preserve that secrecy, the Bankers had been forced to make themselves masters of deceit, maintaining a monstrous collective lie in the face of the governments of the world. Yet to smooth the efficiency of their own operations, the Bankers were also forced to trust each other, as bone trusts flesh and flesh trusts skin, for without such trust the commercial interplay of the various Doors of the Circle would have ground to a halt under the weight of encumbering paranoia.

Here let us compare the Bankers to warriors and to wizards. Now warriors bind themselves to battle with dire oaths made solemnly, and made only after the most cumbersome process of muttering deliberation, accompanied by the furrowing of brows and the grinding of teeth, the clenching of fists and the flourishing of swords. As for wizards, why, every wizard is a lawyer, for one cannot become a full member of the Confederation of Wizards without obtaining a law degree as part of one's preliminary education; and so it is that your wizards cannot agree on the smallest point without five years of niggling debate, and when one wizard tries to buy a horse from another then the animal in question will typically die of old age before the conditions of the sale have been settled.

But — Bankers!

A Banker will see, think, decide, accept and settle, and all that in less time than it takes to snap your fingers, and will do so in any of the five favourite languages of your choosing. The Bankers keep no lawyers and little notation, and will trade in fortunes on the strength of the spoken word alone.

So it is that the Bankers of the Partnership Banks developed the fastest-moving, quickest-thinking and superlatively flexible organization in the entire civilized world, and made themselves masters of the adroit appraisal, the quick consensus and the snap decision. And it is only natural that Guest Gulkan was entirely lost, confused and bewildered when he found himself unexpectedly plunged into the vortex of the Banks' affairs, and whirlwinded into the foreign geography of an alien city, and dungeoned, and interrogated to purposes which were scarcely his to comprehend.

For we must remember always that Guest Gulkan was Yarglat born and Yarglat bred. The strength of his breeding was that he could hack at his father with a sturdy sword, or use the same sword to coerce a wizard of Skatzabratzumon into launching a mountain avalanche at his command, or subsist when necessary upon the blood of a horse — and none of these strengths were suited to a resolution of his present predicament.

We must remember, too, that Guest was only 17 years of

age, having experienced his 17th birthday in Galsh Ebrek in the spring. And here in summary, before our history sees Guest plunged into an uncertain future, let us take a brief moment to recap his past.

Our history picked up the boy when he was aged 14, and foolishly fought the Rovac warrior Thodric Jarl, contending for the possession of the woman Yerzerdayla — and thus offending his own father and securing his own exile to Alozay. On Alozay, Guest had his 15th birthday, and was tempted by the demon Iva-Italis, who offered him the chance to make himself a wizard. After such temptation, he sojourned upon Alozay for another year, attaining the age of 16. The young Weaponmaster was then whirlwinded by airship to the mountains of Ibsen-Iktus, from which he descended to the lowlands, only to be captured by his father's enemies.

Throwing in his lot with those enemies, Guest Gulkan duelled his father in a civil war, only to lose the entire Collosnon Empire to the invader Khmar. Father and son being united in defeat, the Weaponmaster Guest and the Witchlord Onosh retreated to Alozay, chiefest of the Safrak Islands. There Witchlord and Weaponmaster made themselves masters, overthrowing the Safrak Bank by a combination of guile and violence — only to have the sweetness of their victory upset when Sod took advantage of their momentary lapse from unity.

Pursuit of Sod made Guest a refugee in Galsh Ebrek, ruling city of Wen Endex, and so it was that Guest Gulkan saw out the winter in Wen Endex, survived his 17th birthday in the spring, and continued working as a barman in the Green Parrot while spring turned to summer.

Midsummer's Day marked the formal start of the rule of Khmar in the Collosnon Empire, and thus was the first day of the year Khmar 1; and it was the first day also of Alliance 4308 (and also, for those who have an interest in historical cross-reference, the third year of Talonsklavara, and the first year of the rule of Justina Thrug of Untunchilamon).

It was on Midsummer's Day that Eljuk Zala Gulkan reached Safrak, arriving in the company of the wizard Ontario Nol; and it was shortly afterwards that the Witchlord Onosh caused the Circle of the Partnership Banks to be reopened, thus unwittingly making his son Guest the focus of the full and unfriendly attention of all the surviving Banks.

So we find Guest entering into the greatest predicament of his life at the age of 17, and this is a boy's age. Since boys of 17 typically lack wives, and children, and households, and businesses, it has usually been found expedient to use such children as the meat of war; and the historically continuous slaughter of children has given rise to the conceit that a boy of 17 is fit for the adventures of adulthood.

However, this conceit is false, and Guest was certainly most woefully ill-equipped to face the unfriendly face of the world on his own.

To this, the casual reader of this history may object.

One can imagine the objections.

The young Guest Gulkan was a warrior! A hero! A leader of men! A master of revolutions! A lord of the avalanche! A victor in battle! Surely he was a man in his independence, and ready for the world!

Ah, but was he? Anyone who thinks that he was must have overlooked a supremely important fact: the fact being that Guest had ever been guided and supported by the wisdom of wizards. Admittedly, one of those wizards was a mere slug-chef, an unemployed necromancer, a broken-down wizard of Xluzu unable to nerve himself any longer to the full employment of his wizardly powers. But the other wizard! Why, that other wizard was a scholar, and a sagacious scholar at that, and as learned in war as he was in the irregular verbs.

A close reading of this history will show that Guest was never far from the wizard Hostaja Sken-Pitilkin. It was Sken-Pitilkin who preserved the boy's life when he fought Thodric Jarl in Enskandalon Square; Sken-Pitilkin who accompanied the boy to Alozay; Sken-Pitilkin who ensured that the boy was kept well way from the demon Iva-Italis after that demon had first tempted him; Sken-Pitilkin who flew the boy from Ema-Urk when escape from that island was required. It was the sagacious wizard of Skatzabratzumon who then aided the boy in war, who helped both the boy and the boy's father escape from a wrathful Khmar, and who used his wizardly powers directly in the fight for Alozay.

Let the victories of the boy's childhood be placed where they belong: at the feet of the mighty Sken-Pitilkin!

Guest, then, had lived as a child must live — ever guided, assisted, disciplined and educated by adults. And what could he have done without them? Why, nothing — for Guest on his own lacked the skill even to parse a verb or bake a hedgehog.

Even in Galsh Ebrek, Guest had been watched over by a diligent adulthood, for the callow ignorance of this primitive Yarglat barbarian had awakened the maternal sympathies of the worthy Anna Blaume, who had routinely kept him safe in her bed of nights, thus preserving him against the worst consequences of his own native folly.

But now he was truly on his own; and was on his own at the worst of all possible times; and was beset by the jabber of incomprehensible languages; and was fed food which was strange to his tongue; and was dungeoned he knew not where; and was shocked and dislocated by the suddenness of his incomprehensible change of fortune.

But while Guest was bewildered, there is no need for this history to duplicate his bewilderment mimetically. Let his location then be stated with precision. He was held in Chi'ash-lan, a city in that region of ice and snow which is known as the Cold West. Chi'ash-lan lies at the western end of the Ravlish Lands, and it is a city mighty in war, a city ruled by a cruel and oppressive Bailiff. The Bailiff's unfortunate habits were matched by the like traits of the Morgrim Bank of Chi'ash-lan, in which Banker Sod of Safrak held high position; for, though nominally independent, Safrak's Bank had long been subordinate to the disciplines of the Morgrim Bank.

With the Circle open, and with Guest Gulkan a prisoner in Chi'ash-lan, and with Sod likewise restored to the freedoms of Chi'ash-lan, negotiations began between the Partnership Banks and the Witchlord Onosh — who naturally guarded his own

Door in the mainrock Pinnacle with supreme care, making sure there could be no repeat invasion by murderous Zenjingu killers.

The Bankers invited Lord Onosh to come to Chi'ash-lan under flag of truce, telling him that his wizards were not included in this invitation. Sod had made it clear to the Partnership Banks that Lord Onosh had the support of two wizards, Pelagius Zozimus and Hostaja Sken-Pitilkin, and that both these wizards were dangerous.

Lord Onosh accepted the Partnership Banks' Invitation, and ventured to Chi'ash-lan in the company of Ontario Nol — who was introduced as a Yarglat warlord, and who looked the part, for he was dressed in boots of felt and in a coat made out of an old solskin horseblanket. Thus garbed, and armed with a scalping knife at his side, the venerable wizard of the order of Itch looked every bit the bloodstained barbarian.

With Lord Onosh and Ontario Nol went Eljuk Zala, venturing around the Circle to the chamber of hanging skeletons which held the Door of Chi'ash-lan's Morgrim Bank. With some trepidation, they exited from that chamber, daring themselves past the demon Ko, which remained mute in their presence.

Then they were taken to one of the inner offices of the Morgrim Bank, where Guest Gulkan was brought before them.

"Know our price," said Banker Sod, speaking on behalf of the Partnership Banks. "We will let you have Guest if you will surrender to us the rule of Safrak."

"I cannot surrender Safrak," said Lord Onosh, "for I have already surrendered my empire to Khmar, hence have nowhere to go."

"You will be allowed to hold the island of Ema-Urk in fief," said Sod. "That will be your reward if you will only surrender."

"I was told on an earlier occasion that I would be allowed to hold the island of Im-skim-patorta in fief," said Lord Onosh. "Solemn agreement to that effect was followed by your effort to murder me and mine."

"You call me murderer?" said Lord Sod. "You? When you smuggled weapons into the mainrock Pinnacle with murderous intent?"

"The weapons were solely for self-defence," said Lord Onosh. "You must admit that not one blade was used against you until you had started to seize my men."

"But you intended murder," said Sod.

"Intent!" said Lord Onosh. "You speak for intent, do you? Well, I speak for action!"

So the two men argued back and forth; and indeed argue was all they could do, for since each had betrayed the other once there was no firm basis on which they could come to an agreement.

But—

While Sod threatened and blustered, Guest Gulkan looked in such good health that Lord Onosh was hard put to credit any threat to his life. Surely — so thought the Witchlord — the Partnership Banks would have treated the Weaponmaster Guest harshly had they thought of him as anything other than a friend. Believing Guest to be in no serious danger, Lord Onosh decided to call the Bank's bluff.

"You cannot kill my young Weaponmaster," said the Witchlord Onosh to Banker Sod, "for if you kill the boy Guest then you will have no hostages left to barter with. I suggest that you hand him back and negotiate with me as equal to equal on terms of — well, friendship, if you could bring yourself to think of me as a friend."

"Kill him we will unless you come to your senses," said Banker Sod, "and we will give you an invitation to the killing."

Then the conference broke up, with the Witchlord Onosh returning to Alozay with Ontario Nol and Eljuk Zala, and with Guest being dragged away to the cell in which he was to languish until his death-day.

Very shortly, Lord Onosh was served with an invitation to that death-day, which he accepted, still thinking it a bluff.

As Guest Gulkan lay in the shadow-stink of a deathcell in Chi'ash-lan, he thought himself forgotten and abandoned by the world. But in this he was deluded. For Guest Gulkan and the companions of his misfortune were a subject of intense discussion and speculation in places as far removed as Stokos and Tang.

"So he is to die in the arena," said Elch of Stokos, speaking of the young Guest Gulkan. "What does he think about that?"

"One doubts he does think," answered Ibstork. "He is after all a child of the Yarglat, and the Yarglat, if they have brains, have yet to demonstrate any of those behaviours which would prove it."

Elsewhere, in Quilth, Guest Gulkan was again the subject of discussion.

"His bowel motion was healthy," said Physician Floth of the Healer's Guild of Quilth.

He knew?

Of course he knew!

The most detailed bulletins of Guest Gulkan's health and conduct daily circulated through the realms of the Partnership Banks.

Guest Gulkan was vitally important because he was the son of Lord Onosh, albeit a bastard son; and the Partnership Banks still thought that the Witchlord Onosh might intervene and concede the rule of Safrak in order to preserve his son's life.

But no such concession had been made when the day scheduled for Guest Gulkan's death dawned.

On that day the Witchlord and a small party of observers and bodyguards came to Chi'ash-lan, and were escorted through its streets of snow to the arena of Chi'ash-lan.

It was then still summer in Safrak, so Lord Onosh was hard put to see how it could be winter in Chi'ash-lan. He asked of Sod the answer to this mystery, and was told that it was not winter in Chi'ash-lan but summer, but that the "Breathings" of the Cold West made it snow snow and ice ice even in the heartland of summer.

In the cold of that winter-frigid summer, Guest Gulkan sat in a cell, waiting to see what the lord of Safrak would do. Would the Witchlord Onosh surrender the rule of Alozay and liberate his much-beloved son? Or would he not?

Since the "not" was unthinkable, Guest Gulkan tended to concentrate on what he would do once he got back to Safrak.

He had been told that Thodric Jarl was gone. Good. That meant that Guest could make Yerzerdayla his forever. If he could find her. Where was she, that woman of surpassing beauty? In Gendormargensis still — he presumed. Perhaps she could be bought from Khmar.

The young Weaponmaster focused on the image of Yerzerdayla, her breasts his bounty, her lips his pleasure, and her thighs—

His meditations came to an abrupt halt as the turnkey hammered on his cell door.

"Wake up, you in there!"

Guest abrupted to his feet.

"Up against the wall!" said the turnkey, peering through the cell's spyhole.

Guest flattened himself against the wall.

"Turn around!" yelled the turnkey. "Turn around! Turn and face the wall or I put a crossbow bolt through your backside!"

With some reluctance, Guest conceded his will to the voice. Then the door was unlocked and thrown open, and muscle stormed forward and seized him.

"What's this, then?" said Guest, when he was out of the cell. "What's happening? Where are we going?"

But nobody would answer him.

Guest was beefed through the underground corridors by two guards, one a gigantic man whose shoulder overtopped Guest Gulkan's head, the other an iron-muscled dwarf with a grotesque acromegalic face. They brought him to the Door of Death and pushed him out into the snowlight. He fell, and went sprawling on the frozen dirt-curds of filthy snow which had hardened to ice.

Grazed and shaken, Guest Gulkan scrambled to his feet and looked around the arena of Chi'ash-lan, wincing at the brightpuzzle light of the sky. His enemy. Where was his enemy? Nobody was waiting to fight. Instead the arena lay desolate under a low grey sky, scurfed with the sky's discards — heaps of snow and buckled ridges of ice. There must be an enemy here somewhere. But where?

In the snow, of course!

Guest Gulkan bootcrunched over frozen ice towards the most man-shaped of the snowdrifts and kicked at it. His boot uncovered a man, but the man was dead.

"To sword," said Guest, kicking the corpse.

The young Weaponmaster half-expected the corpse to rouse and resurrect, to haul itself up to the challenge and brute it out to the death. But the corpse remained in the snow, stolidly frozen. This was the corpse of no gladiator but that of an alcoholic old man who had frozen to death after falling from the terraces.

Laughter from those terraces drew Guest Gulkan to survey his audience, which was paltry, for the terraces were almost empty. The quantities of unswept snow which lay drifted on the stone ledges of the terraces indicated that they had been largely empty for days, if not for months; which is scarcely surprising, for the operation of a gladiatorial arena is such that even a place as rich as Chi'ash-lan can hardly hope to indulge in the more bloody forms of entertainment right through the year.

The Witchlord Onosh was up there, together with his entourage, but they were hidden behind the veils of the windows of a walled-in box, and Guest Gulkan could not see them, and was not aware of their presence.

"What's going on?" said Guest Gulkan, addressing his audience in the Galish, since that had been the language of his jailors.

By way of reply, the alcoholics in the audience laughed uproariously and hurled snowballs in Guest's direction. The snowballs fell short, for the arena was large and the alcoholics nearly incapably drunk on the dreadful rubbish they had been imbibing, which was a dire concoction fermented from the blubber of whales and the dung of dogs.

Guest Gulkan scanned the rucked surface of the arena's snows for any further enemies who might have buried themselves in ambush, saw none, shivered, stamped his feet, and looked to the box reserved for Bailiff Vok, to which his attention was called by the pair of gilded dragons which flanked it. But Bailiff Vok's box was empty. At that time, the Malf of Chi'ash-lan had bankrupted themselves to buy the right to launch ten days of pogrom against the Zy. The Malf were making the most of it, and Bailiff Vok was doing likewise — patrolling his streets on foot to observe the burnings and lynchings, the tortures and rapes, the savagings and the lootings.

So Guest Gulkan stood desolate in the arena, wondering if he was to be allowed to shiver to death.

He was not.

For, with a scraping squeal of rust and reluctant timbers, a sally port opened, and out from that sally port there ventured a dozen athletes, each armed with a wooden staff. Black was their garb and black the masks which hid their faces. These were yet more of the dreaded Zenjingu warriors, the ultimate killers, the dreaded combat cult fanatics of Chi'ash-lan. It was known in Chi'ash-lan that the Zenjingu could kill with a touch, or a laugh, or a look. It was known in Chi'ash-lan that the Zenjingu could decapitate a man with an adroitly thrown dinner plate, or eviscerate a stalwart warrior with a sharpened toothpick, or take a blacksmith by the foot and shake him till his spine dislocated and his liver fell out of his side.

But Guest knew none of this. So why then did his heart quail when he saw his enemies were a dozen in number? After all, he was a hero, was he not? And is it not written that any hero worthy of his salt can kill a dozen of his enemies single-handed? Here a mystery. But what is certain is that Guest Gulkan did quail. But not for long. For shortly he was far too busy for any quailing. He was trying to defend himself — and he was failing.

The athletic Zenjingu ringed Guest Gulkan and began to whack him with their wooden staffs. He tried to grab one. And did! For a moment the Weaponmaster stood there tussling with a Zenjingu warrior, seeking to wrench the staff from his enemy's grip. Then another staff smashed his wrist. Guest Gulkan opened his mouth in soundless agony.

Obliterating pain.

A staff rammed him in the stomach and down he went. He retched, puking yellow bile to the snow. Hit around the head, he slumped, dazed and struggling. He rolled, kicked, got up on one knee, staggered half-upright. Then was felled by a blow to the kidneys. The alcoholics on the terraces screamed their approval. The staffs rose and fell, smashing ribs and cracking other bones.

Then it seemed the Zenjingu were done, for nobody hit the Weaponmaster any more. Not that this improved his condition much. To move hurt, to breathe hurt, to be hurt. He waited for someone to kill him properly. He waited to die.

But nobody came to give him the *coup de grace*.

Instead, there was some excited shouting in a language he did not understand. He was too wrecked to look around, and so did not see a cylindrical cage being dragged out into the middle of the arena. Once centrally positioned, the cage was anchored with cruel metal spikes which were driven deep into the frozen snow.

Then jailers came for Guest Gulkan, who was being pissed on by half a dozen Zenjingu warriors who were otherwise unemployed. Once the fighting cult heroes had finished, Guest was dragged to his feet. He screamed in lacerated agony as bones rubbed against broken bones. He screamed again and again as he was bundled across the frozen snow then forced into the cage.

Guest Gulkan was made to sit upon the iron bench which bisected the cage. The iron was so cold that, had his captors stripped him of his clothes, his skin would surely have frozen instantly to the metal. But the Zenjingu and the jailers had left the Weaponmaster with his garments.

Humiliation was not what they had in mind.

Once seated, Guest was tied in place. His arms were tied so they stuck out of the cage at the elbow and his legs were tied so they stuck out of the cage at the knee. Then, after a little self-congratulatory backslapping, the Zenjingu and the jailers withdrew, hooting with laughter as they went.

Guest Gulkan sat.

In pain.

In gasping torments.

In wrenching agony too sharp to be delirium, there sat Guest

Gulkan, shocked and shattered, too savaged by his torments to have any comprehension of what was going on. That "what" was nothing. For nothing happened as Guest Gulkan sat, living from breath to breath, from pain to pain, a lifetime passing between each spasm of renewed excruciation.

How long he sat there, he did not know. Perhaps a lifetime, perhaps thrice longer.

Then he heard something.

It was soft but it was big. How big? He could not tell. Not precisely. But the thing was big enough to pad the air with silence, to change the world of sound with the muffling stupendousness of its presence. It was huge. It had to be. But what was it?

It was behind him.

A bigness, a prowling softness, a bulking appetite, a lode of deliberate purpose shifting and sensing, a hungering half-heard and half-smelt. And then. It breathed upon him. Its breath was hot against his neck.

It leaned against the cage. But all its bulk was not sufficient to move that cage. Nevertheless, Guest felt the metal shudder with the strain.

Then.

Then.

It.

It licked his hand.

Its tongue was hot, and heavy, and then it bit.

Guest Gulkan screamed and wrenched and saw. No hand — a bloody wrist, a bloody thing, the swordgrasp gone, the blood. The bulking white which thrust and slammed and heaved its bulk against the cage, and snapped at metal with its teeth, seeking his face, his head.

The cage was built to take such onslaughts. Brute metal withstood the angered white. Which prowled outside, prowled while Guest sobbed his horror, his swordhand gone and more as yet to go. In agony he sobbed. The whiteness bulked and loomed. Reared in silence on its hind legs. So silent in its massiveness. Reared, then dropped again to all fours, and breathed upon his face. Hot breath, hot breath.

"Ah! Gods!"

Thus Guest Gulkan. The words were scarcely words at all. Rather, they were spasms of twisted air wrenched from his gut.

Then the hugeness of the white horror slammed against the cage in earnest, then savaged the surviving hand. No hand surviving.

Impossible.

Impossible.

The impossible possible.

Guest Gulkan looked, and screamed, and it was his leg which was next to go, and the pain was one claw which tore his whole body, so that he was quite incapable of telling whether it was the left leg which had gone or the right.

Later, they—

They unlatched his shocked and sobbing flesh from the cage, and took it inwards on a bloody stretcher, hands gone and both legs shreds beneath the knee.

All this the Witchlord Onosh and his entourage observed from the heights, but they did not quite believe it was real. Not until Guest Gulkan's torn and bleeding body was given to them in a box, the body still breathing but surely doomed to die shortly.

"Take it," said Sod. "For it is yours."

The Witchlord Onosh could not speak. He was beyond all speech. Wordlessly, he signed to members of his entourage, and they took the box and its contents through the Door from Chi'ash-lan to Safrak. Then Lord Onosh, Ontario Nol and Eljuk Zala made as if to go.

"Not you three," said Sod with a smile. "You three stay here."

"But we have a truce!" said Lord Onosh.

"Yes," said Sod, "and I have weapons."

At which he signed his men forward.

And Ontario Nol enraptured the world with a whirlwind, and spun Sod and Sod's men every which way, so some were slammed against the walls in skull-smash spasms and some spiked their fellows with their own weapons.

"Run!" said Nol, as his whirlwinds exhausted themselves.

So Lord Onosh ran, and Nol with him. But Eljuk lagged.

"Eljuk!" said Lord Onosh, meaning to spur his son to the sprint.

And he turned, and saw the demon Ko grab Eljuk Zala.

"Eljuk!" screamed Lord Onosh.

Already the demon Ko had sucked Eljuk Zala into the green of its monolithic blockwork. Eljuk was half-in, half-out. As Lord Onosh watched, invisible tongues within the clear-jade blockwork stripped Eljuk's clothing from his body.

Eljuk vented his wastes in a spasm, excreting those wastes into the depths of Ko, and the demon Ko laughed hysterically and sent the liquid shit squirting out in a fierce torrent which drenched Lord Onosh. Eljuk screamed, only his face now free from the jade.

And Ontario Nol grabbed the Witchlord Onosh by the hair and hauled him through the Door, and once in Safrak closed that Door and its associated Circle by wrenching the star-globe from its marble plinth.

"There is nothing we can do," said Ontario Nol to the Witchlord Onosh. "Do you understand? There is nothing we can do."

But the Witchlord Onosh was not disposed to agree, and went downstairs to confront the demon Icaria Scaria Iva-Italis, Demon By Appointment to the Great God Jocasta. For Lord Onosh had guessed that the demons were in secret communication, and suspected that he could negotiate with Chi'ash-lan's Bank by addressing himself to Iva-Italis.

"So," said Iva-Italis, drawing out the word into a luxuriance of self-indulgence. "Our poor little Eljuk shit himself, did he?"

"You," said Lord Onosh. "Tell Chi'ash-lan I want my son returned."

"Then surrender," said Iva-Italis. "Unconditional surrender. That's what they want now. Nothing more, nothing less."

"Surrender?" said Lord Onosh. "I'll see you in hell first!"

"Hell?" said Iva-Italis with a trickling laugh which scampered round the Hall of Time like rats at race within a sewer. "Why, this is hell, nor am I out of it."

CHAPTER TWENTY-NINE

Plandruk Qinplaqus: ruler of Dalar ken Halvar, aka Silver Emperor, aka Ulix of the Drum. A gnostic manic-depressive who has long ruled the Empire of Greater Parengarenga from the palace of Na Sashimoko. In appearance: a withered Ashdan of great antiquity, his frail form usually supported by a crooked walking stick, the handle of which is silver, and is in the shape of a pelican.

* * *

For Guest Gulkan, arms and legs both shredded by the mauling strength of the Great Mink, there was no blessed darkness, no sovereign relief, no surcease of pain. Instead, spearblade agony — as if repeated jolts of razorblade lightning were being shoved through his lacerated flesh. He screamed, jolting spasms racking his body. His world was an incoherence of razors.

"He is as good as gone," said Lord Onosh, looking down on the racked and ruined body of his son.

Then Hostaja Sken-Pitilkin took Lord Onosh by the sleeve, and drew him to one side.

"My lord," said Sken-Pitilkin, "there is in Dalar ken Halvar a power which commands the cure of the flesh. Our good friend Ulix of the Drum will guarantee that cure if we can but get the boy Guest to Dalar ken Halvar promptly."

"How would we do that?" said Lord Onosh.

"Why," said Sken-Pitilkin, "do but open the Door, and it can be done in moments. Ulix of the Drum will lead the way, and I will follow, and Zozimus with me. With but half a dozen men to bear Guest along, we can shock our way through the Circle before they realize we are upon them."

"I would think rather to shock with an army," said Lord Onosh.

"Shock, my lord, is a tactical jewel more easily possessed by the few than by the many," said Sken-Pitilkin. "If we take an army, thinking to defeat our enemies in war, they will recover soon enough. But Dalar ken Halvar is friendly territory, if we can but get there."

Lord Onosh was so shaken by what had lately happened that he allowed Sken-Pitilkin to persuade him easily.

Then Sken-Pitilkin assembled his forces.

The wizard first thought himself of the witches Bao Gahai and Zelafona. But both refused their assistance.

"Forgive me if I am wrong," said Sken-Pitilkin to Bao Gahai, "but I had thought you tender of the Weaponmaster's life."

"So I am," said Bao Gahai. "But I am old, Pitilkin. My skin is but a thin web cast in fragility across my flesh. My bones are as matchsticks. Such Power as remains to me is scarcely enough to discipline my dreams. I am entering into my final years, Pitilkin. Some time ago, I paid a dreadful price to secure a thing I wanted above all others. Now I am suffering in consequence of that payment. I would help you if I could, but I am wasted beyond recovery, and all that remains to me is to survive."

Seeing that Bao Gahai was sincere in her confession, Sken-Pitilkin immediately renewed his attack on the witch Zelafona.

"If I remember rightly," said Sken-Pitilkin, "then I gave shelter to you and your son when you fled to my sanctuary on the island of Drum."

"It is so," conceded Zelafona.

"In consequence of my hospitality," said Sken-Pitilkin, "I have angered the Confederation of Wizards, and so have been forced to flee from my home."

"I do not deny it," said Zelafona.

"So," said Sken-Pitilkin, "I believe you are under a moral obligation to me and mine."

"I had not thought the life of the Weaponmaster to be of any consequence to you," said Zelafona.

"Why so?" said Sken-Pitilkin. "He has been as much my son as anyone's. Since he was but five years of age, I have counselled him, tutored him, guided him, raised him. True, he has been uncommonly abusive of scholarship, and has tortured the grammars of the foreign tongues in a most dreadful manner, but

I'll not hold this against him. If you will but save Guest Gulkan's life, then I'll count you free of all obligation to me and mine."

"How can I save him?" said Zelafona. "Pitilkin, the Banks will be on guard against us. We cannot hope to storm the Circle as you think. We can but try, and die trying."

"We cannot hope to seize the Circle," said Sken-Pitilkin, "but we can hope to make our way around it. Each Door stands in a chamber, and we need but force our way through three such chambers. The first is that of the Monastic Treasury of Inner Adeer. The second is that of the Flesh Traders Financial Association of Galsh Ebrek. The third is that of the Bondsmans Guild of Obooloo. Then we will be in the Bralsh, in Dalar ken Halvar, and Plandruk Qinplaqus assures us that he will take charge of things from there."

Zelafona thought about it, then said:

"What exactly do you want from me?"

"I know," said Sken-Pitilkin, "that you have powers to delude the minds of men, powers like those of the wizards of Ebber. I want you to use those powers to seize and hold that chamber in the Monastic Treasury of Inner Adeer which holds the Door."

"And," said Zelafona. "And when I am done with holding? How do I get back to Alozay?"

"You don't," said Sken-Pitilkin. "You escape from the Monastic Treasury, not through any Door, but directly into the city of Voice."

"You mean that I should banish myself," said Zelafona. "You mean that I should be parted from my sister and my son."

"Your son you can take with you," said Sken-Pitilkin. "If he is willing to play the hero. As for your sister — these are her final years. She has little time left to live."

"I will consider," said Zelafona.

"Guest Gulkan is dying as you consider," said Sken-Pitilkin, with considerable impatience. "We are driven by the urgency of a dying man."

Zelafona again replied that she would consider, whereupon Sken-Pitilkin hastened to Lord Onosh and explained the problem. The Witchlord promptly told Zelafona that she could consider getting her head cut off, or getting—

But — enough! There is no need to list here the grim and barbarous threats which the Witchlord Onosh made to the elegant dralkosh Zelafona! Suffice it to say that Zelafona was very swiftly shocked into an acceptance of her fate; and that Glambrax consented to accompany his mother into exile.

The wizards Pelagius Zozimus and Ontario Nol consented to fight at Sken-Pitilkin's side. The force was completed by the wizard Plandruk Qinplaqus and his servant Thayer Levant.

"That completes our force," said Sken-Pitilkin, reporting his readiness to the Witchlord Onosh.

"But," said Lord Onosh, "you will need men to carry Guest Gulkan. Rolf Thelemite, for instance."

"No, my lord," said Sken-Pitilkin. "For if we introduce men such as Thelemite to the Circle of the Door, what will we do with them thereafter? I think we will have no recourse but to kill them. The secret of the Door is too great to be shared among many."

"Then," said Lord Onosh, "do what you must, and kill the men if you must! I give you full permission to kill Rolf Thelemite as and when you wish, since I think him born to be killed!"

"If I must kill Thelemite then I will," said Sken-Pitilkin. "But I have no need to do so, therefore I won't. I myself will levitate the box in which Guest Gulkan lies. Speed is of the essence, my lord! If we were to shock uncouth fools like Thelemite with news of the Door, we would lose a whole day to its explanation, and we have not a day, for Guest will be dead in far less time than that."

"Then do as you will," said Lord Onosh. "But do not fail!"

"If I fail," said Sken-Pitilkin, gravely, "then death will surely be my fate, for the Bankers will kill me out of hand."

Then Sken-Pitilkin procured a sandglass of the kind which is used to time a boiling egg, and said Lord Onosh should open the Door and keep it open while the sand ran, by which time the shock-troops would either be in Dalar ken Halvar or be dead.

"Thereafter," said Sken-Pitilkin, "you will open the Door on each Midsummer's Day, that we may negotiate with the Banks. It may take long for us to settle an agreement with the Banks, but they will yield to us in due course."

"And, meanwhile," said Lord Onosh. "What of Eljuk?"

"We cannot help him," said Sken-Pitilkin. "He must suffer his fate. The only counsel I give you in this respect is this: stay away from the demon Iva-Italis! The demon gloats on suffering, and will encourage you to nightmare if you keep its company."

So the storming party assembled in the abditory in Jezel Obo, the Sky Stratum, the highest level of the mainrock Pinnacle. Then the Door was opened, and the shock-assault party stormed through, and when the sands were run out Lord Onosh closed the Door, and took the star-globe into his own possession, and retired to his own chambers to mourn the loss of both his sons, for he counted the pair of them dead.

The storming of the shock-force party was done swiftly. From Alozay went the stormtroopers, bursting into the padded silence of the Monastic Treasury of Inner Adeer. There the witch Zelafona took command, numbing the minds of all those who stood guard in the chamber of the Door. While they were thus numbed, the dwarf Glambrax efficiently slaughtered them with his axe.

While this work of mass-murder was in progress, the stormforce dared through the door to the Flesh Traders Financial Association of Galsh Ebrek. Here, Ontario Nol conjured the powers of the winds, slamming Bankers in all directions, breaking them at will. Thus Guest Gulkan came again to the land of Wen Endex, the homeland of the Yudonic Knights in the north of Yestron. But he knew it not, for he had been dosed with opium, and hence he was "floating on the lotus", as the fragrant Janjuladoola saying has it.

Pelagius Zozimus then took control. The wizard of Xluzu, using his powers as a Necromancer, animated those corpses which Ontario Nol had so freshly produced, sent those corpses through the Door, then followed them through that Door into the Bondsmans Guild of Obooloo.

There, Zozimus fought a brief but bloody battle, pitching the dead against the living.

As the shrieks of horror-struck Bankers fled into the echoing distance, Sken-Pitilkin sent Guest Gulkan wafting through the Door into the Bondsmans Guild. Again, Guest Gulkan knew not of his travels, for he lay in the sweating squalor of sleep, fast-sinking from lotus to dream. He was dreaming still as they went through the Door one last time, travelling from Obooloo to the Bralsh.

The Bralsh was the stronghold of the Good Neighbours, the lords of the insurance industry of Dalar ken Halvar, and it stood in an area of that city known as Childa Go. The Bralsh was a literal stronghold, an ominously solid fortification built to repulse the periodic disorders which saw Dalar ken Halvar ravaged by riot or by revolution.

On arrival at the Bralsh, Plandruk Qinplaqus used his powers as a wizard of Ebber, numbed the minds of the Bankers who stood on guard there, and maintained his authority as the others came through the Door.

Then that Door closed.

Zelafona, of course, was still in the Monastic Treasury of Inner Adeer. On mature reflection, Sken-Pitilkin realized that it would have been possible for her to come through the sundry Doors with the others, escaping in their company to the Bralsh. Had some unacknowledged desire for revenge compelled him to send the witch-woman into solitary exile in Voice?

Perhaps.

But what was done was done, and repenting of it would be of no help to anyone. At least they had escaped through to the city of Dalar ken Halvar.

It had been deep night when the stormforce had abstracted Guest Gulkan from the Witchlord's stronghold on the island of Alozay. It had been night in the Monastic Treasury of Inner Adeer when Guest Gulkan had been delivered to the healers waiting in that Bank. Night had likewise ruled Galsh Ebrek and Obooloo, and night reigned still on his arrival in Dalar ken Halvar, for all these places are to be found on the same side of the planet, and one span of night can encompass them all.

Know you the meaning of "planet"? A planet is a globe roped invisibly to the sun, the sun being a metaphorical giant which whirls this globe around his head at the end of a rope. Such is the length of the rope that a single circuit of the giant's head takes a year. This is the lunatic scale to which our reality is built, from which fact many have concluded that the Gods of Construction were deranged; and your historian sees no reason to bicker some dispute with such conclusion.

So it was by night that the stormforce came forth from the Bralsh, emerging on to the surface of their planet like ants exiting from a tiny fissure in the rind of a rotten watermelon. Bearing Guest Gulkan with them, the stormforce ventured the night from the Bralsh of the Good Neighbours to the halls of the demon-mountain, Cap Foz Para Lash.

Through the streets of Childa Go they went; they skirted the western slopes of Cap Ogo Botch, which hill sustains the ruling palace of Dalar ken Halvar; and then, avoiding Actus Dorum, the commercial centre of the Silver Emperor's city, they took a back way between the yawning abyss of the Dead Mouth and the upthrust fortifications of the Frangoni Rock.

Thus they went, and arrived at the great gate known as the lockway, where Plandruk Qinplaqus secured their admission into the mountain.

The mountain was ruled by a demon, and the demon commanded a place which was designed for the refurbishment of the bodies of those injured in battle. This demon, the genius loci of Cap Foz Para Lash, went by the name of Paraban Senk. Unlike the demon Iva-Italis of Safrak and the demon Ko of Chi'ash-lan, Paraban Senk had no body of green-burning stone, but, rather, was caged invisibly in some hidden part of the cave-works of Cap Foz Para Lash. That much is sure, and all are agreed upon it; but of the demon's true nature it is hard to give a reasoned account.

Now there are demons and demons, just as there are ghosts and ghosts — and, for that matter, gods and gods. To know things in their true categories is hard enough even when we deal with those mundane entities which breathe the same air as we do, and mate and breed and meet their deaths manner like unto that of men. Is the whale a fish or is it (as the eccentric opinion of certain naturalists would have it) a species of cow? Having considered the whale, consider the woman. Is she like a whale in her milk, a scorpion in her wit or a day of moody weather in her humours?

On such questions the greatest intellects have bruised themselves without securing conclusive resolution, so, since such difficulties attend such things as simple as the analysis of organic life, it is only natural that to win a certain knowledge of things demonic is more problematical yet.

Hence your historian stakes out no definite position as regards the nature of the demon known as Paraban Senk, but merely contents himself with here recording the most peculiar account which this demon gave of itself. Senk was a man, or had been. Yet Senk was presently merged with the life of a species of computational device — that is to say, a kind of self-powered abacus so monstrous in its complexity that the intricate shuttlework of its beads could create patterns complex enough to rival those of a human mind engaged in higher thought.

What is certain is that Senk was an entity which had survived from the dark times hidden behind the veils of the Days of Wrath. When questioned, Senk spoke of worlds linked to worlds and locked in war; of ships of destruction which could rival thought in their speed; of living metal which bestrode the field of battle and demolished cities in its wrath; of peoples devastated by fire and plague; of planets shattered and of suns burst asunder — and of Senk's knowledge of pain, and death, and trial by horror, there seemed to be no ending.

While a degree of mystery surrounds Paraban Senk's origins, nature, powers, function and nature, there is no doubt that this demonic entity wielded much power within the underground fortress of Cap Foz Para Lash, even though (and here your historian relies on the testimony of the Ashdan warrior Asodo Hatch, Senk being mute on the matter) it had no way in which to project such power beyond the lockway.

To that lockway, the wounded warrior Guest Gulkan was conveyed; and there he was placed in the healing room run by the demon of the mountain, and his cure commenced.

Then Plandruk Qinplaqus, who had no knowledge of what might have happened in Dalar ken Halvar since he had been kidnapped by Banker Sod and imprisoned in a time pod in Alozay's Hall of Time, set about the business of reinstalling himself in the city which he had formerly been accustomed to rule as emperor.

The task Qinplaqus had set himself was potentially difficult, for, in his absence, there had been a revolution in the city; and civil disorder had seen all power in Dalar ken Halvar fall to an Ashdan warrior named Asodo Hatch, who ruled in the name of the militant religion known as Nu-chala-nuth.

Yet Hatch proved uncommonly relieved at the abrupt re-appearance of Plandruk Qinplaqus, for the difficulties of ruling Dalar ken Halvar — and the realms of the Empire of Greater Parengarenga which were commanded from that city — were of such complexity and intensity that they almost exceeded Hatch's abilities.

So it was that Plandruk Qinplaqus, rightful lord of the Empire of Parengarenga, returned to his capital city, made an alliance with the revolutionary leader Asodo Hatch, and reinstalled himself in the great palace of Na Sashimoko.

And Guest Gulkan's cure proceeded.

Guest Gulkan's cure was slow, because to start with he had no arms or legs to speak of. As his body had been injured, so too had his mind; and night after night he endured nightmares in which he lost both arms and legs, in which the Great Mink mauled the hair from his head while Thodric Jarl swordbooted his cleats into the blood-gash grin of his face. He dreamt of rivers awash with blood and heads made into pyramids, of floods of roiling eyeballs and hailstorms of bloodstained teeth, and of hectic voyages on ships which catapulted themselves skywards then shattered themselves to toothpicks on the grim-beak heights of mountains.

Yet as Guest's body began to heal, and as his arms and legs

began their slow regrowth under the subtle tutelage of the demon of the mountain, his dreams slowly changed; and more and more he dreamt of women rather than of war.

In his dreams he imagined Yerzerdayla, her hair flowing around his ribs, her mouth nourishing his strength, her lips swallowing pearls, her heat-warmth perfume blossoming around her, her whispers hot with admiration, and her unlimited delights matching his ardour.

Thus Guest began to heal, body and mind; and as time went on he had long sessions with Hostaja Sken-Pitilkin, who thought this an excellent opportunity to re-inspire young Guest with a love of the irregular verbs. Much of their time together was given to arguing over precisely what animal it was which had mauled Guest Gulkan in the arena at Chi'ash-lan.

"It was a bear," said Guest, and he said it not once but repeatedly.

"That was no bear," said sagacious Sken-Pitilkin. "That was a mink."

"Not so," said Guest. "A mink is a small animal which bites, and as punishment for its temperament is commonly made into gloves. Or coats, if the man is fool enough and the woman nags long enough."

"There is a Great Mink which is like unto the lesser minks in its temperament," said Sken-Pitilkin, "and which also bites, just as it bit you. It was the Great Mink you met, and not any kind of bear."

But Guest Gulkan was firmly decided. If one is going to be mauled, then it is better for one's honour to be mauled by a bear than a mink, and so in defiance of zoological science he proclaimed his assailant to have been a bear. Though in truth the Great Mink of the snows of the Cold West is a bloodier monster than any bear, for your average bear is bent on grubs and honey, or has its mind on fish, whereas the Great Mink hunts with deadly purpose, and will as lief hunt men as any lesser game.

So Guest Gulkan was a fool to dispute his tutor's wisdom. But Sken-Pitilkin was not distressed at this folly. Rather, it was a relief to see the young man coming into possession of some spark of life.

When Guest had been some months recovering, he had the first of his formal audiences with Plandruk Qinplaqus, lord of the Empire of Greater Parengarenga.

"Is there anything you need?" said the Lord of the Silver Pelican.

"Yes!" said Guest. "To get out of here!"

"That you will not be doing for some years," said Qinplaqus.

"Years!" said Guest in dismay.

"It will take that long for your arms and legs to regrow," said Qinplaqus.

Then Guest was greatly distressed, for he had not realized that his confinement was to be thus extended.

In truth, the young Weaponmaster Guest was prodigiously lucky to have the favour of Plandruk Qinplaqus, and to have the demon of the mountain of Cap Foz Para Lash dedicated to his cure, for it was only in that one mountain of Dalar ken Halvar that the arms and legs of a multiple amputee could possibly be restored to their strength.

But Guest was a poor invalid, and became increasingly importunate and demanding, saying that at least one of his limbs was still in perfect working order, and hence he should surely — if it was at all possible, and surely it was — be provided with some suitable terrain in which that single limb could be exercised.

Upon which the venerable Plandruk Qinplaqus indulgently declared that he would choose out a wife for the boy Guest.

"A wife!" said Guest in alarm. "I said nothing about getting married!"

"But you were talking of a woman, were you not?" said Plandruk Qinplaqus.

"Why, yes," said Guest. "But a woman is not a wife, or need not be. Get me a woman, that's all that I want."

"Am I a pimp, that I should get you a whore?" said Plandruk Qinplaqus.

"As I am the son of an emperor," said Guest warmly, "it

should be an honour for you to pimp for me."

At which sally, Qinplaqus shook with laughter until his belly almost burst; for it had been several centuries since the venerable Ashdan had encountered anyone with Guest's degree of impudence.

And after some negotiation it was at last agreed between them that Qinplaqus would not pimp out a whore for young Guest, since pimping was beneath the dignity of an emperor; but that Qinplaqus would diligently quest out a wife for Guest, and (with luck) find him a woman who would be happy to take him to bed even though his arms were but buds peeping from stumps.

A tall order, one might think!

But Plandruk Qinplaqus was great in power and knowledge, and knew his people well, and already had a wifely candidate in mind.

CHAPTER THIRTY

Name: Penelope Flute

Birthplace: Dalar ken Halvar

Occupation: priestess of an Evolutionary cult

Status: large-scale debtor

Description: woman of Frangoni race, built to a truly magnificent
scale

Hobby: macramé

Quote: "Why do men always get the good things?"

***

During his sojourn inside the minor mountain of Cap Foz Para
Lash, Guest Gulkan was often in contact with the demon which
ran the place, the demon which went by the name of Paraban
Senk. This demon never manifested itself in the flesh, preferring
to restrict its manifestations to a face on a screen.

While the Weaponmaster Guest Gulkan was in no great
hurry to learn the Secret of Secrets and the Wisdom of Wisdom
from a face on a screen which called itself Paraban Senk, the
wizard Sken-Pitilkin was much more forward in having dealings
with this entity.

Sken-Pitilkin was long in discourse with Paraban Senk;
allowed himself to be interrogated by Senk; and did some
intense and detailed questioning of his own. To Sken-Pitilkin,
Paraban Senk explained many things, including the secret of the
Chasm Gates and the nature of the Nexus; though most of what
Senk said was so frankly incredible that Sken-Pitilkin gave it
precious little credence.

Nevertheless, while Sken-Pitilkin thought Senk to be for the
most part a deluded confabulator, the wizard of
Skatzabratzumon still thought it worthwhile to appraise Paraban
Senk of a suggestion once made by the Great God Jocasta —
namely, that airflight could be made a possibility through

management of the sustained destruction of abnormal artefacts exposed to the normalizing effects of the universe.

Sken-Pitilkin then told Senk of the long and danger-fraught process of experimentation which had resulted from this suggestion.

"So you actually got airborne?" said Senk.

"Twice," said Sken-Pitilkin.

"And lived to tell the tale?" said Senk in amazement.

"Unless I died and was casually reincarnated without noticing the fact," said Sken-Pitilkin.

"Tell me the details," said Senk.

"The first flight was from the island of Ema-Urk," said Sken-Pitilkin. "That's an island in the Swelaway Sea. We flew to the mountains of Ibsen-Iktus, where Guest's brother Eljuk Zala met the wizard Ontario Nol, to whom he is now apprenticed."

"And the second?"

"The second flight was from Locontareth," said Sken-Pitilkin. "We didn't get as far that time. I levitated the roof of a hall and flew it to the outskirts of the city where I, ah, landed it. Crashed it, to be honest."

Then Senk took Sken-Pitilkin through a jolt-by-jolt recapitulation of those flights, after which Senk did a great many calculations, ultimately working out how Sken-Pitilkin could harness the powers of destructive magic to make a functional airship.

"This is how," said Paraban Senk, at last displaying upon a screen an illustration of something that looked like an overgrown bird's nest.

"Why," said Sken-Pitilkin, "it looks like a bird's nest."

"So it does, so it does," said Senk. "But I think it will work regardless."

Then, acting on Senk's detailed instructions, the sagacious wizard Hostaja Sken-Pitilkin began to build a functional airship on some flat land by the Yamoda River.

While Sken-Pitilkin went to work on the airship problem, Plandruk Qinplaqus was exerting his talents to resolve Guest Gulkan's woman shortage, with the result that the Frangoni warrior Asodo Hatch shortly introduced his sister Penelope to young Guest, and suggested that they would make a good match in marriage.

Since the woman Penelope was a handsome wench built to generous specifications Guest promptly agreed that marriage would be a very good idea.

So it was that Guest Gulkan was wed to Penelope Flute, to the general satisfaction of all concerned.

Some women might have had reservations about marrying a man whose arms and legs were currently no larger than those of a baby, but Asodo Hatch explained to his sister that Guest Gulkan's condition was due to the fact that he had been born as a fish, and had only lately begun to evolve into a human being. Since Penelope was a dedicated Evolutionist, she believed this without reservation, and was excited and fascinated to be presented with living proof of the Evolutionary theory which had long been preached to her by her personal guru.

Of course the story of Guest Gulkan's fish-to-man transition was a patent tissue of nonsense, as indeed is the whole of the Evolutionary heresy. As everyone with the faintest acquaintance with human history knows full well, there has never been any firm historical evidence to indicate that spontaneous organic transmogrification takes place, for all that tens of thousands of Evolutionists believe in it fervently. In the whole of human history there has never been so much as one single Evolutionist who has ever been able to produce either a grandparent or a grandchild or any other relative who has spontaneously made the transformation to fish, lizard, dog, cat, cow or budgerigar. Furthermore, it can be stated with confidence that no Evolutionist ever will thus be able to match proof to theory.

Admittedly, a change in organic form can be effected by the application of sufficient Power, and this can be done by either occult resource or by sophisticated machinery. But this is difficult. Very difficult. So difficult that the idea of a species-to-species shift occurring naturally must surely be seen as the absurdity it is.

Despite the passion with which Evolutionists defend their

ideas, the whole basis of Evolutionary theory is irredeemably flawed, for the world we live in is simply not possessed of the massive instability which would be necessary for Evolutionary processes to take place.

The truth of the matter is that Evolution never takes place in our day-to-day world, but instead is restricted to the World Beyond, those realms of almost infinitely flexible improbability where gods, demons and devils have their existence. Unlike us, the entities of the World Beyond are not bound to brute matter and the mundane flesh, and hence they are capable of evolving, and do so on a regular basis, and with alarming regularity.

Again, the proof of this is to be found in human history, for the same history which demonstrates that humans have never evolved also serves to demonstrate that the gods are in a state of constant flux. There is not one god known to the human race which has remained stable in its form for so short a time as recorded history; and many are the gods which have radically altered their shapes, powers and attributes in a generation or less.

While the World Beyond is doubtless the site of the most promiscuously fevered Evolution imaginable, Penelope Flute was in error when she believed Evolutionary instability to be a property of the world in which she lived. However, Guest made no attempt to argue her out of her ridiculous beliefs — for the simple and sufficient reason that they had no language in common.

For want of the language of the tongue, Guest and Penelope had to rely much on the language of the flesh, and here they came to swift agreement, so that the buxom Penelope was often to be found sitting astride her champion, thrashing and screaming as she soared towards the crest of her pleasure.

Guest had never before met a woman who thrashed and screamed, for the females with whom he had previously mated had lacked Penelope's taste for melodrama; and he was flattered by the whole performance, quite failing to recognize that a full nine tenths of it was pure theatre.

But, though Guest and his beloved were satisfied in bed, and though they did not argue, it would not be true to say that their marital relationship was entirely harmonious. For one thing, Guest disliked the uninhibited manner in which Penelope would grab hold of his ears in the course of her physical raptures. Not only did she grab them: she was inclined to haul upon them as she forgot herself in her climax, as if anchoring herself to these prominent aspects of reality lest ecstasy claim her forever. Her fingernails were inclined to bite into the flesh as she hauled on it, and the combined effect of all this abuse was that Guest, in his hours of detumescence, usually felt as if he had been attacked by a pack of homicidal man-eating crabs.

Guest also wished that sometimes, just sometimes, he could have been left alone with his thoughts, for as their relationship progressed it seemed that Penelope spent virtually the entire course of every day and night at his bedside.

He often wondered why she never went out into the city.

The reason why Penelope never went out into the city was that her life would have been endangered had she wandered the streets of Dalar ken Halvar, for the Nexus religion known as Nu-chala-nuth was in the ascendant in that city, and its ascendancy was accompanied by the systematic slaughter of every Evolutionist who could be caught.

Since the Frangoni warrior Asodo Hatch was a priest of Nu-chala-nuth, he should by rights have murdered his sister himself, but instead he had chosen to bury her in the Combat College.

While thus buried alive inside the minor mountain of Cap Foz Para Lash, Penelope had nothing to do except sit with her husband and watch entertainment shows sourced in the Nexus, which played endlessly on a screen which took up one whole wall of Guest Gulkan's room.

The shows Guest Gulkan favoured were those featuring the Wild Tribes, a set of barbaric peoples whose lives were a non-stop drama of war, conquest, killing, fighting, looting, pillage, rape, torture, arson and orgies.

Guest was particularly interested in the orgies, and found that he had much to learn. The Yarglat had a very high opinion of themselves, and Guest had always been very proud of himself and his people, but soon he realized that the Yarglat were a dull and conservative people compared to the Wild Tribes. One of the Wild Tribes was given to staging huge orgies in which ten thousand people at a time grappled promiscuously in a gigantic vat of ripe strawberries while cheering spectators pelted them with handfuls of rose petals.

Once Guest's baby-sized hand was strong enough and skilled enough to manipulate the bedside controls which commanded the entertainment screen, he replayed this particular orgy repeatedly, and vowed that he would strive to match this achievement of the Wild Tribes as soon as he had mastered the Collosnon Empire to his will.

Yes, Guest still hoped to be emperor.

He hoped to defeat Khmar, to conquer Gendormargensis, to install himself on the ruling throne of Tameran, and to establish a dynasty that would rule the Collosnon Empire for generations.

While the difficulties of conquering the Collosnon Empire from a bed based in Dalar ken Halvar proved insuperable, Guest thought he should at least be able to set about producing a dynasty. It is said among the Yarglat that a warrior needs ten sons and an emperor needs twenty; and Guest, knowing that his planned war against Khmar might well be long and bloody, suspected that twenty might be barely sufficient for his purposes.

Hence he put his soul into his bedtime efforts — but his woman never became pregnant.

For, unbeknownst to Guest, Penelope had no plans to hatch children, and the demon had obliged her by arranging for its medical facilities to bury in her buttocks a pair of slow-release contraceptive pellets which would guarantee her infertility for a decade.

As soon as Penelope had mastered enough of Guest's native Eparget to her tongue for basic communication to be possible, she learnt that he wanted sons to fight with him in his great war against Khmar, though she was not by any means clear as to who "Khmar" might be. But the purple-skinned Frangoni beauty was not inclined to co-operate with this plan, for she believed it to be sheer folly. Penelope believed that a great Flood was imminent, and that this Flood would swamp the entire world, precipitating a mass Evolution of humans to fishes.

Once Guest and Penelope were united in piscatorial bliss it would be very nice to have a pair of child-fishes to keep them company, but there was no point in idly breeding human children to fight in a war which would never happen. So thought Penelope — and felt guiltless at frustrating Guest's intent.

By the end of his second year in the minor mountain of Cap Foz Para Lash, Guest Gulkan had arms and legs — of a sort. They were not sufficient for his support, but they were adequate for his propulsion. Daily, the Weaponmaster was carried from his mountain cave to Dalar ken Halvar's river, and there he played fish the whole morning through, strengthening his limbs for war by endless labours of swimming. When he was not swimming, he was resting; or was renewing his efforts to establish a dynasty; or was eating, for he found himself possessed of a ravenous appetite.

Before coming to Dalar ken Halvar, Guest Gulkan had known nothing of swimming, and invariably associated water with drowning. But, as his limbs were initially of an uncommonly light weight, he learnt the art easily, for he found himself naturally buoyant.

Later, as his legs lengthened and strengthened, their weight of ever-growing bone and muscle weighed him down, and to stay afloat became harder. But by then he had entirely mastered swimming to a fine art, and sustained himself in the water as if born to it.

Two years of swimming brought Guest to the end of his fourth year of exile in Dalar ken Halvar, by which time Sken-Pitilkin had wrecked his seventy-seventh experimental airship — and had just succeeded in making the seventy-eighth fly.

And Guest was cordially invited to join Sken-Pitilkin on the second test-flight of that amazing device.

CHAPTER THIRTY-ONE

Jocasta: an alleged Great God held prisoner in Obooloo by
Anaconda Stogirov, high priestess of the Temple of Blood.
This entity has faithfully promised to make the
Weaponmaster Guest Gulkan a wizard should Guest secure
its liberation.

* * *

Now during his time inside Cap Foz Para Lash, Guest Gulkan
had heard from the demon Paraban Senk many wild and
wonderful tales of the worlds which were alleged to exist in
other universes. He had heard of the rollercoaster, and the
bungee jump, both devices of terror unimaginable to anyone
who had led the sheltered life of a Yarglat barbarian.

Though Guest was no scholar, he had been trained in
ethnology by Hostaja Sken-Pitilkin, and so had diligently set
himself the task of discovering whether the rollercoaster and the
bungee jump had been instituted as initiation rites — fearsome
tests of manhood to be undertaken as part of the rites of passage
marking the transition from childhood — or whether these
outrageous forms of horrorshock were looked upon as a form
of fun.

After long research, Guest concluded that the peoples of the
high civilizations known to Paraban Senk routinely plunged
down artificial mountains in rickety carts, or hurled themselves
from the heights with elasticated ropes tied to their ankles,
purely for their own pleasure. He was most frightfully glad that
he had not been born into any world where pleasure itself had
the taste of torture, and looked upon Sken-Pitilkin's airship as a
device better fit for such a world than for his own.

Ever since the precipitous flight which had seen Guest and
his companions flung from the Swelaway Sea to an air-wrecking
in the Ibsen-Iktus mountains, Guest had entirely ceased to envy
the birds; and it was only with the greatest reluctance imaginable

that he allowed himself to be cajoled into Sken-Pitilkin's airship to partake of its second flight.

In the end, thinking himself doomed to be reduced to a mess of fractured chicken bones, Guest Gulkan climbed into the gigantic nest of sticks which Sken-Pitilkin declared to be an airship.

To his amazement, it flew.

And Guest, dazzled and bewildered by the wonders of controlled flight (which was entirely different from the absolutely uncontrolled flights which he had previously endured), was returned to the ground in one piece, amazed to find his skull and skeleton intact.

"Now," said Sken-Pitilkin, "since you have recovered your strength, and since I have a functional airship, we can start to plan our campaign."

"Our campaign?" said Guest.

"Our quest," said Sken-Pitilkin.

"Quest?"

"For the x-x-zix," said Sken-Pitilkin.

"It would seem," said Guest, "that I have a lot to learn."

"So you have," said Sken-Pitilkin. "So you have. Very well! Let us start the explanations!"

Then, in tedious detail, Sken-Pitilkin took Guest Gulkan through the tortuous details of the Witchlord's slow and painful negotiations with the Partnership Banks. Since Lord Onosh had suffered so badly from the Banks' deceits, he had not easily been able to bring himself to trust Sod.

But Banker Sod had been given great incentive to make agreement with Lord Onosh, for the Partnership Banks as a whole were unhappy with Sod. It was agreed among the Banks that Sod should never have incarcerated Ulix of the Drum in his time prison; and the Banks were alarmed at the ambition Sod had shown by arranging this incarceration, for it appeared that Sod had imprisoned the rightful ruler of Dalar ken Halvar because he had entertained notions of seizing that city and ruling it himself.

Furthermore, the Partnership Banks were distressed that Sod

had used ineffective treacheries in his dealings with the Witchlord Onosh. Effective treacheries against non-Bankers were acceptable, but the price of failure was ...

Sod had a lively sense of what the price of failure might be, and so exerted himself strenuously to negotiate an agreement with the Witchlord Onosh. Finally, under dire pressure from the Partnership Banks, Sod surrendered Eljuk Zala Gulkan to his father, and then surrendered himself to the Witchlord as a hostage.

Once his son Eljuk had been restored to him, and once he had Sod as a hostage, Lord Onosh at last consented to negotiate with the Partnership Banks in earnest, as a result of which the Doors of the Circle of the Banks were open again.

"Furthermore," said Sken-Pitilkin, "Ontario Nol has recently returned to Alozay through those Doors, there to resume his training of Eljuk Zala."

"I am pleased for my brother," said Guest Gulkan, mightily wearied by the laborious detail in which Sken-Pitilkin had told the tale of the negotiations for the reopening of the Circle.

"There is more pleasure yet to come," said Sken-Pitilkin. "The high point of my story is that we are to be privileged to travel the Circle, just as Plandruk Qinplaqus was in former times when he travelled that Circle as Ulix of the Drum."

"We?" said Guest. "Who are you talking of?"

"Myself," said Sken-Pitilkin, "and yourself, and Thayer Levant, and Pelagius Zozimus."

"And Qinplaqus himself?" said Guest.

"He no longer wishes to risk the Circle," said Sken-Pitilkin. "For after having been once betrayed and imprisoned, he cannot bring himself to trust the Banks. He blames the Partnership Banks as a whole for Sod's delinquencies, and will assist us against them."

"What are we planning?" said Guest. "War?"

"We are seeking leverage," said Sken-Pitilkin. "And once we have it, we will see how much of the Circle we can win. We already rule the Door at Alozay, and Plandruk Qinplaqus is our ally here in Dalar ken Halvar. If we could but win Chi'ash-lan, then we would be well placed to coerce the Partnership Banks as a whole to obedience to our will."

This was a new Sken-Pitilkin, a Sken-Pitilkin whom Guest Gulkan had not previously seen. The Sken-Pitilkin who had been the companion of Guest's childhood had been a broken-down exponent of the irregular verbs, a ragged refugee scraping his living in exile, an irascible master of the classroom.

But Sken-Pitilkin's true history was far greater and grander than anything Guest had guessed at. Sken-Pitilkin had known power, fame, glory, mightiness and mastery, and the appetite for such things had been rekindled during the long manoeuvrings of the past four years.

While Guest had been concerning himself with the exercise of his limbs, the eating of his meals and the rigours of his marital bed, Sken-Pitilkin had been exercising himself mightily in politics, embroiling himself in the affairs of the Witchlord Onosh and the Partnership Banks, acting as translator, as adviser, as diplomat, as interrogator, and as a professional practitioner of international law.

So it was that, for four long years, as Guest had turned inward in the manner of the invalid, his world shrinking till it took account of little outside his own skin, Sken-Pitilkin's world had been enlarging to a point where its complexity could not be compressed into anything less than a volume of ten thousand pages or more.

(Oh, Time! Strength! Cash! Patience!)

So Guest was uncommonly sluggish in responding to Sken-Pitilkin's enraptured enthusiasm for the embroilments of a quest and its consequences. Sken-Pitilkin perceived this sluggishness, but, presuming it would be transitory, he said:

"We were talking of the x-x-zix. The subject of our quest. Have you by chance heard of this device?"

Then Guest Gulkan thought, and by a miracle of memory he recalled an early mention of the thing. (In truth, Sken-Pitilkin must have spoken of the x-x-zix a thousand times in Guest Gulkan's youth, but the Yarglat barbarian was such a poor scholar that it was a very miracle that he remembered so much as a single of these mentions.)

"The Untunchilamons!" said Guest. "That was it! The Untunchilamons! When you were young, you quested for the x-x-zix. You quested on all twenty-six of the Untunchilamon, and you—"

"There is but one Untunchilamon," said Sken-Pitilkin.

"No," said Guest. "There are twenty-six. I remember that distinctly. If you told me that once you told it to me a hundred times."

"No, no," said Sken-Pitilkin, who had long been out of the habit of tutoring young Guest, and so had started to forget how difficult it was. "It was you who told me the number twenty-six, which you got from confusing Untunchilamon with the islands of Rovac. There is but one Untunchilamon, and I can state it as a certainty since I have been there."

"In your youth."

"Yes, in my youth."

"Questing," said Guest Gulkan.

"Verily," said Sken-Pitilkin.

"And now," said Guest Gulkan, "as you launch yourself upon the years of your senility, you wish to take up that quest again."

"Of senility I know not," said Sken-Pitilkin. "But my resolve is certain, and certainly a quest is a part of it."

Then Sken-Pitilkin explained the nature of the x-x-zix, which was a device capable of controlling the Breathings of the Cold West, which were the ancient weather machines which made that region so abominably cold.

"Our good friend Plandruk Qinplaqus desires the use of the x-x-zix also," said Sken-Pitilkin, "and long has he sought it, for Dalar ken Halvar has Breathings of its own, these Breathings being those which make the climate hereabouts so infernally hot."

Then Sken-Pitilkin tutored Guest Gulkan further, explaining that use of the x-x-zix would allow the climates of both Dalar ken Halvar and Chi'ash-lan to be moderated to something close enough to the sensible.

Therefore Sken-Pitilkin proposed that Guest Gulkan join him in questing to Untunchilamon in alliance with the wizard Zozimus, then return with that treasure to Dalar ken Halvar. There the wizard Plandruk Qinplaqus, he who was otherwise known as Ulix of the Drum, would make use of the x-x-zix to remedy the climate of his own city.

"And then," said Sken-Pitilkin, "he will help us bring the Circle of the Partnership Banks to heel."

"How?" said Guest.

"Why, it is obvious," said Sken-Pitilkin. "The Banks exist to make money, and a greening of the icelands of Chi'ash-lan would make more money than you could shake a stick at. If you have the strength of the x-x-zix in your hand and the wisdom of wizards to support you, then you can make yourself master of the Circle of the Partnership Banks. Or so I believe."

"It would help me also," said Guest, shaking off his sluggishness with a rapidity which was consequent upon his upbringing in the household of a ruling warlord, "if I could make myself a wizard in my own right."

"Why, doubtless it would so help you," said Sken-Pitilkin. "But to make you a wizard would take a lifetime."

"Not so," said Guest. "For there is in the city of Obooloo the Great God Jocasta, who has sworn to make me a wizard, powerful and immortal, if I do but liberate the thing from cruel imprisonment at the hands of one Anaconda Stogirov, priestess of the Temple of Blood."

"So you have told me you have been told," said Sken-Pitilkin, "but it is a nonsense."

And it was a nonsense.

Of this Sken-Pitilkin was certain.

Nevertheless, the sagacious wizard of Skatzabratzumon was hard put to dissuade the Emperor in Exile from this folly, and so called for assistance from Paraban Senk, the Teacher of Control who ruled the Combat College in which Guest had been so long a patient.

"Is this going to be a short lecture or a long one?" said Guest, once he was settled with Sken-Pitilkin in front of one of the screens which Senk used to communicate with mere mortals such as wizards and warriors.

"That depends on you," said Paraban Senk, manifesting his chosen face upon the screen. "Tell me, Guest Gulkan, what on earth has persuaded you to this foolishness?"

"Foolishness?" said Guest. "What foolishness?"

"Your intended quest to Obooloo," said the olive-skinned Teacher of Control. "That is what I refer to when I speak of foolishness. Explain yourself!"

By now, Guest had long been accustomed to treating this face-on-a-screen with the dignity due to a person-in-the-flesh, and so responded to this command with due gravity.

"When I was 14," said Guest, "my father went hunting bandits in the mountains near Gendormargensis."

This was ever the Yarglat way of telling a tale — to start way back in the distant past with the egg of its genesis. The Teacher of Control was lucky that the Yarglat barbarian had not started earlier still — with a detailed account of his family's genealogy, say, or with a founding reference to the Yarglat creation myths.

"I asked nothing about you at the age of 14," said Senk, who came from a culture which lacked all fireside patience, and thus restricted its storytelling to an account of proximate cause, crisis and consequence.

By brute interrogation, Paraban Senk extracted the meat of Guest Gulkan's story in record time. In a time of crisis, a time when Witchlord and Weaponmaster were fighting for their lives on Safrak, Guest Gulkan had parleyed with the Great God Jocasta through the mediumship of the demon Icaria Scaria Iva-Italis, had won a victory against his enemies thanks to the Great God's intervention, and so was bound to fulfil his pledge to the Great God.

"In proof of my honour," said Guest, "I must quest to Obooloo to liberate the Great God. Besides — without Jocasta's help, how can I win a wizard's powers?"

Paraban Senk heard this out to the finish then said:

"I think you bound to no quest, for I think Jocasta has lied to you. There are many kinds of god and many kinds of demon, but Jocasta is no god, demon, devil or hero. Jocasta is only a machine, and Iva-Italis likewise. Iva-Italis is a farspeaker designed for use in war, and Jocasta is a thinking machine which once proved delinquent in the exercise of its will. Both are devices of delinquency — fraudulent, scheming, power-crazed and treacherous."

"I think," said Guest, his response so instantaneous as to make it very improbable that any thinking had gone into the framing of it, "that you don't like me and you don't want me to be a wizard."

"The wizards of this world," said Paraban Senk, "have gained their powers by making an alliance with entities of the World Beyond. Since the machine which calls itself Jocasta is no such entity, it cannot make you a wizard. It can however make you a slave. Jocasta can build a web through your body, a web through your brain. With such a web once built, Jocasta can control you, body and brain alike, and project power through you, albeit at a risk to your health."

Guest frowned.

"What web do you speak of?" said Guest. "Is Jocasta a kind of spider?"

"Jocasta," said Senk, "could conjure in your flesh and bone a web of nerves of cunning design. With your body thus adapted to a new pattern, Jocasta could make you flesh of its flesh, mind of its mind. At a distance you would be safe, but if ever near the Great God then you would be its slave. It could control you likewise if you were ever near a farspeaker such as the demon Iva-Italis."

"I don't understand," said Guest, still frowning. "I don't understand this — this web."

"Do you expect to understand?" said Senk, who really thought it over-optimistic to expect a Yarglat barbarian like Guest to understand so much as basic arithmetic, far less the greater mysteries of the world.

"If you'd stop talking in riddles and talk sense for once," said Guest, "then I'd understand soon enough."

"All right, then," said Senk. "Supposing you have a ball of

string which is knotted and ravelled. Can you talk to it? Or with it?"

"That's a nonsense question," said Guest. "String can't talk. It's not in the nature of string to talk."

"Isn't it?" said Senk.

"Of course it isn't!" said Guest.

"Have the Yarglat no music? Have you never seen a harp?" Since the making of music was not one of the strong points of Yarglat culture, harpists had not exactly been thick on the ground in Gendormargensis. But Guest knew of the instrument, and, sensing that for some obscure reason any denial of harp-knowledge might be thought of as a demerit, he staunchily said:

"We Yarglat are mighty in harpwork. We are famous for it."

"So," said Senk. "What is the harp if not a string which talks?"

"But that's a trick!" said Guest. "The riddle wasn't fair!"

"Whoever said we were playing at riddles?" said Senk. "I speak of no riddles but of facts. String in combination with the simplest of devices can talk as a harp, or hear the wind as a windchime, or pull a fish from the sea, or kill a man by triggering a trap, or weave itself to art in the game of cat's cradle. Your body is one knotted, ravelled, snarled-up ball of string, and Jocasta is the weaver who can shape it to a new pattern, then play that pattern with the skills of harpist and fisherman."

"Jocasta is then a thing mighty in power, then," said Guest. "You admit it!"

"Is there no sense to be got out of this thing?" said Senk, in an exasperation which echoed that of the learned Sken-Pitilkin in one of his more frustrated moments.

"I'll take no talk of sense from a schoolteacher, which is all you are," said Guest. "I'm an emperor's son and heir to an empire myself. I'm oath-bound to rescue Jocasta, and so I will."

"You are not oath-bound at all," said Senk. "You are not oath-bound because Jocasta lied to you. The thing cannot make you a wizard. It can only control you, possess you, seize you, subject you. Use you as a tool, a thing."

"But it bound itself to me in honour," said Guest.

"It has no honour!" said Senk. "Honour is — how can I put this? You're mortal, you die, you seek significance in the face of mortality, you seek a meaning. The oath-culture is quest for precisely that: significance in the face of mortality. The honour of a man's death is the meaning of that death. Jocasta shares no such fear of death, hence needs the support of no such culture, hence cannot be trusted to hold to an oath. Do you understand?"

"You are a schoolmaster," said Guest, "hence have an ethnological temperament. But a thing — you're like Sken-Pitilkin. What's it all about, that's what you say. Then you riddle out a meaning, then you say because it's got a meaning it's got no meaning. First you shape the thing in words, then you say the thing's only words so it's nothing. But things are things despite any number of words, and a thing is good in itself. My horse, my woman, my honour, my sword. My honour—"

"Your honour is not a thing," said Senk, with crushing force. "You confuse categories. You confuse your horse with your honour when your horse is a flesh-and-blood animal with mass, weight and an appetite for hay, whereas your honour is a cultural construct, which is something quite different."

"Yes, well," said Guest, not appreciating that he had just been crushed under one of the heavier hammers in the intellectual toolbox, "you're talking categories, but that's just like breaking up a bit of bread, you get big bits and small bits but it's all bread when you're finished with it."

Though Guest had been tutored by the wizard Sken-Pitilkin since the age of five, he had nevertheless ever preserved a sturdy independence of intellect, reinforced by a close observation of a world in which brightsparking intellects (such as that of Eljuk Zala) tended to lose out to solid-muscled swordarms (such as that of Guest Gulkan).

Paraban Senk protracted the argument for another three days, until at last in the despair of reason he recognized the Weaponmaster's implacable resolve, and began to counsel Guest as to how he might (just possibly) be able to bring his mission to a successful conclusion.

This complicated Sken-Pitilkin's plan to quest to the island of Untunchilamon to rescue the x-x-zix: for Guest was determined first to dare to Obooloo, penetrate the Temple of Blood, rescue the Great God Jocasta, and (by way of reward) win the powers of a full-fledged wizard.

"We could manage such a mission," said Sken-Pitilkin at last, "but there is one thing which must be done first."

"What?" said Guest.

"First we must recover the ring of ever-ice which you won from Banker Sod," said Sken-Pitilkin. "For, if you die in Obooloo without revealing its whereabouts, then it will be lost to the world forever."

Guest, who had preserved the secret of this ring's whereabouts as much as an act of independence as anything else — for, as an invalid, what other sphere of independent action had been left to him? — declared the thing to be in the care of one Anna Blaume, proprietor of the Green Parrot, an establishment in Galsh Ebrek. Sken-Pitilkin then undertook the tricky business of recovering this ring, which he handed over to the Witchlord Onosh. Lord Onosh then used the ring to open one of the pods in Alozay's Hall of Time, and to incarcerate within that pod the woman Yerzerdayla.

Lord Onosh then directed Sken-Pitilkin to make one last attempt to dissuade Guest Gulkan from the folly of his planned onslaught on Obooloo: and Sken-Pitilkin reluctantly accepted this commission.

CHAPTER THIRTY-TWO

Obooloo: capital of the Izdimir Empire. Lies amidst mountains in
the province of Ang in the heartland of the continent of
Yestron.

***

In the end, Guest Gulkan could not be dissuaded from his
madcap plan to venture to Obooloo to liberate the Great God
Jocasta. Furthermore, he sought to implicate and involve his
father in this plan; and the Witchlord Onosh, who was
consumed with guilt because he felt himself partly to blame for
Guest's mauling in the arena of Chi'ash-lan, felt constrained to
agree to commit his own strength to the raid on Obooloo.

So Guest said goodbye to Penelope, telling her that he was
going to fly away on Sken-Pitilkin's stickbird, the airborne
contraption which had so lately terrorized the skies above Dalar
ken Halvar.

This was a blatant lie, since Guest was actually going to travel
to Obooloo by way of the Doors of the Circle of the Partnership
Banks; but the Weaponmaster had told his wife nothing of that
Circle or those Doors, and did not intend to.

"When will you be back?" said Penelope.

"As soon as I can be," said Guest, speaking in perfect
honesty.

For, though her womb had proved barren, Guest was
generally satisfied with his wife, and had no thought to abandon
her on a permanent basis. Rather, he wished her to do what the
wives of heroes have always done: to wait.

"You'll be back?" said Penelope, seeking confirmation of the
Weaponmaster's pledge.

It would not be true to say that the purple-skinned Penelope
was passionately in love with Guest Gulkan. Nevertheless, he
had been tolerably civil and attentive to her during four long
years which she had spent as a refugee in the tunnels of Cap Foz

Para Lash, sheltering from the wrath of her home city, which had given itself to the madness of the religion known as Nu-chala-nuth.

Indeed, Penelope would surely have fallen in love with Guest entirely, had she not already pledged her heart to another. That other was a valorous Ebrell Islander, Lupus Lon Oliver by name. To tell the truth, Penelope had once been married to the valorous Lupus, and had never gone through the formality of getting a divorce. The red-skinned Lupus Lon Oliver was currently in insurrection against the city of Dalar ken Halvar and the religion of Nu-chala-nuth. He was leading a wild life in Parengarenga's deserts, fighting with a band of doomed but undaunted revolutionaries led by a female of the Pang, a woman warrior named Shona.

In the absence of Lupus Lon Oliver, her true love, Penelope had developed a strong affection for Guest Gulkan, hence sought his return.

"I'll be back," confirmed Guest.

"Then," said Penelope, "take this."

And, with that, she took from her neck the bright-metal chain which she customarily wore, and passed the chain and its pendant to the Weaponmaster.

"Thank you," said Guest, taking the chain and the amulet which served as its pendant.

This object he had seen often enough, for Penelope wore it always, whether she was clothed or naked. He knew already that the pendant burnt with its own light, and was not surprised by this.

But — the weight!

The amulet was small enough for Guest to conceal in his fist, yet it was so uncommonly heavy that he wondered at its weight. Over the last four years, it had been so much a part of his everyday existence that he had ceased to notice it. But now he looked at it closely. The webbing and weaving of half a thousand filigree threads created the oval of the amulet. The wire of which this work had been fashioned appeared at first glance to be silver, but it was not, for it glistened with a shimmering light like the moon itself made liquid and mixed with mercury.

"What is it?" said Guest.

"It is luck," said Penelope.

Then she kissed him.

So Guest Gulkan departed from the minor mountain of Cap Foz Para Lash, taking with him a mazadath, an amulet of Nexus make. This mazadath — the pendant which Penelope had given to her Weaponmaster — had once been part of a dorgi. And the dorgi was a formidable brute of animated metal which had once guarded the tunnels inside Cap Foz Para Lash.

(At any rate, this is what Paraban Senk told Hostaja Sken-Pitilkin, for that disembodied demon, on realizing that Penelope had given her amulet to the Weaponmaster, and that the amulet was about to depart from Cap Foz Para Lash, was loath to see the thing go; and, speaking privily to Sken-Pitilkin, Senk requested that the wizard relieve the Weaponmaster of his burden. Something Sken-Pitilkin declined to do, for life was difficult enough already without gratuitously enhancing its difficulties by trying to steal a love-charm from a Yarglat barbarian.)

So it was that Guest Gulkan took his leave from his wife Penelope, exited from Cap Foz Para Lash, and made his way through the city of Dalar ken Halvar to the Bralsh — the building which housed Dalar ken Halvar's Door.

According to their plans, Weaponmaster would unite with Witchlord on Alozay, then together they would venture to Obooloo to liberate the Great God Jocasta. By now, Guest was fired up with a great enthusiasm for his mission, and for the quest for the x-x-zix which would follow it.

Witchlord and Weaponmaster would not be venturing alone, for the wizards Pelagius Zozimus and Hostaja Sken-Pitilkin would be daring the dangers with them, together with the knifeman Thayer Levant. The last-named, Levant, was undoubtedly sent by Plandruk Qinplaqus to spy on the others, but they did not resent such scrutiny, since a cheating of the Silver Emperor formed no part of their plans.

Plandruk Qinplaqus came in person to the Bralsh to see

them off.

"One last thing," said Qinplaqus, once all their arrangements had been confirmed and reconfirmed for one last time.

"What?" said Guest.

"Good luck," said Qinplaqus.

That benediction meant a lot to Guest, and it warmed him mightily as he ventured through the Circle of the Partnership Banks, passing from Dalar ken Halvar to Tang, from Tang to Quilth, and then to Stokos, to Chi'ash-lan, and then to Alozay.

On Alozay, the ruling island of the Safrak Islands, Guest Gulkan was greeted by his brother Morsh Bataar, who brought him dire tidings of disease.

"Our father is ill," said Morsh.

"Ill?" said Guest, in startlement.

This was the last thing which Guest had expected!

"You speak as if you doubt my word," said Morsh. "But it is true. As a horse has hair, so our father has an ailment. He cannot quest with you, not yet, for his doctors have pronounced him too sick to stir from his bed."

"What's wrong with him, then?" said Guest.

"He has a cold," said Morsh.

"A cold!" said Guest, scandalized.

They were heroes, were they not? Questing heroes! Truly heroic heroes, their deeds and avowals proportioned like the greatest of those of legend. How then could they be held up by a trifling matter like a cold?

Guest demanded to be shown into the presence of his father, and found Lord Onosh laid up in bed with a bad headcold, which he was endeavouring to treat with a medicinal concoction compounded of lemons, hot water and something strongly alcoholic. As a consequence of the side-effects of the alcoholic component of this medicine, Lord Onosh had reached a stage of pronounced incoherence.

This did not please the Weaponmaster at all, who in his anger was threatening to scalp the Witchlord when the Witch herself appeared. Bao Gahai hustled Guest out of the sickroom, interrogated him at length about all of his doings, then at last consented to leave him in peace.

In the moody solitude of his disappointed brooding, Guest Gulkan took himself off to the Hall of Time. This was guarded by men with spears, and by solid doors which a blacksmith had closed with chains. Both the men and the doors resisted the Weaponmaster's will, but Guest at length succeeded in subduing the men and having the doors broken down.

Then Guest Gulkan stalked into the Hall of Time, expecting to find it a place of dust and cobwebs. It was and it wasn't. True, there were cobwebs in plenty sprawled across the time prison pods. But there was precious little dust, for the open slit windows of the Hall of Time ventilated the place as a draughty cave is ventilated.

Guest Gulkan came to a halt in front of the jade-green monolith known to him as Icaria Scaria Iva-Italis, demon of Safrak and Guardian Prime. At first, the demon did not consent to acknowledge his presence. But at last it spoke.

"Greetings," said the demon.

"And to you, greetings," said Guest.

"You have come by a mazadath," said the demon. "Where did you win such a prize?"

"A mazadath?" said Guest. "What's that?"

"The thing which you have about your neck," said the demon.

"This?" said Guest, lifting his heavyweight amulet from its concealment.

"That," confirmed Italis. "Where did you get it?"

"It was a present," said Guest. "A present from my wife."

"So," said Iva-Italis. "So you are married. Have you children?"

"Not yet," said Guest.

"Your brother Morsh has children," said Iva-Italis.

"Has he?" said Guest, most surprised at this intelligence; for nobody had even suggested to him that his brother Morsh had so much as a woman, far less a child.

"He has," said Iva-Italis. "He has two sons, Yurt and Iragana."

"So you say," said Guest. "But you have been locked in here for years, far beyond any breath of rumour. So how could you rightly claim to know such a thing?"

"I am in communication with demons elsewhere," said Iva-Italis. "Have you not been told of this? I communicated, to name but one, with Koblathakatoria, he who is commonly known as Ko. You know him? Koblathakatoria is the demon of Chi'ash-lan. There is no scrap of gossip about Safrak which does not reach Chi'ash-lan, and usually sooner rather than later."

"So," said Guest. "They spy on us."

"The mere collection of gossip is scarcely a matter of espionage," said Iva-Italis. "Are your matings and breedings a matter of state secrecy? If they are, then all I can say is that you do not act in accordance with any such doctrine. It is a matter of public record that your brother Morsh Bataar maintains a wife on the island of Ema-Urk, and that she has given him two sons. Yurt is aged two, and Iragana is but one year of age."

"This is news to me!" said Guest.

"So," said Iva-Italis. "But I doubt that you have any news for me."

"You didn't know about the — the maza," said Guest.

"The mazadath," said Iva-Italis. "Maz-a-dath. No, I didn't know about that. But I take it to be a recent acquisition. The rest of your past I know. I have followed the saga of your recovery in the city of Dalar ken Halvar. I know, too, that you are now determined to venture to Obooloo."

"They speak of this in Chi'ash-lan?" said Guest.

"Of course they do," said Iva-Italis. "For Sod is held hostage in this very mainrock in which we now stand. Sod's brother rules in Chi'ash-lan, and fears that Sod will be murdered when your father's minions hear of your father's death."

"My father is not dead!" said Guest. "He's got a cold, that's all!"

"Yes," said Iva-Italis, "but soon you and your father will both be venturing to Obooloo. In Chi'ash-lan, they think both Witchlord and Weaponmaster will die in that venture, and that Sod will be murdered once the pair of you are dead."

"And will we die?" said Guest.

"That is for you to say, not me," said Iva-Italis. "Tell me how you are going to rescue the Great God Jocasta, and I will tell you whether you are likely to live."

Then Guest told the demon of the plan which he had hatched with Sken-Pitilkin, drawing on Sken-Pitilkin's by-now-detailed knowledge of the various Doors of the Partnership Banks.

The questing heroes would venture through the Circle of the Partnership Banks to the city of Obooloo. The Door in that city was housed in the Sanctuary of the Bondsman's Guild, a structure which stood atop a tall triangular rock known locally as Achaptipop, from which it was possible to overlook the Temple of Blood.

By studious reconnaissance, Sken-Pitilkin had already determined the layout of the Temple of Blood. It was built around a central courtyard in which stood a Burning Pit into which human sacrifices were periodically cast.

"From the Sanctuary of the Bondsman's Guild," said Guest, "we will overlook that Burning Pit. Sken-Pitilkin plans to improvise a flying ship. He will not build a full-scale stickbird. Rather, he will make a small device good enough for the descent from Achaptipop to the Burning Pit."

"So," said Iva-Italis, "you will float downwards through the air, landing by the Burning Pit."

"Precisely," said Guest. "But we're not sure how to find the Great God Jocasta."

"That's easy," said Iva-Italis. "The great rock Achaptipop stands directly to the north of the Temple of Blood. The central courtyard in which you find the Burning Pit has four sides."

"Most courtyards do," said Guest.

"The sides are orientated to the north, south, east and west," said Iva-Italis, ignoring Guest entirely. "It is easy to orientate yourself. Once you land in the central courtyard, look for the great rock Achaptipop. It lies to your north."

"And?" said Guest.

"Where does Achaptipop lie?" said Iva-Italis.

"To the north!" said Guest impatiently. "As I face that rock, the east will be to my right, and—"

"Go east," said Iva-Italis.

"East?" said Guest.

"Yes," said Iva-Italis. "A single archway is set in the eastern side of the central chamber of the Temple of Blood. Go through that archway and you will find the Great God Jocasta."

"What does the Great God look like?" said Guest.

"The Great God," said Iva-Italis, "looks like a doughnut."

"A doughnut?" said Guest, baffled by this description.

"Take a single link from a chain," said Iva-Italis. "Beat that link into a circle, and there you have your doughnut. The wizard Pelagius Zozimus commonly bakes a kind of sweetened bread in just such a shape. Have you never eaten such?"

"Ah!" said Guest, "now I understand!"

"So," said Iva-Italis. "The Great God Jocasta is a doughnut, a doughnut about the size of your head. The Great God is trapped in a force field. Do you know what a force field is?"

"Tell me," said Guest.

"A force field," said Iva-Italis, "is a wall of light which is hard to penetrate."

"Then how is Guest to penetrate this particular wall of light?" said Sken-Pitilkin.

At which Guest almost jumped out of his skin, for the Weaponmaster had been so engrossed in his dialogue with the demon that he had not heard the wizard of Skatzabratzumon enter the Hall of Time.

"The Weaponmaster Guest can cleave through this particular wall of light by the mere application of his sword," said Iva-Italis.

"Really?" said Sken-Pitilkin, sounding somewhat sceptical.

"Yes," said Iva-Italis, "for these force fields are but poor and trivial devices. Once Guest had hacked the force field apart with his sword, the Great God Jocasta will be free. The Great God will then confer upon Guest the powers of a wizard, and will secure your exit from the Temple of Blood."

"So you say," said Sken-Pitilkin, who still had reservations about this venture.

"Rest assured," said Iva-Italis. "It is as I say. Besides, you will have a demon to help you."

"You're coming with us?" said Sken-Pitilkin.

"No!" said Iva-Italis. "For I am scarcely portable! But a demon stands in the Temple of Blood already. The demon stands beside the imprisoned Great God."

"There's a demon which guards the Door of the Bondsman's Guild," said Sken-Pitilkin.

"The demon Lob, yes," said Iva-Italis. "But that's not the demon of whom I'm speaking. There are two of my siblings in Obooloo. One is Lob, of whom you have spoken. The other is Ungular Scarth, who stands beside the Great God Jocasta."

"Then why can't this Scarth claw away this force field?" said Sken-Pitilkin.

"Because," said Iva-Italis, "a force field of the kind of which we are talking about can only be destroyed by the application of metal. Iron will do, or steel. Bronze. Tin. Whatever. But it must be metal!"

"Then I will remember to leave my wooden sword at home," said Guest.

"Do that," said Iva-Italis. "Go, now! Go! Do as you have vowed to do! Rescue the Great God! And you will be a wizard within the week!"

"The week!" said Guest. "You too know of this business of weeks!"

"It is true," said Iva-Italis, "for I am mighty in knowledge, and anything a wizard knows I know too. Go now! And do well!"

So Guest and Sken-Pitilkin departed from the Hall of Time, paying no heed to the cobwebbed time pods which were set about its walls, and occupied themselves with preparations for their journey.

Guest found the time to seek out his brother Morsh Bataar, and to question him about his alleged wife; and Morsh inspired Guest's jealousy by confessing that he had indeed married one of the women of Ema-Urk, and that he had his own small sheep farm on that island, and had sired two sons.

"I will likewise have sons," said Guest, "for my wife Penelope will bear them for me. Once I have the powers of a wizard, I am sure I will be able to overcome her barrenness."

Comforted by this thought, the Weaponmaster occupied himself by choosing gear, and by climbing up and down the stairways of the mainrock Pinnacle to put a keen fighting edge on his fitness. And, once his father had recovered from his transitory illness, the questing heroes gathered together.

Need the heroes be named?

There was Witchlord and Weaponmaster; there was the servile Thayer Levant; and there were the wizards Pelagius Zozimus and Hostaja Sken-Pitilkin.

Guest had wanted to bring the wizard Ontario Nol, but Sken-Pitilkin had vetoed this.

"If your demon is telling the truth," said Sken-Pitilkin, "then we have strength sufficient for our mission. And if your demon is lying, then the mere addition of another wizard will not help us if we have to fight the city of Obooloo as a whole."

"Of course the demon's telling the truth!" said Guest. "It wants to have Jocasta liberated!"

"Doubtless," said Sken-Pitilkin grimly. "But if the task were so simple, then one suspects it would have been performed long ago. Anyway, let us be going!"

So the questing heroes passed through the Circle of the Partnership Banks to the city of Obooloo, where they enjoyed the hospitality of the Sanctuary of the Bondsman's Guild on the heights of the great rock Achaptipop.

There Sken-Pitilkin improvised a kind of air-raft, a primitive flying device sufficient to sustain the weight of the heroes and moderate their descent from Achaptipop to the central courtyard of the Temple of Blood.

When all was ready, the heroes gathered by the edge of Achaptipop, and, aided by Sken-Pitilkin's air-raft, they floated gently down to the central courtyard of the Temple of Blood. In the gloom of night, they located the archway on the courtyard's eastern flank. The arch opened on to a tunnel of uncommon darkness, a tunnel which could have doubled as part of the gut of a whale. The heroes drew their swords and ventured into that darkness.

It was an uncommonly moist darkness, which smelt alternately of the sewer and the brothel. As he shuffled forward through that absolute blackness, the Weaponmaster Guest started to find it difficult to keep his balance. A momentary dizziness beset him, and he found himself breathing swiftly, too swiftly.

"We should have brought a lamp," said Thayer Levant.

"Hush!" said Guest, who thought that Levant's rightful mission on this quest was to hew firewood, draw water and peel potatoes, not to pass comment on the plans and performance of his social superiors.

Thayer Levant did hush, though in all truth the knifeman felt himself well-qualified to pass comment. Levant had travelled the Circle of the Partnership Banks for a great many years as the servant of Plandruk Qinplaqus, hence thought himself an expert on that Circle and its cities; and, to him, his companions on this present quest were but rank amateurs in the art of travelling the world.

Once Levant had hushed, the silence became oppressive. Each of the questing heroes could hear the steady scrapage of boots against stone, the clinkage of metal, and the tiny sounds made by their tongues and their teeth, by the creaking of their kneecaps and the hush-wash of their breathing.

In the black and oppressive hush, wash after wash of smells assailed them. From somewhere came the smell of dung; then that of camphor; then a sweet, sickly perfume of the kind favoured by women of ill repute, or by young women who have yet to learn the art of sophisticated restraint in matters of self-enhancement. In that darkness—

"Stop," said the Witchlord Onosh.

All stopped.

"What is it?" said Guest.

"Something," said Lord Onosh.

"What?" said Guest.

"Hush! Not so loud!" said his father.

"What is it?" said Sken-Pitilkin.

"A light," said the Witchlord.

It was a dull, red light which lay ahead of them. It was so dull it was almost impossible to see. Sken-Pitilkin stared at it for a long moment, then abruptly strode forward. The light moved.

"The light's moving!" cried the Witchlord.

"Because," said Sken-Pitilkin, with scathing scorn, "it is in my hand. That's why it's moving."

Then Sken-Pitilkin returned to his companions, bearing in his fist a stick of incense, which he waved rigorously before letting it fall. Like a dying star, the incense lay on the stones.

"Light," muttered Lord Onosh. "I wish we had light."

Then the Witchlord bethought himself of the ring of ever-ice which he had taken from Banker Sod long, long ago on his first conquest of the island of Alozay. Lord Onosh now customarily wore that ring on a chain slung around his neck. Bethinking himself of that light, he produced it: but its feebleness could scarcely do more than illuminate his own face.

Not to be outdone, Guest Gulkan produced his mazadath. That amulet was a light more powerful than the Witchlord's ring of ever-ice, but it was insufficient to light the path.

"Hush down your lights," said Pelagius Zozimus. "They can but betray us. They cannot serve us."

Both Witchlord and Weaponmaster accepted this admonishment from the slug-chef Zozimus, and, concealing their futile lights, they pushed on down the tunnel until they saw a familiar green glow ahead.

That steady-burning jadeness was sure sign of the presence of a demon. Or so thought these questing heroes! As it happens, they were right, though some experts hold that the eyes of a basilisk burn with just such a cold and steady green; and certain mariners aver that a kraken encountered at night will be seen to emanate a similar baleful light; and one of the brands of the moonpaint which comes from the city of Injiltaprajura is most definitely a thus-shaded green.

Still, in the confidence of encountering a demon, Guest

Gulkan and his companions advanced, and found themselves in a vaulted octagonal chamber. Ranked around the walls of that chamber were niches in which stood time prison pods identical to those of Alozay's Hall of Time — some occupied, others not.

"Time pods," said Thayer Levant.

"And a demon," said Sken-Pitilkin.

Indeed, in the centre of that chamber stood a jade-green monolith identical in outward form to Icaria Scaria Iva-Italis, demon of Safrak. Thanks to a briefing from Iva-Italis, Guest Gulkan knew this to be the demon Ungular Scarth, a servant of the Great God Jocasta.

Illuminated by the green frostlight of the demon Ungular Scarth was the Great God Jocasta. As advertised, the Great God was a doughnut the size of a man's head. It was floating in the air within two shells of light. The inner shell of light was a dull red, the red of iron which has lately been removed from a furnace, and is cooling. The outer shell was blue — a sharp-burning blue which hurt the eyes and made Guest Gulkan think of the sun, and of teeth. (Why teeth? He could not tell, but that outer shell of blue-burning light made him think most decisively of saliva and teeth.)

"It is a demon," said the Witchlord Onosh, whose attention was given not to the Great God but to Ungular Scarth. "But it is short for its kind."

"Because," said Guest, heavily, "it is standing in water."

So it was, as Lord Onosh saw a moment later. The demon Ungular Scarth was half-buried in oily sewer waters. For the octagonal chamber in which the demon and the Great God were imprisoned was awash with sewer-water.

Fortunately, a metal grille reached from wall to wall, and looked as if it would allow the intruders to dare the approach to demon and god without getting their feet wet. Guest tested the grille, found that it bore his weight, and advanced to the base of the demon. The grille appeared to have been custom-made, and to have been installed long after the demon took up residence in this octagonal chamber, for the demon rose up from a neatly edged square hole in that grille.

Guest Gulkan glanced down into the oil sewer waters, where hunks of unidentifiable material floated on the surface. The water was still, unmoving, fetid. In the chamber's sullen silence, Guest heard his father's breathing, which was uncommonly laboured. He guessed that Lord Onosh was distressed by this place, and found its silence hard to bear.

To break that silence, Guest Gulkan addressed the demon Ungular Scarth.

"I am the Weaponmaster, Guest Gulkan by name," said he. "I am here to rescue the Great God Jocasta in fulfilment of my oath."

"Greetings, Guest Gulkan," said the demon, speaking to him in his native Eparget.

"And to you, greetings," said Guest politely. "OK, what do we do now?"

"You cut through the fields of force which have trapped my master," said Ungular Scarth.

"OK then," said Guest.

Then Guest drew his sword, and, striking with all the confidence of a hairy-arsed barbarian who has hacked off more heads than the world has fingers to count, he struck. He hacked with his sword, striking a mighty blow, a blow sufficient for the decapitation of dragons, the rupture of chains, or the lopping off of the limbs of a giant. But that blow availed the Weaponmaster not, for his sword bounced off the bubbles of force as if off the celestial armour of the greater war-gods.

"Gods!" said Guest.

"Come," said Ungular Scarth. "You did but tickle it. You can do better than that."

"Better!" said Guest. "I have struck with force sufficient for the murder of ten men simultaneously."

"Then strike again," said the demon.

So Guest struck. But his metal bounced from the blue-burning force field which imprisoned the Great God Jocasta.

"What are you?" said Ungular Scarth. "Are you a child? I thought you a man!"

At which Guest was enraged, and hacked again at the force

field. Again his metal bounced harmlessly from the sphere of
force.

"Let me," said Lord Onosh.

Upon which Guest stepped aside, with hot sweat dripping
down his forehead — sweat which was consequent upon the
combination of exertion and embarrassment.

Lord Onosh hacked at the force field. But, just like his son,
the Witchlord made no impression on that blue-burning
armour.

"It is too much for us," said Lord Onosh.

Upon which the demon laughed.

"Ah," said Ungular Scarth, "but what did you expect?"

"We expected to be able to cut it," said Guest, starting to
lose his temper. "Iva-Italis told us that steel would be ample for
the purpose."

"And you believed my dear friend Italis?" said Ungular
Scarth. "Of course you did. For you are but a naive barbarian.
Italis has told me of you. Often. And in detail."

"Naive!" said Guest. "Why am I naive? Am I not your ally?
I came to save the Great God!"

"Then save the Great God," said Ungular Scarth.

"How?" said Guest. "We have tried to cut the force field,
but we cannot."

"Of course you can't," said Scarth. "For your swords are not
metal but wood."

"Wood!" said Guest, in renewed fury. "I'll show you what
kind of wood this is!"

Then Guest chopped at the demon Ungular Scarth. But his
blade bounced harmlessly from the demon's jade-green flanks.

"Cool yourself," said Scarth. "Cool and calm. Enough of
jokes. If you would liberate the Great God Jocasta, then you
must first secure a tool which is ample to your purpose. There
is a kind of knife. Two specimens are known to me. One is
carried by Anaconda Stogirov, the High Priestess of this temple.
The other is in the possession of Aldarch the Third, the
Mutilator of Yestron. You will know these knives—"

"Knives!" said Guest. "I was told that a sword—"

"Italis lied," said Sken-Pitilkin. "I suspected as much. I told you so."

"True," said Ungular Scarth. "A sword is useless for the liberation of the Great God. To cut through the force field, you must first procure this special knife of which I have spoken."

"There are two spheres of force," said Guest. "The outer blue and the inner red. Will one knife cut through both?"

"You need only cut through the outer," said Ungular Scarth. "The shell of blue-burning light was put there by Anaconda Stogirov. It keeps the Great God a prisoner. The inner shell of red light is a field of force which is generated by the Great God itself. That inner shell has preserved the Great God from all attack by the evil Stogirov."

"So the inner shell is armour," said Guest, "and the outer shell a cage."

"Precisely," said Ungular Scarth. "Now if you will but listen, then I will describe to you the knife which you must win to cut through the outer shell. The knife is small. It is curved. It ends not with a point but with a bead. Stogirov has one, and the Mutilator has the other."

"There are only two?" said Guest.

"There was once a third, a fourth and a fifth," said Ungular Scarth. "But three are lost, and only two remain."

"Very well," said Guest, with some bitterness, realizing he was so deeply embroiled in this adventure that there was no easy way out. "Then tell me. Which of these knives is closest?"

"That which is closest is that which is carried by Anaconda Stogirov," said the demon. "For she dwells nearby."

Then the demon directed Guest Gulkan to her chambers, and so to her chambers the adventurers went. They quit the octagonal chamber which was home to the Great God Jocasta, exiting from that chamber by means of an arch set in its northern wall. The arch admitted them to another black tunnel, a tunnel which terminated in a stairway. Up the stairway they went, expecting to find Stogirov's bedroom at the top.

But they were far from the top when Guest — who was in the lead — unexpectedly stepped on a man who was sleeping on the stairs. Guest tripped, and went down. The man awoke with a bellow, and his bellow woke a dozen of his fellows.

Were these sleeping men guards, petitioners or exhausted lovers of the evil Stogirov? Guest had no time to ask, for the men did not stand still for questioning. Rather, they drew weapons and attacked the adventurers.

Such was the disorder of the dark that the men who guarded the stairs were soon hacking at each other in their blindness, while the adventurers tumbled back down the stairs.

"I am wounded," gasped the Witchlord Onosh.

And Guest Gulkan saw it was true. His father had been sorely wounded in the gut. Pain was clearly writ on his face, and Guest doubted him able to run.

"Guest," said Zozimus, speaking with harsh directness. "We must run. If your father cannot run with us, then you must make a choice."

"You could choose to put him in a time pod," said Thayer Levant.

"In a time pod?" said Guest, in amazement.

"Why not?" said Levant. "He'll be perfectly safe there."

"Your servant Levant speaks with good reason," said the demon Ungular Scarth. "Nobody in Obooloo has a ring apt for the opening and closing of these pods, not to my knowledge. Look! To your left! The pod nearest the exiting archway is empty!"

"It is best," said Lord Onosh, scarcely able to speak because of the pain of his wound. "I can hardly stand, far less walk."

So Guest took the ring of ever-ice which hung from a chain round his father's neck, and with that ring he opened an empty time pod. Zozimus and Sken-Pitilkin helped the Witchlord into the pod, then Guest used the same ring to seal it.

Upon which the men who had surprised them on the stairs started to pour into the octagonal chamber.

"Scarth!" bellowed Guest. "Kill them!"

So saying, Guest gestured dramatically at the men who were pouring into the chamber. Such was the drama of the Weaponmaster's gesture that the ring of ever-ice escaped his hand. Still strung on its metal chain, it flew through the air, clittered to the steel grille, slipped through, slished into the oily depths of pungent sewerage, and was gone.

"Pox!" swore Guest.

As if commanded by this Word, the demon Ungular Scarth lashed the air with tentacles of quick-slicing green. But the chamber was too large for the demon's tentacles to command the whole of it, and Guest and his companions were soon sorely oppressed by their attackers.

"Go!" yelled Ungular Scarth.

Taking the hint, the adventurers began to retreat down the tunnel by which they had first penetrated to the Great God's chamber. They retreated through the darkness to the central courtyard which contained the Burning Pit.

"Your airship!" said Guest to Sken-Pitilkin.

"It was not made for ascent," said Sken-Pitilkin. "It was but a crude device made to let us float downwards. We cannot escape."

"Not by that means," said Pelagius Zozimus. "So let us try our strength in combat!"

"Which way to the Temple's outer gate?" said Guest.

"How would I know?" said Zozimus.

"The gate to the Temple of Blood is on the southern side," said Thayer Levant.

Since a few lights shone atop the great rock Achaptipop, and since Guest Gulkan knew that great rock to lie to the north of the Temple of Blood, it was the work of a moment to determine which way was south.

An archway on the southern side of the Temple's central courtyard gave the adventurers access to yet another tunnel, and by dint of the speed of their feet and the bloody commitment of their swords, they shortly found themselves out on the streets of Obooloo.

"Which way now?" said Guest Gulkan.

"How would I know?" said Pelagius Zozimus in extreme irritation, somehow presuming that this generalized question had been addressed specifically to him.

"Now," said Thayer Levant, "we must make for Achaptipop. This way!"

Levant knew Obooloo intimately, since he had been there so often in the past with Plandruk Qinplaqus. And Guest Gulkan, who had initially thought Levant to be the most useless member of their party, was swiftly changing his opinion, and was now more inclined to think Levant likely the most useful of their number.

But the adventurers found the way to Achaptipop was barred against them. For alarm-trumpets blown on the heights of the Temple of Blood had already roused a great number of soldiers into the streets, and roadblocks had been thrown up, dividing Obooloo into a number of small areas between which communication was impossible.

Finding themselves trapped in a small area of the city, and surely doomed to be discovered by search parties, Guest Gulkan and his companions turned again to Thayer Levant, and asked for direction.

"I think," said Levant, "that only one recourse remains to us, and that is to make our way to the House of Conceded Sacrifice, which lies nearby."

"The House of Conceded Sacrifice?" said Guest. "That sounds ominous."

"It is," said Levant. "For it is a place where people go to die, and death is the only way to leave it."

This scarcely sounded inviting, but the inhospitality of the city was such that, in the end, Guest Gulkan and his companions had no alternative but to accept Levant's advice, and to consign themselves to the House of Conceded Sacrifice.

CHAPTER THIRTY-THREE

House of Conceded Sacrifice: an institution in Obooloo which has
the legal right to offer unassailable protection to all and
sundry — for a price. It is nominally devoted to the worship
of the Experimental Frog (also known as the Missing Frog,
the Mouth of Blood, Our Great Lord Hosjabajaba, and as
Jolatarba the Gourmet). Once refugees run out of money
they are invariably dissected, their dissection being dedicated
to the greater glory of the said Frog.

*** * ***

So it was that Guest Gulkan and his comrades escaped from the
Temple of Blood and surrendered themselves to the House of
Conceded Sacrifice, where they were received with the
traditional courtesy extended to all who sought that refuge.

Night was almost done by the time the adventurers were safe
in that refuge. Then came the dawn, bringing the familiar sun,
the familiar sky. Yet despite the renewal of sun and sky, Guest
Gulkan felt as if the world had been turned upside down.

The Weaponmaster had firmly expected that by now he
would have been a wizard, and the honoured ally of a liberated
Great God, with the world at his feet, and enough strength at
his command to allow him to crush the greatest of his enemies
beneath the pad of the smallest toe of his left foot.

Instead, Guest had failed utterly. The Great God and its
demons had been proved to be liars. Guest's father had been
sorely wounded, and was now imprisoned in the unchanging
stasis of a time pod inside the Temple of Blood. The ring which
commanded that time pod had been lost to a pool of sewage
inside the Temple of Blood. And as for Guest, why, he found
himself a prisoner in the House of Conceded Sacrifice, which
offered refugees sanctuary for only as long as they could afford
to pay for their keep.

Once the adventurers had exhausted their supply of ready

cash, they would be dissected, this dissection counting as a sacrifice in honour of the Experimental Frog, the deity to whom the House of Conceded Sacrifice was dedicated.

The priests of the House of Conceded Sacrifice provided the adventurers with a list of temple charges. After consulting with the other adventurers, Guest pronounced the prices reasonable, and announced that he and his companions would stay for twenty-nine days then prepare themselves for dissection by drinking themselves into insensibility.

Guest made this announcement in Toxteth, which was the only language he had in common with any of the priests of the House of Conceded Sacrifice. He made the announcement directly to the High Priest of that House, since Guest and his companions had stirred up so much trouble in the city that no lesser dignitary dared to deal with them.

"I have heard," said Guest, "that there is a spirit of great potency distilled from the crushings of the sugar cane."

"There is," said the High Priest gravely. "It is called rum."

"Very well," said Guest. "On the thirtieth day, we'll drink down a barrel of this — this rum. A barrel between four. Will that suffice?"

"My lord," said the High Priest, "a barrel would suffice for the suicide of thirty. We do not wish you dead."

"I am of the Yarglat," said Guest staunchly. "I will still be fit enough to scream, even should I drink the whole of this barrel to myself. I have but one request. After I have been dissected, I wish my body to be burnt of a pyre of my own making. My companions wish likewise."

The High Priest had no objection to this, so Guest Gulkan and his companions spent twenty-nine days building such a pyre, configuring it in the form of a gigantic bird's nest, and at dawn on the thirtieth day they all four of them piled into this stickbird and took to the heavens.

Up, up, up and away they whirled!

Guest whooped with exhilaration as he looked down upon Obooloo. Then he spat.

Unfortunately, Guest's spittle fell into Lake Kak, a body of water so thoroughly polluted that no act by any human agency could possibly damage it further. Still, this gesture of defiance buoyed up the Weaponmaster; and, thus buoyed, he settled himself down to endure the rigours of air-flight.

From Obooloo they flew to Manamalargo, a lagoon on the seawashed shores of Yestron, the seas of the washing being none other than the waters of the Great Ocean, that bulk of salinity otherwise known as Moana, or (to give its name as do the Yarglat) as the Sea of Salt.

Once all were rested — to the extent that rest is possible on the shores of Manamalargo, a region beset by stench-hole snakes and pestilential mosquitoes — the four took to the air once more, intending to search out the fabled island of Untunchilamon. However, the navigational difficulties of airflight being greater than the groundsman might suppose, their quest for Untunchilamon proved fruitless.

It also proved exceedingly dangerous.

The stickbird was held aloft and velocitated through the air by energies generated by a conflict between its abnormal components and the normalizing forces of the universe. Yet the whole arrangement was so intrinsically unstable that Sken-Pitilkin was taxed to the limit by the demands of managing his unruly instrument. Given the slightest mismanagement, the stickbird would shake itself to pieces, or — quite possibly — explode with force sufficient to rupture the sky from horizon to horizon.

Sken-Pitilkin, then, was subjected to such extreme degrees of physical and psychic stress that he was more than once tempted to crash his creation deliberately, and thus bring his agonies to an end.

In the course of his flyforth across bewilderments of sea and sky, Sken-Pitilkin five times rested and renewed his strength on nameless chunks of coral and rock lost somewhere in the vastness of Moana. Then, his strength almost being exhausted for a sixth time, Sken-Pitilkin at last found something to which he could put a name.

But it was not the island of Untunchilamon.

It was, rather, the continent of Argan.

A sizeable discovery, you might think, but not the kind of thing one can claim by right of salvage and stuff into a spare pocket; and Sken-Pitilkin was not entirely glad to have found it.

Down from the clouds came Sken-Pitilkin and his passengers, hurtling towards the shores of the abovementioned and above-named continent of Argan.

"Brace!" yelled Sken-Pitilkin, as his stickbird went skimming across the waves.

All braced.

The stickbird clipped a wave, spun skywards, plunged, hit the sea with a shatter-splash, bounced, hit the sands, scuffed up the beach with a great flurry of fractured silicon and shell, then skidded. Then flipped. The passengers went sprawling to the sands, from which they picked themselves up — all except Sken-Pitilkin.

"Cousin," said Zozimus. "Are you hurt?"

"Mortally," said Sken-Pitilkin weakly.

Then collapsed into the silence of utter exhaustion, which elicited no sympathy whatsoever from those whom he had so grievously misled across the ocean.

"Dogs and cats!" said Thayer Levant, giving voice to one of the mightiest oaths of Chi'ash-lan. "Where are we?"

"We are now," said Pelagius Zozimus, scrutinizing the beach of their landing, "on the Chameleon's Tongue."

"Tongue?" said Guest Gulkan. "This is a tongue?"

"Indeed it is," said Zozimus. "We are on the Tongue of a certainty. To be precise, we are at the Elbow."

"The Elbow?" said Guest. "Only a moment ago you called it a tongue. What will you have it next? A kneecap?"

"No," said Zozimus "for the Kneecap is elsewhere."

Then Zozimus detailed out the location of the Kneecap, and having thus indulged himself in an entirely gratuitous display of geographical superiority, he suggested that they climb the conical knoll which he identified as the Elbow so they might confirm that they were on the beach known as the Tongue.

Thereupon all but the collapsed Sken-Pitilkin climbed the

knoll, and Zozimus confirmed that they were truly on the Tongue, the white-heat beaches of which stretched away for league upon league to north and to west. Out to sea lay the Teardrop Islands, and inland rose the heights of the Lizard Crest Rises.

"It is true of a certainty," said Zozimus. "That fool Sken-Pitilkin has flown us clean across the ocean."

Later, when finally roused from the sleep of his exhaustion, Sken-Pitilkin confessed as much.

"We have," said that wizard of Skatzabratzumon, "but one option."

"And that is?" said his companions.

"To fly back across Moana," answered Sken-Pitilkin, with swift-reviving enthusiasm for further adventures in flight. "Fly back again in quest for Untunchilamon."

His companions, however, averred that they had several alternative options, some of which were starting to look increasingly palatable. The roasting of Sken-Pitilkin, for instance; or the boiling of him, bones and ungutted flesh together; or the braining of him with heavy rocks; or the feeding of his intellect to a pit of dragons; or the delivery of his walking corpse to the slaveyards of Lesser Narglash.

"Furthermore," said Zozimus, "that does not exhaust our choices. For we have yet another option. We could walk from here to Drangsturm, then book passage on a ship and get to Untunchilamon the fast way."

"The fast way!" said Sken-Pitilkin. "A ship would take months!"

"Months!" said Zozimus. "It would take months, would it? Well, with you stitching your way back and forth across the ocean in the derelictions of your confidence, we look to waste out a lifetime in futility."

As the two wizards argued it out, Guest took himself off into the hinterland, returning much later with a dead lizard. In the evening, that lizard made a meal, once it had been supplemented by fish caught by Sken-Pitilkin and clams dug from the seasands by a reluctant Thayer Levant working under the remorseless supervision of Pelagius Zozimus.

That night, Guest Gulkan dreamt his way through the plunging darkness of blue seas and green, through the kraken depths of the northern wastes and the shallows of the Green Sea.

The Weaponmaster woke from his dreams to find it was late at night, and cold, and dark. A desolate wind blew in from the sea. Guest got up on his four limbs and crouched on the beach, watching the sea suspiciously. Watching. Listening. Waiting. For what? He knew not, but felt fearfully vulnerable.

"There is nothing," he muttered.

Then took a piss. The head of his penis was furry with smegma, and the smell got on Guest's fingers, and he sniffed at the smell, and was comforted by it on this strange and darkened beach. Nothing is more intimately consoling than one's own scent, just as few things can be so repulsive as the smell of a stranger.

But the transitory comfort of Guest's private indulgence was not enough to guard him against the dark, for Guest began to be convinced that he knew what had wakened him. That he knew what was out there. It was the Great Mink. He was sure of it. He could see it! He could see its hulking shadow!

Guest was convinced that he was deluding himself. He was in a land too warm for the Great Mink, a land far removed from ice and snow. Nevertheless, while logic told him that there could not possibly be any such monster lurking in the night, he was simultaneously gripped by the unshakable belief that just such an animal was out there — and that he could see it.

So Guest sat for a frozen eternity, until at last the slow lightbirth of dawn revealed the hulking shadow to be no more than a tree trunk.

And in the relief of the morning, Guest told his companions of his plan for finding Untunchilamon, a plan he had got from brooding on his dream of the night.

"We ride the line of the green," said Guest Gulkan.

"The green?" said Zozimus.

"The green of the Green Sea," said Guest.

Then he explained.

In the course of his flight across Moana, Guest had observed that the shallow waters round islands and reefs appear from the air to be uncommonly green, and are clearly demarked from the blue-black of the deeper waters. It was known that the southern waters of Moana, those waters known as the Green Sea, were uncommonly shallow; and it was consequently obvious that they should be a literal green.

"Furthermore," said Guest, "it is known that the island of Untunchilamon lies on the line of demarcation which separates the depths from the shallows. Therefore, if we do but follow the line of green, then we must necessarily find Untunchilamon."

This sounded so suspiciously like commonsense that Sken-Pitilkin was sure there had to be a thousand things wrong with it. And, apart from all other reservations — since when had Guest Gulkan been a geographer?

But at last Sken-Pitilkin and the others were persuaded to Guest Gulkan's enterprise. So to the air they took, and found their way to the line of the Green Ocean, and followed that line as best they could, until one day Guest Gulkan espied great upthrusts of red rock in the distance.

"Red rocks ahead!" said Guest, announcing the oncoming cliffs.

"The bloodstone of Untunchilamon," said Sken-Pitilkin.

And turned his stickbird north.

"Cousin," said Zozimus, "we seek the city of Injiltaprajura, which lies at Untunchilamon's southernmost point."

"So we do, so we do," said Sken-Pitilkin, "but I hope to make a discreet entry to the island, so let us land a little to the north of the city."

In accordance with this strategy, Sken-Pitilkin brought his stickbird over the coast of the island of Untunchilamon some distance to the north of Injiltaprajura, its one and only city. His stickbird passed over the briskwater surf of the fringing reef at altitude, then over those cliffs of bloodstone. An updraft hit them, flinging the stickbird high to the heavens.

"Wa!" cried Guest, alarmed.

"Pitilkin!" cried Zozimus.

"No danger, no danger, said Sken-Pitilkin, skewing the stickbird across the lurching sky. "Sit back! Relax! Enjoy the view!"

A good view it was, too, for the deserts of Zolabrik were laid out beneath them.

"If this be Untunchilamon," said Guest, "then where be its dragons?"

Even from great altitude, the smallest details of the ground are easily espied from the air. But there were no dragons to be seen in Untunchilamon's desert. There was no sign of life in the desert at all.

"Relax," said Sken-Pitilkin. "Dragons you'll see in plenty when we get to Injiltaprajura."

Injiltaprajura was and is the port which lies at the southern extremity of Untunchilamon; and it was and is the sole concentration of human life on that island. The rest of that rockbeast is an expansiveness of sun-parched desolation interspersed with pits, craters and sundry ruins.

"What's down there?" said Guest, scanning the wastelands below.

"Nothing that need trouble us," said Sken-Pitilkin.

"A city!" cried Guest, making out an extensive configuration of square-walled rock in the desert. "It's a city!"

"It is but ruins," said Sken-Pitilkin, "as you can see from here. Ruins abandoned for millennia. We've no call to go landing there."

In fact, on Sken-Pitilkin's first visit to Untunchilamon it was the very red-dusted ruins which Guest had espied which had brought the sage to something very perilously close to disaster. Those ruins had lured him — not through exercise of magic but simply by existing. For Sken-Pitilkin had been young then, in comparative terms if not in terms absolute; and such had been the foolishness of his (comparative) youth that he had dared himself to those ruins on a whim, and had been lucky to escape from their dangers with his life.

"Maybe we can go to the ruins on the trip home," said Guest, watching them recede in the distance.

"Maybe, maybe," said Sken-Pitilkin, sending his stickbird speeding southward, and hunting the horizon to the south for some sign of Injiltaprajura.

Before such sign was espied, Thayer Levant cried in his native garble:

"Ware! Ware! A claw! A claw!"

"A claw?" said Sken-Pitilkin, addressing Levant in his native Galish. "Enough of your nonsense. Look! That rim of rock! See the glitter-flash? That's the topmost building of Injiltaprajura, for sure. The pink palace. Pokra Ridge."

"Sken-Pitilkin," said Zozimus quietly, or as quietly as the buffeting winds of airflight would allow. "There are two claws in pursuit. I suggest you turn and give them the benefit of your attention."

"Claws?" said Sken-Pitilkin. "Nonsense!"

But then Guest Gulkan took the sage by the shoulders and physically forced him to a confrontation with the pair of levitating claws fast approaching from the rear.

"Claws!" said Sken-Pitilkin in astonishment.

The claws were of a luminously explosive orange. Each was thrice the length of your average rowboat, and each had as many wings as a stickbird — which is to say, none.

"Hold tight!" cried Sken-Pitilkin.

"Why?" said Zozimus. "Pitilkin, you're not thinking of—"

But the brave Sken-Pitilkin was not thinking at all. Rather, he was acting.

As a brawny slave, seeking to free himself from a mine ruined by rockfall, lifts a huge weight at the risk of crushing vertebrae or splitting his spine clean down the middle, so Sken-Pitilkin jerk-thrust the stickbird upward, sending it soaring into the sky.

Up up up up they burst—

Winning a view of Untunchilamon, spread out for league upon league of redness beneath them. In that vastness, Sken-Pitilkin spied a great pit — a pit of such vastness that Sken-Pitilkin was reminded of Argan's notorious dry pit.

"The claws!" cried Zozimus in alarm.

The claws were pursuing.

So Sken-Pitilkin slammed the stickbird down in a spiral which took it plunging into the pit. At the bottom, Sken-Pitilkin braked their fall with levitating energies, looked up and saw—

"Out!" yelled Sken-Pitilkin.

One and all abandoned ship, and moments later the claws fell upon that ship and sundered it, while the adventurers sheltered in a niche in the side of the pit.

When the claws had torn the stickbird to pieces, they did their best to tear the adventurers likewise. But the questing heroes were safe in their niche, which was large enough to accommodate a few humans, but too small to admit the enormity of the claws. So, being frustrated in their destructive whims, the claws began to ascend towards the heights — and were torn to pieces by something invisible which disintegrated them in flame and sundering thunder.

"Grief of gods!" said Guest.

"Can you think of nothing original to say in the face of such a distinctly original encounter?" said Sken-Pitilkin, dusting himself down.

"Original!" said Guest. "I think there to be nothing original about someone or something trying to tear me to pieces! Rather, I think it to be the story of my life, and probably the story of my death as well! Now, how do we get out of here?"

"We climb," said Zozimus, optimistically.

"Climb?" said Sken-Pitilkin, kicking through the wreckage of his stickbird in search of his country crook.

"Why not?" said Zozimus. "Or maybe you could levitate us."

"I will be doing no levitating today," said Sken-Pitilkin, recovering his country crook.

"Why not?" said Guest.

"Because," said Sken-Pitilkin, "even if I were to levitate us to the heights, supposing that feat to be within my power, we would be lost in a waterless desert, and doomed to die in consequence of the strength of the sun."

So spoke Sken-Pitilkin, who, in his youth, had almost died

from thirst in that very same desert. But Guest was not convinced.

"You will levitate us!" said the Weaponmaster, threatening Sken-Pitilkin with his sword.

"I will levitate your weapon, and promptly, unless you lower it," said Sken-Pitilkin. "Remember! You have not an army at your back! Not this time! This is no repeat of Ibsen-Iktus!"

Thus admonished, Guest lowered his sword, declaring that he would climb the walls anyway, and risk death from thirst in the sun, whatever Sken-Pitilkin said about it.

But the walls of the pit were quite unclimbable, leaving the adventurers with two distinctly unpalatable options. One was to sit where they were and shortly die of thirst. The other was to exit from the pit by a shoulder-width hole which looked as if it would make an ideal lair for a large spider of bloody disposition and anthropophagous habits.

"It looks as if it will have to be the hole," said Guest, with great reluctance. "Which of us is the bravest? Let the bravest prove himself, and lead the way!"

Upon which Pelagius Zozimus declared that Guest himself was the bravest. But Guest disputed this.

"No," said Guest, "it is my noble servant Thayer Levant who is the bravest. Lead on, Levant!"

On being poked with Guest's sword, Levant conceded that perhaps he was brave. And he crawled into the hole.

Then screamed.

"What is it?" said Guest, in great alarm, as Levant backed out of the hole.

"A centipede!" said Levant, in panic. "A huge centipede, bigger than you are!"

Guest was greatly alarmed, at least until he realized that Levant was grinning.

"Enough of your jokes!" said Guest, who was in no mood for being trifled with. "Get into that hole before I kick you!"

Whereupon Levant led the way into the depths, with Guest Gulkan following him, and Sken-Pitilkin and Zozimus crawling along after them.

It would be tedious to recount in detail the long wanderings of the adventurers in the complex and seemingly never-ending underworld which they then entered. Tunnels led to tunnels in unceasing succession, until these four wanderers felt like insects lost in a monstrous maze constructed by a zealous child of over-intellectual disposition.

The tunnels were warm and cold by turns. Some were ice-cold in consequence of the actions of noisy machines busy with the production of huge blocks of ice. By drinking the melt water from such ice, the heroes kept themselves from dying of thirst; but they had nothing to eat, and so grew uncommonly hungry. At the peak of his hunger, Guest proposed that they eat the unfortunate Thayer Levant, and Sken-Pitilkin was not at all sure that he was joking.

"Are you serious?" said Sken-Pitilkin.

"Serious?" said Guest. "About what?"

"About eating Levant. You were talking about it only a moment ago."

"Was I?" said Guest. "I might have been talking about Levant, but I certainly wasn't thinking about him."

"Then of what were you thinking?" said Sken-Pitilkin.

"Of women," said Guest.

As if in direct response to this declaration, there came the sound of women singing. Their clear and beautiful voices sounded uncommonly close.

"Good grief!" said Sken-Pitilkin.

"A choir," said Zozimus. "Perhaps they would like to hire someone to cook for them."

"Not you, you lecherous old goat!" said Sken-Pitilkin.

"Lecherous?" said Zozimus, feigning amazement. "Me? Pitilkin, I haven't had a woman for half five hundred years or more."

"Then now's no time to be changing your habits!" said Sken-Pitilkin.

"Yes," said Guest, setting out towards the voices. "Let's each of us keep to our habits."

Zozimus and Sken-Pitilkin followed Guest Gulkan, but

Thayer Levant lingered.

"Levant!" said Sken-Pitilkin. "Hurry up!"

"But," said Levant, diffidently.

"But what?" said Sken-Pitilkin.

"But," said Levant, "they might be ... they might be mermaids."

"What?" said Sken-Pitilkin in astonishment.

Then Levant confessed to his superstition.

Thayer Levant was from Chi'ash-lan, and the people of those parts have many dire superstitions concerning mermaids. It is said among them that these half-human fishes configure themselves as beautiful women, then use the beauty of their voices to lure strangers to a hideous death.

"Levant," said Sken-Pitilkin firmly, "there are no such things as mermaids. They are imaginary creatures, like elves, and orcs, and gnomes, and fairies, and leprechauns, and talking animals. And even supposing that there were mermaids, what then? Would you really expect to find them down here in these tunnels, deep deep deep beneath the earth?"

"By now," said Levant, evidencing an unusual intellectual belligerence, "we may well be deep deep deep beneath the sea, for there is no saying where these tunnels have taken us. So. So maybe they're mermaids, and maybe they'll eat us."

"Well," said Sken-Pitilkin, "Guest Gulkan lately suggested eating you, so if you've got to be eaten by someone it might as well be by mermaids. Come on!"

After considerable further hesitation, Thayer Levant at last consented to follow the others. With Guest Gulkan leading, they braved their way into a huge chamber where there arose a kind of waterless fountain which was adorned with the warm and breathing bodies of a thousand women. Up, up rose this fountain, in tier upon tier, crowded with nubile beauty.

For once, Guest Gulkan was quite lost for words. He just stood there and gaped. As he stood there, a woman danced forth from the company of her peers, positively floating through the air as she tranced towards him. She beckoned to him, and he stepped forward, as if in a dream.

Abruptly—

The women vanished.

The women vanished with a clangour of metal and a burst of shuddering laughter. Immediately, the adventurers realized they were confronted by (and more than partially surrounded by) a huge heaped-up conglomeration of steel, a towering contraption of whispering tubes and slowly grinding tentacles, of rotating disks and spindling toroidal columns, of glowing screens and phosphorescent feelers, of spiked antennae and gleaming chelae.

This thing of coiled and coiling metal sat there in a huge and brooding inertia, sat there with all the mighty weight of an ink-black thundercloud pregnant with hailstones the size of a turtle, sat there in predatory poise. There was no telling what or where its eyes might be, yet the thing saw the travellers, clearly, and these four mortals were the focus of its vulturing regard.

Others had been thus focused upon beforehand, as was proved by the large number of corpses which lay scattered in unmethodical disorder in and about the monster's great colony of threats. The bodies of close to fifty people were thus scattered, and, to judge by what was left of them, they had not died pleasantly.

"I told you!" said Levant fearfully, thinking himself doomed to become another such corpse.

"You told us of mermaids," said Sken-Pitilkin, with a pedantic emphasis which spoke of long years of pedagogical engagement. "But this is scarcely a mermaid! I think this thing to be an octopus, or a very kraken."

So spoke Sken-Pitilkin, and he spoke harshly, for he was more than half-inclined to blame Thayer Levant for their present predicament. For, if Levant had not spoken his utter nonsense about mermaids, Sken-Pitilkin might have given more serious consideration to the possible source of those womanly voices, and might have realized that the unlikelihood of finding a female choir so deep underground most surely spoke of deception and danger.

Do not therefore blame the adventurers' predicament upon

any presumed defect of the wizard Sken-Pitilkin! Recognize Sken-Pitilkin for what he was, an uncommonly sagacious and hypercapable wizard of Skatzabratzumon! And put the blame for the travellers' downfall firmly where it belongs — upon the back of the superstitious Thayer Levant!

"I do not think this is a kraken," said Guest, at last recovering his voice. "I think it is a——"

"Whatever it is," said Zozimus, "suppose we quietly back out of here."

Then Zozimus matched action to suggestion. But a lithe tentacle, green in colour and slick in its glistening, promptly whipped around his ankles and held him fast. It held him with a strength which bruised his flesh and almost broke his bones.

"It has me!" said Zozimus.

"Then — nobody move," said Sken-Pitilkin. "Guest! Don't move!"

"I'm not moving," said Guest, who was still staring at the looming monstrosity which confronted them.

The thing was huge. Guest got giddy just looking at it. Obviously it would be quite impossible to hack it to pieces with his sword. Confronted by such invincible strength, Guest Gulkan was possessed by a sense of angry frustration. He was a Yarglat barbarian! Therefore, hacking things to pieces was a part of his birthright! An essential part of his cultural heritage!

Throughout his childhood, the Weaponmaster had lived with the certainty that if he was brawny enough and quick enough on his feet, then he could hack into bloody pieces anyone and everyone who was intemperate enough to oppose his will. But there would be no such hacking here in Untunchilamon's underworld. Consequently, Guest wished most heartily that he was back in Tameran, back on the flatlands of the Collosnon Empire, sending out his scouts and manoeuvring his cavalry; and, in this time of peril, Guest felt not so much fear as, rather, a sickening sense of homesickness.

Beset by such homesickness, the Yarglat barbarian at last acknowledged that he had been in error when he had wilfully embroiled himself in the affairs of wizards, demons and gods.

But it was too late to turn back!

Then, realizing he was trapped, irrevocably entangled in matters far beyond his competence, Guest Gulkan grew angry, so angry that he challenged the looming monster in front of him, challenged it as if it were a paltry slave, and he a victorious conqueror with his boot on its neck.

"Who are you?" said Guest, with a lifetime of practised self-assertion pouring itself into the challenge.

"I am the therapist Schoptomov," said the monster, answering Guest Gulkan in his native Eparget. "Who are you? Who are you, and what are you doing here?"

Guest Gulkan cleared his throat, as if in preparation for explanation. Sken-Pitilkin covertly stepped on his foot. The Weaponmaster took the hint, and was silent.

"We're, ah, tourists," said Sken-Pitilkin.

"Tourists?" said the therapist doubtfully.

"Yes," said Sken-Pitilkin. "We've come to see the, ah, the dragons. Untunchilamon is very famous for its dragons, is that not the case?"

"Where are you from?" said the therapist, disregarding the question of dragons.

"From Chi'ash-lan," said Sken-Pitilkin, hoping at least to puzzle the monstrosity.

"Ah," said the therapist. "Chi'ash-lan. I have heard of that place. They feed, I am told, on the eyes of the dog."

"You are uncommonly well-informed," said Sken-Pitilkin, astoundingly astonished to find the therapist so well-versed in the ways of such a far and distant land.

By contrast, Guest Gulkan in his ignorance thought the therapist to be in error; for Guest in his confusion thought that it was only in the Safrak Islands that the eyes of a dog are a favoured delicacy. But, while Safrak does use the dog to the fullest, the same gastronomical quirk is found also in Chi'ash-lan.

"You find me informed, do you?" said the therapist smugly. "Well, I make it my business to be informed. And I don't believe for a moment that you're here as tourists. Why did you come here? The truth!"

"The truth," said Sken-Pitilkin, prevaricating, and wishing that Zozimus would say something to help him out.

"Yes, yes, the truth," said Schoptomov. "Truth, the highest virtue!"

"We had business with one Wazir Sin," said Sken-Pitilkin, since nobody else had courage or wit sufficient to help bluff the monster.

"Ah, Sin, Sin," said the therapist. "A delightful man by all accounts. A man very much after my own tastes. He was doing so very well, too. It is most unfortunate."

"You mean he's dead?" said Guest Gulkan.

"Several years dead," said the therapist.

"Then who rules Untunchilamon?" said Guest.

"I do," said the therapist.

"You braggarting liar!" said Guest, still in his mode of wrath. "You are not a ruler! You are just a species of vermin, a species of rat!"

This speech caused Sken-Pitilkin great pain, for had not the venerable wizard Skatzabratzumon laboured for years in an effort to teach Guest Gulkan the arts of diplomacy? All useless, useless, wasted effort — for once a Yarglat barbarian, always a Yarglat barbarian!

"The therapist," said Sken-Pitilkin, seeking to remedy the damage which had surely been done, "is of such sophistication that the rule of Untunchilamon is surely not beyond its capabilities."

"You are right," said the therapist, not bothering to disguise its amused delight, for it had been a long time since anyone had flattered it. "I also have the capacity to kill you."

"Who are you?" said Guest. "And what?"

"I have told you my name already," said the therapist Schoptomov. "If you have forgotten it, then it is fear which is doing the forgetting. As for my function, why, I have told you that, too. I am a therapist."

"A therapist?" said Guest.

"I administer therapy," said Schoptomov. "Algetic therapy."

"What mean you by that?" said Guest Gulkan, puzzled.

"It's a torturer," said Zozimus. "That's what it means."

"You sound as if you despise the Art," said Schoptomov. "Well, my friend, you will despise it less hereafter."

At this threat, Guest Gulkan suddenly bethought himself of the heaviness of the amulet which hung as a pendant from the necklace he wore always at his throat. Paraban Senk, the disembodied entity which had ruled Cap Foz Para Lash in the city of Dalar ken Halvar, had not wanted him to depart with that amulet. Later, the demon Icaria Scaria Iva-Italis had immediately recognized that amulet for what it was.

But what was it?

Guest felt the amulet start to beat in time with his very heart, and, inspired by that beating, knew — he had the gift of Knowing, did he not? — that this amulet was a device which would be proof against the power of the monster which now confronted them.

So Guest seized his amulet, and drew it forth from its concealment, lifting the necklace clear of his head and brandishing its pendant on high as he cried:

"Behold, the mazadath!"

In response ...

In response, the therapist laughed. Which angered Guest intensely, for he was profoundly tired of things laughing at him.

"Why, a mazadath!" said the therapist. "A pretty trinket, but one useless for the concerns of the moment."

In demonstration of this, the therapist swatted Guest with a lazy tentacle, knocking the mazadath from his grasp and sending it skittling across the floor. At which Zozimus said to Sken-Pitilkin:

"Can you?"

Sken-Pitilkin knew what this question meant. It meant: can you lift this therapist? Ordinarily, Sken-Pitilkin would have answered: no. For the therapist was huge. Its weight was surely greater than that of the demons of Safrak, Chi'ash-lan and Obooloo put together. By trying to lift it, Sken-Pitilkin might kill himself.

But Sken-Pitilkin said, without hesitation:

"I will need a moment's distraction, cousin."

"Then you shall have it," said Zozimus.

Then Pelagius Zozimus animated those corpses which lay about the therapist. In creaking swarms they attacked, flesh falling away as they stormed around the therapist, trying to attack the brute's tentacles and chelae.

What good could this do?

None whatsoever!

For the therapist was too much of a brute to be harmed by the belabouring of a few dozen rotting corpses.

Nevertheless, the therapist was momentarily taken by surprise at this attack. In alarm, it flailed at the corpses with its tentacles. The tentacle which had gripped Pelagius Zozimus came free, whipping itself into the battle against the corpses.

"Now!" said Zozimus.

Then Hostaja Torsen Sken-Pitilkin exerted all his power, and wrenched the therapist — tore it loose from its foundations, heaved it into the air then dumped it down.

Hard.

The therapist screamed. Pipes ruptured. Flailing steam gouted into the air. Bursts of lightning crackled. Guest Gulkan seized Sken-Pitilkin — who had quite fainted away on account of the monstrous nature of his exertions — then led the retreat at the sprint.

Pelagius Zozimus grabbed the country crook which had fallen from Sken-Pitilkin's grasp, and sprinted alongside Guest Gulkan. Thayer Levant lagged a footstep in the rear — and was soon lagging even further, for he paused momentarily to scoop up Guest's fallen mazadath.

The therapist lashed at Levant with a tentacle.

Almost caught him!

But Levant gained the safety of the corridor to which his fellows had fled, leaving the therapist behind him. The wounded monstrosity bellowed in a fury close to madness. In the heat of its rage, it forgot which languages the adventurers had used, and swore at them in some uncouth tongue from its monstrous past.

"Gods!" said Guest, coming to a panting halt, and letting Sken-Pitilkin slip unconscious to the floor. "He's heavy. And he's hot!"

Pelagius Zozimus touched Sken-Pitilkin's skin. It was hot, hot as if in a fever. The venerable wizard of Skatzabratzumon seemed to be positively burning up. Zozimus shuddered.

"What is it?" said Guest.

"We are lucky he is only hot," said Zozimus. "That is what it is!"

Guest did not rightly understand the import of this remark, but, sensing it might be something he was better off not to understand, he asked no more about it. Instead, he reclaimed his mazadath from Thayer Levant, slung the chained amulet around his neck, and declared himself ready to go on a reconnaissance mission to find some ice.

By the time Guest had returned with some ice — quite a long time, as it happened — Sken-Pitilkin was conscious again. The wizard of Skatzabratzumon proved strong enough to suck on some ice, though it was a long while before he was strong enough to speak, and longer yet before he was capable of walking.

But at last the adventurers got underway again, and a long and weary journey they had before they at last found their way to the daylight.

When at last the travellers did escape to the outer air, they found the fair city of Injiltaprajura to be in a state of uncommon disorder. For the eminent Wazir Sin had indeed been overthrown, and overthrown something close to seven years earlier, a fact which had escaped the notice of everyone from Hostaja Sken-Pitilkin to Plandruk Qinplaqus; for it must be understood that, while Untunchilamon is regularly visited by travellers bent on trade, the extreme isolation of that island means that news is only slowly disseminated from there to parts as far removed as the northern continent of Tameran and the southern continent of Parengarenga.

Sken-Pitilkin explained as much to his companions.

"But," said Guest Gulkan, "you told me that you travelled

the Circle of the Doors at length while you were acting as diplomat for my father Lord Onosh!"

"So I did, so I did," said Sken-Pitilkin.

"Then," said Guest, "your travels must have taken you repeatedly to Obooloo, where it seems the story of Untunchilamon's wazirless state is well known! Therefore I find myself unable to understand why you did not learn what Obooloo knows all too well!"

Sken-Pitilkin took this criticism hard, but at last admitted — and let this concession be seen as proof of his scholarly maturity! — that he had not enquired too closely into the affairs of Untunchilamon because he had been there once himself. Admittedly, that personal visit had been a long time in the past; but the fact of having made such a visit had tricked Sken-Pitilkin into thinking himself an expert on Untunchilamon, and hence free from the duties of research.

Let this be a lesson to all travellers! The country you visited in your youth is no longer the same nation of which you have such fond recollections! For its government has changed, yes, and its laws, its customs, its currency, and maybe its very language and religion into the bargain!

So, if a moral is to be drawn from this book (and it is said, is it not, that all books should have morals, even if they be books of history like this one?) then let the moral be this: personal knowledge does not secure one's freedom from the burdens of research!

The Untunchilamon which Sken-Pitilkin had visited in his youth had been a well-ordered state ruled by a wazir loyal to the rulers of Obooloo. But the Untunchilamon in which he now found himself was a mutinous state in rebellion against the Izdimir Empire, that hegemonic power which was ruled from Obooloo by Aldarch the Third, Mutilator of Yestron.

Finding themselves in this disordered city, our heroes did the obvious. They pursued their business relentlessly! Using every power and device at their disposal, they strove mightily to win possession of the x-x-zix, the device known to Injiltaprajura as the wishstone.

But, since Sken-Pitilkin had been pitifully weakened by his encounter with the therapist Schoptomov; and since Guest Gulkan's strength proved quite unequal to the difficulties of the task; and since Pelagius Zozimus allowed himself to be shamefully distracted by the various career opportunities available to a master chef; and since Thayer Levant proved absolutely no help whatsoever; and since Injiltaprajura proved to be an uncommonly restless, dangerous, brutal, licentious and anarchic place, the bottom line is quite simple—

They failed.

Our heroes were now in a parlous position. They had quite failed to win control of the wishstone, the x-x-zix, the precious triakisoctahedron which would give them political leverage in the struggle for control of the Circle of the Partnership Banks. Furthermore, they were marooned on Untunchilamon, which might at any day be invaded by the bloodthirsty armies of a victorious Mutilator.

Sken-Pitilkin did the obvious.

He built another airship.

But, since Sken-Pitilkin's efforts to secure possession of the x-x-zix had made him many enemies on Untunchilamon, and since those enemies included certain sorcerers who were resident upon that island, Sken-Pitilkin's airship was promptly destroyed.

"This is not profiting us," said Pelagius Zozimus. "I vote that we build a boat."

"I vote that we steal one," said Guest Gulkan.

"I vote," said Thayer Levant, in disregard of the fact that he was not strictly entitled to a vote, "that we flee to Zolabrik and join Jal Japone."

Jal Japone was an outlaw drug dealer who dwelt in the desert wastelands north of Injiltaprajura. His reputation naturally made him attractive to one with Thayer Levant's criminal propensities, but Levant's suggestion was vetoed out of hand.

"I'll tell you what we do," said Sken-Pitilkin.

Then told.

Sken-Pitilkin would build a decoy airship in public view and

a real airship in secret. It would take time, but time they had —
he hoped.

The days that then followed in Untunchilamon were tense
and desperate. As Sken-Pitilkin laboured to build his decoy
airship and his true escape ship, the various factions on that
fraught and troubled island manoeuvred for advantage. Ships
arrived with the Trade Winds, bringing confusing news, rumour,
raiders, impostors, swindlers, cheats, refugees and free market
entrepreneurs hellbent on making as many dragons as they
could out of confusion and alarum.

And all these alarums ultimately culminated in a riot, in the
course of which Guest Gulkan at last managed to secure the x-
x-zix from Injiltaprajura's treasury, and to make his escape with
the thing on a ship, in the company of Thayer Levant.

Now, one might think this a perfectly reasonable procedure.
For, after all, Levant and Guest Gulkan had come to
Injiltaprajura to steal the x-x-zix, had they not? They had. But
they had come, of course, in the company of the wizards Hostaja
Sken-Pitilkin and Pelagius Zozimus.

And the really unfortunate thing is that, when riot arose,
Levant and Guest Gulkan seized a transitory opportunity to win
the x-x-zix, and departed from Untunchilamon on a ship,
leaving Sken-Pitilkin and Zozimus to make their way off the
island as best they could.

This the two wizards eventually managed to do, for Sken-
Pitilkin did in the end successfully build another airship. But the
really unfortunate thing is that, by the time the wizards escaped
from the island, Pelagius Zozimus had been turned into a
hampster by a delinquent sorcerer of Injiltaprajura.

A hamster?

The mighty slug-chef Zozimus, reduced to a hamster's
estate?

Sad but true!

The details I would tell, but unfortunately it is a long story,
which requires a book of its own, and cannot be fitted into this
one. For this book concerns itself above all else with the history
of the mighty Guest Gulkan, who got away from

Untunchilamon by ship only to run into hideous danger before his ship had got all that terribly far.

CHAPTER THIRTY-FOUR

Moana: the Great Ocean bounded by the continents of Tameran (to the north), Parengarenga (to the south), Yestron (to the east) and Argan (to the west). The southern shallows of Moana are known as the Green Sea, and local names have been given to several of its smaller fractions, so that for example the cold and stormy whale wastes of the north are known in Galsh Ebrek as the Winter Sea, and the more tropical waters east of the Stepping Stone Islands are commonly known as the Ocean of Cambria.

* * *

Injiltaprajura's riots saw the ships in its harbour flee — though most fled slowly, for they were heavily burdened by loot.

Guest Gulkan fled initially on a ship commanded by one Troldot "Heavy-Fist" Turbothot, who had personally looted from Injiltaprajura a female creature named Theodora, and who was intent on taking her home with him to the distant island of Hexagon. Since Hexagon was not on Guest's itinerary, both the Weaponmaster and Thayer Levant soon transferred to another ship, one which was making for Galsh Ebrek.

Guest had fond memories of Galsh Ebrek, that city in Wen Endex where he had once worked for Anna Blaume as a barman. In Galsh Ebrek stood one of the Banks, the Flesh Traders Financial Association. By rights, Guest should be able to win admission to that Bank, and venture through its Circle of Doors to his home on Alozay.

If the Bank denied him the Door, well, even that would not be a disaster, for ships travelled intermittently between Galsh Ebrek and the Port Domax. Once at Port Domax, Guest could take the overland trade route which led from there to the Swelaway Sea; and, once he had reached the shores of the Swelaway Sea, a short journey by boat would take him home to Alozay.

One way or another, he would get there.

Once Guest was safely home in the Safrak Islands, he would be able to bend his mind to the important tasks: to rescue his father from a time pod in the Temple of Blood; to liberate the Great God Jocasta; and to reclaim his wife Penelope from the tunnels of Cap Foz Para Lash in the city of Dalar ken Halvar.

But what of Pelagius Zozimus? And what of Hostaja Sken-Pitilkin? Truth to tell, Guest Gulkan did not trouble his head about either of those dignitaries. They were wizards, were they not? Of course they were! Therefore it followed — did it not? — that they would be able to find their own way back to Alozay without any help from the Weaponmaster.

Thus thinking, Guest relaxed, and repeatedly congratulated himself on his success. He had dared himself to Injiltaprajura, and had wrested the x-x-zix from the treasury of that most perilous of cities. And he had got away scot-free!

Or so he thought.

Actually, he had not got away at all.

Though he did not know it, he was irrevocably trapped, and his doom was almost upon him.

Guest was trapped because the fleet of which his ship was a part was making its way northward between the reefs of Untunchilamon's narrow lagoon; and, simultaneously, a fleet of ships loyal to the Mutilator of Yestron was making its way southward between those same reefs. It therefore followed that a collision was inevitable between the ships bearing the looters and those which were carrying the Mutilator's soldiers; and, in the fullness of time, this collision duly occurred.

As Guest was one day sunbathing himself—he was no fan of washing, but this business of bathing in the sun was much to his liking — the lookout of his current ship announced the sighting of ships coming from the north.

Those oncoming ships soon proved to be ships of war, ships which were flying banners which marked and identified them as the ships of Aldarch the Third, the dreaded Mutilator of Yestron.

Before venturing to Untunchilamon, Guest Gulkan had not been very clear as to the identity of Aldarch the Third. But the

Mutilator had so dominated the imagination of the inhabitants of Injiltaprajura that Guest now felt he knew the fellow as a brother. Aldarch had initiated Talonsklavara, a seven-year civil war which had devastated the Izdimir Empire. The general presumption was that Aldarch had proved victorious in that civil war, and that he was going to celebrate his victory with an orgy of sanguinary destruction.

So Guest was not exactly happy when the lookout announced the approach of the Mutilator's ships. Indeed, he was so unhappy that he felt as if the world itself had been upset.

The sky above was the same blue sky as ever, and the sea the same green and coral-spiked sea. There was no change in the chop of the light which came brisking from the quick-flick waves which slapped and sundered against the ship's creaking sides. Yet all of existence had been subjected to an abrupt reversal; and, in token of this, the sails of Guest Gulkan's ship shuddered as the vessel hove to.

As the ships of the dreaded Mutilator closed with Guest Gulkan's barque, that ship remained hove to. Over its silence there soared a seabird, a white flash briefing away to the life of its own purpose.

With a pang of regret, Guest compared the bird's freedom to his own blighted state. The bird could wish itself away on a wing, free-flighting to anywhere the winds might take it, but Guest was hopelessly embroiled in the toils of his ambition. And after all he had been through, his father was still stranded in a time pod in Obooloo's Temple of Blood. And, if Guest was to be captured and stripped of the x-x-zix, then what profit would he have to show for his adventures in Injiltaprajura? Its horrors were still fresh in memory, and those horrors looked set to be his only reward for his pains.

With all sincerity, Guest wished he had settled for a quiet life — assuming such a thing as a quiet life to be truly possible in a world as disordered as the one we are doomed to live in.

As Guest was thus wishing, Thayer Levant came up to him, and addressed him thus:

"Master."

"What do you want?" said Guest.

He strongly suspected that Levant wanted something which Guest would be in no mood to give, for Levant usually shunned formalities such as "master", preferring an independent taciturnity to anything which might be construed as servility.

"Well?" said Guest.

"I want to help you," said Levant.

"How?" said Guest, further disturbed by this prolonged indirectness.

"I have it in mind to protect your mazadath," said Levant. "That and the x-x-zix."

"Protect!" said Guest. "How could you protect them?"

"By hiding them," said Levant. "I believe myself equal to the task of concealment. I believe I could work my way back to Obooloo then take those treasures through the Door."

"And?" said Guest.

"I could take them to Dalar ken Halvar," said Levant. "There, Plandruk Qinplaqus could put the x-x-zix to work, to modify the weather of his capital city. Furthermore, he could hold in custody your mazadath, keeping it safe for your return."

"If I return," said Guest, who had no certainty of survival.

"Well," said Levant, "if you don't return, then the mazadath could go to your heirs."

"I have no heirs!" said Guest, with some bitterness.

"Your brother Morsh has sons, has he not?" said Levant. "If memory serves, he has sons in duplicate. Yurt and Iragana. May they not serve as your heirs? After all, they're your nephews."

"That is true," conceded Guest, somewhat comforted to think that he was an uncle even if he was not a father, and that he would always have a place in family tradition, even if he was doomed to be slaughtered by the Mutilator's men.

Guest considered Levant's plan.

It was true that Levant had a better chance of hiding the mazadath and the x-x-zix than did Guest Gulkan. For Guest had been too loud-mouthed and open in his dealings with the world. He had led something of a high-profile existence, so that there must by now be a thousand people on Untunchilamon who knew Guest Gulkan to be an emperor in exile. Within the fleet which was trying to escape from Injiltaprajura, and which shortly looked to fall prisoner to the Mutilator's men, there might be ten dozen people or more who knew Guest by face, name and mission, and who knew him to have seized control of the x-x-zix.

But Levant ...

To Guest's knowledge, Thayer Levant spoke no language other than Galish, and so restricted his dealings with strangers to the business of sharping them at cards. Thayer Levant had the lowest of profiles imaginable; and, though many men must have marked him as Guest Gulkan's companion, he might escape attention thanks to his lowly status — for, after all, Levant was in all truth nothing but a ragged serving man.

"Why do you hesitate?" said Levant, as Guest puzzled thus through his options. "The x-x-zix is no weapon of war."

"That is true," conceded Guest.

It was true indeed. The x-x-zix, the famous wishstone of Untunchilamon, granted no wishes to anyone, despite what rumour might say. It was but a heap of cubes and pyramids conglomerated into something approximating the dimensions of an orange; and, on Untunchilamon, its sole use had been ornamental, for it had long been reserved as a bauble set aside for the enhancement of the sceptre wielded by whoever temporarily governed that island.

"As for your mazadath," said Levant, "what use is that?"

Guest thought about it.

His mazadath had sentimental value, for it had been given to him by his purple-skinned Penelope, and in his exiled condition he found he missed the woman. Furthermore, the mazadath was doubtless a thing of Power. But what Power? Guest had tried to use the mazadath as a weapon against the therapist Schoptomov, but the therapist had simply laughed at the shining silver, and had knocked it from Guest Gulkan's hand. The wizards Sken-Pitilkin and Pelagius Zozimus had never thereafter remarked on the thing, a circumstance which suggested that, even if the mazadath were assumed to be possessed of Power, its Power was nothing which could be diagnosed by a wizard.

"I'm not sure," said Guest.

"Of what do you lack certainty?" said Thayer Levant.

"I'm not sure you have wit enough to hide these things from the search which will surely befall us," said Guest. "There are plenty of men in this fleet who know me to be possessed of these toys, and nine in ten of those men will surely be ready to betray my possession to the Mutilator's soldiers. So. We will be searched."

"Then you must show the world you have already hidden the things," said Levant, "and hidden them where nobody can find them."

"What are you talking about?" said Guest, who had ever been irritated by riddling.

In response, Thayer Levant smiled, and gestured at the sea.

"What are you on about?" said Guest.

"Come down below decks," said Levant, "and I'll tell you."

So the Weaponmaster and his servant disappeared below decks. When Guest Gulkan shortly thereafter manifested himself on deck, he was possessed of a purposeful air. After glancing at the oncoming fleet of ships which was loyal to the Mutilator, Guest Gulkan dived to the waters of the sea.

This sparked an uproar on the ship he had quit. For that ship had hove to as an act of submission, thus declaring its loyalty to the Mutilator. Hence Guest's rebellion was not to the taste of the ship's crew, which promptly launched a boat and pursued him.

But Guest Gulkan, after the long exercise which had marked his years of convalescence in Dalar ken Halvar, could swim with the fluency of a fish. Indeed, swimming was now as natural to him as the act of riding (an act which is ever far more natural to a Yarglat barbarian than the tedious business of walking). So Guest had gained the shores of Untunchilamon before he was caught.

Thus it was that Guest Gulkan was taken prisoner by a fleet of ships loyal to the Mutilator of Yestron, a fleet of ships which had been sent to return the rebellious island of Untunchilamon to the Izdimir Empire. In due course, Guest was interrogated; and confessed himself to be the Guest Gulkan who was notorious for having stolen the wishstone from Injiltaprajura's treasury during a riot; and confessed further that he had ditched this treasure in Untunchilamon's reef-waters when pursuit was close upon him.

As to what really might have happened to the wishstone and to the mazadath — why, since Guest was parted from Thayer Levant, and had no news of him, he had no way of telling whether that shifty master of devices had successfully concealed these treasures, and no way of telling whether Levant might ultimately make good his promise to deliver those things to Dalar ken Halvar.

Thus the Weaponmaster fell to the forces of the Izdimir Empire. He was returned to the city of Injiltaprajura, there to endure a weary confinement, a muchness of interrogation, several beatings and a wastefulness of impossible requests. To Guest's dismay, rumour had marked him as a wizard, and so he found himself asked to serve his new masters with his wizardry, and beaten anew in consequence of his failure to serve.

With the Mutilator's men at last convinced that Guest was no wizard, and convinced that he would be of no further use to them on the island of Untunchilamon, he was consigned to a ship that was travelling eastwards, and so was conveyed across the vastness of the oceans as a prisoner in the company of other prisoners.

Thus the Weaponmaster Guest Gulkan voyaged to the continent of Yestron as a prisoner.

Since his ship was no seagull's wing, it was a long time before Guest was landed at Bolfrigalaskaptiko, that city which lies upon the shores of the river Ka, just upstream from the great lagoon of Manamalargo. From there, he was taken inland to the mountainous region of Ang, where he arrived at last at Obooloo, capital city of the Izdimir Empire and home of Aldarch the Third.

Such were the rigours of this journey that Guest was

suffering from both dengue fever and dysentery by the time he was brought into the notorious prison known as the Fulch, and his condition was such that it was a full six months before he was in a fit state to be presented to Aldarch the Third, the Mutilator of Yestron.

The day before Guest was due to be so presented, a kindly jailor who spoke a little Toxteth exercised his skills in that language to advise the Weaponmaster that it would be best advised to commit suicide rather than to endure such presentation. But Guest distrusted the jailor, and so rejected this perfectly sound advice, and so on the morrow was conveyed uphill to the knoll which sustained the Mutilator's palace, that building known as Ubazakura.

Guest was checked through the gates of Ubazakura, and thus passed from the world of men, entering the lair of a demon-beast best fitted for a life in an otherworld hell.

But, as yet, the Weaponmaster was still far from despair. For, as yet, the Weaponmaster Guest Gulkan had not met the Mutilator, and so was inclined to discount nine-tenths of that which rumour had conveyed to his ears — whereas the truth of the matter was that Guest, rather than discounting rumour, should rightly have amplified it.

As he was soon to find out.

CHAPTER THIRTY-FIVE

Aldarch the Third: the Mutilator of Yestron, he who by genius of terror won the vicious civil war known as Talonsklavara. His joy is to supervise the scourging of the Izdimir Empire, which he governs from the province of Ang in the heartland of the continent of Yestron. His capital city is Obooloo, where he resides in the palace known as Ubazakura, which affords him a splendid view over Lake Kak.

* * *

As Midsummer's Day approached, Guest Gulkan was dragged from the dismal depths of his imprisonment. The tangled matting of his long-grown hair was shaved to a hedgehog's prickling. He was bathed, scrubbed, deloused and perfumed. His rags were burnt — sending up a thick and oily smoke to the heavens — and he was dressed in a loincloth and openweave sandals.

Then, on a hot day near the summer's uttermost height, the loincloth-clad Weaponmaster was escorted to the palace of Ubazakura. This monument to power stood upon Obooloo's heights, and was the home of Aldarch the Third, Mutilator of Yestron and ruler of most of it.

The Mutilator's reign was by then near the end of its Second Year of Peace. The year Peace 2 in the Izdimir Empire was the year Khmar 7 in the Collosnon Empire. Guest Gulkan's birthday had been and gone; he had already attained to the great and ancient age of 24; and shortly it would be Midsummer's Day again, and the Third Year of Peace would begin, and with that beginning the eighth year of the rule of the Emperor Khmar would likewise commence.

In the long darkness of his imprisonment, Guest Gulkan had steeled himself for his confrontation with Aldarch the Third. It is a mark of his upbringing that Guest had seen this confrontation to have been inevitable since the moment of his capture — for Guest was the son of an emperor, was he not? Hence he had never expected death through anonymous execution, but, rather, had braced himself for an edge-to-edge face-off with the very lord of the Izdimir Empire himself.

Now the long-expected showdown was at hand, and so Guest expected to be led into realms of patent doom, of screaming shadows and blood-reek dungeons. He expected to be confronted with assorted tableaux of gaping corpses and truncated torsos, of gibbering victims and crawling wreckage bloody in its writhings.

But no signs of any such provincial barbarism were to be seen as the young Guest Gulkan was escorted into the palace of Ubazakura. The Izdimir Empire can be called many things, but by no stretch of the imagination can it rightly be called provincial; and Aldarch the Third, the ruler of that empire, was one of the most civilized and highly cultivated rulers in all the world.

Hence the palace of Ubazakura was no gross place of wreckage and threat. Rather, it was typified by peace, grace and balance. It was a home to the arts and a monument to interior design.

Guest was led through a courtyard where diamond-gilled catfish whiskered through a lily pond which was deep — deep as drowning. The Weaponmaster slowed and lingered, lingered in the sun, lingered under the beating sky. He was conscious of the delicacy of the moment, of the fragility of his own existence. He felt the blood sifting through the smallest and most intimate sacs of his lungs. He felt the cobwebbed construction of his bones and the subtle dance of the very particles of air which wafted in and out through the great wings of his nose.

In those moments of heightened consciousness, the Weaponmaster heard a woman begin to sing. Her song echoed through the sprawling bat-wings of his ears, and, making its way through the tubes of flesh to which his ears gave access, caused the small and delicate bones deep inside his ear to thump out a message suitable for interpretation by his brain.

The beauty of the song suggested to Guest that a beautiful

woman was responsible for its generation. This was not the case. Rather, the day was bright with the golden song of one of the imperial dragons of Yestron — creatures of gentle nature and spectacular musical talent.

"Who is the woman?" said Guest, hearing the dragon, and thinking from its song that it must be a woman at least as beautiful as his long-lost Yerzerdayla.

"Hush," said the translator who accompanied him. "We are entering the Presence."

With that, they left the courtyard's sun behind them, venturing into the airy shadows of a series of chambers interconnected by arched doorways. They walked across hexagonal tiles, each of which was decorated with a representation of one of the body's internal organs. By contrast, the tapestries which adorned the walls were devoted to abstraction, to interweaving glyphs and helixes utterly removed from all realities of the flesh.

While passing through these chambers, Guest smelt camphor. Camphor. What did that remind him of? It reminded him of the tunnel which had led him into the depths of Obooloo's Temple of Blood. He had smelt camphor there, along with other things.

But—

There was some other memory, older, deeper, more compelling. It was — it was—

Camphor, camphor and the bright spires of golden song ... a supremely evocative combination ... so evocative that, somehow, Guest was certain that he had been here before. Here! In these very same chambers! Walking over these very same tiles! But this was his first visit to this palace. Surely.

Guest Gulkan had no absolute index to his past, for his memory had been jumbled by the many shocks of his life, by his rending at the hands of the Great Mink, by the displacements of war and exile, and by the sheer complexity of the press of ever-changing faces which had been a feature of his journey. Yet, even though he could not unscramble every detail of his past with any certainty, Guest Gulkan was sure that this was his very first visit to the palace of Ubazakura.

And yet ...

The golden song of the imperial dragon soared skywards with increasing passion, and again Guest Gulkan was assailed by the smell of camphor. Smells are the great memory-triggers, for smell is the most primitive of all the senses, the sense which is closest to animal existence.

Camphor!

Guest halted, for his skin prickled, and his very hair stood on end. He shuddered, and his heart pounded, and hot blood flushed through his veins.

For he remembered!

The Weaponmaster remembered a distant day on which he and his father had conquered the mainrock Pinnacle, and had secured admission to the abditory which housed the Door of the Safrak Bank. Plandruk Qinplaqus, the Silver Emperor of Dalar ken Halvar, he who had then been concealing his true identity by calling himself Ulix of the Drum, had told Witchlord and Weaponmaster that a globe of stars must be procured if that Door in the mainrock Pinnacle was to be open.

Suspecting that Banker Sod had fed just such an artefact to Icaria Scaria Iva-Italis, Guest Gulkan had challenged the demon Italis, at last persuading it to give him the star-globe.

But on taking that globe into his possession, Guest Gulkan had been plunged into a visionary world in which he had heard a woman's soaring song, in which he had smelt camphor, and in which he had met a man who had back-knuckled him across the face. That back-knuckling had precipitated Guest's return to the Hall of Time, where he had then been put to the trouble of staunching a nose made bloody by the back-knuckle blow delivered to him during his visionary adventuring.

"Come on!" said the Janjuladoola interpreter who had been assigned to Guest Gulkan. "Come on! We've no time to linger!"

But Guest still stood, staring at all around him, taking in the details with a heightened awareness close to that of hallucination. This was the very place! He was sure of it! This was the very place to which his vision had taken him when he had first seized control of the star-globe!

In the time since that visionary experience, Guest had deliberately striven to forget all that unsettling displacement, for he had been truly terrified by that displacement, and so had sought to suppress all memories relating to it.

But—

Here he was!

Here he was in a place identical to that which he had seen in that long-ago vision which he had endured in the mainrock Pinnacle!

"You," said his Janjuladoola interpreter, poking him. "Weren't you listening? Come on!"

On being poked, Guest at last bestirred himself, and allowed himself to be hurried into the next chamber, where the interpreter encouraged him to kneel.

Guest was a little slow in reacting to the encouragement.

"I said kneel!" said the interpreter, who was starting to get flustered. "Now! Now! I say it again! Kneel! Kneel! Down on your knees!"

"Why?" said Guest. "Is this my execution?"

"It will be, if you don't find your manners, and fast. He's almost upon us!"

The interpreter's panic managed to communicate a sense of urgency to Guest, and so the Yarglat barbarian went down on his knees, and had no sooner got down on those frugally padded lumps of bone when Aldarch the Third entered upon the audience chamber.

Aldarch proved to be a small man of the Skin who increased his apparent height by wearing shoes with platform soles. It is traditional for the emperors of Yestron to walk on stilts, thus demonstrating their social superiority in an even more pronounced fashion. But Aldarch had been methodically tortured by his father while he was still a child, and the damage then done to his legs made it unwise for him to attempt any feats of stilt-walking as an adult.

Aldarch spoke; Guest's translator interpreted; and Guest, in conformity with the Mutilator's orders, seated himself in the visitor's well. This square-cut recess in the floor contained a stool padded with a goose-feather cushion, and when seated upon that cushion Guest found nothing but his head and shoulders above floor level. The Mutilator took his own seat upon a modest throne set back from the visitor's well, and the dignity of this throne set the Mutilator's knees at a height greater than that of Guest's head.

This cunning arrangement neatly indicated the social gap between Mutilator and prisoner, while making it virtually impossible for Guest to launch a surprise attack upon his captor.

"You have lately come from Untunchilamon, I hear," said Aldarch the Third.

"It is so," said Guest.

"You know," said Aldarch, "I have heard that they were walking on stilts."

Guest Gulkan, who did not know precisely how he was supposed to respond to this intelligence, assumed a grave demeanour.

"Well?" said Aldarch. "Is it true, or is it not? I have heard that the one called Pokrov was particularly noticeable for getting above himself."

"For getting above himself?" said Guest.

"For elevating himself above the height appropriate to his class!" said the translator to Guest. "For walking on stilts!"

"Well," said Guest, who was properly confused by now, "it may have happened. I can't say that it didn't."

"What does he say?" said Aldarch.

"My lord," said the translator to Aldarch, "he confesses that with his own eyes he saw such people as Pokrov walking on stilts."

"You saw," said Aldarch, "yet you made no move to stop it?"

This accusation was translated to Guest. The Yarglat barbarian was so ignorant of the customs of the civilized world that he had not yet absorbed the full import of this business of stilt-walking, yet even to such a limited soul as Guest Gulkan it was obvious that something of importance was afoot, so in puzzled confusion he responded to the Mutilator by saying:

"I, ah ... as a foreigner, I..."

"He says, my lord," said the interpreter to Aldarch, "that as a poor and ignorant foreign-born barbarian he did not see fit to interfere in the internal affairs of the Izdimir Empire, hence did not murder the stilt-walkers for their impertinence. He further says that he thought such acts of murder would be to you a pleasure, and he had no wish to cheat you of such pleasure."

"Well," said Aldarch, who was pleased to receive this news, "that was well-spoken. Suppose we pause for a moment to indulge ourselves in a lesser pleasure?"

The interpreter not demurring, Al'three gave a command; a woman entered with a tray; and cups from this tray were served to Mutilator, interpreter and prisoner. The cups were of bone china and in them was the warmth of a greenish fluid which Guest Gulkan tentatively identified as tea.

"You are familiar with this drink?" said the Mutilator.

Aldarch the Third once again spoke through the interpreter, since Weaponmaster and Mutilator had no language in common. Guest Gulkan was no linguist, and hence had not the slightest competence in any truly scholarly language. He could make himself known in Ordhar, the command language of the armies of the Collosnon Empire; he could speak Eparget, the native tongue of the Yarglat; and apart from that he could only use Toxteth and the Galish Trading Tongue. The various barbarous and primitive languages which were at the command of Guest Gulkan's tongue were virtually useless in the heartland of the Izdimir Empire. As for the Mutilator, why, he was a scholar great in learning, but his wisdom was exclusively restricted to Janjuladoola, the infinitely subtle and fiendishly complicated language of Yestron's master race.

"The drink," said Guest, half-sure of its nature yet wary of committing himself to an error, "the drink is ... ah, something from Chay, perhaps?"

"No," said the Mutilator. "It is jade tea. The jade tea of Obooloo, much sought after both here and in foreign parts."

Guest did not think it healthy to be consuming hot drinks

on such a sultry day, but drank without arguing about it.

"So," said Aldarch, when Guest had drunk. "You have been adventuring on Untunchilamon."

"I have," said Guest, who hoped they were not going to get back to the subject of stilts, because he could not in the least understand it. "Would you like to hear more of it?"

"My interrogators did their work well," said the Mutilator. "And you have not been the only person to be interrogated. Consequently, you have no secrets from me and mine."

Guest wondered if this meant that Thayer Levant had been caught and questioned. But he did not dare to ask. Simply to ask that question would be to betray Levant, who — if he was still at liberty — might still be trying to make his way back to Obooloo and escape to Dalar ken Halvar by way of the Door of the Bondsman's Guild. In any case, the Mutilator was still speaking.

"We know what you did in Injiltaprajura," said the Mutilator. "We know it in detail. Likewise, we know what you did earlier in this city of mine. You raided the Temple of Blood, and your father lies there yet, sheltered in a time pod to which we have no access."

Guest's interpreter had a little difficulty placing the words "time pod" into the Toxteth tongue, but did the trick by calling it "the egg which does not change". Upon puzzling out the meaning of this phrase, Guest remembered the time pod, and remembered the day of the raid, and the ring of ever-ice which had fallen to the oily waters of the innermost sanctum of the Temple of Blood. He deduced that the ring had not been found.

Since the whereabouts of the ring had not been betrayed, this meant — surely — that the demon in the Temple of Blood had kept silent about it. So the demon Ungula Scarth was Guest's ally! This thought heartened the Weaponmaster greatly.

"It is true," said Guest, "that I came to the Temple. There is a Great God held prisoner in the Temple, a—"

"A demon," said Aldarch. "There are two things in the Temple, and both are demons. Both are old, old things, and dangerous. One is too big to move. The other — only a fool would seek its liberation. The high priestess of the Temple is Anaconda Stogirov. She is — she is my friend. My only friend. She tells me much, and she has told me all about those demons."

"Then," said Guest, carefully, "I congratulate you on the possession of such a knowledgeable friend."

"Anaconda Stogirov has also confirmed to me the nature of the cornucopia, that device which features so largely in legend. Do you know of the cornucopia?"

"No," said Guest.

A shameful confession, this! But, thanks to the derelictions of his scholarship, the young Weaponmaster was uncommonly ignorant of many things which others were apt to take for granted.

The ignorance of one's associates is not always painful, particularly not to those who derive a delicious sense of superiority by indulging in the act of enlightenment. Being enamoured of such indulgence, Aldarch the Third lectured Guest Gulkan at length, telling him all about the cornucopia, the horn of plenty which had for so long been lost in the Stench Caves of Logthok Norgos. The tale took quite some time, particularly as the Mutilator dwelt in detail upon the horrors that some unsuccessful questing heroes had spoken of as they died. The tale began—

But the reader is surely familiar with the tale of the cornucopia of Logthok Norgos, for that story is a part of everyone's basic education, and the sagacious Sken-Pitilkin had told it at least thrice to Guest Gulkan when the pair of them were respectively tutor and student back in the city of Gendormargensis.

Still, the Mutilator told the story in something close to its full detail, for the story was one of his favourites.

"You understand?" said the Mutilator, when he was done with telling his tale.

"My lord has been very clear," said Guest. "I understand."

"Then know your duty," said Aldarch. "You will liberate your father from the time pod. Then you will quest to the Stench Caves in his company, and retrieve for me the cornucopia."

"My lord," said Guest, "I cannot free my father since —
there is a ring, and it is lost. I had a ring, but I lost it, and without
the ring I can't open the pod."

"If ... if you speak the truth," said Aldarch, "then you ... you
may regret your limitations hereafter. Come. Bring your skin and
your scalp to my bathroom, and I will ... I will show you
something which will interest you."

This was said very calmly, which disturbed Guest, who had
expected to be ranted at, and had prepared himself accordingly.
In absence of all rant, the Mutilator abandoned his throne and
limped through the palace with Guest and his ever-shadowing
interpreter trailing along behind.

The Mutilator led the way to his bathroom. This was not by
any means a narrow chamber. No, it was a room so extensive
that one could comfortably have drilled a company of armed
men within its confines. It was a spacious chamber of bright-
bathing light which played upon white marble bare of ornament.
The light came in through the windows, which were open, and
which afforded a view of the high mountains. Those mountains
were white with snow, as they were all through the year, and
upon their heights—

But let us not be distracted by scenery. Let us attend to those
matters to which Guest attended. He attended first of all to the
bath, which sat in one corner of the bathroom. It was an entirely
regular and unremarkable bath made of three or four ox-weights
of solid gold; and it was daily filled with warm water so that the
Mutilator might perform his ablutions.

In the centre of the room, however, was something not quite
so conventional. It was not particularly startling, but it was odd.
Under the circumstances, Guest Gulkan found anything odd to
be ominous. The thing which had attracted his attention was a
shallow rectangular well, square-cut, and of no great depth —
for had it been filled with water (or with blood, or milk, or liquid
honey) then Guest could have jumped into it without getting
wet above the knees. For the moment, though, the well was
entirely empty of all fluids, so Guest was able to see that its floor
was pierced by many drainage holes.

In the centre of that well there stood a brazier, which was lit; and above the brazier hung what appeared to be a coffin, suspended from the roof on metal chains. The coffin had the milky whiteness of porcelain.

"We have a man in the coffin," said Aldarch.

"So," said Guest, affecting a calm which he did not quite feel. "So you're boiling him alive."

"Oh no," said the Mutilator. "The brazier is ... it's for his health, you could say. This room gets cold, especially at night. If he wasn't kept warm then he'd die. Shall we look at him?"

"By all means," said Guest.

The Mutilator took Guest Gulkan by the elbow in a companionable manner and guided him forward till they both stood on the edge of the well, where they were able to look down upon the coffin and observe its contents.

Might there perhaps be snakes in the coffin?

No, there were no snakes.

Instead, there was a man.

A modest opening in the coffin allowed for an inspection of the man's face. The man's nose stuck through the gridwork bars, and the bridge of that nose had gone septic where the skin had been chafed away by the unprotected iron. The man's complexion was olive; his pores big; his eyebrows black; his lips full and sensual.

Guest absorbed all these details as he looked down on the man. There seemed to be no hurry. Aldarch the Third seemed prepared to stand here all day. The more Guest stood there, the more ... the more he was disturbed. Something ... something was not quite right.

A fluid of dire darkness, a fluid filthy with bodyscum, a fluid hinting of oil and eels, bathed the man with the quiescent menace of a quicksand swamp, and bathed him so generously that it almost swallowed his face.

With a little more fluid ...

If a little more fluid were to be poured into the coffin then the man would surely drown. Now Guest saw the nature of the torture. The man was kept here for many days, and each day a little more fluid was added. In the end, someone would pour in one last jar, and the victim would be helplessly choked. The horror would be to wait for day after day, trapped, helpless and immobile, knowing the nature of the death that was to come.

"How long has he been here?" said Guest.

The moment he asked, he knew the question was a mistake. Because Aldarch smiled. The smile was thin but satisfied. Aldarch knew that Guest had begun to appreciate the horror of the victim's situation.

"He has been here for forty days," said Aldarch. "He has fed well. We have fed him upon figs and we have fed him upon almonds. That is sufficient."

"Figs, nuts ... and ... and water? Do you feed him water? Is he lying in his urine?"

"What makes you think that?"

"It would be a way to drown a man," said Guest, making an incontinent confession of the workings of his mind. "Trap him in a coffin like this, then ... he has to piss, and in the end he drowns of it."

Aldarch snorted with laughter.

"What a mind!" said the Mutilator. "But, no. We do nothing so crude. From the first day, the coffin is filled to the level you see now. The bathroom attendants adjust the level as necessary. The fluid, of course, is sesame oil." As this was translated, the Mutilator watched his prisoner's face. When Guest did not react, the Mutilator said, softly: "So. So you really don't know. You really don't understand. Very well."

The Mutilator raised his hand and gave an order — an order which was not translated. Guest Gulkan listened in confusion to the slick-sliding vocables of Aldarch the Third's Janjuladoola. He could not even guess what was going to happen next. But obviously something was going to happen, and Guest feared that—

Guest wished he was elsewhere.

While Guest was still wishing, a girl-slave with symbolic chains dangling from her wrists stepped forward to remove the brazier. Once she had exited with her burden, an executioner approached, bearing a sledgehammer. He looked at the Mutilator.

"Proceed," said Aldarch Three.

The executioner tapped the coffin with his sledgehammer. The ceramic coffin cracked. The executioner hit it again. The coffin shattered. Down came the coffin in a bursting of fragments, a leapage of filth. In the middle of this downburst flopped the prisoner, who hit the marble, clawed at it spasmodically, then lay still in the accumulated slime of forty days of his own filth.

Guest flinched, and slashed at his own face with the flat of his hand, abolishing a splash of filth which had landed there.

"Watch," said the Mutilator. "You will find this very interesting."

At first it seemed that nothing was happening. Guest raised his eyes to the blue sky and the high mountains, to the impeccable white of the distant snow. He had a great yearning to be free from this place of self-important steel and degrading spectacle, to be free to walk in those mountains and to leave his footprints in those snows. He remembered the far-distant mountains of Ibsen-Iktus, remembered the blackrock razorblade of those uppermost heights, remembered the high-altitude winds which had stripped away the snows in pluming streams which—

"Watch," said the Mutilator, with something of the corkscrew in his voice.

Guest, called back to the filthy spectacle before him, forced himself to study the wretched thing which lay before him in the crippled eloquence of its squalor. It lay on its belly. He could see its ribs moving with the lizard-quick panting of its breathing. It was going nowhere, yet it was exhausted by the rigours of the journey.

Guest caught a whiff of the stench from the slime-coated body, and he almost gagged.

He controlled himself.

He struggled to understand.

What was the true import of this spectacle? What was the

significance of bathing a man in his own filth? Was this some insult to the pride of the Janjuladoola? Some insult based on the transgression of protocols and the breach of taboos? Was this the ultimate punishment of the Izdimir Empire? To be made to lie helplessly for day after day in the putrid stench of one's own dung and urine?

Aldarch the Third, who had been covertly watching the Weaponmaster, grunted with satisfaction. He gave an order. This time the translator rendered it into Toxteth for Guest's benefit:

"Wash the man."

A bevy of slave girls approached, each bearing a wooden bucket brimming with water. Aldarch dipped his fingers into each bucket in turn, then signified his approval. The buckets were emptied over the man, were emptied one by one, and as the downpour washed away the slime it became possible to see, and as it became possible to see—

"Watch," said Aldarch softly, as Guest Gulkan looked away. "Watch. Look closely. Watch and learn."

By an effort of great self-control, Guest forced himself to watch, forced himself to look closely, and forced himself to see, to learn, and to understand.

The forty days of immersion in sesame oil had caused the skin to be eaten away from the body, exposing the bare flesh and the blood vessels. Little remained of the face except those parts which had been free from the fluid. The rest was gone. As for the head, why, the sesame oil had eaten away the skin of the scalp. The bald bones of the skull were bare, their sutures clearly visible. Across the bare bone there laced a webwork of arteries.

"Soon," said the Mutilator. "Soon it will begin. As the water dries, so it will begin. He is tender after his long confinement, and the air is painful."

"The air?" said Guest, not quite understanding.

"As you see," said Aldarch, indicating the specimen on the floor in front of them.

Even as Guest watched, the anatomical specimen before him began to tremble as if shivering. Then it began to move, warping in slow-motion agony. Guest was reminded of a spider crumpling in a flame. But this was a slow, slow fire. This fire did not quickly consume the flesh.

The man on the floor jerked in spasms. His wet slithering spasms reminded Guest obscenely of orgasms. Aldarch the Third watched with intense interest. Even for him, this was a special thing. He did not see this every day. The Mutilator's attendants were, one and all, frozen into a hieratic stillness.

"It hurts him," said Aldarch, speaking with a softness which the interpreter translated in a bare whisper. "He is burning. It hurts him to breathe. It hurts him to be."

As if in response, the writhing man began to mutter, speaking in choked intakes, speaking in the language of drowning, speaking of pain, of strangulation, of the utterable unutterable.

"Always," said Aldarch, intently. "Always. It always happens this way. He is speaking."

"Of what?" said Guest.

"Of his pain," said Aldarch. "He begs for his mother in her mercy. He begs. But. But if you ask — he can tell you the future if you ask."

"This I — I don't need to know the future," said Guest. "I'll face the future when I come to it."

"The man will die anyway," said Aldarch. "Since the man will die in any case, you might as well have the knowledge of his wisdom. I will ask your future for you."

Then, abruptly, the Mutilator stepped down into the well. Disregarding the stench and the filth, he straddled the writhing man. Then, to Guest's utter horror, the Mutilator seated himself on that appalling figure. The living corpse screamed in a high-pitched whistle. The Mutilator slapped it. Slapped it hard. Splatters of filth flew in all directions. Then the Mutilator spoke to the thing, spoke with a snarling savagery, as if to a delinquent dog.

At which—

At which the man either did or did not begin to speak.

Guest was not sure whether the dying man was speaking, but

he knew for a certainty that he could hear a voice of some description, a withered voice which was warped with agony, a voice outgulping words in gouts, words of terrible import.

Then the voice fell silent.

Aldarch the Third rose from his victim, who had ceased to move. The Mutilator scrambled out of the shallow well. He looked uncommonly ungainly as he climbed out of that pit, but his ungainliness did not detract from his dignity.

A slave girl approached, bearing a canary-yellow hand-cloth which steamed slightly. Aldarch took it, wiped his face, cleaned his hands, then tossed it into the pit. Despite this token cleansing, the Mutilator was still besmeared with filth. He stank. But he did not seem to mind. He looked the Weaponmaster in the face, and he said:

"He says you will kill your father."

Guest shuddered.

For it was hard to deny the likelihood of any prediction by such a terrible creature.

"That is what he says," continued the Mutilator. "He says that you will kill your father. And I say this — if you cannot or will not liberate your father from the time pod in the Temple of Blood, then you will most certainly be the death of your father. For I will put that pod in a fire then heat it until it bursts."

As Guest absorbed this threat, the Mutilator enhanced it with one last statement:

"I have done as much before."

Guest shuddered.

And, with that, the Mutilator exited, leaving the Weaponmaster to contemplate the final twitchings of the man who lay dying at his feet.

CHAPTER THIRTY-SIX

Stench Caves: complex of caverns from whence that thin and putrid flux known as the Nijidith River outflows and courses west to Lake Kak. The Nijidith River affords pigs and such with a constant source of nourishment, and was the original attraction which caused Obooloo to be founded on the shores of Lake Kak.

* * *

Choosing to quest to the Stench Caves and thus save his father from incineration, Guest Gulkan confessed to the location of the ring of ever-ice which had the power to open and close the time pods in the Temple of Blood.

Once Guest had confessed, the sewer-flavoured waters in the Temple of Blood were siphoned dry, and the muck at the bottom of the octagonal chamber which housed the Great God Jocasta and the demon Ungula Scarth was sieved until the ring was found.

Then Aldarch the Third used that ring to open the time pod which held the Witchlord, and the man fell from that pod, and was received by the Mutilator's healers. Thereafter, the Mutilator wore the ring of ever-ice on his own hand.

Now since Lord Onosh had been sorely wounded when Guest had first consigned him to the safety of a time pod, and since no time whatsoever had passed for Lord Onosh since then, he proved grievously wounded when liberated, and was some months recovering.

But, with the Witchlord Onosh being finally recovered, and reconciled to joining the quest for the cornucopia to which his son had pledged himself, Witchlord and Weaponmaster left the palace of Ubazakura, accompanied by the Mutilator and a great host of his people.

They went on foot, this being the traditional manner in which the Stench Caves are approached from Obooloo, since those caves are holy, and therefore to approach those caves is to undertake a kind of pilgrimage.

While they pilgrimaged, Aldarch the Third led that multitude in a holy chant. His voice was not so melodious as that of one of his imperial dragons, but his power and status compelled Guest Gulkan to attend to him with such concentration that the Weaponmaster soon began to feel that he had never heard a more affecting plaint in all his days.

Even so, Guest did not feel very much like a pilgrim. On the night before, the Mutilator had honoured Witchlord and Weaponmaster with a feast, and Guest's head was aching from all the wine he had drunk, for liquor of all descriptions had become unfamiliar to his flesh during his days of imprisonment. Yes, despite Guest Gulkan's great constitutional strength, the stress of imprisonment had weakened him bitterly, and today he felt his weakness in the length of the road, the sharpness of the light, the invincibility of the sun.

The day was hot, and in its heat the greenflies of Ang were at their pestilential worst. A hot shimmer of dragonflies flickered between the processioning pilgrims and went winging out over the Nijidith River — a slow and oozing flux of filth in which pigs were diligently rooting for their sustenance. The pigs were not by any means alone, for keeping them company were ducks which went filleting through the muck with their beaks; and, ignoring both pigs and ducks, multitudes of barefoot peasants stood up to their knees in the rivermud, and sieved it for unimaginable treasures (fish? bugs? worms? eggs? tadpoles? gemstones? coinage? bones?).

It might have been thought that the Weaponmaster would have occupied himself on that journey by making plans for resistance or escape. But he did not. The fight had gone out of him, for he had suffered too many setbacks and defeats — starting with the tearing of his arms and legs in an arena in Chi'ash-lan. That had marked him. The demon of Cap Foz Para Lash had repaired the damage done to his flesh, but his psyche had been deeply damaged. He knew his own vulnerability, and knew it too well, for all that he tried to deny that knowledge.

And, having found that all his resources of strength had failed him in Chi'ash-lan, he was less sure of those resources than he had been on that foolish day of youthful bravura when he had faced the Rovac warrior Thodric Jarl in a duel in Enskandalon Square.

Consequently, though Guest had functioned well enough when questing in the company of the wizards Pelagius Zozimus and Hostaja Sken-Pitilkin, he had found it harder to play the hero without them. So when endeavouring to escape from Injiltaprajura, and finding his escape ship confronted by a fleet loyal to the Mutilator, he had found himself entirely lacking in initiative and resource; and it had only been the intervention of his servant Thayer Levant which had saved him from tamely surrendering the x-x-zix and the mazadath to the Mutilator's forces.

Since then, imprisonment and threat had further sapped Guest's confidence; and, of course, he was nursing a dragon, as the cognoscenti of Obooloo term a hangover. He was further depressed by the fact that his new boots — a personal gift from the Mutilator — were giving him blisters. Therefore he made no plans for mayhem, and he attempted no touristic appreciation of the novel sights and scenes which greeted him on the way to the Stench Gates, though he did take note of a young woman breast-feeding a piglet, which (much to the Weaponmaster's envy) nuzzled against her flesh in an utter contentment of gluttony.

As the procession drew nearer to the Stench Gates, the river became more obviously polluted — for nuggets of floating filth and lengths of what looked like intestines came floating downstream on its oily waters. These delicacies were salvaged by the bucketload by industrious peasants, who carted much away for their own use, yielding up token portions to be burnt as offerings at the several temples of the God of Bounty.

The God of Bounty, a minor god who had Zoz the Ancestral as his patron, was worshipped by the banks of the Nijidith River, and nowhere else. The largest of his temples occupied the huge portal cavern which linked the world of daylight with the inner dark of the Stench Caves, and, at the end of their journey, Witchlord and Weaponmaster were led into this Prime Temple. It was dominated by a huge carving which depicted the God of Bounty graciously vomiting into the begging bowls of His worshippers.

It was then explained to the two that they must convert to the worship of the God of Bounty if they would venture deeper into the Stench Caves. Since both were agreeable to being converted, the rites of conversion immediately began: and took a full three days to complete.

Neither Lord Onosh nor his son Guest either felt or expressed any impatience at this display. For, while those who read histories are commonly eager to know What Happens Next, those who have the misfortune to be making history in their own right would usually rather not know, or at least not just yet. Guest in particular welcomed the respite, for it allowed him to drain and dry the blisters which he had got from his new boots on the march to the Stench Caves.

Witchlord and Weaponmaster endured the three days of ritual with such perfect patience that the high priest of the God of Bounty, impressed by their manifest piety, told them that there were two vacancies in the priesthood.

"You are candidates," said the high priest. "Say the word, and you will be accepted."

"Ah," said Guest, "but we are doomed on a quest."

"No," said the high priest. "Do but say the word, and you will be inducted into the priesthood. Priests do not quest."

Encouraged by this — for the longueurs of three days of ritual had failed to give him any enthusiasm for finding out What Happens Next — Guest asked for details. He was told that the two positions currently vacant were those of the Collector of Alms and the Blesser of Turds.

"The one, by tradition, is always a blind man with his male attributes removed," said the high priest, licking his lips. "The other has no ears, and is likewise bereft of the attributes specific to his gender."

On getting a painfully precise explanation of what was meant by the removal of "male attributes", Witchlord and Weaponmaster decided that (unfortunately) neither of them was worthy to be inducted into the priesthood of the God of Bounty.

"A pity," said the high priest, who had looked forward to the task of making these potential new recruits eligible for the priesthood. "A great pity."

Then he supervised the arming of Witchlord and Weaponmaster. They were equipped with swordbelts, with swords, with knives, with throwing stars, with eye-gouging hand-screws, with darning needles and with packets of pepper. All the weapons were firmly lashed to their swordbelts (but for the darning needles and packets of pepper, which were enclosed in leather purses which had been stitched tight, the purses themselves then being bound to the swordbelts). The idea was that the questing heroes would not be given any encouragement to run amok in the temple — but, once free in the Stench Caves, they would be able to liberate a full complement of weapons at their leisure.

And so at last — much to the relief of Aldarch the Third, who lacked the infinite tolerance for ritual which Guest and his father had so capably demonstrated — Witchlord and Weaponmaster were conveyed to the innermost door of the Prime Temple which occupied the portal cavern of the Stench Caves. The Nijidith River exited from the Stench Caves by means of the gap beneath that innermost door, which was opened in a long ceremony involving much wailing, and the laceration of priestly noses, and the banging of calabashes, and the ceremonial sacrifice of a rat.

Having been sacrificed, the rat was then cooked, and portions of it were served to both Witchlord and Weaponmaster. They ate it without any qualms whatsoever (while confined in the Fulch, Guest Gulkan had several times eaten raw rat, therefore had no objection to the same article when cooked), and found it perfectly palatable, for it was not a filth-eater, but, rather, a pampered creature which had been properly raised expressly for the purpose of consumption.

Having thus fed, Witchlord and Weaponmaster were escorted through the Gates of Filth (for thus was the innermost door named), where they were ordered to halt in front of a small altar set amidst a sea of mud. A greenish phosphorescent light shone dimly down from the roof, and this was supplemented by flaring torches.

"Halt!" said the high priest.

For the ceremonies were not yet over! Before the questing heroes could be allowed to proceed any further into the inner depths, Aldarch the Third must first consecrate their mission by sacrificing a frog.

A frog was produced. It was a brown frog spotted with purplish strawberry-shaped markings. It had been securely trussed with threads of gold, and of silver, of purple, and of crimson. Guest Gulkan and his father were invited to kiss this animal, which they duly did, pressing reverent lips to the coldness of its skin. Then the high priest placed the sacrifice on the altar, and withdrew.

Aldarch the Third then stroked the frog with his finger, and hummed to it, then sucked on his finger, then let a glob of saliva fall to its cool flesh, then used his finger to spread his spittle across the animal's skin. Guest watched closely, for the Mutilator was wearing the ring of ever-ice on the very same finger which was stroking the frog, and Guest wished he could think of some way to win possession of that ring.

Then the Mutilator drew his knife.

It was a small knife, a weapon made with a backbreaking curve which ended not in a point but in a bead. A bluish bead. Bluish? Greenish? It was hard to tell, for, after all, the Stench Caves were lit by the green glow from the roof combined with the flaring torchlight, which — as any interior designer will tell you — is scarcely the kind of illumination to be using when one is trying to match colours. But, despite the limitations of the light, Guest Gulkan was fairly sure that the bead on the end of the Mutilator's knife was a kind of blue or green. It looked to be made of porcelain, and so reminded him of the hideous coffin in the Mutilator's bathroom. Yet. The sight of that bead stirred a deeper memory. What?

The Mutilator jabbed at the frog. The animal convulsed. And Guest remembered.

Standing there at the Stench Gates, Guest Gulkan once again remembered the vision which had long ago beset him in the mainrock Pinnacle. His vision had transported him to a room where a grey-skinned stranger had slapped him, then had jabbed him with a hooked knife, terminating his vision, and precipitating his return to the realities of the mainrock.

Aldarch was the grey-skinned stranger.

The knife which had sacrificed the frog was the same knife which had assailed Guest during his visionary transportation.

And.

And!

The demon Ungula Scarth had said—

In the Temple of Blood, in the octagonal chamber which housed the Great God Jocasta, the jade-green demon had told Guest that a special knife was needed to cut through the force-field which imprisoned the Great God. Anaconda Stogirov, High Priestess of the Temple of Blood, was in possession of one such blade.

The other—

"Wah!" said Guest.

And his father, who had been waiting for a cue which would tell him his son was ready for violence, slammed the Mutilator with his elbow. Down went the Mutilator! Guest grabbed for the Mutilator's knife.

"Mazara!" screamed the Mutilator, rising from the mud.

Guest slashed him across the cheek. The Mutilator reeled backward, and Guest kicked him in the crutch. As Aldarch doubled over, Guest grabbed the man's head. Slammed it with his knee. He ripped the ring of ever-ice from the Mutilator's finger, and crammed it on to his own hand.

"Come on!" cried Lord Onosh.

So, realizing he did not have time to decapitate the Mutilator, or to skin him alive, or to organize his roasting, Guest chopped him on the neck — hoping the blow would kill — then went pelting into the darkness.

Witchlord and Weaponmaster fled at full pace. A dozen paces took them to the first of a multitude of corkscrew turns in an ever-branching tunnel. Then the Stench Caves widened from tunnel to cavern, and the Witchlord tripped, and went down. He fell heavily, winding himself.

Guest, conscious of the cries of the guards who were in hot pursuit, grabbed his father. The cavern was lit by the unearthly green phosphorescence from overhead, but here and there were patches of darkness. Guest dragged his father towards the nearest such patch, not knowing whether it was a maw or a womb.

It proved to be a pocket of rock-shadowed mud. Cold mud. Wet mud. Slickery mud which absorbed Guest and his father as they plunged into it, going in up to their waists, and going in just in time — for moments later a good two dozen of the Mutilator's guards came pounding into the cavern.

As the guards raced into the cavern, Guest noticed that the chip of ever-ice in the ring on his hand was gleaming in the darkness, vibrant with its own inner light. Hastily, he plunged it under the mud.

The guards went pelting past. One slithered, slid, then went sprawling with a belly-flop. One of his fellows kicked him, swearing in fear, rage and panic. Green light slick-sliced from the guards' swords, making Guest uncomfortably aware of the fact that his own weapons were as yet unavailable for his use, since they were firmly attached to his swordbelt. In his hand, he still had the little knife he had won from Aldarch the Third, but he doubted the wisdom of cutting anything free while he was waist-deep in mud, for he might loose his steel to the slime.

Abruptly, the leading guard halted.

Then cried out.

Guest thought he had been discovered.

A moment later, with a roar, a thing with a great many tentacles lunged from the mud and seized the guard who had halted and shouted. The guard screamed, then screamed no more, for a tentacle forced its way down his throat. Even as

Guest watched, aghast, the tentacle abrupted through the guard's back.

The guard thrashed in spasms. Then the monster of the murk tossed him to one side. He hit the wall with a sick glap-slup of bursting organs, then folded up in a crumpled heap on the mud of the cavern floor.

And while all this was going on, the murkbeast had simultaneously grabbed most of the other guards, and was variously squeezing them, crushing them, waving them about, or munching them down to satisfy its appetite.

As far as Guest could make out by the dim green phosphorescent light from the roof of the cave, the murkbeast had no feet, no legs, no means of perambulation. Rather, it appeared to be rooted in the muck on a thick stalk. It made him think of a toad which had been grafted on to a sea anemone and equipped with the tentacles of an octopus (tentacles dreadfully reminiscent of those of the therapist Schoptomov).

While Guest was still staring in fascinated horror, the murkbeast finished its feast.

Then the cavern was still, but for the noisy vomiting of a cowering survivor, and the groaning of a man — a man who had been crushed but uneaten.

When the survivor had finished vomiting, he started crying, then exited from the cavern, exiting from this scene of living nightmare. But no such easy retreat was available to Witchlord and Weaponmaster. For if they retreated, they would run into Aldarch the Third; and, all things being equal, Guest would far rather take his chances with the murkbeast.

The guard who had been crushed was still groaning. As if annoyed by the noise he was making, the murkbeast swatted him with a tentacle. He screamed, and thrashed, and was slapped again. Several times. Guest heard the crunch of breaking bones, a crunch like that of rock being quarried. Again, a tentacle slapped living flesh, making a sound like a canoe grounding itself on a coral reef.

And, thus slapped, the man screamed no more. Rather, he panted, his breath a matter of heaving gasps, a strenuous fighting. He was fighting for his life, and he was losing.

Guest was reminded of a dying woman he had once encountered on the stairs in the mainrock Pinnacle. That had been on a night of battle, the night on which Witchlord and Weaponmaster had wrested control of Alozay from Banker Sod. Guest had encountered a dying woman, had paused to pity her, then — compelled by the necessities of war — had passed on. Ever since then, he had not once thought of that woman. But now he remembered.

Half-thinking to help or comfort the man, Guest started from the muddy pit in which he was mired. But his father pulled him back.

"Wait," said the Witchlord. "Guards may come in search of their dead."

"We'd hear them," said Guest.

"Not if they were quiet," said his father. "Not while our friend out there is making such a racket."

So Guest, acknowledging the truth of this, subsided into the pit.

He waited.

At length, Lord Onosh grunted, the loudness of his grunt emphasizing the silence in the cavern — for the man who had so recently been dying was now dead.

"Time for us to be moving," said the Witchlord.

But by this time, Guest was in no mood to be moving. The wait had served to sap his courage, for the obvious and irrevocable truth of the green-glowering depths was that the Weaponmaster was way out of his depth. He was not equipped to wage war on a murkbeast — and that creature was the very first of the dangers encountered in those depths!

In this cold, wet, muddy place, there was nothing which was familiar. Guest had precious little to pad him against the cold, and was afforded no padding of habit or familiarity which could protect him against the full knowledge of the fragility of his own vulnerability. This was an alien place, a place which by no stretch of the imagination could be considered home, and it made him conscious of the pain, the death, the agony which was implicit in the configuration of his flesh and bones.

Guest remembered squatting on a beach by night on the Chameleon's Tongue, on the shores of Argan, convinced that the Great Mink was on the loose in the night. He remembered comforting himself with his own familiar, personal, private smell. The gesture had served. But no such comfort would avail him here. For there was no denying that a monster waited in the dark, a murkbeast built for the rending of men.

"It will eat us," said Guest, trying to keep the fear from his voice.

"It has left one uneaten," said Lord Onosh, "therefore it has fed sufficiently. Come. Have you a knife?"

"Take this," said Guest, passing his father the weapon he had won from the Mutilator. "But be tender of the point."

"The edge will serve," said his father, starting to saw at the fastenings which bound his weapons to his swordbelt.

Then Lord Onosh passed the knife back to his son, who used it to liberate his own weapons. They were well-made and serviceable, though the possession of sword, knives, throwing stars, eye-gouging handscrews, darning needles and packets of pepper gave Guest no confidence in the face of the murkbeast. It did not look to be the kind of creature which would take much notice of weapons. So thinking, Guest discarded one of his knives, and used the buckle-down sheath thus freed as a repository for the blade which he had stolen from the Mutilator.

"You threw away a knife!" said his father, in tones of accusation.

"So I did," said Guest. "And it is a crime, yes, but I would do it again, and, what's more, I have done worse in the past and will do worse again in the future."

Guest spoke with some heat, for fear was converting itself to anger. His fear was all of the murkbeast.

Though the murkbeast had been initially hidden in the mud, it had made no move to withdraw to that shelter. Its stalk was severely distended, suggesting that its glutting of itself had made such withdrawal a physical impossibility. Perhaps it would lie there for days, quiescent, digesting, its sprawled tentacles lying heedless in the muck.

Perhaps.

And then again ...

"I'll go first," said Lord Onosh, when his son made no move to venture forward.

Then the Witchlord matched action to his words.

Guest watched as his father stepped forward, moving carefully, keeping close to the walls of the cavern. The green light from above shone on the Witchlord's gouged and slanting forehead, lit his high Yarglat-bred cheekbones with a fever sheen, and emphasized the darkness of the shadows which pooled in the bigness of his ears. Moving thus, Lord Onosh looked more like a creature from myth than a man; and Guest felt fragile, incompetent and childish by comparison.

So the Witchlord ventured forward. He drew level with the murkbeast.

And—

And took another step.

And abruptly lurched, and fell.

"Father!" shrieked Guest.

The cry was torn from him, as if with hooks. The murkbeast had the Witchlord! Had him, had seized him!

And Guest, in shamed horror, found himself rooted to the spot, paralyzed by his own terror. He could not do the manly thing. He could not dare the forward step, even though his father was down, was—

Was—

Was getting up ...

"Uh," said Lord Onosh, grunting.

Then he spat out mud.

Then he turned to Guest, and said:

"There are little brutes in imitation of the big one. A little one grabbed me, but my hand was enough for its strangulation."

Guest was still unable to speak, but grunted, hoping his grunt did not betray too much of his wet and shit-sliding terror.

"Come," said his father. "It's safe."

Obedient to this encouragement, Guest drew his sword and

began to venture toward his father.

The mud in the cave was particularly sticky, or so it seemed to Guest. His boots bogged deep with every footstep, and it was a physical effort to pull each foot free from the morass.

"Slowly," said Lord Onosh, sensing or seeing Guest's distress. "Slowly does it. Slow and steady."

"Slow and steady," said Guest, his voice trembling involuntarily as he took up that refrain.

Even as he said it, a tentacle uncurled itself in lazy leisure and reached out in Guest's direction.

"Careful," said his father, thinking the tentacle was but feinting.

Then the heavy weight of the tentacle slammed itself down on Guest's shoulder, slapped home in a positively convivial manner, then abruptly whipped itself around his neck and started to tighten.

"Gah!" said Guest, with a choked cry barely a hair's-breath from strangulation.

The tentacle was pulling on him. Not with any unduly monstrous force, but with a sufficiency of effort to shortly secure his death.

Guest had been judged by the murkbeast, and condemned, and sentenced to death by hanging!

When he realized that, the Weaponmaster became icy calm. The worst had happened. The murkbeast had him.

So.

When a dog seizes upon your hand, you must not pull it away, for that is what the dog is expecting. Rather, you must plunge that hand fiercely down the dog's throat, and use the other hand to destroy the brute which has seized you.

So thinking, Guest ceased to resist. With a mighty lunge, he hurled himself at the murkbeast. Taken by surprise, its tentacle momentarily slackened. By rights, Guest should have used the slackening to attack the murkbeast. But — weakened by fear, and by long habit of irresolution — the Weaponmaster yielded to the entirely human impulse to free the slack of the tentacle from his neck.

By trying to do so, he lost his chance. The murkbeast recovered itself, fed strength into the tentacle, held Guest tight, then abruptly jerked him off his feet and hauled him towards its gaping toad-mouth.

"Father!" screamed Guest.

But his father could not help him now. The murkbeast had him, and would engulf him in moments, sucking him down to a suffocating doom, or breaking him with its bone-munching strength.

CHAPTER THIRTY-SEVEN

Cornucopia: horn of plenty rumoured to lie in the Stench Caves of Logthok Norgos. Many people have died questing for this legendary generator of wealth, most notoriously Uri the Valorous, far-famed master of insouciant courage. It is possible that the murkbeast which dwells near the entrance to the caves bears much of the responsibility for the 100 per cent fatality rate among cornucopia-questers. The above-mentioned murkbeast currently has Guest Gulkan by the ankle, is dragging him towards its maw, and looks set to munch him down in moments.

* * *

As Guest Gulkan screamed, the murkbeast wrenched him towards its maw. With one convulsive spasm of strength, it got his booted foot inside its mouth.

Then stopped.

"Gods, gods, gods," sobbed Guest.

Lazily, the murkbeast tasted his boot.

So there was Guest Gulkan, down on his elbows in the muck, his sword in his hand but in no position to strike. His foot was in the murkbeast's mouth. And it was ... it was making up its mind. Thanks to its prodigious strength, the murkbeast could tear its prisoner from limb to limb had it so wished. But the thing had bruited down a sating surfeit of the Mutilator's soldiers, and had no true appetite for further human flesh.

Even so, the thing was seriously considering gulleting Guest Gulkan as well. The murkbeast was like a small child which has stuffed itself with sweetmeats to the point of vomiting, but is still tempted by the gross and slimy glitter of a candied cherry, and deludes itself into thinking it can munch down that cherry while still escaping the painful and inevitable consequences of further gluttony.

"Help me!" said Guest, in a very whimper of uncontrolled and uncontrollable terror.

The cut-thrust heat of action was over. Time had slowed to a slow ooze, and in that ooze the Weaponmaster had all too much opportunity to consider the dreadfulness of his situation. Here we must remember that Guest Gulkan had already lost his limbs on one occasion, arms and legs having been torn away by the Great Mink in an arena in Chi'ash-lan. That being so, he knew the truth of pain, and knew that there is nothing worse.

"Be still," said Lord Onosh, urgently.

This was the most useless of all conceivable advice, for Guest was already being still. Very still. Furthermore, he had absolutely no intention of being anything else. But his studied quiescence did him no good at all. The tentacle wrapped round his ankle tightened. Then wrenched. Then pulled off his boot.

Guest screamed.

"Has it hurt you?" said the Witchlord.

That sobered Guest sufficiently to allow him to give voice to an obscenity. Upon which the murkbeast swallowed his boot, decided it liked leather, and helped itself to the other.

"The boots have gone," said Guest flatly. "It will be flesh and blood next."

At which, Lord Onosh hesitated. Then kicked something. Stooped. Grabbed something from the muck, and began to haul it towards the murkbeast.

"What are you doing?" said Guest.

"I'm—"

The murkbeast sucked roughly on Guest's feet.

"God's grief!" said Guest, sobbing in uncontrollable terror.

"Hold on, hold on," said his father. "I'm coming."

Indeed, the Witchlord was floundering through the mud with all the speed he could muster, dragging with him the corpse of one of the Mutilator's guards. As he closed the distance, Lord Onosh sheathed his sword and held the corpse in front of him as a shield.

The Witchlord's approach put the murkbeast in something of a minor quandary. If this dumb two-legged animal was going to walk right into its mouth, then there was no need for the murkbeast to waste time by capturing it. But what if it changed its mind? Best to make sure ...

So thinking, the murkbeast extended a lazy tentacle and grabbed the corpse which Lord Onosh was holding in front of him as a shield. Lord Onosh heaved mightily on that corpse. Thinking it held a living animal with its tentacle, and thinking that animal was struggling to get away, the murkbeast heaved mightily on the corpse, wrenched it from the Witchlord's grasp and hauled it towards its mouth.

Lord Onosh then tried to attack, thinking to close with the monster and kill it while it was corpse-consuming. But the mud was too thick, too clutching, and he was still floundering even as the murkbeast opened its mouth wide enough to swallow both Guest Gulkan and the corpse simultaneously.

Guest felt himself being sucked into the murkbeast's mouth.

"Your sword!" yelled his father. "You still have your sword!"

True.

Clutching his sword, Guest fought savagely, turning himself on to his back as he was sucked into the murkbeast's mouth. Clasping his sword with both hands, he turned the blade upwards.

Even as the murkbeast bit down.

The murkbeast munched down with full force, munched without thought, driving Guest Gulkan's sword upwards through the roof of its mouth. The pain of this unprecedented wound sent it into spasms. Caught still in its mouth, Guest was trapped by the wet, pumping lubrication of the murkbeast's spasming organ of absorption. He was being stifled, pulped, crushed. He could not breathe. A huge heat was drowning him, was—

"Ya!"

The shout was the Witchlord's, a shout of wrath, a shout so loud that Guest heard it even in his confinement. With that shout, the Witchlord drove his sword deep into the murkbeast's guard-glutted stalk.

This rupture of its belly was more than the murkbeast could stand. Insane with pain, it vomited up the contents of its gut. Guest was ejected in a hurtling spurt which saw him thrown to the mud, with a rain of corpse-mash splattering down on him.

Then the murkbeast collapsed in a shuddering heap, and Lord Onosh grabbed his son and dragged him to safety.

"Gods," said Guest, when his father released him. "I'm—"

"Hush down," said the Witchlord. "Hush down, and still. Lie still, and rest ..."

Whereupon his son, needing no further introduction, flopped like a rag doll. A very muddy, wet, dishevelled rag doll. A barefooted rag doll.

Even after all the trauma he had so recently suffered, the Weaponmaster had wit enough to lament the loss of his boots, for an underground warren like the Stench Caves was sure to be prodigiously productive of things which could tear the feet.

"Well," said Lord Onosh, at length, "at least we're through the worst of it."

"Are we?" said Guest.

"We got past the — the thing," said Lord Onosh.

"The murkbeast," said Guest.

"You had heard of it?" said Lord Onosh.

"I had not heard of it," said Guest, "but my many travels have made me adroit in putting names to unknown things. We will call it the murkbeast."

"The eater of many men," said Lord Onosh.

"Doubtless," said Guest. "But it can hardly have eaten everyone."

Many people had quested into the Stench Caves in search of the cornucopia. None had survived. Guest doubted that a mere murkbeast could have been sufficient for the destruction of so many heroes — for, after all, the murkbeast had not proved a match for two brawny Yarglat barbarians, and some of those who had quested into the Stench Caves had gone in great companies, strongly armed and surely proof against all but the worst of violence.

"You are very much the pessimist today," said Lord Onosh. "So I hope you won't be too offended if I give you some good news."

"What good news?" said Guest.

"I spy light," said his father. "White light. Over there."

With that, Lord Onosh pointed in a direction which might have been north, south, east or west — there was no telling precisely which, for both Witchlord and Weaponmaster had got hopelessly turned around in their underground adventuring.

"It is white light, yes," said Guest. "A good change from this liquid vomit of green which pours down upon us. Very well, then. I am ready for the journey."

"So let's be going," said his father — spuriously, but the Witchlord found himself reluctant to let his son claim the initiative.

With that, the pair set off towards the white light, which grew to a steady promise, a promise which was fulfilled when they gained the safety of a tunnel smooth-walled, level, flat and warm. In that tunnel, there was music — quiet music, not like the roiling measures of the musicians of Sung, but subtle easings reminiscent of the drift of the sea, and backed by a leisured pulse which spoke of the womb at midnight.

The light which lit this tunnel was that of mother-of-pearl: a gleaming gloss with something of the restfulness of grey about it. Into this restfulness there ventured the two Yarglat barbarians. Both had lost their swords in the battle with the murkbeast, though they still had knives, throwing stars, eye-gouging handscrews, darning needles and packets of pepper. And Guest still had — it was safe in a buckle-down sheath — the bead-tipped blade which he had stolen from the Mutilator.

Thus armed, the pair proceeded down the corridor, looking like two mud-splattered lunatics who had escaped from an asylum by way of a swamp. They had the wary look of men for whom the world has become a place of hallucinatory shock, of untrustworthy delusion, of tripwire and deadfall.

Yet ...

The swooming music continued its sundering lunder-munder melody, drowsing all with restfulness; and the tunnel was pleasantly warm, with the nondescript grey tiles assuming a similar warmth beneath Guest Gulkan's naked feet; and the way was clear, and ...

"Stop," said Lord Onosh.

Guest stopped immediately.

"There's a ... a rat or something," said Lord Onosh.

"Where?" said Guest, looking down the corridor, which curved subtly as it disappeared into the distance.

"There's a door," said Lord Onosh. "Do you see it?"

Even as the Witchlord spoke, an animal ventured from a door some thirty paces away.

"It is a rat," said Guest.

"A tame rat, perhaps," said Lord Onosh.

"We'll see," said Guest.

And with that, the two advanced upon the small creature, which made no move to run away. It was certainly built along the general lines of a rat, but as they approached it sat up on its hindpaws, and seemed quite comfortable in that posture. Guest studied the beast with caution, knowing that a wild animal that is over-friendly may well have rabies.

He remembered an episode from way back in his past, when, in the early years of his youth, he had ventured down from the Ibsen-Iktus Mountains in the company of the witch Zelafona, her dwarfson Glambrax and others. Glambrax had been bitten by a dog believed to be rabid, which had occasioned a great lecture from Sken-Pitilkin on the subject of rabies.

"This thing may be diseased," said Guest. "As the fox from the forest which licks your hand may be dooming you to death by rabies, so too may this thing."

"Perhaps," said Lord Onosh. "But it looks a pleasant enough creature."

This was so odd, coming from the Witchlord, that Guest Gulkan half-wondered whether the soothing background music had addled his father's head. But ... well, it had to be admitted that the thing in front of them was certainly layered with cuteness, so much so that Guest was hardly sure whether it was any kind of rat at all.

"It's soft," said Guest, who was by now almost within grabbing distance of the thing. "And a little bit plump."

"A rat well-fed," said his father.

"I'm not a rat," said the beast, sounding very offended.

The quokka spoke in Eparget, the very Yarglat tongue in which Witchlord and Weaponmaster had been conversing. To hear the creature speak shocked both barbarians to silence.

Lord Onosh sucked in breath through his teeth.

And Guest—

Guest found himself sweating. He reminded himself that there are no such things as talking animals. Guest remembered Sken-Pitilkin telling him as much. There are no talking animals, just as there are no orcs, elves or leprechauns. They are things of fantasy, things which have no place in our world of mud and blood and toil and disease, of sickness and failure, of human frailty and invincible death.

Yet!

"You," said the Witchlord, heavily, "you are a rat."

"I am not!" protested the beast.

"What are you, then?" said Guest, feeling himself dragged into this conversation rather against his better judgement.

"I'm a quokka."

"A quokka?" said Guest. "What in the name of Behenial is a quokka?"

"What, for that matter, is Behenial?" said his father.

"Behenial," said Guest, "is one of the gods my good friend Rolf Thelemite used to swear by. Now, by the name of Behenial — what are you, quokka-thing?"

"I'm a philosopher," said the quokka.

"I asked not of your profession but of your species," said Guest. "Of your species, your kind. What manner of thing is a quokka?"

"It is a marsupial," said the quokka.

"And," said Guest Gulkan, unable to keep himself from asking the next and most obvious question, "what then is a marsupial?"

"A kind of rat, obviously," said his father. "Shall you kill it or shall I?"

"I will," said Guest.

"No!" squealed the quokka.

And fled.

Now it might be thought that Witchlord and Weaponmaster had better things to do than hunt after a small furry animal — even an animal which spoke. But both were in a mood for a meal, and both remembered the most excellent taste of the roast rat which had been served to them before their entry into the nethermost depths of the Stench Caves. Accordingly, they set themselves to pursue the quokka-rat, which fled down a side tunnel which led into a—

Witchlord and Weaponmaster halted at the end of the side tunnel, and gaped at the vast chamber into which it led.

It was a huge chamber, lit by trumpeting radiance, and dominated by a gigantic multi-tiered banqueting table, the most enormous banqueting table which ever was. It was gorgeous with the orange of oranges, the red gloss of apples, a cascade of cucumbers awash in a river of rain-flushed lettuce leaves. Wine winked in a constellation of crystal vases. Milk and honey ran in rivers. And there were cakes, cakes loaded with cherries, bulging with almonds, adorned with marzipan. And there were cones of sugar, absolute cones of it, fantastically expensive, the height of luxury.

"Grief of a dog!" said Lord Onosh in astonishment.

Then made as if to enter.

But to Guest, this place had an ugly familiarity. It was familiarity by analogy. The Stench Caves were an underworld, a veritable Downstairs, and in this underground was something possessed of an uncommon linguistic fluency, and associated with this was an intoxicating allurement which was analogous to—

"No!" said Guest, grabbing his father.

He grabbed so roughly that the Witchlord at first feared his son to be intent on murder, and tried to break free.

"Let go!" said Lord Onosh.

"No, no," said Guest desperately. "You can't go in, it's murder."

"If it will make you happy," said Lord Onosh, with an ill grace, "then I'll stand here all day and slaver. But come tomorrow, I'll go in and eat!"

"Tomorrow?" said the quokka. "Why wait for tomorrow? What's the matter? Come in! Come in! There are good things to eat!"

"Then, little thing," said Guest, watching the animal closely, "pray be so kind enough as to fetch me a small portion of one of those good things."

The quokka hesitated. Its nose twitched nervously. Guest detected this petty betrayal and knew the thing to be a liar.

"We know what this is," said Guest.

"It's a feast," said the quokka.

"No it isn't," said Guest.

"It is, it is!" said the quokka, with insistent fervour.

"No," said Guest, stamping the word with definitive negativeness. "It's not a banquet. It's a therapist."

"A therapist?" said the quokka innocently. "What on earth is a therapist?"

"Come here," said Guest. "Come to my clutches, and I'll show you exactly what a therapist is!"

At that, the quokka ventured forward. In the most affecting manner imaginable, it ventured to place its very paw upon Guest Gulkan's mud-clad shin.

"Will you starve yourself for suspicion?" said the quokka. "As I trust you, won't you trust me?"

The animal was so trusting, and so surpassingly cute, that it was enough to make the heart melt. Any civilized person would have trusted it immediately. But Guest was a barbarian, a Yarglat barbarian, and one who had lately been terrorized by a murkbeast, and so was in no mood to be merciful. He snatched at the quokka, seized it and shook it — his hand at its throat! — then squeezed it so hard that it squealed. Red blood stained its teeth.

At which, a voice of moiling thunder spoke, a voice underwritten with subsonic threat:

"Let it go!"

Guest did no such thing, but turned to view the banqueting chamber. The banquet had entirely disappeared. In its place stood a towering conglomeration of slowly evolving windmills, of spindling bones and twirling tapes of metal, of skeletal steel and huge beams around which spheres and cones went twining.

"Wah!" said Lord Onosh, taken aback. "What is it?"

"I am a Great God," said the dull-roar voice. "You have displeased me! Fall down on your knees and repent!"

Now when one is confronted by a Great God, and a Great God which is manifestly some ten thousand times larger than an elephant, then one's natural reaction is to do what it says. So Lord Onosh quite naturally went down on his knees.

But Guest Gulkan — who had had far more to do with gods and demons of all descriptions than had his father — gripped his father by his muddy black hair and wrenched him to his feet. Then Guest spat on the floor. Lord Onosh expected that the Great God would retaliate by obliterating them on the spot, but it did no such thing.

Guest Gulkan then addressed the apparition in front of him.

"You are no god," said Guest. "You are but a wretched therapist, a torturing machine, and once I get out of here then all the world will know of you."

Then, as the therapist roared with anger, and thrashed at the Weaponmaster with every spike, prong, hook and tentacle at its disposal — finding him, however, some several paces beyond its grasp — Guest retreated, taking the quokka with him.

Once Guest and his father were safe in the main tunnel, Lord Onosh asked the obvious question.

"That thing," said Lord Onosh. "How did you know what it was?"

"Because," said Guest, "I met a great family of such things on the island of Untunchilamon. They breed there in their thousands, as do huge crabs some ten times the height of a man, and the flying bubbles which men call shabbles."

Then, having delivered himself of that geographical information, Guest Gulkan set about interrogating the quokka.

"Thing," said Guest, "I suspect that the therapist bred you."

To this, the quokka made no answer.

"In nature," said Guest, "there are no such things as talking animals. It follows that you speak through some resource of the therapist. Either you are an extension of the very therapist itself, or else it has somehow tutored your animal brain to enhance it to the point where speech is one of its capabilities."

Lord Onosh could not quite follow this argument. This is hardly surprising. For Lord Onosh was but poorly educated, whereas his son had long been tutored by Hostaja Sken-Pitilkin, most excellent and sagacious of all the wizards of Skatzabratzumon. Furthermore, Guest Gulkan had resided for four years in the halls of Cap Foz Para Lash, where he had been introduced to many notions which were alien to his father — such as the idea that a machine of sufficient subtlety could insinuate its processes into the brain of an animal then animate that animal as a puppet.

"If you are but an extension of the therapist," said Guest, in a conversational tone of voice, "then doubtless your death will mean nothing, for you are but a fingernail."

"Quokka," said the quokka, getting that word out in defiance of Guest's choking pressure.

"I was speaking by way of analogy," said Guest. "You know the analogies? My good tutor Sken-Pitilkin was very big on the analogies, though I must say I never saw their use till today."

Ah!

Take note!

It is said that, as we go through life, we slowly accumulate wisdom. In Guest Gulkan's life there had so far been precious little sign of this process — till now! On this day of days, he had saved his own life by arguing by analogy, and had saved the life of his father too. Had Guest not been adroit with his analogies, then both Witchlord and Weaponmaster would surely have already been dangling upside down while a chortling therapist gouged out their eyes.

Let us then open the Book of Morals, and record in that Book the supremacy of the philosophies, for it was the application of philosophy that had saved Guest Gulkan's life, saving him from a doom against which the strength of his sword would have availed him not (even presuming him to have had a sword, and of course he had none, having lost his steel to the murkbeast).

Doubtless, had Guest been philosopher sufficient, he could have resolved all his other difficulties with equal ease, sliding past the murkbeast without getting so much as the smallest splattering of mud upon his hide, discovering the cornucopia and then securing his exit from the Stench Caves.

But, since Guest's wisdom had yet to reach its full flowering, he had to solve his remaining problems by using a non-philosophical mode of operation. This he did by further squeezing the quokka.

"Quokka," repeated the quokka.

"A quokka, are you?" said Guest. "Then I tell you this. You will very shortly be a dead quokka unless you bind yourself to my service. I once hung three men. In the village of Ink, that's where it was. I hung them high in a consequence of the damage they did to me and mine. They brought our lives into peril by selling us rotten boats. Just as I hung those men, so I will hang you, for I think you a menace as great, if not greater."

"Quokka," said the quokka.

"Are you pretending to be imbecile?" said Guest. "Well, if you are, then you will die as an imbecile. Father! A bootlace! I will hang this thing, and now!"

Then Lord Onosh consented to free one of his bootlaces, something not easily done, for the thing had tightened after getting wet, and the Witchlord broke two fingernails getting it free. But with the bootlace free, Guest Gulkan made a hangman's knot — he had learnt that art from Thodric Jarl — and placed the noose around the quokka's neck.

At which the animal broke down entirely, and began to cry.

Have you seen a rat cry? No? Then imagine it. It is the most lugubrious of sights. But it left Guest Gulkan entirely unmoved.

"Since you weep," said Guest, "then I presume you to be a creature in your own right, presumably one tutored beyond its natural temperament by injection of nanotechnological manipulators."

By this phrase "nanotechnological manipulators", Guest

Gulkan meant "very small insect-like working-things made of steel". To say this, he did not use the Eparget of the Yarglat, for the Yarglat have little use for nanotechnology. Instead, Guest inserted into his conversation a fragment of alien nomenclature which he had absorbed in the halls of Cap Foz Para Lash in the city of Dalar ken Halvar.

On hearing the words "nanotechnological manipulators" phrased in that alien nomenclature, the quokka flinched as if burnt.

"Aha!" said Guest. "It confesses its nature, does it?"

"I confess nothing," said the quokka sullenly.

"Then I will hang you," said Guest.

"If you hang me," said the quokka, "then you'll die. You can't get out of here alone."

"Well then," said Guest, "if I must die, I'll at least have the satisfaction of having one last meal before I do die."

With that, the Weaponmaster rose to his full height, and raised the bootlace. The quokka was dragged upwards on to the tips of its toes. It squealed as the noose tightened. Guest eased off the pressure — just a trifle.

"All right, all right!" said the quokka. "I'll show you, I'll show you! I'll show you the way out! But. But. You have to promise me. You have to promise not to kill me."

"You have my word," said Guest. "I give you my oath upon it. I swear by my honour. I will not kill you, nor do you any other harm. But — but! This oath is conditional. To be honoured with your life, you must find us the cornucopia."

"The cornucopia?" said the quokka scornfully. "There's no such thing."

"Then," said Guest, again tightening the bootlace, "you will very shortly find yourself equally non-existent."

At that, the quokka was at last persuaded, and, with uncommonly little fuss and difficulty, it guided them first to the cornucopia — which was hidden in the heart of a three-dimensional maze which would have perplexed the intellect of any five dozen mathematicians put together — then led them to a gnarled flight of derelict stone stairs which led upward.

"Your liberty is at the top of these stairs," said the quokka. "But as for me — this is as far as I go."

"Very well," said Guest. "Father mine, it is time for you to hang this quokka."

"Hang me!" said the quokka, in great distress. "But you swore to preserve me!"

"I swore to do you no harm," said Guest, demonstrating his rapidly advancing philosophical prowess by a strict application of logic. "That is not the same as preserving you. I will be true to my oath. I will do you no harm. It is my father who will do you harm."

"I doubt it," said the Witchlord.

"What?" said Guest, startled.

"You may amuse yourself by hanging this rat, if you wish," said Lord Onosh, "but I think it beneath my dignity."

"Dignity!" said Guest. "We're not talking dignity. We're talking of law! This thing has led men to their deaths, I'm sure of it. Are we to let it free to lead more men to destruction?"

Here Guest had a point. It was undeniably true that the quokka had tried to lead both Witchlord and Weaponmaster to their deaths; and, in all probability, if released it would encompass the death of anyone else who found their way into the Stench Caves. So it was necessary to hang it. Hanging is an ugly business, and in an ordered society there would be no need for it, since an ordered society would have an Inspector of Boats to regulate the sale of boats and an Inspector of Caves to regulate the governance of Stench Caves.

But as Guest Gulkan lived in a singularly disordered age, a great age of darkness in which competent Inspectors and other regulatory bureaucrats were singularly thin on the ground, he must necessarily be put to the trouble of undertaking the singularly brutal business of hanging in order to serve the ends of justice and preserve the lives of the unwary.

So the quokka was duly hung; and, having been hung, it was eaten. Raw. For Witchlord and Weaponmaster did not have a tinderbox between them; and, besides, they were in no mood to waste time on unnecessary cookery.

Having eaten the quokka — not all of it, for they were not hungry enough to trouble themselves with the guts, and they discarded the fur and the bones — Witchlord and Weaponmaster ventured up the stairs.

At the top of the stairs, the two Yarglat barbarians found themselves at the bottom of a huge pit. Honest sunlight beamed down on them from the top of the pit — it was by Guest's reckoning late afternoon — but the walls of the pit were quite unclimbable.

Witchlord and Weaponmaster climbed to the small mound of rubble in the middle of the pit, a mound made of rocks and of bones, of stones and of dirt, of the droppings of bats and the feathers of vultures. Guest saw something which he thought he recognized. He picked it up. It was a skull.

"So much for that!" said Guest, tossing the skull away.

The quokka had betrayed them!

Realizing this, Guest greatly regretted having persuaded his father to hang the brute. He had discovered one of the great drawbacks of hanging, which is this: supposing you hang a person, and that person then proves to be a greater criminal than you thought, why, it is impossible to recall them so you can escalate their punishment. This is why, under many of those regimes which do practise hanging, convicted criminals are kept under lock and key for as much as ten or twenty years, to allow the authorities time to prove out any greater crimes of which they may be guilty.

"We have at least the cornucopia," said the Witchlord, trying to be encouraging.

"So we do," said Guest. "So we do."

But he thought of the possession of this magical device as a totally inadequate compensation for being marooned at the bottom of an unclimbable pit somewhere in the Stench Caves of Logthok Norgos.

So thinking, Guest let the cornucopia fall, then kicked it as it fell. It flopped into the air then sprawled flat on the ground.

The cornucopia was a piece of wrinkled green leather the length of Guest's forearm. It was shaped like a hollow cone, and nothing could be seen within it except a voluminous blackness. It was flexible, and could be comfortably folded up and stuck in one's pocket, and it worked as advertised — that is to say, it duplicated anything which might be put into it. Guest had already tested it by spitting into it and getting it to duplicate his dribble in a constant stream.

"Since we've got time on our hands," said the Witchlord, "you might make use of that thing to make me a ring."

"A ring?" said Guest.

"Yes," said his father. "A ring of ever-ice. Or are we to fight over the one you're wearing on your finger?"

"That's a thought," said Guest.

So he took the ring from his finger, sucked on it to remove all crusted mud, spat out the mud, picked up the cornucopia, held it upright, then popped the ring of ever-ice into the voluminous darkness.

Then Guest turned the cornucopia upside down.

Out fell the ring of ever-ice.

Followed by a twin of itself.

Then a triplet.

Then, in a cascading rush, some seven or eight thousand rings came pouring from the cornucopia, piling up around their ankles in a clickering chittering turbulence.

"Whoa!" cried the Witchlord in alarm.

Guest jerked the cornucopia to the upright, thus cutting off the flow of rings.

"Wah!" he said.

Then stooped to inspect the hoard at his feet.

"Why," said Guest in disgust, picking up a handful of rings, "they're rusted!"

And it was true.

The rings were rotten rounds of rust, each with a glob of rust where the original had displayed a chip of ever-ice. But where was the original?

"Where is my ring?" said Guest.

"It was probably the first to fall out," said his father. "It fell at your feet, so — don't move!"

Then Guest stooped to the scrapmetal nightmare at his feet, and rummaged through it with an avaricious diligence. Not all of the rings proved rusty, and some were tolerable counterfeits of the original. But Guest eventually located the one true ring of ever-ice, which could be told from all the others because only the true ring shone with its own inner light.

"Gods!" said Guest, kicking his way clear of the trash-dump rubbish heap. "What a let down!"

And so it was.

"Have you a coin about you?" said Guest.

"No," said his father.

But Guest had already guessed that the cornucopia would not prove an adequate counterfeiter of coinage.

"Time for us to be going," said the Witchlord.

"Where?" said his son.

"If we presume that this treacherous quokka has done its best to defeat our escape," said Lord Onosh, "then our best bet is to go back the way we came."

"If we can remember it," said Guest. "Well then! Lead on! I'm ready!"

But Lord Onosh chose to take a piss before leading on, making Guest realize that it was time for him to do the same himself. Obedient to nature's necessities, Guest pissed ... and was childish enough to try to fill the cornucopia with his outflow.

"What are you doing?" said Lord Onosh, when he turned to see Guest at play with a pissing cornucopia.

"I am—"

Guest was about to come up with some justification for his behaviour, but did not, for the trickle of urine which was exiting from the cornucopia in his hands suddenly abrupted into a vomiting outflow which made the cornucopia plunge and buck, so that it took all his strength to hold the thing.

The outflow knocked the Witchlord off his feet, and he went rolling away for a dozen paces before he recovered himself and stood. Lord Onosh tried to find words for his rage:

"You — you — you—"

The Witchlord was so profoundly angry he was quite speechless. And Guest—

"Gods!" said Guest, half-shocked, half-intrigued by the strength with which the flux of fluid was bolting from the cornucopia. "It's increasing!"

Indeed, the force of the outsurge from the cornucopia was increasing to such an extent that dirt, stones and entire rocks were blown away where the yellow flux impacted.

"Guest!" said Lord Onosh. "Will you stop that!"

"I will not!" yelled Guest.

"Then if you don't—"

"Yes!" said Guest. "Tell me what happens if I don't!"

"If you don't," said Lord Onosh, raising his voice to make himself heard over the pounding shock-splatter of the cornucopia's high-pressure vomiting, "then I'll — I'll—"

Then the Witchlord fell silent.

He was starting to think.

The Witchlord stared with wild surmise at the ever-intensifying torrent which was blasting from the cornucopia. A veritable stream of urine was pounding away, trying to escape from the nearest tunnel, and already it was plain that the tunnel would be hard put to drain the flux if it increased any further.

There then followed a long and very tedious siege of automated pissing, as father and son took turns at holding the cornucopia, keeping it pointing downwards so it would continue to output its surges.

Sitting atop the small mound in the centre of the great pit, father and son worked the evening through, and maintained this great labour of hosing all through the following night. But when dawn came, they at last admitted defeat, and raised the cornucopia to the vertical, thus cutting off the flow of urine.

"It is no good," said Guest, sadly folding up the cornucopia. "There are too many holes in this pit."

So there were, so there were.

Though the whole pit was one reeking yellowish pool of piss, in which the central mound was a small and forlorn island, there was no hope of the flood filling the pit as a whole and thus floating Witchlord and Weaponmaster to freedom. Even as they watched, the piss-level began to drop by perceptible degrees.

"It is escaping," said Guest.

"Yes," said his father. "But where?"

"All waters from the Stench Caves drain from the Nijidith River," said Guest. "Or so I was told."

"I was briefed likewise," said his father. "So, if there is but one outlet from this hell-hole, then the waters will surely lead us out of it."

"A man would have to be very brave to venture this flood," said Guest speculatively, looking at the sinuous lines of strength which marked the currents generated by the swift-draining urine.

"A man would have to be braver yet to stay here and starve," said his father. "I am thirsty, and I have not drunk. I am hungry, and I have not eaten. I am tired, and I have not slept, nor do I expect to sleep in a pit which stinks as much as this one."

"You are right," said Guest, conceding his own hunger, thirst and fatigue. "We'd best be going, and now."

There were three things which Guest wished to preserve in the journey ahead. One was the ring of ever-ice, which should be safe enough on his finger. The second was the knife he had stolen from Aldarch the Third, which ... well, it was in a buckle-down sheath, and if that was not good enough then there was no way Guest could improve its security.

But what of the cornucopia?

How was he going to keep that safe?

"I'll keep that in my boot," said Lord Onosh, seeing Guest looking speculatively at the cornucopia.

Guest was most reluctant to surrender the thing, but could not think of a safer way to manage its transit. So he handed it over to his father, who took off his right boot. On his right foot, Lord Onosh was wearing two pairs of woollen socks. In their own lands, the Yarglat are accustomed to prepare the foot for the boot by winding a long bandage around it, but such foot-bindings were not the fashion in the Izdimir Empire, and it was that Empire which had equipped the Witchlord for this particular mission.

Lord Onosh took off his own socks, then forced his foot into the cornucopia. Guest thought this a most unwise procedure, but his father came to no harm from it.

With the cornucopia acting as a singularly odd and ill-fitting sock, Lord Onosh crammed his foot back into his boot — not without difficulty! — and laced up that boot with the very same bootlace which had recently been used to hang a quokka.

Then father and son plunged into the swirling waters — they both of them tried most strenuously to think of the flux which faced them as being a flux of water — and began a journey into nightmare. Down they went, sucked away by the swirling currents of drainage, plummeted down a huge sewerpipe where darkness ground darkness in a throttling cacophony of buffeting backspray and jolting collision. Skleetering rats screamed and clawed in the frothing upswirl which rammed them against the roofs of caverns then slammed them down drop-pipes, floated them through caverns loud with the guttural glorp of sideline discharges, then sent them screaming over impromptu waterfalls.

Sometimes Guest saw — or thought he saw — his father's green-sheened face. But sometimes he saw nothing, for sometimes the hot flux plunged him into a roaring darkness where breathing was an intermittent luxury, where rocks rubbed him, where rapids tried to kick him to bits with a billion boots, and where Things with leathery wings went screeching overhead — for all the world as if Guest Gulkan's ears had liberated themselves and, each taking flight from its perch, multiplied themselves in flight until their strength was legion.

After a while, Guest Gulkan no longer knew whether he was alive or dead, awake or awrath in nightmare. He was swept from one passage of temporary strangulation to the next, was boiled, vomited, plunged, purged, gobleted, zorded, rambleskinned and rumped, was battered by the slurping outpour of a million billion bowls of soup, was shocked by the sundering waves of five oceans and a dozen seas, was—

Was shocked at last to the daylight, was vomited out from

the dark, was plunged down the boiling thrash of the Nijidith River, and then was swashed away downstream in the company of shattered bits of tables, chairs, doors, gates, gods and shrines, dead kittens and half-chewed cockroaches, dishrags and begging bowls, the underwear of drowned priests and the straw sandals of doomed peasants.

Floating on his back, Guest was slewed around by the sun, cartwheeled by the hallucinatory daylight, overawed by skies of a blue so wide it was beyond his imagination.

Was this life?

It seemed it was.

But—

What a world! And what a life!

The banks of the river were a wasteland of the torn and tattered, a wasteland of mulched houses and slewed shacks, of canted temples and drowned corpses, of groaning cattle and struggling pigs half-drowned in pits of morass. Finding his strength, or what was left of it, Guest struck out for the nearest shore, and hauled himself up on to the bog of undry land, there to grapple with the oppressive physicality of cold slime and stinking slush.

He was unslaked, unfed, and overwashed, and his father was missing, was nowhere to be seen, so what should he be doing first?

As Guest was still wondering, a body came floating downstream, face upturned to the sun, and he realized it was his father, and realized the man was dead.

CHAPTER THIRTY-EIGHT

Nijidith River: a flux of filth which flows out from Stench Caves and down to Lake Kak, that singularly unpristine body of water on the shores of which stands the city of Obooloo, capital of the Izdimir Empire.

* * *

Guest Gulkan dragged his father from the river. It was him! It was him! Guest smoothed his hand over the steep slope of his father's forehead, feeling beneath his fingers the corrugations of the deep ridges gouged in the bone of that forehead, ridges which ran from hairline to eyebrows. He was too devastated to weep.

As Guest sat there on the banks of the Nijidith river, kneeling beside his father's corpse, that corpse opened its eyes.

"Wah!" said Guest, taken very much by surprise.

"So you too are dead," said Lord Onosh.

Guest thought about it a moment, then declared that, in his considered opinion, neither of them was dead, as unlikely as that might seem.

"I think you wrong," said Lord Onosh. "I think the pair of us certainly dead, for where could this be if it is not in hell?"

Now the Witchlord was being perfectly reasonable when he delivered himself of this opinion, for in all truth the landscape in which the two Yarglat barbarians were marooned did look very much like one of the uncouth outlands of hell.

Guest conceded as much.

"Yet," said Guest, "I believe us to be alive."

"Then all I can say," said his father, "is that it would be much more convenient if we were dead."

To this gloomy sentiment, Guest voiced no opposition. For survival was sheer depression in such a brutalized landscape, and all the Weaponmaster really wanted to do was to collapse. He was ragged with lack of sleep, his throat was sore, his belly was griping, and he was so severely bruised that to move was to inflict upon himself a savagery of suffering.

Yet, being disciplined in the necessities of war, both Witchlord and Weaponmaster did get themselves moving, and shambled along the riverbank, heading downstream until they saw what looked to be a surviving hut atop an unwashed knoll.

"The hut," said Guest, pointing it out.

"Huhn," grunted his father.

And no debate more complicated than that, the two bent their footsteps towards the hut, where they found a peasant family engaged in taking a meal.

There were eight or nine peasants — it was hard to count them exactly, since three or four of the smallest were sitting under an outside table at the feet of their elders — and one of these was a young woman who was breastfeeding a piglet. This scene of indulgence reminded Guest of another young woman — perhaps the very same one — whom he had seen performing a similar action while he was on his way to the Stench Caves.

"Hello," said Guest, trying to smile, and doing his best to look more like a man and less like a zombie.

He was greeted with blank incomprehension.

"Speak you the Galish Trading Tongue?" said Guest, voicing the question in that language.

The same mute, uncomprehending stares were echoed back to him by way of reply.

"Toxteth?" said Guest. "Galsh Ebrek. Wen Endex. Understand?"

In educated company, the names of places often rouse a response where other vocabulary fails, but none of these peasants was geographer enough to have heard of any place so foreign as Wen Endex.

"Never mind," said Lord Onosh. "We don't have to talk to them. We can take what we want."

"Can we?" said Guest, casting hungry eyes on the chickens which were grucking around under upturned baskets of loose-woven cane. "We have no swords, and I for one am in no mood for war."

"Never mind," said Lord Onosh.

Then the Witchlord took off his boot, pulled the cornucopia from his foot, and wrung out the cornucopia as best he could. None of the peasants reacted to the sight of this device, so Guest presumed they did not realize its import.

Having thus readied the cornucopia, Lord Onosh reached out and took a handful of soy beans from a cast-iron bowl which sat in the middle of the peasants' table. None of the peasants made any move to stop him, for he was bigger and brawnier than they were. Indeed, from the paralyzed steadfastness of their silence, Guest deduced that they thought both Witchlord and Weaponmaster to be ghouls or demons, and not creatures to be challenged or otherwise trifled with.

Having seized a handful of soy beans, Lord Onosh let them fall into the cornucopia, then upended the thing.

A dribble of soy beans spilt from the cornucopia's crumpled green cone. Then, with a rustling hiss, a cascade of beans slewed forth, piling up around the Witchlord's feet. Suddenly, Lord Onosh began to laugh. Despite his fatigue, his hunger, his unappeased thirst, he was enraptured by the sheer childish pleasure of working a miracle. Such was his engrossment in this task that he walked right round the hut, spilling out a track of soy beans.

"Enough!" said Guest.

At which his father brought the cornucopia to the vertical. It made a terminal grockling sound as it swallowed anything that was left inside it, then was silent. Empty.

At all this, the peasants sat and stared, for these shenanigans were totally beyond their experience, and they had no repertoire of reaction which was adequate to the occasion. Then a full-grown pig came porking up the slope to the hut, and began to trough its way through the spilt soy beans, eating with a sanguine confidence which persuaded the peasants to follow suit.

As the peasants started in on the soy beans — tentatively at first, as if fearing that what was undenied to a pig might yet be denied to them — Witchlord and Weaponmaster seated themselves at the table and helped themselves to long and greedy draughts of potable water. As if realizing that their guests might be human beings, and human beings sorely beset by adversity, the oldest of the female peasants — a venerable materfamilias with a face seamed like a grey mudswamp in a time of drought — began to fuss around them. Before she was through, a pair of straw sandals had been procured for Guest's sore feet, and the food on the table had been supplemented by a bowl of boiled potatoes and a plate of raw mushrooms.

Comforted by this attention, both Witchlord and Weaponmaster began to start to feel human again. They ate prodigiously, downing handfuls of soy beans. Working away at the munchiness of those beans, Guest found they brought back memories of Dalar ken Halvar, where he had often eaten the same provender.

The peasants relaxed, chattering away to each other in their own language. Listening to these grey-skinned Janjuladoola people talking in the Janjuladoola tongue, the two Yarglat barbarians were painfully reminded of the fact that they were marooned on a foreign continent where they spoke not a word of the dominant language, and where they were unlikely to run into more than an occasional smattering of people who spoke their own native Eparget.

Consequently, there was absolutely no point in whoring off into the hinterland in the hopes of somehow finding a way off the continent by land or sea. They did not know the language; they had no money; and they would draw undue attention to themselves if they went around routinely performing miracles with the cornucopia.

There remained to them but one sensible course of action: to follow the Nijidith to Obooloo, which city could reasonably be expected to have been disordered by flood, and in that city to venture to Achaptipop, the great rock which sustained the Sanctuary of the Bondsman's Guild. If they could only win admission to the Bank, then the Circle of the Partnership Banks would take them to Dalar ken Halvar, where Guest's wife Penelope was surely waiting for his return, and then on to Alozay, where Lord Onosh had his kingdom.

"If," said Guest, as they discussed this, "your kingdom has not been somehow subverted or overthrown in your absence."

"I doubt very much that it has been," said Lord Onosh. "For Sod was a hostage on Alozay, and Bao Gahai was in charge of his custody."

Guest thought this a less than adequate guarantee of the security of his father's kingdom, but did not dispute with him. Nor did he dispute with his father when Lord Onosh retained the cornucopia — seeming to think it his own property. While Guest was greatly displeased at his father's presumption, he thought that now was not the time for a confrontation over the matter, so held his tongue on the journey to Obooloo.

Witchlord and Weaponmaster travelled cautiously, taking time to rest, sleep and scavenge in accordance with their requirements, and so it was dawn on a summer's day when they finally entered the city of Obooloo.

The city was beset by a dreadful desolation. The whole city was one reeking morass of urine, and nobody moved in the streets. One might have thought the population dead, but for constant and unnerving wailing which arose from ten thousand buildings. It was the wailing of sinners beseeching the gods for mercy.

For the people of Obooloo knew nothing of Guest's discovery of the cornucopia and his use of it. All they knew was that the gods had pissed on their city, filling the Nijidith with a torrent of filth which had caused Lake Kak to rise and storm the city with sundering pollution. Now, in dread, the people of Obooloo tried to stave off a repeat performance, or to advert the imminent end of the world which so many of them feared.

So Witchlord and Weaponmaster proceeded without opposition into the heart of the city, guided by the great rock Achaptipop, which landmarked the way when they were confused by the backstreet bafflings of this alien urbanisation. But their progress towards Achaptipop took them inevitably closer to the Temple of Blood, and when Guest realized he was in the presence of that building — which was unmistakable, since there was no other great building immediately south of

Achaptipop — he drew his father's attention to the fact.

"You're not thinking of going in there, are you?" said Lord Onosh.

To Lord Onosh, the Temple of Blood was the place where he had been sorely wounded, then captured. To Lord Onosh, the Temple of Blood was the scene of one of the worst traumas of his life. But to Guest, the fighting in the Temple had been but a trifling incident. After all, what was a swordpoint brawl to a hero who has faced the Great Mink in a gladiatorial arena, who has dared the wrath of two therapists, and who has escaped alive from the very mouth of a murkbeast?

"If you're in such a great big hurry to get home," said Guest, "then go ahead. If that's what you want, I'll dare the temple on my own."

Whereupon his father produced the cornucopia, spat in it, and declared himself armed for the expedition. Carrying the cornucopia upright, the Witchlord then headed towards the Temple of Blood, declaring that any opposition would see the entire city digested by the outflux of his saliva.

Guest Gulkan thought his father's spittle to be but a poor weapon with which to defy the strength of a Temple, let alone the undiluted might of an entire city, but it was the best weapon they had. Their swords had been lost in the Stench Caves of Logthok Norgos, and since that loss they had met nobody from whom they could beg, borrow or steal any replacements. In particular, soldiers were so short on the ground that it was possible that perhaps the army had committed suicide en masse as an act of contrition for presumed offences against the gods.

With Lord Onosh bearing the cornucopia, Witchlord and Weaponmaster won their way to the Temple of Blood, and, entering by the unguarded southern gate, found the interior of that sacred place to be eerily silent.

They found their way to the central courtyard which held the Burning Pit, which was today very much an unburning pit — for it was full of squelched ashes. Amidst those ashes, Guest saw a ribcage, a cracked skull and a thighbone. Turning his face from these grim tokens of piety, he looked up — and realized that the southern face of the great rock Achaptipop was covered with crawling figures. Like so many spiders, dozens of penitents were scaling the face of the cliff, as they always do when the city of Obooloo has suffered some great misfortune.

Those human spiders were climbing without ropes, and, even as Guest watched, one slipped and fell. In utter silence. Guest listened, but heard no scream, no sound of impact — nothing but the unending wail of ten thousand mourners and the hoarse gutturals of a distant shout which might have been entirely unrelated to the fallen climber.

"Come," said the Witchlord, leading the way into the tunnel which exited from the courtyard's eastern side.

Guest followed, splashing through rank puddles of his own urine, which further soaked the ruinous wads of his straw sandals. In such manner, Guest ventured the fumbling darkness till he saw ahead the green glow of the demon Ungula Scarth.

Witchlord and Weaponmaster found that the octagonal chamber which housed the demon was still graced with a metal grille which allowed one to walk across the pool of liquid filth which dominated that room.

When that pool had been temporarily drained so a ring of ever-ice could be recovered from the floor of the chamber, a small portion of the metal grille had been removed to admit a man, but this portion had been replaced, and the once-drained pool had been flooded again. It occurred to Guest that maybe Anaconda Stogirov, the notorious High Priestess of the Temple of Blood, had arranged for the chamber to be flooded with liquid filth as a way of demeaning the untouchable demon which dominated the room with its green icelight.

"Greetings," said Guest Gulkan.

"And to you, greetings," said Ungula Scarth. "I see you have the knife. Is it Anaconda's knife, or did you take it from the Mutilator?"

"I took it from the Mutilator," said Guest.

"And you have the cornucopia," said Scarth, speaking to the Witchlord. "So! That explains the misfortune which has beset Obooloo!"

"One would have thought you would have guessed that much already," said Lord Onosh.

"I should have," admitted Scarth. "But I am as other people are. When legend speaks of the cornucopia, it speaks of the generation of silver, of gold, of wealth beyond imagining. It says nothing of pissing."

"That is the difference between legend and life," said Guest.

"Yes," said the demon. "And there is a further difference. The people of legend have more sense than the people of life. Why are you wearing those gutter-tread sandals when your father has boots?"

"Am I to kill my father for his boots?" said Guest.

"It may well be that you will end by killing your father," said Scarth, "but I was not talking of murder. The cornucopia, man! If the boots are folded, they will fit!"

Then Guest felt properly foolish, for he knew his father's feet to be a match for his own.

"Never mind that," said Guest, unbuckling the sheath which held the Mutilator's hooked knife. "We'll see about boots later."

With that, Guest Gulkan withdrew the Mutilator's blade from its sheath.

And wondered.

How had the demon Ungula Scarth detected the presence of that weapon when it had been hidden from sight inside the buckle-down sheath? Maybe ... maybe by logic alone. For, after all, Guest would not have ventured idly into the Temple of Blood. His presence in that Temple implied that he had secured resource sufficient for the liberation of the Great God.

With knife in hand, Guest Gulkan advanced upon the Great God Jocasta, who hung silent and unchanging in the air. While Guest advanced, his father hung well back, taking care to keep well out of reach of the demon Ungula Scarth. For Lord Onosh did not trust the demon further than he could throw it.

While Lord Onosh had profound reservations about the demon and the Great God it served, Guest Gulkan had none such. He smiled upon the Great God, which presented the same aspect to the world as it had done when Guest had seen it first.

It was a doughnut the size of a man's head, floating in the air within two shells of light — a dull red inner shell of its own production, and a sharp-burning outer shell of blue which constituted its imprisonment.

"Hail, Jocasta," said Guest, with due formality.

The Great God made no reply, and the demon Ungula Scarth did not speak on its behalf.

Then Guest applied the blue-green bead at the end of the Mutilator's hooked knife to the surface of the blue-burning shell which imprisoned the Great God.

As the knife touched the force field, it began to vibrate, setting Guest's teeth on edge. He had expected the knife to slice apart the transparent shell, but instead it twisted wickedly and skidded across the surface.

"More strength!" said Scarth.

"More!" said Guest. "I am using strength enough to open a coconut!"

"More," affirmed Scarth. "Use your muscle!"

Then Guest gritted his teeth and applied his full strength to the task. His hands, his arms, his entire body shook with vibratory energy. A thin line of white fire appeared, and widened to a slit.

"I've done it!" said Guest.

And withdrew the knife.

The slit promptly healed itself.

"The force field is self-sustaining," said Ungula Scarth. "Self-sustaining, self-healing."

"Now you tell me!" said Guest.

"Try again," said the demon.

"Again!" said Guest, who was sweating heavily, and who could feel his forearms shaking with the effort of his exertions.

"Are you a weakling?" sneered the demon.

"Am I weak?" said Guest, with an ill temper. "Well, yes, I am, because I have suffered in the dungeons of the Mutilator, and suffered in the Stench Caves, and suffered from bedless wandering since, and I am in no mood to be trifled with!"

"I do not call the liberation of gods a matter of trifling," said

Scarth, softly. "Look! The Great God is ready!"

At which Guest saw that the red glow of the Great God's self-protective force field was dying away. Where there had been two spheres of light, now only one remained: the outer sphere of imprisoning blue. Guest realized that the Great God was preparing to exit, was preparing to escape.

"Your strength, now," said Ungula Scarth. "Use your strength, and liberate a god!"

Thus encouraged, Guest scraped the ruinous mess of his straw sandals from his feet, and braced his bare feet against the rigidity of the metal grille. Then, with all the brutality at his command, Guest hacked a great slice through the blue-burning skin of the force field. Before the slit could heal, the Great God pushed its way to liberty, birthing itself with a sound like a breaking harpstring.

"Ha!" said Guest, his face alight with a grin of triumph. "So! You are free! Well, here I am!"

There he was, indeed, and the Great God Jocasta was duly conscious of the fact. Liquid fire ran through Guest Gulkan's veins. Images swirled through his head in a dementing turmoil. He felt dizzy, and almost dropped the knife he was holding. A hand which was not his own forced that knife to the challenge, but the hand was his own, his own hand but not his own to control, and his head was turning, his body was turning, he was turning on his father, the knife was poised to kill—

Then Guest found tongue enough to cry and yelled:

"Run!"

Lord Onosh took the hint, and fled.

Then Guest Gulkan, hopelessly possessed by the Great God Jocasta, was puppeted into the pursuit of his father.

With his son in hot pursuit, Lord Onosh raced into the central courtyard, slipped in a puddle of urine and went down. And before he could rise, his son was upon him.

Guest felt his own hand wrench at his father's hair. Felt his own strength smash his father's face to the reeking urine. Felt his knotted fingers haul his father's face from the splash-puddle, then twist it, exposing his life to the blade.

Then — compelled by the Great God Jocasta, which had him in firm possession — Guest Gulkan raised his knife for the slaughtering of his father.

CHAPTER THIRTY-NINE

Guest Gulkan: the Yarglat barbarian otherwise known as the Weaponmaster. Under the compulsion of hubristic ambition, he has dared his way into the Temple of Blood. There he has liberated the Great God Jocasta. By way of reward, he expected to be given the powers of the wizard. Instead, the Great God has taken possession of him. His father, the Witchlord Onosh, lies at his feet. And Guest is poised to kill his father. He does not want to, but he cannot help himself!

* * *

So there was Guest, about to slaughter his father, when with a whoosh a high-pressure flood of saliva came barrel-bursting from the cornucopia, knocking him down and rolling him over and over till he ended up in a thrashing heap against the temple wall. The Great God Jocasta lost control of Guest's body, for its contortions were too quick to be followed by the God's mechanism of control — and Guest abruptly found himself free.

Free from possession, Guest fought through a swiftly rising flood-rush of foaming spittle, grappled with the pumping cornucopia, and brought it to the upright, thus cutting off the outflow of his father's spit — which otherwise would surely have continued pumping until it had digested the world.

This was no sooner done than Guest realized that the Great God Jocasta was moving in on Lord Onosh, humming ominously.

"Run!" said Guest.

But, even as he said it, a voice of thunder roared in outraged anger:

"Halt!"

Guest momentarily thought it was the Great God Jocasta

speaking, but it was not.

"*Halt!*" roared the wrath-thundering challenger, "*Halt! Throw down your sword! Or you will be eliminated!*"

For a moment, Guest was all confusion, then he saw the challenger who owned that voice which mountains would surely have envied. The loud-mouthed challenger was a woman who was dressed in an armour fashioned from the same painfully bright blue transparency which had imprisoned the Great God Jocasta.

Guest had never seen this woman before, but he had heard the odd snippet of news about Obooloo while he had been incarcerated in the Mutilator's dungeons — and knew enough to surmise (with absolute accuracy, as it happened) that this was none other than Anaconda Stogirov, High Priestess of the Temple of Blood.

Stogirov had a weapon in her hand, a weapon of contorted metal which ended in a nozzle tipped with white light. Guest had barely caught sight of it when it spat flame.

The firebolt which jolted from Stogirov's alien weapon slammed into the Great God Jocasta. That blast of raw energy struck the Great God, sending the free-floating thing crashing backwards. The Great God was sent slamming into the rearward wall. It caromed off the blank-faced stone, tumbled through the air, then steadied itself.

The Great God spat fire at Stogirov, who ducked.

She ducked too slowly!

She was hit!

But not vaporized — for her armour absorbed the fireshock. Stogirov coolly levelled her own weapon and returned the Great God's fire.

Guest acted.

He grabbed his father, who was in no condition for independent heroics, then he slung the unconscious man over his shoulder like a sack of severed heads and positively sprinted from the central courtyard.

Behind him, Stogirov and the Great God engaged in a firefight which the Great God lost — for Stogirov's weapon-power was greater. So Jocasta followed Guest Gulkan's lead and fled, exiting from the Temple of Blood in the wake of the Witchlord-burdened Weaponmaster.

"Come back, you!" said Stogirov, firing yet once again at the retreating Great God.

The echoes of the amplified boom of Stogirov's voice died away, to be replaced by the truncheon-beat of her boots trampling over the heat-cracked rock as she moved in the pursuit of the fast-fleeing Great God. Out of the Temple of Blood went Anaconda Stogirov — out of the temple and into the streets of Obooloo.

Guest Gulkan most naturally fled up Lopdoptiskop, that narrow street which winds its way uphill in the shadow of Achaptipop, the massive rock which sustains the Sanctuary of the Bondsman's Guild. Up the street he laboured, sweating under the burden of his father's weight. Then that burden began to gasp and croak. Hoping that if Lord Onosh was well enough to complain then he might be well enough to walk, Guest dumped the man down.

Panting and sweating, Guest Gulkan turned. And looked downhill. And saw. He saw a floating doughnut, which he knew immediately to be the Great God Jocasta. And in pursuit of that doughnut was a figure bulbous in blue-burning armour — the wrathful Anaconda Stogirov, High Priestess of the Temple of Blood! Guest, in his supreme innocence, had thought those two would happily spend the rest of the day fighting it out in the temple.

"Grief of gods!" said Lord Onosh, staggering to his feet. "There's no way out for us now!"

But Guest still had the cornucopia.

Nearby was a cow which was fortuitously lifting its tail. As a great gush of urine gouted from its backside, Guest filled the cornucopia. Then he upended that horn of plenty. A limitless surge of bovine urine slammed forth from the cornucopia like a spout of water erupting from a hole at the base of a mighty dam.

In moments, the plunging street of Lopdoptiskop was being pillaged by a flood of drenching urine. Anaconda Stogirov clutched at a doorway but was knocked away. With a scream, she was swept downhill, vanishing in the millrace of the cow's multiplied bounty. But the Great God Jocasta floated clear of the jouncing flood.

Guest abruptly brought the cornucopia upright. He held it firmly upright, to let the horn of plenty swallow what urine remained within it. Guest stowed the cornucopia, then father and son hurried on up the street to gain the gateway of the Sanctuary of the Bondsman's Guild.

"You can't come in here!" said a guard, addressing the pair in the Janjuladoola tongue, which language neither of them spoke.

Whereupon Guest Gulkan knocked him unconscious, and hurried into the Sanctuary with his father in his wake.

To penetrate the precincts of the Sanctuary had been easy, but to get into its Holy of Holies was (theoretically) rather more difficult. For that Holy of Holies was guarded by a jade-green block of stone, a block of stone which ate people who had not permission to pass. This monster was of course the demon Lob (in whose honour the street of Lopdoptiskop had been named).

Lob was but one of the far-scattered demons loyal to the Great God Jocasta, and of course Lob was under the impression that Guest Gulkan had set himself the task of rescuing that Great God. So when Lob saw Guest approaching with Jocasta bobbing along behind, why, Lob naturally thought that Guest had fulfilled his mission of rescue (as he had) and that the Weaponmaster was now Jocasta's beloved friend (or slave).

So the man-eating demon let Witchlord and Weaponmaster pass, unwounded and unrestrained, and so they entered into the Holy of Holies where the Door of the Bondsman's Guild was kept safe from all prying eyes.

There was the Door!

The gate to the Circle of the Partnership Banks!

In all his life, Guest had seldom been so relieved as he was when he saw that metal archway standing on its marble plinth, and confirmed that the span of the archway was filled with a screen of shimmering, hard-humming silver.

In front of that archway stood a Banker, and he did not look happy to see Witchlord and Weaponmaster intruding on his domains. He held up a single finger in a gesture of admonition. The Great God Jocasta fired a bolt of energy at the Banker, and it burnt off that upraised finger. The Banker looked at the roastmeat scar where his missing digit had been but a moment earlier, then he fainted clean away. He fell face forward. There was a solid crunch as his face smashed into the marble of the plinth, teeth splintering, jaw breaking.

Remorselessly, the Great God glided through the air towards the humming silver screen.

"No!" shouted Guest, horrorstruck.

But it was far too late for protest.

For the Great God slipped through that screen and was gone.

It had escaped! It had got away from Obooloo, going through the Door to — why, to Dalar ken Halvar, of course! For Dalar ken Halvar was the next place on the Circle of the Partnership Banks.

Witchlord and Weaponmaster did not hesitate. They scrambled up on to the plinth and hurried through the humming screen of vertical quicksilver, arriving instantly in the Bralsh, the Bank of Dalar ken Halvar. In the Bralsh there was a smell of scorched flesh and a scene of panic-stricken disarray. The Great God Jocasta was briefly glimpsed — vanishing out of the main exit.

"Guest Gulkan!"

So cried Yubi Das Finger, the leading Banker of the Bralsh. But Guest had no time to spare for idle conversation. Instead, Witchlord and Weaponmaster charged from the Bralsh, striving out into the hot sun of Dalar ken Halvar. Precisely what they hoped to accomplish is a mystery, for surely they must have known themselves to be unequal to the powers of a Great God.

But charge they did.

And got out into the streets of Childa Go, the fishing quarter of Dalar ken Halvar. There the Great God lurched to a halt, and turned to confront them. And, to his horror, Guest Gulkan felt his mind again slipping into the possession of his enemy.

CHAPTER FORTY

Name: Paraban Senk (aka the Teacher of Control)

Birthplace: Charabanc

Occupation: teacher

Status: head of the Combat College of Dalar ken Halvar

Description: disembodied entity which typically manifests itself as an olive-skinned face, male and of middle years

Age: Senk claims an age in excess of 20,000 years

Hobby: Senk personally schedules the entertainments which appear on the Eye of Delusions at Dalar ken Halvar, and this voluntary activity may be the nearest thing which Senk has to a hobby.

Quote: "The Stormforce exists for the controlled application of force."

* * *

"No!" shouted Guest Gulkan.

His voice was a wing-broken squawk of protest.

But it was too late for protest, for the Great God Jocasta was bent on taking over the Weaponmaster's mind, and was in no mood to argue about it. Yet Jocasta did not find the act of possession as effortlessly easy as before, since this time Guest was forewarned and fighting — and the Great God itself had been damaged in its battle with Stogirov.

There in the hot sun, Guest Gulkan felt bright-spark slivers of memory sharping out of his mind's darkness as Jocasta probed for a hold, a grip, a secure possession of the Weaponmaster's will. Cold. That was what Guest felt. Despite the heat of the day, he shivered, for Jocasta's probing had recalled to mind the frozen heights of the mountains of Ibsen-Iktus. Guest remembered—

The impossible clarity of the mountain heights. Breathless heights where every step is a staircase. Blue transparencies of sky. A drift of snow grown grey with wind-blown grit. A bridge of ice, humped across a river. The chickling trickle of melt-water sheeking and sharking beneath sheets of ice. A windless day with an unfelt wind high, high above blasting dragon-licks of snow from sky-scarp heights.

And he remembered—

Avalanche!

A roiling roll-roar of rocks went toiling in spuming plummets from the heights, causing the ground to shake beneath his feet. A real memory, this. Caught by the living life of that memory, Guest saw the wizard Sken-Pitilkin. There was blood on the wizard's forehead — blood beaded in drops. The wizard Sken-Pitilkin was literally sweating blood, and his face was pallid as unbaked dough.

Guest remembered.

Under a swordpoint's compulsion, Sken-Pitilkin had sent an avalanche rolling downhill, and then had retched violently, bringing up green bile from an empty stomach.

"But I had to!" protested Guest.

And with that protest, the Weaponmaster was free from the Great God's efforts at possession.

The Great God Jocasta had tried to sound out Guest Gulkan's most potent memories, seeking thus to make an accurate index of the Weaponmaster's mind, and so to facilitate his possession. But Guest's most potent memories were memories of shameful deeds which he had later repudiated.

Guest had invested a lifetime's effort in protecting himself from his own memories by suppressing them, justifying them or minimizing them. So when Jocasta probed Guest's deepest memories, the unfortunate Great God ran into defensive structures built up by a lifetime's effort. And so, weakened as it was by Stogirov's onslaughts, the Great God was unable to possess the Weaponmaster.

"You will yield," said Jocasta, trying to sound convincing.

"Yield!" said Guest. "The hell I will!"

Then the wrathful Weaponmaster grabbed a sword from a vacillating soldier who was trying — and failing — to figure out just what was going on here.

Having grabbed that sword (and accidentally breaking several of the soldier's teeth in the haste of his grabbing) Guest Gulkan attacked the Great God with that weapon. Guest attacked with all the vigour of a musician of Sung assailing that elephant-sized metal drum which is known as a klambakora. Steel clanged uselessly against the Great God's flanks. But Guest's defiance served to convince the Great God Jocasta that possessing the Weaponmaster was not a possibility, at least not for a shaken and battle-weakened Great God. Accordingly, Jocasta decided upon retreat.

Jocasta lurched through the air, bumped the Weaponmaster, hit him hard. Guest went down. Jocasta hesitated. Having been hit so heartily, might the Weaponmaster perhaps be weaker than before? The Great God hung over its fallen prey, humming.

And Guest felt cold again.

Very cold.

The coldness solidified to actual ice, and he found himself back in the arena of Chi'ash-lan where once the Great Mink had torn off his arms and legs at the behest of Banker Sod. Once upon a time. But once upon a time was now! He screamed as the mauling strength savaged his perfections. The glunching bones broke slick and wet, smunch and crunch. Flesh to pulp, bone to slivers.

Then the image faded, and Guest found himself being bounced along the dirt under the harsh sun of Dalar ken Halvar. His father had him by the hair, and was dragging him away from the Great God Jocasta.

"Enough!" yelled Guest, as the pain of being hauled by his hair washed away the pain of the waking nightmare he had just endured. "Let me go!"

So the Witchlord let go of the Weaponmaster, and Guest slumped to the ground. He felt a twinge of cold, a touch of frost, an insinuation of ice, as the Great God Jocasta again made a determined effort to seize control of his mind.

"You won't," said Guest grimly, recovering his fallen sword and getting to his feet. "You can't."

But before Guest Gulkan could mount yet another fatuous attack on the Great God Jocasta, Yubi Das Finger came out of the Bralsh. A striking figure was Yubi Das Finger! For this Banker was dressed in motley, with the motley being rigorously littered with shiny ceramic animals, his whole outfit being topped off by a damaged face and a golden skullcap fringed with tiny glass beads. Yet Guest spared him only the briefest of glances — for he had encountered the man before in his various sparse yet informative dealings with the Banks. Rather, Guest concentrated his attention on those who were following on behind Yubi.

The honourable Das Finger was leading a dozen sweating slaves who were carrying a huge black cauldron, a cauldron which looked to be one of the orking pots of Galsh Ebrek. On Yubi's command, they upended the pot and dropped it over the Great God.

"We have it," said Yubi, with satisfaction.

Guest gaped.

It had never occurred to the Weaponmaster that something as mighty as a Great God could be secured and imprisoned by any expedient so simple as dropping a pot on top of it. But of course the Great God Jocasta had been direly injured by the firebolt weapon so generously employed against it by Anaconda Stogirov, and Yubi Das Finger's tactic appeared to be working.

For Jocasta strove against the pot, trying to lift it directly upwards. But the Great God could not raise it from the ground by more than a fingerlength. Next, Jocasta tried to burn a hole in the black iron. The metal grew red hot, but it did not melt or yield.

Yubi Das Finger spat on the glowing iron. His saliva sizzled into silence.

"Let me out!" roared Jocasta, using the Galish Trading Tongue.

Yubi knew that language, but made no reply. Instead, the scar-faced Banker giggled maniacally.

Thwarted, Jocasta lifted the iron pot clear off the ground — only a fingerlength clear, but a fingerlength was sufficient — and began to carry that burden on an erratic course of retreat which sent the iron pot caroming into a succession of ox carts and bamboo huts.

"It's getting away!" said Guest in alarm.

"Yes, my friend," said Yubi Das Finger. "The thing is getting away from us. So tell us, little friend — what is it, exactly? A friend of yours? You brought it through the Door, didn't you?"

Yubi Das Finger had spoken of the Door! Admittedly, he had spoken in the Galish, which few people in Dalar ken Halvar were likely to know. But even so! A Banker does not speak of Doors or of Circles in public, and Yubi was a Banker born and bred. The error was a measure of the extreme stress of the moment.

"The — the thing is a god," said Guest. "A Great God, that's, that's what it says, it alleges. But we didn't bring it here, it, it followed us!"

"A god, is it?" said Yubi dubiously.

Yubi Das Finger was no theologian, but he thought it most unlikely that any god of any description could be confined under an upturned orking pot for even as short a time as half a heartbeat. He presumed, therefore, that the thing under the pot was an artefact of some description, possibly a weapon of war left over from the Days of Wrath or from some conflict more ancient yet. That then was how Yubi described it to the public.

"It's a mad machine," said Yubi, to all who wanted to know. "A mad machine, which we'll have to destroy."

Whereupon assorted heroes did their best to kill the thing, or at least to disconcert it. They beat its iron pot with the butts of spears, setting up a great racket. The pot lurched, crushing a soldier against an ox cart. As he screamed piteously, the pot continued on its way, navigating hazard by hazard through the streets of Childa Go.

Childa Go, Dalar ken Halvar's fishing-shack quarter, was heavy with the smell of drying fish. As Guest plodded along behind the iron pot, keeping at a respectful distance — for he had no wish to be burnt or crushed himself — the smells awakened strong memories of his past adventures in Dalar ken

Halvar. He heard a sharp explosion as a piece of bamboo burst in a cooking fire, and remembered the excited hubbub of Dog Day festivities, when the city was one uproarious turmoil of competitive confusion.

He remembered other things, too.

His legs kept remembering the injuries they had suffered on that terrible day in Chi'ash-lan: the day of the Great Mink. Those memories were idle folly, for Guest's legs were new legs, grown for him in the minor mountain known as Cap Foz Para Lash. Still, he remembered what he remembered. He could not deny it.

The procession of people trooping after the Great God steadily swelled. Guest realized they were skirting the slopes of Cap Ogo Botch, the minor mountain atop which stood the palace of Na Sashimoko. The imperial palace — for Dalar ken Halvar was the capital of the Empire of Greater Parengarenga. Who ruled now in Dalar ken Halvar? Thanks to his embroilment in the affairs of Untunchilamon and Obooloo, Guest's knowledge of current affairs was years out of date — a failing which could be potentially fatal.

As Guest was worrying about it, the Great God Jocasta slipped through the streets, making its way between the Grand Arena and Cap Uba. It gained Scuffling Road. The broad avenue was just as Guest remembered it — still lined for the most part with the impoverished bamboo buildings which typified Dalar ken Halvar. It was still unpaved, surfaced with the soft red dust of the Plain of Jars. Guest remembered often, often making his way through red dust rutted with cart tracks, going on crutches to the Yamoda River or to Lake Shalasheen to swim, back in those long-ago days when his new-growing legs had been too weak to sustain him.

In those years, his home base had been the underground stronghold within the minor mountain known as Cap Foz Para Lash, so after his swim he had always returned to that place. And Guest realized that — whether by accident or design — the Great God Jocasta was making a similar journey.

At the end of Scuffling Road was the kinema, the natural

amphitheatre outside the lockway. The lockway, with its twin doors of kaleidoscope, guarded the way into Cap Foz Para Lash. Guest had the uneasy suspicion that the Great God knew where it was going, and intended to link up with Paraban Senk, the formidable demon who ruled the depths of Cap Foz Para Lash.

Was Senk then a friend of Jocasta?

Certainly the demons of Guest's acquaintance seemed to have the ability to talk to each other at a distance, silently communicating across oceans and continents. The demon Iva-Italis on Alozay maintained relationships with Lob in Obooloo and Ko in Chi'ash-lan. So — was Paraban Senk a member of this strange and long-enduring partnership?

By now, a very considerable procession was trailing after the Great God Jocasta. It was joined by a company of armed and armoured men moving at a pace which had them gasping in the heat of the day. The leader of those men was a Frangoni giant who challenged the Weaponmaster by name:

"Guest Gulkan!"

"My lord," said Guest, speaking in the Galish.

Yubi Das Finger, who had been keeping pace with Guest, translated and elaborated that courtesy.

Meantime, Guest summed the stranger, who had muscles of a hugeness indicative of a fondness for pumping iron rather than water, who wore robes of flowing purple, and whose uncut hair was most curiously heaped on top of his head to amplify his height further. A Frangoni warrior. A tall, big, purple-skinned Frangoni warrior. An impressive figure, certainly, but to Guest they all looked alike, these Frangoni.

Then the Frangoni warrior said — and Yubi Das Finger translated, for Guest and the purple-skinned stranger had no language in common:

"What's going on here?"

"My lord," said Guest. "We're chasing a Great God."

This Yubi Das Finger translated, deadpan.

The Frangoni was more learned in theology than was Guest Gulkan, and so, like others before him, the purple-skinned warrior decided that whatever was lurching along under the iron orking pot was most definitely not a god. Possibly it was a turtle, or a large crab, or an injured Shabble, or a low-powered Sword, or a bad-tempered dwarf of prodigious strength. But a god? Never!

"Stop it!" said the Frangoni.

In response to his order, his men surrounded the orking pot, and braced their shields against it, and tried to sweat it to a halt in a scrum. While they sweated and strained, Guest used his Galish to ask a discreet question of Yubi Das Finger:

"Who is the — the big one?"

"The big one, as you so nicely put it," said Yubi Das Finger, "why, that is Asodo Hatch. If memory serves, you were once married to his sister Joma."

Now that Hatch had been named, Guest felt foolish for not having recognized him, for they had met often enough in the past. Guest's failure to recognize the Frangoni was surely an index of his fatigue, his disorientation, and the pounding he had suffered during his long wanderings. But Guest was not troubled by this hint of mental deterioration. Rather, he was troubled to hear Yubi say that he had been "once married". For was he not married now?

"Joma?" said Guest. "Why, I have a wife, big, yes, tall and purple, but her name—"

"Penelope," said Das Finger. "That was the other name. You may have known her as that, but now we call her Joma, for she — but never mind that."

"What?" said Guest. "Never mind what? Why? And — and where is she?"

Guest was sorely alarmed, for during his entire absence — which had involved him in a trip to Alozay, a preliminary raid on Obooloo, a journey across Moana, prolonged difficulties on Untunchilamon, imprisonment in Obooloo and the hazards of his venture into the Stench Caves — he had imagined Penelope to be faithfully waiting for his return. It had never occurred to him that the woman might have an independent existence, a life which could be separated from his own wants and desires. So he was shocked to hear Yubi use a form of words which suggested the possibility that his long-anticipated reunification with his purple-skinned true-heart might not proceed with automatic ease.

"There is no time for the first question," said Das Finger, who was unwilling to waste time on lecturing Guest in ethnology. "And as for the second question, why, I suspect it one better answered by Asodo Hatch himself."

But the Frangoni warrior Asodo Hatch was too busy to be free for such questions, since he was playing referee, overseeing the duel between his soldiers and the runaway orking pot. The pot, which had once more grown red-hot as Jocasta filled it with flames of wrath, was driven into a bamboo house. The house caught fire, and Hatch's men were driven back, leaving the pot to blunder blindly in the flames.

Asodo Hatch had the house surrounded. His men tore down its pitiful bamboo fence, giving access to the back yard. Guest Gulkan was close to the fore, and almost accidentally buried himself in the yard's copious rubbish pit, which was mired with festering unpleasantness.

As the burning house collapsed, the god-driven orking pot emerged from it uncertainly. Somewhere a woman was screaming. The pot wobbled, then thrust its way towards the waiting soldiers. They made a wall of shields and stood ready to receive the pot.

But the rubbish pit lay between the soldiers and the pot.

The pot hovered over the pit—

Then halted.

It settled.

It was half-over and half-off the rubbish pit.

The Great God Jocasta promptly dropped down into the bottom of the pit and escaped upwards through the uncovered portion of that pit.

Asodo Hatch gave a curt order, and a hail of spears assailed the Great God. Most missed, and sent murder hurtling into the crowd of over-eager spectators. Some clanged home, bouncing off the Great God in a demonstration of futility.

The Great God hung in the air, humming.

Asodo Hatch held his ground, and challenged the thing in all the languages he spoke. Guest Gulkan understood none of them, and had to tug at Yubi Das Finger's sleeve to get a translation. Had the Weaponmaster been more diligent in his linguistic studies, he would have known most of those languages — such as the Code Seven of the Nexus.

It is widely believed in Dalar ken Halvar that many of the greatest artefacts available to our own age were sourced in the Nexus. This "Nexus" is said to have been a grouping of interlinked worlds, an association comprised of more worlds than this world has fingers to count. It is believed in Dalar ken Halvar that the stars of those worlds are not green, red, blue and yellow like the stars of our own sky, but, rather, burn with a cold and uncanny ice-chip white. Under such stars — this at least is Dalar ken Halvar's ruling superstition — metal beasts such as the dorgi were once made.

Asodo Hatch, presuming the Great God Jocasta to be a creature from just such a world, challenged Jocasta in the Code Seven which Dalar ken Halvar believes to have been spoken by the Nexus.

"You!" said Asodo Hatch, bellowing like a water buffalo as he endeavoured to imitate that dreaded Nexus monster known as a dorgi. "You! You! Halt! Halt right there! Or I will eliminate you!"

"You have no idea who I am, or what," said the Great God Jocasta, responding to Asodo Hatch in the same Code Seven in which Hatch's challenge had been phrased. "Know that I am a god, and a Great God at that. Many are my servants. Their number is legion. I command heavens of ice and hells of living needles. You will bow down and worship me. Here! Now! Or you will end up in hell, where you will be constrained to burn your own liver as a sacrifice to the Lesser Slime Toad."

"I know precisely who you are, and what," said Hatch, who had no patience with such nonsense. "You are a delinquent asma from Gorbograd. If you are who I think you are, then you were employed in Gorbograd as a person in charge of cart parks."

This is what Hatch said, or at least the sense of what he said, for his words cannot be translated precisely into any of the languages of our world. For example, the "carts" of which he spoke were not precisely carts as we understand them, for they had no wheels. Rather, they hovered. But in their hovering they were not like birds or butterflies. The "carts" of which Hatch spoke were more like ghosts than vehicles made of actual wood and actual leather, for these "carts" could dissolve themselves, and could travel in a state of dissolution through stone and through steel, later coagulating themselves out of the thin smoke of their ghosthood to come to rest in the ordinary domains of the physical world. Even so, they could carry humans, or take water from place to place, just like the carts of our world.

This at least is what was believed by Asodo Hatch, and by many others in Dalar ken Halvar. And it was believed, too, that the Nexus had so many of these carts that, even though they could not jam the roads as do the carts of our own world, they caused appalling city-blighting traffic jams whenever a great number of them tried to simultaneously come to rest in the same place.

Hatch's slander was that Jocasta's function in the world of the Nexus had been to supervise the "parking" of these "carts". At least, one gathers that it was a slander, though why this should be so is not clear. After all, in our own world we think the pilot's art to be a great and worthy one. A ship's pilot who supervises the docking of ships is surely discharging a function similar to that of one who is in the cart-parking business; and the pilot has ever been saluted as one of civilization's most useful minor functionaries.

Yet on being likened to such a pilot, Jocasta declared: "Slander! Slander!"

Then spat fire at Asodo Hatch — though weakly, for the Great God had exhausted its strength in the struggle with the orking pot.

Seeing the weakness of the flame spat by the Great God, Hatch ordered his men to seize clothing from civilians, and to use it to manhandle the still-hot orking pot. But even as those futile efforts at capture got underway, the Great God Jocasta began to escape by air, and all Hatch's efforts to hold it firm by engaging it in debate were ignored.

Jocasta fled down Scuffling Road, reached the doors of kaleidoscope which led into Cap Foz Para Lash, and uttered a high-pitched command which caused those doors to dissolve away to nothing. With the way thus clear, Jocasta fled into the tunnels of the mountain, with the barriers of kaleidoscope reforming in its wake.

Asodo Hatch came to those doors. They opened for him. Hatch entered, and the doors closed behind him.

Guest Gulkan did not know whether he himself still retained any right to enter that mountain, the place which had sheltered him during four long years of convalescence. Would the doors open for him? Hard on the heels of Asodo Hatch, Guest approached the first of the barriers of kaleidoscope. It dissolved away to nothing, admitting him to the interior of the mountain. The inner door then followed suit.

Once past the double doors of kaleidoscope which guarded the interior of Cap Foz Para Lash against unrestrained intrusion, Guest Gulkan swiftly caught up with Asodo Hatch, and the pair hunted down the mountain tunnels in the wake of the Great God Jocasta.

The Great God made its way to Forum Three, a lecture theatre with a roof layered thickly with kaleidoscope. The Yarglat barbarian Guest Gulkan and the purple-skinned Frangoni warrior Asodo Hatch followed in hot pursuit.

"Halt!" said Guest, doing his best to imitate the wrathfulness of a dorgi or a Stogirov.

But the Great God paid him no heed.

Instead, it rose to the roof, buried itself in the kaleidoscope above their heads, and disappeared.

"Senk!" roared Asodo Hatch.

There was a pause, then Senk's features appeared on the screen which dominated Forum Three.

Guest noticed that Paraban Senk, the demon who ruled the mountain of Cap Foz Para Lash, chose to paint that magical screen with a face of features olive-skinned. On their first encounter, when Guest had been a legless and armless patient of the demon's clinic, Guest had thought how very unusual those olive-skinned features were.

Now, on reacquaintance, that skin-shade reminded Guest very much of two individuals he had encountered on Untunchilamon: Ivan Pokrov (the master of an analytical engine which had been housed on a minor island in the harbour of Injiltaprajura) and Odolo (a conjurer in the service of one Justina Thrug, who had been Untunchilamon's *de facto* ruler at the time when Guest had been questing in that territory). Guest was inclined to think there might be some more than spurious relationship linking the olive-skinned Senk to the equally olive-skinned Pokrov and Odolo.

But a relationship of what kind?

Somehow, this hardly seemed to be the time to ask.

"Greetings, Guest Gulkan," said Senk.

While Guest had been away from Dalar ken Halvar long enough to have had trouble recognizing such a personage as Asodo Hatch, Paraban Senk instantly recognized Guest Gulkan. Like Yubi Das Finger and other such sharp-minded personages, Senk never forgot.

Senk addressed the Weaponmaster in the Galish. On this occasion, Senk's linguistic mastery reminded the Weaponmaster uncomfortably of Schoptomov, the therapist based Downstairs in Injiltaprajura. Just like that therapist, Paraban Senk had dwelt underground for generation upon generation, gathering wisdom — and gathering evil with it? Guest's long prejudice against scholarship had been reinforced by his encounter with the therapist Schoptomov, and made him cautious in his renewed dealings with Paraban Senk.

"And to you, greetings," said Guest formally. "I am here in pursuit of my enemy, who has violated your neutrality by taking refuge here."

As he spoke, Guest was aware of an unobtrusive sound-source speaking in a language which he took to be Frangoni. Paraban Senk was giving Asodo Hatch a simultaneous translation of Guest's comments. Guest was familiar with Senk's tricks, since a similar convenience had allowed the Weaponmaster to argue with his wife Penelope when they lacked all common language. Still, on this occasion he found such facility positively sinister.

"I have noticed the intrusion of your enemy," said Senk, "but think you owe me a full explanation."

Then Guest Gulkan and Asodo Hatch collaborated on that full explanation. So Senk learnt that Guest Gulkan had assaulted the Mutilator of Yestron, thus winning the specialised knife needed to cut the Great God Jocasta free from imprisonment; that Guest had duly freed the Great God; that the Great God had tried to take possession of Guest's mind; that the intrusion of Anaconda Stogirov had saved Guest from possession; that the Great God had fled through the Circle of the Partnership Banks, leaving Obooloo to come to Dalar ken Halvar; and that both Guest and Hatch wanted Senk to collaborate in the thing's destruction.

"I would gladly help you," said Senk, "but help is beyond my power."

"But you are the ruler here!" said Guest, with explosive anger.

"Ruler?" said Senk. "I long ago had to concede true mastery here to Asodo Hatch. For all my functions are failing. I need the help of human agency if I am to fulfil the most basic of my missions."

"But," said Asodo Hatch, "you can at least cause this ceiling of kaleidoscope to dissolve itself. I recall you doing just that during a riot."

"I could," said Senk. "But it would not help you. The thickness of the ceiling's kaleidoscope conceals privileged tunnels likewise packed with kaleidoscope. Jocasta has fled down those tunnels, penetrating to the innards of the mountain."

Then Senk explained to Guest that the realms within the mountain were only partly given over to human domination. Large parts of those underground domains were reserved for mobile artefacts such as Jocasta. Without the aid of allied artefacts, Senk could not hunt Jocasta out of hiding.

"The thing will shelter there," said Senk, "repairing the damage done to it by Stogirov. Only then will it venture forth again."

"Only then?" said Guest. "But when will that be? A day? Two days? Three?"

"Twenty or thirty days, perhaps," said Senk. "Or twenty or thirty years. Or maybe longer. The thing has been grievously injured, otherwise you would not have been able to force it to run."

So spoke Senk.

Naturally, neither Guest Gulkan nor Asodo Hatch were easily satisfied, for both found this outcome of their conflict with Jocasta to be intensely unsatisfying. But Senk had no cure for their dissatisfaction, so in the end there was no help for it. They had to concede defeat, and to leave the Great God Jocasta uncaught and unkilled.

"Then," said Guest, "if we can leave aside the question of Jocasta's fate, perhaps you can tell me the fate of my wife. Where is Penelope?"

"Penelope?" said Senk. "Oh her! No, I can't tell you what happened to her. She left here a year ago, and I've had no news of her since."

Meanwhile ...

While Guest Gulkan was pursuing the Great God through the tunnels inside Cap Foz Para Lash, his father allowed himself to be seated in the kinema and tended to by Yubi Das Finger. Lord Onosh was feeling his age, and was feeling the effects of the battering of disorientations and disconcertments which he had so recently endured.

So Lord Onosh seated himself, and was fed by Yubi Das Finger, who had bowls of soup and polyps brought for him, and fried locusts as well, and curried worms served on thin slices of unleavened bread, and other things that were likewise good for the belly and comforting to the psyche.

While the Witchlord ate his soup, his polyps, his locusts, his curried worms and his unleavened bread, he watched the entertainments being shown on the Eye of Delusions. That great Eye, set above the lockway, was proof that the Nexus (presuming it to have truly existed) must have known of one or more barbarian tribes very like the Yarglat. For the Eye showed repeated scenes of scalping, of disembowelling, of axe-blade battles and outright cannibalism.

Watching such familiar scenes, Lord Onosh was comforted, for they reminded him of his youth, his homeland, his people. He began muttering to himself in Eparget for the sheer pleasure of hearing the Yarglat tongue, and he was muttering still when Guest Gulkan at last emerged from the mountain to rejoin him.

Asodo Hatch came forth from the mountain with Guest Gulkan, and hustled Witchlord and Weaponmaster away from the kinema.

"Where are we going?" asked Guest of Yubi Das Finger, who was keeping pace with them so he could do duty as an interpreter.

"To the palace," said Yubi. "To Na Sashimoko."

"Then," said Guest, "I would like to know who rules from that palace."

So Guest began an interrogation of Yubi Das Finger, trying to get a grip on what had happened in Dalar ken Halvar during the years in which he had been adventuring in Untunchilamon or enduring imprisonment in Obooloo.

"Things are much as they were," said Yubi, "except that Nuchala-nuth gathers strength by the year."

"That," said Guest, "is nothing to me. So much for Dalar ken Halvar. What of Safrak?"

"Bao Gahai rules it still in the Witchlord's absence," said Yubi Das Finger. "Or so I have heard."

Guest had learnt little more by the time they reached Na Sashimoko and were shown into the presence of Plandruk Qinplaqus.

Though Guest at first had trouble in recognizing Asodo Hatch, he had no such trouble in identifying Qinplaqus. For, after all, Qinplaqus was firmly seated on his throne with the

Princess Nuboltipon upon his knees, hence the elderly Ashdan could scarcely be mistaken for one of his own servants.

Besides, the Silver Emperor still had at his side the same pelican-headed walking stick which he had been carrying when Guest had first met him, back in the days when Plandruk Qinplaqus had been in the habit of travelling the Circle of the Doors of the Partnership Banks, his identity disguised by his travelling name: Ulix of the Drum.

(Ulix of what Drum? After all these years, Guest finally realized that the name had been designed simply to mislead, and that there was no literal drum to be identified with the name. A small discovery, but a certain one — and the Yarglat barbarian felt quite pleased at working it out.)

"Greetings, Guest," said Qinplaqus.

"Greetings, my lord," said Guest, pleased to be recognized.

But, just as Guest Gulkan had no trouble in recognizing Plandruk Qinplaqus, so Qinplaqus had no trouble in turn in recognizing him. For, after all, how many Yarglat barbarians were there in Dalar ken Halvar? A definitive answer to this question cannot be given, but it is reasonable to presume that precious few such savages soiled their feet with the red dust of the Plain of Jars from one generation to the next. And, besides that, there was the matter of Guest's ears. Even among the Yarglat, his ears were of such a largeness that they would have been considered unique had not his father been similarly disfigured.

Even though Plandruk Qinplaqus these days allowed Asodo Hatch to have practical day-to-day control over the management of the Empire of Greater Parengarenga, Qinplaqus remained the ultimate power in Dalar ken Halvar. He dismissed Hatch, and Hatch went, departing without complaint.

Qinplaqus similarly dismissed Yubi Das Finger, sent Lord Onosh away to a bedroom for some much-needed rest, then set about interrogating Guest Gulkan.

For Guest to tell of his adventures was no easy matter, and it was evening before he was finished even a fraction of it.

"You have not mentioned Untunchilamon," said Qinplaqus

at length.

"Haven't I?" said Guest. "I must have!"

"Well," said Qinplaqus, "you may have said one or two words about it, but I think there's more to tell. Still. It grows late. The rest can wait till tomorrow. Meanwhile — have you any pressing questions of your own?"

"The x-x-zix," said Guest. "I left it with Thayer Levant. Have you had word of him?"

"Yes," said Qinplaqus. "He reached my palace with that very device barely three months ago."

Then Plandruk Qinplaqus explained that all the skill of Dalar ken Halvar had not yet proved able to compel the x-x-zix to its proper purpose, which was to control the Breathings which made the weather of Parengarenga so fearsomely hot.

"But," said Qinplaqus, "Hatch has some people working on the problem, and we hope to crack it within the year. Once we have our own Breathings under control, the device will be yours to use against the Cold West."

"I'm glad to hear it," said Guest cordially, doing his best to conceal his mounting distress.

Guest Gulkan had always presumed that the x-x-zix, the fabled wishstone of Untunchilamon, was a magical device of some description which could merely be waved at a Breathing to change its weather. The idea that ancillary machinery was necessary, and would take a year to build, was upsetting. Guest hoped to use the x-x-zix to persuade the Partnership Banks to his will — or, at a minimum, to win control of the city of Chi'ash-lan. After his long exile and the many difficulties of his wandering, he was in no mood to wait.

"I would do things quicker," said Qinplaqus, seeing something of Guest's distress, "but speed is not in my power. Unfortunately there is, ah, a shortage of people apt for the construction of the devices which Hatch is supervising."

What Plandruk Qinplaqus did not say was that he himself had for generations compelled the murder of all "mad scientists", that is to say all people who were prepared to put to some practical use the knowledge they won from Paraban Senk and the mountain of Cap Foz Para Lash. After long generations of diligent murder, Qinplaqus was at last prepared to admit that he might have made a mistake — but the effects of his bloodthirsty predations could not be easily reversed.

"It can't be faster?" said Guest.

"It can't," said Qinplaqus.

Now Plandruk Qinplaqus was a wizard of Ebber, and there are many men who will not trust such a wizard, fearing any hint of trust to be a proof that the wizard himself is dabbling with the contents of their minds. But, to Guest's knowledge, this wizard had never played him false. So the Weaponmaster said:

"I trust you."

"Any more questions?" said Plandruk Qinplaqus.

"One," said Guest. "Where is Penelope?"

"Penelope?" said Qinplaqus blankly.

"Yes," said Guest, "Penelope, Penelope, you remember! A Frangoni woman. Tall. Purple. She was married to me. She was my wife. Where is she?"

"I would presume that she is where you left her," said Qinplaqus.

Guest was offended at this bland dismissal of his concerns. True, Plandruk Qinplaqus was an emperor, so the domestic affairs of a wandering swordsman were unlikely to be prominent among his concerns. Yet Guest — who felt himself a ranking emperor in his own right, albeit an emperor temporarily displaced from his realms — considered that he was being slighted.

"I left her here," said Guest. "I left her here in Dalar ken Halvar when I went questing to Untunchilamon. Yet Senk tells me she's gone."

"But you went away ages ago!" said Qinplaqus. "A woman isn't something you can leave like a lump of gold you buried in a dungheap, charting its burials with maps and plans. In any case, the governance of an empire is our concern, not matters of marriage and such."

With this rebuke, Qinplaqus dismissed the Weaponmaster.

Guest's sole consolation was that the mazadath was

delivered to his quarters in the evening. It was delivered by a servant who spoke no language which Guest could understand, but, in the absence of explanations, Guest supposed that Thayer Levant had brought that amulet to Dalar ken Halvar just as he had brought the x-x-zix.

So thinking, Guest put on the mazadath, vowing never to take it off again, for it had been given to him by his wife Penelope — whose perceived value had been increased tenfold by their long separation. But where was Penelope? This was all most unsatisfactory!

We need but turn our backs and the world changes. Guest had done far more than turn his back, and he passed a night in nightmares, for the distress of the world's transitions came home to him in full force during the night.

The next day, Guest was reunited with his father, who proved to be in possession of the cornucopia — which Guest had succeeded in forgetting about during the upsets of the previous day.

"Where did you get that?" said Guest.

"You dropped it," said his father, making no move to give it back. "You dropped it in the dust."

"But where?"

"Outside the Bank."

"Dalar ken Halvar's Bank?" said Guest.

"The same," said the Witchlord.

Guest had indeed dropped the horn of plenty in the dust outside the Bralsh while duelling with the Great God Jocasta. But he had been so badly upset by attempted possession, by battle, by a disconcerting adventure into Cap Foz Para Lash and by Penelope's disappearance that — surprising as it seemed to him in the calm of the new day — he had entirely overlooked the cornucopia's loss.

"What about the ring?" said the Witchlord.

"The ring?" said Guest. "Oh, the ring!"

The ring of ever-ice which Guest had taken from the Mutilator was still on his finger. But the knife—

There was no sign of the Mutilator's knife. After thinking

about it, Witchlord and Weaponmaster realized that Guest must have lost it in the inner courtyard of the Temple of Blood when grappling with the saliva-spitting cornucopia. Guest counted this a sore loss. Still, better to lose such a knife than suffer the loss of the entire world to a great Flood of his father's digesting spittle.

Guest said exactly that to Plandruk Qinplaqus when that wizard put in his appearance, and suggested that the cornucopia might make a potent weapon.

"For," said Guest, "were we to threaten to digest the whole world with spittle, or, better still, with hot acids taken direct from the stomach itself, might we not compel the whole world to obedience to our power?"

"One suspects," said Plandruk Qinplaqus, "that the world is larger than has been computed by your mathematics. One would take longer than a lifetime to flood the world, even with such a thing as a cornucopia. Besides, there may be a limit to its production. And, further, just as there exists something which can produce, so too may there be something which can swallow."

As the wizard was thus denting Guest's pretensions to Power, Thayer Levant arrived, expecting to be overwhelmed by the Weaponmaster's gratitude. For, in obedience to his master, Levant had ventured all the way from Untunchilamon to Dalar ken Halvar — in the face of hardship, danger and difficulty — and had brought both the wishstone and the mazadath safely to the palace of Na Sashimoko.

"Now that we are all here," said Plandruk Qinplaqus, who took more cognisance of Levant's arrival than did Witchlord and Weaponmaster, "let us turn to the problem which confronts us."

"Yes," said Guest, "Penelope."

"Penelope?" said his father.

"My wife!" said Guest. "She's missing!"

"Your wife?" said his father.

"Yes, wife, wife," said Guest. "We were married, in love, we were—"

"In love"? said Lord Onosh. "I think it lust."

But the Witchlord was wrong. Guest Gulkan's concern for Penelope's whereabouts was no mere matter of lust. After the rigours of his journeys, his imprisonments, his battles and his knife-edge struggles, the young Weaponmaster was not feeling particularly lustful. Rather, he was feeling lonely, isolated, and nostalgic for the past.

Penelope was very much a part of the Weaponmaster's past, for she had comforted him over four long years of convalescence. She had been his woman when he had been scarcely a man, having no arms and no legs. He had plans for her, plans which involved a proper life — family, home, security, stability, and an end to this mad and maddening wandering.

Hence Guest was very much concerned to find out where Penelope was, and what had happened to her. But Plandruk Qinplaqus was entirely unmoved by Guest's concerns.

"Penelope is of no account," said Qinplaqus. "We have greater matters to worry about."

"Yes!" said Guest, with a flash of animation. "The business of the Banks! Now that we have the x-x-zix—"

"We're not yet ready to take on the Banks," said Qinplaqus.

"But," protested Guest, "you said, you promised—"

"Guest," said his father, trying to shut him up.

"No," said Qinplaqus. "Our young friend is right to press his case. The Banks have sorely offended him, just as they have offended me."

Guest was momentarily hard put to think what offence the Banks might have given Qinplaqus. Then he recalled that Banker Sod had imprisoned Qinplaqus in a time pod on Alozay, meantime fomenting revolution in Dalar ken Halvar in the hope of adding that city to his own possessions. But — what was a trifling matter of imprisonment compared with the far greater damage which Guest had suffered?

"You acknowledge my rights," said Guest, "but I'm not sure that you acknowledge my impatience."

"In this case," said Qinplaqus, "remedy may not lie in my province, even if acknowledgement does."

"What are you riddling about?" said Guest.

"Have you heard," said Qinplaqus, "of an entity known as Shabble?"

"Shabble?" said Guest. "Why, yes, I have heard of, uh, Shabble. But — here? Is Shabble here, here in — in—"

In his stumble-tongued confusion, Guest found he had temporarily mislaid the very name of the city in which he was presently stationed. An unlikely mishap, one might think! But when one travels the Doors of a Circle, one can skip continents in an instant, and it sometimes happens that the mind is left behind in one city while the body is in another.

"No," said Qinplaqus. "Shabble is not here in Dalar ken Halvar. Shabble is on Alozay."

And Guest almost fell from his chair with the shock of sheer surprise.

CHAPTER FORTY-ONE

Name: Shabble

Place of manufacture: Nadokov (a city on the planet Sendak IV, a part of the Musorian Empire)

Occupation: High Priest of the Cult of Cockroach

Status: messiah

Description: a full-sized sun contained in its own miniature cosmos, and linked to the worlds of human action by means of a transponder the size of a fist

Hobbies: ventriloquism; the making of music

Quote: "Loneliness, loneliness, that's the worst thing. Be kind to the cockroach and you'll never be lonely, that's as firm as a promise."

* * *

Of Shabble's genesis and of Shabble's true nature no certain account can be given. But one thing is sure. This free-floating globular pyrotechnist was intrinsically more irresponsible than a sea dragon — which is saying something! — and was potentially far more dangerous.

Therefore, on hearing that Shabble was on Alozay — Alozay, of all places — Guest Gulkan was much disturbed.

"Alozay!" said Guest.

The Witchlord Onosh then demanded to know who Shabble was — and what might this personage be doing on Alozay.

Then Guest explained that Shabble was a playful ball he had met on Untunchilamon, a ball which could shine at will with a brightness fit to rival that of the sun itself, and which could fly. Lord Onosh, who was inclined to doubt the truthfulness of this intelligence, then demanded to know the full story of Guest's travels on Untunchilamon, of which he had heard but the barest fragments since his liberation from a time pod in Obooloo's Temple of Blood.

"Well," said Guest, "it's, it's a long story."

"Then suppose you hurry up and start it," said his father, "because the day's getting shorter by the moment."

But Guest was reluctant to begin, for he had no idea how he could possibly go about telling the full story of his exploits on Untunchilamon. For so many things had happened on that distant tropical island, and to explicate those happenings would require the telling of a tale so tangled that Guest could not so much as sort it out in his own head.

In truth, the Weaponmaster felt like someone who has been embroiled in a riot, and is put to the difficulty of reconstructing its events in the cold light of day for the satisfaction of a court of law. When one is placed in such a situation, it is very difficult to imagine that one ran around without any trousers, assisted in the skinning of a tax collector then proceeded to the local temple to have intimate connections with its vestal virgins.

Just as a person put in such a predicament is hard put to know where to begin their explanations, so too was Guest beset with perplexion when his father challenged him to outline that part of his history. Indeed, the Weaponmaster's hesitation was so great that Plandruk Qinplaqus was moved to violate the norms of civilized behaviour by using his powers as a wizard of Ebber to look inside Guest's mind.

The Weaponmaster did not notice this wizardly intrusion into the intimacies of his psyche, hence did not resist it; but, despite the lack of resistance, Qinplaqus got no profit from his adventure. For Guest's mind was a moiling confusion in which images of Penelope's nakedness were entangled with sharks, dungeons, coral reefs, fireflies, mosquitoes, monkeys, coconuts, the claws of a crab and the shadow of a bablobrokmadorni stick, the leering teeth of Bao Gahai and (sheer randomness, this) a memory of a long-ago day on the island of Spradley Rock, which had been converted to one gigantic scrub-bath by the invasion of a horde of Yarglat barbarians.

Only Guest himself could possibly be the equal of sorting out such a mess, so, Power having failed, Qinplaqus resorted to interrogation.

"The salient points," said Qinplaqus.

"Uh, myself and the wizards," said Guest, "we ventured to Untunchilamon."

This brief preamble served to offend Thayer Levant, who considered that he had been an equal partner in that venture, and was aggrieved at being overlooked. Of course, Levant was being unrealistic, for a man does not say "I and my servant went venturing" any more than he says "I and my walking stick went venturing" — but his hurt was genuine, even if it was totally unreasonable.

"So," said Qinplaqus, "what did you find on Untunchilamon?"

"A therapist," said Guest. "A therapist, a dorgi, a Crab, a conjurer, a large number of bad-tempered sorcerers, the analytical engine, a madhouse, a slaughterhouse, a dosshouse ... that's about it. Oh, and Shabble."

"What about a Cockroach?" said Qinplaqus.

"A cockroach?" said Guest in puzzlement, wondering if the Silver Emperor was at last lapsing into outright senility.

"Yes, yes, a Cockroach!" said Qinplaqus. "A Cockroach which commanded the worship of men, yes, and women too, and dogs, cats and monkeys for all I know!"

"Oh," said Guest, belatedly remembering. "Yes, there was a Cockroach. It was a god, at least that's what Shabble said, and there were tax advantages — but that was long ago, and in a different country, and the insect must be dead by now."

"It is not dead," said Qinplaqus. "It is an immortal god which successively reincarnates itself in a series of cockroach bodies."

"Are you — are you then a worshipper?" said Guest, wondering if he had mortally offended the Ashdan's piety.

"No!" said Qinplaqus, hammering his pelican-headed walking stick against the floor. "I have no time for this trifling nonsense! But the problem with nonsense is that it becomes serious when enough people believe in it. Shabble and Shabble's god have installed themselves on Alozay. And this—"

"A god!" said Lord Onosh, interrupting with intemperate

force. "Since when is a cockroach a god?"

"Oh, many things can be gods," said Qinplaqus. "Why, this walking stick of mine was once a god in its own right, though it is a god no longer. So. As I was saying, the world's worst nonsense must be taken seriously if enough people believe in it. Shabble has set up a god upon Alozay, and we have no choice but to treat with this problem in a serious manner."

Lord Onosh shook his head. He was still having trouble adjusting to the news. His home island — invaded by a cockroach! The Witchlord Onosh had often feared that the Safrak Islands might be invaded by the Red Emperor, the fearsome Khmar, whose horsemen currently dominated the Collosnon Empire. He had feared, too, that he might be betrayed by the treachery of the Partnership Banks, or face an intemperate challenge from his son Guest. But never in his wildest dreams had he thought himself likely to suffer invasion from a talking ball and an immortal cockroach.

"You say that Shabble is installed upon Alozay," said Guest. "Do you mean that this Shabble-thing is there as a conqueror?"

"Not yet, not yet," said Qinplaqus. "At the moment, Shabble is but an uninvited guest. But I fear that it will be but a matter of time before Shabble declares itself the lord of Alozay, and the lord too of all the Doors of the Circle."

Then Plandruk Qinplaqus called for tea, for coffee, for wine, for chocolate, for sweetmeats, for roast polyps and boiled water, to afford them a break in which they could chew over their difficulties as they chewed over their food.

Guest chewed with some anger.

The Weaponmaster had thought of Untunchilamon as a mere waystation in his life; and, though he had sojourned there for some considerable time, and though a great many things had there happened to him, he had never expected any of the strangers encountered on Untunchilamon to intrude into his future. Least of all on Alozay! After all, there was an entire ocean between Untunchilamon and Alozay.

While chewing, Guest suffered the most horrendous sense of overwhelming difficulties. As a hero whose multiple heroics had no precedent in myth, legend or affidavit, the Weaponmaster had dared unimaginable dangers (including the temptations of therapists and a great Flood of his father's saliva), and had succeeded where many had failed. In the face of all the odds, he had won the wishstone from Untunchilamon and had got it as far as Dalar ken Halvar — but now the wishstone didn't work, or not yet at any rate, and his return home was problematical.

During his earlier sojourn in Dalar ken Halvar, when he had spent four years convalescing from injuries, Guest had learnt something of the rise of the religion of Nu-chala-nuth, which was now the dominant faith in Parengarenga. If Shabble was intent on seizing the Circle of the Doors of the Partnership Banks and converting the world to the doctrines of the Holy Cockroach, then there was surely the potential for a horrific holy war when the adherents of the Cockroach clashed with the Nu-chala-nuth.

So, with a potential religious war added to his own problems, Guest felt positively depressed. And things were all the worse because he was facing his current difficulties without the help of his wizards.

So where exactly were those dignitaries?

When Guest had escaped from Untunchilamon by ship, he had left behind the wizards Pelagius Zozimus and Hostaja Sken-Pitilkin. At the time, Sken-Pitilkin had been trying to build another of his flying machines.

Assuming that he had succeeded ...

"Is Sken-Pitilkin on Alozay?" said Guest, with a note of intense suspicion in his voice.

"Why, yes," said Qinplaqus. "I forgot to mention that. Sken-Pitilkin arrived with Shabble."

"I knew it!" said Guest, speaking like a man who has just discovered a scorpion beneath his pillow. "Only Sken-Pitilkin could have tempted that bubble to Alozay. Shabble could never have got there by accident, not ever! What would Shabble know of Alozay, Safrak, demons, Doors? It's Sken-Pitilkin, he's the one!"

"Yes," said Lord Onosh, relieved to find they had an obvious target to blame for the mess they were in. "I blame it all on Sken-Pitilkin. Him and his flying machines!"

"Yes," said Guest, "if he hadn't got into this business of flying, we'd never have been in this mess. I knew right from the start that those stickbirds of his were bad news. Why, back at Locontareth he wanted to build one especially to drop bombs."

"Bombs?" said Lord Onosh.

"Those rock-things which fly from volcanoes," said Guest. "He wanted to build a stickbird to drop bombs. Drop them on people's heads."

"No, no," said his father. "It was nothing to do with volcanoes. It was donkeys! He was going to load them up then — then drop them on people. He almost killed me with one of his infernal experiments. He dropped a donkey from a roof."

"It might be," said Plandruk Qinplaqus, "that the donkey was a beast of burden which he intended to transport by air, and that its fall was an accident."

"Nonsense!" said Lord Onosh. "For we were preparing for war. And — and there was an armchair on the donkey! One does not go to war with an armchair, not even if one is a sotted old wizard like that worthless Sken-Pitilkin."

Then Guest remembered Sken-Pitilkin talking with the demon Icaria Scaria Iva-Italis about flight. Sken-Pitilkin's intensity had helped convince Guest that the demon was truly a creature of Power. Consequently, Guest was more than half-inclined to blame Sken-Pitilkin for all their subsequent disasters.

And had it not been Sken-Pitilkin who had been truly enthusiastic about questing to Untunchilamon for the x-x-zix? Of course it had been! And why? Perhaps — this was Guest's dire thought — perhaps Sken-Pitilkin had not been intent on winning the wishstone. Perhaps Sken-Pitilkin had bethought himself of the Shabble which lived on Untunchilamon.

So ...

If Sken-Pitilkin had seen Iva-Italis on Alozay, and if Sken-Pitilkin had then gone to Untunchilamon, then might it not be that the wizard's true intent had ever been to introduce Shabble to the demon Italis?

Guest could not help but think that, while a Shabble in isolation was not necessarily particularly dangerous, a Shabble in combination with a demon — or in combination with all the demons of the Circle of the Partnership Banks — might prove an alliance capable of dominating the world.

"We will not be contending with Shabble," said Guest grimly. "Rather, we will be contending with Sken-Pitilkin, for I fear him in conspiracy against us."

"How so?" said Qinplaqus.

"I fear that Sken-Pitilkin may have deliberately sought out Shabble on Untunchilamon with the sole purpose of introducing that delinquent to the demon on Alozay," said Guest. "I fear that Shabble and the demon may now league with Sken-Pitilkin, matching their powers with his powers of flight, and producing a world-dominating combination."

"Then," said Lord Onosh, with the ferocity which befits a Yarglat warlord, "we must hurry to Alozay and cut off Sken-Pitilkin's head!"

But it was not till three days had passed that they were conveyed at last to the Bralsh in covered palankeens.

By this time, Yubi Das Finger had obtained clearance from all the Banks through which Witchlord and Weaponmaster would travel on their way home. They were free to travel.

Plandruk Qinplaqus then assigned Thayer Levant to Guest Gulkan's service, partly so Levant could later bring Qinplaqus an independent account of the activities of Witchlord and Weaponmaster, and partly because Qinplaqus thought that Levant might be of use to those Yarglat barbarians.

After all, had it not been for Levant's audacity and endurance, the x-x-zix would never have reached Dalar ken Halvar and the mazadath would not have been saved for Guest Gulkan. Instead, both those treasures would have fallen to the Mutilator of Yestron.

Levant was not particularly keen to be of service again to Guest, for the Weaponmaster had proved singularly ungrateful for the magnificent service which Levant had rendered him. The shifty-eyed knifeman was beginning to think he had had quite enough of this adventuring business, and that it was time for him to be thinking of settling down in his native Chi'ash-lan, or perhaps in Dalar ken Halvar itself.

But Qinplaqus was adamant.

Levant must go!

"Then we will take Levant," said Guest. "And we will leave you the cornucopia which we won from the Stench Caves of Logthok Norgos. On our behalf you may use it to generate wealth, piling up the treasure which we may need for the financing of our future wars."

So spoke the Weaponmaster. For his part, the Witchlord Onosh was not at all sure that he wished for Plandruk Qinplaqus to take charge of the cornucopia. Nevertheless, the offer could not be unsaid, so the cornucopia was handed over to Qinplaqus. But — to the mutual dismay of both Witchlord and Weaponmaster — the thing had been corrupted by over-use.

For it proved capable of generating nothing but an outflux of black slime, regardless of what was put into it — silver, gold, grapes, chocolate, sand, water, urine, cockroaches, mice, kittens, steel, copper, zinc.

A great disaster, this!

So died all visions of world-conquering wealth; and, depressed at realizing they had won no profit from their raid on the Stench Caves, Witchlord and Weaponmaster prepared to leave Dalar ken Halvar.

In accordance with the insistence of Plandruk Qinplaqus, Thayer Levant accompanied Witchlord and Weaponmaster as they travelled to the Bralsh. There, the three adventurers were admitted to its weirding room; and stepped on to the marble plinth in that weirding room; and stepped through the archway sustained by that plinth; and found themselves in the Singing Dove Pensions Trust of Tang.

Again through the Door, and they were in the Taniwha Guarantee Corporation of Quilth. Another passage through that humming silver screen took them to the Orsay Bank of Stokos. Then to a room of hanging skeletons — the weirding room of the Morgrim Bank of Chi'ash-lan.

The next step would take them home.

Home to Alozay, the ruling island of the Safrak archipelago.

Witchlord and Weaponmaster braced themselves. Levant saw their bracing, anticipated swordplay, and sighed.

They stepped through the Door.

And found themselves in the weirding room in the uppermost chamber of the mainrock Pinnacle, the great spike of rock which dominated the island of Alozay.

And there—

CHAPTER FORTY-TWO

Alozay: ruling island of the Safrak archipelago of the Swelaway
Sea. On Alozay stands the mainrock Pinnacle, home to the
Door of the Safrak Bank. This Bank was formerly ruled by
Lord Sod, who is now a hostage on Alozay, which has been
ruled by the dralkosh Bao Gahai in the absence of the
Witchlord Onosh. Also in residence on Alozay is Guest
Gulkan's scholarly brother, Eljuk Zala Gulkan, he who is
disfigured by a birthmark which dribbles from the corners
of his mouth then spills to a merging at his neck; and Ontario
Nol, a wizard of the order of Itch, who has long been Eljuk's
tutor.

* * *

Through the Door came Witchlord and Weaponmaster, with
Thayer Levant trailing but a footfall behind them, and there they
found Shabble waiting for them.

Lord Onosh was so disconcerted that he almost turned and
fled back through that Door. For, though Guest had by this time
described Shabble often and at length, the Witchlord was hard
put to maintain his composure when he found that the truth of
this flying ball lived to the tale which Guest had told.

"Hello," said Shabble, speaking in the Toxteth which was
used by so many of Alozay's inhabitants.

But Lord Onosh made no reply.

Shabble drifted through the air towards the Witchlord. The
fist-sized bubble pressed itself against the Witchlord's cheek,
rolled up the Witchlord's face, bumped over the ridges of the
Witchlord's slanting forehead, shone a tightly focused beam of
light into the mysterious recesses of the Witchlord's bat-wing
ears, then rolled down his back, ducked between his legs, and
slid upwards through the air till they were (so to speak) face to
face once more.

"Welcome to my island," said Shabble. "I welcome you. You

and my son.”

Then Shabble turned on Guest Gulkan.

Shabble drifted through the air to hang hot and humming by the Weaponmaster’s ear. Shabble was warm, warm as a cat’s yawn, a bath-sponge sea. The warmth was suggestive of magma. Guest thought of scar tissue, of welted burns, of buckled flesh, of molten distortion, of hot-poker pain.

“You have a ring on your finger.”

“A ring?” said Guest.

“A pretty ring,” said Shabble. “Light within and light without. I have heard of this ring. Yilda!”

At that, one of Shabble’s people approached. A woman. A hard-bitten woman named Yilda, whom Guest had last seen on Untunchilamon. At that time, he had scarcely remarked her face, for he had not thought her made for great destiny. But obviously he had been wrong.

“Give her the ring,” said Shabble. “Do not — do not! — swallow it. The corpse master Uckermark is somewhere in this rock, and his skill is ample for dissection.”

Guest knew this Uckermark also. The thus-named corpse master had been another of the denizens of Untunchilamon, another of those people whom Guest had never expected to see ever again in his entire life.

Guest handed over the ring of ever-ice, the ring which could open and close time pods.

Yilda slipped it on her own finger.

Guest then expected Shabble to ask for the mazadath, the silver-gleaming amulet which hung round Guest’s neck, against his skin and hidden from the world.

“Guest,” said Shabble, singing the name with lilting sweetness. “Guest. There is something else.”

“Is there?” said Guest.

He was very conscious of the mazadath’s weight. He did not want to give it up. Why? He knew of no certain use for it. But if he could only retain its possession, concealing it from this Shabble, then he would feel he had won a victory of a kind, if only a moral victory.

"Guest, Guest," crooned Shabble. "My dear friend Guest. The wishstone. You had it. Where is it?"

"Did I have it?" said Guest.

"You did!" said Shabble. "And the Cockroach has need of it!"

"Then," said Guest, "you'll have to ask Thayer Levant where it got to, because he was the one who had it last!"

"Levant?" said Shabble.

Guest indicated the ever-faithful Thayer Levant. Shabble sang out for guards, and Levant was taken away for interrogation — while Witchlord and Weaponmaster were escorted to the lower depths of the mainrock Pinnacle.

Guest and his father fully expected to be promptly thrown into a prison cell. But, instead, they were shown to the best of all available quarters, and were told that they were to be guests of honour at a banquet.

And, that very evening, Guest Gulkan and his father dined in the banquet hall which was such a prominent feature of Dolce Obo, the Pillow Stratum of the Grand Palace of Alozay. Guest was surprised to find the bounty of the autumn harvest gracing the banquet table, for the Weaponmaster had been chronologically disorientated by the pressure of recent events, and by his rapid translation between the differing climates of Obooloo, Dalar ken Halvar and Alozay.

But autumn it was.

Guest Gulkan had spent so much time adventuring in Untunchilamon and counting the shadows in a dungeon in Obooloo that the Witchlord Onosh had not been liberated from his time pod in the Temple of Blood until that Midsummer's Day which had been the first day of the Third Year of Peace in the Izdimir Empire.

That day was now three months in the past; the season had turned from summer to autumn; and Alozay was feeding on all that came to the Safrak archipelago from the lands surrounding the Swelaway Sea. Plums, pumpkin, apples, cucumber ... Guest lost track of the number of fresh good things laid out to eat.

Yet the Weaponmaster found he wished to satisfy his

appetite for conversation more urgently than he wished to appease any demands made by his belly.

At the banquet table he could see his brother Eljuk, and after their long separation Guest found himself longing to talk with Eljuk. Eljuk had stayed on Alozay when Witchlord and Weaponmaster had departed, meaning to raid Obooloo and rescue the Great God Jocasta from Anaconda Stogirov's Temple of Blood.

While Guest had been adventuring, Eljuk had remained on Alozay, studying under the tutelage of Ontario Nol, the wizard of Itch to whom he was apprenticed. Guest found the thought of such a quiet, steady and uneventful life quite incredible, for it seemed to him that the whole world had been the scene of unrelenting alarums for years on end.

Yet the truth is that the world had been a fairly peaceful place in the last few years. At least, the part of the world inhabited by Eljuk had been peaceful. After the departure of Witchlord and Weaponmaster, Bao Gahai had ruled Alozay with an iron hand, managing the affairs of the Safrak Bank efficiently, and managing too the matter of Alozay's relationships with the other Partnership Banks.

To Guest, Eljuk represented — among other things — the confidence and security of the life he had enjoyed before becoming entangled in the world of gods and demons. So he longed to talk with his brother. But he was denied opportunity for such conversation, for he was seated between the wizard Sken-Pitilkin and Sod's daughter Damsel. Damsel, who had once perched upon the Weaponmaster, squealing like a wounded mouse as she crested to her ecstasy, spent the whole meal practising her seductive wiles on the corpse master Uckermark, who was seated on her left. So Guest was left at the mercy of Sken-Pitilkin.

While both Witchlord and Weaponmaster had come to Alozay with the idea of administering a degree of discipline to that wizard of Skatzabratzumon (with Lord Onosh being determined to remove his head, while Guest was more inclined to think the cropping of his ears would be sufficient) they had both now set aside thoughts of such punishment. For both had focused their thoughts firmly on their true enemy: Shabble.

Shabble the usurper!

In any case, it soon became clear that the suspicions of Witchlord and Weaponmaster were unfounded, and that Sken-Pitilkin had not wilfully conspired to bring Shabble to Alozay. This became particularly clear to Guest at that banquet, for, speaking with all the zeal of a born lecturer, Sken-Pitilkin took the Weaponmaster through a full account of the vicissitudes of his recent life.

After fleeing from Untunchilamon, the sagacious Sken-Pitilkin had eventually arrived at Port Domax with Shabble. No easy journey, that! For, just as Guest had suffered unanticipated complications to his journey from Injiltaprajura to Dalar ken Halvar, so too had Sken-Pitilkin endured a number of the most perilous and extraordinary embroilments imaginable. And the wizard told the Weaponmaster of all of these embroilments — and told of them at full length.

At last, however, Sken-Pitilkin had reached Port Domax, the famous free port on the southern shores of Tameran. There, Shabble had founded a Temple of Cockroach, a temple to be presided over by two natives of Untunchilamon, a young man named Chegory Guy and a young woman named Olivia Qasaba.

Thereafter, Shabble had taken to exploring the surroundings, eventually venturing as far as Safrak.

"It may well be," said Sken-Pitilkin, "that Shabble knew of this place from earlier encounter. But in any case, little can be hidden from a bubble so versatile in its curiosity. The fact is that Shabble won every secret of the Safrak Bank, and then prevailed upon Bao Gahai to establish a branch of the Cult of Cockroach upon Alozay."

Adroitly blackmailed by Shabble — who threatened to expose the secret of the Doors of the Circle of the Partnership Banks to the whole world — Bao Gahai had conceded the Cockroach a temple. The dralkosh had hoped that Shabble would be content with that, but by slow and remorseless degrees Shabble had built up an organization on Alozay and had taken all power on that island into (so to speak) its own hands.

"Well," said Guest, when Sken-Pitilkin's story was finished. "This is all much different than what we were led to expect by Plandruk Qinplaqus."

"Dalar ken Halvar cannot hope to have any certain knowledge of Safrak," said Sken-Pitilkin, "for Shabble has not allowed the Banks any unrestricted use of the Door. The bouncing bubble is feckless when its attention wanders, but right now it is flushed with the first enthusiasm of a new toy. I think the Circle will hold its full attention for some time to come, and it will be hard for anyone to distract it. These days, Shabble spends the daylight with the Door, examining all those who come through it, and sleeps by night with the star-globe on the floor beside it."

"You mean," said Guest, "that the Door is closed by night?"

"I do," said Sken-Pitilkin.

The wizard needed to say no more on that subject, because Guest could imagine how such nightly closure would distress the Banks, which were accustomed to make full and never-ceasing use of the Circle of Doors to shift their merchandise from one place to another.

"Have you more to tell?" said Guest, still unclear as to whether or not Sken-Pitilkin had thrown in his lot with Shabble.

"No," said Sken-Pitilkin. "That's it. That's the story of our lives since last we met. Your own story, I hazard, is more of a saga in its shaping."

"So it is," said Guest. "But before I tell it, pray tell me this — where is our friend Zozimus?"

"Why," said Sken-Pitilkin, "he is still in Port Domax, still the pet of the sweet Olivia, since he is still incarcerated in the flesh of a hamster."

"Still!" said Guest.

"I fear," said Sken-Pitilkin solemnly, "that his transformation may be permanent."

"So," said Guest Gulkan, "Zozimus is doomed to serve a hamster's flesh, and we in our turn are doomed to be slaves in the service of Shabble."

"You have truthed about Zozimus," said Sken-Pitilkin, "but declare your own fate in error. You will be no slaves for Shabble. Rather, you are far likelier to be emperors, since Shabble plans nothing less than the conquest of the world. The smallest part of Shabble's domains will then be an empire, and each of you likely to have charge of such."

Though Guest had feared that Shabble might have designs on the very world itself, it was one thing to fear as much and quite another to hear it stated of a certainty.

"You spoke of the Circle!" said Guest, in unconcealed alarm. "You said nothing of the world!"

"No," said Sken-Pitilkin, "but I am saying it now. Shabble, my friend, in truth plans nothing more or less than the conquest of the world."

"Who told you that?" said Guest, wondering if the wizard had perhaps been reading his mind.

"Why, Shabble, of course!" said Sken-Pitilkin — who, as a wizard of the order of Skatzabratzumon, had absolutely no mind-reading powers whatsoever.

Then Sken-Pitilkin elaborated Shabble's plans. The bubble of bounce planned to use the Circle of the Partnership Banks to spread the Cult of Cockroach throughout the whole world.

Guest did not like this idea one little bit, because he was unwilling to bow to a bubble. Or to propitiate Cockroach! He was still not sure where Sken-Pitilkin stood — so took a risk, and made his displeasure plain.

"I would rather see the world burn than see it fall to Shabble's possession," said Guest.

Sken-Pitilkin looked around the banquet hall to see where Shabble was. Shabble was chasing in and out of the smoke-rings which were being blown by a pipe-smoking Yilda. Safrak's banquet hall was dominated by the braying hubbub of a heavy-drinking dinner in its bone-picking phase. Sken-Pitilkin looked around to make sure no servant was standing behind him, then masked his mouth with a wineglass full of red, then leaned close to the Weaponmaster and said:

"If you wish to overthrow Shabble," said Sken-Pitilkin,

"then you will need allies for the purpose. I suggest you speak to your tutelary demon to see how that dignitary views our bubble."

Guest Gulkan did not like this idea at all, but after some persuading by Sken-Pitilkin he left the banquet early and took himself off to the Hall of Time. Thus did the lordly Weaponmaster come once more into the presence of Icaria Scaria Iva-Italis, Demon by Appointment to the Great God Jocasta.

The jade-green monolith of cold-glowing stone stood exactly where Guest had left it — at the eastern end of the Hall of Time. Little had changed in that Hall. It was larger than Guest remembered, for his recent past was so tainted by dungeon confinements and underground endurance tests that his memories of the entire world had been claustrophobically squeezed. Yet the oval Hall cut in the granite of the mainrock Pinnacle had undergone no such crushing, and was still its full hundred paces in length, its full three dozen paces in width. And the jade-block demon was still its original height, which was twice Guest Gulkan's own.

"So," said Iva-Italis, when Guest presented himself. "It's you. Have you come to beg forgiveness of my lord and master?"

The demon addressed Guest in Eparget — a courtesy which was much appreciated. In many ways, Guest had found the worst and most effortful part of his travels to be the weary business of dickering with strangers in languages of which he lacked a perfect comprehension. To be addressed in the Eparget of his Yarglat upbringing was a great relief, and Guest felt a surge of positive gratitude. Even so, he did his best to hide that emotion.

"No," said Guest staunchly. "I have not come to beg forgiveness. It's you who should be begging me. And I wouldn't forgive you even if you did. You never told me I needed a knife!"

By this remark, Guest was referring to the special knife he had needed to cut the Great God Jocasta free from force-field imprisonment — the knife which he had been forced to win from the Mutilator of Yestron in battle.

The knife which — he did not like to remember it! — he had subsequently lost in the Temple of Blood.

But, though the need for such a knife had not been explicated to Guest before his first venture to the Temple of Blood, and though Guest had suffered much at the hands of the Great God Jocasta since then, the demon Iva-Italis did not so much as bother to acknowledge the Weaponmaster's discontent.

"If you are not here to beg forgiveness," said Iva-Italis, "then what are you here for?"

Guest, seeing that the demon was quite shameless about the way in which it had misled him about the nature of the task it had wanted him to perform in Obooloo, dropped the subject and got down to business immediately.

"I have come to seek your aid against Shabble," said Guest. "I don't know if you've heard, but Shabble has seized Safrak. Shabble's a ball, a ball which flies. It throws fire, too, and speaks in prophecy of the teachings of a Cockroach."

"I know of Shabble," said Iva-Italis. "And I know of Shabble's recent doings. Do not trouble your head about Shabble, dear friend, for Shabble is but a toy, a thing of trifles."

"A toy!" said Guest.

"Just so," said Iva-Italis approvingly.

"This ... this toy of which you speak so lightly, this toy has set its heart on global conquest, a feat one thinks within its powers."

"Undoubtedly," said Iva-Italis, entirely unperturbed by this probability. "So Shabble seizes. So Shabble conquers. But, having seized, will Shabble hold?"

"I don't see what can stop the thing," said Guest.

"It's not a question of stopping," said Iva-Italis. "The thing is a toy, as I have said. It is trifling in its nature. It has fads, fashions, passing fancies. The preaching of religion, the conquest of the world — Guest, the thing is but a bubble. It will tire of its games. Come back to me when Shabble is gone, and then we will talk business."

Privately, Guest thought as did Iva-Italis. Shabble would tire of the game of world conquest sooner or later. But it had by now occurred to Guest that the people Shabble had been installing on Alozay — many of them piratical refugees who had fled from Untunchilamon and had arrived by diverse paths at the Temple of Cockroach which had been founded in Port Domax — would not tire so readily.

By the time Shabble abandoned the Circle of the Partnership Banks to find new toys elsewhere, Shabble's followers might have consolidated a regime which could rule the world with or without the bubble of bounce — a regime which would have precious little use for Guest Gulkan, and precious little time for his pretensions to power.

So Guest wanted Shabble abolished — and now!

Guest had expected Iva-Italis to be angry rather than calm; and, finding the demon not angry, Guest presumed the thing to be ignorant of the fate of its master Jocasta, and hence vulnerable to bluff.

"My lord," said Guest, seeking some way to bend Iva-Italis to his will. "You may not have heard, but your master Jocasta is in desperate peril in Obooloo. Shabble has chosen to close the Door which gives us access to Obooloo from Alozay. If we could but reopen that Door, and promptly, then—"

"You are a liar," said Iva-Italis calmly.

"A liar?" said Guest, affecting surprise. "Me? My lord, the Yarglat are noted for their honour."

"You," said Iva-Italis, "are noted for the weight of your turds and the bigness of your ears. I am in daily contact with the Great God Jocasta. Even now, that Great God languishes in Dalar ken Halvar, recovering its strength after an encounter with the evil Anaconda Stogirov."

"So you will not help me," said Guest.

"I will do nothing precipitate," said Iva-Italis. "If you cannot control your suicidal urge to over-hasty action, then you must find your death in your own time, in your own way, and without any help from me."

Rebuffed, Guest Gulkan withdrew, and began to brood his way around the Hall of Time, pacing a slow and steady track around its echoing oval. While he tried to think of a way to coerce Iva-Italis to his service, he began an idle inspection of the time pods, smearing away the dust and spiders to gaze on the visages inside.

Most were unchanged from the first inspection he had made of this facility — long, long ago, in the years when he had been but a boy hostage on Alozay.

But to his surprise, when he had scarcely begun his inspection, Guest found someone who was — was it? — yes! — it was her! Yerzerdayla! Yerzerdayla, yes, the woman whom he had won from Thodric Jarl in combat! Yerzerdayla the fair, locked in her time prison!

Guest Gulkan thought this the greatest of all imaginable mysteries, for he had long been under the impression that Yerzerdayla had been left in Gendormargensis when Witchlord and Weaponmaster had gone to war with each other. As the interloper Khmar had taken advantage of that civil war to conquer first Gendormargensis then the entire Collosnon Empire, Guest believed that Yerzerdayla had surely fallen to Khmar's possession. He had heard, after all, that Thodric Jarl had chosen to enter Khmar's service specifically so he could reclaim the luscious Yerzerdayla.

So how had Yerzerdayla come to be on Alozay?

A great, great mystery!

Of course it was really no mystery at all. For the simple fact was that the Witchlord Onosh, insulted to find Thodric Jarl leaving his service on account of a woman, had arranged by secret treaty for Yerzerdayla to be covertly brought to Safrak.

The Weaponmaster — who had entirely forgotten about his beloved Penelope now that he had sight of Yerzerdayla — caught himself licking his lips.

He broke away from the time prison pod, since staring at the stasis-frozen woman was getting him nowhere. From past experience he knew full well that the pods could not be broken by brute force — they could only be opened or closed by application of ever-ice. And the sole chip of ever-ice on Alozay was in the ring which had fallen to Yilda's possession!

Well.

Guest Gulkan was not about to confess his need for that ring, since such confession would give Yilda a hold over him, and give Shabble a hold too.

As Guest turned away from Yerzerdayla, a thought occurred to him. He returned to the ever-patient block of jade which represented the corporeal form of Icaria Scaria Iva-Italis.

"My good lord Italis," said Guest.

"Iva-Italis," said the demon, as fond of its proper name as any person-in-the-flesh.

"Iva-Italis," said Guest. "Can you ... have you any idea how long Shabble usually maintains an interest in ... in a new sport?"

"Shabble," said Iva-Italis, "never maintains an interest in anything for more than half a thousand years at a time."

Half a thousand years!

That prospect was enough to push Guest into swift and decisive action, and soon afterwards a gathering of seven met in conspiracy. Those seven were Vernon Brigadoon Sod, Onosh Gulkan, Guest Gulkan, Eljuk Zala Gulkan, Thayer Levant, Ontario Nol and Hostaja Sken-Pitilkin.

"Half a thousand years!" said Sod, when he knew the worst.

"One suspects," said Lord Onosh, "that it is but the blink of an eye to a demon."

"An eyeblink!" said Sod. "I have been on Alozay far too long to suffer another eyelash of it!"

Banker Sod had of course been taken hostage before Witchlord and Weaponmaster went questing for the x-x-zix. Sod had expected his hostagehood to be brief, but instead it had stretched out almost to eternity.

"So the demon will wait," said Ontario Nol. "It will wait rather than help us. Very well. Then we must wait likewise. Or else we must steel ourselves to action, and tackle this Shabble on our own. However ... do we have the power to destroy this Shabble? One doubts it."

"The thing can be broken," said Sken-Pitilkin.

"Surely," said Guest Gulkan, remembering back to his adventures on Untunchilamon, and a crisis of combat in the wormways deep beneath the equatorial city of Injiltaprajura. "It can be broken, and knows it, and fears its own breakage."

"How do you know that?" said Eljuk Zala, he who in his prideful days as a wizard's apprentice was inclined to doubt very much that his warworthy but ignorant brother Guest could be an authority on anything as arcane as a Shabble.

"We fought this Shabble on Untunchilamon," said Guest. "There was an iron dog, underneath the city. A dorgi. The iron dog, the dorgi, the dorgi made the bubble run. Later, there was a demon."

"Like Iva-Italis?" said Eljuk.

"No," said Guest, glad to be able to lecture his scholarly brother for once, instead of enduring the reverse position. "The demon on Untunchilamon was greater by far. Not a rock but a spirit. It's name was Binchinminfin."

Then Guest indulged himself by giving his wide-mouthed brother Eljuk a terse but melodramatic account of the doings of the demon Binchinminfin on the island of Untunchilamon.

"We were underground when the demon raided Untunchilamon," said Guest. "We were held prisoner by Shabble. But by the time Shabble got us to the surface, why, this demon Binchinminfin had seized the island's ruling palace. So we decided to attack it. Shabble set us at liberty, and we launched ourselves on an assault of the palace."

"And?" said Eljuk.

"And we were lucky not to be killed!" said Guest. "The demon was mightier than any of us! It almost killed Shabble! There was a firefight, Shabble and the demon. Then Shabble ran, because the bubble was too scared to fight with Binchinminfin any further."

"So what did you do then?" said Eljuk.

"Why," said Guest, "we left the demon in possession of the palace. Then we went downhill and we all got drunk."

This was the truth, but it was not at all what Eljuk had expected to hear. He had expected to hear that his warworthy brother had somehow challenged the demon and defeated it — though the sorry truth was that the mastery of Binchinminfin had proved beyond Guest Gulkan's means, and in the end the task of getting rid of it had been accomplished by an Ebrell Islander named Chegory Guy, whose later destiny had been to serve the Cockroach in a temple in Port Domax.

Seeing that he was in danger of losing some large fraction of his brother's esteem, Guest hurried past the subject of getting drunk in the face of a demon's danger.

"Anyway," said Guest, "enough of Binchinminfin! Suffice it to say that the demon, why, it could take people in possession then change their form to whatever monstrosity suited its purposes. That demon — why, that one made Shabble run."

"How?" said Eljuk, wishing that he himself had been privileged to see the doings of Binchinminfin on Untunchilamon.

"I don't know," said Guest. "Maybe Iva-Italis could tell us, after all, Italis is a demon of sorts, but Italis doesn't want to help."

With a brute force confrontation being eventually ruled out by careful debate, the conspiracy then discussed the character of Shabble's trusted associates, and in particular the character of Yilda and Uckermark.

"Uckermark is a corpse master," said the Weaponmaster. "He's a pillager and a pirate to boot. A booty-hunter with the morals of a mosquito. If we can bribe him to our purpose, then he'll turn from Shabble's service sharply enough."

"But Shabble is bent on world conquest," said Lord Onosh. "What could we offer Uckermark which would over-shadow the potential rewards of association with a world-conqueror?"

"I think," said Eljuk Zala. "I think—"

"About time, young man," said Sken-Pitilkin. "I always thought you had some thinking in you, if you would but give yourself a chance. Tell us now, what do you think?"

"We may perhaps lack the slaughtering of this Shabble," said Eljuk. "But I think its displacement still within our power."

"Displacement?" said Guest, who knew not that word in its Galish incarnation.

"Maybe he means we could kick it," said Thayer Levant.

"I have," said Eljuk Zala carefully, "something very close to that in mind."

Then Eljuk explained what he had in mind.

CHAPTER FORTY-THREE

Name: Vernon Brigadoon Sod (aka Banker Sod)

Birthplace: Latimore (a small town near Chi'ash-lan)

Occupation: merchant banker

Status: owner of the Morgrim Bank of Chi'ash-lan; claimant to the Safrak Bank; sometime Governor of the Partnership Banks; owner of the wondrous Pazabantsen mansion (most notable building in all of Chi'ash-lan); father of the voluptuous Damsel

Description: florid male of iceman race, with the black fingernails and thick white bodyhair so typical of that breed. Hair, eyes and teeth all similarly yellow.

Hobby: breeding snails

Quote: "The world's one great hidden secret is that we live in a great Age of Agiotage. This is the real significance of the Circle of the Doors."

* * *

The conspirators required a night of cloud and fog, something they could not wish into being by mere force of will alone. The right conditions first came some five nights after the banquet which had greeted the return of Witchlord and Weaponmaster to the island of Alozay.

With a night of cloud and fog having been secured to their satisfaction, the conspirators gathered in the banquet hall in Dolce Obo, the Pillow Stratum of the mainrock Pinnacle. In that great gloom, they confirmed their federation.

Sken-Pitilkin had a stickbird airship waiting on the Palace Docks of Alozay. The wizard of Skatzabratzumon, accompanied by Ontario Nol and Eljuk Zala, would fly the airship to the heights. As a wizard of Itch, Ontario Nol had powers to command the winds, and Nol's ability to summon up a miniature tornado or a minor whirlwind could conceivably prove useful if things went wrong and they found themselves locked in outright battle with Shabble.

With those three confirmed in their roles, they departed, going downward towards the Winch Stratum, where bribed washerwomen were waiting to lower them to the docks where Sken-Pitilkin's stickbird waited.

For his part, the Witchlord Onosh would play no active role in the assault on Shabble. Rather, he would withdraw and wait. Once the star-globe had been stolen, Lord Onosh would stay on Alozay and play at being innocent. If Shabble chose to remain on the island even with the star-globe gone, why then, Lord Onosh would accept Shabble's authority.

But if Shabble left the island, then Lord Onosh would seize power — easy enough to do, since everyone on the island was loyal to him but for a few bandits such as Yilda and Uckermark who gave their allegiance to Shabble.

"Unfortunately," said Lord Onosh, "I do not think it wise to barbecue this Uckermark, or pull his teeth out one by one, lest Shabble hear of it and one day take revenge. But you can be assured that his authority will cease the moment the bubble flees this realm!"

"Yes," said Guest. "All well and good. But remember that Yilda has my ring! Don't let her swallow it!"

"I won't," said Lord Onosh. "I'll make very sure I get hold of that ring."

It had already been agreed among the conspirators that the star-globe would not return to Alozay until three years had passed. That should prove long enough for Shabble to lose interest in the island and depart.

Banker Sod had insisted on accompanying the star-globe into exile, hence was to accompany the raiding party which would shortly venture upstairs to steal treasure from Shabble.

"You realize," said Lord Onosh, who did not trust Banker Sod any further than he trusted the demon Italis, "that if you do not return at the end of three years, then I will execute your daughter Damsel."

"I know it," said Sod.

Sod had pledged his daughter Damsel as a hostage — without consulting that young woman on the matter.

That, then, was the plan.

The star-globe would be stolen, and carried far from Alozay, and kept away from that island for three years. To safeguard the star-globe, those who stole it would not decide upon their place of exile until three years had passed. That way, even if Shabble interrogated Lord Onosh, the Witchlord would not be able to say where the star-globe had gone to.

At the end of three years, with Shabble having departed — back to Port Domax and its Temple of the Holy Cockroach, or back to Untunchilamon perhaps — Sken-Pitilkin would return the star-globe to Alozay by stickbird, and the Circle of the Partnership Banks would once more be reopened.

With all confirmed, Lord Onosh took himself off to his bed — not to sleep, but to worry.

That left three.

Sken-Pitilkin, Ontario Nol and Eljuk Zala Gulkan had gone downwards to the docks of Alozay. All going right, they should have claimed Sken-Pitilkin's stickbird already, and have lofted the thing to the air. Lord Onosh had taken himself off to bed.

So the only people left in the banqueting hall were those who were going to tackle Shabble head on head: the Weaponmaster Guest Gulkan, his faithful servant Thayer Levant, and Banker Sod of Chi'ash-lan.

"Well," said Guest, uneasily. "Let's get on with it."

Then, with Thayer Levant lighting the way with two lanterns carried on a bablobrokmadorni stick — an implement unknown on Alozay until it had been imported by some of the piratical refugees from Untunchilamon — they made their way upward through the mainrock. As they went, Guest Gulkan worried. In particular, he worried about Sod, and the difficulties of guarding against Sod's treachery for three long years of exile.

And where would they spend that exile?

The idea of not deciding on a destination until they had quit Alozay was a good one. It secured them against accidental betrayal. But it also made Guest profoundly unsettled not to know where he would spend the next three years.

Where could they go?

Galsh Ebrek? Possibly, but rumours from Galsh Ebrek reached Port Domax by way of trade. Ashmolea? A highly civilized place, by all accounts, but also another place which traded with Port Domax. Dalar ken Halvar? Too dangerous, since Shabble knew that Witchlord and Weaponmaster had lately been in that city. Drangsturm? Sken-Pitilkin could go nowhere near Drangsturm, since he was a renegade wanted by the Confederation of Wizards. Sken-Pitilkin's home island, then? No, for Shabble would surely think to seek for the wizard of Drum on the island of Drum. What about Chi'ash-lan itself? Too dangerous, for it would put them in Sod's power.

So where?

Sken-Pitilkin seemed so confident that he would be able to hide in a place beyond Shabble's reach that Guest was slowly coming to the conclusion that the wizard of Skatzabratzumon intended to fly them to Argan South, and land them in the terror-lands of the Deep South, those wastelands which were commanded by the monsters of the Swarms.

He did not like that idea at all.

Revolving such complexities in his mind, Guest Gulkan walked as rearguard behind Sod and Thayer Levant as they quit Dolce Obo, the Pillow Stratum, home to the mainrock's living quarters.

Quitting Dolce Obo, they ventured upward through the office layer of Inic Obo, the enforcement layer of Brondon Obo and the paper-storage layer of Trilip Obo. At Trilip Obo, they paused for long enough to set fire to the outer wooden staircase which led upwards to the weirding room. Then they took the inner stairway which led upwards from Trilip Obo to Zi Obo, the Pod Stratum.

Zi Obo had but the single room, this being the Hall of Time. As the three made their way across the skull-pattern tiles to the stairway at the eastern end of the Hall of Time, Guest Gulkan was not at all sure whether the demon Iva-Italis would allow them to pass. If not, their plan would be doomed to failure, for they had already set fire to the wooden outer stairs which connected Trilip Obo with the weirding room of the Safrak Bank.

But Iva-Italis maintained a glow-worm's silence, and allowed them to pass without challenge or comment.

As they went up the stairs, Guest Gulkan took the lead, with Sod and Thayer Levant falling behind. At the head of the stairs, the Weaponmaster halted, and surveyed the weirding room of the Safrak Bank, which was lit by a lantern hung from the very arch of the Door itself. On the floor of the weirding room, Shabble was sleeping, nestled beside the star-globe, like a kitten at sleep beside a sister-kitten.

While sleeping, Shabble dreamed. Dreaming, the immortal bubble changed colour, glowing first silver then gold. A fragmentary image of sleek-sea depths brightened on Shabble's surface. A dolphin flashed across the sea then shattered to diamonds. The diamonds fell, tinkling sharply as they burst to a brightness of blood. The blood darkened. Shabble darkened. Became black blood. Black opal. Coral black in the night-dark depths of a whale-belly sea.

In darkness, Shabble was silent.

Guest Gulkan found the spectacle of this dreaming Shabble aroused in his soul a delicate sense of wonder. But Banker Sod was dead to the minor enchantments of this spectacle-in-miniature. Sod most certainly had a soul of his own — though the asset in question was mortgaged three times over to the tutelary gods of Chi'ash-lan — but there was no seat for a sense of wonder in the frosty iron from which the dourness of that soul had been forged. Banker Sod was a banker indeed, banker in blood and banker in bone, and when Sod saw the Shabble asleep with the star-globe he wailed:

—Loss loss loss loss loss!

While Shabble slept, the Doors were denied to the Banks, and while the Banks were banned from the Circle they could not proceed with the transit of chocolate and opals from Dalar ken Halvar, of Stokos steel from the Orsay Bank, of leeches from Wen Endex and silk from Tang, of rice from Voice, of snow and ice from Chi'ash-lan. Sod's commercial sense was geared up to accommodate the intricacies of contractual order, so Sod could not begin to encompass the calculations necessary to assess the financial devastation wrought by Shabble's piratical irresponsibility.

As Sod calculated — despite the impossibility of the task, he could not keep himself from trying — smoke from the burning staircase began to fill the room.

As the room started to fill with choking smoke, Thayer Levant cocked his crossbow. Then Levant lay down — carefully, for his crossbow had a hair-trigger, and could easily be set off by accident — and loaded the crossbow with a quarrel. Levant lay flat, and took aim at Shabble, lining up Shabble with one of the open floor-to-ceiling windows which connected the weirding room with the night of fog and clouds outside.

Then Levant fired, unleashing a blunt-tipped quarrel which went hurtling in Shabble's direction.

The quarrel smashed into Shabble.

Shabble was slammed across the room and knocked through the nearest arched window.

"Go!" yelled the Weaponmaster.

Sod charged across the room, grabbed the star-globe, then rushed to the window. Guest Gulkan followed, as did Levant. Levant gave a piercing whistle. In response to that whistle, Sken-Pitilkin's airship swooped down.

Guest, Sod and Levant joined Sken-Pitilkin, Eljuk and Ontario Nol in Sken-Pitilkin's stickbird. Sken-Pitilkin took the star-globe into his own hands — for he thought Sod an unreliable custodian of such a treasure — then sent his stickbird whirling to the skies.

As Sken-Pitilkin and his passengers climbed towards the heights, there glowed in the fog behind them an arc of fire, an arc which marked the wrath of the burning of the exterior stairway built out from the side of the mainrock Pinnacle.

* * *

For Shabble, it was all very confusing. Shabble was happily dreaming, bobbing up and down in seas of silver-sharded dream music, when the world suddenly bucked and buckled, and the bubble of bounce found itself unceremoniously smashed into wakefulness.

"Squa!" squeaked Shabble, in shocked amazement.

The entire world appeared to have unaccountably vanished. Gone was the mainrock Pinnacle, gone the kitten-friendly company of wishstone and star-globe. Instead, Shabble was lost in a formless blackness-in-greyness-in-blackness, a nothing-in-nothing, a primordial pre-Creation chaos.

The world had ended!

The universe had ceased to be!

Time was at an end, and Shabble had suffered the misfortune of surviving that end!

Shabble had time to think just this:

—Woe!

Then Shabble realized that Shabbleself was falling.

A moment later, the bubble was struck by the slam-shock impact of the Swelaway Sea. The falling bubble hit the waters hard and fast, and plunged deep into the watery darkness.

Lost.

Bewildered.

Utterly confused.

In many ways, Shabble was much smarter than any human, but Shabble had been short-changed in the matter of unreasoned orientation. A human shocked awake in unfamiliar circumstances will orientate itself to new surroundings almost instantaneously. A cat or dog will do likewise. But Shabble had been designed to run on logic — albeit the logic of a child rather than that of an adult — and hence was poorly equipped to deal with any alogical ellipsis.

And what is more illogical than to go to sleep in a tower and wake to find oneself in water?

—But it is water.

So thought Shabble, still sinking, and still trying to work out what had happened and where it was.

—I'm in water.

—I think.

—But what kind of water?

Then Shabble steadied itself. Once stable, Shabble spat out a fireball to mark its place, then let itself sink again. Using the quick-fading fireball as a watermark, Shabble computed the rate of sinkage, deduced the salinity of the water, and pronounced the water fresh.

—I'm in fresh water.

—The Swelaway Sea is fresh not salt.

—So maybe.

—Maybe ...

The hard-thinking bubble decided that maybe — indeed, probably — it had been violently displaced from the main-rock Pinnacle and precipitated into the waters of the Swelaway Sea.

Which meant ...

Why, it meant that in all probability someone had attacked poor Shabble with a weapon from the Nexus or the Technic Renaissance. Perhaps a force-shock projector such as a Maverick IV slam-gun.

"Well," said Shabble, loudly, "you're going to pay for that."

Having issued that threat — easy enough to do underwater, since Shabble lacked any mouth or other orifice, and hence could speak as easily to the fishes as the birds — Shabble quested upwards to the surface.

Won the night air.

Spun thrice, to rid itself of excess water.

Then started to climb.

Somewhere out in the fog of the night, a fire was burning, high, high above the water. Shabble sent flame flaring through the baffling fog, fire answering to fire. Then Shabble homed in on the flames, and found the stairway outside the mainrock Pinnacle to be burning.

It had been the hope of the conspirators that Shabble would be confused by the fire, and would waste valuable time in searching the burning stairway for clues as to the loss of the star-globe. But Shabble had lived through much human disorder, and on the grounds of grim experience the bubble of bounce had come to associate arson as a customary and essentially motiveless manifestation of all other forms of disorder.

Therefore, when Shabble saw the stairway burning, Shabble thought thus:

—Oh, the stairway's burning!

And having thus acknowledged the fact, Shabble wasted no further time on it, but instead did a swift-search sprint up and down a quick half-dozen stairways.

The search ended when Shabble dropped down to the Palace Docks of Alozay and found Sken-Pitilkin's stickbird missing. Then Shabble guessed! Then Shabble knew!

The bubble sprinted outwards, whizzed upwards, shot through one of the windows of the Hall of Time, and spun to a hovering halt in the presence of Icaria Scaria Iva-Italis, Demon By Appointment to the Great God Jocasta.

"Where's Sken-Pitilkin?" said Shabble. "Him and whoever's with him! Where are they?"

"They are fled by air," said Iva-Italis.

Since Shabble's arrival on Alozay, the quarantine which had previously isolated the demon had ended entirely, and Italis had since made up for lost time. Icaria Scaria Iva-Italis knew much, heard much, guessed much, was nourished in wisdom by spies and informers, and had wit sufficient to deduce what was not told by direct presentation. "They are fled — Sken-Pitilkin, Sod, Levant, Guest Gulkan, and possibly others. They have fled by air, and if you are swift you will catch them."

"Which way have they gone?" said Shabble.

"Seek!" said Iva-Italis. "Seek, seek! For as you bubble in your folly they are cleaning their heels with the moon's doormats."

"The clouds, you mean," said Shabble.

"Of course," said Iva-Italis, indulging in a moment's smug pride. "For I am a poet among other things, poetry being—"

But Shabble was gone already.

Through a slit window shot Shabble, slicing with speed towards the north. Then Shabble climbed, and scanned. But all was cloud, impenetrable cloud which hid the thieves who had made off with the star-globe. Shabble blasted fire in all directions. Clouds bloomed red. Water steamed as bolts of Shabble-wrath struck home.

But all was useless, useless, for the night was vast and Shabble but a pinprick lost in that night. Shabble was most upset. Everything had been going so well! It had been so much fun!

But now—

Shabble returned to Alozay, and in the Hall of Time the bubble of bounce again sought counsel from the demon Icaria Scaria Iva-Italis.

"What's happened, little friend?" said Iva-Italis. "Couldn't you catch them?"

"No," said Shabble. "They got away. Where have they gone?"

"Come closer," said Iva-Italis, "and I'll whisper it in your ear."

"Shabbles don't have ears," said Shabble, keeping well out of reach of Iva-Italis. "Just tell me where they've gone and I'll — I'll, um—"

"You'll do me a favour," said Iva-Italis.

"Yes!" said Shabble.

"Then," said Iva-Italis, "listen closely, little friend. I don't know for certain where they've gone, but Sken-Pitilkin, you doubtless recall, is not known as the wizard of Drum for nothing."

That was all the clue that Shabble needed. The wrathful bubble promptly launched itself into the night skies, making for the Penvash Channel, for the island of Drum, and for a confrontation with those who had stolen the star-globe.

CHAPTER FORTY-FOUR

Drum: Sken-Pitilkin's home island in the Penvash Channel (otherwise known as the Penvash Strait) from which he has long been exiled. In spring of the year Alliance 4293, the peace of Drum was disturbed by the arrival of fugitives, these being Pelagius Zozimus, the dralkosh Zelafona and the dwarf Glambrax. All three were running from the wrath of the Confederation of Wizards. Sken-Pitilkin gave them shelter, only to find that pursuit was hot on their heels. Fearing for his life, Sken-Pitilkin fled from Drum with the others, and after two years of wandering all four arrived in Gendormargensis, in spring of the year Alliance 4295, at which time Guest Gulkan was only five years of age. It is now Alliance 4315, but Sken-Pitilkin has not returned to Drum in the 22 years since he first fled from that island.

* * *

To make a swift transit to Drum, Shabble soared high above fog and clouds, then navigated by the stars. But Sken-Pitilkin kept his stickbird firmly in the mist, and flew throughout the night in those realms of obscurity.

In the grey of dawn, the exhausted wizard of Skatzabratzumon set his stickbird down in a swampy clearing somewhere in the woods. Which woods? Sken-Pitilkin and his passengers could not tell.

"We don't know where to find ourselves," said Sken-Pitilkin, "so it's most unlikely that Shabble can hunt us. Therefore I pronounce us safe. Guest. Look to our security. For I must sleep."

Sken-Pitilkin was as good as his word. He curled up in the bottom of his stickbird, shrouded himself with a solskin horse blanket, and in moments was as dead to the world as a hedgehog wrapped in clay.

Whereupon Guest marched across the soft and yielding turf,

making for the nearest tree. The over-bright luxuriant green went squidge-slush-slurk beneath his boots. He grasped the lowest branch of the nearest tree then began to climb, forcing his way upwards to the heights which rustled with the dry rasp of leaves growing brittle-brown as their autumn change beset them.

Guest expected his survey to reveal a clutch of bloodthirsty saurian monsters, or mayhap a crocodile. But all he saw was swampland and the glimmer-glip of water clipped by the sun.

In such a setting, it was hard to take seriously the possibility of pursuit. But of course there would be pursuit. Shabble would hunt for the star-globe, because if there was one thing Shabble loved it was a toy, and the Door of the Partnership Banks was surely the greatest toy of all.

Guest, then, was doomed to be hunted by an immortal bubble. And how exactly could one hide from such a bubble for three years, particularly when rumours sweep tracks out a radius measured in leagues by the hundred? Shabble would be monitoring rumour. And so too might the various demons such as Italis of Alozay and Ko of Chi'ash-lan.

If the demons conspired with Shabble, and dedicated themselves to sifting the news which filtered through cities such as Obooloo and Chi'ash-lan, then Guest and his companions would have to shun all of civilization for fear of discovery. And, speaking of demons — how many of the things were there exactly? There were two of the jade-green monsters in Obooloo alone: the demon Lob in the precincts of the Bondsman's Guild and the demon Ungula Scarth in the Temple of Blood.

Demons and Shabble.

A dire combination, if it ever came to pass.

Meantime, Shabble alone was formidable enough.

Human pursuit is constrained by time, weather, money and mortality, but Shabble acknowledged none of those. Only boredom would bring Shabble's hunting to an end — and would a three-year hiatus be long enough to guarantee such boredom?

What if Shabble found the very hunt itself to be an eternally rewarding game?

So thinking, Guest tried to rouse himself to a state of concern. But all was autumn drowsiness.

Sunlight.

Shadow.

Peace.

Somewhere a bird called:

"Kil-klop! Kil-klop!"

Its song was bright-metallic, a slither of sharpness needling through the utter relaxation of the day.

After his ravaging journeys, the Weaponmaster had at last entered upon a phase of utter peace and oozing time. He felt strangely at a loss; and then, in his idleness, gradually became conscious of his overwhelming fatigue. So he descended from his tree and joined Sken-Pitilkin in sleep; and he slept like a baby until roused for a conference.

Sken-Pitilkin kicked off that conference.

"I had thought to run to Drum," said Sken-Pitilkin, "but on mature reflection that seems too obvious. After all, I am known to all of Safrak as the wizard of Drum."

"You are?" said Guest, by no means certain that Sken-Pitilkin was as famous as he thought.

"At the very least," said Sken-Pitilkin, "the demon Italis knows me as such, and it may well be that the demon will tell Shabble where to look for me. So we must not go to Drum. At least, we must not go there directly. As we know, the bubble's weakness is its capacity for boredom. It lacks persistence. If it does not find us in a season, then, having searched Drum and found it empty, it is unlikely to return."

"We hope," said Sod.

"We hope, yes," said Sken-Pitilkin. "In any case, we know that we must at a minimum secure our disappearance for our season. Therefore we must choose some place which is less than obvious."

"Ema-Urk," said Guest, naming the island on which his brother Morsh Bataar had wife, children and sheep farm.

"You jest, I hope," said Sken-Pitilkin, "for Ema-Urk is far too close to Alozay."

Then the wizard of Skatzabratzumon pulled out a map of Tameran, a weathered map of parchment which had dirt seamed in its folds.

"As you can guess from the condition of this document," said Sken-Pitilkin, "it is no map of mine. I abstracted it from a room of maps in Trilip Obo, the Archive Stratum of the mainrock Pinnacle."

Then Sken-Pitilkin pulled out a handful of coins.

"What's this?" said Guest. "Divination?"

"In a manner of speaking," said Sken-Pitilkin. "We must each write down the name of one of the destinations shown on this map, then choose a destination by the tossing of coins."

"Why?" said Guest.

"Because," said Sken-Pitilkin, "Shabble is smart enough to out-guess us if we work by logic. Therefore we must call chance to our assistance."

Then Sken-Pitilkin demanded that they each choose a destination.

Guest Gulkan vacillated between Stranagor — the place of his birth — and Gendormargensis. He settled on Gendormargensis. His brother Eljuk opted for Qonsajara, high in the mountains of Ibsen-Iktus. Thayer Levant decided upon Favanosin, while Ontario Nol chose the uplands of the Balardade Massif. Sken-Pitilkin himself then chose Stranagor.

"And you?" said Sken-Pitilkin to Sod.

"I," said Banker Sod, "choose Alozay itself."

"Alozay!" said Sken-Pitilkin. "Why, but that's impossible!"

"Why?" said Sod. "Shabble will surely have left Alozay to seek us elsewhere. If we return, then we can revenge ourselves upon Shabble's creatures. Furthermore, we can glut our pockets with gold, which would see us better prepared for a journey than we are at present."

Sod's plan was extremely dangerous, but Sken-Pitilkin, though he thought Sod over-audacious, nevertheless accepted that plan as one possible option.

Then Sken-Pitilkin tossed the coins that the coins might decide which plan they would opt for.

The coins directed them to Guest Gulkan's choice: Gendormargensis.

This occasioned uneasiness among all of them, even Guest Gulkan himself, for Gendormargensis was ruled by the Red Emperor Khmar, who had won his name by slaughtering so many of his enemies that the rivers ran red with their blood.

"I have another plan," said Nol. "It lacks the virtue of being randomly chosen. But, even so, I do not think that Shabble will divine this plan."

Then the wizard of Itch pointed at Sken-Pitilkin's map. He pointed at the south-west of Tameran. He pointed at a tongue of land which sprinted out into the sea, terminating in a bulb of rock. He pointed at the bulb itself.

"There," said Ontario Nol, softly. "The bubble will not seek us there."

"There?" said Sken-Pitilkin, in patent alarm.

While thoughts of venturing to Gendormargensis had made Sken-Pitilkin uneasy, this new suggestion made him positively alarmed.

"What place is that?" said Guest Gulkan.

Sken-Pitilkin looked around, then said, albeit with some reluctance:

"We will not speak its name. Not here. But Nol is right. It is a good destination."

So Sken-Pitilkin flew his stickbird to Lex Chalis, a place of caverns where the rock is fluid and warm beneath the touch. It is a place of ghosts, a place of hallucinatory dreams and waking delusions. Do you wish to hear more? Then you must seek elsewhere for the telling. For Lex Chalis awakens things which the mind has deliberately put to sleep. It stirs the old things to life, cracks the inner coffers of the psyche, incarnates the dead.

Worse, in the caverns of Lex Chalis, the thoughts of one person's mind create half-perceived shadows in the minds of that person's companions. Assume, then, that you are in Lex Chalis in the company of Guest Gulkan, he who was once mauled by the Great Mink in an arena in Chi'ash-lan. Assume that Guest is asleep, and dreaming, and that you are dreaming too. Can you imagine what your condition will be when you finally wake, heart pounding, eyes bulging, skin drenched with sweat?

In the great days of the Empire of Wizards, when all of Argan was ruled by the eight orders of the Confederation, then many wizards ventured north to Tameran, and dared their way to the caverns of Lex Chalis. But it is not recorded that any of them had any profit from such venture. For the place is beyond the understanding of wizardry; and, as far as history can tell, there has never been anything made of flesh or blood or stone or steel which has been able to grapple with its mysteries.

During the season in which the travellers sojourned in Lex Chalis, Ontario Nol was once moved to theorize on the nature of the caverns of Lex Chalis. He claimed those caverns to be the work of a theoretical breed of Experimenters.

"It is said by those who claim to know," said Ontario Nol, "that Probability is a single sheet of fabric pockmarked here and there by those patches of embroidery which mortal creatures know as the Realms of Time.

"It is further said that Probability is the great Enablement which permits the existence of the gods. Enabled by Probability, a god such as the Horn may master a small patch of this great fabric to its own purposes, just as a woman may master a small patch of a great bedsheet for her own embroidery."

Listening to this theorizing, Guest Gulkan thought it disgraceful that a Yarglat male as mighty as Ontario Nol should use reference to a woman's work to describe things so weighty. Nevertheless, he followed the metaphor.

"If the gods, then, are those who embroider worlds on the raw fabric of Probability," said Ontario Nol, "then the Experimenters are those who move from patch to patch to rearrange each piece of embroidery to something closer to their own liking."

At which, Guest Gulkan began to lose track of Nol's explanation, finding the metaphor to be growing obscure. So Nol switched metaphors.

"Supposing we talk of the soil as a great Enablement which

permits life," said Nol. "Suppose we then think of a god as an entity which can create a seed — an entity which can create life. This is a mighty act, and it takes a god to do it. But what then do we call the farmer who takes the seed and breeds it down through the generations to a plant reshaped to his own requirements. Is the farmer a god? No. He is but a technician, albeit great in his field. And those who claim to know of such things construe their theoretical Experimenters as just such a breed of technicians."

Guest Gulkan had difficulty following this metaphor, too, since it was an agricultural metaphor, and the Yarglat have precious little understanding of farming. So Ontario Nol was put to the labour of explaining that farmers can selectively breed plants to reshape them to their own requirements — a datum which was new to Guest, and one which he was inclined to regard with great scepticism.

Yet that was the best metaphor which Ontario Nol could provide, so, whether Guest could understand it or not, he had to put up with it.

"We have, then," said Ontario Nol, "three levels of Power. There is the original Enablement, which some call Probability. Then there are the gods, the creators-of-life, those who shape spheres of existence from raw Probability. Then there are the technicians, those who do but remould that which the gods have created."

"What of demons?" said Guest. "And ghosts?"

"They are the creatures of the sub-categories," said Nol, using one of those airy generalizations which a teacher employs when he is in no mood to plunge into complexities. "Let us not bother with sub-categories. Let us stick to our main division, which is the Enablement, the gods and the technicians. The Experimenters, then, are a theoretical race of technicians much given to wholesale remoulding."

"And," said Guest, "you claim these caverns of Lex Chalis to be a part of their work?"

"I claim nothing," said Ontario Nol. "I merely retail the theories of others. Those others claim the very configuration of our world to be the result of a wholesale remoulding undertaken by the Experimenters. It is said by these theorists that Lex Chalis is a communicator of sorts — an artefact which the Experimenters once used to communicate from world to world."

So said Ontario Nol.

But it must be clearly stated that there are well over a thousand different theories which purport to explain Lex Chalis, and that all of these theories are in conflict. The only thing which all theories are agreed upon is that Lex Chalis is a singularly unpleasant place in which to take up residence.

In that singularly unpleasant place, Sken-Pitilkin and his companions passed the winter season, grubbing a living from the seashore and studying the irregular verbs. Yes! Let it be stated as a fact! Before that season had run its course, Guest Gulkan had grown so desperately bored by the tedium of his refugee existence that he had permitted Sken-Pitilkin to tutor him in one or two or the milder of the foreign irregular verbs.

So passed a season of hardship, in which the refugees of Shabble searching the continents for their shadows, interrogating the buttercups of X-zox Kalada and the humming birds in the southern jungles, bathing in the red dust of Dalar ken Halvar or rolling in the snows of Chi'ash-lan.

Then, in the spring, Sken-Pitilkin at last declared that he was ready to fly them to Drum.

"Will that be any improvement?" said Guest, who knew of Sken-Pitilkin's island only that it was rocky and infested by sea dragons.

"A great improvement," said Sken-Pitilkin. "For we will be able to sleep in peace, without alien intrusions vexing our nights."

"You mean, then," said Guest, "that your island has no ghosts."

"That is not all I meant, but it is part of it," said Sken-Pitilkin. "Yes, take it from me, there are no ghosts on Drum."

That was a lie, for Drum was haunted by a number of ghosts, and Sken-Pitilkin knew at least seven of them by name. But, since their visitations were infrequent, Sken-Pitilkin thought he could get away with this lie.

Then Sod declared that, ghosts or no ghosts, he was in no mood to fly to Drum, and thought it would be far better for them to make for Chi'ash-lan.

"Impossible," said Sken-Pitilkin flatly. "For once you have been in Chi'ash-lan for a day or less, the demon Ko will know of it. And once Ko knows of it, then so too will every other such demon, and Shabble may well be in alliance with these demons by now even if Shabble was not in alliance with them before."

At last, Sod was persuaded — coerced is perhaps a better word for it — into Sken-Pitilkin's stickbird. Then Sken-Pitilkin sent this airship whirling skywards, and headed south.

Guest Gulkan, who had grim memories of a traumatic journey across the wastewaters of Moana, predicted of a certainty that Sken-Pitilkin would lose them somewhere over the sea. But in this the Weaponmaster was entirely mistaken, for Sken-Pitilkin knew Drum and its surrounding geography to a nicety. Thanks to his intimate knowledge of the area's geography, the wizard had already worked out a fail-safe method of finding his way to Drum by air.

The sagacious wizard of Skatzabratzumon flew south, navigating by the sun alone. Since Lex Chalis is barely a hundred leagues north of Argan, Sken-Pitilkin soon picked up the coast of that continent. Then it was a simple matter to continue down the coastline, keeping a lookout to the west.

As Drum lies barely thirty leagues west of Argan, and as it is a considerable island (for an ant must walk for twenty leagues to cross from its northern coast to its southern), the island is easily seen from the air on a clear day.

Had Sken-Pitilkin gone too far south, he would have realized his error as soon as he reached Larbster Bay, an unmistakable landmark which should serve to safeguard the aerial navigator against error. That at least was the theory — but there was no need to put theory to the test.

For, as Sken-Pitilkin flew south, he sighted Drum to the west, and headed in that direction.

On reaching the island, Sken-Pitilkin did not immediately land at his castle, but ventured on a circumnavigation of the shore. From the heights, Sken-Pitilkin and his companions checked the rocky shores for boats, ships, rafts, canoes and wreckage, but saw none such. All they saw was a number of sea dragons, variously sea bathing and sun bathing.

"It is safe," said Sken-Pitilkin with satisfaction, "at least as far as I can see."

Then the wizard sent his stickbird scudding downwards towards his castle. But, while the airship was still high in the air, it began to shake, as if in the grip of an enormously powerful invisible monster.

As the air adventurers clutched at the sticks of the airship in outright panic, it tore apart entirely — leaving them hanging in the air with nothing between them and the rocks below but the clear blue sky.

CHAPTER FORTY-FIVE

Confederation of Wizards: the organization which represents the interests of the eight orders of wizards. The strongholds of the Confederation are the strongholds of Drangsturm, the flame trench which divides Argan North from Argan South. The Confederation dedicates itself to guarding that flame trench, which protects the lands of the north from the Swarms — monsters of the southern terror-lands which are controlled by an entity known as the Skull. The Confederation looks upon the maintenance of Drangsturm as a holy trust. And a very profitable holy trust it is, too, since the Drangsturm Road is an important trade route, and the wizards tax every scrap of merchandise which moves along it.

* * *

So Sken-Pitilkin's stickbird tore apart, leaving the sagacious wizard of Skatzabratzumon and his passengers hanging in midair — with nothing between them and the rocks below but the clear blue sky.

Much to Sken-Pitilkin's surprise, they did not fall.

"Are you keeping us up?" yelled Guest.

"No!" said Sken-Pitilkin, clutching the star-globe tight to his chest and keeping a firm grip on his country crook.

Sken-Pitilkin's powers of levitation were by no means equal to the task of supporting so many in midair so far above the ground.

"If you're not keeping us up here," said Sod, kicking his legs in midair, "then how about getting us down?"

"I'll think about it," said Sken-Pitilkin.

But he had not the slightest idea of where to start. Usually, to descend after levitating, a wizard of Skatzabratzumon simply eased off the application of Power, and gravity (that force of universal suction exerted by the planet on which we live) then secured a certain descent.

"Get us down!" yelled Sod, kicking his legs in fury.

At which — without Sken-Pitilkin doing anything about it at all — they began to rotate. Swiftly they grew dizzy, and in their dizziness they were sucked downwards through the air, which thickened to an impenetrable white fog, which hardened to something as cold as glass.

They ceased rotating, and found themselves sitting in a small teardrop-shaped chamber which glowed with its own cold white light. The light was that of sunstruck snow.

"Where are we?" demanded Sod.

Sken-Pitilkin made no response to this demand, for he had not the slightest idea where they might be. He was disorientated — and more than a little frightened.

Then the opacity of the walls began to clear, easing away to a lucid transparency, and Sken-Pitilkin and his erstwhile passengers found themselves sitting inside a tiny teardrop in the centre of a three-legged table. Abruptly, the teardrop was seized, and hoisted skywards. Eljuk screamed in involuntary terror, and Sken-Pitilkin almost joined him in that scream.

A giant — it was a giant, wasn't it? — was holding the teardrop on the palm of his hand. The giant brought the teardrop close to his face so he could peer inside. He grinned. Sken-Pitilkin stared at the vastness of the giant's slab of a face, at the stalks of his stubble poking through his skin, at the yellowness of his gravestone teeth and the white fur of unscrubbed detritus between the top of those teeth and the gums, and the whale-flank rubbberiness of the giant's lips and the snarling crevices by his nose. In the wet overlay of reflections which slicked across the giant's nearest eye, Sken-Pitilkin saw the teardrop and its captives caught in reflection.

Then the giant began to move, jolting the teardrop severely. Eljuk Zala was sick, spewing vomit all over Sod, who swore at him. In response, Guest Gulkan braced himself in the swaying teardrop then bloodied Sod's nose with a blow from his fist. Nothing daunted, the Banker struck back, and the two of them began to fight in earnest. Thayer Levant and Ontario Nol fell on the fighters, struggling to separate them, while Sken-Pitilkin lashed out at knees and elbows with his country crook.

All the frustrations of a long season of confinement in Lex Chalis came out in that fight, which left all of them panting, besmirched by blood and vomit, stinking of bile and digestive juices. At which point the teardrop was set down on another table, this one being inside—

"Why," said Sken-Pitilkin in amazement, looking at the vastly enlarged geography outside the teardrop. "This is my living room! My very own living room inside my very own castle!"

Thus did Sken-Pitilkin belatedly come to realize that he had not fallen to the possession of giants. Rather, he and his companions had been shrunk.

While Sken-Pitilkin was still savouring this discovery, another giant picked up the teardrop, then fiddled with a ring on his finger. Even as the giant twisted the ring, Sken-Pitilkin caught sight of a small yellow bottle on a nearby table, and guessed that the giant, the teardrop and the people trapped inside that teardrop would shortly be sucked inside that bottle.

And so it came to pass.

By now, both Sken-Pitilkin and Ontario Nol realized — more or less — what had happened. The stickbird had been destroyed by a subtle act of wizardry. And, caught by some new and unprecedented advance in the wizardly arts, the stickbird's passengers had been sucked down from the sky and encapsulated in miniature in a small teardrop of some kind of imitation crystal. And now they were inside a bottle — and the nature of such bottles is well known to all wizards.

So Sken-Pitilkin and Ontario Nol, being orientated to their surroundings, tried to calm and reassure their bewildered companions. But they had barely begun this labour when the teardrop began to expand. Then, with dizzying velocity, Sken-Pitilkin and his companions expanded likewise — upon which the teardrop abruptly dissolved away to nothing.

So it was that Sken-Pitilkin and his companions were caught by a device of some description when their stickbird challenged the skies above the island of Drum; were sucked into a teardrop; were carried into the castle on Drum; were transported into the interior of a yellow bottle; and were then restored to their full size.

They found themselves the prisoners of a force of some five dozen of their enemies. There were a handful of the Confederation's wizards, who were in charge of the operation, and these were backed by a strong force of the mercenary soldiers of the Landguard which served the Confederation in the realms of Drangsturm.

Ever since Sken-Pitilkin had fled from Drum — which was a mighty long time ago — a force from the Confederation had been waiting for his return. Sken-Pitilkin was at first hard put to believe this, as he had been gone for 22 years; but it was explained to him that those who were keeping guard on Drum had been relieved every three years.

What had compelled the Confederation to make such strenuous and unprecedented exertions? Sken-Pitilkin did not know. His only recent crime against the Confederation was the assistance he had given to the wizard Zozimus, the witch Zelafona and the dwarf Glambrax. Some 22 years ago, he had helped them escape the Confederation's wrath.

Obviously, that trio must have committed some truly appalling crime against the Confederation. But as Sken-Pitilkin's captors refused to say exactly what it was that Zozimus and company had done, Sken-Pitilkin was denied the satisfaction of knowing the true reasons for the state of arrest in which he found himself.

Sken-Pitilkin and his companions were not the only ones to be imprisoned in the yellow bottle, for in that same bottle was Shabble, held captive inside a restraining net which was woven from a white-glittering substance which Sken-Pitilkin could not identify.

The yellow bottle, by virtue of the way in which it was fabricated, quelled all powers of magic. Sken-Pitilkin could not work his magic in that bottle, and neither could Ontario Nol. But Shabble was not a magical device: Shabble was a technic, a machine. That being so, additional precautions had to be taken to restrain Shabble, who (when unrestrained) was capable of spitting forth fire in great quantity. So Shabble was caught in a net, and the net restrained by a tethering rope; and, though Shabble could still play bubble, floating like a balloon, the imitator of suns could spit fire no more.

Once Sken-Pitilkin and his companions had been caught, they were swiftly interrogated.

On interrogation, Banker Sod claimed himself to be a Banker from Chi'ash-lan, a Banker who had travelled to the Safrak Islands to buy the star-globe. He claimed the thing to now be his rightful property.

"What, then," said an interrogating wizard, "is this star-globe?"

"Why," said Sod, "it is a globe into which one can look and reach the future."

The interrogator was unimpressed by this, and attributed Sod's claim to sheer superstition. For, though witches and others have often demonstrated Gifts of Seeing, wizards are reluctant to believe in the validity of such. For all wizards of all the eight orders believe that the will is free — and, consequently, believe that the future is beyond prediction.

Having satisfied themselves that Sod was nothing but a fool of a traveller with more money than sense, the wizards said he could go, and take his star-globe with him.

At this, Sken-Pitilkin and his companions seethed. But they did not betray Sod, or the secret of the star-globe — and neither did Shabble. For it was clear to one and all that, supposing their escape to be ultimately obtained, it would be easier to wrest the star-globe from Sod than it would be to wrest the same device from the Confederation of Wizards.

Now, on overflying Drum, Sken-Pitilkin had seen no sign of ships or boats, so was at a loss to know how the force currently in occupation of his island proposed to leave it. He was told that they were visited monthly by a fishing boat from the port of D'Waith, and would take advantage of that boat's next call to arrange transit to D'Waith.

"And from there?" said Sken-Pitilkin. "I think it difficult for you to make any swift passage from D'Waith to Drangsturm. Therefore I propose to build a stickbird, and fly us all to Drangsturm in a few short days."

But this generous offer was turned down, for the wizards who had caught Sken-Pitilkin had no plans to let him out of the yellow bottle in which he was caught.

So they did things the slow way.

When next they were visited by a boat from D'Waith — a small town at the eastern end of the Ravlish Lands — they arranged for a shuttle service to take one and all to that port. There, Banker Sod was liberated, and was allowed to leave for the west. A long and chancy journey, that march to the west! But, supposing Sod to ultimately be able to complete that journey, why, he would find himself in his home city of Chi'ash-lan.

With Sod went the star-globe, its secret still unbetrayed.

Then those who held Sken-Pitilkin and his companions captive settled down to wait until they were able to arrange to leave by sea.

Now any sea voyage out of D'Waith is a risky procedure, for the waters are made dangerous by sea serpents, and by the shoals of the Lesser Teeth and the pirates of the Greaters.

But the journey overland was generally considered impractical. True, convoys of Galish merchants routinely travelled the overland trading route known as the Salt Road, and that led all the way south from Larbster Bay down to the Castle of Controlling Power at the western end of Drangsturm.

But in those days — and of course, while we are here talking about recent history, the world has changed out of all recognition since then — the Galish had their own agents in every town of substance. So supposing one of the Galish were to break a leg, or suffer some other misfortune, why, it would be the easiest thing in the world for shelter to be arranged, and for the victim to be left to heal, in the certainty of being able to join another Galish band at some time in the future.

A combination of armed strength, willing agents, assured

credit and sustained goodwill made it possible for the Galish to hazard overland journeys which others would blanch at. Thus blanching, the wizards who had caught Sken-Pitilkin and his companions patiently waited until they were able to procure passage by sea from D'Waith to the city of Runcorn, a free port to the north of the Harvest Plains.

From Runcorn, another sea voyage took them to Androlmarphos, a port which serves the Harvest Plains. From there, it was easy to arrange passage to Cam, the ruling city of the island of Stokos.

All this time, Sken-Pitilkin and his companions were trapped in the bottle, and found their imprisonment to be exceedingly wearying.

Sken-Pitilkin busied himself with the revision of some of the more intricate irregular verbs, but his companions lacked the same intellectual resources. Even Ontario Nol swiftly grew restless in his prison, and swore a great revenge on his jailors. And even Sken-Pitilkin had to admit that a diet of siege dust and water — for on such the prisoners were typically fed — was less than satisfactory.

In the days of their confinement, the prisoners made elaborate plans for tricking, deceiving, bluffing, ambushing and overpowering their jailors, for seizing the ring which commanded the bottle, and for wreaking their revenge on those who had so unjustly deprived them of their liberty.

But these plans came to nothing, for the jailors treated their prisoners with the greatest of caution, and never came near them unless it was absolutely necessary, and then only approached them in force.

Denied all possibility of escape, the prisoners began to use the undisturbed possession of their peace to co-ordinate stories which would protect the secret of the Door — a secret which none of them wished to yield to the Confederation of Wizards.

"What will we say, then?" said Guest. "How will we explain away Shabble?"

"Why," said Sken-Pitilkin, "we will say that we were living on Safrak when a demon in globular form rose unexpectedly from the depths of the Swelaway Sea and began burning and raping everything on the islands. The Confederation will take this Shabble to be a demon, and destroy it."

"That's hardly credible," said Guest.

"Of course it is!" said Sken-Pitilkin. "That's what demons do, you know. They arise when they're least expected. As for their depredations — boy, a very Yarglat barbarian would blanch at them."

Guest ignored the implicit accusations of boyhood and barbarism, for he had long since grown out of taking either seriously. Instead, Guest said:

"Stories are all very well, but Shabble will give the lie to them if challenged in interrogation."

"But who would believe anything Shabble says?" said Sken-Pitilkin. "If Shabble tells the truth of what happened on Untunchilamon, and of all that has happened since, why, nobody will believe so much as the smallest fraction of it, since it is all so frankly incredible."

"Perhaps," said Guest. "But there yet remains the problem of how we are going to escape from the Confederation ourselves."

"I think," said Sken-Pitilkin, "you will find escape to be no problem at all. I think you are merely being held as a witness."

"A witness?" said Guest.

"Yes!" said Sken-Pitilkin. "Have you not understood? We are heading towards Drangsturm for a trial. My trial! I am to be put on trial for crimes against the Confederation. For sheltering Zozimus and Zelafona when they came to me for help. You will be but a witness at that trial, and then, doubtless, you will be released."

"And Eljuk?" said Guest. "And Levant?"

"The same," said Sken-Pitilkin. "And, unless he has somehow offended the Confederation in some way which is not known to me, Ontario Nol will also be released. Be of good cheer, boy! The problem is mine, and mine alone!"

A few days after Guest Gulkan had been given this intelligence, the jailors got passage out of Cam. And thus began the final stages of the journey down to Drangsturm.

By now, Shabble was getting on famously with Eljuk. Eljuk was a born student, and Shabble, when all else failed, was a patient teacher. Shabble taught Eljuk origami, and, before the bubble was through with his teaching, Eljuk's nimble fingers could shape paper dragons, or configure a scrap of paper to an imitation of a Neversh.

The Neversh is the greatest of the brutes of the Swarms, the monsters which then dominated the lands south of Drangsturm. The Neversh has two spikes which can suck the juices from a man or a water buffalo, and both Sken-Pitilkin and Guest Gulkan had bad dreams about those spikes.

Drangsturm was now close.

From Cam, the jailors took the yellow bottle south to Narba, then travelled down through Provincial Endergeneer to the realms of the Far South, the realms of Drangsturm.

"Right!" said Guest, who longed for their arrival and for his release from the bottle. "Just wait! As soon as I'm out of here, heads will roll!"

But, when Guest Gulkan reached Drangsturm, he was dismayed to find that he was not to be liberated from the yellow bottle. Instead, there was to be (eventually) a trial. The renegade wizard Hostaja Torsen Sken-Pitilkin would be put on trial for high treason. As Sken-Pitilkin had predicted, Guest Gulkan would be a witness at that trial, and both the trial and the pre-trial interrogations would be held in the yellow bottle itself.

Sken-Pitilkin, who did not want to see Guest Gulkan put to death for perjury, advised him to tell the truth in his pre-trial interrogation.

"But what should I say about Shabble?" said Guest. "And about the star-globe? And about Doors?"

"Of Shabble you need merely say that you are ignorant," said Sken-Pitilkin. "This will be readily accepted."

"But, but what about Doors?" said Guest. "What about when they ask me about Doors?"

"Will they ask if you've got a dragon in your pocket?" said Sken-Pitilkin. Then, when Guest looked at him blankly:

"They've no reason to suspect we've a Door on Safrak, so won't ask after such. Anyway, if they ask you any question too sensitive, just say you don't remember."

"But I do remember!" said Guest.

"I'm not sure that you do," said Sken-Pitilkin, who, in long conversation with the Weaponmaster, had found that Guest's memories of the past were selective in the extreme. "Tell them you were tortured. Tell them about your time in the dungeons of Obooloo. Tell them you were driven into the Stench Caves and washed out in a great Flood. Once they know the number of your traumas, they'll not expect you to remember much."

Such was Sken-Pitilkin's counsel.

But Guest Gulkan was still greatly worried about his pre-trial interrogation until that interrogation actually began. Then he found he had no problems at all.

For Guest was a barbarian, was he not? Of course he was! And does one ask a barbarian a question of any complexity? Of course one does not! For a barbarian's brain is small, and his intellect is slow, and his wit is sufficient for nothing more than the riding of horses and the skinning of his enemies.

So those who interrogated Guest Gulkan were careful only to ask him small questions, easy questions, questions which would not confuse and jumble his poor and untutored brain.

Was he a Yarglat barbarian? Yes, he was. Was he acquainted with Hostaja Torsen Sken-Pitilkin? Yes, he was. And with the wizard Pelagius Zozimus? Again, yes. And the witch Zelafona? Yes, without a doubt. And her son Glambrax? Yes. And had he seen these three in company? Why, yes. And where was that? In the city of Gendormargensis. And when? Why, during the final years of the reign of the Witchlord Onosh.

That was all the interrogators really wanted to know from Guest Gulkan. It was sufficient to tie Sken-Pitilkin to the criminals Zozimus, Zelafona and Glambrax. It was sufficient, therefore, to damn Sken-Pitilkin and ensure his execution.

With Guest Gulkan, Ontario Nol, Eljuk Zala and Thayer Levant having been interrogated, the trial did not immediately start, for Sken-Pitilkin had demanded to be given time in which to prepare for that trial.

So Guest, being of no further interest to the Confederation's prosecutors, was turned over to the wizards of the Ethnological Commission, who were delighted at having a real live Yarglat barbarian to interrogate.

Much the ethnologists asked, and much Guest told — though he did not tell all. In particular, Guest in his shyness preserved in secrecy some of the sex customs of the Yarglat. For example, he did not confess that the woman in her ecstasy will often haul upon the ears of the man, and leave those ears a mass of bruises on the following day.

"No sex customs?" said his interrogators, when Guest tried to stonewall them on that point. "But you must have sex customs! Everyone has sex customs!"

This is the thing about ethnology. It is very much a science of the bedroom, for your average ethnologist is nothing but a thwarted pornographer. Since the ethnologists were so insistent, Guest at last found he had no alternative but to invent new sex customs for their delectation. So he described louche orgies in which a great congress of men, women, dogs and horses took place in a gigantic bowl of strawberries and cream.

"From where are so many strawberries obtained?" said one of the more sceptical wizards.

"Well ..." said Guest.

Frankly, though the Weaponmaster had long had the image of a strawberry-and-cream orgy in mind, and was determined to stage such an event at least once before he died, he still had absolutely no idea as to how one could come by so many strawberries and so much cream — even supposing that the resources of an empire were placed at one's disposal.

Guest proving unforthcoming on this subject, the interrogators turned their attention to Eljuk Zala.

"You were of the Yarglat in your youth, were you not?" said they.

"So I am told," said Eljuk. Then, venturing on a blatant lie to preserve himself from dissection: "But I was taken from those barbarous realms when I was but a baby, hence have no memory of them. But — but some little I have heard. When Guest spoke of strawberries and such, he spoke by way of euphemism. For cream read blood, and for strawberries read the organs of sacrificial victims."

"Brother!" said Guest, evincing shock. "These things are not to be spoken of in the presence of the unclean!"

The ethnologists were delighted, and in particular they were exceedingly pleased by Guest Gulkan's shock. For it is counted a great feat of ethnology to penetrate to the most secret, sensitive part of an alien culture, then display the intimacies of those secrets for public view, like the organs of a dead chicken.

Finally, the ethnologists compelled Guest Gulkan to undress for them, so that his physique might be sketched. For they had observed the largeness of his flap-handle ears, and wondered whether other organs might be similarly distended.

The undressing of the Weaponmaster — a grievous breach of the taboos of the Yarglat, but one which he was past caring about — proved him to be uncommonly battered and scarred. It also proved him to be in possession of an amulet, the mazadath which he had come by in Dalar ken Halvar.

"What is that?" said Brother Fern Feathers, the wizard who headed the Ethnological Commission.

"It is the liver of a dog," said Guest.

"A dog!?" said Fern Feathers.

"Yes, yes, a dog," said Guest. "An iron dog, a dog of a kind known as a dorgi. I slaughtered the thing in Dalar ken Halvar, hacked it with my sword then gulleted its ruins with my fingernails. It is from that corpse which I have this prize of mine."

Naturally the wizards did not believe this farraginous mix of fact and fantasy, so examined Guest's amulet. But they dismissed it as a trinketing piece of silverwork, though a proper Investigation would have proved its metal to be much, much harder than silver.

"It is a pretty thing," said Fern Feathers, giving a final verdict on the mazadath, "but it has no potency."

This was true, at least as far as the wizards were concerned, and so they left the thing in Guest Gulkan's possession, having done no more than sketch it for their ethnological records.

With his interrogation at last at an end, Guest Gulkan was able to exercise his own ethnological curiosity by first participating in and then spectating at the trial of Hostaja Torsen Sken-Pitilkin, which was presided over by three judges. Those judges were all wizards of Arl: being Heenmor, Phyphor and Garash. It may be argued that the last-named was still technically an apprentice. However, though Garash had not yet been released from the service of his master Phyphor, he still commanded a wizard's full powers.

It would be a grievous labour to recount in full the laborious processes of a trial of a wizard by wizards. It was a trial of truly historical length, and most of it was spent arguing points of law.

The bare facts of the case may be stated with the utmost simplicity. Sken-Pitilkin was accused of high treason, in that he had aided and abetted certain enemies of the Empire of Wizards, those enemies being things belonging to or allied with the Sisterhood of Witches. It was said that the witch Zelafona had fled from the justice of the Empire of Wizards. Fleeing in company with the dwarf Glambrax and the wizard Zozimus, the witch had sheltered upon Sken-Pitilkin's home island of Drum. Shortly afterwards, Sken-Pitilkin had departed from Drum with witch, wizard and dwarf, fleeing to the northern continent of Tameran, where he made his home in the city of Gendormargensis, and earned his living as a tutor.

Those were the facts, at least as the Confederation's lawyers stated them. But Sken-Pitilkin accepted none of it, and disputed vigorously on each and every point. He was accused, was he, of aiding and abetting enemies of the Empire of Wizards? Then surely it was logical to ask — what Empire?

Running along the track of this logic, Sken-Pitilkin argued that the Empire of Wizards had fallen to ruin long generations previously, which was undeniably true as a matter of literal fact. But the lawyers representing the Confederation argued, rather, that the Empire still existed as a legal entity, even if the Empire had entirely vanished from the world of the flesh and the fact.

With the judges deciding for the Confederation on that point, Sken-Pitilkin tried another tack. Sken-Pitilkin claimed the Confederation must prove that he had known Zozimus, Zelafona and Glambrax to have been in flight from justice.

"For," said Sken-Pitilkin, "the law does not allow you to assume me to have had such knowledge. On the contrary. You must summon your witnesses and prove it."

"We need do nothing of the kind," said the lawyers in opposition to him. "For common sense does all the proving the law requires."

"Common sense!" said Sken-Pitilkin, scandalized. "Since when has common sense had anything to do with the operation of the law? Ten thousand years of legal tradition deny the legitimacy of common sense! Will you set yourself against such tradition?"

But his enemies were unmoved. They claimed that the mere application of common sense was sufficient to prove that Sken-Pitilkin — whom all of them knew of old — would never have left Drum except under dire pressure. Sken-Pitilkin was a creature of habit, known to be very fond of his home island; and, furthermore, no wizard would willingly go to a place so barbarous as Tameran unless driven by extreme necessity. It followed that Sken-Pitilkin had known his guests — Zozimus, Zelafona and Glambrax — to have been criminals. By rights, he should have chopped off their feet and handed them over to the Confederation. Since he had not done so, he was guilty of treason.

"Common sense proves as much," said the chiefest of the prosecutors.

Sken-Pitilkin thought this a low and scurrilous blow. To allow common sense into a case before the courts! Surely there was no precedent for such a thing! Not in all the annals of legal infamy!

But, condemned by no evidence saving that of common sense alone, Sken-Pitilkin was ultimately found guilty of high treason, and was sentenced to death.

The manner of his sentence was this: he was to seek his death by taking the thing called Shabble, and by disposing of it in the depths of the Warp, the depths beyond the Veils of Fire.

For, after long interrogation of Shabble, the wizards of the Confederation had decided that this thing was dangerous; and, not being sure as to how it might otherwise be disposed of, they had decided to consign Shabble to certain doom which waited beyond the Veils of Fire.

CHAPTER FORTY-SIX

Shackle Mountains: a range of mountains on Argan's eastern seaboard, inland from the Breach and the Bitterwater Coast. In these mountains is the Warp which apprentice wizards enter to endure the Trials which will decide whether they graduate (or whether they die). In the Warp itself lie the Veils of Fire, and no person has ever penetrated beyond those Veils and returned to tell the tale. Accordingly, the wizards of the Confederation believe that the enigmatic but doubtlessly dangerous Shabble can be destroyed by being taken beyond those Veils.

* * *

It would be a long and weary business to give an account of the process of appeal whereby Sken-Pitilkin sought to challenge his conviction for high treason. The case dragged on for years.

During that time, Ontario Nol was at liberty, since no crime could be proved against him. He had led a blameless life, first at the monastery of Qonsajara in the mountains of Ibsen-Iktus, and later on the island of Alozay. His long but voluntary exile was regarded as eccentric, but not criminal. So Nol was assigned quarters in the Castle of Controlling Power, the great stronghold at the western end of the flame trench Drangsturm, and was allotted that portion of the Confederation's profits to which he was rightfully entitled.

Sheltered and sustained by Nol's benevolent patronage, Guest Gulkan, Thayer Levant and Eljuk Zala lived out the years in the same Castle. There was yet a hope that Sken-Pitilkin might win his case and be set at liberty; and, sustained by that hope, Guest Gulkan was reluctant to venture to Chi'ash-lan on his own account to mount a solitary challenge against Banker Sod and the might of the Partnership Banks.

But at last Sken-Pitilkin's final appeal failed, and the effective death sentence against him was confirmed.

By this time, Eljuk Zala Gulkan had progressed so far in his studies under Ontario Nol that he was ready to enter the Warp and endure the Trials which would see him graduate as a full-fledged wizard (if he survived!).

So it was that Eljuk Zala and his master Ontario Nol joined Sken-Pitilkin on the journey eastward from the Castle of Controlling Power. With them went Guest Gulkan and Thayer Levant; for Guest still hoped to liberate Sken-Pitilkin somehow during the journey, even though Ontario Nol had warned him that in all probability this would be impossible.

At the eastern end of the flame trench Drangsturm, the party took passage on a ship which set forth from the Castle of Ultimate Peace and began to cruise eastward in the direction of the Stepping Stone Islands and the Ocean of Cambria.

Once the ship was past the Stepping Stone Islands, its eastward course took it into the waters of the Ocean of Cambria. On that voyage, Guest Gulkan was granted a second look at the Chameleon's Tongue, that hook of beach-fringed land on which he had once made a landing when Sken-Pitilkin had botched the job of navigating to Untunchilamon.

To Guest's disappointment, nobody was much interested in the view. Sken-Pitilkin was incarcerated in the yellow bottle, brooding on the certainty of his death, and was in no mood to trifle with memories. Thayer Levant had taken up residence in that same bottle, where he passed his time by practising knife fighting, and proved uninterested in reminiscence. As for Shabble — why, to Shabble, flight was a way of life, so the bouncing bubble could scarcely be expected to be impressed by Guest's recollections of his aerial voyage across Moana. Meantime, Ontario Nol was busy soothing Eljuk's nerves, and giving him some last-ditch tutoring, and had no time to play tourist.

This might seem a small matter, but it left Guest singularly disgruntled to find himself reduced to such a marginal role that he could find nobody willing to take an interest in his reminiscences of the past.

Once the ship was eastward of the Elbow, it turned for the

north, taking care to stand well off shore.

As the ship sailed north, the west was landmarked by the jagged stubble of the Lizard Crest Rises, blue-toned by distance. The ship was so far from shore that it was impossible for uninitiated landlubbers to tell when they were passing Seagate, the entrance to the Sponge Sea. But thereafter the mountains to the west became more formidable — great slab-sided thunderbolts of rock rising to crags which were peaked with patent snow.

The eastern coast of Argan — that coast which now lay to the west of the ship — is a mix of the lightly populated and the entirely desolate. Even from a distance, and even to such a poor geographer as the Yarglat barbarian Guest Gulkan, those mountains effortlessly clarified the demographical dynamics which had populated the west while leaving the east to the woodlouse and the bumble bee.

It is commonly said that the great geographical determinant is water, and by and large this is true. Any large city must be built by water; and those rulers who have commanded construction in defiance of this imperative are usually forced to abandon the works of their ego shortly thereafter. But, while water is the one great essential, the lie of the land must not be overlooked.

The sagacious Sken-Pitilkin, though doomed to death, was still a compulsive pedagogue. Therefore, when Guest Gulkan entered the yellow bottle in which Sken-Pitilkin was held captive, and there reported on the view, Sken-Pitilkin took advantage of the report to lecture Guest Gulkan on the Demographic Theory of Contours, and was lecturing still when their ship sailed into the Breach, ending its voyage by the Shores of Glass which lie on the dawnside of the Shackle Mountains.

The shore was made of billows of glass in blue and yellow. Hard glass it was, and great heat was required to melt it, and sundry scratchings near the shore gave evidence of the efforts of generations of over-optimistic entrepreneurs who had bankrupted themselves by trying to mine the stuff.

It is true that a profit could be made from the Shores of Glass were they to be located near any centre of civilization, despite the hardness of the substance and the difficulties of smelting it. But the dangers, isolation and barrenness of the Breach increased all expenses unreasonably.

There was no water, hence all must be imported; there was no food, and the waters of the Breach were unaccountably impoverished from a fisherman's point of view; there were storms in winter; there was a danger of dragons all through the year; and the Malud marauders from Asral were so rapacious in their plunderings of the sea-trade that no ship that made passage through the Ocean of Cambria could possibly get insurance for its voyage.

Hence the wizards of the Confederation naturally expected to find the Shores of Glass deserted, and were disconcerted to find a small colony of purple-skinned Frangoni warriors established by the sea. These Frangoni were from the Ebrell Islands, and to a man they were sages who had chosen to devote themselves to dith-zora-ka-mako, the Mystical Way of the Nu-chala-nuth.

In any religion there is typically a triple dynamic at work. There is the dynamic of political power, which attracts those who infiltrate religious organizations with the motives of cold-blooded careerists. These will typically be found advising Banks, Bankers, emperors, warlords and kings. Then there is the pastoral dynamic, which attracts those who, as a solution to their personal inadequacies, seek to bring into their own lives (or into the lives of men in general — and, sometimes, the lives of women also, although this is usually optional) — the light of such Living Gods as the Great Frog, the Holy Goat-Rapist, the Smock-Smock and the Vodo Man.

Then there is religion of the third kind.

Religion of the third kind is the mystical religion which concerns itself with the burning moment when heart and mind are consumed by an incandescence which cannot be captured in words — or when, in the peace of a raindrop, a rock becomes a rock and a tree becomes a tree, each known in the fullness of its own nature.

The Frangoni from the Ebrells were bent on practising that

third kind of religion, but their theory and praxis meant but little to the wizards. The entire religion of Nu-chala-nuth counted as nothing as far as the Confederation of Wizards was concerned.

Still, the travelling wizards admired the dedication with which these ascetic Frangoni mystics were building their colony. They had made small hutches for themselves by gluing together fragments of glass. With enormous labours, they were wresting further fragments from the local terrain, with a view to constructing an enormous monastery; and, judging by the size of the foundation-lines which had been scratched out on the ground, if ever completed this monastery would be one of the wonders of the world.

By cunning employment of solar stills, the religious colonists provided themselves with fresh, clean, potable water. Already they had piled up great heaps of byproduct salt; and, since the Confederation of Wizards is, among other things, a commercial operation, it was entirely natural for the travellers to dicker with the mystics, trading olives and oranges for sacks of salt which could be sold elsewhere for enormous profit. Thus a dozen days passed in preparations and barter. But at last trade was finished and the expedition was ready to set forth.

This business of trade was entirely logical, moral and unobjectionable, yet it infuriated Guest Gulkan beyond measure. He believed (this was the rationalization by which he sustained his own ego against the buffeting of misfortune) that his life was heading towards some culminating crisis; and he took it as a personal affront to find the wizards so casual as to postpone this crisis by a whole twelve days of mercantile dickering.

At last, leaving behind a strong contingent to guard their ship, the wizards went inland on foot, bearing great stocks of food, water and firewood in the yellow bottle in which both Shabble and Sken-Pitilkin were still held as prisoners. Thayer Levant chose to keep Shabble and Sken-Pitilkin company, for the knifeman had absolutely no interest in tramping at great length through the mountains. But, compelled by pride, and by a rational soldierly interest in maintaining his own fitness, Guest

Gulkan chose to march the long leagues rather than ride them out in the bottle.

The wizards marched to the north-west corner of the Breach, where the blue and yellow billows of the Shores of Glass gave way to honest rock. From there, they followed a steep and ancient train marked with cairns and with ancient grey-white banners mounted on bamboo poles.

The trail climbed precipitous slopes by means of stairways a league or more in height. They crossed engulfing gorges by ancient bridges. In places, Eljuk had to be blindfolded and led with a piece of rope, for he was too terror-stricken to proceed with his eyes open. Some of the paths, after all, consisted of nothing but flags of rock inserted into man-made slots in a sheer cliff face.

Eljuk's brother Guest was more disturbed by the long tunnels which pierced entire mountains, and which were a necessary and unavoidable part of the route. In those sometimes-humming, sometimes-hot wormways through the living rock, Guest experienced grim intimations of doom, particularly when passing certain great iron doors which were sealed against intrusion.

The more lengthy and many-branched tunnels reminded Guest of the mazeways Downstairs, the labyrinth beneath the city of Injiltaprajura on the far-distant island of Untunchilamon. At times — when black grass was growing underfoot and cold green lights were burning overhead — the resemblance was so close that he more than half-expected to encounter a dorgi or a therapist.

But every venture through the long succession of such complexes delivered them again to the sky, and each time the sky was higher, and colder, and more beset by wind.

In the dry and wind-ravaged heights of the Shackle Mountains, environmental stress — the height, the dryness, the grinding wind, the poor food and the labour of travel — began to take their toll on Eljuk Zala. Under the influence of that stress, cold sores broke out, and their crusted presence added a further disfigurement to the purple birthstains which marred his lips. Spreading beyond those lips, the sores took hold on his cheeks.

Eljuk had to be reminded not to touch those sores, with Sken-Pitilkin doing the reminding repeatedly when Eljuk entered the yellow bottle in the evenings to study irregular verbs and origami. If the hands wander from lips to eyes, then the disease can endanger the sight, as Sken-Pitilkin had learnt during those years of his youth in which he had practised as a pox doctor.

"He saved our brother Morsh," said Guest Gulkan, reminding Eljuk of the manner in which Sken-Pitilkin had secured a cure for Morsh Bataar when that young man's leg had been grievously broken, "so you should trust to his counsel."

Guest was solicitous of Eljuk's health, and tried to convince him that he should travel inside the yellow bottle. But Eljuk would not. Since his brother Guest chose to march the mountains, Eljuk was determined to do likewise. Besides, the bottle was claustrophobic, and from previous confinement Eljuk had grown to hate the thing.

Once, when Shabble was busy chasing shadows in the depths of the yellow bottle, and when Eljuk had fallen asleep in the middle of construing a particularly irregular verb — the verb trizon, which varies according to astrological influences — Guest ventured to share with Sken-Pitilkin his concerns for Eljuk's safety.

"He's — he's got these Trials to face, hasn't he?" said Guest. "He has to go into this, this Warp thing. Maybe he'll die."

"Maybe he will," said Sken-Pitilkin.

"Well," said Guest, "isn't there any way I can help him? Maybe I could persuade him to rest, you know, to gather his strength."

"I didn't know you to be so tender of your brother," said Sken-Pitilkin.

"Why," said Guest in surprise, "but I saved him from drowning at the risk of my own life."

"Eljuk?" said Sken-Pitilkin.

"You remember!" said Guest. "The battle, you know, down

by the Yolantarath. Oh, but you weren't there. It was Zozimus, that's right, he was all dressed up in his armour, he had a falcon, you were back in Gendormargensis. Anyway. Eljuk was in the water, he was crying out for help, so I raced down to the river, I jumped in and pulled him out."

Guest was emphatic in his account. Clearly the Weaponmaster believed himself to be telling the truth. But Sken-Pitilkin, even though he had not been there on the day, knew otherwise. For Guest had confessed the full story in drunken reminiscence with the Rovac warrior Rolf Thelemite and the dwarf Glambrax, and Sken-Pitilkin had overheard some of those drunken confessions.

True, Guest had jumped into the Yolantarath River to save a man. But — Eljuk? Sken-Pitilkin had a very distinct memory of Guest saying:

"Eljuk! I'd not so much as sponge my face for Eljuk!"

Furthermore, though Guest plainly retained no memory of the occasion, the Weaponmaster had once made a sober confession to Sken-Pitilkin, admitting to a precognitive vision in which he had seen his father drown in the Yolantarath. In consequence of that vision, when Guest had seen someone floundering in the river he had naturally thought it to be his father — and, identifying the man thus on the strength of his vision, had risked his life to save the poor fellow who was in difficulties, only to find to his disgust that it was actually Eljuk.

Guest Gulkan had confessed the whole truth of the matter to Sken-Pitilkin on an evening when he had sat at the confluence of the Pig and the Yolantarath, waxing sentimental about the fate of some men he had hung some days earlier.

Sken-Pitilkin was interested to observe how systematically Guest misremembered his own past — not wilfully, but entirely unconsciously. We are often the least reliable witnesses to our own lives, for so much in memory later changes as we reconfigure ourselves in the light of future experience.

"You saved your brother once," said Sken-Pitilkin, who saw no point in challenging Guest's misremembering of the past, "but now he must save himself. There is nothing you can do to help your brother face his Trials. The Trials are as much a test of will as anything. Your brotherly solicitude can scarcely help strengthen his will."

"I'm afraid he's going to die," said Guest.

"I know for a fact that I am most definitely going to die," said Sken-Pitilkin pointedly.

This forced Guest to face up to a fact which he was most reluctant to acknowledge: the fact that he was in the presence of one who had been sentenced to death.

"Couldn't you escape?" said Guest. "I mean, they've got to let you out of this bottle when we get to this Warp. You can't take the bottle into the Warp if you're still inside it."

"Some of these wizards are wizards of Arl," said Sken-Pitilkin. "When I'm let out of this bottle, they'll be watching me. One false move, and I'll be crisped to a cinder."

Guest Gulkan accepted this.

In the arrogance of his early youth, the Weaponmaster would never have accepted such a gloomy prognosis. For, in his extreme youth, the Weaponmaster had thought himself equal of anything the world could bring about him. But, ever since being mauled by the Great Mink, Guest had been unable to muster up the same invincible confidence.

So the trek continued, with each day taking Guest Gulkan and his travelling companions higher and higher into the Shackle Mountains. The heights were cold, and silent. The lichen of long centuries grew on cairns where dirt-grey banners hung from grey bamboo. The path crossed slopes where rock had once run liquid.

Eljuk began to turn inward, no longer responding to his brother. In the face of his silence, Guest sought advice from Ontario Nol.

"Is he sick?" said Guest Gulkan.

"Sick?" said Nol.

"You know," said Guest. "Like all of us were at Ibsen-Iktus, you know, the first night in Qonsajara."

"Your sickness was caused by climbing too high too fast," said Nol. "Here we have gone slowly, hence height is not a problem."

"But Eljuk's so quiet," said Guest.

"What would you expect?" said Nol sombrely. "Of course he's quiet! He's preparing himself for tomorrow."

"Tomorrow?" said Guest.

"We should be there tomorrow!" said Nol. "At the Warp. At the Place of Testing. Then — Guest, many try, but few succeed."

"Why?" said Guest. "What happens? These, these Tests, what makes them kill people?"

"That is not for you to know," said Nol.

And the eminent wizard of Itch quite refused to talk about it any further.

That evening, Guest Gulkan tried to discuss the matter of Eljuk's Tests with Sken-Pitilkin.

"It's those — those Mahendo Mahunduk things," said Guest. "That's what it is, isn't it? They'll kill him!"

"Quiet!" said Sken-Pitilkin, in shock. "Quiet, lest a wizard hear, and kill you!"

It had now been so long since Sken-Pitilkin had heard Guest speak of the Mahendo Mahunduk that he had hoped the Weaponmaster to have forgotten all about them. The Mahendo Mahunduk, the sometime soldiers of the Revisionary Gods, were creatures of destruction who were half-demon and half-deity. Their old masters were dead, or else had evolved, since evolution is one of the fatal flaws to which the gods are prone; and so the Mahendo Mahunduk were at liberty to make alliances with wizards.

As a slave can enter the service of an emperor, and gain a measure of power and protection from his association with such a dignitary, so too can a wizard make an alliance with one of the Mahendo Mahunduk. But, just as a cruel and demanding emperor may subject a candidate slave to a potentially destructive test of will, so too do the Mahendo Mahunduk test all candidate wizards.

To make contact with the Mahendo Mahunduk, a candidate wizard must enter the Warp in the Shackle Mountains; and this, as Sken-Pitilkin painstakingly explained to Guest, exposed the Confederation to danger.

"For," said Sken-Pitilkin, "to maintain its strength, the Confederation needs an infusion of new blood. Were anyone to use armed force to close the road to the Place of Testing, then the Confederation would have no means to replenish its strength. Hence the secrets of the Warp are exceptionally sensitive."

"But," objected Guest, "it is widely known that wizards make pilgrimage to the Shackle Mountains."

"Perhaps," said Sken-Pitilkin. "But further publicity will be less than welcome. If you preach to the world of the Mahendo Mahunduk then the Confederation will kill you."

"I was hardly preaching!" protested Guest.

"Be deaf, dumb and mute," said Sken-Pitilkin. "Else you will die in these mountains, and soon."

Guest Gulkan obeyed.

But the Weaponmaster was far from happy at being told to shut up and do nothing. While Guest Gulkan had stoically endured the long journey from Drum to Drangsturm, his subsequent interrogation by ethnologists and the longueurs of Sken-Pitilkin's trial, the cumulative effects of these insults to his autonomy had bred in his breast a savage frustration.

Guest Gulkan had desired to make himself the conqueror of the Circle of the Partnership Banks, or at least of some small portion of that Circle. To that end, he had quested for the x-x-zix, had dared himself into the Stench Caves, had gone head-to-head with Aldarch the Third and Anaconda Stogirov, had contended against Great Gods and demons, and had put himself through more torment than most people endure in a lifetime.

And what was the end result of all this?

Why, the end result of this was the total perversion of all his expectations — so that, rather than ruling an empire, he found himself tagging along behind a band of wizards, a refugee dependent on the charity of Ontario Nol, a ragged swordsman without power or authority or status or recognition.

And now, as a crisis neared, as his brother Eljuk looked likely to die, as Sken-Pitilkin looked certain to die, as Shabble was to be wastefully consigned to whatever destruction waited behind the Veils of Fire, why, Guest Gulkan's sole role was apparently to be a gawking spectator.

Now Guest no longer had the confidence to believe that he could successfully challenge the strength of a parcel of wizards armed and ready for action — but, as his frustration mounted to a head, he began to think himself ready to take on the world regardless, even if his certain doom was to be the result.

The next day, with Guest still brooding darkly on the collapse of his hopes and the many insults which had been done to his dignity, the travellers laboured to the top of a sharp ridge, and found themselves looking across a steep but narrow valley.

"On the other side of this valley," said Ontario Nol, "is the Cave of the Warp."

Guest Gulkan looked across the valley and saw not one cave but an array of gaping holes opening to realms of darkest shadow.

"It looks like a perfect lair for dragons," said the Weaponmaster.

"Dragons would not live here," said Ontario Nol. "They must live near their food. Hence you will find them near the sea, where they can fish for the whale; or close to our cities, where their food runs two-legged; or else living near volcanoes or similar, for they can diet upon sulphur at a pinch."

Having received that intelligence, Guest Gulkan studied the prospect further, then said:

"These caves have been artificed by the hands of men."

"What makes you think that?" said Ontario Nol.

"The spacing is regular," said Guest, holding out his hand and measuring the gap between each cavemouth with his fingers. "Nothing in nature is so regular of formation."

"The caves were made," acknowledged Ontario Nol. "But I would not say that they were necessarily made by men."

"By who, then?" said Guest. "Gods? Demons?"

"I cannot say," said Nol.

"Why not?" said Guest.

"Because," said Nol, "I do not know."

And, with that, the wizard of Itch headed downwards into the valley.

By evening, the travellers had reached the cave of the Warp, which proved singularly disappointing. It was a big cave, true, but no monsters lurked in the velvety blue-black of its shadows. Instead, at the far end of the cave — some fifty paces from the opening, in Guest's judgement — there was a wall of interwoven rainbow. This twisted slowly, sinuously, throwing off occasional sprays of lights.

"That," said Ontario Nol, in portentous tones, "is the Veils of Fire. Many have ventured beyond those Veils, but none has returned to tell the tale. Tomorrow, Sken-Pitilkin will take Shabble beyond those Veils, and both will die."

"So you say," said Guest, who was effortlessly unimpressed by this cave and its Veils.

"I say it because it is the truth," said Nol. "Now come away. And stay well away from this cave, for sometimes the denizens of these shadows have reached out to kill those who idle outside by the entrance."

"Is that so?" said Guest.

"It is so," affirmed Nol, and drew Guest away from the cave, and compelled him to the campsite the wizards were setting up a stone's throw distant from that cavern.

By this time, Guest was more than half-convinced that the wizards were the victims of a communal hallucination; and that, if anyone had truly died inside that cave, then their deaths had more to do with autosuggestion than with the Mahendo Mahunduk or any similar creatures.

That night, Guest Gulkan did not sleep. Neither did most of the rest of the adventurers. The wizards for the most part sat muttering through their Meditations. For them, the Cave of the Warp was a place of the utmost significance, whatever Guest might think of it, and to be in its presence awakened old dedications, old ambitions, so that the most slovenly among them was compelled to fresh endeavour.

Eljuk sat apart, keeping a solitary vigil, and when Guest

approached him Ontario Nol was quick to head him off.

"Eljuk needs to be by himself tonight," said Nol.

"But I'm his brother!" protested Guest.

"Eljuk is a wizard now," said Nol. "Or will be if he survives tomorrow."

After this uncompromising brush-off, Guest wandered away from the campsite and sat sulking in the dark of the upland night. But it was too cold to sit sulking for long, so he was soon on his feet again.

Natural curiosity, combined with a childish desire to defy Ontario Nol, soon drew Guest back to the Cave of the Warp. In that Cave, the rainbow-flickering Veils of Fire still burnt in silence.

Guest stood outside, looking in.

Inside this cave, or so he was told, apprentice wizards struggled with the Mahendo Mahunduk, and died if they were not equal to the struggle. To step over the threshold of that cave was to precipitate such a struggle.

So he was told.

Guest was strongly inclined to doubt the truth of any of this. The cave simply did not look dangerous. Rather, it looked spectacularly empty.

"I am the Weaponmaster, am I not?"

So muttered Guest. Then he hesitated.

Then—

Then stepped inside.

Once inside, Guest shuddered at his own audacity. But, with shuddering done, he felt no different. He ventured another step. Where was the danger? Where was the challenge? This was but an empty cave. There was no murkbeast inside, no simulacrum of the Great Mink, no dorgi, no therapist.

"Anyone home?" said Guest.

Not even an echo answered him.

Gaining confidence, Guest boldly ventured all the way to the Veils of Fire, where he again hesitated. Now this, this wall of cold-burning rainbow, this was most definitely something new. But was it dangerous?

As Guest was wondering, the rainbow lashed out. It coiled around his feet and spun in threads of kaleidoscopic lightning, accelerating upwards in wreathing coils until his whole body was alive with multi-coloured light. Wreathed in that light, he felt buoyant, exhilarated — even a little drunk.

Alarmed to find himself growing slightly lightheaded, Guest backed off, and the coils of light relinquished their grip and sank back.

"So," muttered Guest.

So what? What was he to make of this?

Guest had dared himself into a cave which wizards thought of as a place of death and terror. And inside he had found — well, really, precisely nothing.

"Weirdness," said Guest.

Then made his way back to the cavemouth, and made his exit.

Guest had barely exited when he was challenged by Ontario Nol, who was advancing on the cave from the direction of the campsite.

"What are you doing here?" said Nol, when he recognized Guest, whose face was lit by the cold-burning veils of rainbow located fifty paces away, deep in the depths of the cave.

"Investigating," said Guest.

"Investigating?" said Nol. "What are you talking about?"

"Investigating these caves of yours," said Guest. "I don't think much of them. I went right inside, but—"

"Inside!" said Nol. "Enough of your nonsense!"

"It is not nonsense," insisted Guest. "I went inside! Look, I'll show you, I—"

With that, Guest made as if to enter the cave. But Ontario Nol gripped him with fingers which could have demolished stone, and, trapped by Nol's invincible strength, Guest had no option but to bend to the wizard's will.

"Go back to bed!" said Nol.

"I don't have a bed to go to," said Guest.

"There's comfort sufficient inside the yellow bottle," said Nol. "Come. We'll go there."

And such was the insistence of the wizard of Itch that Guest Gulkan was compelled to enter the yellow bottle, where he found that Sken-Pitilkin was already soundly asleep, dreaming opium dreams thanks to the chemical benediction which had been provided to him by a fellow wizard.

Guest was much disgusted by Sken-Pitilkin's stuporous state, and found he could not sleep. In the end, he spent the night talking with Shabble, who seemed unfussed at the prospect of imminent destruction. The truth was, Shabble quite frankly did not believe in the existence of this Warp, or its Veils of Fire, and was perfectly confident of surviving the morrow.

"Perhaps you will," said Guest. "But, one way or another, these wizards will destroy you, because they've set their hearts on your destruction."

"No they won't," said Shabble. "They like me too much."

"They like you!" said Guest.

"Eljuk likes me," said Shabble. "I taught him paper dragons, he likes that. Oh, and the ethnologists like me. I was months and months teaching them sex customs."

"Ethnologists are always in the market for sex customs," said Guest grimly. "But that doesn't stop them being a bunch of cold-blooded vivisectionists."

But Shabble would not believe a word of it.

As for Levant, he was asleep, and protested strenuously when Guest tried to wake him for a tactical discussion.

All in all, Guest Gulkan began to get the impression that he was the only person who was capable of making a sane and rational response to the demands of the moment. Sken-Pitilkin, who had retreated to the unpardonable comfort of a drug-stupor, had resigned himself to death with disgraceful ease. Eljuk, with his uninterruptible vigil, had chosen a like-minded retreat into mystical silence. Shabble was fecklessly unconcerned with the future, and Ontario Nol quite flatly refused to accept the results of Guest's Investigations into the Cave of the Warp.

And Levant! Well, Levant had proved his nature with a vengeance. Useless, useless, dead weight and ballast.

So thinking, Guest at last got to sleep, and endured a few

brief and troubled dreams before he was roused for the morning's ceremonies.

On the rocky ground outside the Cave of the Warp, those who had made the pilgrimage to these inland heights assembled, with a fair amount of coughing, scratching, hawking and yawning. Guest looked around, and saw that Levant was missing. Thayer Levant, who had no interest whatsoever in Eljuk's Trials or Sken-Pitilkin's execution, had chosen to stay in the depths of the yellow bottle and sleep in late.

But everyone else was there.

Sken-Pitilkin was most definitely there, looking much the worse for wear. Indeed, the sagacious wizard of Skatzabratzumon looked almost as shattered as he had at times on Untunchilamon — particularly after the encounter with the therapist Schopotmov, in which Sken-Pitilkin had almost killed himself by over-exertion. Seeing the state Sken-Pitilkin was in, Guest saw at once that the wizard would be no use in a battle.

As for Shabble, why, given freedom, Shabble could have incinerated all the wizards with a single blast of fire. But the bubble of bounce was still caught in a web of silver, and tethered by a chain of silver, and whatever the nature of this restraint it most certainly prevented Shabble from throwing any fire whatsoever.

In the cold light of morning, Shabble hummed softly, doing a gentle imitation of the skavamareen.

As Guest surveyed the scene, one of the wizards began to speak. Unfortunately, his entire discourse was in the High Speech of wizards, of which Guest knew not a word; and nobody was in the mood to provide the Weaponmaster with a translation.

After a long and supremely tedious speech, the wizard beckoned to Eljuk, who stepped towards the Cave of the Warp. Eljuk stumbled even before he entered the cave. But enter he did. He took one step, two, three — and Guest began to feel faint.

Realizing he was holding his breath, Guest Gulkan forced himself to breathe. Even as he did so, Eljuk shrieked. Eljuk screamed as if he were being nailed with needles. He collapsed. Then, to Guest's disbelief, Eljuk's body began to float upwards from the floor of the cave. White fire began to flicker around Eljuk's limbs.

From the sombre, funereal silence of the watching wizards, Guest deduced that Eljuk had failed his Trials, and was going to die.

"Well," said Guest staunchly. "That's what you think, but—"

Then, abandoning speech for action, the Weaponmaster pushed through the wizards and strode into the cave.

"Guest!" yelled Nol.

Heedless to the cry from Ontario Nol, Guest Gulkan walked right into the cave. As he touched his brother, the white fire which had been flickering along Eljuk's limbs abruptly died away to nothing. Whatever force had been levitating Eljuk's body ceased to operate, and the full weight of it fell into Guest's arms.

Guest grunted as he took the weight.

"Eljuk?" he said.

Eljuk was still breathing, but he was unconscious.

So Guest quite naturally carried him out of the cave.

As Guest exited from the Cave of the Warp, the wizards fell back before him, regarding him with horror. He was no wizard, but he had ventured into the Warp! He had ventured, and had emerged unscathed! Could he then be human?

Guest stood before them, an inscrutable Yarglat barbarian, a creature with huge ears and painfully high cheekbones, the embodiment of alien mystery. He had done what nobody else in recorded history had ever succeeded in doing: he had ventured into the Cave of the Warp without a wizard's training to support him, and had come out alive.

As Guest stood there, a voice of thunder boomed:

"I am Lorzunduk, lord of the Mahendo Mahunduk! Behold! And know your doom!"

The voice cried thus in the High Speech of wizards. On hearing the cry, Sken-Pitilkin promptly collapsed.

"See!" said the thunder. "The evil Sken-Pitilkin has been killed! You likewise will die!"

Under the circumstances, this seemed so probable, so easily believable, that the wizards broke and ran. Even Ontario Nol fell back before this combination of inexplicable mystery and patent threat.

One wizard ran too slowly, for Guest grabbed and smashed the wizard who was carrying the yellow bottle — knocked him senseless with fist and elbow, tore the bottle from his possession, then wrested from his finger the ring which allowed one to enter and leave the bottle.

Guest lowered Eljuk to the ground.

"Shabble!" said Guest.

The bubble of bounce, which had so recently scattered the wizards with a threat couched in the High Speech of wizards — for of course it was Shabble, the world's most reckless ventriloquist, who had breached the morning with a voice of thunder — came drifting towards Guest Gulkan.

Shabble was free-floating in the air, the silver-braided tethering rope having been dropped by the wizard who had been holding it. Shabble responded to the Weaponmaster's summons because long and amicable acquaintance had led the shining bubble to think of Guest Gulkan as a friend.

Guest promptly grabbed the tethering rope. Then he strode to Sken-Pitilkin and seized the wizard by the scruff of the neck. The wizard was not dead at all — merely unconscious. Guest twisted the ring on his finger, and was carried into the yellow bottle in company with Sken-Pitilkin and Shabble. With no time to waste, the Weaponmaster released the bubble and let the wizard fall, then used the ring to make a solo return to the outside air.

In that outside air, the wizards were already beginning to rally, with Ontario Nol shouting:

"It was Shabble! It was Shabble who shouted! There's no god, no demon, just Shabble!"

Seeing the wizards were no longer running, Guest did a swift calculation. He had hoped to bundle his brother Eljuk into the yellow bottle then head for the hills. But the wizards were no longer running in panic, so Guest could not hope to flee across the mountains.

And he had no time to pick up Eljuk.

"Guest!" yelled Nol. "Drop the bottle! Drop the bottle, or you're a dead man!"

So.

So Nol had chosen to throw in his lot with the Confederation.

Well.

He'd have to try something better than threats if he wanted to catch Guest Gulkan!

So thinking, Guest began to back into the Cave of the Warp, carrying with him the yellow bottle which contained Sken-Pitilkin and Shabble (and, presumably, the shamefully oversleeping Thayer Levant).

"Guest," said Nol, advancing to the mouth of the cave. "Come out of there. I don't know why you're still alive, but I don't expect you to live much longer. It's dangerous in there!"

Guest thought this a singularly futile threat, since he was surely a dead man if he came out of that cave to face the wrath of the wizards.

So thinking, Guest retreated to the very end of the cave, to the rainbow wall which the wizards knew as the Veils of Fire.

"Guest!" yelled Nol, as rainbow-weaving coils of cold fire began to weave around Guest Gulkan's limbs. "Guest! Guest! Come out of there!"

But, instead, Guest took a single step backwards.

And vanished right through the Veils of Fire.

"Blood of a goat," said Ontario Nol in disbelief. "Now I've seen everything."

Those wizards who had been quick enough in the recovery of their courage to have witnessed Guest Gulkan's departure joined him in his disbelief.

Then one, at last accepting the evidence of his eyes, hawked, and spat, and said:

"Well. It's over. He's dead of a certainty."

And, the destruction of Guest Gulkan, Sken-Pitilkin, Shabble and the bottle now being entirely assured, nothing remained for the wizards but to pack up and make their return to Drangsturm — and there to report the death of the inscrutable Shabble and the terminal disposition of the renegade wizard Hostaja Sken-Pitilkin.

CHAPTER FORTY-SEVEN

Warp: the rift in reality into which apprentice wizards venture to pact with creatures of the World Beyond. All such apprentices know there is one thing they must never do: they must never ever tread beyond the Veils of Fire. What lies beyond the Veils of Fire, nobody knows, but this much is for certain: nobody has ever returned alive from an inspection of its mysteries.

* * *

With all the insouciant ease of a drunken man stepping off the top of a cliff, Guest Gulkan stepped backwards through the Veils of Fire. Cold-burning rainbow leapt around the Weaponmaster as he stepped backwards. On the third step of his retreat, his back bumped against a wall.

Since he was safely out of sight of the wizards — there was nothing to be seen in front of him but veil upon veil of impetuous rainbow — Guest turned to face the wall. It was a dark, velvety, purple-black wall which yielded slightly beneath his touch.

Guest, being the Yarglat barbarian he was, responded to this mystery by subjecting it to an exercise of brute force. He pushed. Hard. And shouldered right through that purple-black wall.

The world plunged to black.

The world plunged to black as Guest's feet plunged to water, with something fragile smashing and shifting underfoot as he sought for his balance.

He was—

He was standing ankle-deep in cold water in a place which was very dark, very cold and very quiet. He could no longer see the slightest trace of rainbow fire. In fact, he could hardly see anything at all. The largest sound was his own harsh breathing.

Since he was temporarily blind, or near enough to blind, Guest stood absolutely still and listened. As he listened —

658

hearing nothing of consequence — he closed his eyes. A long moment later, he opened them.

Then looked around.

As Guest's eyes began to acclimatize to the gloom, he began to see ... shapes. What kind of shapes? Not ghouls, ghosts, werewolves, vampires, sorcerers or necromancers. Not armoured marauders armed with weighted lead and bloody iron. No. These were strange shapes — and their totally unprecedented nature told Guest Gulkan that he was very much out of his depth.

In the dim and half-formed netherworld which confronted the Weaponmaster, he saw fluid obfuscations of liquid dark, saw glowing hoops and senile suns, saw twisted helix-shapes and toroidal follies. At first blush, it looked like the kind of place that would in the very nature of things be singularly unproductive of beds and bawds, of horses and kitchens, or anything else which would make it a worthy refuge for an emperor in exile.

"Grief of a bitch," said Guest. "What have I got myself into now?"

For once, the Weaponmaster thought he might have gone a little bit too far. Having seen what was here, he quite wished he could go back where he came from.

But where was the wall through which he had pushed?

Guest turned, looked back, and saw no wall. Instead, he saw a prospect of — of—

He groped for words, then decided he was looking at dimly shadowed free-floating versions of some of the more abstract paperwork creations which Shabble had taught Eljuk to conjure to life. Certainly there was no sign of any kind of wall, door, or other exitway which would take him back to the Cave of the Warp — a cave for which he now felt a considerable nostalgia.

Meantime, he was standing in water, and the water was leaking into his boots, and his feet were getting exceedingly cold. A faint trace of violet light gentled round Guest Gulkan's feet as the current teased around his battered leather.

Guest shuddered.

At least he still had the yellow bottle. Inside that bottle was food, bedding, shelter, comfort. Sken-Pitilkin was inside that bottle. And Thayer Levant. And Shabble.

Well.

Was that really a matter for comfort?

Were the companions of his death to be a mad wizard addicted to opium and the irregular verbs, a servant lately grown sullen, and a childish bubble which played with equal happiness with cockroaches and bits of folding paper?

Still, he did have the bottle. He did have the ring. The ring was comforting in its rigidity. And the bottle — best to make the bottle safe.

So thinking, Guest tied the bottle to his belt with a thong designed for the secure retention of scalps — a moligok, to use a word from the Eparget.

Now.

Where was he?

At second and third blush, the place to which the Weaponmaster had ventured looked every bit as uncomfortable and uncomforting as it had from the start. It was a cold place, a quiet place, a place without smells. Bone would be at home here. Rock would be content. But a Yarglat barbarian?

Guest was more and more inclined to think he had made an irretrievable mistake, for the place looked uncommonly like a prison, and a prison from which escape was likely to prove impossible. It was cold; it was gloomy; and there was nothing to eat, not even a mushroom or a lump of fungus or such. The crunchy things underfoot were snail shells. Were they edible? They glowed faintly — glowed variously red and green.

While there is nothing written in the Book of Survival concerning the edibility of things that glow in the dark, Guest was inclined to the opinion that the consumption of such things is inadvisable. He presumed, therefore, that he was going to starve, or die from eating poisoned monstrosities. After all, even if he retreated to the yellow bottle, the food inside that bottle was bound to run out in due course, and probably sooner rather than later.

All in all, the hole to which he had fled was a singularly useless place, good for no purpose whatsoever, unless one wished to retire from life for a couple of thousand years to study the intricacies of the irregular verbs — something impossible for Guest, who as ever was travelling without the companionship of a copy of Strogloth's Compendium of Delights.

"But," muttered Guest, "Sken-Pitilkin will surely have such a book."

Then he checked himself.

Verbs? Irregular verbs? He must be growing mad to think of reducing his life to the study of such!

"I am the Weaponmaster," said Guest, more to cheer himself up than anything else. "An emperor in exile! Rightful lord of the Collosnon Empire!"

So said Guest, then felt uncommonly silly for having said it, for this was a place where the greatest of his pretensions was likely to count for absolutely nothing.

Meantime, his feet were growing ever more chill thanks to the cold water which was leaking into his boots. As he was slowly beginning to recover from the shock of his abrupt precipitation into this den of strangeness, he was ready to do something sensible, and so began to wade towards the nearest rock.

Guest Gulkan had almost reached the safety of the rock when someone spoke to him. Someone spoke to him, using the High Speech of wizards.

Once he had assured himself that he had not actually leapt right out of his skin, Guest cleared his throat — which was exceedingly dry — and spoke into the darkness.

"Who's that?" said Guest, using the Galish.

Nobody answered, so Guest presumed the voice to have been but a figment of his imagination. He made as if to sit on the rock. But the voice forestalled him, saying — and this time it used the Galish—

"You're not going to sit on me, are you?"

It was the rock that was talking.

Now the Weaponmaster Guest was in no mood to be lectured to by a rock. He had been tramping through the mountains for an unconscionable length of time, enduring all manner of hardship as a consequence of geology's heaping up of great stoneworks, and saw no reason why he should suffer a lecture on top of the other insults and injuries done to him by rock, stone and mountain.

"Sit on you?" said Guest, with a boldness which suggested that holding converse with rocks was nothing but a commonplace of life, "why shouldn't I sit on you?"

"You should not sit on me," said the rock, with a sorrowful heaviness, "because I would be upset if you were to prove yourself so thoroughly impertinent."

"And what do you do when upset?" said Guest. "Do you bite?"

"No," said the rock. "I do not bite. But I do get unhappy. You would not like me if I were to be unhappy."

"This implies," said Guest, "that you think yourself happy right now."

"Of course I am," said the rock. "Nobody is sitting on me, therefore I am happy."

It struck Guest that the rock was uncommonly easy to satisfy. Naturally, Guest himself was unhappy when someone was sitting on him, or standing on his head, or jumping up and down on his ribcage, as the case might be. But for positive happiness he required rather more than mere freedom from unwelcome encumbrance.

"Some people," said Guest, hinting heavily, "Increase their own happiness considerably by helping others. I'm standing in the water, and the water is exceedingly cold."

"Then the cold," said the rock, "is something you will just have to endure."

"Who are you to tell me what I will or won't?" said Guest, starting to become a trifle truculent.

"I," said the rock, "am the Lobos."

"Then know that I am Guest Gulkan, the Weaponmaster in person, lord of war and rightful heir to the mastery of the

Collosnon Empire and the rule of Tameran."

"You are a young thing, then," said the Lobos.

"Young?" said Guest. "I'm — I'm—"

But, to his dismay, the Weaponmaster found he had quite lost track of his birthdays. He was shocked. How could he possibly have come to such a pass? Obviously the world had rejected him, had ignored him, had overlooked his needs, his celebrations, his festivals.

So thinking, Guest began to feel very sorry for himself. But he was not willing to confess to a rock either his distress or the source of that distress.

"I'm old enough," said Guest. "I've reached a — an age of maturity."

"Maturity!" said the rock, positively snorting with derisive amusement. "Why, you are but a toothpick to a tree, a lump of last year's ice boasting to the mountain of its antiquity."

"You are older, then," said Guest.

"Older!" said the Lobos. "Why, I was here before the Experimenters!"

Here Guest was at a loss, for he had forgotten what he had been told at Lex Chalis. Had Guest Gulkan been in the possession of a disciplined and scholarly memory, then he would have recalled that the Experimenters are a hypothetical race of creatures, lesser than gods but greater than anything human, who are thought by some to have influenced the shaping and the populating of worlds.

"So you're old," said Guest, accepting this assertion without proof since he saw no point in arguing about it. "Even so, old man, you should acknowledge authority when you find it. You stand in the presence of Guest Gulkan, the Weaponmaster himself, the conqueror of Safrak, the lord of the Collosnon Empire!"

This was the windiest of all possible rant, and, as the sound of his own voice died away to nothing, Guest became uncomfortably aware of that fact. For once, he felt embarrassed by his own empty boastfulness.

"So," said the Lobos, speaking into the silence. "You are like all of your kind. You are a most vulgar race of trivial creatures. A vulgar race of murderers."

"Murder!" said Guest, seizing upon this unjust accusation. "You speak of murder, do you? Well, know this. It was me who almost got murdered! It was wizards, you see, they were set to kill me. That's why I ran."

"So," said the Lobos. "You came here for the most vulgar of all possible purposes. To preserve your miserable skin."

"Why else would I come here?" said Guest.

"Most people," said the Lobos heavily, "come here in search of wisdom. Usually they have deep questions to ask of me. I do my best to answer them before they die."

Guest did not like this talk of death at all. He was about to ask how the rock's inquisitive visitors usually met their deaths, and why. But the rock was still talking.

"Even though you have proved yourself a vulgar and ignorant barbarian," said the Lobos, "I will still extend to you the customary courtesy. All is known to me. All things in the earth and under the earth. If you wish to know, then ask!"

Guest Gulkan thought about it. He was not sure that there was really any question he needed to have answered. He had learnt much from his own experience; Sken-Pitilkin had ever been at pains to teach him more than he really wanted to know; and encounters with such knowledgeable creatures as Paraban Senk and Shabble had allowed him to answer just about every question he really wanted to have answered.

"Well?" said the Lobos. "Do you have a question?"

"OK," said Guest, "let's try this for size. I've got this ambition, a big one. I want to stage an orgy, OK, with, let's see, maybe a thousand women, men to match, some horses, and a few dead sheep for those who are truly perverted. I can see my way clear to getting hold of the flesh, but there's just one complication. I want the whole thing to take place in a big bowl of strawberries and cream. How do I go about that?"

The Lobos gave a very heavy sigh. Its every prejudice had been confirmed. Guest was just the barbarian he seemed to be.

"If you really wish to stage such an orgy," said the Lobos,

"then you must begin by recruiting a caterer."

"A what?" said Guest.

"A caterer," said the Lobos. "Don't you understand the word? A caterer is someone whose profession is the provisioning of parties."

Guest Gulkan grappled with this concept, which was a new one to him. So far, the Weaponmaster had gone through his entire life without meeting a caterer, an interior designer or a hairdresser. But the Lobos was quite patient, and explained the business of catering in detail.

"But," said Guest, when he understood, "there's a problem. We, ah, we don't have caterers, not in Gendormargensis. Not that we're short of people, it's a big city, a hundred thousand people or more."

"A hundred thousand," said the Lobos. "Is that your biggest city?"

"It's the biggest I know of," said Guest.

"Then," said the Lobos, "if you are in search of that material wealth which a civilization requires to sustain a vigorous catering industry, I would earnestly suggest that you increase your population base."

"Get more people, you mean," said Guest.

"Yes."

"How would I do that?"

"To begin with," said the Lobos, "make sure that all your people boil all their water and wash their hands every time they go to the toilet."

Guest Gulkan considered this eccentric advice, but was quite unable to make the connection between washing one's hands and staging a mass orgy with cream and strawberries. He concluded that the rock was quite mad.

"Is there anything else you want to know?" said the Lobos.

"Well," said Guest, "what do people usually ask?"

"They commonly ask how they can come by great wealth," said the Lobos.

"That's easy," said Guest. "I can pick up my sword and take it."

"You do not seem to be in possession of a sword," said the Lobos.

"A temporary problem," said Guest. "What else do they ask?"

"They ask the secret of satisfaction," said the Lobos.

"That's easy," said Guest. "Any pimp can help you."

"For a wizard," said the Lobos, "things are not quite so — so impromptu."

"I'm not a wizard," said Guest.

"So I'd noticed," said the Lobos. "Most wizards ask after the secret of immortality."

"Oh!" said Guest, "immortality! Well, now you mention it, what is the secret of immortality?"

"There is no true immortality," said the Lobos. "This is because of the inevitability of entropy. Do you wish me to explain entropy for you?"

"Not if it will delay my next meal unduly," said Guest.

"It might delay your next meal considerably," said the Lobos. "If we leave aside the question of entropy in the interests of your stomach, know that you can make yourself temporarily immortal by putting yourself through an organic rectifier. That is a machine which can extend life indefinitely by inserting self-correcting codes into the genetic material. That is how you make yourself immortal. Of course, you would not have the slightest idea what an organic rectifier is, or where to find one."

Guest Gulkan, rather offended to have a rock speak to him in tones of insufferable intellectual superiority, was quick to rebut this claim.

"Yes I would," said Guest. "There was an organic rectifier on Untunchilamon."

"There was?" said the Lobos dubiously.

"There was!" said Guest. "It rectified a Crab."

"A crab?" said the Lobos.

"Yes, yes, a crab," said Guest. "You know, one of those things that lives by the sea, it's got two claws and six legs, no, eight legs, eight legs and a pair of pincers, there was a big one of Untunchilamon but the organic rectifier made it into an Ashdan, it called itself Codlugarthia."

"You," said the Lobos, on hearing this disjointed story, "are quite mad."

And the more Guest told, the more the Lobos thought him to be quite insane.

"Mad and a murderer," said the Lobos sadly.

"A murderer?" said Guest. "How so?"

"Why," said the Lobos, "the evidence of the murder is at your neck."

Then Guest was moved to put a hand to his neck. He felt the dry warmth of his own skin, the lumpiness of his thyroid cartilage, and the thin chain which sustained the weight of the amulet he wore.

The amulet.

Of course.

"Are you talking about — about the mazadath?" said Guest.

"You see!" said the Lobos. "You play ignorant, but you know the thing, and know it by its proper name."

Now Guest began to understand. Slowly. Dimly. Partially.

Guest Gulkan had always supposed his heavyweight silver amulet to be a device of Power, but until now he had never known what it might possibly be good for. It had proved useless in a confrontation with the therapist Schoptomov, and no wizard had recognized its virtue. Yet, now his attention was drawn to the thing, the obvious conclusion was that it was the mazadath which had preserved his life when he ventured into the Cave of the Warp. For all he knew, it might well be preserving his life right now.

"I know the thing by its name," said Guest slowly, "but I know no reason why I should be called a murderer on account of being in its possession."

"You know where it came from!" said the Lobos.

In the face of this accusation, Guest bravely acknowledged the truth.

"Why, yes, I do," said Guest. "The mazadath is a thing taken from the body of a dorgi. But a dorgi is nothing but an iron dog. It is a machine, a technic, a device. That's all."

"A dorgi!" said the Lobos, with invincible scorn. "Is that where you think that thing came from? Do you really expect me to believe that for so much as half a heartbeat?"

"Why, yes, I do," said Guest, with some heat, "for it is the truth."

"The truth!" said the Lobos. "Is that really what you believe? Well, bless my toes! I think you do!"

"It is the truth as I have been told it," said Guest stubbornly. "This — this trifle is a piece of a dorgi. I got it as a present. A wedding present. A present from my wife."

"A wedding present!" said the Lobos in fury. "You chop up bodies then make presents of their pieces!"

"I chopped up nothing!" protested Guest. "There was a dorgi, an old one, it fell to pieces, and this was what was left."

The Lobos chewed over that claim in silence, then said:

"So. You really don't know."

"I am but a poor barbarian from the north of Tameran," said Guest bitterly. "I know scalping and killing and fighting and torturing. Oh, and sex customs, any ethnologist could tell you that, us barbarians have got plenty of sex customs. But as for what you're on about, why, I couldn't begin to understand it. This is a bit of a dorgi, that's all I know, and I don't know why you should be so upset about it."

"I was upset," said the Lobos, now sounding sad rather than angry, "because the thing which you have about your neck is a thing stolen from one of the Zelamith. Know you the Zelamith?"

"I have never heard of them," said Guest.

"The Zelamith," said the Lobos, "were a race of whispering dragons which lived in the places which do not exist, the places which lie between cosmos and cosmos. For each of the Zelamith there was a mazadath. And a mazadath, dear child of man, a mazadath is a token of identity. In vulgar parlance, a mazadath is a soul. It is like a harp: as the harp is nothing on its own, yet comes to life when in concord with the harpist, so the mazadath is nothing on its own, yet comes to life when in a synergetic relationship with one of the Zelamith. The Zelamith were slaughtered by the Shining Ones, the Vangelis, who butchered them, then sold their souls to humankind for trifles."

"For what purpose?" said Guest. "I mean, why would people buy these things?"

"To allow people and machines to survive in zones of instability," said the Lobos. "Were you not in possession of the mazadath, then the Mahendo Mahunduk would have taken you in the Cave of the Warp. Were you not in possession of the mazadath, then you would have smoked away to nothing right in front of me."

"Is that — is that what usually happens to the people who come here?" said Guest.

"Usually," said the Lobos.

"And, uh, the unusual people?" said Guest.

"There is a way out of here," said the Lobos. "I take it you do have some idea where you are?"

"Why, yes," said Guest. "I'm at the back of a cave in the Shackle Mountains."

"No!" said the Lobos, obviously distressed. "Don't you know anything?"

"It seems not," said Guest. "If I'm not in the Shackle Mountains, then where am I?"

"You," said the Lobos, with heavy emphasis, "are very much in the World Beyond."

Guest tried to absorb this. Did it mean he was dead? He certainly didn't feel dead.

"You don't understand," said the Lobos.

"What makes you say that?" said Guest.

"Your silence says it all," said the Lobos. "Listen. The world in which you live is but a bubble of invention afloat in the great seas of Probability. Now you are outside that bubble. You have entered a much greater realm of existence where, technically speaking, you are not equipped to exist."

"Then, uh, how do I leave?" said Guest.

"Look around you," said the Lobos. "Some of the things of your world have a partial existence of sorts even here in the World Beyond. You see that violet light over there? No, no, to your left, look to your left!"

Guest looked, and did make out a dull violet light place half a league or so in the distance, and said as much.

"That," said the Lobos, "is the local star which lights your home planet. I would, by the way, strongly advise you against interfering with it. Now. Watch."

"Watch what?" said Guest.

In response, several dozen dull red hoops began to glow in the dark. They were scattered in all directions, none close enough to touch, but none further than a slingshot's distance from where he stood.

"How did you do that?" said Guest.

"Ah," said the Lobos, sounding very pleased with itself. "A slight rearrangement of the nature of time and space, that's all."

"Then," said Guest, "are you a god, that you should be playing tricks with time and space?"

"I'm not a god," said the Lobos. "I'm a Lobos. The Lobos. I've told you that all ready. A Lobos is not a man, god, devil or demon. It's a category in its own right."

"But—"

"Is a cow a cuttlefish?" said the Lobos. "Well?"

"No," said Guest.

"So," said the Lobos, "when you go to the seashore, will you start calling the cuttlefish a cow simply because you haven't any other word for it?"

"What do you know of the sea?" said Guest.

"I know most things about most things," said the Lobos, "though you are something new in my experience, because in all my life I've never met anyone as ignorant as you before."

Very much stung by this, Guest started to lose his temper. He struggled to control himself, suspecting that this was no time to be playing the berserker.

"All right," said Guest. "So you're a Lobos, I'll concede that much gladly. Not a cow nor a cuttlefish, but a Lobos. So. So what are those hoop-things?"

"Those," said the Lobos, "are the Doors of the Circles of your world."

"Doors?" said Guest. "You mean, like the Doors of the Partnership Banks?"

"Ah!" said the Lobos. "So it does know something! It's not as ignorant as it acts! Yes, those are the Doors."

"But," protested Guest, "there's, there's uh, maybe a hundred, maybe more."

"Yes," said the Lobos. "And you can exit through any of them."

"But, uh, how will I know which one to choose?" said Guest.

"You can look through them," said the Lobos. "Or, if you have a special one in mind, I can pick it out for you."

Guest thought about it.

Thinking made him feel more than a little bit dizzy.

"If I leave," said Guest, "can I come back again?"

"Only by again venturing through the Veils of Fire in the Cave of the Warp," said the Lobos.

"So," said Guest. "So I've got to choose. Uh. Well. There's Dalar ken Halvar. Uh. I've got a wife there. Or I did have, but where she's got to I've no idea. Then. Safrak. Alozay, I mean. There's a Door there. I suppose my father's still in charge. But, really, it's the star-globe, that's what I really want."

"Star-globe?" said the Lobos.

Guest explained.

"The device which controls the Doors of the Circle of the Partnership Banks is currently in Chi'ash-lan," said the Lobos.

"How do you know that?" said Guest. "I mean, you can look through the Doors, or what?"

"I see as if through a glass darkly," said the Lobos. "I hear as if through a wall. It is enough. If Chi'ash-lan is your destination, then there is your Door."

As the Lobos was so saying, the light of all but one of the red hoops died away to nothing. Guest waded through the wet, cold water to that last remaining hoop. When he peered through it, he seemed to see — as if through thick mist — the weirding room of the Morgrim Bank in Chi'ash-lan. It was identifiable on account of the skeletons which hung from the ceiling.

"Go ahead," said the Lobos, as Guest hesitated. "It's

perfectly safe."

"Maybe I should think about this a little longer," said Guest.

"Then, then," said the Lobos. "But don't spend too long about it. You've been here too long already."

"What do you mean?" said Guest.

"Look at yourself!" said the Lobos. "Look at your hands!"

Guest did look at himself. He looked at his hands. And saw, to his horror, that they had grown transparent. He could see right through them.

"Don't worry," said the Lobos. "The condition's not irreversible. As long as you leave now! Go! Go! Quick! Quick! Or you're doomed to be a ghost forever, mazadath or no!"

Compelled by this command, Guest took one last look around, then stepped through the red hoop, leaving the world of the Lobos and entering the weirding room of the Morgrim Bank in Chi'ash-lan.

CHAPTER FORTY-EIGHT

Chi'ash-lan: city at western end of Ravlish Lands. This city was the birthplace of Banker Sod (sometime Governor of the Safrak Bank) and of Thayer Levant (Guest Gulkan's servant, who previously served Plandruk Qinplaqus). The Bank in Chi'ash-lan is the Morgrim Bank. In this Bank is a monster twice man-height. The monster is of jade green stone, and is known to the world as the demon Ko (or, to give it the dignity of its full and formal name, as the demon Koblathakatoria). This demon is not actually a creature of the world of gods and shadows — rather, it is a machine, a military farspeaker of Nexus make.

* * *

Guest stood on the marble plinth, momentarily uncertain as to whether it was the real thing or an illusion. Then he was abruptly shoved from behind by an unruly Banker who came pushing through the humming silver screen which filled the arch of Chi'ash-lan's Door.

"Time is money!" said the Banker, as Guest went stumbling.

Then the Banker promptly turned and made his way back through the Door, pushing on to the Safrak Bank on the island of Alozay.

Guest realized he truly was in Chi'ash-lan, and that its Door was in use, and that there was no telling who or what might come through that Door unless he acted quickly. He jumped down from the marble plinth. Water squelched in his boots as he landed, for his boots were still soaking wet from the water in which he had lately been standing.

That squelching water assured Guest that at least some small fraction of his recent experience had been for real. Otherwise, he might have dismissed the Lobos and its cave as sheer hallucination.

He checked. Did he have the yellow bottle? Yes, it was still tightly tied to his swordless swordbelt with a moligok. Presumably, Sken-Pitilkin and Thayer Levant were still safe inside that bottle. And the ring which controlled it was still safe on Guest's finger.

Right, then.

Guest looked for the niche in the plinth of the Door, found it, and found it occupied by the star-globe, as he had expected.

He hesitated.

As soon as he seized the star-globe and pulled it from that niche, the Circle of the Doors of the Partnership Banks would abruptly close. Then Guest would be stuck in Chi'ash-lan, and would be put to the trouble of fighting his way free from the Morgrim Bank — if he could. He was sorely tempted to take an easier course: to abandon the star-globe and simply jump through the Door, making the passage to the island of Alozay in the tricing of an eyeblink.

But—

But did Lord Onosh still rule on Alozay?

That was the first question which troubled Guest Gulkan. And the second was this: what would his father say if he knew that Guest had been within grasping distance of the star-globe, but had declined its challenge?

Guest came to a quick decision.

He seized the cold cool of the star-globe and snatched it from its niche. The silver-buzzing hum of the Door died away on an instant. When Guest rose, the star-globe in his hand, no screen of shimmering silver remained in the arch. Instead, the arch was but a loop of metal.

Now to get out of here.

Guest hastened towards the exit of the Morgrim Bank's weirding room. But halted abruptly, for of course the demon Ko stood on guard in that exit.

"Ko," said Guest, challenging that monolith of jade-green stone.

"I see you and hear you," said Ko. "You are welcome, thrice welcome. You are free to pass — with or without that which you have won."

All this was said with immaculate courtesy, and was said moreover in Guest's native Eparget, which in itself was sufficient to tell Guest that he was recognized. Ko knew who he was, and what. And Guest remembered a terrible day on which that very demon had seized his brother Eljuk, had torn away his clothes, had—

Remembering, Guest realized he could not trust Ko for so much as half an eyeblink. Courtesy was not the custom of demons, which meant that this demon meant to seize him and tear him.

Guest had a rough and ready idea of the demon's reach. It could extrude quick-striking tentacles, smash him and mash him, grip him and clutch him, drag him in and slaughter him. Or hold him prisoner — as Eljuk had been held. Eljuk had eventually been released. But would Guest be so lucky? Somehow, he doubted it.

Guest glanced back at the arch of the Door. He was half-minded to open it, then make his retreat, leaving the star-globe in Chi'ash-lan. But if his father still ruled on Alozay, then—

"Come to me," said Ko, softly. "Come to me. It's perfectly safe."

Guest looked back to the demon, which saw his hesitation, his fear, his intense suspicion. In response, it laughed.

"Now you see," said Ko, with a sudden change of tone. "Now you realize. There is no way out."

Then the demon laughed again, with brutal frankness.

But—

The thing's laughter was so frank that Guest thought it to be too frank. One could trust a demon in nothing. The brutality of the laughter was so theatrically overstated, so brilliantly triumphant, that Guest was immediately sure that the demon must be trying to distract his attention from something.

But what?

Guest remembered Sken-Pitilkin's performance on the day of the battle for the mainrock Pinnacle. Sken-Pitilkin had levitated above the demon Icaria Scaria Iva-Italis, taking advantage of the headroom between the demon and the roof.

There was just as much headroom between the demon Ko and the ceiling of the doorway it guarded.

While Guest was still deliberating, he heard footsteps approaching. He had no sword, hence did not even momentarily think of fighting his way out of difficulty. Rather, he turned the ring on his finger — and was promptly sucked into the yellow bottle.

It was the work of moments for Guest to retrieve Sken-Pitilkin from the yellow bottle, but unfortunately such was his haste that he accidentally retrieved Shabble as well.

As Guest and Sken-Pitilkin emerged from the yellow bottle, sweeping out as so much smoke, and solidifying to their proper forms instants later, Shabble swept and solidified likewise. True, Shabble was still secured in a net of silver — but the bubble was free!

"Where are we?" said Sken-Pitilkin.

The yells of a dozen Zenjingu fighters instantly gave him the answer to that question.

Sken-Pitilkin could not for the life of him work out how he had been abruptly transported from the Shackle Mountains to the Morgrim Bank, but the sight of the black-clad Zenjingu, combined with the sight of the demon Ko and the skeletons which dangled from the ceiling, orientated him instantly.

As the Zenjingu charged around the flanks of the demon Ko, Sken-Pitilkin threw up his hands and cried out a Word.

The Zenjingu were scattered in all directions, seized by levitational energies and smashed against walls and against skeletons.

"Into the bottle!" said Sken-Pitilkin. "In, and I'll have us out of here in instants!"

Then Guest made a grab for the silver rope which was trailing from the silver net which secured Shabble. But he missed, and Shabble promptly drifted out of reach.

"This is no time for bubble-hunting!" said Sken-Pitilkin. "Get in the bottle! And stay there!"

With that, Guest turned the ring on his finger, and was again transported into the yellow bottle, thus leaving the responsibilities of initiative to Sken-Pitilkin.

Then Sken-Pitilkin exerted his Power and levitated himself, endeavouring to preserve a grave dignity as he did so. But it is an unfortunate fact that this business of levitation tends to be singularly ridiculous, particularly when one is wearing fisherman's skirts as Sken-Pitilkin was. For, while the skirt is a most practical form of dress, it is most definitely not one which is meant to be viewed from below.

Carrying the yellow bottle, Sken-Pitilkin drifted with due deliberation above the demon Ko, thus making his escape from the room which held the Door of the Morgrim Bank. Shabble confidently tried to follow. But the bubble of bounce had forgotten that it was trailing a rope of silver — and this the demon caught!

On hearing a wail of distress from Shabble, Sken-Pitilkin turned to see the demon dragging Shabble closer and closer towards its own cold green substance.

Then Sken-Pitilkin paid no more heed to Shabble, for he had other problems to worry about.

Need we give here an account of the manner in which Sken-Pitilkin fought his way free from the Morgrim Bank? Need we mention the arrows which were fired at him, and the supreme skill which he demonstrated in coping with their onslaught? Of course we need not! For it may be taken for granted that any wizard of the order of Skatzabratzumon is more than a match for a rabble of Zenjingu fighters. And, further, it would be injurious to Sken-Pitilkin's dignity to suggest that he had (or has) any need for history to take account of the splendidly satisfying manner in which he crunched bones, shattered flesh, and sent the bravest running in all directions in bawling terror.

Let it then merely be recorded that Sken-Pitilkin escaped from the Morgrim Bank, which is set in the approximate centre of the city of Chi'ash-lan, and he was levitating towards the outskirts of the city when—

When a cloud formed in the air close at hand.

Sken-Pitilkin had barely time sufficient to gape at the cloud before it configured itself as a Yarglat barbarian. Judging from the bigness of his ears, that barbarian was Guest Gulkan. And, on this occasion, the bigness of his ears was matched by the bigness of his mouth. For, when Guest emerged from the bottle to find himself poised in mid-air above the city, his jaw dropped in outright horror.

"The ring!" bawled Sken-Pitilkin.

But it was too late.

Guest was already falling, and by the time he had wit sufficient to turn the ring on his finger, he was too far removed from the yellow bottle for the ring to compel him within it. Thus he fell, with Sken-Pitilkin — his own power nearly exhausted by battle and flight — helpless to save him.

Guest did not fall far.

After all, Sken-Pitilkin was no seagull, hence had not soared to any great height. Rather, he had been levitating — and not without difficulty, for it is a business far more tricky than it may appear to the uninitiated, this fine art of levitation — about four storeys above the ground. Guest fell but three storeys before his fall was intercepted by a roof. He crashed through the roof and disappeared from sight.

In the face of this disaster, Sken-Pitilkin did not have to make any fine ethical calculations. The best he could do was to ensure his own survival, so that was what he did. He got himself to the outskirts of the city, landed, and took to his heels and fled.

Need we give here an account of Sken-Pitilkin's escape? No, surely not. For it was only Zenjingu fighters who were pursuing him, and any fieldsman who cannot elude five thousand of the Zenjingu or more is not worthy of his bootleather.

While Sken-Pitilkin was a wizard, he was other things as well. Among other things, he was a fisherman. He had not adopted a fisherman's skirts as his customary attire by random choice! No, he had studied the Art of Arts for generations, and from its study he had learnt his fieldcraft thoroughly.

Thus Sken-Pitilkin was able to elude the Zenjingu, and get himself away from Chi'ash-lan — and, eventually, to improvise a stickbird of sorts and go limping back to the island of Drum.

A fine predicament, this!

For Sken-Pitilkin was still in possession of the yellow bottle, which he took with him all the way to his home island of Drum, but he did not have the ring which allowed one to enter or leave that bottle. The sole ring to command that bottle was in Guest Gulkan's possession, and, for all the wizard knew, Guest might well be dead.

Well.

We all have to die sometime.

But the truly tragic part was that Thayer Levant, Guest's long-serving, long-suffering and totally unappreciated servant, was trapped in the yellow bottle, unable to get out through his own exertions, and with Sken-Pitilkin (for all his undoubted sagacity) in no position to help him.

And suppose one is trapped in a wizard-made bottle, as was Thayer Levant. What then will one have to drink? And what to eat?

As a rule, drink is no problem, for wizards take care to stock such bottles well with water. And food? Well, this yellow bottle had lately been used as a portable storehouse on a journey into the Shackle Mountains, so it contained rations sufficient to feed one person for a few months or so. But supposing those few months pass, what then? Why, a prisoner trapped in a wizard-made bottle and beyond succour by outside forces must necessarily resort to the siege dust which is so commonly found in such bottles.

Of siege dust, it may be said in its favour that it can last for upwards of five thousand years while still remaining as good to eat as it was to start with. The problem is that, even to start with, siege dust is no more palatable than ordinary dust.

So Thayer Levant was doomed to suffer a cruel and unusual punishment, for his ordinary food must inevitably run out unless Guest could make it back to Drum in six months or less.

But six months passed and there was no sign of Guest. A year passed, and still there was no sign of Guest. Sken-Pitilkin had every right to presume the Weaponmaster to be dead — but, not content with taking such a position, the wizard of

Skatzabratzumon had built a fully serviceable stickbird, and had several times flown it the full length of the Ravlish Lands in search of the Weaponmaster.

However, despite Sken-Pitilkin's exhausting and exhaustive endeavours on his account, Guest Gulkan had to do it all on his own. Having survived the fall through a roof — he had after all fallen a mere three storeys, and what is three storeys to a stoutly built Yarglat barbarian? — Guest escaped from Chi'ash-lan and fled east through the Ravlish Lands.

For a year and a day he fled, with the Zenjingu fighters ever close on his heels. And, a year and two days after Guest's intemperate materialization in the skies of Chi'ash-lan, the sea dragon Hobagamandrik came to Sken-Pitilkin with the news that a fishing boat had arrived from D'Waith, and that Guest Gulkan was a passenger on that fishing boat.

(Two Zenjingu fighters arrived the very next day, and were shortly thereafter eaten by Sken-Pitilkin's sea dragons, who pronounced them to be rather stringy, and of a flavour midway between that of cat and that of pig.)

Thus Guest Gulkan returned to Drum, and was able to use his ring to liberate Thayer Levant from the yellow bottle. For all that time, Levant had preserved the star-globe, which Guest had left behind in the bottle when he had exited to the skies of Chi'ash-lan. Levant — rightly enraged by a year of imprisonment — declared that Guest could count himself supremely lucky that the star-globe had not got itself flushed down one of the vents which allowed wastes to exit from the yellow bottle.

In the light of what later happened, it may be seen in retrospect as being very unfortunate that Guest did not take the time to address Levant's complaints in depth and in detail, to soothe him with flattery and to balm him with promises. But instead, Guest belittled Levant's sufferings, saying they had all taken place indoors, free from the wind and rain, the wasps and thorns, the rockburn and sunburn which had bedevilled the Weaponmaster on his year of flight from Chi'ash-lan.

Then Guest promptly launched himself into a conference

with Sken-Pitilkin, making plans for returning to Alozay with the star-globe, and, assuming his father still to be in possession of that island, using Alozay as a base for a struggle which would surely see him end as master of the Circle of the Partnership Banks.

CHAPTER FORTY-NINE

Lord Onosh: the Witchlord, the sometime lord of the Collosnon Empire who retreated to Alozay after his defeat at the hands of the Red Emperor Khmar. On Alozay, Lord Onosh made himself master of the Safrak Bank. His regime suffered a setback when Shabble temporarily usurped his authority; but, when Shabble left Alozay, Lord Onosh was easily able to restore his authority, and has governed the Safrak Islands and the Safrak Bank ever since.

* * *

Of Guest Gulkan's return to Alozay, there is no need to give a detailed account.

Lord Onosh had long been separated from Guest, the most warlike of his sons. So, when Witchlord was reunited with Weaponmaster, the celebrations were considerable. Horses were slaughtered, and their meat cooked in great barbecues. A babble of storytelling was followed by bout upon bout of drunken boisterousness.

The celebrations went on for a full ten days; the hangovers lasted a further three; and it was not until the fourteenth day after Guest's return to Alozay that a council of war was held to consider the reopening of the Circle of the Doors.

"After all I have endured," said Guest, "I will settle for nothing less than the rule of the Circle."

"That may be difficult," said his father.

"Nevertheless," said Guest, "it is what I have set my heart on."

"Then," said Sken-Pitilkin, "perhaps our first move should be to talk with the resident demon of the Hall of Time."

Guest was most reluctant to do this. But he knew the importance of the demons to the Banks. Had it not been for these silent, ever-watchful jade-green monsters, then Bank security would have been a much more difficult proposition.

The Circle of the Banks could still be run — and perhaps dominated — without the assistance of such monsters. But their co-operation would make Guest's schemes of conquest infinitely easier.

"But," said Guest, "what can I offer them?"

"You can offer," said Sken-Pitilkin, "to give material assistance to the Great God Jocasta when that dignitary eventually emerges from the tunnels of Cap Foz Para Lash."

"I can what!" said Guest.

"You heard me," said Sken-Pitilkin.

Then they began to argue the rights and the wrongs of offering to aid the Great God Jocasta, the delinquent controller-of-carts which was currently sheltering inside one of the minor mountains of Dalar ken Halvar.

During this debate, Sken-Pitilkin reminded both Witchlord and Weaponmaster of some uncomfortable facts. Both were Yarglat born and Yarglat bred, but they were cut off from their own people. Few of the Yarglat had followed Lord Onosh to Alozay, most choosing instead to desert to the Red Emperor Khmar. Lord Onosh had won the rule of Alozay with a rabble of mercenaries, slaves and other such underlings.

"You have no natural constituency on Alozay," said Sken-Pitilkin. "You have no natural constituency in the Safrak Islands. The society you rule has no internal cohesion. It is not unified by language, or by race, or by religion. By personal strength, by studied alliance, by careful management and with the assistance of a fair measure of luck, you have managed to reach an accommodation with the Partnership Banks in the past."

"With difficulty," said Lord Onosh, remembering the many vicissitudes of his relationship with those Banks.

"Yes," said Sken-Pitilkin. "You know the Bankers can be cunning, treacherous, and totally ruthless in the application of power. Your own resources have served to let you deal with them. But if you and your son are resolved to conquer them, why, then you must have something greater to stand behind you in support. If you can win the aid of the demons of the Circle by promising support to the Great God, then you have that something."

"But what do we do then when this Great God comes forth from the hiding place where it is licking its wounds?" said Guest.

"The licking of those wounds may take generations," said Sken-Pitilkin. "Don't worry about it."

Here Sken-Pitilkin showed his great wisdom, for he no longer sought perfect solutions. If Guest Gulkan was determined to make himself master of the Circle, then he might have to settle for a regrettably imperfect alliance with a treacherous Great God. Even such a flawed solution would be safer than trying to challenge the might of the Banks single-handed — and Sken-Pitilkin knew full well that it was useless to suggest that Guest might care to abandon thoughts of such challenge and make his retreat to a monastery.

Sken-Pitilkin said as much, and at length. After long deliberation, the wizard's wisdom prevailed, and so Guest and his father went in Sken-Pitilkin's company to the Hall of Time, where they bearded the demon Icaria Scaria Iva-Italis.

Guest Gulkan did the talking. He made a frank confession of his desire to conquer the Circle of the Banks; he declared his intention to seek an alliance with the demons of the Circle, using their brute strength and intelligence to his advantage; he offered in return to declare himself for the Great God Jocasta; and then he asked, quite openly, how long it would be before Jocasta returned to the world of daylight.

"The Great God Jocasta will come forth from the tunnels of Cap Foz Para Lash in due course," said Iva-Italis. "But the Great God's renaissance will not take place for many years yet. The Great God was grievously injured by the evil Stogirov in the Temple of Blood."

"I'm sorry to hear that," said Guest, who was not sorry at all, and wished upon Jocasta a thousand years of painful convalescence.

"However," said Iva-Italis, "while Jocasta will not be seen by the sun for many years yet, there is work to be done even now. Should we conclude a satisfactory alliance, then there would be much for you to do in preparation for the Great God's renaissance. There are for example many machines which should be built — machines designed to aid comfort supplement and support the Great God in its endeavours. The contrivance of such mechanisms is not easy. You would have to build lesser machines to construct greater machines, and even with guidance from myself and my colleagues, this task could not be accomplished in anything less than two or three generations."

Then Iva-Italis paused.

Guest Gulkan promptly answered the unstated but implicit question, which was this: can you, mere mortal, make any meaningful commitment to a task which may well last generations?

"My brother Morsh Bataar has bred sons on the island of Ema-Urk," said Guest. "Though my brother Morsh is slow in his wits, his sons by all accounts have proved worthy of their grandfather. I have sired no dynasty myself, but will pledge myself to the support of Morsh Bataar's sons. Yurt and Iragana can be the founders of a dynasty which would see your machines constructed as you wish."

"Very good," said Iva-Italis, positively purring. "Very good."

Sken-Pitilkin was almost inclined to purr himself. This was all going very well. Guest Gulkan had spoken with uncommon reasonableness, and the demon had matched him in that.

But there was more to come:

"I have conferred with the Great God Jocasta," said Italis.

"That was quick!" said Guest.

"It is over a year since you stole the star-globe from the Morgrim Bank," said Italis. "We have had a full thirteen moons to consider the possibilities. Where would you come to if not to here? We have had a year to talk this matter out in full — and to discuss it with Shabble."

At that, Guest and Sken-Pitilkin exchanged glances. It is significant that Sken-Pitilkin should look to his former tutor rather than to his father. Despite the rapturous reception which Lord Onosh had given his long-lost son, the plain fact was that Guest had spent much more of his adult life in Sken-Pitilkin's company than he had in his father's house, and wizard and Weaponmaster knew each other to a nicety, whereas Guest had inevitably become something of a stranger to his father.

"What are you talking about?" said Lord Onosh, addressing his question to Italis. "What's this about Shabble?"

Guest and Sken-Pitilkin had already realized what Italis was going to propose, and had acknowledged the realization to each other by no more than a wordless glance. But then, both Guest and Sken-Pitilkin had endured long and deep acquaintance with Shabble, who had been to Lord Onosh but a transitory phenomenon briefly encountered and thereafter unknown.

"We feel," said Italis, "and here by we I mean both the Great God Jocasta and the conference of demons which serves that god — we feel we need an immediate deity under which the Circle can be united."

"Shabble, you mean?" said Lord Onosh. "If that's how you feel, why do you come by the notion now? Now and not formerly?"

"Formerly," said Italis, "we did not have the pleasure of Shabble's company. Shabble has only kept us company for the last year or so. It is Shabble who now forms the focus of our plans. Let me make it clear that your offer of dynastic support for the Great God Jocasta is not sufficient to tempt us to support you in a conquest of the Circle."

Translation: you are mortal, we are not. You will be gone in a hundred years, whereas we will be here in a thousand.

"In addition to your dynastic support," said Italis, "we feel we need an immediate deity. The peoples of the Circle are wedded to the superstitious worship of that which they can see, touch, hear and feel. They are not yet ready to bow down and worship Jocasta, who is distant, and wounded, and temporarily unavailable to worshippers. We need a god."

"The Yarglat have gods," said Lord Onosh. "There is the horse god, Noth. Would Noth suit your purposes?"

"I have another god in mind," said Iva-Italis. "This god was born upon Untunchilamon."

Guest knew what was coming. But, fearing his father was

going to make a fool of himself by an undue display of ignorance, Guest intervened with a preemptive question.

"You're not talking about, uh, a certain Cockroach, are you?" said Guest.

"But what else?" said Italis. "What else would I be talking about? You know it, you know it all, even if your father does not."

By that response, Icaria Scaria Iva-Italis, demon of Safrak, showed the intimacy with which it knew Guest Gulkan. The thing had divined the reason for his slow-on-the-uptake question. Just as Guest and Sken-Pitilkin could confirm shared perceptions with no more than a glance, so too the demon Italis could as good as read Guest Gulkan's mind.

Intimacy was the key to this skill.

Sken-Pitilkin, Italis, Guest Gulkan — they had shared so much of the recent years that they had no secrets from each other. Guest certainly had very few secrets from the demon Italis, for, while formerly incarcerated in the yellow bottle with Shabble, Guest had shared many intimacies with that ever-talkative bubble, and the demons of the Circle had had a full year and more to extract the history of those intimacies from Shabble.

In a way, Guest Gulkan could not help but be gratified by the manner in which the demon Italis understood him. For Guest, the mainrock Pinnacle had become a place of stability, and his easy familiarity with the demon Italis was an index of that stability. The demon had prevailed, unmoved, unchanging, while the rest of existence had shifted beyond recognition.

One of the terrors of human existence is that, as we get older, the world loses the solidity and stability which it possessed during childhood, when the existing order seemed absolute. Indeed, to a wizard, the world seems at times a sheer phantasmagoria, in which empires shift, deform, and melt like fog in the sun, and in which the very gods themselves change the faces which they show to humanity as they endure their evolution.

While Guest had yet to suffer that terror which a wizard

suffers when he first realizes that all of living creation, saving he alone, has forgotten the names and genesis of his parents, he had nevertheless seen so much change, evolve or perish that he had lost any confidence in the stability of the existing order.

In many ways, the demon Italis had become a foundation stone of Guest's existence; and, though he half-hated the thing, and feared it more than a fraction, he nevertheless felt an inevitable dependency upon it. For if the demon Italis were to cease to exist, then who but for Sken-Pitilkin would truly know, recognize and understand the Weaponmaster?

"The demon," said Lord Onosh, taking Guest by the shoulder. "It says you know something. What is it you know?"

"You remember Shabble," said Guest.

"Of course," said Lord Onosh. "Of course I remember. Shabble, the Cockroach, that rabble of piratical filibusters — how could I forget?"

"Well," said Guest, "our good friend Iva-Italis has plans for Shabble, and for that Cockroach."

By this stage, Guest Gulkan, Sken-Pitilkin and the demon Italis understood exactly what was on the agenda, but to bring the Witchlord Onosh to the same state of understanding was the work of a full week.

Lord Onosh, like a diligent student of the higher peevishness, seemed perversely reluctant to understand the obvious; and Guest, his mind sharpened by matching wits with Crabs and inquisitors, with wizards and ethnologists, with Great Gods and demons, and with the very Lobos itself.

Despite the Witchlord's reluctance to concede that he understood, the facts were simple. After long millennia of imprisonment, the Great God Jocasta had at last been liberated from the Temple of Blood in Obooloo: and, even though the Great God was temporarily recuperating from battle-damage inside a mountain in Dalar ken Halvar, Jocasta would eventually be able to sally out to assume the rule of the world.

To prepare the way for the Great God, the demons of the Circle of the Partnership Banks were willing to help Guest Gulkan seize control of that Circle — if he would pledge to use it for the benefit of the Great God.

As Guest would probably be dead of old age by the time the Great God completed its recuperation, he was more or less prepared to assent to such a deal. But there was a hitch. The demons wished to enslave the populations of the cities of the Circle by imposing upon them a new god: the Holy Cockroach. In the name of the Cult of Cockroach, the peoples of the Circle would build the new technologies which the Great God Jocasta would (in the fullness of time) painlessly inherit.

At last Lord Onosh conceded his understanding, after which he debated the matter with Guest and Sken-Pitilkin.

It was Guest who was given the task of delivering their decision to the demon Italis.

"We thought about your proposition," said Guest, "and we have decided that your notion of inflicting this Cult of Cockroach upon the world is intolerable."

"But," said Italis, "you will surely need our help if you are to conquer the Circle. Mere possession of a single Door and a single star-globe is nothing in itself."

"Quite right," said Guest. "But we have thought it through, and we have decided that, if the Cult of Cockroach is to be the price for victory, then we will not attempt any such conquest. All things considered, we would rather not reopen Alozay's Door. We would rather live out our lives in the modest contentment of these our Safrak Islands."

"But what is your objection?" said Italis. "I did not know you to be in possession of a religion. If you are not a religious person, then why does it matter to you what god is or is not worshipped?"

"If the peoples of the world wish to worship rocks, trees, stones or toads, then let them," said Guest. "It's nothing to me. At least, not in itself! But, in the city of Dalar ken Halvar, a city of the Circle, the militant religion of Nu-chala-nuth holds sway. If you are bent on forcing the Cult of Cockroach upon all the world, then you will spark a religious war, when Cockroach clashes with Nu-chala-nuth. I have been in that city, I have met that religion, and I think it better for the world if the doctrines of Nu-chala-nuth be confined to the wastelands of Parengarenga."

"You fear this religion?" said Italis.

"You know as much of it as I do," said Guest, "and probably much more."

"Ah," said Italis, "but has this Nu-chala-nuth a bubble which speaks, which squeaks, which flies, which burns with a fire as bright as the sun, which can blast towers and maim cities at a firestroke?"

"No," said Guest, "but—"

"So it is mere superstition!" said Italis. "Whereas the Cockroach is fact, a proven god, with living hellfire ready to strike down his enemies! Holy holy holy! Holy is the Cockroach! Unholy are his enemies! They will burn! Their flesh will blister, will char, will crisp! The smoke of their burning will be as incense unto the nostrils of heaven!"

Much more in the same vein followed. To which Guest responded thus:

"You can and will defeat the forces of Nu-chala-nuth in a clash of war. But to defeat this religion in war will be to scatter it, for the refugees of war will carry it to every horizon. Once scattered, it is sown. As you sow, so shall you reap. I think to use a vicious war as an instrument to sow the seeds of Nu-chala-nuth broadcast through the world would be — in time — to reap the whirlwind."

"Brave rhetoric," said Italis. "But the rhetoric veers from the truths of your Yarglat birth, your Yarglat upbringing. The Yarglat say nothing of sowing and reaping. They are a nation of hunters, and you a hunter in the manner of your kind. For all your crop-planting rhetoric, I cannot imaginatively configure you as a farmer. For all your rhetoric, I cannot imagine you much concerned if Dalar ken Halvar were to run awash with blood and every person in Parengarenga be slaughtered by religious war."

This was perceptive, though not uncommonly so.

In the course of his life, Guest Gulkan had not shown himself to be any great humanitarian. His true fear — which he had shared with Sken-Pitilkin, though he had no intention of sharing it with the demon Italis — was the dilution of his own authority.

Long exile, defeat and disappointment, combined with fear, suffering and gruelling endurance tests of all descriptions, had hardened and strengthened the Weaponmaster's will to power. His ambitions had become focused on the overthrow of his enemies and the mastery of the Door. He had no wish to share such mastery with a priesthood in the service of the Cockroach, or with a Shabble; and he saw that a Conference of Demons allied to such a priesthood and to such a Shabble would find it the easiest thing in the world to push aside a mere Yarglat barbarian once he had outworn his use.

"Come," said Italis, as Guest remained silent. "My terms are surely reasonable. After all, you're offering me nothing, but I'm offering you the rule of the world."

"Out of the goodness of your heart," said Guest.

"I would choose you as my instrument rather than anyone else," said Italis, "for I know you better than I know any other. I would rather give employment to an old friend than to a stranger. But you must understand that I speak of a whim. It's not, after all, as if you had anything I want."

"On the contrary," said Guest. "We must have something you need, else you would not have bothered talking with us."

"What, then?" said Italis. "What is it you have that I need?"

"We have Sken-Pitilkin's power of flight," said Guest. "That and the yellow bottle, yes, and the ring which commands that bottle. In the bottle we can carry an army, and Sken-Pitilkin can fly it anywhere at will. With Shabble's strength combined with your own, and with that strength matched with the ability to ship an army by air, we can in combination bring the Bankers to their knees."

"If we have to," said Italis, "then we can rule the Circle in our own right with assistance from Shabble alone."

"Shabble is not reliable," said Guest.

The Weaponmaster did not think that even demons such as Ko of Chi'ash-lan and Italis of Alozay could succeed in bending

Shabble to their will on a permanent basis. True, it seemed that the demons had had Shabble as a prisoner for a year. Much could have been done in that time to make the bubble amenable to their discipline.

But, as Guest had learnt from the side-chatter of Untunchilamon, and from long conversations with Shabble itself, a thousand attempts at ruling Shabble had been made in the past, and all had come to disaster in the end. Shabble could not be permanently coerced by threats, promises, oaths, temptations, for Shabble was one of nature's born delinquents, and Shabble's only ultimate allegiance was to a creed of self-indulgent anarchy.

"Shabble might not prove permanently reliable," conceded Italis, "but a priesthood of the Cockroach would be. Us demons, we'd be the high priests. The rest follows naturally."

"I will think about it," said Guest.

And with that, the Weaponmaster withdrew.

There then followed a long and tense conference between Witchlord and Weaponmaster, with Sken-Pitilkin in attendance.

"We've faced this problem before," said Lord Onosh.

They had indeed.

On fleeing Untunchilamon with Sken-Pitilkin and others, Shabble had come to the island of Alozay, and had made a brief-lived effort to install upon that island the rule of the Cult of Cockroach.

But Guest and Sken-Pitilkin had defeated such efforts by stealing the star-globe. Shabble had chased after the stolen star-globe, and, on venturing to the island of Drum in pursuit of it, had been captured by certain wizards of the Confederation who had long maintained a vigil there, hoping for Sken-Pitilkin to fall to their snares.

"That net thing," said Guest Gulkan, referring to the silver net with which the wizards of the Confederation had restrained Shabble. "How did that work?"

"I've no idea," said Sken-Pitilkin. "But most things of wizard make can be destroyed by application of brute force, if the force is sufficient. We must assume that the prodigious strength of the demon Ko would surely have been adequate to destroy that net and liberate the Shining One for flamethrowing, regardless of the make of that net."

"So," said Lord Onosh, "if the demons have truly suborned Shabble to their service, if only temporarily, then they may send the bubble against us to coerce us to their service."

"That is a strong probability," said Sken-Pitilkin.

"Then," said Lord Onosh, "we must seek to apply the same remedy that we applied before. We must send the star-globe away from here so that the Circle of the Doors remains closed. Once deprived of all possibility of playing with these toys, Shabble may well seek amusement elsewhere."

"Shabble may well," said Sken-Pitilkin.

"But," said Guest, dismayed at the prospect of further exile, further wandering, further hazard and suffering, "this will take years!"

"What alternative is there?" said Lord Onosh. "I am no wizard, and I have not wandered the world as widely as you have, but I think I know enough of Italis and such similar demons to know that they cannot in any way be trusted."

With Guest coming to reluctant agreement, preparations were made for the Weaponmaster to depart once more with his tutelary wizard. Thayer Levant agreed — with some considerable reluctance — to accompany the Weaponmaster once again. The yellow bottle was heavily provisioned. The demon Italis was placed under interdict once more, with the doors to the Hall of Time being sealed and guarded. Sken-Pitilkin took charge of the star-globe.

All these arrangements took no more than the length of a day. And, on an evening of fog and low cloud, Guest and Sken-Pitilkin took to the skies, accompanied by a somewhat surly Levant.

They had flown no great distance from Alozay when the darkening mists behind them were torn apart by rupturing fire. Either a dragon was assailing Alozay, or else the mainrock Pinnacle was coming under attack from a very, very angry Shabble.

"We got away only just in time," said Guest, soberly.

"We are not away yet." said Sken-Pitilkin, "for we have yet to reach a place of refuge."

And, with that, the wizard of Skatzabratzumon guided his stickbird through the night, wondering just how much damage Shabble might have done on Alozay, and just how much more damage Shabble might do in the future, and what manner of place might give the refugees some kind of reliable sanctuary.

CHAPTER FIFTY

Penvash: peninsular in the north-west of Argan. To the south, at the base of this peninsular, is Estar. To the north, across the waters of the Pale, is the rockthrust of Lex Chalis. To the west is Sken-Pitilkin's home island of Drum.

In Penvash are the ruins of the Old City, which house dangerous arcana which have killed many an unwary treasure seeker. The construction of the Old City is a feat variously attributed to an extinct race of intelligent dragons, to a breed of men possessed by malign demons, or to an entirely hypothetical breed of land-dwelling octopuses. In fact, the Old City was a creation of the Technic Renaissance, and so is the work of ordinary humans.

The Old City is superficially similar to the mazeways Downstairs beneath Untunchilamon's ruling city of Injiltaprajura. But there are profound differences. Much Downstairs — lights and ice-makers in particular — is reliable in its fulfilment of an obvious and useful purpose. Whereas the Old City is the ruinous habitation of mad destruction, a place unfit for human flesh.

* * *

As on their first retreat from Alozay, Sken-Pitilkin and his companions flew through the night in the roughest of directions, so that by dawn they had lost themselves entirely. As on their first retreat, they settled in the wilderness of Tameran.

"But this time," said Sken-Pitilkin, "we cannot make Lex Chalis our next stop."

"Good!" said Guest, who had the direst of memories of that place of extreme unpleasantness.

"That is an entirely inappropriate reaction," said Sken-Pitilkin sternly. "Lex Chalis is a very interesting place. Possibly, our one and only proof of the existence of the Experimenters of old."

"Which Experimenters were doubtless very fond of irregular verbs," said Guest.

"One would expect so," said Sken-Pitilkin, "for scholarship and greatness typically go hand in hand. However, much as we would all like to return to Lex Chalis, Sod may have betrayed its secrets to Chi'ash-lan, and Chi'ash-lan may have betrayed its secrets to Shabble."

This was a sobering thought.

"Sod knew all the thinking which guided our earlier retreat," said Guest.

"Precisely," said Sken-Pitilkin.

"So Shabble may have been granted a disclosure of that thinking," said Guest, "if only at third or fourth hand."

"Exactly," said Sken-Pitilkin. "So what would you do if you were Shabble? What would you do if you knew it to be our policy to choose directions at random?"

Guest puzzled over the question, but could come up with no answer. It was his servant Thayer Levant who, abandoning the business of scratching the green fungus which grew on his scalp, delivered himself of the answer:

"Shabble will quarter the skies."

"Exactly," said Sken-Pitilkin. "Perhaps in circles, perhaps in spirals, perhaps in a cross-hatched pattern. But that is certainly how Shabble will search for us."

"Then we must fly by night," said Guest promptly.

"But how are we to navigate?" said Sken-Pitilkin. "This business of night flying has perils of which you are not properly aware. We have come so far with good fortune, but if we press our luck too often then we must sooner or later fly into the side of a mountain."

"Or the mouth of a dragon," said Thayer Levant.

"Yes," said Sken-Pitilkin testily, "though I think a mountain the more likely danger. Anyway. Shabble is searching for us, so I think we must do what Shabble does not expect. We must fly to Drum."

"Drum!" said Guest, in startlement.

"Well, yes, yes," said Sken-Pitilkin. "It's perfectly safe. I've lived there a year with not a sniff of any other wizard anywhere. The Confederation thinks me dead, you realize. As far as the Confederation's concerned, we're all dead. You, me, Shabble, our good friend Levant here. We vanished beyond the Veils of Fire, vanished into the Cave of the Warp. Nobody ever comes back from there alive."

"But Shabble will look for us on Drum," said Guest.

"Not if Shabble thinks us choosing destinations at random," said Sken-Pitilkin.

"But Shabble may not think us thus choosing at all!" said Guest. "We're making assumptions! We're assuming that Sod blabbed our strategies in Chi'ash-lan. We're assuming, too, that Shabble heard of those strategies. Then we're making yet another assumption — which is, that Shabble will act on that which Shabble has heard."

All this was uncomfortably logical.

But the logic of Guest Gulkan's argument tended inevitably towards more wandering, more deracinated exile. And, while the Weaponmaster might yet have stomach sufficient for more such adventuring, Sken-Pitilkin did not. He wanted his bed, his armchair, his cats, his kitchen, his established routines and the comforts of his library.

So, in the end, since Sken-Pitilkin was in charge of the stickbird, it was Sken-Pitilkin who prevailed.

So the adventurers flew south till they picked up the coast of Tameran. They crossed the wind-thrashed waters of the Pale, the strait which separates the northern continent of Tameran from the southern continent of Argan, then flew towards Drum, that island which lies off Argan's western coast.

But in the skies above Drum, Guest Gulkan spied a spark of fire.

"Fire?" said Sken-Pitilkin.

"It is fire, yes, fire," said Guest, whose eyes were sharper than those of the wizard of Skatzabratzumon.

Then Sken-Pitilkin realized that his emotional weariness might have overmastered his sagacity; that the spark of fire might be Shabble making a display of wrath above Drum; and that the stickbird could be even now flying towards its doom.

So Sken-Pitilkin abruptly swung his stickbird into a tight turn.

"Where are we going?" said Levant.

"To Penvash!" said Sken-Pitilkin. "I have it in mind to hide out in the Old City, at least for tonight."

"The Old City?" said Levant.

"A set of ruins," said Sken-Pitilkin. "A place of no particular consequence."

"Oh," said Levant.

The knifeman's nondescript response showed that he had heard nothing of Penvash and its terrors, though these — as the reader may well be aware — are known to the rumour of as many as fifty lands.

"Penvash," said Guest, savouring the word. "Why Penvash? Why ruins?"

"There is a Door in these ruins," said Sken-Pitilkin. "If we are to be denied Drum, then I have it in mind to open this Door."

"But why?" said Guest.

"To see where it goes," said Sken-Pitilkin.

And flew onwards.

Quite apart from any other consideration (such as sheer curiosity) Sken-Pitilkin had in mind the possibility that Shabble might have spotted them already, and might shortly pursue them, in which case a Door in the Old City would give them (possibly) the means of escape.

So Sken-Pitilkin dared himself to the Old City in Penvash.

Much the wizard knew of this Old City. Before his exile to Tameran and his embroilment in the affairs of the Yarglat barbarians, the wizard of Skatzabratzumon had dwelt for generations on the island of Drum, and had come to know the surrounding geography in detail.

In particular, he had learnt much of Penvash from the questing heroes of Sung, a mean and provincial place in the Ravlish Lands, not far from Drum. The Melski — a breed of pacific but formidable green-skinned creatures which live in

Penvash — had once defeated the people of Sung in a great war. Ever since then, the Old City of Penvash had possessed a peculiar fascination for the more warlike of Sung's inhabitants. For it was known that the Melski shunned that city, which led the optimistic to presume that something potent against the Melski could conceivably be recovered from that city.

Consequently, down through the generations, a great many questing heroes of Sung had ventured to Penvash, with all of them having the Old City as their goal; and, though few had returned to tell of their venturing, most of the survivors had at one time or another discussed their experiences with Sken-Pitilkin. In the course of his debriefings, Sken-Pitilkin had made great heaps of maps, charts and diagrams, and so had recorded the existence of a Door in the Old City long before he ever knew what a Door might be good for.

Being in possession of a star-globe capable of opening such a Door, Sken-Pitilkin therefore headed for the Old City, a heap of ruins in the Penvash Peninsular, well north of Lake Armansis.

In Sken-Pitilkin's stickbird the heroes hustled across the horizons, making for the continent of Argan, for the Penvash Peninsular, and for the dangers of the Old City.

They had actually caught sight of the ruins of the Old City when Guest spied a flash of fire in the sky in front of them. He cried out in alarm.

"What is it?" said Sken-Pitilkin.

"Shabble!" said Guest.

"Where?" said Sken-Pitilkin, looking back. "Where?"

"Not behind us!" said Guest. "In front of us! Look!"

"He's right!" said Levant. "It's either Shabble — or a dragon!"

Sken-Pitilkin looked, and, on squinting, did indeed see something which might well be Shabble, spitting out volleys of fire in non-stop spasms of incontinent anger.

For once, Sken-Pitilkin was hard put to believe the evidence of his own eyes. For Drum was by now more than an eyeshot distant. They had flown over the ocean, had crossed the coast, and were now almost ready to spit upon the Old City. How then could Shabble be in front of them?

The wizard of Skatzabratzumon deduced that Shabble must have been flying in a great circle of scrutiny designed to accommodate the visual inspection of the vastest possible area of land, sea and sky. He marvelled at Shabble's speed, and realized that he had previously underestimated the bubble's capacities.

"Don't just stand there gawking!" said Guest. "Put us down! Put us down!"

Realizing that the Weaponmaster had reason, Sken-Pitilkin sent his stickbird into a downward spiral.

"It's stopped," said Levant, clutching tight to the rail of the stickbird.

"What's stopped?" said Sken-Pitilkin.

"The flame-spitting," said Levant. "Shabble's stopped flame-spitting, I can't see the thing. So that means—"

"Ten to one it means that Shabble's seen us!" said Guest.

At that, Sken-Pitilkin began to make his final approach, for he had spied the Door of the Old City. It was set in a muddy clearing, in which Sken-Pitilkin shortly made his landing in a shower of filth and spray.

On landing, the stickbird spun thrice in a sickening fashion, exhausting the last of its momentum in a flurry of flying mud. Then it ceased to spin. It rocked twice or thrice, then was still. They had landed.

"Out! Out!" said Sken-Pitilkin.

Guest jumped to the mud. Thayer Levant snatched the star-globe from Sken-Pitilkin and followed.

"Hey!" said Sken-Pitilkin. "The globe!"

"Tell Shabble you lost it," said Levant, holding the thing close. "Try for the sky. Try fly the horizon, we'll hide in the trees. When Shabble catches you, then bluff like crazy."

"It's a plan," said Guest. "It's not much, but something."

Guest was right.

It was not much of a plan.

But Sken-Pitilkin could think of nothing better.

Sken-Pitilkin took to the skies in his stickbird, while Guest and Levant ran for the nearest trees. They sprinted through the mud towards the shelter of the foliage — but before they reached it, that foliage erupted into fire.

"Halt!" yelled a voice from the sky. "Halt right where you are! Or you'll be incinerated!"

Guest and Levant looked up.

There was Shabble, hovering high above them.

"I will not be captured," said Guest. "Not by that thing. I have it in mind to run."

"Where?" said Levant.

"The Door!" said Guest, snatching the star-globe from Levant. "Where it goes I don't know, but I'll chance it."

Then Guest sprinted for the plinth on which stood the Door of the Old City. He slammed the star-globe into the niche in the marble base of that plinth. A screen of living silver hummed to life, filling the metal arch which rose from that plinth. Guest leapt on to the marble plinth, and positively rolled through the silver screen, disappearing from sight.

"How dare you!" roared Shabble, furious to see his quarry escaping.

And Shabble swooped down from the skies, and flashed through that silver screen, following Guest Gulkan.

Upon which, Thayer Levant did a quick calculation. Sken-Pitilkin had fled to the skies, and Shabble had pursued Guest Gulkan through the Door. So if Levant were to close that Door, why then, he would be in undisputed possession of the star-globe.

So thinking, Levant ran to the marble plinth, snatched the star-globe from its base, and thus closed the Door. At which a voice challenged him from the sky.

"Hoy! Shabble!"

Thayer Levant looked upwards, and saw Sken-Pitilkin's stickbird go scudding overhead at speed. Sken-Pitilkin, realizing that Shabble had not chosen to chase him, had returned, and was trying to tempt the bubble into pursuit.

Of course, Shabble was in no position to pursue, for the bubble had vanished through the Door to some place

Elsewhere, some place doubtless far over the horizon. But if Sken-Pitilkin was not going to flee, then soon he would land. So, if Levant wanted to keep the star-globe for himself, he would have to persuade the sagacious wizard of Skatzabratzumon that it had been lost.

What then went through Levant's head?

Did this disgruntled servant think he could persuade Sken-Pitilkin that the star-globe had been carried off by a large magpie, say, or eaten by a hungry porcupine?

We cannot tell.

But what is certain is that Levant swiftly buried the star-globe at the base of the marble plinth, and, having concealed this buried treasure, he hastened himself towards the treeline, doubtless working to contrive an excuse to explain the loss of the precious globe.

Meantime, Sken-Pitilkin swooped back and forth across the clearing, endeavouring to tempt Shabble to pursuit. On his second swoop, Sken-Pitilkin saw Levant running for the treeline. And on his third swoop, Sken-Pitilkin saw Levant thrashing in the jaws of a gigantic scorpion.

In long interrogation of some of the questing heroes from Sung who had ventured to the Old City of Penvash, Sken-Pitilkin had heard many stories of the monsters which haunted those ruins. He had heard, for example, of just such a giant scorpion. Even so, it was a shock for him to see Levant twisting in his death-agonies in the jaws of such a monster.

Sken-Pitilkin did not hesitate.

The wizard of Skatzabratzumon, who was as courageous as he was sagacious, threw his stickbird into a tight spiral, and brought it down in the clearing of the Door. The scorpion promptly dropped Levant, who fell writhing to the ground. The monster then advanced on Sken-Pitilkin.

Sken-Pitilkin raised his country crook and cried out a Word. A flare of levitational energy caught the scorpion, which was blasted backwards, and sent tumbling into a tree. It smashed into the tree trunk, then flopped to the ground. An ooze of yellow slime issued from its twitching body.

Warily, Sken-Pitilkin advanced, seeking to succour the fallen Thayer Levant.

But, by the time the wizard reached Levant, the man was dead. His body had been hideously crushed. His shattered ribs had pierced outward through his skin, and the froth of unbreathing blood on Levant's lips told Sken-Pitilkin that the man's lungs had been pierced by those same cruel-edged bones.

Dead, dead, finished, doomed, beyond all chance of cure, beyond all chance of resurrection.

In the aftermath of the crisis, Sken-Pitilkin started to shudder. He felt weak. He felt his age. As he stood there in the clearing, rain began to fall, pattering on the leaves of the trees, splattering on the mud of the clearing. Amidst that rain, something large and yellow began to ooze out of the forest, and Sken-Pitilkin realized it was a slug. A huge slug. A slug as big as an ox. Behind it was another slug. And another. A veritable armada of the things was cruising through the trees.

Sken-Pitilkin remembered stories told by some of the questing heroes who had ventured from Sung to Penvash. Those yellow slugs ate men.

But — before Sken-Pitilkin quit the clearing — where was the star-globe?

"You had it last," said Sken-Pitilkin, addressing Levant's corpse.

Then Sken-Pitilkin hastily searched the corpse, for such was the importance of the treasure. But Levant did not have it, and the slugs were swift closing in on Sken-Pitilkin and his stickbird. Sken-Pitilkin used his Power to test the weight of one of the slugs. It was as heavy as it was huge. In a battle with such monsters, he must necessarily exhaust himself, and be swiftly overcome by their numbers.

Realizing this, Sken-Pitilkin hobbled to his stickbird, supporting himself with his country crook. He hauled himself into the stickbird and took to the skies, leaving behind him the clearing, the marble plinth, the steel archway of the Old City's Door, the slow-cruising yellow slugs, and the untenanted corpse of Thayer Levant.

Where was Guest?

Sken-Pitilkin cruised backwards and forwards across the Old City, hunting for the Weaponmaster. But there was no sign of him. And as there was likewise no sign of Shabble, Sken-Pitilkin deduced that in all probability the pair of them had gone through the Door. And as to where they might be now, he had no idea whatsoever.

CHAPTER FIFTY-ONE

Guest Gulkan: the Yarglat barbarian otherwise known as the Weaponmaster. He duelled his father for possession of the Collosnon Empire — this civil war so weakening that empire that it was conquered by the interloper Khmar. Guest Gulkan then united with his father to fight Khmar — but lost.

Retreating in defeat, father and son sought refuge on the island of Alozay, which they were constrained to conquer. Conquest of Alozay made them masters of one of the Doors of the Circle of the Partnership Banks, embroiling them in an unrelenting struggle for the mastery of that Circle.

The latest entity to enter this struggle is Shabble, the miniature sun which has lately made an alliance with those demons which serve the Great God Jocasta. Shabble itself is a servant of the Holy Cockroach, is determined to conquer the world for that Cockroach, and wishes to use the Circle of the Partnership Banks to expedite this conquest.

* * *

For Guest Gulkan, the flight from Drum to the Old City was terrifying. He was bucked across the sky without the slightest hope of controlling his own destiny, and in hot pursuit was the outraged Shabble.

The Old City came into sight below them. Sken-Pitilkin sent his stickbird hurtling down out of the skies. As they slammed into the earth, Guest Gulkan threw himself out of the stickbird and raced for the Door. He slammed the star-globe into the socket of the marble plinth on which stood the steel arch of the Door. The archway filled with humming mercury.

Guest Gulkan bounded up on to the plinth, drew his sword, then leapt through the Door, with his sword braced to strike down whatever enemy confronted him. He found himself alone in a hot and insect-humming eucalyptus forest. Without tarrying for further inspection, he dared his way through the Door again.

Of course he did not return to the Old City, for the Door was not like one which opens into a bar or a brothel. Rather, it is best construed as a series of one-way valves arranged in a Circle, and by bearing this model in mind one can easily understand the Weaponmaster's progress.

On leaping through that Door a second time, leaving the eucalyptus forest behind him, Guest emerged on to a sunstruck desolation of sand. He mistook it for desert — then blinked at the sundazzling sea, and realized it was beach. Beach? A quick scan proved it to be an island.

Guest Gulkan had time for no more than that one quick scan, for Shabble came bursting through the humming screen of the Door before he could engage in a more elaborate survey of his surroundings.

"Maraka daga dok?" said the seething Shabble.

Guest knew Shabble to be fast-striking, able to outpace a human in any martial endeavour. Yet if he could somehow distract the impetuous bubble of wrath, then perhaps he could plunge back through the Door and make his escape.

As Guest was so thinking, that Door snapped out of existence. The shimmering silver screen in the metal archway vanished, and was replaced with hot and cloud-less sky.

"Daga!" demanded Shabble. "Daga dok!"

"What?" said Guest, afraid for his life and so striving mightily for comprehension.

"I said," said Shabble, reverting to Toxteth, "Where is my toy?"

Guest Gulkan was quite out of the habit of speaking Toxteth, so it took him a disconcerting interval to comprehend even this simplicity. But with comprehension achieved, Guest gladly explained that the star-globe was — most naturally! — back in the Old City of Penvash.

"And you," said Guest, "should be heading for that Old City immediately, for obviously the globe has been taken out of its pocket, and every moment you waste here sees the thing slip further from your grasp."

"I can still spare a moment to burn you alive!" said the wrathful Shabble.

"If I am to be firewood," said Guest, "then burn away."

In answer, Shabble stung the Weaponmaster with a bolt of singing fire. It burnt a smoking hole in his skin. The stench of burnt flesh and singed hairs rose hot to his nostrils. For a moment, Guest gaped at his wound. Then the pain hit hard, driving him into the sea. But all the waters of Moana were not sufficient to quench the pain of that wound. As Guest soaked it, Shabble hummed round his head like a mutant wasp. The buzzing globe of malevolence bobbed and bounced, hitting the water repeatedly, sending stinging spray in all directions.

But Guest paid no heed to Shabble because his pain was so great. Indeed, the Weaponmaster was in such palpable agony that Shabble backed off somewhat. Guest, divining that the bubble might have realized it had gone further than it truly wanted to, began to recover a degree of self-possession. As he began to master his pain, he took advantage of his recovering self-possession to stage deliberate theatricals of ever-intensifying agony.

"Are you hurt?" said Shabble anxiously.

Guest responded with groans, as if the Great Mink itself was in the process of tearing off his toes one by one.

"Are you really really hurt?" said Shabble.

Guest fell to sand and thrashed in an agony which was nine-tenths simulated. All the while he watched Shabble covertly from the corner of his eye.

The response surprised even the Weaponmaster.

For, after a bare ten breaths and a heartbeat, Shabble lost interest in the Weaponmaster's prolonged suffering, and went to investigate the sea, disappearing from sight beneath the waters.

This stunned Guest, who did not quite follow Shabble's reasoning. Shabble saw that Guest appeared to be in grievous pain; and, knowing humans in such condition were no fun at all, Shabble had gone to look at the coral and play with the fishes. Shabble's earlier anxiety had not been feigned. But Guest had been wrong to assume that anxiety to be symptomatic of vast reserves of empathy. Shabble had been designed and built as a toy, and so had the emotional resources appropriate to the nursery rather than those befitting grand opera.

While Guest did not quite realize how and why his tactics had failed, he did see that his operatic performance was getting him nowhere. So he gave up his groaning and sat on the sand clutching his arm — which still hurt like hell.

Then Guest waited.

He waited for Shabble to emerge from the waters.

But Shabble did not emerge.

Guest was profoundly puzzled by this, for Shabble's behaviour was contrary to human experience. A human, on arriving abruptly on a coral island in the company of a grievously wounded companion, does not proceed immediately to extended underwater tourism. But, again, Shabble's performance would not have been out of place in the nursery, for Shabble had been made as a toy for children, not as a replacement for a parent.

In the absence of any mature adult concern from Shabble — who surfaced briefly once or twice, but immediately splashed down under the water again — Guest at last got to his feet and sauntered over to the Door. In the white coral sand — sand whiter than eggshell, whiter than bone — he saw only one single set of footprints. They were his own.

Guest confronted the Door.

"Open!" said Guest, in his most commanding voice.

But the Door remained firmly closed.

With some difficulty — his arm was grievously sore, and hampered his movements — Guest climbed on to the plinth and examined the Door in detail. He was careful not to let any part of his person intersect the plane of the arch, since he had no wish to lose head or hand to a sudden reopening of the Door.

On a whim, Guest took the heavy mazadath from around his neck, and displayed it to the Door, and tried to command it again:

"Open!"

But, as he had expected, nothing happened. He slung the mazadath round his neck once again, feeling its heavy silver glissade across his sweat-slick skin. The use of the thing, it seemed, was to preserve his life in the realms of the World Beyond which lay beyond the Veils of Fire in the Cave of the Warp in the Shackle Mountains; and Guest, not for the first time, was intensely irritated that a thing which he had carried so far and for so many years should be possessed of such a specialized use — and was totally useless in his present circumstances.

The lancing sunlight blinked sharps of light from the scattering of sand on the marble of the plinth. On impulse, Guest Gulkan touched his lips to the outer metal of the arch, finding it strangely cool. He licked it. Tasted salt. The arch had been salted by the tropical sea.

As far as Guest could tell, the arch and the island alike showed no sign of prior use.

Or did it?

Towards one end of the island, a bare stone's throw distant, was the turtle-hump of a rowing boat, which Guest had not noticed at all in the first startlement of his shocked arrival and Shabble's subsequent attack.

Now, Guest jumped down to the sand and strode towards the rowing boat. He was conscious of the heat, which brought back memories of Untunchilamon and Injiltaprajura. But Injiltaprajura had been lush with sprinting water, alive with monkeys and tropical birds, aswarm with cockroaches and mosquitoes. This island, by comparison, was tiny. Bare as a picked bone.

Guest reached the overturned rowing boat. A few streaks of blistered ochre paint had yet to be elementally stripped from the weathered grey of its planking. Guest lifted it, flipped it over, and revealed bare bones and a broken oar. Guest estimated the bones. Skull, vertebrae, ribs, pelvis, thigh bone and shank bone, carpals and teeth. A man had died here, and Guest was uncomfortably reminded of the possibility that he might die likewise.

Guest stood in the sunblind quiet, taking stock. The shit-brown mud of the Old City was still smeared on his shins, though it was wet no longer, for it had dried and hardened swiftly in the heat. Guest stood stork-like on one leg, brushed at the mud, and peeled away a leaf. It was a mottled brown and yellow, its substance frayed, its skeleton showing through its flesh.

"Grief of a bitch," muttered Guest.

Then kicked away the bones, used the broken oar to prop up the rowing boat — there was nothing else by way of shade on the island — and took shelter. He still had the yellow bottle, and still had the ring which commanded it, so it would have been the easiest thing in the world to take refuge within. But Guest was waiting for Shabble.

After an unconscionable delay, Shabble grew bored with exploring the island's coral reef, and came to see how the Weaponmaster was faring.

"How are you?" said Shabble.

"What would you care?" said Guest.

It was not at all what he had planned to say, but the words came out anyway. His burnt arm felt as if a continuous branding operation was in progress, and Guest was hard-put to ignore the pain. It brought back uncomfortable memories which he had done his best to suppress rigorously — starting with the spiking of his foot in the Battle of Babaroth and working through to some of the more life-threatening of the beatings he had suffered at the hands of the soldiers of the Mutilator.

"I'm your friend," said Shabble. "Of course I care."

"My friend!" said Guest.

"Why, of course," said Shabble. "I came to Alozay in friendship, didn't I?"

"You could have fooled me!" said Guest, thinking the bubble quite mad in its delinquency.

But, as Shabble's story began to emerge in full detail, Guest slowly started to understand.

Shabble and Guest had first met on Untunchilamon, during the Weaponmaster's wild adventures on that island. Guest's days on Untunchilamon had been so confused, so hectic, so full of turmoil, that he these days found it hard to connect their scattered fragments in any coherent fashion. To the Weaponmaster, Shabble had been just one more of the many spectacles of that island, something to rank alongside the Crab, the wealth fountains, the analytical engine, the therapist Schoptomov, the bullman Log Jaris, the flying claws, the demon Binchinminfin, and the pink-eyed albino who had been such a mighty sorcerer.

Yet Shabble, it seemed, still remembered in detail every moment of that long-ago encounter, and thought that the deeds in which they had been involved (they had, for example, raided the Pink Palace of Injiltaprajura together, seeking to put an end to the transitory rule of the demon Binchinminfin) made them comrades in arms.

Later, Guest and Shabble had been incarcerated in the yellow bottle during their transit from Drum to Drangsturm. On that journey, Guest had spent a great many days in exhaustive conversation with Shabble. Guest had simply been passing the time, but Shabble had been doing something entirely different. Shabble, it transpired, had been nourishing the development of a beautiful friendship.

As Shabble's tale unfolded, Guest began to understand how the jade-green monsters of the Circle of the Partnership Banks had been able to suborn Shabble to their will. They had not discovered a new method of torturing or coercing Shabble. No. They had got to the bubble through its weakest point — its need for friends and friendship.

In Chi'ash-lan, the jade-green monster which named itself the demon Ko had indoctrinated Shabble. The demon Ko had told the bubble of bounce that the star-globe had been restored to the island of Alozay (which was true), that Guest and Sken-Pitilkin planned to seek the control of the Circle (which was also true), and that they were eagerly waiting for Shabble to assist them by bringing the Cult of Cockroach to the populations of the lands of the Doors.

The demon Ko and its colleagues had obviously

miscalculated. They must have thought that Shabble would arrive on Alozay, hot with enthusiasm for missionary work, and that the combination of Shabble's eagerness and flamethrowing abilities would leave Guest and Sken-Pitilkin with no choice but to co-operate.

But of course, by the time Shabble reached Alozay, Guest and Sken-Pitilkin had fled with the star-globe. This had been the bitterest of all possible disappointments for Shabble. The bubble had precious little use for power, or gold, or women, or opium, or any of the other things men commonly fight for. But Shabble wanted friendship. Needed it. Valued it above all else. And Shabble, having been told that friends awaited on Alozay, was furious to realize it had been victimized by lies.

"You realized the demons had been lying to you?" said Guest.

"Of course," said Shabble.

"So what did you do?"

"I blasted the demon!" said Shabble, positively squeaking with excitement. "I blasted that thing Italis! I blasted it!"

"Really?" said Guest.

"Really and truly," said Shabble.

"So it's dead."

"Well," said Shabble, guardedly. "Not exactly."

"What do you mean, not exactly? What happened? What happened when you blasted it?"

"Well," said Shabble, "what happened was that it laughed."

"It laughed?"

"Yes," said Shabble, sounding mightily crestfallen. "It laughed at me. It told me to go bounce."

"So what did you do then?"

"I blasted it again. But it didn't make much difference."

"So then you chased me," said Guest. "That wasn't very fair, was it? To get angry with the demon then go chasing after me on that account?"

Shabble tried to avoid the question, but Guest pressed the bubble hard, and in the end it had to concede that it had been naughty.

"Naughty!" said Guest. "You were rather more than naughty! I'm stuck here on this hellhole of an island, and there's no way off that I can see!"

"You've got the Door," said Shabble.

"But it's closed!" said Guest.

"Well," said Shabble, "there's, uh, there's this boat."

"This rowing boat?" said Guest, "are you mad? It's got cracks in it which I could just about crawl through."

"Well, someone came here in it," said Shabble.

"From a sinking ship, maybe," said Guest. "Or maybe they were marooned. But judging by the evidence, they didn't get much further!"

With that, Guest indicated the bones which he had found beneath the rowing boat.

"Well, I don't see what you're so worried about," said Shabble. "You've got the bottle, you've got the ring, there's food, there's water, they told me that on Alozay."

"Who told you?" said Guest.

"The one with big ears," said Shabble. "Your father."

"Neither of us has big ears," said Guest. "We have normal ears. Everyone else has an undersized issue."

"If you say so," said Shabble. "But you've still got food, you've still got water, what else do you need?"

"All kinds of things!" said Guest. "Women, to start with."

"Oh," said Shabble, crestfallen.

Shabble knew that men liked women, and had a theoretical knowledge of the reasons why, but Shabble remained unconvinced of the validity of the theories. Shabble had once maintained a small harem, but many nights of sleeping with women and exploring their intimacies had convinced the bubble that the whole experience was grotesquely overrated. Shabble much preferred sleeping amidst the flames of a fire (for fire was pretty, and gave Shabble melodious dreams), or sleeping with a balloon (for Shabble thought balloons were happy creatures), or sleeping alongside a billiard ball (which gave Shabble the comforting illusion of having the company of one of its own kind).

"You wouldn't understand," said Guest moodily.

"Oh, I understand," said Shabble. "You miss your Yerzerdayla."

"Yerzerdayla?" said Guest.

"The woman," said Shabble. "You know! She was locked in a pod, you were all set to rescue her!"

"Oh," said Guest. "Yes, yes, so I was."

But the truth was that the Weaponmaster had long ago forsaken Yerzerdayla. She was a figure from his adolescence, and in these the years of his maturity he had almost forgotten her. The woman Penelope meant much more to him, for it was Penelope who had comforted him during the four years of his convalescence in Dalar ken Halvar — but even Penelope, it seemed, was lost to him.

As for Yerzerdayla — why, on his latest sojourn on Alozay, Guest had been so busy getting drunk and eating horse meat, or planning strategy and dealing with demons, that he had never thought of the woman for so much as a moment. Long ago, he had conceived the notion of rescuing her from the pod in the Hall of Time in which he had seen her last, but all such thoughts had long since passed from his head.

Still, Guest thought it unwise to confess as much to Shabble, for he feared the bubble might be a romantic. If so, then it would think less of Guest for his forgetfulness. So Guest put his head in his hands and moaned, in what he hoped was a convincing manner:

"Oh! Oh! My poor Yerzerdayla!"

Then much more of the same followed, until Shabble gallantly declared that it would fly back to the Old City in the Penvash Peninsular and find the star-globe (wherever that might have got to) and reopen the Door so Guest could continue round this particular Circle.

"Or," said Shabble, "I could find Sken-Pitilkin and get him to fly here."

"But that's impossible," said Guest. "For a start, you don't know where we are to start with, and even if you did, you'd never be able to get here again."

"I know exactly where we are," said Shabble.

"How?" said Guest, wondering if Shabble perhaps had some anciently derived knowledge of the previously unexplored Circle into which Guest had so precipitately ventured.

"From the sun," said Shabble simply.

Then the bubble declared that they were some hundreds of leagues north-west of Untunchilamon; that it had calculated their position to a nicety: that its agility at celestial navigation would permit it a swift passage back to Penvash; and that it would have no trouble whatsoever in guiding Sken-Pitilkin back to Guest Gulkan's island.

Guest then expected the bubble of bounce to go whistling up into the heavens, hastening with all possible force to the Old City. But Shabble did not. Shabble wanted to chat, to talk, to play some more in the water, to invent names for the fishes, to speculate on the size of the clouds. And Guest, realizing that he was dependent upon Shabble for his rescue, had no alternative but to play along with these games.

At last, after a full two days of play — an excessive indulgence, doubtless, but Shabble had been held prisoner by the demon Ko for upwards of a year, and so was in a mood to enjoy its liberty to the full — Shabble gave Guest a parting present. The parting present was a full-length massage of the Weaponmaster's back, and Guest had to admit that Shabble did it very well.

Then the bubble set forth.

It did not soar upwards, but, rather, went bouncing across the sea, skip by skip. On seeing Shabble adopt this slow and self-indulgent mode of transport, Guest groaned. He had a vision of the bubble slow-hop-skipping all the way across Moana, a process which would surely take days.

"Grief of gods!" said Guest.

Then made a moody promenade around his minuscule island, then withdrew — not for the first time — to the yellow bottle. With Shabble gone, Guest began to make a methodical assessment of his assets. He had food, including more siege dust than he could have eaten in a thousand years, and he had water.

And, towards the end of his search, Guest realized he also had a book.

The book was a book of verbs.

To be precise, the book was Strogloth's Compendium of Delights, that hateful manual of irregularities which had vexed, perplexed and persecuted Guest's boyhood. Guest glared at the thing, then laid rough hands upon it, determined to rend it and tear it, to rough it and burn it.

Then he stopped himself.

He was all alone, marooned without women or companions, deserted by even Shabble. In this exile, nothing remained to him but the exercise of his sword and this one, single, solitary book.

"But," said Guest, "Why did it have to be this book?"

Why not a pillow book, or a potentially useful Book of Maps, or a great Book of Battles, or (he had raw materials in plenty) a great Book of Cookery?

"I blame Sken-Pitilkin," muttered Guest.

For who else did he know who was in love with the verbs? Who else had the motive, the means and the opportunity to smuggle such a reprehensible object into the yellow bottle? But, regardless of who was to blame, the facts were the facts, and Guest was stuck with the facts. He was marooned on a desert island, and the sole companion of his maroonment was the most hateful book in all the world: Strogloth's monomaniacal compendium of the world's irregular verbs.

Oh doom of dooms!

Oh fates worse than death!

Guest Gulkan saw the future, and he shuddered.

CHAPTER FIFTY-TWO

Moana: aka Great Ocean: that mighty body of water which has
to its west the continent of Argan, to the east Yestron, to the
north Tameran, and to the south Parengarenga. The several
notable islands of the Great Ocean include Ashmolea
(homeland of the formidable Ashdans), Asral (home of a
breed of semi-piratical traders) and Untunchilamon.

* * *

Mighty is the Great Ocean of Moana and many are its islands.
Lost on a speck of sand anchored somewhere in the vastness of
that ocean, Guest Gulkan endured his solitude, feeding on black
slime from the cornucopia and living under the rowing boat.

The Door remained steadfastly closed.

And Shabble—

Shabble did not return.

Guest was not exactly surprised by the bubble's
disappearance. He could well imagine Shabble swimming in the
sea with the dolphins and the sharks, or browsing through the
forests of Ashmolea, or flirting with dragons amidst the higher
mountains of Argan.

But what had happened to Sken-Pitilkin? And to Thayer
Levant? Even without Shabble to inform them and summon
them, surely they would have reopened the Door to rescue the
Weaponmaster. Wouldn't they? Or were they too scared of the
unknown dangers of the Door? Or too scared of discovering an
angry Shabble? Or — had something happened to them?

Guest could only guess, and though he guessed a thousand
times he never struck precisely at the truth, for it never occurred
to him that Levant might have had sufficient independent will
to betray his master. Though Levant had kept Guest company
for a good many years of wandering, Guest had never really got
to know the man. He had always thought of Levant as a creature
owned and operated by Plandruk Qinplaqus, and had never

given him that uncompromising trust which is necessary for the fullest friendship.

In the absence of rescue, Guest languished on his island through day after day of sterile frustration, with nothing but Strogloth's Compendium of Delights to comfort him.

Guest's long marooning was doubtless of great benefit to his scholarship, for, with Strogloth as his guide, he at last (and with great resentment, and with many sighs, moans and whimpers) began to explore the highways and byways of foreign linguistic irregularities. He studied in the Geltic, for instance — Geltic being the language of the Rice Empire.

Now Geltic is not one of the world's most complicated languages, and its irregular verbs are distressingly few in number. However, the verb "jop", which means "to be", is worthy of the scholar's attention. The present tense of jop, for example, runs thus:

Po ojop — I am
Skobo hunjasp — thou art
Soth jopskop — he is
Mo sadithjop — she is
Parakama ipjop — mother is
Yem opdop — father is
Zodo nop — we are
Bara jolp — you are
Haji jijop — they (friends or associates) are
Aski jujop — they (strangers or neutral parties) are
Jili jilijop — they (enemies) are
Bo jo — they (slaves, inferiors, animals or things) are

Ah, how sweet it is to contemplate this spectacle! The barbarian has been tamed! His sword has failed him, and so, with the sweet resignation of a milkmaid, he bends himself at last to the Book!

And so the days passed; and the weeks; and the months; and sun piled up on sun, and moon on moon; and Guest began to mutter to himself in the foreign tongues, and found his dreams beset by their verbs, hooked verbs and winged verbs, verbs which crawled and verbs which tunnelled, verbs with antennae and verbs with teeth. He imagined himself becoming a monstrous creature like the demons Ko and Italis, or like the therapist Schoptomov: a thing which sits and waits and broods and conjugates its verbs.

Surely, on release — if release ever came — he would be a master of all the languages of the world. He would be as adroitly fluent in his linguistics as one of the jade-green monsters of the Circle of the Partnership Banks, or those lurking torturing machines which skulked variously in the mazeways Downstairs beneath Injiltaprajura or in the Stench Caves of Logthok Norgos.

So thought Guest.

But — alas! — the Weaponmaster had yet to start upon the complexities of Janjuladoola, or of Slandolin, or of the High Speech of wizards, when the peace of his scholarly studies was rudely interrupted.

Guest was sitting one day beneath his fishing boat, with a fishing line laid out along the beach. He was fishing. No, he was not mad. Though his baited hook lay upon the sand rather than in the water, he was still fishing in earnest. He was not fishing for fish — he had eaten fish sufficient to feed a whale, and had no wish to catch another fin for as long as he lived. Guest Gulkan was fishing for seagulls; and, though you would be right in thinking this a cruel and vicious sport, it was the only way he could get himself any fresh meat.

While Guest was so fishing — idly, for seagulls were few and far between that day — his peace was shattered by a battle-cry scream. Guest was jerked away from a semi-doze dream. He sat up in such a hurry that he cracked his head against his rowing boat. He swore, then rolled out into the sun, crouched on all fours then looked to the Door.

There was a small group of people on and around the marble plinth of the Door. And Guest realized he could hear the hum of the Door in action — a hum which he had not noticed in his earlier drowsiness. The arch of the Door was filled with a screen of liquid silver.

Hastily, Guest concealed the yellow bottle beneath his rags, then strode down the beach towards the strangers. If they had come to hunt him, then they would find him soon enough, since he had no caves or jungles to hide in. And, if they had come to rescue him, why, all he wanted was time sufficient to make a ceremonial burning of Strogloth's Compendium of Delights. Then he would be ready to leave his island.

As Guest closed the distance with the strangers, he was confronted by the largest of them, a whale-built thing larger than any two-footed creature in all Guest Gulkan's experience. It towered above him. Its height was equal to that of the monsters Ko or Italis, and it towered over him all the more because it was standing on the plinth whereas he was standing on the sand. It had bulging cheeks and a skin which had the yellowness of vomit. Its eyes were small: glimmering buttons bright with malign suspicion. It had no ears.

Not wishing to show any fear — and afraid he was, for the monster was armed with a monstrous species of crowbar, fit for the pulping of a hippopotamus — Guest jumped up on to the plinth, an act which made great demands on his courage.

In response, the monster opened its mouth.

Then it spoke, and, to Guest's surprise, its speech proved surprisingly intelligible. It spoke in a roughwork variant of the Galish Trading Tongue, that language which Guest had formerly been accustomed to use in his converse with Thayer Levant.

"Who you be?" said the thing.

Of all the questions it could have asked, this was the most surprising. In his exile on the island, Guest Gulkan had thought himself very much the focus of the world's concerns. He had imagined that his fate, whereabouts and destiny would be vigorously debated in Chi'ash-lan and Molothair, on Drum and in Obooloo. He had imagined demons, Bankers, wizards and warriors studying maps and debating his whereabouts. He had imagined quests, searches and hunts, all focused on him.

To console himself when he had nothing else but the verbs

as his comfort, Guest had studiously inflated his own sense of his own importance, until it had come to seem entirely logical to him that the whole world must surely be aflame with the news of his loss, and must surely be hunting for him.

So, of all possible questions, the one addressed to him by the monster was the most surprising. For what was the thing doing on this desolate island if it was not hunting for the great Guest Gulkan, the famed and fabled Weaponmaster, the hero of the Stench Caves, the Emperor in Exile?

Seeking to buy time so he could puzzle over this conundrum, Guest braced himself for possible action, and said:

"Who asks?"

But before he could be answered, a monster came bursting through the Door — a brute of a thing as grey as one of the Janjuladoola, its neck frilled with a collar of ruffled armour from which great man-tearing spikes projected.

Moments later, the monster was dead, killed by the swift reactions of those it had incontinently assailed. The speed of the battle-blades of his new companions told Guest they were all trained for war. Dangerous men, then. He scanned the dead monster, noting the heavy-duty claws on its feet, and the mud on those feet, and the dead leaves plastered to its underbelly. On the slender evidence of the mud and leaves, he guessed that the thing had come from the Old City in Penvash.

But—

"What is it?" said Guest.

"No member of my family, you can be sure of that," said one of the bloodthirsty ruffians who had helped kill the thing.

Guest summed the man. An Ashdan. Beyond his prime. Bald. Hard death in his weathered blue eyes. A battleworthy confidence in his shoulder-width stance. A warrior's training confirmed by the methodical cleansing of his blooded blade. Guest realized that blood was still dripping from the blade of his own sword, which had taken its share of the grey-skinned monster's lifeforce. He should clean it, but—

Guest wanted time, time to think, time to question, to find out who and what and when and where and why. But the

Ashdan was already ordering his men through the Door. But to where? Where were they going, and why?

"Where does this Door go to?" said Guest.

"You know about Doors, do you?" said the Ashdan.

Guest almost gaped at the question. How could the fellow be so stupid? Of course he knew about Doors! Else how could he have arrived on the island?

Even as he was thus thinking, and parrying the question with a joking reply, Guest remembered the rowing boat. Of course! The Ashdan had seen the rowing boat, and had presumed that Guest had arrived on the island by means of that vehicle! So he didn't know who Guest was! Or how he had got here!

Even as Guest was figuring that out, his companions were bustling through the Door at the scramble.

"What did you say?" said Guest, realizing the Ashdan had said something.

But the Ashdan, having done with dialogue, went plunging through the Door himself.

It was like a battle. Everything was happening too quickly, with not enough time to sit down and figure out what was going on, or why, or who was involved.

As Guest was thinking then, two more men came through the Door. The first hacked at Guest, who almost died then and there. But his sword was in his hand, and a short and vicious battle saw him hack down both of his would-be murderers.

"What the hell is going on?" said Guest.

Then, unable to answer that question on his own account — and realizing that he was now alone again, if corpses be not counted as company — the Weaponmaster plunged through the Door.

To his shocked surprise, Guest found himself by Drangsturm. Drangsturm, of all places! Yes, and the wrong side of Drangsturm at that!

During his time at the Castle of Controlling Power, Guest had studied the fortifications of Drangsturm with a battle-commander's diligence; and, on a march from the Castle of Controlling Power to the Castle of Ultimate Peace, he had taken every opportunity to back up study with scrutiny.

So Guest could place himself with a great degree of exactitude, and was surprised to find his small group of new companions were entirely ignorant as to where they were. He started to explain, and, as he gave his explanations, he realized one of his companions was — why, it was Rolf Thelemite!

Wasn't it?

It was now so many years since Guest and Rolf Thelemite had last seen each other that Guest was not certain of this identification. When Rolf had bodyguarded Guest in the city of Gendormargensis, both had been mere striplings. Since then, the battering of the years had seen them mature, age, thicken and change. Yet—

Guest caught Rolf's eye, and Rolf gave him half a wink.

So it was Rolf!

Then Guest began to conjecture wildly. Maybe Rolf was engaged in a plan to rescue him. Maybe Rolf had been directed to the island by Shabble, or by Sken-Pitilkin, or by Thayer Levant. Maybe there was conspiracy here, and danger. Maybe Rolf was rescuing the Weaponmaster in defiance of his Ashdan master, the bald-headed warrior who seemed to be in charge of the party. Maybe—

But at this point Guest was forced to abort thought in favour of action, for a gigantic green centipede came trundling across the landscape, forcing all to retreat through the Door.

They came out on a mountainside of precipitous ice and driving cold, a mountainside so high and bleak that Guest was more than half-convinced it was a part of Ibsen-Iktus. There they thought themselves safe, but the centipedes attacked them through the Door.

They fought viciously with one of the monsters, by brute strength precipitating it from the plinth of the Door, and sending it hurtling down the mountainside in an avalanche of snow which saw it precipitated over a cliff. Guest realized he was fighting in the company of great warriors, for none shirked combat. But one of their number was dead by the time the silver-shining screen of the Door suddenly snapped out of existence, amputating the head of one of the monsters.

Then Guest asked the obvious question:

"Who was controlling the Door for you?"

"Nobody," said the Ashdan. "We had a star-globe. We left it where we started out."

Guest was all the more perplexed to know who he was dealing with. Who were these people? Adventurers? Bandits? Pirates? Deserters? How come they were so organized for action, yet so disorganized in their management of the Door? If they were bent on exploring the Circle of the Old City of Penvash, then why hadn't they left a party to guard their star-globe? And who were the people whom Guest had fought on his own desert island?

Guest was about to ask about this last point when he checked himself. For a dreadful possibility occurred to him. Two men had assailed him on his desert island, and he had killed both. But maybe those men had been in the service of the Ashdan with whom he was now in dialogue! If so, then what would happen if this whole party went right round the Circle of the Door and discovered the corpses?

Realizing he might have some explaining to do, Guest wondered if he should make his escape. He clutched the yellow bottle under his rags. He could toss it to the snows. Then, as it slid down the mountainside, following the path of the avalanching centipede, he could turn the ring on his finger, which would cause him to get sucked into the bottle.

Should he do it?

Guest flexed his fingers, which were rapidly losing all sensation. If he was going to act, he must act soon, else he would be quite incapable of turning the ring. The shock of transit from tropical heat to iceland mountainside was telling on him, and quickly. All warmth had been stripped from his body already, and he would be a casualty of the cold unless he did something, and quickly.

Meantime, his companions were arguing angrily, arguing in a babble of voices, discussing the possibility of killing and cooking one of their number. Grief of gods! What manner of people was he mixed up with?

No sooner had he asked himself this question than the Door abruptly reopened. One of the adventurers — apparently in danger of being immediately slaughtered and cooked — bolted for safety. Guest expected his companions to go yahooing after him, hot for slaughter. But they hesitated.

Why?

Everyone was going to freeze to death unless they moved quickly!

Then Guest took a better look at his new companions, and realized that all of them were dressed for cold weather. He caught sight of bits of grass sticking out from the lumpy jackets of one or two of that number, and realized that some of them had used vegetative padding to supplement the warmth of their clothing. A good trick, but not one Guest could emulate, not when he had nothing but snow available as padding.

Guest flexed his fingers. Or tried to. His gloveless digits were so stiff he would be hard put to turn the ring.

Decisions, decisions!

He was right out of the habit of making quick decisions, but the weather was giving him a helping hand. The bottle or the Door! Choose! Choose now! Or die!

Guest chose, and led the way through the Door, through to—

"Mother of god!" said Guest, in disbelief.

He was on a battlefield. A battlefield, of all places!

Some of Guest's new companions shared his shock, so he did his best to steady them, speaking as a leader should.

The earth was dusty, and the sky was black with thunder. The air boomed with drums, wailed with screams, roared with fear. But battle had not yet been joined. As Guest's companions mobbed around him, he realized he was standing slap bang between two armies, and that war was about to be joined.

"There is war here," said Guest, wondering if his own self-possession might allow him to displace the bald-headed Ashdan as the leader of this band, "hence there is opportunity."

So he said. But what he did not add was that the opportunity was mostly for death, for maiming, for capture and imprisonment, for suffering and thirst, for fear and for terror, for trauma and regrets.

A warrior rode from the army to the west. He was mounted on a heavyweight black horse, and from his accoutrements Guest summed him as a Yudonic Knight of Wen Endex. One of Guest's new companions said something to the rider. Guest failed to catch the words, but they must have been mightily provocative, for those few words precipitated a fight.

Moments later, the rider was dead, and his horse likewise. One of the killers started drinking the blood of the horse, and another — not to be outdone — started drinking the blood of the man. Guest realized the monster with the oversized crowbar had gone through the Door, with one or two of his fellows. The others — those of them who were not greeding on blood — had fallen to arguing.

Guest took the opportunity to grab Rolf Thelemite by the arm and drag him out of earshot of the others for a private word.

"Rolf," said Guest. "It's Rolf, isn't it?"

"Who else would it be?" said Rolf Thelemite.

"Then — good to see you, man!" said Guest, gripping his erstwhile companion by the shoulder. "Now, tell me, what's going on here?"

"Well," said Rolf Thelemite, "it's a long story."

A long story, and one which Guest was not to be favoured with. For, as Rolf Thelemite geared himself up for the telling of his tale, a savagery of pale-skinned warriors came leaping out of the Door. They were barefooted, had leather breeches, had sheepskin jackets, and were armed with spiked clubs, with spears, and with swords.

In the *mêlée* which followed, Guest was separated from Rolf Thelemite. And, as the fighting ended, Guest realized that the two armies of the battlefield were starting to march towards each other, bent on starting a larger war.

"Rolf!" said Guest.

"Here!" said Rolf Thelemite, who was standing on the plinth of the Door. "I'll see you later!"

And, with that, the Rovac warrior vanished through the shining silver screen of the Door.

Guest hesitated.

He had two choices, both unpalatable. He could pursue Rolf Thelemite and his mob through the Door. Or he could stand here and get himself embroiled in a battle.

Another horseman came riding from the west, bearing down on the Door. And Guest, realizing this horseman might be riding for revenge of his fallen colleague, fled precipitately through the Door. He found himself in a huge darkness. A cave? He caught sight of the moon, and realized it was night. Then someone or something moved in the night, and Guest, fearing attack, plunged back through the Door.

No sooner had Guest plunged — jumping through to searing sunlight — than the silver screen of the Door snapped out of existence.

Guest glanced back to confirm what his ears had told him. The Door was closed! So here was sun, here was sand, he was back on his island, but the blood—

The sand stretched away.

Thirty paces away, a totem pole.

Sand hot in the sun.

Sand scattered with bodies.

Corpses of men and corpse of monster.

And the sand was fringed with a circular arena, the walls of which were of white marble. The arena's steeply-sloped tiers of seating — packed with people, all of them yelling and roaring — reminded Guest of Forum Three, the lecture theatre in Cap Foz Para Lash. Then, with a shock of recognition, he realized where he was. He was standing in the Grand Arena of Dalar ken Halvar (otherwise known as the Great Arena, and, to scholars, as the Kilsh Dilsh Dalsh Tantasand).

He saw the corpses of those death-lizards known as striders, their heads pulped. He saw dead men. And he saw crocodiles. Crocodiles very much alive! By the look of them, they looked hungry! And they were coming in Guest Gulkan's direction!

Guest looked around at the packed arena.

"It's me!" he roared. "Guest Gulkan! Friend of Plandruk Qinplaqus!"

But the Weaponmaster's shout was drowned by the maelstrom of the crowd's rioting enthusiasm. Dalar ken Halvar recognized him not. He was in the arena, alone in the arena, alone with his sword, and the crocodiles were closing in on him. There were dozens of the monsters.

But could they climb the plinth?

Guest glanced around, and saw that the sand had been ramped up at the back of the plinth. He guessed that the ramping had been done especially for the convenience of the crocodiles. The steel arch looked unclimbable. But just thirty paces distant was the totem pole.

Guest gathered his wits and ran for the totem pole. But a man stepped from its base and challenged him with a sword. The man was barefooted, wore leather breeches, wore a sheepskin jacket — and was, Guest realized, one of those who had so lately been engaged in a melee on the battlefield Guest had fled. Moreover, now that he examined it closely, he realized the totem pole was jam-packed with such savages.

Even had the savages been cooperative, there was simply no room for Guest Gulkan on that totem pole. And, to judge from the attitude of the man at the base of the pole, they were in no mood to be cooperative.

Guest backed off.

The crowd went wild.

Here was a great spectacle! One man, alone in the arena against a horde of hungry crocodiles! The totem pole is crowded, so he cannot climb! The gates are closed, so he cannot run! One side of the plinth has been ramped with sand, so it is useless as a fortress! He has nothing between him and monstrous death but the strength of his sword!

The crowd cheered with a passion. Whooped, hollered, yelled, stamped, clapped, applauded!

Ah, drama!

Blood, death, fear, pain, anguish!

But the man in the arena was undaunted.

For the man in the arena was no ordinary mortal. Rather, he was the mighty Guest Gulkan, the Weaponmaster, the Emperor in Exile. If Crabs, Bankers, therapists and Shabbles were not sufficient to encompass his doom, how then could any mere rabble of crocodiles hope to pull him down, however great their numbers?

Guest Gulkan strode grimly across the burning sands of the arena. He raised his sword on high. With a felicity beyond the command of any ordinary mortal, the Weaponmaster took the measure of his target. Then he struck. A mighty blow he struck, for the training of a lifetime went into that single swordstroke.

Down came the Weaponmaster's sword. The very sun itself burnt hot-white in the brightness of its steel. With heroic force the blade descended. Impact! The sword hacked into flesh! The sword struck clean, struck true, and hacked the head away from one of the human corpses with which the burning sands were littered.

Guest seized the head by the hair and lifted it. The head was heavy. The hair started to slip through his fingers, till he clutched it tighter.

With his grip secure, Guest raised the head on high, scattering droplets of blood.

Then he locked eyes with the nearest crocodile, which paused in its waddle and regarded him suspiciously.

"Here, big boy," said Guest.

Then tossed the head to one side. It flew, it fell, it hit, it rolled. It rolled in the direction of the totem pole, leaving a splattering of blood upon the sand.

As the crocodile hesitated, Guest hacked off a hand, and threw it so it fell nearer the totem pole than the head.

At which the savage who was standing on the sands in the shadow of the totem pole waited no longer. He saw what must inevitably happen. There was no room for him upon the totem pole, therefore he must inevitably meet his doom when the Weaponmaster's treacherous tactics betrayed him to the arena's monsters. Choosing to meet his death as a hero, the savage screamed, and charged towards the crocodiles.

Inspired by this example — and perhaps realizing that some adroit flesh-hacking and flesh-throwing could disperse their small-minded enemies so as to make them easy game for organized human onslaught — his comrades came scrambling down from the totem pole to join him in his efforts.

Now it happens that the crocodile is a very expensive beast, for Dalar ken Halvar lies in the heartland of the great continent of Parengarenga, and the crocodile must be brought there at enormous cost from the Crocodile Coast, which lies some 1,500 leagues to the west of the city. There are in Dalar ken Halvar people who devote their entire lives to this business of bringing crocodiles from the sea to the city for the annual gladiatorial games. Consequently—

As Guest and his *de facto* allies started scattering the crocodiles by the simple process of throwing lumps of dead meat in all directions, those in charge of the arena started doing their calculations.

The crocodile is a beast of very little brain, and knows not the virtue of alliance. So, compelled by simple hunger, the brutes were already scattering to glut themselves on the chunks of ragged meat which Guest and his savages were so freely delivering. It was inevitable that Guest and his well-armed little army would soon start the slaughter of the beasts.

This would have been a disaster for Dalar ken Halvar's entertainment industry, since the Arena's schedule called for those very crocodiles to eat a great many unarmed slaves, heretics, common criminals and juvenile delinquents in the days which yet lay ahead.

So, fearful of their investment and the despoilment of their timetable, those who commanded the Grand Arena threw open the gates which led to the burning sands, and crocodile-handlers poured out in force to defend the poor animals against the merciless Weaponmaster and those with whom he had leagued himself.

Even as the crocodile-handlers started pouring out on to the sands, the silver screen of the Door hummed into life again. The savages cried out in excitement. Abandoning their corpse-hacking efforts, the savages fled for the Door, and vanished through it. But Guest stood his ground, for he thought himself as safe in Dalar ken Halvar as anywhere.

Or was he?

As Guest was rethinking it, the Door snapped out of existence once again — and he realized the decision had been made for him.

CHAPTER FIFTY-THREE

The Penvash Circle: the Circle accessed by the Door in the Old
    City of Penvash runs thus:
    —the Old City of Penvash
    —an unmapped forest of eucalyptus
    —an ocean cay at anchor in Moana
    —the fringes of Defelfankarzosh
    —an unmapped mountainside
    —the Plain of Tazala
    —a jungle a night away from the Old City's Penvash day
    —the Grand Arena of Dalar ken Halvar
    —a cold cannibal beach
    —and back again to the Old City of Penvash

* * *

So the bewilderments of rescue brought Guest Gulkan to the
city of Dalar ken Halvar. In later conference with Plandruk
Qinplaqus, the Silver Emperor who was master of Dalar ken
Halvar and lord of the Empire of Greater Parengarenga, Guest
eventually decided that Thayer Levant must have escaped from
the Old City with both the star-globe and the secret of the
Doors.

"That," said Guest, "would explain why I was found by a
gang of bandits. For Levant must have sold them the star-globe
and the secret of the Doors."

Being thus satisfied that he had fully and properly explicated
the manner of his rescue, Guest debated long and diligently with
Plandruk Qinplaqus, endeavouring to decide what he should do
next.

The Weaponmaster still wished to make himself master of
the Circle of the Partnership Banks.

"But," said he, "the last time I tried to make alliance with the
demons of the Banks, they betrayed me."

"Of course," said Qinplaqus. "For they had Shabble. But it seems Shabble has lost itself, so now they have the bubble not. If you can win the star-globe and make your return to Alozay, then you may find Italis and its kind more amenable to your discipline."

If.

Could Guest find the star-globe? Could he return to Alozay? Could he find a way to break Italis to his will?

He could only try, for, as he saw it, he had precious little by the way of alternative.

So Guest Gulkan sat with Plandruk Qinplaqus, endeavouring to chart out his destiny, and, by application of cunning and intelligence, to find a steady course into the future — a course which he would be able to hold regardless of the buffets of fortune.

In order to minimize his liabilities as he ventured to Argan to pursue the star-globe, Guest Gulkan decided to leave the yellow bottle in Dalar ken Halvar. It had saved his life during his maroonment on a desert island; but, during his brief travels with Rolf Thelemite and his fellow bandits, Guest had realized the bottle to be as much of a danger as it was an asset. It was such a prize that it could not be openly held by anyone less than an emperor.

So Guest divested himself of the bottle and the ring which commanded it. Plandruk Qinplaqus declared that the bottle would, in future, be used for the transportation of crocodiles from the coast to the city. This would allow great economies, and give a valuable boost to the city's entertainment industry. The Silver Emperor even drew up a formal contract under which Guest leased the bottle to Dalar ken Halvar for that purpose.

"So," said Qinplaqus, "you now have a source of earnings here, which will guarantee your financial security during the years of your retirement if you meet with failure in your quest."

This was all very reasonable, but it dismayed Guest thoroughly. Retirement! Was he to think of retirement? He was in his maturity, was at his peak, was ready for the rule of the

Circle, the rule of the world! How then could he think of retiring to Dalar ken Halvar? To live by the Yamoda River; to swim in the waters of Lake Shalasheen; to eat polyps and soy beans; to live in a bamboo hut ... no, it was scarcely a vision of paradise.

Having divested himself of the yellow bottle and its controlling ring, Guest then decided to leave his mazadath in Dalar ken Halvar. He knew what it was for, and knew it was no good to him.

This left Plandruk Qinplaqus holding the profits of the struggles of Guest Gulkan's life. The Silver Emperor had become the guardian of the yellow bottle and its controlling ring; the mazadath; and the cornucopia, which steadfastly refused to generate anything whatsoever except black slime. The Silver Emperor was ruler too of the x-x-zix, the fabled wishstone of Untunchilamon, which still refused to control the Hot Mouth. Despite all the efforts of a team of mad scientists supervised by Asodo Hatch, this weather machine remained beyond human control, and it was supposed that it might take two or three generations to discipline the thing.

Guest thought of these treasures as tokens of defeat. Rightly or wrongly, he had derived one great lesson from their possession: he was not adequate to the difficulties of contending against demons and gods. The great error of his life had been when he had first trusted the demon Italis.

Icaria Scaria Iva-Italis, demon of Safrak and Guardian Prime, had promised Guest that he would be granted the powers of a wizard if he would only liberate the Great God Jocasta from imprisonment in Obooloo's Temple of Blood. But the demon had been lying. The Great God Jocasta had been lying. At great personal cost, Guest had succeeded in liberating Jocasta from the Temple of Blood — and Jocasta had immediately possessed him, and had tried to make him kill his father.

Thanks to the intervention of Anaconda Stogirov, Guest lived free of possession, his father yet survived, and a badly damaged Jocasta was hiding out in the nethermost depths of Cap Foz Para Lash. In preparation for his onward journey, Guest visited Cap Foz Para Lash himself, and paid his respects to Paraban Senk, the disembodied entity which commanded that troglodytic realm.

Inside Cap Foz Para Lash, Paraban Senk organized running repairs on the Weaponmaster's teeth. His teeth were treated in the same room of miracles which had secured the regrowth of his arms and legs after his long-ago mauling by the Great Mink of Chi'ash-lan. That same room of miracles cured the Weaponmaster of threadworm, roundworm and ringworm, treated him for dandruff then sampled his blood.

After his blood had been sampled, Guest Gulkan was told he had been infected by yaws, a tropical disease transmitted by the contact of skin with skin. If left untreated, it would — or so he was told — deform his bones and damage his joints. But treatment was offered to him in the form of a dose of chemicals, and this he took.

He was also told—

But enough is enough!

It would be wrong to intrude upon the Weaponmaster's privacy by itemizing the various diseases with which he had infected himself in the course of his travels. Let us remark only that, while many questing heroes have died by the sword, and an equal number have fallen to dragons, a far greater proportion of such creatures have been ultimately struck down by syphilis, or by other diseases similarly acquired and yet more fearsome in their operation.

With this visit to Cap Foz Para Lash having come to its conclusion, Guest was ready to leave. Or, not exactly ready — for he was daunted by the difficulty of the task which yet awaited him. But there was nothing more to be secured by lingering further in Dalar ken Halvar.

Plandruk Qinplaqus organized Guest's transport as far as the realms of Drangsturm. A military convoy escorted him from Dalar ken Halvar to the seaport city of Estro Sex. From there, an imperial ship took him to the Ebrell Islands, then through the Stepping Stone Islands to the Inner Waters, landing him in due course at the Castle of Ultimate Peace, the stronghold which guarded the eastern flank of Drangsturm.

Guest landed with some trepidation.

For, as far as the Confederation of Wizards was aware, Guest Gulkan had died in the Cave of the Warp in the Shackle Mountains, when he had ventured beyond the Veils of Fire. There was a danger, then, that he would be recognized; that recognition would lead to arrest; that arrest would lead to torture; and that, having been rigorously tortured for his secrets, he would be handed over to a cabal of wizardly ethnologists for lethal dissection.

Yet, as Guest knew well from his earlier sojourn in the realms of Drangsturm, the management of trade along the Drangsturm Road (the road between the Castle of Ultimate Peace and the Castle of Controlling Power) was routinely controlled by the soldiers of the Landguard. Since Guest was presumed to be dead, no member of that garrison force would be on the lookout for him, so he thought the danger of his capture was minimal.

In practice, Guest proved right in this. He was able to travel the Drangsturm Road unmolested, thus reaching the Salt Road which ran up Argan's western seaboard.

Guest headed towards Narba, feeling rather more hopeful now he had negotiated the dangers of Drangsturm. But, en route to Narba, he began to hear the most troubling news from the north. There were wild rumours of war; of dragons; of a Power which turned the living to stone; of battles of wizards; of the overthrow of cities; of a wholesale piracy which looted entire provinces; of plague; of mad dogs; of living rainbows; of werewolves; of outbreaks of contagious vampirism; of blasphemy; of revolution; of treason; of treachery; of floods; of orcs and ogres; and (ah! fearsome threat!) of rates of inflation running at a thousand percentage points per day.

Giving support to the probability of threat was the fact that the roads were clogged with refugees; and, on reaching Narba, Guest found that many of the people there were sailors and merchants customarily based in Androlmarphos, people who had been away from that city when it was struck by war, and were unable to return there because the city had fallen to an alliance of pirates.

From what Guest could make out, it seemed that the city of Androlmarphos had been invaded by pirates from the Greater Teeth. The Harvest Plains, the nation which owned the seaport of Androlmarphos, was arming for war — seeking to displace the pirates from their seaport. In the Rice Empire, the armies were likewise arming for war, and — if rumour was to be believed — Lord Regan of the Rice Empire hoped to profit from disturbance in the Harvest Plains by launching an invasion of those Plains.

This gave Guest a problem.

How was he to go north in the face of such a concatenation of difficulties? And if he did go north, how was he to preserve himself against being mistaken for a spy, or for a pirate, or for a bandit?

Fortunately, an easy solution to Guest Gulkan's difficulties was at hand. Narba had long traded with the pirates of the Greater Teeth; and, now that those pirates had ambitiously seized the city of Androlmarphos, Narba continued to provide them with every facility they could pay for. So pirate recruiters were working freely in Narba, recruiting mercenaries, and pouring out the treasure of Androlmarphos to build an army which could contend against the might of the Harvest Plains.

So Guest volunteered himself for war, and thus was shortly shipped north to Androlmarphos, so avoiding the dangers posed by whatever part of rumour could be substantiated by fact.

Thus it came to pass that the Weaponmaster was in the city of Androlmarphos when that city was assailed by the armies of the Harvest Plains. Since the forces of ordered civilization triumphed on this occasion over the lawless forces of piracy, the Harvest Plains reclaimed Androlmarphos; the pirates retreated north to the Greater Teeth; and Guest Gulkan found himself very well advanced on his journey to the Old City of Penvash.

At this stage, an inexperienced adventurer would have incontinently flung himself into a direct assault on the Old City itself. Guest could have done as much. He could have stolen a boat, and shipped himself from the islands of the Greater Teeth to the shores of Argan. From there, he could — if all else failed — have simply walked north to the Old City.

But the Weaponmaster doubted very much that the star-globe which had been used to control the Door in the Old City in Penvash was still to be found in those ancient ruins. After all, during Guest's sojourn in Dalar ken Halvar the Circle of Doors which was based in Penvash had not been reopened. The Door in Dalar ken Halvar's Grand Arena had been diligently watched by the Silver Emperor's minions, and not once had it shown the slightest flicker of life.

Guest presumed, then, that the bandits who had won possession of the star-globe had carried their treasure away from the Old City. He presumed, further, that they would naturally seek to recruit the aid of a prince, a king or an emperor before they attempted to reopen the Circle which was based in Penvash.

For, if you find yourself in possession of a device which can open Doors to places as dangerous and as various as a battlefield and a Grand Arena, then it necessarily follows that you must be rather more than a bandit to exploit such a device successfully in defiance of the lords of the territories to which such Doors open.

Hence Guest suspected that those who currently held the star-globe would be seeking to enlist the support of some territorial power in or near Penvash. Thus thinking, the Weaponmaster ventured no footsore journey to the Old City, but, instead, set about the business of suborning a territorial power for his own purposes.

To this end, Guest set himself the job of getting close to the leader of the defeated pirates, a Rovac-born warlord by the name of Elkor Alish. Being jealous of the secret of star-globe and Doors, Guest did not immediately reveal all to Alish. Indeed, he revealed nothing. Guest thought he should first learn the temper of this man, and assess the degree to which his oath was trustworthy, and should only then suggest to him an alliance of purpose.

So Guest sought audience with the black-bearded Elkor Alish, he of the elegant dress, the bright gleaming jewels. On being granted audience, Guest sought employment as a bodyguard.

"Explain yourself," said Elkor Alish.

Upon which the Weaponmaster gave a heavily circumscribed account of his own life. He declared himself to be the son of Onosh Gulkan, the ruler who had been overthrown so many years ago by the barbarous Khmar.

"My childhood was spent in Gendormargensis," said Guest, "where I was tutored exclusively by Rovac warriors. Thus I learnt the manners of the Rovac, and something of their tongue. After my father lost his empire, I was exiled into the world. Thereafter, I put my sword at the service of the world, until I wandered too near Drangsturm and fell victim to the Ethnologists who dominate the castles of wizardry."

"The Ethnologists?" said Alish. "I have long studied the Confederation of Wizards, for I count that Confederation as the greatest of my enemies, but I have heard nothing of these Ethnologists."

"They are a new and horrible kind of evil," said Guest. "They are a cabal of wizards which specializes in the destructive interrogation of selected individuals from every race and nation. They seek to gain intimate knowledge of the strengths and weaknesses of each breed of men, so that by possession of such knowledge they can conquer the world."

This news was of intense interest to Elkor Alish, who was widely famed for his hatred of all wizards. So the mighty Rovac warrior demanded a full account of Guest's experiences at the hands of the Ethnologists, and Guest happily obliged, ending with a graphic account of the heroic manner in which he had finally fought his way out of the Castle of Controlling Power, leaving seven wizards dying in his wake.

"All this is well and good," said Alish, pleased to hear a tale so greatly to his taste. "But you have yet to explain why I should hire you as my bodyguard. I am of the Rovac and have others of the Rovac in my entourage."

"Yes, my lord," said Guest. "And my father was of the Yarglat, and had many mighty Yarglat warriors in his entourage. Yet his bodyguards were of the Rovac. For the Rovac had no power base in Tameran, therefore could not be a threat to his rule. Likewise, as a single Yarglat barbarian in the Greater Teeth, I have no power base. Hence I can be trusted."

"Are you accusing my Rovac compatriots of harbouring thoughts of revolution?" said Alish.

"I remark only that my lord is said to have lately been in dispute with one of his valued Rovac compatriots," said Guest Gulkan. "While serving in Androlmarphos, I have heard much of the tale of Elkor Alish and Morgan Hearst. The details are all in confusion, yet it seems clear that here were two Rovac warriors, and that bad blood led to battle between them."

This was undeniable.

Still.

"There are many refugees like yourself," said Alish. "Masterless men without power base. If I make a choice of such for my bodyguards, why should I trust you, and not one of them?"

"Because of my familiarity with wizards and their ways," answered Guest. "Wizards are your enemies, or so it is said. As their prisoner, I have learnt of their ways, and of their devices. My lord has sought to command such devices, and to use them against their originators. Yet many of his men have a superstitious dread of such things, and no knowledge of their powers and limitations."

"Good, but not good enough," said Elkor Alish. "There are a thousand people a day petitioning for my patronage. You will have to do better than that if you want to be my bodyguard."

"Then," said Guest, "know this. I had a special motive for seeking to serve you."

"What?" said Alish.

"I am Guest Gulkan, the son of Onosh Gulkan, and the rightful heir to the Collosnon Empire. My lord Alish is engaged in a struggle which has as its ultimate aim the control of the western seaboard of Argan and the destruction of the

Confederation of Wizards. With such ambition secured, his thoughts will turn north. Surely. With his ambition contented by the digestion of Argan, he will want allies in the north. I do not ask my lord to give me an army. Not now. Not this month, or next. But I suggest to my lord that it might be to his ultimate advantage to accept my offer of service, that he may sound out the degree to which my oath is trustworthy, and learn my temper."

This speech was greatly pleasing to Elkor Alish.

It was true that Alish had grotesquely grandiose visions of conquest, and entertained these visions still, even though he had lost the city of Androlmarphos and had been driven back to the Greater Teeth. In defeat, few believed that Alish could do more than hold those bare and barren rocks against the onslaughts of his enemies. So Guest made the sweetest of music when he confidently stated that Alish would secure Argan as his own — and then have the strength to look for greater influence to the north.

Alish considered at length.

Then said:

"I can offer you nothing now."

"I ask for nothing now," said Guest. "I wish only to serve, that we may measure each other's temper. When we have tested each other's temper, then we may talk of power, of conquest, of alliance. Till then, my sword is yours."

With that persuasive argument, Guest Gulkan entered the service of Elkor Alish. Flattery had helped win him that position; and his knowledge of the works of wizards; and the fact that he had personally murdered seven wizards in the course of escaping from the vile and hideous ethnologists who had turned the Castle of Controlling Power into a grim place of screaming evil and of bloodcurdling torture. Added to this, it must be acknowledged that a person of royal birth is always of potential use to any ruler; for the superstitions of the world are such that it is commonly thought that an emperor's son has a heaven-sent claim to great destiny, and Elkor Alish must surely have been aware of the political potential of such superstition.

So Guest was installed in the court of Elkor Alish, who was then making a diligent effort to acquire whatever devices of wizardly power he could gather in by purchase, by bribery, by search and by theft.

Having thus placed himself at the heart of the information nexus, Guest was ideally placed to learn of the destiny of the star-globe. And his manoeuvring was duly rewarded on the day when Rolf Thelemite himself was produced before Elkor Alish, and was commanded to tell the tale of his adventuring in Penvash.

One can imagine the shock, astonishment and consternation of Rolf Thelemite when he was brought before Elkor Alish and found the Weaponmaster standing as bodyguard at the warlord's side. Rolf had last met up with Guest on a desert island on the Circle of the Door of the Old City, and had last parted from him on a battlefield to which one of the other Doors of that Circle had opened.

How then had Guest come to be standing on the Greater Teeth, in company with Elkor Alish? And in what capacity was he there? And with what intention?

"Be not afraid of me," said Elkor Alish, seeing Rolf Thelemite's confusion. "I am merciful. All I want is the truth. Do but grace me with the truth of your history, and I will be content."

Then Guest intervened.

"My lord," said Guest. "If I may make so bold."

"Be bold," said Alish. "It is a virtue in a warrior, though it be a vice in a chambermaid."

"Then, my lord," said Guest, "let me say that I know this man. This Rolf Thelemite, he was bodyguard to my father in the days when he served my father in Gendormargensis. He was a mighty warrior in my father's armies, and covered himself in glory in the battles of our empire. His confusion is perhaps because he thinks I have placed myself at your side by subterfuge."

"Is this so?" said Elkor Alish.

"It, uh, it's true," said Rolf Thelemite, whose true terror

came from the fact that he was an oath-breaker accursed of Rovac, and was sure to be dead meat if Elkor Alish learnt of the details of his history.

"Then know that Guest Gulkan has declared himself to us properly as the son of Onosh Gulkan, the Witchlord of Tameran," said Elkor Alish. "He has declared himself further to be the son of Bao Gahai, a witch — and, as all the world knows, the witches are the sworn enemies of all wizards. My enemy's enemy is my friend, and the wizards of the Confederation are most definitely my enemies."

This set Rolf Thelemite to gaping, for, if there was anything Rolf was sure of, it was that Guest Gulkan was not and could not possibly be the son of Bao Gahai. For the dralkosh Bao Gahai was surely a thousand years beyond the age of childbearing, hence could not have mothered Guest. But — well, Elkor Alish had never set eyes on Bao Gahai, nor was he likely to. And doubtless Guest had stretched the truth at the corners to win himself the confidence of the doughty Elkor Alish.

Very well.

"My lord," said Rolf. "I, uh, you're — it's this globe you're interested in."

"This globe of stars," confirmed Elkor Alish. "This Door of Doors."

"You've, ah, heard some of this story," said Rolf Thelemite. "From Drake Douay, I mean. Did you speak to him? They said you met him in 'Marphos, they said—"

"Just the truth," said Alish, cutting off Rolf Thelemite's verbating.

Then Rolf controlled himself, and gave a plain account of his doings.

"I was engaged in this diplomacy business," said Rolf. "There was a mission, a mission from the Greaters to Ork."

"So I've heard," said Alish.

"There was a sea-wreck," said Rolf.

"Is there any other kind of wreck?" said Alish.

Rolf Thelemite was about to answer in the affirmative. Rolf

Thelemite was about to say that a person could be airwrecked as easily as they could be sea-wrecked. But then Guest Gulkan caught Rolf Thelemite's eye, and conveyed a warning by the grimness of his expression.

Only then did Rolf Thelemite catch himself. He was in the presence of Elkor Alish, the scourge of the Confederation of Wizards. It might well be death for Rolf if he was to confess his long association with the notorious Hostaja Torsen Sken-Pitilkin, wizard of Drum, wizard of the order of Skatzabratzumon, and master of controlled flight. Much has been written about the hazards of the battlefield, and the dangers of the sea, but the terrors of a court can be worse than storm and battle put together; and Rolf, realizing how dangerous his long association with Sken-Pitilkin might yet prove to the integrity of his liver, was hard put to know what to say next.

"You were saying?" said Alish.

"There's, ah, carts," said Rolf Thelemite. "Carts can be wrecked, yes, wheels came off, Drake told me once, a cart, it was Cam, there was coal, a whole building demolished, there—"

"Just the facts," said Alish. "The facts of your journey. Briefly. Not the whole of your life in vomiting detail."

"Ah," said Rolf, relieved that this dangerous business of wrecking was done with. "I was diplomat, then. But wrecked. Wrecked on Penvash. There was capture and battle beforehand, a big ship, a metal ship, but the wrecking was the end of it, and, ah — inland, we went inland, north was the start and the south to be the finish, and the Old City in the middle."

"Tell on," said Alish.

"We reached this Old City," said Rolf, "and it was Drake, Drake Douay, you've met him, I'm told. He found the globe, it was full of stars, he put in this hole, and then this Door opened, a Door between countries."

"Then?" said Alish.

"We closed it," said Rolf. "Because it was, ah, there were crocodiles, there were big lizards, a battle, all kinds of stuff, giant centipedes, a mountainside. So we got back to the Old City, we closed it, that was enough. But then there was a fight."

"I'm sure there was," said Alish. "So?"

"The, the globe," said Rolf, "it got lost in the river. Because of the fight, I mean."

"Then?" said Alish.

"Then we came back," said Rolf, lamely. "Back home. Back to the Greaters, I mean."

"And that's it?" said Alish.

"That's it," said Rolf.

And that was the end of the interview.

Guest Gulkan then expected Elkor Alish to rush an army to Penvash to filter that region's rivers for the star-globe. But Alish remained singularly unmoved by Rolf Thelemite's revelations. And, on mature reflection, Guest Gulkan realized the reason why.

Elkor Alish desired to conquer Argan. The Door in the Old City started in no place in which he wanted to be, and went to no place to which he wanted to go. Ultimately, he desired to make war on the wizards of Drangsturm, true — but there was no point whatsoever in opening a Door which debouched into the territory of the Swarms on the wrong side of Drangsturm. Alish was searching for devices, yes, but he wanted things he could use immediately as weapons of war.

Unlike Guest Gulkan, Alish did not know of the existence of the far more valuable Circle of the Partnership Banks. Unlike Guest Gulkan, Alish did not have a father who ruled Alozay, where one of the Doors of the Banks was located. Unlike Guest Gulkan, Alish did not have the hope of eventually making an alliance with gigantic and invulnerable jade-green demons like Ko of Chi'ash-lan and Italis of Alozay.

So Guest Gulkan began to plan an expedition into Penvash on his own account, and to this end he renewed his acquaintance with Rolf Thelemite, and tried to meet and covertly interrogate all those who had been in Penvash when the star-globe was lost to the river. For Guest had already realized that the difficulties of finding a small star-globe in a large river could well be extreme; and that he could easily exhaust his life in futile search unless he could pin down the location of loss with some degree of exactitude.

In the end, Guest realized that research would not be sufficient in itself. To have any hope of success, he would have to take Rolf Thelemite or one of Thelemite's companions to Penvash, together with several hundred people equipped to search rigorously whatever stretch of river Thelemite indicated as the site of star-globe's loss.

To this end, Guest Gulkan began to sound out the temper of some of the other chieftains on the Greaters, concentrating in particular on the most lordly of the pirates.

When Guest was not thus engaged, he spent much of his time in a green bottle which had fallen to Elkor Alish's possession. In the secrecy of that bottle — the commanding ring of which was retained in Alish's possession — Guest spent most of his time writing a detailed account of the fortifications of Drangsturm, and of the Castle of Controlling Power in particular. Since Guest had studied those fortifications in detail, he was well-equipped for the task; and, since he still held a grudge against the Confederation, and against its ethnologists in particular, he had no hesitation in honourably discharging that duty.

Thus Guest was hard at work in the green bottle when that treasure of treasures was stolen from Elkor Alish by a sneak-thief named Togura Poulaan; and Guest was still helplessly imprisoned in the same bottle when that Poulaan carried it away from the Greater Teeth in a small boat which was shortly struck by storm.

CHAPTER FIFTY-FOUR

Togura Poulaan: a would-be questing hero from Sung who became one of Sken-Pitilkin's protégés at a time when Sken-Pitilkin was living alone on Drum (Guest Gulkan having disappeared through a Door in the Old City of Penvash)

* * *

Now Guest Gulkan was a questing hero, a survivor of encounters with Crabs and with therapists, a mighty swordsman whose daring had defeated both the murkbeast and the crocodile. Yet being such a person is no defence against ignominious disaster, for the world's greatest warlord may yet step by accident in a dogturd, or have a chamber pot emptied on his head by a careless chambermaid at work in the upper storeys of a building which overshadows the route of his promenade.

So it was that Guest, he who had confronted the dreaded Ethnologists in their lair yet had lived to tell the tale, he who had suborned the imperial strength of Plandruk Qinplaqus to his service, he who had duelled with the Great God Jocasta and had survived the treachery of the demon Italis, fell victim to the lowest and meanest specimen of scuttling cowardice to be found west of Galsh Ebrek and east of Chi'ash-lan.

The vile and villainous Togura Poulaan, a native of the pork-eating nation of Sung, stole the bottle in which Guest was hard at work on his self-interrogation; and, by the time Poulaan had managed to carry the bottle home to his lair in Sung, he had succeeded in damaging the bottle so badly by long abuse that it ultimately broke, liberating Guest Gulkan from its interior.

That, at least, is the story as told by the Weaponmaster. It must be admitted that the above-mentioned Poulaan has given a different account of the matter, and claims that Guest destroyed the bottle from within by incontinently tampering with a subtle wizardly mechanism he found in its depths.

Be that as it may, the outcome was that Guest Gulkan was carried north of the Greaters to Sung, a barbarous province of the Ravlish Lands. In some quarters, it is alleged that he did not leave Sung before committing a number of murders. Indeed, Poulaan is said to have blamed the Weaponmaster for the death of his much-beloved brother Cromarty, who was put to death in the town of Keep in a singularly sanguinary manner.

Whatever the truth of the matter, it is certain that Guest, having been abstracted from the Greater Teeth by the villainous Poulaan, ended up in Sung, a dismal land of bogs and rockdumps in Ravlish East, where peasants with provincial mudpuddle minds dedicate themselves to the practice of obscure yet hideous abominations. The inhabitants of this depraved place eat offal (in addition to pork), rape sheep, commit vile abominations with toads, and abominate themselves also with liquid dung. Nor is this the limit of their delinquencies, for the people of Sung have disgraced themselves down through the generations by systematic inhospitality, the worst manifestation of which is that they frequently mistake wandering scholars for lepers and endeavour to stone them to death. They further display their debased iniquity by giving houseroom to the skavamareen, an instrument of aural obscenity which has long been outlawed in every civilized nation from Tang to Chi'ash-lan. It must also be said that a debasement equal to that of their morals has from time to time afflicted their coinage; and that this great injury has been suffered by innocent persons.

The capital of Sung is Keep, which has been mentioned above as the site of the alleged murder of Cromarty, and Keep is notable inasmuch as it is a town much undermined by gemrock tunnelling, to the point where its very existence has been for some time threatened. One has read that anciently great civilizations were destroyed by the very processes which produced their wealth; and, while Sung is neither great nor (properly speaking) an abode of civilization, one foresees that its destruction will ultimately befall it thanks to a similar dynamic.

However, despite the sundry derelictions of Keep, of Sung, and of the people of Sung, Guest Gulkan escaped from that barbarous province with skin and foreskin yet intact, and got himself down to the coast.

He then headed toward D'Waith.

D'Waith is the seaport at the easternmost end of the Ravlish Lands, and hence is the port which is handiest to Drum. One might therefore have presumed Guest Gulkan to be making for the island of Drum, intent on discovering whether the sagacious Sken-Pitilkin yet survived on that island; and intent, too, on recruiting Sken-Pitilkin's power, might, wisdom and all-round sagacity to his cause.

But — not a bit of it!

Though Guest Gulkan had reached the full years of his maturity, he had yet to acquire wisdom; and the proof of this is that he had no thought of seeking the help of his tutelary wizard, but planned instead to get transport from D'Waith to the Greaters, and there to present himself once again to Elkor Alish, and this time to make a full confession of the existence of the Circle of the Partnership Banks.

Guest had been grievously shaken by his kidnapping. Having been swept to Sung by the villainous Togura Poulaan, he had been forced to acknowledge that the slow, elegant ballet of carefully choreographed politicking in which he had been engaged on the Greaters was fatuous. For Guest was not living in any great Age of Peace in which slow measures might yet win the day. Instead, he was living in an Age of Darkness, which favoured the roughness of the fist and the sharpness of the swordblade.

So Guest, who had previously been working on intricate plans for the confidential recovery of the star-globe from the rivers of Penvash, now planned to abandon subtlety and secrecy altogether, and to confront Elkor Alish with the truth.

This is what he would say:

"Just south of here, a short voyage distant from the Greaters, a Door awaits us on the island of Stokos. It is the Door of the Stokos Bank, a Door which is linked to similar Banks in places as far afield as Chi'ash-lan and Dalar ken Halvar. Command of this Circle of Banks would answer your most crying need; possession of a source of wealth equal to the demands of financing your war against the Confederation of Wizards. If you will but give me an army, a small one, then I will wrest from the waters of Penvash the device which commands these Doors, and place both the device and myself at your service."

This was what Guest planned to say, for he had been compelled to an acknowledgement of his own limits, of the uncertainties of his previous elaborate scheming, and of the need to cut his ambitions down to size, so his capacities would be equal to those ambitions. Thus, whereas the Weaponmaster had previously set his heart on mastering the Circle of the Partnership Banks in his own right, now he was prepared to compromise, to make an alliance with Elkor Alish, and to accept a subordinate role in any conquest of that Circle.

But he was too late!

For, on reaching D'Waith, Guest found that a ship from Androlmarphos was in port, and the news which had been brought by the ship had already infected the whole town.

Drangsturm had fallen.

Words cannot encompass the enormity of this disaster.

Drangsturm, of course, was the trench of flame which the wizards of the Confederation had built to guard the north of Argan from the monsters of the south.

In earlier discussion with Elkor Alish, Guest Gulkan had asked the Rovac warrior how he planned to master the defence of the continent once he had overthrown the Confederation of Wizards. To this, the black-bearded Rovac warrior had given a two-part answer. First, he planned to compel a certain number of wizards to serve him as his slaves, and to maintain the flames of Drangsturm against invasion by the monsters of the Swarms. Second, he intended to quest later to the heartland of the terror-lands of the Deep South, and there to overthrow the Skull, the entity which commanded the Swarms.

Such was the hubris of Elkor Alish, he who is said to have been ultimately overpowered and slaughtered by certain of the monsters of the Swarms — for, if rumour is to be believed, Alish was killed by one of the Neversh while attempting to stem the invasion of the monsters which forced their way to the north after the destruction of Drangsturm.

When Guest Gulkan first heard the news of Drangsturm's fall, Elkor Alish yet lived. But Guest did not think for a moment that Alish, or any other warrior, could hold the Swarms in battle. During his earlier adventuring round the Circle that began in the Old City of Penvash, Guest had gone through a Door which opened on to the wrong side of Drangsturm, the southern side, that side which had always been the province of the monsters of the Swarms. There he had encountered huge centipedes, from which he and his companions of the moment had fled.

And Guest knew, in his-heart of hearts, that there was little to be done in the face of the Swarms except to run.

So, when Guest heard that Drangsturm had fallen, and that the Confederation of Wizards had destroyed itself in a civil war which had set one wizard against another, he realized that all of Argan was doomed. Words could not encompass the enormity of this disaster. The cities of Narba, Voice, Veda, Selzirk, Androlmarphos and Runcorn lay open to the onslaught of the worst of mindless marauding monsters — mindless monsters which were commanded by the malign intelligence of the Skull of the Deep South.

So Guest knew then — and rightly knew — that all would perish. The hotlands of the Far South would be overwhelmed. The ricelands and the wheatlands, all would go. The forests of the Chenameg Kingdom, the horselands of the Lezconcarnau Plains, the walls of Selzirk the Fair and the boulevards of Voice — all would fall to the forces of living death.

For three days, Guest Gulkan lingered in D'Waith, until he had exhaustively researched the news of Drangsturm's fall. Meantime, discreet enquiry established that Sken-Pitilkin yet lived, and lived on Drum.

With news gathered, and with nothing of use yet left to do in D'Waith, Guest Gulkan persuaded a fisherman to dare the ugly waters of the Penvash Strait, that body of water which lies between the Ravlish Lands and the continent of Argan. It is toothed with rocks, haunted by sea serpents, and frequently beset by storms of great severity — all of which threaten to drown the mariner, or to wreck him upon shores where he will surely fall victim to the savagery of the harp seal (or so it is said, though, despite their bloodthirsty reputation, even harp seals have their occasional defenders).

This was the body of water which Guest Gulkan dared, and the dare brought him home to Drum, where the fisherman was rewarded by Sken-Pitilkin (and was rewarded, too, by being made guest of honour at a three-day poetry reading given by Sken-Pitilkin's sea dragons — though whether he was entirely appreciative of this compulsory honouring of his courage is debatable).

And on arrival—

On arrival in Drum, Guest Gulkan was seven days in conversation with Hostaja Torsen Sken-Pitilkin, the wizard of Skatzabratzumon who had been the tutor of his childhood and the guide of his later years.

Now Sken-Pitilkin was a mighty wizard, the greatest wizard of the order of Skatzabratzumon, and the first wizard in the history of the world to have mastered the arts of controlled flight. But the sorry truth is that Sken-Pitilkin had no remedy for the misfortune which had befallen Argan. For he could not repair Drangsturm, nor could he see any way in which the Swarms could be prevented from sweeping north through Argan.

Sken-Pitilkin's gloomy prognosis was predictive of events. For, in the months which followed, the Swarms completed the conquest of Argan's western seaboard. Only a tiny fraction of the populated flatlands held out against the monsters. This tiny fraction was the province of Estar, where mountainous defence, coupled with great force of arms, allowed the Swarms to be checked and held.

For the moment.

During these months of disaster, Guest Gulkan and Sken-Pitilkin were by no means inactive. Do not imagine that they sat idly on Drum while the world went down to disaster! No, they exerted themselves mightily, and a chronicle of their mutual exploits would fill an encyclopedia.

Their exploits began with a monumental air adventure which took them to the city of Dalar ken Halvar, where Guest recovered the cornucopia, and recovered too the yellow bottle which had been devoted to transporting crocodiles for the benefit of Parengarenga's entertainment industry.

Armed with the bottle, and with the cornucopia, and aided by Sken-Pitilkin's mastery of airpower, the Weaponmaster and his wizard then made war upon the Swarms to the extent which they could.

But the cornucopia proved a singularly ineffective weapon for use against the Swarms. Wizard and Weaponmaster had anticipated unleashing floods of black slime against the armies of the Swarms, but found these monsters scattered widely rather than bunched in tight formations like the armies of humankind. Protected by their very dispersion, the Swarms had no great concentrations which could be destroyed by human agency.

Still, wizard and Weaponmaster did their best, until the very cornucopia expired from sheer over-use — shrivelling to a warped strip of something which looked like burnt black leather.

Then the pair essayed what rescue they could with the aid of the yellow bottle. And one would think, given the enormous capacity of that bottle, and given Sken-Pitilkin's command of the air, that they should have been able to evacuate entire cities. But it was not so. For the human material which they were endeavouring to help was unruly in the extreme.

And here one is tempted to give a catalogue, that it may be clearly understood by all of history that wizard and Weaponmaster did not shirk their duty when the world was in need. But such self-defensive exculpatory cataloguing would fill many pages needlessly, and add nothing to the body of wisdom. Let it merely be recorded that, of the people whom wizard and Weaponmaster saved, at least one in ten responded by trying to murder them in an effort to win possession of the yellow bottle and its commanding ring.

And inside the bottle itself — well, the behaviour of the refugees is better imagined than described. Like so many rats trapped in a cage, they fought, they raped, they stole, they murdered, and they waged warfare against each other. They fought over religion, race and language. They came to blows over matters concerning personal odours, and the food which one breed ate, and the food which another breed didn't eat. Men killed each other in fights over women and women killed each other in fights over men.

And when these refugees were set down on hard land — usually in the Ravlish Lands — they were at the mercy of the sundry bandits, warlords, slavers and professional murderers who made the plunder of the helpless their speciality.

Furthermore, Sken-Pitilkin's stickbird began to be increasingly menaced by the Neversh. The wizard of Skatzabratzumon could outfly the Neversh, the lumbering winged monsters which were the greatest of the Swarms, but they seemed to be anticipating his movements. He would fly from one, only to find his flight intersected by another at a distance of a hundred leagues. As the danger increased, Sken-Pitilkin realized that the Skull of the Deep South was distantly aware of the tiny stickbird which was nimbling in and out of the lands of its conquest, and was doing its best to destroy this adversary.

So Guest and Sken-Pitilkin were forced to become selective, to plan their raids carefully, to limit their flights, and to fly for the most part by night, when the Swarms did not fly.

It was then that Sken-Pitilkin began to hatch a grandiose plan — which was, to gather in as many wizards as he could, and base them upon Drum, and set up a new Confederation with himself as its head.

To the sagacious wizard of Skatzabratzumon, this seemed the most logical plan in all the world. The Swarms were conquering Argan, and were threatening the northern continent of Tameran and the eastern Ravlish Lands. It was therefore surely supremely logical that the surviving wizards of the Confederation should base themselves defensively upon Drum, a substantially fortified island set in a wild wash of water which was at or near the intersection of Argan, Tameran and the Ravlish Lands.

But this scheme met with little success.

One fraction of the Confederation, finding the city of Androlmarphos to be defensible, had made that city its own, and declined to exchange its comforts for the windswept barrens of far-distant Drum. Others had fled east, taking ship, and voyaging across the Inner Waters and past the Stepping Stone Islands to the Ebrell Islands. They declared the Ebrells to be a base more logical than Drum, for it was closer to the Breach (and, therefore, closer to the Shackle Mountains and the all-important Cave of the Warp).

And when Sken-Pitilkin did meet isolated wizards who had not thrown in their lot with the rival Confederations arising in Androlmarphos or on the Ebrells, why, he found that many bore a grudge against him for things he was alleged to have done in the past, and for crimes he was alleged to have committed against the Confederation; and more than one held Sken-Pitilkin to be personally responsible for the downfall of Drangsturm, and (though there was neither truth nor logic to any such accusation) tried to kill him on that account.

In the end, Sken-Pitilkin was able to bring a bare one dozen wizards to Drum. That dozen included the ethnologist Brother Fern Feathers. Fortunately, Guest failed to recognize Fern Feathers; and Sken-Pitilkin, who was fully aware of Guest's attitude towards the scientific researches of wizards, warned the ethnologist that he should do his best to conceal the scholarly labours of his past. Therefore, when Guest asked Fern Feathers to declare his history, that wizard said he had long laboured as a slug-chef; and with this declaration Guest was contented.

The dozen wizards brought to Drum also included (much to Guest's delight) the Yarglat wizard Ontario Nol; and (to Guest's yet greater delight) Eljuk Zala Gulkan. In the years in which Guest and Eljuk had been separated, Eljuk had attempted his Tests for a second time: and, in the Cave of the Warp, had succeeded in making the necessary alliance which made him a wizard in his own right.

But what could a dozen wizards do against the Swarms? What could they do when they were refugees upon Drum, a bare and barren island which was hard-pushed to feed itself and its sea dragons? On their own, they were nothing.

Guest therefore bent his attention once more to the business of recovering the star-globe, and to this purpose he dared the hazards of the Old City of Penvash, and spent many days up to his neck in the waters of the river which ran south from that Old City. But, search as he might, Guest never managed to recover the star-globe which could have opened the Doors of the Partnership Banks — even though he coerced Sken-Pitilkin and his fellow-wizards into assisting him in this hunt.

Concluding that the star-globe might well have been removed from the river by an earlier treasure hunter, Guest then realized the thing might be anywhere in the world. And how was he to find it when the world was so vast, and in such disorder?

It was then that Guest, for the first time in his life, began to make a systematic effort to exploit the Gift of Seeing which was a part of his inheritance. But in these efforts he failed absolutely.

For, whereas in early youth Guest had routinely had premonitions, and had from time to time endured visions of the future, and had seen things-which were yet to be, and had seen too those things which were distant, in his maturity this facility had perished entirely.

There is nothing unusual in this.

For the Weaponmaster's life had been, in many ways, one long exercise in selective amnesia. If he had not been able to suppress the memory of the pain of his wounding at Babaroth, when his foot had been cruelly wounded by a bamboo spike, how then would he have been able to prosecute his later battles valorously? If he had not been able to subdue the memories of a mighty avalanche which he had used to crush, grind and pulverize his father's army during the course of Tameran's civil war, how then would he have been able to sleep at nights?

Guest had forced himself to suppress his memories of the mauling he had endured in an arena of Chi'ash-lan, when the

Great Mink itself had shredded his arms and legs, sentencing him to four long years of humiliating convalescence.

So.

To remember was terror. To be aware was to suffer. And, after a lifetime of blunting self-awareness and suppressing memory, Guest was entirely shut off from those wild and undeveloped Powers which (given the tutelage of a shaman or similar) he might potentially have developed into something useful.

So it was that Guest was forced to fall back on routine method for his interrogation of the world; and, year after year, he was often to be found in D'Waith, or in Favanosin, or in Port Domax, or in the other cities to which he persuaded Sken-Pitilkin to fly him.

And, at last, Guest learnt of the location of the star-globe. It had been uplifted from a river in Penvash by one Yen Olass Ampadara, and was presently said to be on the island of Carawell.

And Carawell, the chiefest island of the Lesser Teeth, was virtually on Guest Gulkan's doorstep.

CHAPTER FIFTY-FIVE

Lesser Teeth: a group of sandy, low-lying islands north of the
Greaters, south of the Ravlish Lands, and an eyeshot or so
east of the continent of Argan.

* * *

So Guest Gulkan raided Carawell, chiefest of the islands of the
Lesser Teeth. He came from the sky, swooping down from
above in a stickbird piloted by Hostaja Sken-Pitilkin, and he
brought with him a half-dozen fighting men and two sea
dragons.

Guest Gulkan expected war, battle, screams and terror. His
thoughts had been focused on the star-globe for so long that he
automatically imagined that the whole world shared his lust for
the thing. But of course to the people on Carawell the star-globe
was nothing but a useless bauble. Suppose a gang of bloodthirsty
cut-throats broke into your house, and proclaimed their
intention to make off with your deceased grandmother's teeth.
It is not likely that you would risk murder, rape and arson to
defend this dubious treasure — and, similarly, the people of
Carawell put up no fight to defend the star-globe.

Quite apart from everything else, the chiefest warlord of
Carawell, a Rovac warrior named Morgan Hearst, had taken
himself and his gang of cut-throats to Estar, where he had
embroiled himself in some dubious provincial power-struggle,
the details of which were of no interest to Guest Gulkan.

On Carawell, Guest Gulkan interrogated a young Rovac
warrior named Altol Stokpol, and learnt from this source rather
more than he cared to know about the affairs of Morgan Hearst.
From this interrogation, Guest learnt only one thing of interest:
there was a Yarglat barbarian named Nan Nualador in Hearst's
dungeons.

Guest naturally rescued his fellow countryman, and asked
him why he had been persecuted by Morgan Hearst.

"We quarrelled over a woman," said Nan Nualador.

Guest readily accepted this, for, like many another man who has outgrown the age when lust is dominant, he had come to think of the female sex as being little more than an endless source of trouble and provocation.

It would be wrong to say that the Weaponmaster had an ascetic temperament. Nevertheless, he had led a life which had made ruthless demands on his resources; and, concentrating on the needs of raw survival and the pursuit of power, he had quite got out of the habit of sensual relaxation. If he was hungry, then he ate; but, if one of his appetites needed appeasing, then he satisfied that appetite merely to free himself for undistracted action.

Guest Gulkan, then, had become a more limited creature as he had grown into his full maturity. He had lost sight of certain possibilities and potentialities. In his lustful youth, he had been prepared to fight to the death to secure the prideful possession of the woman Yerzerdayla. Later, during four long years of convalescence in Dalar ken Halvar, he had been faithful to the woman Penelope, exchanging the satisfaction of unbridled lust for those of domesticity.

But now, in the years of his maturity, the Weaponmaster thought little of either lust or domesticity. The rigours of his life — its many defeats, setbacks, disappointments and assorted traumas — had pruned away many possibilities. In maturity, he had focused his life on one great task: to reopen the Circle of the Doors of the Partnership Banks.

Thinking like a soldier, Guest Gulkan invited Nan Nualador to come with him to the island of Drum, for Nan Nualador looked like the kind of person who would be handy in a battle.

But Nan Nualador refused.

"Why?" said Guest Gulkan in surprise.

"I have other business," muttered Nan Nualador.

"That's not good enough!" said Guest.

Then the Weaponmaster interrogated Nan Nualador at length, at last coming to understand that the Yarglat barbarian's refusal was made up of one part of defiance to nine parts of stark terror. Nan Nualador had a positive horror of Guest, this mighty warlock who had descended from the sky with dragons at his feet.

At last, despairing of the man, Guest Gulkan turned Nan Nualador loose, then rounded up the sea dragons (with difficulty, for those delinquent beasts had become engrossed in the hunting of chickens, which they thought to be great sport) then flew back to the island of Drum (taking with him some 275 dead chickens which his sea dragons had incontinently slaughtered).

Shortly thereafter (after the greatest chicken-meat banquet ever held upon Drum) Guest Gulkan and Sken-Pitilkin convened a conference of all Drum's resident wizards.

Sken-Pitilkin was first to address that council of war. He gave his address in the Galish Trading Tongue, for, even after all these years, Guest Gulkan had yet to master even a smattering of the High Speech of wizards to his tongue (and, despite his desert island maroonment in the company of a copy of Strogloth's Compendium of Delights, remained lamentably ignorant of all the other great scholarly languages, such as Janjuladoola and Slandolin).

"We have the star-globe," said Sken-Pitilkin, once he had given a detailed account of Guest's latest exploits. "Therefore, it follows that we can open up the Circle of the Doors of the Partnership Bank."

Then Sken-Pitilkin produced a map, a composite map which he had drawn himself, working partly from documents, partly from conjecture, partly from logical surmise, and (in great part) from his wealth of personal experience. He pointed out the location of the nine Doors of the Circle. These were:

—the Safrak Bank of the Safrak Islands;

—the Monastic Treasury of Inner Adeer, in Voice;

—the Flesh Trader's Financial Association of Galsh Ebrek;

—the Bondsman's Guild of Obooloo, capital of Aldarch III;

—the Bralsh, of Dalar ken Halvar;

—the Singing Dove Pensions Trust of Tang;

—the Taniwha Guarantee Corporation of Quilth;

—the Orsay Bank of Stokos;

—the Morgrim Bank of Chi'ash-lan.

"Unfortunately," said Sken-Pitilkin, "Voice has been overrun by the Swarms. It therefore follows that to open the Circle will mean confronting the Swarms. This we can do, because we need but defend a single Door. Still, we will need to have an army to back us before we dare open the Door."

"Perhaps," ventured Brother Fern Feathers, one of the mildest wizards of Guest Gulkan's acquaintance, "it would be unwise to open the Door at all. Why provoke a war with the Swarms when we've no need for such a war?"

"Being intelligent people," said Sken-Pitilkin, "we will fight no wars ourselves. We will get warriors to fight them for us. Furthermore, the Swarms are sure to force us to the point of war in any case. The Swarms are not settled in Argan. Rather, they are singularly unsettled. They are hot upon the borders of Estar. Furthermore, numbers are rumoured to have been washed up on the shores of the Ravlish Lands, and Guest has lately brought me fresh news of an invasion of the Lessers."

Then Guest Gulkan related a third-hand tale which he had had from the Rovac warrior Altol Stokpol, concerning a number of baby monsters which had made a landing on the beaches of Carawell.

"As you see," said Sken-Pitilkin, "regardless of our pacific intentions, we are sure to find ourselves at war with the Swarms, later if not sooner. If Estar falls to the Swarms, then so too will Penvash. Penvash, gentlemen, is but an eyeshot from the shores of Drum. Attack will come from the sea, from the sky. Doubtless we have the strength to resist such attack, but make no mistake about it — it will be war."

This sobered his audience, because most of them chose not to think about the Swarms unless they absolutely had to. As the ordinary citizen of Obooloo shuns and suppresses all knowledge of the temperament of the Mutilator, so too the wizards resident upon Drum chose to be wilfully ignorant of the menace upon their doorstep.

This initiated a long debate. And the debates of wizards are of a length and complexity which cannot easily be imagined by those who have not had personal experience of such deliberations. Indeed, the debate went on for so long that, before it was over, Drum had news of the latest developments to the south.

Morgan Hearst, the greatest warlord of Carawell, had made an alliance with a southern barbarian named Watashi, and with a number of pirates, and with those forces of the Collosnon Empire which currently occupied Estar. The long and the short of it was that a southern alliance was bent on installing upon the throne of Gendormargensis a child named Monogail, a female child who was alleged to be the offspring of the Red Emperor Khmar (he who was said to have died so long ago in the forests of Penvash).

The greater number of the wizards on Drum were inclined to treat this news as a happy coincidence. They needed an army. Very well! Here was an army! An army organizing for invasion!

"They have ships," said Brother Fern Feathers. "They have ships, swords and men. They have leaders who are mighty in war. They have this child to be a figurehead for an invasion of Tameran. Very well. We can make an alliance. We can use this army to liberate the Circle of the Doors."

But, to Guest, the fact that an army was preparing for invasion on their very doorstep was but idle coincidence.

Since Sken-Pitilkin had an airship, and since Guest Gulkan was in possession of a yellow bottle sufficient for the carriage of an army, and since their goal was not (oh vulgar ambition!) to conquer a continent but, rather (the future beckons!) to reopen the Circle of the Partnership Banks, any Door on that Circle could (potentially) serve as a base for action.

To most of the wizards, the Circle was but a theory. But, to the Weaponmaster, that Circle was a living reality. In particular, he had the most lively memories of Dalar ken Halvar, the city where he had once spent four long years in convalescence.

"It is said that the Rovac are mighty in war," said Guest. "But our war for the Circle will not be as other wars. We have no use for the slowness of ships or the slow ooze of infantry. We have the rule of the air and the capacity of the yellow bottle. The wind's reach is ours. We need no strategy of mud, and of stone, and of wood, and of water. Rather, we must think as the wind, as the sun."

"Very pretty poetry," said Brother Fern Feathers, interrupting Guest Gulkan as he was winding himself up for revelation. "But you have no soldiers."

"I have allies," said Guest, displeased to be interrupted in his rhetoric.

"What allies?" said Fern Feathers. "You are but a homeless barbarian."

"What makes you say so?" said Guest.

"Why!" said Fern Feathers, "I say so because I know so! I know your curriculum vitae in depth and in detail."

"Do you?" said Guest.

As the Weaponmaster had never lately found time for any detailed biographical revelations, he thought it exceedingly bizarre for any wizard to be claiming a knowledge of his past.

"Don't you remember?" said Brother Fern Feathers. "I was head of the Ethnological Commission which interrogated you all those years ago when you were fresh-arrived at Drangsturm."

"Ah!" said Guest, in the tones of a man who has stepped barefooted on a wasp. "Now I remember!"

Now Guest remembered with a vengeance!

Though Brother Fern Feathers was mild (as wizards went) and not arrogant (or not at least by wizardly standards) and politely spoken (or as polite as could be reasonably expected) Guest Gulkan had never been able to bring himself to like the fellow. For some inexplicable reason, Guest had always found himself possessed of a mysterious but ineradicable dislike for Fern Feathers.

Now the inexplicable was explained, the mysterious was made bare and plain. Fern Feathers was an ethnologist! Worse, he was the very ethnologist who had led Guest Gulkan's interrogation in the Castle of Controlling Power!

"Sex customs!" said Guest, slamming his hand on the table. "That's what it was! You had sex on the brain, like all ethnologists!"

"Have I somehow offended you?" said Brother Fern Feathers.

"Somehow!" said Guest. "Where does somehow come into it? My scrotum, my foreskin, the hairs of my arse — are these not meant to be private? Yet — you and your committee!"

"We did but ask a few questions," said Fern Feathers, starting to get defensive.

"Yes," said Guest, "but what questions?"

"Scientific questions!" said Fern Feathers.

"Oh, so it is science, is it?" said Guest. "When I hear someone talk of science, then I reach for my sword!"

So saying, Guest suited action to words.

"We were but enquiring after knowledge," said Fern Feathers, starting to grow fearful of his life.

"Then if you truly wish to receive knowledge," said Guest, in his coldest and grandest tones, "then hearken to me mightily, and perhaps you will live. Or perhaps not. For I am the Emperor in Exile."

Then Guest began to rant — a strong word, true, but the word is apt — about his greatness, his mightiness and his superlativeness. He inflicted upon that gathering a veritable catalogue of the exploits of his steel. He itemized the battles he had won, not neglecting to mention even his boyhood battle against Thodric Jarl in Enskandalon Square. He named the monsters he had faced or fought — the Great Mink of Gendormargensis, the murkbeast of Logthok Norgos, two therapists and a certain Crab of Untunchilamon, a dorgi of the depths Downstairs beneath the city of Injiltaprajura, a giant centipede, a number of crocodiles, and the bright-burning Shabble.

Guest grew positively hoarse from boasting. Down through the long years, the memories of all the provocations he had endured at the hands of the Ethnological Commission had festered in the darkness of his mind, unacknowledged and unaddressed, and now their poison was spurting forth with a vengeance.

"All this I have done!" said Guest, in the fullness of his hoarseness, "yet it is not enough for an ethnologist, no, not battles, not monsters, not travels, not the mastery of languages, not the braving of prisons and the survival of torture chambers. All this I have done, yet he calls me barbarian and doubts my fitness to rule. So my question is this. What must I do to win his esteem? When so many feats have been accomplished already, what yet remains to my sword? I have asked myself this question, and have decided that only one task yet awaits me: the slaughter of an ethnologist!"

Seldom in the course of history has a barbarian been able to turn the tables on an ethnologist! Believe me, it is most uncomfortable for the ethnologist, particularly when the barbarian in question has a sword in his hand, and looks more than half-minded to use it!

Brother Fern Feathers positively grovelled before the Weaponmaster, and assured the gathering that he believed Guest Gulkan to be the most accomplished and civilized of gentlemen, yes, a winner of battles, a slayer of monsters, and (in all probability) a master of the irregular verbs.

"I have no need of the verbs," said Guest, glowering at the mention of these the most ancient and intractable of his enemies. "I have no need of the verbs, no, nor of grammars neither, nor of dictionaries. You can burn your verbs and have done with them!"

Whereupon Brother Fern Feathers declared himself to be of identical opinion. He denounced the High Speech, yes, and Slandolin, and Janjuladoola, and all other tongues not regular to a nicety in their formation.

"They are but twisted toys for sapless pedants," said Fern Feathers, growing passionate in his denunciation. "They should be burnt, cindered, reduced to ashes, grammars and dictionaries together."

"Good," said Guest, somewhat mollified by the whole-heartedness of this capitulation. "Good, good. It is good to see that at least one person has won enlightenment today!"

Then the Weaponmaster shot a meaningful look at Hostaja

Sken-Pitilkin, who, of course, did not (and would not! not ever! regardless of the threat or provocation!) denounce the verbs, no, nor any of the other parts of speech.

With Brother Fern Feathers thus having capitulated before the Weaponmaster (but with the sagacious Sken-Pitilkin remaining as staunch in his scholarship as ever) Guest Gulkan then wound up his speech by making a brief recapitulation of all his exploits, then said:

"So you see, I am well talented enough to undertake the tasks which lie before me. Furthermore, I am a personal friend of Plandruk Qinplaqus, the Silver Emperor who rules the Empire of Greater Parengarenga. In the past, he has received me in the palace of Na Sashimoko, the ruling palace of Dalar ken Halvar. Furthermore, I am a boon companion of Asodo Hatch, the greatest of the emperor's warlords. Upon him I bestowed the woman Penelope, who is now his wife. As a token of their friendship, Plandruk Qinplaqus and Asodo Hatch have kept safe for me the x-x-zix, the mighty wishstone which I won from Untunchilamon. Likewise they have preserved for my benefit the mighty mazadath, a charm of protection which makes a warrior immortal in battle."

This last comment about the mazadath was made by Guest in a spirit of outright deceit, for, since he did not entirely trust the wizards who were assembled on Drum, he thought it best to conceal some of his subtler resources under a camouflaging layer of braggarting barbarism. So, while denying primitive barbarism, Guest yet deliberately aped it; and wizards such as Fern Feathers, who were not equipped to be theatre critics, accepted his gaudier performances as the inner truth of his nature, and thus were led to underestimate the Weaponmaster.

Naturally, Ontario Nol did not underestimate Guest Gulkan, for the wizard of Itch had known the Weaponmaster long enough to form a proper opinion of his abilities. But, even so, Nol did not know Guest well enough to realize that his boastful arrogance was, in part, a self-protective reaction to long defeat and disappointment. So, after listening to Guest boast at length of the high regard in which he was held in the city of Dalar ken

Halvar, and the manner in which he planned to overthrow his enemies and rectify the world, Nol said:

"Brave words for a man who cannot even tell us who his mother was."

This was a low blow. It is usually one's father who cannot be known of a certainty. But, since Guest's gigantic batwing ears marked him as his father's son, it was only his mother's identity which remained a mystery. Guest knew he had been born in Stranagor, but all questions as to his mother's identity had been met with evasions.

But, over the years, Guest had had time in plenty to puzzle out this problem. In the tunnels of Cap Foz Para Lash, in the dungeons of Obooloo, in the Stench Caves of Logthok Norgos, in Drangsturm's Castle of Controlling Power, he had pondered the problem. And he thought he had solved it.

"I know who my mother is," said Guest, with equanimity. "And if in this company you choose to declare her, why, I will not disown her, for I am no wizard, hence do not share the prejudices of wizards."

Upon which Nol, impressed for once by the Weaponmaster's performance, gave the slightest of bows and made no further objections.

"So," said another wizard, "our Yarglat friend knows his mother. If his boast is to be believed, he also knows the emperor of Parengarenga and the greatest of Dalar ken Halvar's warlords. The question then arises. Why is he living here in exile upon Drum? Why is he not living as a prince in Dalar ken Halvar, as the governor of one of Parengarenga's provinces, or perhaps as heir to the very Empire of Greater Parengarenga as a whole?"

Guest did not like the tone of this address. There were several responses he could have made. He could, for example, have mentioned the fact that most of Parengarenga is uninhabitable wasteland, and to be made governor of one of Parengarenga's provinces is not by any means a fate to be greatly desired.

But instead he said:

"Until now, my thoughts have been all for the recovery of

the star-globe. To encompass the search for this globe, I have needed to have mastery of the skies, hence I have of necessity been based upon Drum. For, of all the wizards in the world, only Sken-Pitilkin has mastered the secret of controlled flight, therefore it is natural that he should be the greatest of my allies. Plandruk Qinplaqus is mighty in power, but his power is that over the mind and that over the body politic. Of the skies he knows nothing, hence I count Sken-Pitilkin the greater wizard."

At this, Sken-Pitilkin could not help but feel a wine-smooth warmth envelop his soul; and it occurred to the sagacious wizard of Skatzabratzumon that, however delinquent Guest's scholarship, the Yarglat barbarian had learnt at least the bare essentials of the great art of politics.

"So," said Guest, who was not finished with his speechifying, "till now I have been engrossed with the search for the star-globe. Now I have won that globe. Therefore I turn my attention towards Dalar ken Halvar, seeking help to aid me in the conquest of the circle."

"But what," said another wizard, "makes you think that Dalar ken Halvar will want to participate in such a conquest?"

Guest looked at the wizard in amazement. To the Weaponmaster it was a self-obvious truth that any nation will naturally and inevitably seize any opportunity for conquest which presents itself. However, rather than drawing attention to this truism, Guest said:

"There is in Dalar ken Halvar the militant religion known as Nu-chala-nuth. It preaches the equality of all men and the inferiority of all women. It worships but one god, and is utterly intolerant of all others."

"For what purpose do you lecture us on theology?" said Brother Fern Feathers, who had at last plucked up the courage to match his wits again with Guest.

"Because," said Guest, "Nu-chala-nuth is a militant religion. One of its basic tenets is the righteous necessity for the conquest of all Unbelievers. A religion possessed of such a dogma is a potent weapon for conquest."

"Then why will the believers of a religion so intolerant have anything to do with you?" said Brother Fern Feathers.

"Because," said Guest, "while I was living in Dalar ken Halvar I made a nominal conversion to Nu-chala-nuth. I will be a Believer leading other Believers. Here note that each Believer is thought to be the equal of all the others, presuming his sex to be male."

Brother Fern Feathers wrinkled his nose, trying to grasp this notion. The idea of a god who was equally accessible to all people was something of a novelty to the wizard. Take for example the deity known as Zoz the Ancestral, the ruling god of the Janjuladoola. Anyone can worship Zoz the Ancestral, but it is commonly accepted that Zoz is essentially a racial god, the god of the grey-skinned Janjuladoola people, and that worshippers of other races must therefore be second-class worshippers.

"Are you trying to tell me," said Brother Fern Feathers, "that the god of the Nu-chala-nuth has no natural racial or cultural constituency? Are you trying to tell me that this god is so thoroughly deracinated that anyone can be a leader of its Believers?"

"Deracinated," said Guest, puzzling over the word. "Oh! You mean, exiled. Yes. The god of the Nu-chala-nuth is most thoroughly exiled, for it comes not from this world but from another."

"That, one might have thought, is part and parcel of the definition of the nature of a god," said Brother Fern Feathers.

Whereupon Guest did his best to explain that the god of the Nu-chala-nuth was a god of the Nexus, and that the Nexus was a confederation of worlds existing in a series of inter-linked universes where the stars were (for the most part) an alien white rather than the familiar red, green, blue, yellow and gold of the stars of our world.

With much labour, Guest tried to explain all this, but Brother Fern Feathers plainly thought him wildly deluded in entertaining any notion so improbable.

"So," said Fern Feathers, when Guest was finished, "our Yarglat general is prepared to put his trust in the unifying onslaught of religious war. I think this a very dangerous strategy. True, we must have an army, but why not seek alliance with the army which is on our very doorstep? In the Greaters, in the Lessers, in Estar, in Garabatoon, in Androlmarphos and in Stokos, a great alliance is forming, uniting for invasion. We have heard of this Morgan Hearst, of this Watashi, of the woman Ampadara and the child Monogail. Since they are arming for invasion, why not match our airpower to their swordpower?"

This was so patently logical that the proposal was met with a smattering of applause. But Guest flatly declared:

"I do not trust them."

This was but the smallest fragment of a great and terrifying truth to which Guest did not dare give voice. There were two parts to this truth, one small, one great. The small and secret revelation was that Guest, in his own right, did not have power sufficient to match the potential treachery of the demon Italis and its kin. As for the great revelation—

What Guest did not, could not, would not say was that forces of change were being liberated in Dalar ken Halvar — forces so enormous that all powers of wizardry would be an irrelevance beside them.

Guest had seen machines. He had seen two therapists in their might. He had met with a dorgi in its rampaging wrath. He had seen Shabble. And Shabble, though a mere toy to its makers, could fly, and spit fire, and sing, and calculate income tax, and imitate demons, and tell jokes, and do a dozen other things besides.

Guest knew that a machine culture was on the rise in Dalar ken Halvar. In that city, Asodo Hatch had long been at work, supervising a machine which could command the x-x-zix which Guest had won from Untunchilamon. Guest knew that things would not stop there. The old order was passing, and the rule of wizards was but a passing quirk of the old order.

This Guest knew.

Unlike any wizard, Guest Gulkan had the advantage of having endured four years of convalescence in the tunnels of Cap Foz Para Lash, in the heart of Dalar ken Halvar, where he had enjoyed the company of Paraban Senk, a thing versed in the ways of an anciently powerful machine culture. Later, he had had long acquaintance of Shabble, sharing incarceration with Shabble in a yellow bottle which had been taken by a laborious route from Drum to Drangsturm. Adding stories of the past to his own experience, Guest believed he could see something of the future, though he saw through a glass darkly.

Guest had praised Sken-Pitilkin, the master of the skies. But a machine culture would bring machines which could out-perform a wizard a thousand times over, so that Sken-Pitilkin's stickbird would seem but a ludicrous eccentricity beside the huge ships of the air which circumnavigated the planet, which flew between planets, and which crossed the gulfs between the very stars themselves.

So thinking, Guest realized Sken-Pitilkin was watching him.

"There is much which Guest is leaving unsaid," said Sken-Pitilkin. "In Dalar ken Halvar, they have — potentially — the power to unlock the greatest secrets of the past."

"You mean," ventured Brother Fern Feathers, "to subject us to a repeat performance of the wars of the Days of Wrath?"

"That is part of it," said Sken-Pitilkin, making no attempt to shy away from that possibility. "But what is the alternative? Are we to bow to the Swarms and thus to condemn all unborn generations to a life of skulking terror? And even if we somehow defeat the Swarms by our own devices, what then? The world is a place comfortable enough for wizards, but is it paradise? Perhaps more power will simply see us better armed for our own destruction, but are we on that basis to deliberately choose to see ourselves defeated by the Swarms? With the Swarms upon our borders, I think it reasonable for us to make an alliance with Dalar ken Halvar, and use first its militant religion and later its more secret strengths to right the world to something closer to our hearts' desire."

"We can right the world by making an alliance with these people to the south of us," said Brother Fern Feathers. "With this Rovac warrior Morgan Hearst and his cohorts."

"Yes," said Sken-Pitilkin. "We can do that, but in two or

three generations a greater power will arise in Dalar ken Halvar and sweep away everything we have made."

So said Sken-Pitilkin.

There then followed a full three days of sometimes disorderly debate, during which Guest wished most heartily that he had had Shabble to aid him. The bubble was but a toy, but it had actually lived through the years of the Nexus. It had seen at first hand the wonders of a machine civilization, and it could be most persuasive in describing wonders of which Guest could give but faltering second-hand accounts.

However, at the end of three days of debate, it was formally agreed that Sken-Pitilkin and Guest Gulkan could take themselves off to Dalar ken Halvar to seek an alliance with Plandruk Qinplaqus and the militant religion of Nu-chala-nuth — the purpose of this alliance being to reopen the Circle of the Doors of the Partnership Banks and wage a destructive war against the Swarms.

So, this having been decided, Sken-Pitilkin set forth for Dalar ken Halvar, with the Weaponmaster as his sole companion — and with the rest of the wizards more than half-convinced that these two would get themselves killed either during the journey or shortly after their arrival in Parengarenga.

CHAPTER FIFTY-SIX

The Swarms: diverse breeds of monsters which were confined to the south of Argan until the destruction of the flame trench Drangsturm. The Swarms are controlled by an entity known as the Skull of the Deep South. The unfortunate truth is that wizards once awakened the enmity of the Skull when they made an ill-advised and abortive attempt to enslave it; and, in the thousands of years since then, the Skull has harboured a deep-seated hatred of humankind.

* * *

At this juncture, the lowlands of Argan's western coast had fallen almost entirely to the occupation of the Swarms. Pockets of exception included Androlmarphos, Hok and Estar.

The seaport city of Androlmarphos, defended by tidal marshlands and by a web work of rivers, as yet preserved its integrity, and had become home to many wizards. In the mountains of Hok, the former rulers of the Harvest Plains had taken refuge, together with some of their people. In the north of Argan, the province of Estar was guarded by mountains, and a refugee army had mounted a sturdy defence of those mountains, and had so far defeated the Swarms. The defence of Estar automatically protected the uplands of Penvash.

But, by and large, the entire western seaboard of Argan was dominated by the Swarms. On his previous flight to Dalar ken Halvar, that flight which he had made with the Weaponmaster to recover the yellow bottle from Dalar ken Halvar, Sken-Pitilkin had dared a transit due south from Drum, and had overflown the wreckage of Drangsturm, thus crossing Argan at its narrowest point. But he thought the Neversh to be too numerous by now for him to dare a repeat performance of this feat; and he was well aware that the conscious malignity of the Skull of the Deep South had to be added to the sheer numbers of the Neversh when one sought to calculate their danger.

In the centre of the continent, the mountainous wastelands were as yet free from the monsters. But that high and desolate continental hinterland was the preserve of dragons. Here we are not talking about sea dragons, those idle and talkative creatures who inhabited Sken-Pitilkin's home island of Drum. No, we are talking about land dragons, those crude and hideous beasts of infinite malignity which have so haunted the imagination of humanity.

Since dragons, unlike the Swarms, lack a coordinating general like the Skull, it happens that dragons have never yet proved a serious danger to the survival of humanity. If a dragon should happen to take up residence in your neighbourhood, then its exactions may prove expensive, but the bottom line is that the average dragon does far less damage than the average war, plague, famine or flood; and there is many a region which has stoically gone about its business for generations, despite the informal taxation of that business by one dragon or by a brood of the things.

Nevertheless, Sken-Pitilkin had absolutely no intention of putting himself in the way of a dragon unless he had to; and, on adding the dangers of dragons to the dangers of the Swarms, he decided to shun the continent of Argan entirely, and to chart a passage which would keep him well clear of its shores.

Being thus wary of all winged monsters, Sken-Pitilkin first flew himself and the Weaponmaster north to Lex Chalis, that rock-tip of Tameran where caves still preserved the stone circles in which Guest and Sken-Pitilkin had cooked their fish, their shellfish, their kelp and their lobsters during a long winter's season which they had spent hiding from Shabble.

After resting for a day in that place of unpleasant memories, they flew east towards the island of Ork, eventually arriving there in good order. They were now on the fringes of the Great Ocean of Moana. Imagine Moana to be a box, with Tameran at its top and Argan on its western edge. The island of Ork then lies in the north-west corner of the box.

The eastern side of the box is the continent of Yestron, and the southern side is formed by the continent of Parengarenga.

Guest Gulkan and Sken-Pitilkin therefore had to go far, far, far to the south on their way to Dalar ken Halvar.

They made the trip by island-hopping, landing and resting on the islands of Ashmolea and Asral. Their next stop was the Ebrell Islands — of which, the less said the better. This is no place for a thesis detailing the twenty different degrees of stench which can be generated by rotting whale blubber!

From the Ebrells, Sken-Pitilkin flew to Parengarenga, a target so large it was impossible to miss. But, having picked up the coast, how then was the wizard to reach his way to Dalar ken Halvar? That city is, after all, but a speck in the midst of an enormous wasteland.

Sken-Pitilkin, who still had-occasional nightmares about the crossing of Moana which had seen him miss the island of Untunchilamon entirely, followed the stratagem which had seen him get safely to Dalar ken Halvar on his most recent visit. He took the trouble to scout up and down the coast of Parengarenga till he located one of its few seaports.

All of Parengarenga's seaports are linked by road directly with Dalar ken Halvar, so, having found such a port, Sken-Pitilkin was able to scout down the road for league after weary league, until at last he saw the city of Dalar ken Halvar amidst the red dust of the Plain of Jars.

As one approaches Dalar ken Halvar from the air, the first thing to be seen from a distance is Lake Shalasheen, which lies to the north of the city's centre. One might think that the Caps, the city's minor mountains, would be the first thing to catch the eye. But those lumps of rock, formidable as they are, tend to blend into the landscape of dust, particularly when there is a wind to stir that dust to a haze. It is Lake Shalasheen which landmarks the city, for it catches the sun like a coin tossed from palankeen to gutter, and it was that wink-blind of bright-blazing silver which assured Sken-Pitilkin of his target.

Since it was in Dalar ken Halvar that Sken-Pitilkin had first trialed his stickbird, and since he had revisited the city since the fall of Drangsturm, he knew the place from the air. After all these years, he could still locate a variety of places where he had crash-landed while perfecting his airship. In particular, he had no trouble at all in placing the spot where he had crash-landed in a funeral pyre.

Just as Sken-Pitilkin knew Dalar ken Halvar, so Dalar ken Halvar knew Sken-Pitilkin. In particular, the City of Sun still remembered the long and universally dangerous series of trials in which the sagacious wizard of Skatzabratzumon had mastered the business of controlled flight. The chickens he had killed! The roofs he had torn off! The women he had caused to scream and faint! He had crashed in the river, had crashed in the lake, had crashed in the streets and in yards both public and private. Once, he had even been forced to put down hastily in the very Grand Arena itself.

On this occasion, as on his last visit, Sken-Pitilkin announced his return by circling over the city. At a leisurely pace, he sent his stickbird whirling over the fishing shacks of Childa Go, while Guest Gulkan leaned out and scrutinized the fortifications of the Bralsh. He flew over Cap Ogo Botch, on which stands the palace of Na Sashimoko. And, having circled and spiralled, and having noticed a gratifying stir in the streets of the city, Sken-Pitilkin landed his airship on the heights of Cap Foz Para Lash.

Then the wizard and the Weaponmaster waited.

At last, after a very lengthy delay, a single purple-skinned warrior came scrambling up to the heights. It was Asodo Hatch himself — Hatch the warlord, the man who was subordinate only to Plandruk Qinplaqus himself.

And, after only the briefest of conversations, Guest and Sken-Pitilkin knew that they had not misguessed their welcome.

So it was that Guest Gulkan returned to the City of Sun in the company of Hostaja Torsen Sken-Pitilkin. They were received with dignity, and with speeches in Pang, in Frangoni, and in the Motsu Kazuka of the Nu-chala-nuth.

Then Guest and Sken-Pitilkin were long closeted with Asodo Hatch and Plandruk Qinplaqus. Being uncertain of how much Asodo Hatch knew of the Circle of the Partnership Banks, Sken-Pitilkin placed the star-globe on the negotiating table, then treated that purple-skinned Frangoni warrior to a full exposition of its place in the scheme of things; then updated both Hatch and his wizardly master on the current state of affairs in Argan, and outlined a grand scheme for conquering the Circle of the Banks.

Both Asodo Hatch and Plandruk Qinplaqus had grave reservations about unleashing Nu-chala-nuth upon their own planet. A militant religion like Nu-chala-nuth had endless potential to generate grief, suffering and war.

But what was the alternative?

The Swarms were threatening the invasion of Tameran and the Ravlish Lands, and, ultimately, there was no guarantee that any part of the world would be permanently safe from these monsters. A unifying force was needed to rally humanity against these monsters, and the militant monotheistic religion of Nu-chala-nuth fitted the bill. The unifying force of Nu-chala-nuth, combined with the knowledge of Cap Foz Para Lash and the resources of the Circle of the Partnership Banks would provide all that was needed for the defeat of the Swarms.

As debate proceeded, Asodo Hatch was won over long before his master, Plandruk Qinplaqus. Ever since Guest Gulkan had brought the x-x-zix to Dalar ken Halvar, Asodo Hatch had been masterminding the research project which had been trying to make that ancient weather machine functional. Since then, his life had been one long exercise in frustration. Paraban Senk, the unembodied entity which ruled the underworld of Cap Foz Para Lash, had been able to give Hatch most of the technical advice he needed, but this advice amounted to a heart-breaking recipe for never-ending labour.

For, to build a machine capable of mastering the x-x-zix, one must first build a series of lesser machines; and to build the lesser machines one must first fabricate a thousand different kinds of materials, such as various kinds of metal alloys; and to fabricate each of these thousand different materials one must first build a set of fabricating machines. And—

And the whole heart-breaking exercise had very much confirmed to Asodo Hatch that which he had long suspected: namely, the fact that the impoverished city of Dalar ken Halvar was too poor to emulate the arts of the ancients. It could not support the number of specialists which a machine civilization required; it could not command an adequate supply of energy; and it was short even of the basic metals such as iron, tin, copper, gold and silver.

Since Plandruk Qinplaqus was not likely to yield in his determination to have the x-x-zix made functional, Hatch was doomed to waste the rest of his life in futility unless he could capture the resources needed to exploit his knowledge.

"Stokos can give us iron, and coal, and steel," said Hatch, as he began to appreciate the potential of this Circle. "On Stokos, the mines have been dug already, the forges built, and generations of craftsmen have refined the arts of working metal. If we open this Circle, then the ruling city of Stokos becomes a suburb of Dalar ken Halvar, which means that we have steelworks on our doorstep."

Thus did Asodo Hatch signify his conversion to Sken-Pitilkin's plan; and, though the conversion of Plandruk Qinplaqus was by no means as simple, eventually the Lord of the Silver Pelican was brought to the same opinion.

There then followed long days of preparation, for all were actually conscious of the fact that the Door in Voice opened to a region long overrun by the Swarms, hence there was the possibility that such monsters would muscle through to Dalar ken Halvar as soon as the Door in the Bralsh was opened. The problem was solved — at least as far as Dalar ken Halvar was concerned — by placing huge blocks of stone on either side of the steel arch within the Bralsh. These blocks constricted the approaches to the archway so that, while a man could get to the arch, a monster in its hugeness would not have been able to get out into Dalar ken Halvar.

Nor were these brute physical preparations the end of the matter, for the city of Dalar ken Halvar as a whole had to be briefed as to what was afoot, and prepared for the opening of the Circle. For there was no way that it could be held secret. Not when it would be necessary to use hundreds of men to guard and fortify the Door at Voice, and hold it against the Swarms.

Then came the day.

In the Bralsh, Plandruk Qinplaqus ceremonially placed the star-globe in its niche in the base of the marble plinth which supported the steel arch of the Door. Immediately, there came a hum as of wasps or of bees. The seductive silver shimmer of the screen of the Door came to life, filling the arch. And Guest Gulkan — accompanied by Asodo Hatch, by Hostaja Sken-Pitilkin and by a dozen spearheading heroes — was gone through that screen in moments.

A single footfall took Guest from the Bralsh in Dalar ken Halvar to the Singing Dove Pensions Trust of Tang. He found himself in a well-remembered conical chamber hung with silken ropes and scented with incense. It was utterly empty.

Onward!

Back through the Door went Guest, his onslaught taking him to the Taniwha Guarantee Corporation of Quilth. Here was a similar conical chamber, but this one had been sealed with doors of steel. It was lit — but dimly — by small barred windows high overhead.

No time to linger!

Guest went through the Door again, this time stepping to the Orsay Bank of Stokos. He found the Orsay Bank's Door unattended but for the fresh-made corpse of an elderly Banker who had dropped stone dead at the shock of seeing the Door so unexpectedly reactivated.

Press on!

Guest plunged through the Door again, this time stepping through to the Morgrim Bank of Chi'ash-lan. He found the chamber of Chi'ash-lan's Door to be in utter darkness but for the unearthly green light emitted by the demon Ko. The glowing green shone sick and wet on the skeletons which hung from the ceiling of Chi'ash-lan's weirding room. By that same light, Guest saw that the entrance to the room had been bricked up.

The demon Ko said nothing, but Guest supposed the thing saw him, and supposed too that it would immediately communicate its knowledge to every other demon in the Circle of the Partnership Banks.

Time to go!

Guest dared through the Door again, to Alozay. He arrived in Alozay's weirding room in the highest level of the main-rock Pinnacle. It was bright with sun, and it was empty.

That high and airy chamber was not empty for long, for Asodo Hatch and Hostaja Sken-Pitilkin came pushing through the Door in Guest's wake, with armed men following. As Guest lingered — for he had given himself the task of introducing Alozay to the new realities of the renascent Circle — Hatch and Sken-Pitilkin pushed onward. More and more men came pouring through the Door, stepping into Alozay then stepping back through the silver screen so they could push through to the ruins of the Monastic Treasury of Inner Adeer, where a Door opened to the ruins of the city of Voice.

They would hold Voice in strength, and fortify it against the Swarms.

Once this great press of men had hastened in and out of Alozay, Guest Gulkan was left alone in the weirding room in the mainrock Pinnacle. He had thought it best that he confront his father alone, rather than with armed men at his back, for he wanted the Witchlord Onosh as an ally rather than a slave. He wanted no taint of coercion to contaminate their relationship. He sought an alliance of equals: himself and his father, united against the world.

So Guest was alone when he ventured to the outer stairway which led downwards from the Sky Stratum of Jezel Obo to the Archive Stratum of Trilip — bypassing the Hall of Time where the demon Italis maintained its vigil. But he found that outer stairway hanging in tatters, splinters of sky interpolated into its shattered fabric.

Then Guest ventured out on to the living rock of the main-rock Pinnacle, and scanned the view to north and south. To the south was the city of Molothair, which was inhabited still, for smoke was rising from its chimneys. To the north, the broad expanse of the Swelaway Sea was dotted with fishing boats. So. The island of Alozay, the ruling rock of the Safrak Islands, was still inhabited. Was still at peace. That knowledge cancelled one of Guest's fears: for in recent days he had endured a nightmare in which the Swarms had made a covert invasion of the Safrak Islands.

There had been no such invasion.

Alozay still maintained its integrity.

But the outer stairs had fallen to ruin, so Guest had no choice but to descend the inner stairs, and thus to precipitate a confrontation with the demon Italis — a confrontation which he had wished to defer until after he had met his father in conference.

So down Guest went, descending the inner stairs until he came in sight of that monolithic block of rock, twice his own height, which was as green as jade, that smoothest and hardest of stones, which the Ngati Moana call—

What is the word?

Pounamu.

Remembering that word, Guest remembered Untunchilamon. And so, as he looked around the Hall of Time — trying to see past the demon Italis — the Weaponmaster's head was alive with incongruous memories of tropical heat, of monkeys and of coconut palms.

There was nobody in the Hall of Time.

Not as far as Guest could see.

The Hall was empty. Its walls were terribly scarred by fire, and its tiles, which had once been patterned with skull-shaped designs, were scarred and blistered. Turning his attention back to Italis, Guest realized that there was a spark of brightness moving within the demon. A spark? Watching the lurid light which flashed and pulsed inside the demon, Guest realized it was a sphere about the size of a fist, and realized this was Shabble. That explained why nothing had been heard of the shining one since it had left Guest on his desert island.

"Greetings," said Guest, addressing himself to Icaria Scaria Iva-Italis, the jade-green monolith which stood before him.

The demon did not respond. It heard him, surely. It saw him, surely. But it said nothing. Within its substance, Shabble batted from side to side, trapped, caged, irrevocably imprisoned. And

Guest, his memories of Untunchilamon fading fast, remembered instead the night when he and his father had fought against Banker Sod, striving for control of the mainrock Pinnacle. It was an alliance with Italis which had allowed Guest to win that battle and make himself master of Safrak.

Guest waited.

He refused to be intimidated by this thing, or by its silence. It could say nothing to disturb him, nothing to upset him, nothing to make him afraid. He was past all that.

So thought Guest.

Then the demon spoke.

"So," said Italis. "You have come to kill your father."

The words had weight. They were backed by an infinity of perception, of thought, of analysis, of years of study and of silent interrogation of probability.

And Guest, absorbing the words, felt his eyes become hot with tears. Then his mouth was wrenched open, and he found himself gasping for air. In huge, heaving gasps, he dragged in the air as his grief claimed him. For he had seen his doom, and had seen his father's doom, and had seen that there was no avoiding it.

CHAPTER FIFTY-SEVEN

Safrak Islands: group of islands in the Swelaway Sea, the inland
sea of the continent of Tameran. The chiefest of the Safrak
Islands is Alozay, long the headquarters of the Safrak Bank.
The Safrak Islands have long lived by trade, having
commercial intercourse with the free city of Port Domax (on
the shores of the Great Ocean of Moana) and with the
Collosnon Empire. The great city of Gendormargensis, the
capital of the Collosnon Empire, lies to the north of the
Swelaway Sea.

* * *

This book has concerned itself primarily with the life of the
Yarglat barbarian known to the world as Guest Gulkan, the self-
styled Weaponmaster.

Now Guest, in his confrontation with the ethnologist
Brother Fern Feathers, was hot to deny his barbarous
disabilities. Yet, whatever one thinks of the science of ethnology
and its sundry stupidities and iniquities, it must be admitted that
Guest was very much a prisoner of his barbarous upbringing.

Guest Gulkan was born into the household of a warlord, and
received the upbringing appropriate to a warlord's son, and
therefore lived and thought as a warlord. His imagination
revolved around power and struggle, and swords and horses,
and the clash of armies. And, as he butchered his way from one
disaster to another, Guest comported himself very much like the
archetypal swordsman. He dared his caverns; he slew his
monsters; he slaughtered his crocodiles; he bedded his women;
and he did grievous damage to the irregular verbs wherever he
encountered them.

So it was that the Weaponmaster lived in ignorance of his
true historical significance — which was, to be an instrument to
unlock the power which lay latent in the city of Dalar ken
Halvar.

783

It was Guest, after all, who decided that the world should be conquered by the militant religion of Nu-chala-nuth rather than by the Swarms. When the wisdom of wizards could see no way into the future, it was Guest who bethought himself of Plandruk Qinplaqus, and of Asodo Hatch — so diligently supervising the construction of a machine designed to tame the x-x-zix and bring effective weather control to Dalar ken Halvar — and of the wealth of knowledge protected and preserved by Paraban Senk in the caves of Cap Foz Para Lash.

Only when Guest had unlocked the Circle of the Partnership Banks did he really realize what he had done. Only then did he realize that he had put an end to the old and ancient cyclic dynamic of feudal history which had for so long dominated the world.

It is a new world now.

Precisely what kind of world?

It is hard to say.

It is early days yet, and we cannot tell what shape the future will take. But this we know: the forges of Stokos, matched to the knowledge of Dalar ken Halvar, looks in its own right to be a combination which will prove potent against the Swarms.

As for Guest Gulkan's story, that has been told, at least to the extent which it can be told. There may be more yet to come, for Guest has declared his intention of venturing once more to the Shackle Mountains, and there entering the Cave of the Warp for a second time, and passing again through the Veils of Fire, protected by the mazadath which he yet wears around his neck. For Guest wishes to have further knowledge with the Lobos, a thing which does not figure in the writings of wizards, a thing which is unknown to demons such as Iva-Italis, and of which Paraban Senk can give no explanation.

As to the rest of Guest's life, why, no account need be given of it. For, as soon as Guest had opened the Circle of the Partnership Banks, he had initiated a new phase of history — a phase in which a dynastic struggle between father and son is of little consequence.

Still, for the sake of mere completeness, let us spare a few words to sketch out an account of events which seekers of sensation have elsewhere dealt with at weary length.

On opening the Circle of the Doors of the Partnership Banks, Guest Gulkan returned to Alozay, as has been recounted; and on Alozay he learnt of the doings of his father.

While Guest and his allies had been preparing for the reopening of the Circle, a rabble of pirates and Rovac warriors had been preparing to invade the Collosnon Empire from the south. Dim rumours of this impending invasion had reached as far as Gendormargensis, a city then in some considerable disorder as a consequence of the brawling disorder of its Yarglat rulers, who had been making coups and counter-coups against each other for the better part of half a year.

Hearing of the disorder in Gendormargensis, and of the threat of invasion from the south, the Witchlord Onosh thought the moment ripe for his return.

This may be thought presumptuous.

For, surely, Lord Onosh had been defeated, disgraced and discredited. Lord Onosh had lost his empire to Khmar, and had been reduced to the rule of the Safrak Islands, paltry pieces of rock in the wash of the Swelaway Sea. How then could he aspire to reconquer the Collosnon Empire?

The answer is simple.

During the long years in which he had lived in exile on the Safrak Islands, Lord Onosh — ever counselled by the wisdom of Bao Gahai, the steadfast companion of his defeat — had prepared for his return.

Preparation had been difficult during the reign of the Red Emperor Khmar, whose rule of terror had restricted speech, thought and movement. But, under the rule of Khmar's son Celadric, the Collosnon Empire had become a milder place; and the Witchlord's agents had taken advantage of freedoms of speech, assembly and movement to sound out inclinations, to spy, to suborn, to bribe and to subvert.

In particular — ever remembering the cause of the disorder which had precipitated his overthrow! — Lord Onosh had cultivated the leaders of Stranagor and Locontareth. He had studied at great length the question of taxation, and had covertly promised the provinces a just share of fertilization.

Regarding the question of taxation, it must be admitted that Khmar's son Celadric had been no better than any of the rulers who had preceded him. There were many good things which could be said of Celadric — one notes in particular his scholarship, and the courageous manner in which he subdued even the most wickedly barbed of the irregular verbs — but it has to be admitted that he had one or two exceedingly vicious vices.

The most vicious of all Celadric's vices was that of architecture. Much has been made of the manner in which so many great men have destroyed themselves with strong drink, or with opium, or with gambling, or with an overindulgence in orgasmic pursuits — but the great vice of architecture is potentially as ruinous as all of these put together.

There are many individuals, families, companies and cities which have come to ruin through over-indulgence in oak, cedar, granite, marble and mortar; and, though Celadric had not exactly ruined the Collosnon Empire through such indulgence, it must be allowed that he had grievously over-taxed such provincial centres as Locontareth and Stranagor to pay for the aggrandisement of his capital.

Furthermore, the very length of time which Lord Onosh had been away from his former empire had worked to his advantage. Memories had mellowed and softened to his advantage. Compared to Khmar, he was a golden saint, and his reign a time of peace and plenty. Those who were threatening the invasion of Tameran from the south had made Khmar's daughter Monogail their figurehead — which meant, in effect, that they were proposing the conquer in the name of Khmar. However rational and reasonable that may have seemed in Estar, it met with little favour in the empire's heartland.

So, with Gendormargensis disordered by coup and countercoup, and with a bloodthirsty invasion threatened from the south, Lord Onosh decided to make his move.

Locontareth declared for Lord Onosh, and raised an army

for him; and, by the time Guest Gulkan reopened the Circle of the Partnership Banks and made his way to Alozay, Lord Onosh was once more ruling the Collosnon Empire from Gendormargensis.

Had Bao Gahai survived to see the Witchlord's triumph, things might thereafter have turned out differently. But Bao Gahai died within sight of the walls of Gendormargensis. Years earlier, she had made a terrible sacrifice to fulfil the greatest desire of her heart; and this sacrifice had so aged and weakened her that it is a wonder that she had survived for so long.

In sight of the walls of Gendormargensis, Bao Gahai perished, falling victim to one of those contagious fevers which are so much a part and parcel of campaigning. Therefore, when Lord Onosh learnt that his son Guest was upon Alozay, Lord Onosh lacked Bao Gahai's counsel.

As was noted at the outset of this history, the Witchlord Onosh had been at odds with the world for so long that he had quite lost the art of showing the world kindness and affection. This was the flaw which doomed him to destruction.

For, when Lord Onosh heard that Guest was on Alozay, and was leagued with wizards, and was often in conference with the demon Iva-Italis, and was in discourse with the Shabble whom Italis held as a prisoner, and was arming the soldiers of Parengarenga with the swords of Stokos, why, Lord Onosh did not think to praise his son, or congratulate him on his success, or make him a gift of some of the more transportable pieces of Celadric's architecture.

No.

When Lord Onosh heard that Guest had arrived upon Alozay, he interpreted this arrival as invasion, and feared the conquest of Alozay to be but the opening move of the conquest of Tameran. And, once Lord Onosh began assembling an army to strike against Alozay, what option was then left to his son?

Of course, Guest defeated his father with ease.

For, as has been made plain by this history, the greatest and most difficult part of the art of war is the manoeuvre of armies. But Guest Gulkan had a yellow bottle which was equal to the accommodation of an army; and Sken-Pitilkin had an airship which was equal to the transport of the bottle.

I remember.

It was in spring that Guest Gulkan shattered the Witchlord's forces in the Battle of Sipping Cross, and marched on Gendormargensis.

Since the slow and weary business of loading an army into and out of the yellow bottle was one which could take days to accomplish, Guest Gulkan did not dare try such a stratagem when he was so closely engaged with his father's forces. He expected his father to leave men in ambush; or to turn and meet him in force; or, at the very least, to stand at Gendormargensis and fight.

So, shunning air transport, Guest Gulkan took his army overland for the last few leagues which stood between himself and the city.

On reaching Gendormargensis, Guest found that Lord Onosh had fled, taking his army with him. The city was in no state to stand in siege against the invaders, for it was in the grip of a cholera epidemic, cholera being one of the recurrent scourges of the Collosnon Empire. And here it must be admitted that, regardless of Celadric's great expenditure on architecture, Gendormargensis remained a city in which sewage disposal was of a very rudimentary nature.

On account of the epidemic, the victorious Weaponmaster did not enter the city, but pitched his tents on the mudlands beyond the walls. On Sken-Pitilkin's advice, those tents were pitched a good half-league upriver from the city.

"Cholera," said Sken-Pitilkin, "is spread by filth within water. It would be far less common if you could train your people to boil their drinking water and wash their hands after going to the toilet."

"Are my people babies that I should be teaching them how to piss and dung?" growled Guest.

"Why," said Sken-Pitilkin, staring at Guest as if the Yarglat warrior was a new and remarkable species of frog, "it is a barbarian! It growls in the face of science and bares its fangs at wisdom."

"I," said Guest, with dignity, "lack a pox doctor's perverted interest in the functions of the anus."

"Ah," said Sken-Pitilkin, "then you renounce all claims to civilization. For civilization is essentially a device for the tidy disposal of bodily excretions."

"Really!" said Guest. "I thought the name for such a device was a brothel!"

Thus Guest and Sken-Pitilkin debated outside the walls of Gendormargensis. They continued the debate long into the night, for Guest was too tense to sleep, and too much the professional to drown his tensions with drink.

The next morning, Guest Gulkan pursued his father's retreating army, and at noon he came upon his father's baggage train. It was an incredible scene of spilt rubbish, mud, mired waggons, slaughtered oxen, bonfires, drunks and deserters. Guest Gulkan knew at once that his father's army had given up, for many of the bonfires were made from bunched spears, from arrows, and from other gear of war. It is difficult to accept the surrender of men who can simply snatch weapons from the battlefield, and in consequence of this difficulty it is common to murder those who surrender. By making sure that not one whole weapon remain to them, the Witchlord's men were endeavouring to have their surrender accepted.

"They have disarmed themselves," said Guest, surveying the scene.

"Yes," said Sken-Pitilkin. "As your father disarmed himself before venturing to Alozay."

"I remember," said Guest.

Of course he remembered. His father had caused weapons to be hidden in treasure chests, then had used those weapons against his hosts. But where were the treasure chests now?

"It would be most economical of time," said Guest, "if we were to slaughter these prisoners."

"Doubtless," said Sken-Pitilkin. "But you have cholera in your capital, and an invasion yet threatens from the south. Have you soldiers so many that you can be murdering them?"

"True," said Guest.

Then took the trouble to accept the surrender of those who sought his mercy. Having accepted their surrender, he then went to the much greater trouble of searching them for weapons, and digging in the mud, and launching great interrogations.

At last, Guest declared himself satisfied.

"There are no weapons here," said Guest. "I've looked. I've looked everywhere."

"There are the bonfires," said Sken-Pitilkin.

"Fires?" said Guest. "Fires, yes, doubtless, but — what can one hide in a fire?"

"Think," said Sken-Pitilkin.

Guest Gulkan obeyed, and, after due consideration, ordered that the ruins of the bonfires be raked apart. His subsequent excavations discovered swords, spears, helmets, shields, chain mail, knives, clubs, throwing stars, caltrops and battle-axes. Enough for an army.

Once Guest's inevitable reprisals had added another field of blood and butchery to history's scenery, the Weaponmaster pursued his father, and the pursuit soon took him into the hills.

I remember.

It was cold in the hills.

By now, Lord Onosh was running in earnest. But however he ran, he could not escape from his son. In desperation, the Witchlord Onosh split his forces, sending parties in five different directions in the hope of evading pursuit. But the Witchlord's doom was so patent that some of his people deserted with the express intention of betraying him.

Guest Gulkan accepted the intelligence which was brought to him by the deserters, then had them put to death.

"For," said Guest, "treason is a capital crime, and, besides, it is these deserters who are putting me to the necessity of killing my father."

In the face of these judicial murders, Sken-Pitilkin said nothing, for Guest's mood had become changeable, and the wizard thought it unwise to challenge him when he had entered into one of his sanguinary phases.

And you think you would have done otherwise?

Well, perhaps you would have. But perhaps you would have died on account of your attempted diplomacy. In any case, this is not the tale of what might have been. This is the story of that which was. I remember.

I remember it was cold.

It was cold in the hills, cold in those days of spring, and colder yet by night. In the weariness of the long pursuit, men slept in the saddle. The pursuit went on by day and night, until bad weather set in, bringing abolishing rain, and clouds which reduced the night to an utter darkness.

I remember.

The trees, by night, wrathed by the rending winds. The campfires, driven and shriven by the bone-bleak wind. The muttered discontents of the fingerjoints, old bones protesting against the cold, against the unrelenting rigours of campaigning. Bao Gahai had died in the course of the Witchlord's war with the Weaponmaster, and was there any guarantee that a wizard would prevail in health where a witch had failed and perished?

Dawn, at last.

Dawn, and the rain dying away, and a weak light filtering through the breaking clouds. The ground mired with mud, and wet with petals, the petals of spring blossom brought down to earth by the drenching rains of the night.

Then Guest Gulkan took the saddle and led his people in pursuit. And many men marvelled to see the confidence with which he led the way, wasting no time on spying for tracks.

But of course Guest Gulkan had often hunted in these hills. He had hunted with his father, back in the days when Lord Onosh had sported after bandits. Guest knew the habits of the hunted, and knew too the lie of the land. Lord Onosh had fled through the hills in a great arc, and that arc had taken him into a valley which led down towards the Yolantarath River. The steep scarps of the valley's rocky sides meant that Lord Onosh would now be inevitably channelled down towards the flatlands, like many parties of bandits before him.

So Guest pursued, leading his men with a certainty which the ignorant attributed to precognitive powers — powers which came, or so said a wild Rumour, from the fact that he had been mothered by a witch.

But, as they drew nearer and nearer the Yolantarath, Guest allowed the pace to slacken; and Sken-Pitilkin, deducing from this slackening a lessening of Guest's wrathfulness, ventured to open a conversation.

"You remember this," said Sken-Pitilkin, opening a conversation with the Weaponmaster in the hope of later being able to raise the matter of his execution of the men who had betrayed his father.

"Perhaps," said Guest carelessly. "Or perhaps I dreamt of it. Have you ever thought this might be a dream, and you but a dream in a dream?"

It goes without saying that Sken-Pitilkin had heard of this tired old philosophical conceit some twice times ten thousand times in the past.

"A dream has a purpose," said Sken-Pitilkin. "Its purpose is the cleansing of the mind. Having a purpose, it is simple. Since life is both complex and disordered, we can say of a certainty that it has no purpose, hence is no dream."

"So you say," said Guest, "but your philosophy opens you to deception. If the world were a dream, perhaps it might have been designed for your own deceiving, in which case it would have been purposely designed to be complex and confusing, in order to convince you that it had no purpose."

Thus argued Guest Gulkan and his erstwhile tutor as they made their way down towards the Yolantarath River. Sken-Pitilkin, naturally, was able to defeat his every argument easily and adroitly; but Guest in his ignorance was unable to realize that he had been defeated, and repeatedly declared that a world undreamlike might yet be a dream, assuming it to have been designed for deception.

"That much you've said some three times already," said Sken-Pitilkin, when Guest had said it for the seventh time.

"Which makes it true," said Guest.

"No, not at all," said Sken-Pitilkin. "A thing said thrice is no more true than a thing said once, and to propose otherwise is a nonsense."

"On the contrary," said Guest Gulkan. "Words are the shaping of the world. You told me that yourself. It follows that to say is to shape, and a thing thrice-said gains truth by repetition."

This is typical of the Weaponmaster's erratic style of debate, which, for all it owed to formal logic and systematic learning, resembled nothing so much as an energetic washerwoman trying to hammer home a nail by flailing at it with a wet eel.

"You are confounding a theorem of Practical Politics with a theorem of Axiomatic Philosophy," said Sken-Pitilkin. "And thus it is proved that you are talking nonsense, whether you know it or not."

"Knowledge is unitary," said Guest. "You told me so yourself."

Knowledge is unitary. What does that mean? Guest Gulkan was not sure. But his tutor had often used this grand-sounding phrase to win their debates (or at least bring them to a conclusion) and Guest thought there was no harm in trying it.

"Knowledge is unitary, yes," said Sken-Pitilkin, "but even so, books are not fishes, songs are not sums, and politics is not philosophy, nor did I ever tell you it was."

"On the contrary," said Guest. "You have several times named philosophy as the very heart of politics, which is a nonsense, but is still what you told me."

"The nonsense is not mine but yours," said Sken-Pitilkin, striving with imperfect success to preserve an amiable tolerance in the face of such intellectual folly. "Political method is not philosophical truth, and I never said it was."

"The heart," said Guest, stubborn in dissent. "You claimed philosophy to be the heart of politics."

"One thing becomes not another simply by being placed inside it, whether at the heart or elsewhere," said Sken-Pitilkin. "A stone ditched in the river does not become water. Likewise, your sword would win no degree of equanimity by being thrust the fullness of its length into the flesh of a horse, even if it should penetrate to the very heart."

"But that heart itself would be horse," persisted Guest. "Heart, kernel, pith, gist, essence. The heart of a thing is the essence of a thing, and you claimed philosophy as the heart of politics."

"That is sophistry, and you know it, or should know it, or will know it by the time I'm finished with you," said Sken-Pitilkin. "In any case, I never said that philosophy is at the heart of politics, merely that it should be, which is quite a different matter entirely. I am a philosopher. Am I ruling Tameran? Am I so much as listened to when I venture political advice?"

"You'll be listened to ardently," said Guest, "if you can tell me how to make a peace with my father."

"If we are in luck," said Sken-Pitilkin, "then your father will out-distance you, and you will have no need to worry about either war or peace."

So spoke Sken-Pitilkin, for he was sure by now that Guest was deliberately easing off the pace of the pursuit in the hope that his father would run, and would make his escape, and would not force father and son to a final confrontation.

But, when Guest and his forces eventually reached the Yolantarath, there was Lord Onosh, braced for a final stand. And as for the course of that final stand — why, we have seen that already.

Years earlier, when Guest had been but a boy, the Witchlord Onosh had hunted bandits from the hills, and had encompassed their slaughter on the banks of the Yolantarath. As Lord Onosh had hunted, so he now was doomed to be hunted in his turn.

The Witchlord Onosh was possessed of the Gift of Seeing, and though it was a small gift, and one which was erratic in operation, he had been right in thinking himself doomed to die, and had been right in thinking his son Guest Gulkan was the man who would encompass his death.

And so our history comes full circle, and we end as we began, with a battle by the river, and with a death. But, of course, between the first battle and the last, the world has changed entirely; and I cannot read the future, or know where the changes will end. I know only that one Age is finished, and we are launched into an uncertain future, the perplexities of which are beyond the foresight of man, or woman, or wizard.

The End

The Lost Chronicles
of an
Age of Darkness

The Chronicles of an Age of Darkness are not over...

Paraban Senk ripped away the wires. A needle tore loose from his arm with a sharp pang of silver-bright pain. The ground shuddered. An earthquake? Perhaps.

At the door, a guard. Startled to see Paraban emerging from the chamber. Reacting too slowly. Paraban's hand slammed upwards. The guard went reeling, jaw broken by the fierce blow which Paraban had delivered with the heel of his hand.

"Now," said Paraban. "Where am I?"

The answer came at once. He knew where he was. And how to get where he wanted to go. He needed to get where he had almost succeeded in getting before. He needed to find Antasy. To find out what they had done to him. He needed to find the truth about jumpback.

"Hey!" yelled someone.

Turning, Paraban saw another guard. This one armed with a gun. A gun which was pointed right at him.

"Don't shoot!" yelled Paraban. "I surrender!"

ALSO BY HUGH COOK

Volume 1: The Wizards and the Warriors
Volume 2: The Wordsmiths and the Warguild
Volume 3: The Women and the Warlords
Volume 4: The Walrus and the Warwolf
Volume 5: The Wicked and the Witless
Volume 6: The Wishstone and the Wonderworkers
Volume 7: The Wazir and the Witch
Volume 8: The Werewolf and the Wormlord
Volume 9: The Worshippers and the Way
Volume 10: The Witchlord and the Weaponmaster
and
The Lost Chronicles of an Age of Darkness

To find out more about
Hugh Cook
and the
Chronicles of an Age of Darkness
please visit:

https://www.zenphospress.com

Chronicles Facebook Group:
https://www.facebook.com/groups/hughcook

Hugh Cook Subreddit
https://www.reddit.com/r/hughcook

www.ingramcontent.com/pod-product-compliance
Lightning Source LLC
Chambersburg PA
CBHW070146310726
48976CB00001B/3